The
LAST JUMP

A Novel of World War II

JOHN E. NEVOLA

Outskirts Press, Inc.
Denver, Colorado

The Last Jump
A Novel of World War II
All Rights Reserved.
Copyright © 2010 John E. Nevola
v6.0 r2.0

Cover Photo © 2010 JupiterImages Corporation. All rights reserved - used with permission.
Photos by John E. Nevola.

Outskirts Press, Inc.
http://www.outskirtspress.com

Paperback ISBN: 978-1-4327-5561-4
Hardback ISBN: 978-1-4327-5665-9

Library of Congress Control Number: 2010923837

Outskirts Press and the "OP" logo are trademarks belonging to Outskirts Press, Inc.

PRINTED IN THE UNITED STATES OF AMERICA

**Most men lead lives of quiet desperation
and go to the grave with the song still in them.**

Henry David Thoreau (1817 – 1862)

Dedicated to my mother who was my champion,

my wife who is my miracle

and

my children who will always be my inspiration.

Thank you all for helping me sing.

With all my love,

j.n.

Preface

I knew they were the "Greatest Generation" long before the Tom Brokaw book and well ahead of *Saving Private Ryan* and *Band of Brothers*. One only had to grow up with a father and nine uncles who served in World War II to realize how special these people were who served in "The War".

My father and his five brothers served in the United States Merchant Marine. My four uncles on my mother's side were footslogging GIs in the United States Army, as were most of their friends. They were all just barely Americans, being the first American-born generation from Italian immigrants. Some were drafted, some volunteered, but they all served. They filled my head with their experiences and spurred my curiosity about the great adventure they had embarked upon. In all the stories they told, numbering in the dozens, they always left out the emotions of their fear and how they dealt with it. Also missing were the dangers they faced and how they survived.

My indoctrination was sterile, devoid of all the barbaric savagery of war or accounts of men who never returned. These veterans were proud of their service but never boasted or bragged about themselves. They reserved that for others. To a man, they were modest about their own contribution. As a youngster I listened in awe of what they experienced and accomplished.

It was only later in life, as I studied the conflict, did my aperture widen sufficiently to view this struggle on a global scale and understand how ubiquitous the contributions and sacrifices of all Americans were. The United States was spared the destruction seen by much of Europe and the world. Nevertheless, this conflict consumed America. The young men of this nation, many just boys, went off to the far-flung battlefields of the world for the duration, never knowing if and when they would ever see home again.

They went to places they never heard of, couldn't pronounce or even find on a map. Men and women from all social classes pitched in. The American military included the sons of Senators and Congressmen, movie stars, sports heroes, celebrities and men and women from all walks of life. Most Americans viewed this conflict as a fight for the survival of their country. They were fighting two of the most militaristic nations in history who had already built tremendous war machines and had been fighting for years. Germany and Japan seemed invincible and in the beginning of America's involvement in the war, the outcome was seriously in doubt.

Those who stayed behind went to work in the war factories and struggled to keep up with the incessant demand for war material and supplies. President Franklin D. Roosevelt called America the "Arsenal of Democracy" and the production might of this country went into overdrive. The women of America put down their aprons and picked up riveting guns and welding torches. These housewives built the fighting ships and sleek planes in unimaginable numbers. Massive shipyards and aircraft factories were constructed to build the ships and planes. An unprecedented effort to build an Atomic Bomb consumed immeasurable resources. And to tie all of this together, significant improvements were required to the nation's roads, rail and communications infrastructure. It was a monumental conversion of peacetime manufacturing to urgent wartime production.

Even the children became involved as they collected scrap metal, tin foil and rubber bands to help the war effort. Rationing of goods reached into every home. The lives of everyone in America were touched by this great world conflict. No one was spared from the storm of change. Almost as an afterthought, today's generation began to realize and recognize the Greatest Generation. It may have started with the Brokaw books or Spielberg movies but I have a sense the veterans themselves began it. Dying at the rate of 1,500 per day, they realized time was running out and they had to tell their stories lest they be lost forever.

Encouraged by Public Law 106-380, The Veteran's Oral Histories Project Act of 2000, World War II veterans were moved to action. They began showing up in the classrooms of America, to relay and record their own oral histories. They consented to interviews that just a few years before would have been unthinkable. Veterans Associations reached out to them on the Internet and some published books of their wartime memoirs. These World War II veterans, motivated by their desire to pass on their truths to future generations and driven by their own mortality, finally stirred, awoke and broke their silence. Those personal accounts, the last parting gifts from the Greatest Generation, have had a profound affect on the people of this country.

After years and years of controversy, the World War II Memorial was finally completed in Washington D.C. and opened to the public on 29 April 2004. Previously, the National D-Day Memorial, in Bedford, Virginia, was dedicated on 6 June 2001 and the National D-Day Museum in New Orleans was unveiled on 6 June 2000. Even these tributes do not adequately acknowledge the gift this generation has made to America and the future of the world.

Sixteen and a half million Americans served in the Armed Forces during the Second World War. While we owe them all an incalculable debt of gratitude, within this large group of individuals was a select group of men who served on a higher level. They were the men of the U.S. Marine Corps and U.S. Army Infantry. Many were just young boys not yet past their teens.

Some volunteered for this dangerous duty but most were just assigned to the dubious distinction of becoming riflemen. It was a dangerous job few wanted and most successfully avoided. The relative few who became combat infantrymen did their job well enough to beat back some of the most highly trained, professional soldiers in the world. The American citizen-soldier faced hardships and depravations not seen since Valley Forge. To the infantryman, the fighting and killing was up close and personal. Close enough, at times, to smell an enemy's breath or hear his last gasp as he died. The Infantry, "The Queen of Battle", bore the brunt of the dirty fighting, endured the horrendous living conditions and suffered the preponderance of casualties. Out of the sixteen million who served in all the branches of the services, only about 800,000 were combat infantrymen.

They were America's spear.

Within this group was a unique subset of men who stepped forward to volunteer for special training and hazardous duty. Their motivations ranged from a thirst for adventure to a desire to be part of an elite unit. Whatever their reasons, they would ultimately find themselves in the most crucial, dangerous, and sometimes hopeless situations throughout the war. Among the more celebrated special units were The 5307th Composite Unit (Provisional) codenamed "Galahad" but widely known as "Merrill's Marauders", the First Special Service Brigade, "The Devil's Brigade", the Marine Raider Battalions, the U.S. Army Rangers and the U.S. Army Airborne Infantry more commonly known as paratroopers.

They were the best among America's warriors. Their enemies knew them and feared them. After the early military setbacks at Pearl Harbor and the massive surrender of the American and Filipino forces in the Philippines, these superbly trained specimens of America's youth inspired the people on the Homefront. They built and nurtured the reputation of being America's toughest tough guys. In the dark days of 1942 they were this country's most visible and tangible hope. In the years to follow they became the shining example of American courage and pride.

These gallant men were the tip of the American spear.

This story honors them and is a belated but heartfelt "thank you" to all Americans who contributed to the victory.

Chapter One

The White House – February 16, 1996

"All I want is compliance with my wishes after reasonable discussion."

Winston Churchill (1874 - 1965)

The President stood by the window of the Oval Office staring at *Marine One*, a Sikorsky VH-60N helicopter, squatting patiently on the helipad. The huge dark green craft with its long drooping rotor blades was crewed by the elite members of HMX-1, better known as Marine Helicopter Squadron One. The ungainly machine was poised and ready to carry him and the First Lady to their weekend retreat. It would be a relief to get away for a few days. But there was one last piece of unfinished business before he could leave.

It had not been a particularly good week for him. His poll numbers were down and the news of the grounding of the oil tanker *Sea Empress* on the Welsh coast was particularly irksome as it spilled seventy thousand gallons of crude oil into the Atlantic Ocean. He looked forward to a working weekend at Camp David away from the press and the daily grind of the White House.

"Mister President," his personal secretary stepped through the door. "The Chairman and the Secretary are here."

"Send them in."

The Chairman of the Joint Chiefs of Staff and the Secretary of the Army filed into the Oval Office and the President motioned them to one of the two white facing sofas across from his desk. "Charlie, Aaron, please sit."

The President stood across from them, holding a piece of paper. He handed it to the Secretary of the Army, Charles Radcliffe, as they all sat down.

"Charlie, this letter was given to me by Congressman Williams of the Congressional Black Caucus." The meeting would assume an informal tone, at least to start.

"He asked for a formal review and personal response from me. The Black Caucus is way up my ass on this issue and I really do not want to deal with this with the election coming up." The President looked at both men.

General Clayton raised his eyebrows. "Issue, Mister President?" The general was in his dress green uniform with a chest full of colorful ribbons and four shiny silver stars perched proudly on each collar.

"This is a big issue for these people, Aaron," replied the President pointing to the letter. "Do you know there was not a single Medal of Honor awarded to a black serviceman in World War II? There were four hundred and thirty two of them presented in that war and not a single one to an African-American!" He paused. "I did my homework." The President stood up and walked to his desk. He picked up a small black cloth covered metal case about the size of an envelope and placed it on the glass coffee table between the two couches. "Open it, Aaron."

Clayton reached down and flipped open the lid revealing a Medal of Honor. He carefully lifted the Medal by the dark blue eight-sided pad, adorned with thirteen small white stars. It was a tremendous honor to hold it, even for a moment. All three men stared intently at it. It was the Air Force version, the largest of all the services, featuring the head of the Statue of Liberty in the center.

The Chairman was again the first to speak. "As you know, Mister President, this Medal is sacred to everyone in the military. Officers of every rank salute the bearer. Most of the roughly thirty-four hundred Medals awarded were done posthumously."

"But none to African-Americans, dead or alive," responded the President.

"Mister President," Secretary Radcliffe chimed in. "As you know there have been Medals of Honor awarded to black Americans in the Civil War, World War I, Korea, Vietnam…"

"But none to the black servicemen of World War II, Charlie," the President interrupted. "And the World War I Medal was just awarded a few years ago to, what was his name…Stover?"

"That would be Corporal Freddie Stowers, sir," General Clayton corrected, "in 1991. President Bush presented that Medal to his surviving sisters."

"Right," said the President with an edge in his voice. "Imagine that! A Republican president remedied that injustice and it was over seventy years after the fact. So tell me why we can't fix this World War II problem?"

Radcliffe handed the letter to General Clayton and continued, "We've been reviewing this, sir. We have a study team already in place doing the research and combing the National Archives but it's a delicate and difficult issue. There were few black combat troops in that war and therefore, fewer opportunities."

"Fewer, perhaps," the President again interrupted, "but I cannot accept the suggestion there were none!"

"But we all know there was a good deal of institutional racism in the military back then," Radcliffe continued ignoring the interruption. "So I'm sure there were some acts of valor that were, shall we say, intentionally overlooked."

"Like that one?" the President asked pointing to the letter.

"Sir, we don't know if this letter is accurate," said a skeptical General Clayton after reading it. "There were no black GIs in the paratroopers and the Eighty-second Airborne wasn't even at Bastogne. This letter was written by the granddaughter of a black soldier who supposedly participated in this action." General Clayton shook his head negatively. "The battle history and the facts don't support this claim. It simply cannot be accurate."

The room fell silent for a moment while the President stood, walked to his desk and sat down behind it. He had thought this through. He was about to order a delicate maneuver that had to be done perfectly. If he was successful, he could lock up the African-American vote for the Democratic Party for years to come. The rest of the discussion would be more formal.

"Mister Secretary…General…here is what I need you to do," the President began while he ran a hand through his thick gray hair. "It is my fervent belief there has been a great injustice done to black American servicemen during World War II. I want you to rectify those injustices."

"Yes sir, Mister President," Radcliffe replied.

"Continue with whatever you've been working on but the process must withstand the greatest scrutiny. The last thing I want is to be accused of doing this for political reasons. Is that clear?"

"Yes sir," both men responded.

"Therefore, I would like your recommendations. As long as I can demonstrate the awards are deserved." The President stood up, signaling the end of the meeting.

"Understood, Mister President," General Clayton replied. The Secretary and the General stood up to leave. The general placed the Medal back in its case and handed it back to the President along with the letter.

The President smiled slightly. "It's important to do this thing right, gentlemen. Find a way!" He handed the letter back to the general. "Start with this!"

"Yes sir," said Radcliffe. "We'll get it done right, sir."

The two men made their way toward the door.

"One more thing," called out the President.

"Sir?"

"When President Bush awarded that Medal of Honor, it was to surviving relatives. When you complete your work I don't want to be handing out Medals to someone's son or daughter because their father or grandfather died getting the damn thing…or because they survived the war but didn't live long enough to accept it. That is not exactly the front page photo I'm looking for," the President said tapping the case on his desk.

"Sir?" asked Secretary Radcliffe.

"Find me a live one!"

Chapter Two

Bedford, Virginia – February 2, 1941

"A good and faithful judge ever prefers the honorable to the expedient."

Horace, (Quintus Horatius Flaccus) (65 BC - 8 BC)

"I know you came up hard, Jake," Judge Frank Draper admonished as he addressed a youthful Jake Kilroy in the Bedford County Courthouse. "But you have been before me too many times and I have just about lost my patience with you, son."

Jake stood handcuffed in silence alongside Sheriff Leslie Abbott, directly in front of the judge's bench. He was born John Kilroy and like so many boys named John; he quickly became Jack, ultimately corrupted to Jake. He was born in Bedford in 1923, an only child of Margaret and Clyde Kilroy who were both killed in an automobile accident when Jake was nine years old. Martha Tidrick, his mother's sister, tried her best to raise him but times were tough as the Great Depression gripped America. Eventually, Jake had to be given up to the County Orphanage followed by a series of foster homes administered by the First Baptist Church of Bedford.

Jake was industrious and hard working but grew up with a huge chip on his shoulder and was quick to settle disagreements with his fists. Everyone who met him liked him at first but only had to see his hair-trigger temper once before they decided it was prudent to steer clear of him.

For a while Jake thought he might end up working in the coalmines since they seemed to be the only jobs available until he realized he was claustrophobic. He was lucky his cousin Harley Tidrick got him a part-time job in the Norfolk and Western Railway yards cleaning out boxcars, sweeping the offices and running errands. Harley had since left for the army and Jake moved up to a full time job. It seemed like he might have finally caught a break and would be able to scratch out a living when the most recent fight occurred.

It wasn't exactly a fight. He had beaten Curley Stevens senseless. Nobody in Bedford had much use for Curley. He was a mean drunk and drank more of the moonshine he made than he sold. Jake lived with Curley and his wife in foster care when Jake was thirteen but was removed to another foster home rather abruptly. Jake claimed the bruises on his face were a result of a fall he took while working around the still and though Curley didn't explain his own bruises, the inference was clear.

That incident over four years ago was not the reason Jake had recently returned to the Stevens home. For a long time Curley and his wife continued to take in foster children, one at a time, each lasting no longer than a year until the latest young girl, Macie Vance. Jake had known Macie from the orphanage since they were both ten years old. She was a timid, beautiful little girl with black hair down to her waist. There was a hint of mischief in her saucer-like deep brown eyes. Young Jake instantly came to like her and eventually became extremely protective. They would often be seen walking down the dark dreary halls of the orphanage holding hands.

When she came to see Jake at the rail yard early that morning she was still visibly shaken. Macie was frightened to death of Curley Stevens.

"Did he touch you or hurt you?" Jake angrily asked.

"No Jake," she explained. "Last night he came into my bedroom after Mrs. Stevens went to sleep. I told him to leave but he just sat there, at the foot of my bed. I could smell the stink of liquor on his breath. He rambled on and on about how we could be good friends." Macie wiped a tear from her cheek. She was having a difficult time explaining this. "I really don't know what he was saying. He was rambling," she continued. "I was just too scared to pay attention."

Jake pulled her close to him and hugged her. She was still shaking in his arms. He looked at her tenderly. "Don't you worry 'cause he won't scare you no more. Go have some coffee at the diner, give me half an hour."

"What are you going to do?" she asked.

"I'm going to take care of this the only way Curley Stevens understands," he replied. "Just don't ever tell anyone you came to see me about this, okay?" She nodded quickly, wiped a sniffle with her handkerchief and headed off toward the diner. Jake stuck his head in the office door and yelled to the yard boss, "Be back in thirty minutes."

He never came back.

Mrs. Gail Stevens was dialing the sheriff's office as soon as she saw Jake walking up to the front door. By the time the sheriff arrived it was all over.

Jake crashed through the front door and went straight to the bedroom. He found Curley asleep and threw a bucket of water on him. It wasn't difficult to drag the groggy man into the front yard. As hung over as Curley was, he initially put up a credible fight. He swung his fists wildly. Jake sidestepped the long punches easily and threw jabs at Curley's eyes. He had learned long ago, when fighting a man bare-fisted, to never throw a punch at the mouth or jaw where his teeth could chew up your hands. It didn't take long before Curley's eyes were swollen shut by Jake's powerful jabs. Even though Curley was still swinging blindly, Jake had no trouble sidestepping and throwing short but hard hooks into Curley's ears further disorienting him. Sensing Curley was about to fall, Jake threw the last few punches aimed purposely to break his nose, splattering blood onto the green grass. It was a beating Curley Stevens would never forget. As Jake stood over him, hands covered in blood and oblivious to the screams of Gail Stevens, the sheriff and a deputy grabbed him by the arms and pulled him toward the police car.

"Why, Jake?" screamed a hysterical and distraught Gail Stevens. "Why?"

Jake yelled back over his shoulder as the sheriff and deputy cuffed and tucked him into the back seat of the police car. "He knows why!"

Judge Draper peered over his bi-focal glasses. The courtroom was otherwise empty except for the court reporter. It had the smell of wood polish mixed with sweat. The walls seemed to be closing in on Jake and he suddenly felt so alone. He didn't even have a lawyer.

"You are gonna' do some time, son," said Judge Draper. "But before I pass sentence, tell me, since Curley is in the hospital, was there a reason for this?"

Jake stood before the judge; head bowed concealing his angry gaze. He would not implicate Macie. He lifted his head ever so slightly. "Goes back aways," he answered.

"Goes back aways, *your honor*," barked Judge Draper.

"Yes sir, *your honor*." Jake was surprised and taken off guard.

"I figured this was bad blood simmerin' for a long time, Jake," the judge began, putting his eyeglasses down on his bench. "But that ain't no excuse. This was not self-defense. You went to the man's home and beat him stupid. I know Curley is not exactly a role model, but he has rights too."

Jake decided the judge was right. He had no defense. At least none he wanted to put forward. He would just shut his mouth and take the punishment. The silence was interminable.

"Assault and battery," continued Judge Draper, "and since you've been before my court before, carries a sentence of eighteen to twenty-four months." For the first time since he stepped into the courtroom, Jake looked directly at Judge Draper.

The judge raised his gavel, about to formalize the sentence by a stroke when he hesitated. "Or," and he waited.

Sheriff Abbott nudged Jake. "Or what?" asked Jake.

"Or what, *your honor*," responded an exasperated Judge Draper as he put the gavel down gently. He motioned to the court reporter to stop recording, clasped his hands and leaned forward. "This country will be at war soon, or haven't you noticed what's goin' on in the world. I'll make this simple. You are probably going to get drafted as soon as you get out of jail. You were probably going to get drafted anyway. The choice I'm about to give you today son is… county jail or the army."

Jake thought for a few seconds and said, "Your honor, sir. Are you saying if I go into the army I won't have to do any time in jail?"

Judge Draper took a deep breath. "Look Jake, you're a young man who's made mistakes. Your life will be much harder in the future with a criminal record. I think it's a waste for you to be in jail when your country needs you. So, go into the army and your record stays clean. Simple."

Jake felt pressured to make a fast decision but he wanted time to think it through. He looked over at Sheriff Abbott who nodded back at him. Jake needed to stall for time, to think. "How long, *your honor*, will I be in the army?"

"That is not the point, Jake," sighed Judge Draper, "The point is you stay out of jail. And we have our own National Guard company right here in Bedford. Company A of the One Hundred and sixteenth Infantry Regiment, Twenty-ninth Infantry Division. I'm sure the National Guard recruiting office down the street can arrange to take a Bedford boy into the Company. So, what will it be?"

"It's a fine regiment with a great tradition," offered Sheriff Abbott.

"I don't know anything about it, your honor. I never heard of it," Jake lied. He was stalling for time. His cousin Harley was in Able Company of the 116th Infantry Regiment.

Judge Draper let out another audible sigh. "That is the trouble with you young people these days, you have no sense of history. Let me tell you about the roots of the One Hundred and sixteenth Infantry Regiment. Their nickname is the 'Stonewallers'. Know why?" Judge Draper didn't wait for an answer. "Even though they trace their roots back to Seventeen-sixty, truth be known, what the boys are really proud of is the fact that the Second Virginia was the senior regiment in Stonewall Jackson's First Virginia Brigade of the Army of Northern Virginia. At First Manassas, the Yankees called it Bull Run, the brigade held firm like a stone wall. That is how Stonewall Jackson got his name and how the One Hundred and sixteenth Infantry Regiment, direct descendents of the Second Virginia, became known as the Stonewallers. The regiment has twelve rifle companies all over Virginia and Able Company is made up of mostly Bedford boys, so you'll be serving with some of your friends, I'm sure."

Jake didn't have any friends. Times were hard and many young men were either going into the service or joining the Civilian Conservation Corps. The only appeal this offer had was it kept him out of jail. Jake was far removed from the wars ravaging Europe and raging in China. He never considered enlisting when those foreign wars started and never thought much about getting drafted. And he was a little embarrassed he knew so little about the culture and history he was born to. He stood there, head bowed, mind racing, trying to make a decision.

"In fact," Draper continued, "the Twenty-ninth served with tremendous distinction in France in the Great War. It can trace all three of its infantry regiments way back to the Revolution. But here in Virginia we're partial to the Stonewallers."

Jake shuffled his feet nervously and looked back down at the floor.

"Tell you what, son," said the judge finally, "the sheriff here is gonna' walk you out the door. Down the street to the right is the recruiting office. To the left is the county jail. You got until you get out the door to decide which direction you're gonna' go."

Jake nodded and turned. Sheriff Abbott walked him to the door and out into the street. The air was cold and crisp but the sun warmed his face. They stood in silence in front of the old red brick building alongside the tall white columns that graced the entrance. "You know, Jake, the judge and me both have sons serving with the Stonewallers. That's how come he knows so much about them." Abbott turned to face Jake. "Whatever you decide to do, I'll keep an eye on Macie for you."

For the first time that day, Jake smiled slightly. Abbott had a reputation in town for being fair. Jake sensed Macie would be all right. And the prospect of spending so much time confined in a small jail cell sealed his decision. Without saying a word, he held out his hands so the sheriff could unlock his cuffs. He turned right toward the recruiting office.

Judger Draper stood by the window and watched young Jake Kilroy *join* the army. He wouldn't be the first felon the judge steered in that direction. He had been doing this same thing for years and most of those would-be criminals had decided not to squander their youth on some work gang. However, in this case he felt particularly gratified. He was taking a quick-tempered young hothead off the streets of Bedford and at the same time putting him into the fight with his country's enemies. Somehow, where Jake Kilroy was concerned, the judge felt just a little bit sorry for his country's enemies.

The next day, 3 February 1941, the 29th Infantry Division (National Guard) was activated into Federal service.

Chapter Three

The Pentagon – July 10, 1996

"The sweetest of all sounds is praise."

Xenophon (431 BC - 352 BC)

"**W**ell, sir, I have some good news and some bad news," reported Colonel Carlton Chase, United States Army Awards Branch, to General Aaron Clayton, Chairman of the Joints Chiefs of Staff. Chase sat in the general's Pentagon office. His high and tight haircut rendered his light blonde hair almost invisible. His boyish good looks were marred only slightly by his wire-rimmed glasses and his Class-A uniform was impeccable, as usual.

Colonel Chase was assigned the task of reviewing records to determine if Medals of Honor should be awarded to African-American servicemen in World War II. It was Chase who, working with a specially selected team of historians from academia, developed the evaluation procedures used to analyze World War II combat records for possible medal upgrades.

In Carlton Chase, the general found a person of integrity, high principle and great respect for military honor and tradition. It was important to the general, on many levels, that outsiders perceive the results of this review board as a fair and deserved outcome to remedy prior injustices, and not motivated by political expediency.

When Secretary of the Army Charles Radcliffe and Clayton left the President's Oval Office back in February, it took Radcliffe all of five minutes to punt this mission to the general.

"Well General, this is entirely in your sweet spot," Radcliffe began as soon as the limousine made a right turn onto Constitution Avenue. "Have your team do the same thing they did with that World War I Medal and let me know when you're done so we can schedule a follow-up meeting with the President. I'll advise the SecDef but I suspect this will be an army show, so please handle it."

Clayton pondered for a moment. He was about to explain how much more difficult and complicated this task would be when Radcliffe's cell phone rang. With a dismissive wave of the hand he slipped his phone from his inside pocket, turned his body toward his side window and began speaking.

As the limo approached the Theodore Roosevelt Bridge, Clayton could see the outline of the Iwo Jima Memorial Statue on the Virginia side of the Potomac River. It was just one of the many symbols he saw in and around Washington, D.C. every day. Those symbols silently, yet incessantly, testified to the unbroken chain of sacrifice made by generations of Americans from the Revolutionary War to Desert Storm. They represented the price paid in American blood to preserve and protect this country and defend its liberty. Honoring and remembering their dedication and sacrifice was the only way to appropriately acknowledge that great debt; a debt that could never be truly repaid. Aaron Clayton lived by that creed.

A West Point graduate and teacher at the War College, General Clayton was both a warrior and an ardent student of military history. Three tours in Vietnam, a Silver Star for gallantry and two Purple Hearts later he found himself on a fast promotion track. It had all happened so fast, one successful command after another, promotion after promotion when suddenly he realized the pinnacle of his ascension as Chairman of the Joint Chiefs of Staff with four silver stars on his shoulders.

Shoulders, he thought. *Whose shoulders have I stood on to get here?*

The student and teacher in him reminded him constantly so many others paid dearly for him to be where he was. He knew military history extraordinarily well, particularly the history of the United States Army. He knew black Americans had served with distinction in every war since the Revolutionary War but more often than not their deeds had been overlooked or minimized. The Hollywood movie *Glory* brought some long deprived attention to the 54th Massachusetts Volunteer Infantry, who fought with distinction during the Civil War, but there were many other all-black units and individuals who fought bravely for this country. What the movie *Glory* did not portray, and what Clayton knew all too well, was the first Medal of Honor awarded to a black soldier was given to Sergeant William H. Carney of Company C, 54th Massachusetts, for bravery and wounds received at Fort Wagner, South Carolina in July of 1863. The movie also did not accurately portray that over 160 all black regiments, nearly 180,000 soldiers, served the Union in that bloody strife.

After the Civil War, Congress authorized the establishment of six Negro army regiments, two cavalry and four infantry, whose billets were quickly filled by Civil War veterans. The 38th, 39th, 40th and 41st Infantry Regiments served well as the nation pushed westward and encountered the hostile Native Indian tribes. These four units were eventually consolidated into the 24th and 25th Infantry Regiments.

Clayton also knew the 9th and 10th Colored Cavalry Regiments helped to open the American West and served alongside Teddy Roosevelt's Rough Riders in Cuba during the Spanish American War. The 10th fought courageously in the battle of Las Guasimas and both regiments were with the Rough Riders in their famous charge up San Juan Hill a few days later. However, the contemporary media as well as the War Department ignored their accomplishments. These black units were never adequately recognized for their contributions nor were they particularly well known anywhere outside of military circles.

Clayton authored a paper for the War College detailing how the 369th Infantry

Regiment of the 93rd Division established an outstanding fighting reputation in World War I. He was surprised how few knew of its existence.

In the Second World War, the 99th Fighter Squadron and the 332nd Fighter Group, known as "The Tuskegee Airmen", were given some recognition by a made-for-TV movie but the 92nd Infantry Division, "The Buffalo Soldiers", and the superbly trained 761st Tank Battalion, "The Black Panthers", remained virtually unknown to the American public. Clayton believed these units held the best possibilities for the Medal of Honor. From September 1944 until the end of the War in May 1945, the 92nd was in continuous combat as part of the IV Corps of the Fifth United States Army in Italy. The 761st Black Panthers fought with great distinction while attached to the 26th Infantry Division, "The Yankee Division", in General George S. Patton's Third United States Army. In combat for 183 consecutive days, the Black Panthers participated in the relief of Bastogne in the "Battle of the Bulge" and was eventually awarded a Presidential Unit Citation. If there were to be any medal upgrades or previously overlooked awards for bravery, it would invariably come from these units or from the lesser known, almost anonymous, "5th Platoons".

Clayton considered the saga of the 5th Platoons one of the most shameful episodes in the history of the United States Army. After D-Day, as American forces pushed across France toward Germany, the casualty figures began to mount at a terrifying rate. As the number of killed, wounded and missing approached 350,000, General Dwight David Eisenhower took drastic action to replenish the depleted ranks of riflemen. Back in the United States, units not immediately scheduled to deploy to the European Theatre of Operations (ETO), were stripped of their trained cadres who were sent to front line units as replacements. Non-combatant units were combed for anyone who could shoot an M-1 rifle. Training cycles were shortened. Aviation cadets and Army Specialized Training Personnel were re-assigned and trained as infantry replacements. Any warm-blooded GI who could carry a rifle was snapped up for frontline infantry duty. Despite those efforts, the shortfall still could not be fully met.

Eisenhower was already seriously concerned about being able to field an adequate force for the final push into Germany when the Germans surprised the Allies with an offensive through the Ardennes in Belgium just before Christmas of 1944. The Battle of the Bulge yielded another 80,000 casualties. Eisenhower was now absolutely desperate for any solution to the chronic shortage of trained riflemen.

Lieutenant General John Lee was the commander of the Service of Supply troops in the ETO. He saw the hundreds of thousands of black troops under his command as a solution to the infantry shortage. He suggested some be trained as replacement riflemen. The American high command rejected his suggestion. They were not yet ready or willing to integrate the army at the individual unit level. They would, however, accept segregated platoons to augment their battle-depleted companies and regiments.

Thus the concept of the 5th Platoon was born. Under-strength combat infantry companies would receive an extra platoon of black infantrymen, led by white officers, to function as a separate unit under the company commander. Despite having to give up their stripes for this combat duty, there were over 2,200 volunteers, enough to train fifty-three rifle platoons. By March of 1945, most of them were assigned to one of eight infantry and two armored divisions.

In spite of the apprehensions of the high command, these units were readily accepted on the front lines. Most white soldiers reduced the assignment of Negro troops as reinforcements to the simple math of the battlefield; just another target for the Germans to shoot at, other than themselves.

Insofar as performance, Clayton also knew the battlefield execution of these units was essentially the same as with all-white units. Some units performed better than others. Some were better trained and better led. They spanned the performance spectrum from excellent to adequate; exactly the same as their white brothers-in-arms. There was nothing in their racial make-up or culture that made them any better or worse at bleeding or at making the enemy bleed. While the 5th Platoons represented only a fraction of the nearly one million men of color who served as drivers, stevedores and other non-combat roles, these volunteers served under fire with distinction. They did the dirty, personal job of killing the enemy. For a few months, near the end of the War in Europe, they were American combat soldiers and would forever wear the coveted Combat Infantryman's Badge (CIB).

General Clayton held this ignominious chapter in the history of the United States Army in great disdain. But not because the troops were prevented from being assigned as individual replacements; not since the Revolutionary War were black soldiers incorporated into white units. What disturbed Clayton most occurred after the fighting stopped. The 5th Platoon units were ordered disbanded. To many, this was the ultimate indignity. Even though each one had earned his CIB, they were separated from the units they fought with and returned to their prior non-combatant service units. They would not be allowed to take their earned and rightful place alongside their white brothers-in-arms and they would be denied the public recognition they earned. There were virtually no records kept of their performance. As a result, the deeds of these brave men and their heroic sacrifices were largely forgotten to history.

This little known chapter in the annals of the United States Army in World War II appalled the sensibilities of General Clayton. The inaccurate and often-exaggerated claims of some contemporary black spokesmen on behalf of previously overlooked exploits of black military men bothered him as much.

As if revising history and embellishing the record somehow compensated for deserved recognition never received. Two wrongs never made a right in Clayton's mind and he held those who ignored great achievements and those who purposefully overstated them with equal contempt. He could not afford to have any exaggerations in determining the worthiness of black men to receive the Medal of Honor.

What he currently sought was a fair shake for these African-American warriors. It was the same thing every American soldier who went into harm's way expected; trustworthy leadership, fairness, and the opportunity to be judged solely by his actions under fire.

Radcliffe didn't get off his cell phone until they were both well inside the Pentagon and heading toward their respective offices. It was clear General Clayton had the ball on this project. Balancing the objective fairness of any action with the public relations benefit was paramount. Honoring the duty and sacrifice of some, without disrespecting or diminishing the sacrifice of others would be the challenge. He would have the unique opportunity to correct past injustices. For the sake of everything he believed in he had to get this right.

Clayton was also acutely aware of other similar injustices. He was especially sensitive to the Japanese-Americans who served with distinction in World War II and the tragedy of Master Sergeant Llewellyn M. Chilson, the greatest American combat soldier who never won the Medal of Honor. He both wondered and worried if he would someday be able to correct all of these omissions but decided to deal with that later. Right now, he was faced with a particularly treacherous political high-wire act and all the pressure was squarely on him.

Especially since he himself was African-American.

"Give me the bad news first, Colonel."

Chapter Four

New York City – March 31, 1942

"When we assumed the soldier, we did not lay aside the citizen."

George Washington (1732 - 1799)

John Patrick Kilroy bounded up the steps of the Whitehall Street-Broadway subway station in New York City into a damp and dank March day. Ever since the Japanese attacked Pearl Harbor an overwhelming sense of despair had gripped the country. The War news from far-flung battlefronts was often late, heavily censored yet always bad. Americans eagerly consumed the daily newspapers and gleaned the weekly Movietone Newsreels in the theatres for the slightest tidbits of information. The steady stream of dreadful news continued through the hard, cold winter months and depressed the morale of the entire population.

Before the nation could digest the significance of the defeat at Pearl Harbor, Germany declared war on the United States. Then, after weeks of hope against all hope, the American outpost on Wake Island fell to the Japanese on Christmas Eve.

America's Allies were not faring much better. On Christmas Day, the British surrendered Hong Kong to the Japanese, followed in February by the surrender of over 100,000 British soldiers in Singapore. The civilians of Darwin, Australia were subjected to numerous air raids in February and March from Japanese carrier based bombers. The Battle of the Java Sea on 27 February was another serious defeat for the Allies as they lost ten ships including the United States heavy cruiser USS *Houston*.

On 19 February, in response to the pervasive fear and paranoia, President Franklin Delano Roosevelt signed Executive Order 9066. The order gave the United States military the authority to define certain areas of America as "exclusionary zones". The army was granted the power to relocate German and Italian-Americans from the East Coast and Japanese-American civilians from the West Coast. American soldiers began immediately relocating Japanese-Americans, most of whom were citizens, to camps as far away as Texas and Arkansas. Their numbers would eventually swell to over 120,000 detainees. In addition, 11,000 German-Americans and 3,000 Italian-Americans were incarcerated under this order. Irrational fear gripped the country.

By early March, the Dutch East Indies also surrendered to the Japanese and the American and Filipino forces in the Philippines were trapped on the Bataan Peninsula. With a severely depleted Pacific fleet there would be no effort to reinforce or resupply the Philippines. The ragtag army of Filipinos and Americans were expendable and had no hope of relief or reinforcement. Annihilation or surrender was imminent. Their commander, General Douglas MacArthur, was evacuated to Australia in early March by order of the President. His widely published promise of "I Shall Return" seemed both boastful and hollow.

John Patrick Kilroy remained well informed on world events. As each bastion fell, most Americans would run to their maps to find out where these places were and how close they were to the United States. They were far away places, to be sure, but creeping ever closer and closer. John already knew where most of them were.

The early months of America's entry into the global conflict were both depressing and frightful. These were the black and gray days of the War, typified by this gloomy, chilling Tuesday in lower Manhattan.

John was a handsome young man with brown hair and dark brown eyes. He was called Johnny at the City College of New York (CCNY) where he was a student. When the Japanese attacked Pearl Harbor, he was twenty years old and in the middle of his third year of college. Immediately after the attack, the Burke-Wadsworth Selective Service Act, the first peacetime draft in American history, was amended by Congress to make all men twenty through thirty-seven eligible for the draft. Johnny registered and passed his physical. At six-foot tall, 175 pounds, he was in better-than-average physical condition. He was a brilliant student and followed world affairs closely but was conflicted about joining the service because he was married. However, the stigma of not serving, of being considered a draft-dodger, was more humiliating than most young men could endure.

While he discussed his options with his wife, Rose, he received his draft notice in the mail. Being a street-wise New York City kid, he considered enlisting to assure his pick for branch of service. His college education may even qualify him for some military specialties. In any event, he was told by friends and relatives alike to avoid the infantry. That was the plan.

The Induction Center at 39 Whitehall Street was a fortress-like stone building on the corner of Broadway and Whitehall near the southern tip of Manhattan. With his brown envelope containing his induction orders in hand, he joined a stream of other young men as they entered the building. The main staircase was wide and ascended through the center of the structure. Officers and enlisted men in uniform from every branch of the service were hurrying busily about. Military posters adorned some of the walls. One poster in particular grabbed his attention and he stopped on a landing to observe it more closely. At the top center of the poster was a rendition of Columbia, a beautiful young woman wearing white silk garb enshrouded by an American flag. She held her hands out above seven soldiers at attention. There was a laurel wreath in one of her hands. The seven soldiers in echelon were all bearing rifles. They stood shoulder to shoulder, each one representing a generation to have fought a war in defense of America. At the far end was a Revolutionary War soldier, followed by one from the War of 1812, The Mexican-American War, The Civil War, The Spanish-American War, World War I and finally World War II. Beneath the soldiers was a banner that read:

THE UNITED STATES ARMY
THEN - NOW - FOREVER

He contemplated the sign. *We certainly have been in a lot of wars in our history. Why don't they just leave us alone?*

When he reached the fourth floor he queued up in line behind the main information desk. The army clerk behind the desk, a corporal, was directing each man to a different floor or room based on the information in his folder. The line moved quickly and as he approached the desk he stepped out of line, walked over to a water fountain and bent to take a drink.

"Back in line!" The voice startled him. He felt a twinge in his stomach, stood up and turned to see a Marine gunnery sergeant towering over him.

"Hey, I'm not in the service yet so I don't have to take orders from you," Johnny replied and instantly realized by the look on the Marine's face he said the wrong thing.

"Oh, a wise-ass? We'll see, you little piss-ant son of a bitch." The sergeant turned and walked to the information desk. He leaned over to the clerk, whispered something in his ear while pointing to Johnny. The clerk looked up, nodded and wrote something down.

The sergeant walked back to Johnny. "You'll be a puke boot by noon, wise-ass." The voice was low but strained. His eyes were bulging and the veins were popping in his neck. "And you can travel to Parris Island on the same train with me 'cause I just happen to be leaving for there later today. Your sorry ass is all mine!"

Johnny tried to keep a straight face but felt his knees buckle just slightly. He didn't reply.

"Welcome to the Marines. And don't try to join the navy today, cupcake. I'll make sure they don't take you." The sergeant had his hands on his hips and moved to within inches of Johnny's face. "You can get back in line at your convenience, sweetheart. I got all day. Semper Fi." The gunnery sergeant turned and walked away.

Johnny took a deep breath and exhaled slowly. So much for staying out of the infantry!

Chapter Five

Georgetown – August 10, 1996

"Footfalls echo in the memory,
down the passage which we did not take,
towards the door we never opened."

T.S. Eliot (1888 - 1965)

*E*nter mother's maiden name.

He had never thought so often about his mother until he started establishing accounts on the Internet. It seemed like each time he filled out an application online, he was asked for this information as a security question. John Patrick Kilroy Jr. had established a small number of accounts using this new technology and had even purchased a few items last Christmas. The more he used it, the more he liked it and the more websites he signed up for.

From the comfort of his Georgetown condominium, he typed in S-C-A-L-I-S-E.

Kilroy already felt guilty enough for not visiting his mother's grave as often as he should. He knew he should take some time off from his job as a reporter for the *Washington Times* and make the trip to Mount Olivet Cemetery in Queens. If he didn't do it nobody else would. He was an only child. His mother had no siblings. His father abandoned them years before and they had no contact since.

He finished establishing an account on a new website called *eBay*, signed off his PC and leaned back in his chair. Staring at the ceiling he swiveled around and looked again at the cardboard box he had carefully placed on the top shelf of his floor-to-ceiling bookcase. It was hard to believe his mother was actually gone for an entire year. When he first received this package from her a week before she passed away, he immediately opened the letter attached to it. As soon as he finished reading it he dialed her number.

"Hi Mom, it's me."

"Hello J.P. How's my darling boy?" He picked up the nickname early in life. It made it easier to distinguish between the two 'Johns' in the Kilroy household.

"I'm sorry I haven't been up to see you, Mom." He was more than just sorry. He had only been up to see her once since she was diagnosed. Between his job and his own personal problems, he just couldn't get away. At least that is what he told himself. "But…"

"It's all right son," she interrupted before he could make his excuses. "They're very attentive here at the facility and I'm comfortable. No worries." She was smiling through the pain. He could hear it in her voice.

"That's good, Mom. Look, I got your package and I read the letter and I just wanted to say…"

She didn't let him finish. "Did you call your father?"

"No Mom, I just got the package today. I read the letter but I didn't open the box yet."

"J.P., listen to me." He sensed the urgency in her voice. "You need to promise me after you open the box you'll go to your father and get this family business out in the open."

"Ma!" J.P. complained. "He left us thirty years ago. I have no use for him. For the life of me I don't understand why you don't hate him as much as I do." J.P. knew why. His mother was a saint and she was all about love and forgiveness, even to the man who abandoned them so abruptly so long ago.

"Son, listen to me," she replied. "First of all, I don't have room in my heart for hate, especially now." She was referring to her terminal cancer. "But more importantly, there cannot be family secrets which span generations. Some things should not remain unknown or misunderstood for so long. You *must* speak to your father. Promise me."

John sighed. "Why don't *you* just tell me?"

"Perhaps I should. But you really need to talk to your dad."

"All right, Mom. I'll find out where he is and I'll contact him."

"He's in Bedford, Virginia. Promise?"

"Yes, of course. I promise."

"Very good. One more thing. Can you get up to see me? Soon? We'll talk. Maybe I can share some things with you. Make it easier when you talk to your father."

"Sure Mom, I'll be up this weekend."

J.P. didn't visit his mother that weekend and he never spoke to her again. She died the following week. He was beset with a fair amount of guilt, but his own worries and challenges eventually reclaimed his attention and his life returned to a semblance of normalcy. This Internet thing and the often requested *mother's maiden name* immediately brought him back to those precious last few days. He couldn't help but recall his guilt at not seeing her before she died and at not visiting her grave often enough. It was also a merciless reminder to him that he never even tried to contact his father.

J.P. reached to the top shelf and slid the box off into his hands. The envelope was attached under the strings that tied the box closed. Inside the envelope were two photographs and a letter. Both photos were black and white, dog-eared and faded. One was of two American soldiers. Both were smiling broadly, one wore a helmet at a jaunty angle with the signature paratrooper chinstrap dangling loosely. The other was holding his helmet under his arm. Each had a hand on the other's shoulder. They were standing in front of a tent in a desert. The helmeted soldier on the left appeared slightly taller. He was holding an M-1 Garand rifle. The other trooper had a Browning Automatic Rifle, also known as a B-A-R, slung over his shoulder.

Both young men had similar dark hair and facial features but they were standing far enough away from the camera to render specific details somewhat inscrutable. J.P. could not tell which one was his father. Neatly written on the back of the picture was, "Jake and I, Oujda, June 1943". Every time he looked at this picture he wondered, *where the hell is Oujda?*

The other picture was of two soldiers standing on either side of his mother. He recognized his father but not the other soldier. There was a familiar looking bridge in the background. On the reverse side in faded blue ink was scrawled, "Jake, Johnny and me, September 1943".

J.P. read the short letter again for what had to be the fiftieth time. It was obvious his mother had written it, but it raised more questions than it answered. Despite his ambivalent behavior, he knew what she wanted him to do.

What was it he told her? *I'll find out where he is and I'll contact him.* He never did it. Then, of course, there was that other reason why he dreaded confronting his father.

Chapter Six

New York City – March 31, 1942

"The real man smiles in trouble, gathers strength from distress,
and grows brave by reflection."

Thomas Paine (1737 - 1808)

Johnny Kilroy looked in the mirror in the second floor men's bathroom of the Armed Forces Induction Center in New York City. He repeatedly wet his hands with cold water and massaged his reddened face and back of his neck. He had smart-mouthed a gunnery sergeant and was about to be inducted into the United States Marine Corps.

He stepped outside the bathroom into the hallway and sat down on a thick, sturdy wooden bench along the wall. He needed a moment to collect himself and clear his head. The temptation to walk out the door and take the subway back to his apartment in Washington Heights was overwhelming. The physical act would be easy. Just walk out the door, down into the subway and take the train to his apartment on 165th Street and Fort Washington Avenue directly across from Columbia Presbyterian Hospital. He could be home in thirty minutes. As much as he wanted to stay out of the Marines, however, he could never willfully avoid serving his country in her time of need. But at that moment, the comfort of home was beckoning him.

Johnny grew up in "The Heights". He was raised in a working class family of Irish immigrants from County Cavan, Ireland. His father held jobs as a bricklayer and a laborer while his mother worked for a doctor cleaning his office and house. Johnny helped by working a newspaper route after school.

Although the family struggled to make ends meet during the Great Depression, Johnny always felt well taken care of. His parents placed great emphasis on education and he was conditioned at an early age to attend college.

The neighborhood was as close-knit as it was diverse. The east side of Broadway, known as the "shanty" side, was a mixture of ethnic groups which included Irish, Italian, German, Eastern European and small but growing Hispanic and Black populations. All shared the same problems and challenges of survival and the same hopes and dreams of a better life for their children. Shared activities strengthened the already strong sense of community. Saturday afternoons were spent in the local movie theatres where a nickel would buy two B-Western movies, twenty-five cartoons and a cliffhanger serial which kept the kids coming back week after week. Among Johnny's favorites were the *Buck Rogers* and *Flash Gordon* serials with Buster Crabbe. It was at one of these Saturday matinees he met Rose Scalise.

The west side of Broadway was an affluent middle-class Jewish community. Johnny's mother often referred to it as the "lace" side of the tracks. Many of the residents on the "shanty" side aspired to someday move to the "lace" side. Someday.

The Heights was a thriving, bustling community. On any given day, trucks could be seen delivering coal on shiny chutes into the basements of the tenement buildings. Vendors in horse-drawn wagons flocked the crowded streets selling ice, vegetables and sharpening scissors and knives. The sounds of children playing were ever-present. It was a neighborhood where people watched out for each other and everyone felt safe.

Johnny's parents were not thrilled when he married her but they eventually accepted it. In time they actually became quite fond of Rose even though she was of Italian decent at a time when Irish-Italian marriages were frowned upon. When his parents moved to New Jersey, Johnny and Rose took over their apartment. There they began their lives in earnest. Rose worked as a nurse's aide at Columbia Presbyterian Hospital and Johnny attended CCNY while working part-time as a taxi cab driver. They were planning to start a family when he graduated. Like so many others, their plans went to hell when the Japanese attacked Pearl Harbor.

Johnny and Rose often discussed the possibility of him joining the military. He gave the Army Air Corps serious consideration but Rose was not keen on him flying. To most, the navy seemed like a reasonable choice, but Johnny was prone to getting seasick and was not a good swimmer. Besides, if he were going to serve on ships, the Merchant Marine paid much better and he would be assured of getting back home to New York about every six to eight months. The army seemed like the logical choice. If only he could get into a specialty that took advantage of his intellect. They probably didn't need a history major but he was conversant in French, fluent in Italian and could get by in German. Languages came easy to him because of his photographic memory. He was hopeful he might leverage those skills into a relevant military occupational specialty.

They discussed, contemplated and mulled over all these questions until finally time ran out. The orders for a pre-induction physical were followed by orders for induction by only a few months. And here he was, induction letter in hand and just a few minutes away from being impressed into the United States Marines.

As he sat on the bench, hunched over with his elbows on his knees, his hands on his temples and staring at the floor, a pair of boots stepped into his line of sight. Olive drab military trousers were tucked up into the boots, which were the shiniest he had ever seen. Johnny sat back to look up at an army officer standing above him. He was immediately impressed by the stature of the soldier. He was well over six feet tall with wide shoulders and a broad muscular chest. Johnny noticed the thick neck of a football player and the single silver bar of a first lieutenant on his collar.

"I overheard your little chat with the sergeant," said the officer. "Maybe I can help."

Johnny was about to stand up when the officer sat down beside him. "I can get you into the army."

"What?" Johnny was surprised by this unexpected turn of events. "How can you?"

"My name is Lieutenant Wolff, and I have priority here," he replied. "Just sign this form and I'll walk you up to the desk and you'll be inducted into the army. Just like that!" The lieutenant snapped his fingers and smiled.

"What am I signing?" asked Johnny.

"It doesn't matter, you'll be out of the Marines," replied Wolff holding out a piece of paper. "Just sign it."

Johnny hesitated for a moment. "I just need to know what I'm getting into. If you wouldn't mind taking a minute to explain, I'd appreciate it."

Wolff let out an impatient sigh. "I'm a recruiter for Army Airborne Command. My job is to recruit volunteers for the paratroopers." Wolff pointed to the jump wings pinned above his pocket. "The reason I can get you into the army is simple. Volunteers for the airborne have priority over every other branch. The reason I can't spend all day answering your questions is I'm about to leave New York for my next recruiting assignment." Wolff glanced at his watch. "But I have about five minutes so you have that much time to decide. Even though it really doesn't matter."

"Thanks, Lieutenant," Johnny replied. "I read an article in *LIFE Magazine* about this experimental outfit of parachutists. I'm not so sure I want to jump out of a plane and I'm pretty damn sure I don't want to be in the infantry so why would I sign up?"

"As I said, it doesn't matter but let me tell you a few reasons why this is a good deal for you." Wolff again glanced at his watch and went into abbreviated sales mode. He held up one finger. "There's jump pay. An extra fifty bucks a month." He held up two fingers. "All paratroopers are trained as combat infantrymen but we also have medics, combat engineers, signalmen and artillerymen. You seem like a smart guy so perhaps your primary job won't be as a rifleman. Finally," he held up three fingers, "I don't think you really want to go to Parris Island with that gunnery sergeant. I don't know what you said but you managed to really piss him off. You sent him into a rage in just a few seconds. I think he hates your guts." Wolff smiled and held out the form.

"What's in this for you?" Johnny asked.

"I told you, I'm a recruiter. I have a quota."

Johnny had to think quickly. If he did nothing he was sure to be drafted into the Marines. That meant he would be a rifleman for sure. If he signed the form and volunteered for this new airborne outfit, there seemed to be some slight chance he might do something other than just haul a rifle around. However, if he had to become a rifleman, he might as well take the extra pay. The additional money would help in supporting Rose and justifying the decision to her. Finally, Lieutenant Wolff was right. That sergeant definitely hated his guts.

"Let's do it," he said and took the form and scribbled his signature. Both men got up and walked up the stairs to the fourth floor. The line was still queued up in front of the main desk and the gunnery sergeant was standing a short distance away.

Johnny stopped at the end of the line but Wolff grabbed his arm and led him to the front. "I told you son, I have priority."

Lieutenant Wolff took the brown envelope with Johnny's orders and the form he just signed and placed it on the desk in front of the army clerk. "Yes, sir," the corporal began collating, stapling and stamping the various forms.

The sergeant glared at both of them. "Sorry, Gunny," smiled Wolff. "This one's mine! Better luck next time."

The clerk handed the forms back to Johnny. "Right through there," he pointed to a doorway. Johnny took the papers, avoiding the eyes of the sergeant and walked toward the door.

"Thank you," Johnny whispered. "But just one more question before you go?" Wolff nodded. "When you asked me to sign the form, you said a number of times, 'it doesn't matter'. What did you mean?"

Wolff hesitated for a moment. He put his hand on Johnny's shoulder and leaned over so only Johnny could hear his answer. "The paratroopers are an elite and a very selective outfit."

"And?" Johnny asked.

"And *you* won't make it."

Chapter Seven

The Pentagon – September 23, 1996

"It is not the titles that honor men, but men that honor titles."

Niccolo Machiavelli (1469 - 1527), *Discourses*, 1517

Colonel Carlton Chase arrived in the 1E801 Conference Complex, Room 3, in the Pentagon's outermost E-Ring a good fifteen minutes before the scheduled start of the meeting. Arriving early gave him the opportunity to make and place the seating name cards in the configuration of his choice. It always amazed him how people, regardless of their position or rank, went immediately to the seat with their name card, usually without protest.

After placing his presentation foils and a stack of handouts at the front end of the rectangular polished oak wood conference table, he switched on the overhead projector. Nothing! He fished a spare bulb out of his uniform pocket, flipped over the projector and replaced the bulb.

As he worked on the projector, Cynthia Powers walked into the conference room. She was a civilian who worked in the Public Affairs Office of the U.S. Army Military District of Washington. She was currently assigned to the Chairman of the Joint Chiefs. Colonel Chase looked up at her and smiled, then lowered his head to continue what he was doing. Cynthia was an extremely competent, attractive brunette with a killer body.

"Hi, Colonel," she began. "Looks like we're a bit early."

"Hello Cynthia," he answered without lifting his head. "Good thing, too. Darn bulb burned out." He turned the projector to its upright position and flipped on the switch. It worked.

He reached for the name cards and marker. "Where would you like to sit?"

"Next to General Clayton," she smiled. "Where is he sitting?"

"I'll sit him next to you. He'll probably have a lot of takeaways for you, anyway." He handed her a neatly printed tent card with her name on it.

"Who's coming to this meeting?" she asked.

"General Clayton, Secretary Radcliffe and his aide Francis Blossom." He was writing out the other name cards as he spoke. He handed her the name cards and indicated where he wanted them placed. Chase just finished placing a thick handout in front of each seat as General Aaron Clayton walked into the room.

"Good morning, everyone," he greeted pleasantly, glanced at the name cards and slid into his seat at the head of the conference table. "Are we ready, Colonel?"

"Yes, sir. We'll start as soon as the Secretary arrives."

"He was right behind me in the hallway." Just then Secretary Radcliffe walked into the room with Francis Blossom in tow. Chase smiled to himself as they both went immediately to their assigned seats.

After greetings were exchanged, Chase stood up on one side of the screen. He reached for the wall switch and lowered the room lights. With his wire-rimmed glasses and intelligent deep-set gray eyes, he easily assumed a professorial persona. The room suddenly seemed smaller and more confining with two of the most powerful men in the Department of Defense sitting at the table. He took a deep breath to help shake off the butterflies. He moved to the side of the table that would allow an unobstructed view for Secretary Radcliffe, thereby partially blocking the view of Francis Blossom. Chase switched on the overhead projector, which already held the title page of the presentation in focus.

World War II Medal of Honor Reevaluation
Analysis and Recommendations

"The objective of this meeting," began Chase looking directly at Radcliffe, "is to secure your approval for our recommendations. Let's get right to the bottom line. After six months of intensive review and analysis by my team, we recommend awarding Medals of Honor to seven African-Americans who served in our Armed Forces in World War II."

"Is that all?" interrupted Blossom. "Why so few? How many were considered? How did you come to these conclusions?" The meeting was only a few seconds old and Blossom was already disrupting it, as was his reputation. Chase remained calm.

"Those questions will be answered during the course of the presentation and all the background material to support the conclusions are in your handout packets," answered Chase. He paused for a moment while Blossom began flipping through his handout.

Radcliffe reached across the table. "Not now, Francis." Radcliffe turned to Chase. "I have only one question at this time, Colonel, if I may. Are any of these gentlemen still alive?"

"Yes, sir. One of the men is presently still living." Chase had the feeling he had just answered the only question of importance to Radcliffe. "However, I do believe it's important that you understand and agree with how this process unfolded and how we reached the conclusions we came to, before you endorse our findings."

"I agree. Please proceed." Radcliffe was not a novice to politics and realized he may someday have to explain his decision at a press conference or a Sunday morning news program.

"Let me begin with a brief history of the Medal for background, then I'll discuss the process and finally the results and recommendations." Chase flipped to the next foil. "I'll move quickly so please stop me if you have any questions." Chase paused for a moment and then continued. "The Medal of Honor has a somewhat checkered history and endured many growing pains before it became the revered sacred icon it is today. Only a little more than thirty-four hundred were ever awarded and only about one hundred and fifty recipients are still alive. The Medal of Honor was first authorized by Congress and approved by President Lincoln in 1862 during the Civil War. Up until that time, there were no medals or awards in existence to recognize individual military gallantry, to speak of."

"None at all?" asked Powers.

"You're a good straight man, Cynthia," Chase said as he slipped another foil onto the projector. "During the Revolutionary War, General Washington authorized the Badge of Military Merit in 1782. It was intended to recognize the lower ranks for acts of unusual gallantry. All recipients were permitted to wear the badge over their left breast. The actual badge device was a cloth or silk figure of a purple heart. Only three were awarded near the waning days of the Revolution and the Badge of Merit fell into disuse and was never awarded again until 1932. At that time the award was revived and redefined by then Chief of Staff General Douglas MacArthur into what we know today as the Purple Heart." Chase changed the foil.

"The Certificate of Merit was introduced by Congress for enlisted men during the Mexican-American War of 1847," Chase continued. "There was no badge or other medal device to be worn, just a certificate and an extra two dollars a month in pay. This award was unpopular because it was abused, misused and eventually discredited and also fell into disuse."

"Question," Cynthia called out. "Why no medals?"

"It appears the military at that time considered medals to be associated with European nobility and those symbols of aristocracy had no place in a new democracy," answered Chase. "As we will see, all that changed in the Civil War." He flipped another foil.

"First the navy, then the army had bills introduced in Congress for the creation of a Medal of Honor. The intent was to inspire men to their duty. The Medal was for both enlisted ranks and officers who distinguished themselves by 'gallantry in action' and other soldier-like qualities. Congress approved the bills and President Lincoln signed them on 12 July 1862. The Medal of Honor quickly became very popular and a victim of its own success, as we shall see in a moment." Chase paused. "Questions?"

Francis Blossom was the first to speak. "This is all very interesting, Colonel, but I don't see how this is pertinent to the issue at hand. We didn't attend this meeting for a history lesson." Blossom glanced furtively at his boss for some sign of approval.

What a worm, thought Chase but before he could respond General Clayton replied to the comment speaking directly to Secretary Radcliffe. "Sir, it will become clear in a moment how this background supports the efforts of this Review Board and more importantly, the credibility of their recommendations."

Radcliffe nodded and gestured for Chase to continue and he positioned the next foil. "Today," he began, "the criteria for winning the Medal of Honor are extraordinarily high. One must demonstrate conspicuous gallantry that places his or her life at great risk. Most present-day recipients do not survive the action for which they were recognized. You may not know this but a person *cannot* receive this award for acting under orders. In the beginning it was not exactly this way.

"There were no specific criteria for the early awards. Since it was the only medal available, it was conferred for good as well as great accomplishments. Medals were awarded en masse to whole units for simply extending their enlistments as well as for acts of great courage. Initially about twenty-five hundred Medals were awarded in the Civil War alone. There was such a wide disparity in the justification for the Medal in the first forty years that the recipients formed the Medal of Honor Legion in 1890 to protect the integrity of the Medal. They campaigned Congress for more stringent guidelines, received them and then an extraordinary thing happened."

"And that was?" Blossom interjected as Chase changed foils. "That was, Mister Blossom," Chase responded, "the Purge of 1916. With the passage of Section 122 of the National Defense Act of 1916, a board of five retired generals was convened to review every Medal of Honor previously awarded under the new, stricter requirements. They reviewed the citations without knowing the individual names and what do you think they did?"

"No clue," answered Blossom. Chase smiled to himself. *You never have a damn clue, Francis.* "They revoked nine hundred and ten Medals previously awarded. That caused quite a stir at the time but it was done nevertheless. On 9 July 1918, Congress passed an act that stated..." Chase pointed to the screen.

> *...the President is authorized to present, in the name*
> *of Congress, a Medal of Honor only to each person*
> *who, while an officer or enlisted man, in action*
> *involving actual conflict with the enemy,*
> *distinguish himself conspicuously by gallantry*
> *and intrepidity at the risk of his life*
> *above and beyond the call of duty.*

"This is the criteria for the Medal of Honor that exists today," continued Chase. "I might point out this act also established a *precedent*. That precedent was that a duly authorized panel could change the criteria. Now, fast forward to the present time."

Radcliffe shifted slightly in his chair. His body language indicated he was suddenly much more interested in this part of the presentation.

Chase placed the next foil on the projector. "It's the late 1980s and two Congressmen, one a black Democrat from Texas and the other a white Republican from New York, petition the Secretary of the Army to investigate the lack of Medals of Honor for African-American soldiers in World War I and World War II. This was a sensitive issue. No one wanted to appear arbitrary or unfair to either African-Americans or to the high standards of the Medal. Upon investigation, it was discovered that four African-American soldiers had been recommended for the Medal of Honor in World War I. Three of the awards were processed, reviewed and downgraded to a Distinguish Service Cross, the second highest military honor. This in itself is not unusual; many DSCs start out as Medal of Honor requests. But given the time period and a segregated military, these decisions remain controversial."

"You said *three* of the recommendations were downgraded to Distinguish Service Crosses. What about the fourth?" asked Blossom, now more interested.

"The Department of the Army dispatched a team to France to review the circumstances of that recommendation for Corporal Freddie Stowers. He served with the Three hundred seventy-first Infantry Regiment which was attached to the French Hundred and fifty-seventh Infantry Division."

"And the result?" asked Blossom again.

General Clayton interjected. "The Army Decorations Board approved the award and Corporal Freddie Stowers was awarded the Medal of Honor in the East Room of the White House by President Bush on 24 April 1991. The Medal was presented to his two surviving sisters. He was killed in the action for which he was recognized. The citation is truly extraordinary. You should read it. It's in your package." Clayton pointed to the handout. "Also, there's a street and an elementary school in Fort Benning named after Corporal Stowers," he added with just a tinge of pride in his voice. "Sorry for the interruption, Colonel. Please continue."

"Which gets us to the current issue," Chase continued, "the absence of Medals of Honor for World War II African-American soldiers. The previous Secretary started down this road in 1993. He wanted an independent investigation and a fair review process so he recruited some academics and historians from Shaw University in Raleigh, North Carolina and teamed them up with some combat veterans. We'll call them the *Process Team*. The first rule they established was any solution had to follow *established precedent*. That way there could be no accusations the military made up new rules that were custom-designed for just this situation. The second rule was to find that precedent. They found two." Chase paused a moment to heighten the curiosity, changed the foil and continued.

"The first precedent was not at all well known. After the First World War, General Pershing was deeply disturbed only four Medals of Honor were awarded primarily because of the slow moving military bureaucracy. So he ordered an immediate review of all Distinguish Service Awards and seventy-eight were subsequently upgraded to Medal of Honor awards."

"So, most of the Congressional Medals of Honor awarded in the First World War were based on an after the fact review of DSCs?" asked Blossom.

Chase stared directly at Blossom. Now he would have some fun. "For the sake of accuracy, Mister Blossom, the correct and appropriate title is simply 'Medal of Honor'. There is no *Congressional* before it even though it is awarded by the President in the name of Congress." Chase smiled to himself. He loved to tweak Blossom.

"Of course. I knew that. Slip of the tongue," responded Blossom as he glanced over to his boss with a sheepish grin.

Chase continued. "The second precedent turned out to be the most relevant and more important one. In 1943, after the Mediterranean campaign, General Eisenhower noticed there were relatively few Medals of Honor awarded to his soldiers, so he ordered a review. Subsequently four DSCs were upgraded to Medals of Honor. The Process Team concluded if the army could review awards for possible upgrades based on geographical imbalance they certainly could review awards for administrative or racial imbalance. These are our two precedents. Now we had to develop fair review procedures and the Process Team recommended the 'double blind' approach."

"Would you explain that approach, Colonel?" asked General Clayton.

"Certainly sir, I have a foil here somewhere." Chase fished through his pile until he came up with the correct foil.

"Our Review Board consisted of four senior army officers and one enlisted man. Three white, two black. All combat veterans. One was a Medal of Honor recipient." Chase used the pointer for the first time as he discussed each bullet on the foil. "They were given twenty-one citations to review. The names, locations and unit designations were carefully disguised and not disclosed. Ten of the citations were from previous Medal of Honor winners and ten were from lesser awards presented to African-American servicemen. The last one was entirely new. We told the Review Board to evaluate the citations and unanimously agree on which ones deserved the Medal of Honor. They had no idea which ones were already awarded and which ones were for lesser awards…which, by the way, included nine Distinguished Service Crosses and one Silver Star."

Chase changed a foil. "Here are the results. First, the Review Board recommended all ten who had previously been awarded the Medal. We were very pleased with that outcome. In addition, they recommended the Medal for six of the ten black soldiers who had been originally put in for lesser awards. Of these six men, three died in the action for which they received the award and the remaining three have subsequently passed away. He looked directly at

Radcliffe. "Obviously, sir, we concur with these findings of the Review Board and are soliciting your approval."

"Certainly, of course I approve," answered Radcliffe, "But if I'm not mistaken, at the start of the meeting you mentioned seven awards including one living recipient. Your math doesn't add up. What am I missing?"

"Of course, I apologize sir. Let me explain," replied Chase. "Six of the ten are upgrades from lesser awards. The seventh, and only living recipient comes from a separate review of an after-action investigation and report for which no commendation was ever originally sought. This seventh award was a result of the letter the President gave to you back in February."

Radcliffe quickly swiveled his chair and faced General Clayton. "Aaron, I thought you said the claim in that letter was not supported by the historical facts."

"The letter contained many of the right facts, sir, but in the wrong sequence," Clayton responded. "The soldier involved did not become part of the Eighty-second Airborne until some time *after* the action at Bastogne for which he won the Medal. At the time of the action, he was a Red Ball driver, a support services soldier. His name is Lincoln Abraham and his citation is also in your package."

"Was he put in for any medal?" asked Radcliffe.

"No," answered the general.

"Since there was no original citation or any award, it was extremely difficult to track down the facts," offered Chase, "but we found a sufficient number of eyewitnesses to verify this action. It turned out to be one of the most extraordinary acts of courage to save others in the entire War. It also has a bit of an unexpected twist to it."

"And that is?" asked Radcliffe.

"Well, there was a white soldier with him," answered Chase.

Radcliffe contemplated this bit of unexpected news for a moment and asked, "So, they will both be receiving Medals of Honor?"

"That is our recommendation, sir. The Review Board approved the Medal based on the description of the action, not on who or how many were involved in it," answered Chase. "That makes a total of eight Medals of Honor to be awarded, seven to black soldiers, of which only one is alive."

"Is there a precedent for awarding two Medals of Honor for the same action?" asked Blossom.

"I'm afraid so, Francis," answered Chase. "Somalia, 1993. Sergeants Gordon and Shugart." He was referring to the two Delta Force soldiers who volunteered to protect the crew of a downed Blackhawk helicopter and were killed in the effort. Many Americans still shuddered at the images of the two Special Forces soldiers' bodies being dragged through the streets of Mogadishu.

"Right. Of course," said Blossom.

"Aaron, I'm not sure this is what the President had in mind when he handed us that letter," said Radcliffe to General Clayton. Radcliffe was thinking of the photo op and wondered if the presence of a white soldier among the black recipients would somehow dilute the intent of the ceremony.

"I'm sure it wasn't," answered the general. "It surprised us too. But, if it's any consolation, the white soldier, John Kilroy is his name, recently passed away."

"I'm sorry to hear that," feigned Radcliffe. "So we'll have only one living recipient, this Lincoln Abraham fellow, at the awards ceremony and seven other posthumous awards." Radcliffe contemplated that prospect for a moment. "I think the President will be pleased, especially since you acted positively on the letter from Congressman Williams." Radcliffe looked over to Francis Blossom. "Comments, questions, Francis?"

"Do we have a date for a formal presentation ceremony?" asked Blossom.

"We have a hold for 13 January pending approval," Chase nodded toward Radcliffe. "We have a lot to do between now and then. Notification of the recipients and the invitations to the surviving relatives."

"Sounds like you have all the bases covered Colonel," said Radcliffe. He turned to General Clayton. "This is a fine piece of work. Please pass along my appreciation to your team. I'll notify the SecDef and I believe the President will also be extremely pleased."

"Thank you, sir," replied Clayton. "We feel good about the credibility of these results."

Radcliffe turned to Colonel Chase and asked, "What do we have to do to formally authorize and approve these awards, Colonel?"

"Mister Secretary, yours is the final approval." Chase placed a stack of approval forms in front of the Secretary of the Army and pointed to the signature line. "Right here, sir."

Radcliffe began signing the first of eight forms. He muttered, "What's today's date?"

Blossom answered. "September twenty-third."

Chapter Eight

Fort Jackson, South Carolina - April 1, 1942

"A decent boldness ever meets with friends."

Homer, *The Odyssey*, c. 800 BC

Johnny Kilroy wondered exactly how he wound up in the middle of an army barracks in South Carolina surrounded by a group of crazed Alabamans who were about to beat the crap out of him. Was this some cruel April fool's prank or were they serious about doing him grave bodily harm?

When he left the Induction Center in New York City a few days before, the United States Army gave him subway fare, a meal voucher and a train ticket. With a small group of other young men from New York, he made his way by subway to New York City's Penn Station to await his train to Fort Jackson, South Carolina. He was now a bona fide *GI (Government Issue),* the universal label given to every grunt who ever served in the army in World War II and after.

In a corner of the waiting room in Penn Station, he and his new found New York acquaintances discussed advice about never volunteering for anything and never acknowledging you had special skills or attended college. The Non-Commissioned Officers (NCOs) would absolutely torture anyone who appeared smarter than them.

"Try not to get noticed," was another tidbit of good advice offered by a hulk of a kid from Brooklyn named Vinny Larini. "Those sergeants will crucify you if you answer back or if they think you're a wise-ass. They're always looking for scapegoats to show us how tough they are. And those southern sergeants hate New Yorkers." Vinny had a year at Brooklyn College and Johnny took a liking to him right away. They had some things in common. Here was somebody he might be able to buddy up with.

The conversations continued until late in the afternoon when the announcement was made over the loudspeakers for their train. Like so many condemned prisoners, they morosely ambled toward their track number. Rose asked Johnny to call her so she could come down to Penn Station to say good-bye. It was a farewell Johnny could not endure and he knew it. He never called.

Once on board the train, he was directed to a cramped private compartment, called a Roomette, which served as his sleeping berth. The conductor took great pains to explain how unusual this was, that most of the inductees were assigned to bunked beds in Pullman sleeping cars. But with the shortage of rolling stock in America – steel had to be used for more important purposes – exceptions had to be made to squeeze every ounce of space from every trip. Johnny felt fortunate he didn't have to share this closet-sized room with another GI. After a few minutes, the train jerked and lurched and got underway to begin their long trip to South Carolina.

Johnny brought a small gym bag that contained his shaving kit, a few chocolate bars, soap, toothbrush and toothpaste along with two paperback books; *The Robe*, a novel by C. Lloyd Douglas and the non-fiction comedy, *See Here, Private Hargrove* by a reporter named Marion Hargrove. He had hoped to gain some insight into the military by reading about the adventures of the author regarding life in the army. Johnny always tried to gain some advantage or get an edge by simply knowing more and being better prepared than the next guy. He sat back on the bed, his back against the wall, and gazed out the window.

The train started out in darkness under Manhattan and remained so as it crossed under the Hudson River. It emerged in New Jersey to a bright setting sun perched on the distant western horizon. Johnny shaded his eyes as he watched the landscape race by. His mind wandered as he took in the scenery. Eventually the huge oil storage tanks and refineries gave way to wooded pinelands and a broad landscape of budding trees in emerging forests. The wheels raced like galloping steel as the train bounced along the rails and the bumpy, swaying motion of the train merged with his conscious thoughts. He wondered what Rose would think of this turn of events? *What did that lieutenant mean when he said, 'You won't make it'?*

A sharp knock on his door interrupted his thoughts. "Dinner served in the dining car, " said the anxious voice of the conductor.

Johnny locked his berth and made his way to the dining car. While it was obvious most of the passengers on this train were young male inductees, there were a number of civilians. The dining car was emptying out as the meals were served in shifts. It was an old World War I era railroad car with a pot-bellied stove at one end for heat and old-fashioned oil lamps for light. Every last bit of the rolling stock in America was being pressed into service.

Johnny took a seat by the window and continued his solitary gaze out into the scenic panoramic view as if the answers to his questions were written somewhere out there for him to find. He noticed a small sign propped up on the table. It politely exhorted diners to finish their meal quickly so as to make room for the next shift of diners. He smiled to himself. Every place he looked he could find evidence of how profoundly life in America had changed in just a few short months. An entire nation had been joined together with one purpose, one goal, and one mind. Because America had been so far behind the rest of the world militarily, it had to be inventive and creative to overcome its many deficiencies. He wondered how long it would take his country to catch up and surpass its enemies in men and material. *Not long,* he concluded.

The conductor seated a family at his table, a couple and their daughter who looked to be about ten years old. Introductions were brief and Johnny politely resisted the small talk the father was trying to engage in. Seeing he preferred not to engage in conversation, the parents stopped talking but the young girl continued to ask questions.

"Where are you going?" she asked.

"South Carolina. A place called Fort Jackson."

"We're going to Florida. Will you be going to fight overseas?"

"Millie," her mother interrupted. "Please leave the nice young man alone."

Johnny suddenly realized how rude he must have appeared and for the first time cracked a small smile. "It's okay," he said to the mother and then looked right at the young girl. "I don't know where I'm going yet Millie, or what I am going to do. Today is my very first day."

Dinner was simple and served quickly. Rationing had already begun to take hold and various foods were hard to come by. They were served bean soup and roasted chicken with broccoli. Dessert consisted of a small slice of apple pie with ice cream. Millie devoured hers before Johnny was even served his piece and he graciously offered it to her. She accepted despite the frowns from her parents. As the family left the table the mother clutched his arm and said, "Good luck to you, son. God bless."

The dining car was emptying out. As Johnny made his way through the car he noticed a card game at the last table. The young men from New York City were playing poker. There was some money on the table. Vinny Larini noticed Johnny walking down the aisle and said to him, "Hey, Johnny. Can I borrow a sawbuck?"

"For that?" Johnny replied pointing to the cards on the table. "Not a chance."

Johnny continued back to his compartment. He had brought twenty dollars with him. That was a whole month's pay in the army. He decided he would use it only for essentials or emergencies. The card game was neither.

When he returned to his compartment he decided not to take any more meals in the dining car. He fished out his *Private Hargrove* paperback and began reading. At midnight he finished the book and tried to get some sleep but he was too wound up to sleep for long.

The train sped along through the night, stopping only in Philadelphia, Baltimore, and Washington D.C. At each stop more young men boarded. The stop in Washington D.C. was a long one. It was there the yardmen replaced the electrified locomotive with a steam-powered one. There were no electrified rails south of the nation's capital. The rest of the journey would be just as harsh as crossing the Great Plains in the era of the Westward Expansion. After the train left Washington D.C. he tried unsuccessfully to sleep. He would doze off for an occasional catnap but never to a sound slumber.

After a fitful night, the dark gave way to the dawn. He took a partially melted chocolate bar from his bag for breakfast and devoured it. Once they were beyond Washington, the view barely changed. He was traveling through the rural South and it reminded him of a jungle compared to the sparse vegetation of the North. As the train traveled deeper into the South, he would periodically see a shanty or shack alongside the tracks and was amazed to realize people actually lived in them. The structures were small, ramshackle and dirty. The roofs were made mostly of tin sheets cobbled together. Laundry hung from clotheslines and blew in the breeze like the surrender flags of the pitiable and the destitute. There were no windows, only openings and the brief glimpses he had of the interiors revealed more squalor than he had ever imagined. He wondered if most southerners lived like this or just the Negroes he saw living alongside the railroad tracks.

The train moved on late into the afternoon. Finally, at dusk, the conductors began pounding on the doors of the compartments.

"FORT JACKSON, FIVE MINUTES!" They yelled over and over as they walked the length of the train.

Johnny began to collect his belongings. Everything went back into his gym bag except the paperbacks. No reason to let on he was a reader. He stashed the books under his bed. Just as he finished, the train began to slow and pull into a station. As the train crept to a stop, what he saw out the window shot a bolt of fear through his stomach.

About a dozen NCOs were standing, waiting, hands on hips, staring up at the slowing train. They were spread out across the length of the train platform. They all had the cocky swagger of men with the authority to hand out mischief and mayhem. Near the center of the platform was a group of white circles painted on the ground, four deep and half the length of the train. Stark, bare floodlights illuminated the whole scene. They were *inside* Fort Jackson.

The train stopped and the boys began to get off. The NCOs immediately began yelling and screaming at the recruits as they directed them onto the white circles. Johnny couldn't hear much through the window of his compartment but it was obvious all hell was breaking loose outside. Satisfied he had a sneak peek at what was going on, he left the room and stepped off the train and into the pandemonium. Boys were shuffling around trying to find an open white circle as the NCOs screamed insults and obscenities at everyone. The circles were filling up fast, but not fast enough for the agitated NCOs. It wouldn't be a good thing to be milling about after everyone else had found a spot. Johnny saw an open circle just a few feet away inside the ranks and made a move toward it. Suddenly, a large foot from an adjacent circle stepped over and covered the open spot.

"Reserved for a friend," said Vinny Larini as he leaned toward Johnny and blocked him.

Johnny was surprised. "I thought we *were* friends," was the only thing he could think of in reply.

"If you want to *have* a friend, you need to *be* a friend," answered Vinny obviously referring to the fact Johnny didn't lend him money back on the train.

Johnny just nodded. He was angry but certainly didn't want to do or say anything to attract attention. He stepped away just as another soldier stepped in to take the spot. "I'll keep that in mind," he said to Larini as he stepped toward the back of the rapidly forming ranks.

The stream of recruits pouring from the train had slowed to a trickle. Two NCOs on either end of the group began closing down on both ends. They quickly compressed the formation by squeezing out empty spaces. Johnny worked his way along the back of the formation, closest to the train. He found an empty circle and quickly hopped on it.

Once the NCOs had tightened up the formation, they signaled to the NCO in charge. There were roughly 200 recruits in the formation.

"Do not speak and do not move," he yelled at the assembled boys. He signaled to the conductor and the train hissed, bucked and pulled out of the station through a cloud of steam.

"We lost a few yesterday because they didn't listen to orders," he barked at the formation. "Running around like chickens without heads and went right under the train's wheels. Crushed 'em so bad there was hardly enough to send home to Mama." Johnny didn't believe him but it was a good attention getter.

"Listen up, ladies," the chief NCO continued. "I'm Sergeant Lupton and I own all of you sorry swinging dicks! When I give the order we'll move out. Then, we're going to feed you, because we have to. After that, we will issue you GI gear, skivvies and sheets and find you a rack. Pay attention and we'll get this over with before dawn. Left face!"

Most of the men turned to their left but a few turned to the right and quickly corrected themselves. "I see we have a bunch of goddamn idiots in this train load," screamed Lupton. "You all must be from New York or Philly. Only Yankees can be that stupid." Lupton was on a roll. "It's getting dark and I know y'all are afraid of the dark so let's all hold hands as we march to the mess tent." Some of the men were reluctant to reach for the hand of the man next to him. Lupton went apoplectic. "If I catch anyone *not* holding hands, I will make him sorry he was ever born." All the men quickly grabbed a hand.

The formation walked, rather than marched, despite the "left-right" cadence being called out by one of the NCOs. After a few minutes, they were ordered to halt. Then the ranks formed a single file that wound its way into a large mess tent.

Inside the tent was a long table behind which were soldiers with large shiny stainless steel pots containing the ingredients of the meal. The first item each man took was a steel tray with shaped food compartments, then a spoon and fork. As they filed by the long table, the servers would ladle the food into the tray.

At the first station a server dropped a piece of toast onto the tray and then ladled a creamy glutinous mixture on top of it.

"What's this?" asked one boy.

"Chipped beef," barked the server.

"Looks like shit", answered the same boy.

"Funny you should say that," laughed one of the cooks. "The unofficial, official name of this meal is SOS. 'Shit on a Shingle'. Enjoy."

"I can't eat this crap."

Sergeant Lupton was observing this scene. He stepped in at that moment and turned the soldier around. "You're right, girlie. You can't eat this." He grabbed the tray and flung it across the mess tent. "You go hungry tonight." The recruit proceeded without saying another word.

After that, everyone else took his chipped beef, peas and carrots, and mashed potatoes without protest. Johnny gulped down his meal. At least it was hot. If one could ignore the metaphor, he concluded, it wasn't all that bad. He ate standing up or walking as everyone else did. There was no place to stop and sit. After just a few bites, the order was given. "Move out!"

The line quickly exited the mess tent. Once outside the men disposed of their steel food trays and whatever morsels of food might be left in appropriately marked cans. Johnny wiped his mouth of the last vestiges of food just as he noticed the first lightning bolt in a deep, dark sky. A thunderstorm was brewing and it was not far off.

The line of men then snaked into a long warehouse. Again, there were long tables with army personnel lined up on the other side. At each station, the recruit would be issued some element of military gear. The first few stations were easy. The men were issued folded sheets, pillowcases, blankets, a poncho and a barracks bag. They all were folded flat and the bundle formed a foundation for what was to come next. Then it got harder.

The next station doled out fatigue shirts and pants. A sergeant would eyeball the recruit and say "small, medium or large" to a private who would reach into a stack and pull out shirts, pants and a web belt. The next soldier would pile underwear and undershirts onto the rapidly mounting pile of gear. A field jacket would come next. By now the pile was agonizingly clumsy as the men would have to support the weight with one arm, contain and balance the pile with the other arm all the while not being able to easily see in front of themselves. Almost everyone had a small personal travel bag they had to support as well.

At the final station each recruit was issued socks and a pair of boots. Another sergeant would ask the recruit, "What size shoe?" and proceed to issue a different size boot. That any boot fit any soldier at all was a minor miracle. Johnny began to experience the sinking feeling of the abandoned. He didn't like it one bit.

Once he was issued his socks and boots, Johnny made his way out of the building along a blacktop path marked by overhead lights. It was pouring rain under a black sky filled with thunder and flashes of lightning. The raindrops were thick and heavy and he was soaked to the skin within seconds. The next stop would be the barracks and he could not get there soon enough. He struggled with his load as he strained to see where he was going.

The line of GIs went off into the distance. To the right of the path was a series of buildings lined up side by side as far as he could see in the dark. It appeared the line of men was entering the fifth or sixth building ahead. At least he would be reunited with his buddies from New York. Although already drenched, it would not be long now.

Johnny noticed a soldier dressed in a poncho standing in front of him alongside the path. The soldier said something to the GI in front of Johnny but he could not hear what was said. Then the soldier addressed Johnny. "Where y'all from?" he asked.

"New York," answered Johnny still moving clumsily along.

"Come with me," the soldier, whose rank Johnny could not see because of the poncho, grabbed his arm and pulled him toward the first barracks building, almost spilling his delicately balanced load of equipment. "I have one open bunk in here."

"But..." Johnny decided not to continue his objection as he assumed this voice of authority was probably an NCO.

The soldier all but dragged him into the dimly lit barracks. It was after curfew and the main lights were out. They walked past the stairs that led to the upper floor of the barracks. There was no noise except for the rain pelting the windows. On the lower level the double bunks were lined up side-by-side pointing inward from the windows. They ran along both sides of the barracks. The space between the two lines of bunks created an open corridor, which ran down the center of the barracks. On the near side, to the right of the entrance hallway, was a single double bunk nestled against the end wall perpendicular to the length of the barracks. It was obvious this placement was not normal but rather a function of trying to squeeze more recruits into an already overcrowded situation.

The soldier pushed Johnny toward that bunk and said, "Bottom rack," turned on his heels and abruptly walked back out of the barracks area.

Johnny Kilroy shook his head in disgust. *How the hell did he wind up in here?* He was drenched to the skin. His hair was matted from the rain and partially covered his eyes. He was still hungry and dog-tired. When he carefully placed his pile of clothes on the bare mattress of the bottom bunk, he noticed the upper bunk was occupied. A young soldier in a white T-shirt was lying on top of the covers writing a letter in the dim light. His face was friendly despite his bushy eyebrows and lantern jaw. He put down his pen and reached out his hand. "Hi, my name is Tom Swanson. Where you from?"

Johnny detected a slight Midwestern accent. He swept the wet from his eyes with his forearm, blinked a few times and squinted. He wiped his hand on his bunk and shook the outstretched hand. "Johnny Kilroy, New York City," he sighed.

Tom Swanson let out a big smile and a small laugh. "Son of a bitch," he muttered to himself.

"You too?" asked Johnny hopefully.

"Oh, no," answered Tom. "I'm from Idaho...Boise." Tom picked up his pen and continued writing. "Welcome."

Johnny sat down on his bare mattress. He pushed his hair out of his eyes and began to sort through his pile of clothes. First he would find his bedding and try to make up his bunk. Then he would shove everything else into his barracks bag, shed his wet civilian clothes, dry off and hit the sack. Reveille, he knew, would come early and he was beat. In the morning, he would try to fit into his misfit uniform the best he could.

Suddenly, through the faint light of the barracks came a sharp high-pitched voice in a deep southern drawl. It pierced the shadows like a knife. "Like ah was sayin', I was up there in New York once and them boys up there are all pussies." There was a smattering of quiet laughs and chuckles. "Why, they would even try to fight dirty, just break off a car antenna and try to use it on you. I would take it away from them and whip those poor boys like their Pa taking em' to the woodshed." More snickers and laughter followed.

Johnny was sitting on his bunk and looking down the length of the corridor in the center of the barracks. Shafts of moonlight slipped through the windows and crossed the corridor floor providing just a flicker of illumination. The voice was moving along the far wall, crossing back and forth from one side of the central corridor to the other. A bolt of lightning lit up the room and then another. Johnny saw a young soldier of medium height with blazing bright red hair. He could see the brightness of the hair even in the faint light. The redheaded soldier continued to talk to his buddies but in a voice intentionally loud enough for everyone in the barracks to hear. The thunder drowned out his words but not the laughter from the rest of the barracks. He was walking back and forth, into and out of the flashing glow of the lightning, talking and laughing in a scene, which was both macabre and surreal.

"So, ah must say," he continued, "if a New Yorker ever showed up in this barracks, ah would have to spank his ass and send him back home to his Mama." Some boys in the barracks were laughing loudly and making exaggerated sounds of rebel yells.

At first, Johnny assumed this just might be a silly coincidence. He figured it was just some goober popping off for the benefit of his redneck friends. He was about to let it all pass but that last comment seemed to be directed at him. In fact, there was something about this bizarre scene that convinced him all the remarks were aimed directly at him.

Johnny was not a tough kid as tough New York City kids went. Nevertheless, he learned how to fight at a young age and was capable, if not proficient at it. But there were other lessons he learned on the streets of Washington Heights that transcended the ability to fight. He easily remembered those hard-earned lessons. *Never show fear! Never back down! If you sense fear in the other guy, be aggressive! Swing first while everyone else is talking!* If any situation in his entire life screamed out for him to apply those lessons, this was it.

He weighed his options quickly. There were two choices; either ignore the provocation or confront it. If Johnny challenged him, there would be a fight. There was no telling how many others would jump in. More than likely, he would get in a few good shots before some NCO would eventually show up and break up the brawl. Then there would undoubtedly be disciplinary action taken against all the participants. His army life would instantly turn to shit. He might even be thrown into the stockade. So much for not being noticed.

To do nothing, on the other hand, meant he had backed down. He would have to live here, in this barracks, with all of these guys for the next four or five days with that stigma hanging over his head. It was a humiliation he couldn't handle.

The shrill voice of the redhead, punctuated by the laughs of the other soldiers, continued to pierce the darkened barracks. Johnny was now focused on what he had to do. He continued to hear "Red" talking along with the howls and laughter of the men but could no longer understand the words. Their meaning was lost in his tunnel vision. His focus was entirely on Red and he glared at him through the darkness. Johnny stood up slowly and took off his wet jacket. His heart was pounding and the adrenalin was surging as he began walking down the central corridor toward Red. It had already been a long day and he would end it by taking on half of the state of Alabama.

Red continued to pace back and forth spouting his rancor, oblivious to Johnny slowly walking toward him. Someone quietly said, "Oh shit," and the barracks went silent. Johnny continued walking deliberately toward Red who had stopped and was facing him.

"I'm from New York City," Johnny said in a firm and steady voice, "and I don't have a car antenna, " he held out his hands palms up. "So come and whip my ass." Johnny wagged the fingers on both outstretched hands in a 'come-to-me' gesture.

Red wasn't expecting this. He froze and then took a step back. Through the dim light Johnny thought he saw fear in Red's eyes. That was all he had to see. He kept closing the distance. In a few seconds he would be all over Red. Suddenly, he heard some of the recruits hop off their bunks behind him. He figured he was about to get jumped by Red's friends and he sensed someone directly behind him. Johnny quickly turned ready to defend himself.

Tom Swanson came up behind Johnny swiftly. He positioned himself solidly between Johnny and Red before Johnny could do anything. "Whoa," he said in a booming voice. He had one hand lightly on Johnny's chest and was pointing at Red with the other. "This is not going to happen. Not here. Not tonight." Swanson was obviously trying to prevent the fight. He wheeled around to the few boys who had jumped off their bunks and pointed at them. "Get back on your racks," he commanded. Swanson was an intimidating figure at nearly six foot five. The men quickly jumped back into their bunks.

"There's not going to be any fight in this barracks tonight," Swanson continued. "I don't need this trouble."

Emboldened by Swanson standing between him and Johnny, Red suddenly recovered his bravado. "Ah was only foolin' with you *Yank*. Can't you take a joke?"

"This is not over between us, Bubba," Johnny called out over his shoulder as Swanson guided him back to their bunk.

"Fuck you, Yank," Red managed to respond in a weak and squeaky voice once Swanson had maneuvered Johnny back to their bunk.

"Remember, it ain't over between you and me," Johnny pointed back at Red.

Suddenly, the NCO who brought Johnny into the barracks appeared in the doorway. He wasn't wearing his poncho and Johnny could see he was a corporal. "Everything all right in here?" he yelled rather than asked.

"Yeah, Corporal. Everything is fine," answered Tom Swanson. "No trouble here."

"Well keep it down. It's past lights out," he said as he left.

Tom Swanson climbed back up onto his upper bunk. He was as calm as he was when Johnny first showed up. Tom resumed writing his letter as Johnny was still trying to come down from the adrenalin high.

"I suppose I owe you a debt of thanks," Johnny finally said after a few minutes.

"They set you up," Tom replied not looking up from his writing pad.

"What?" Johnny asked.

"The corporal is from Alabama too," Tom said, putting down his pencil. "Apparently, they all got along famously since this morning. I came in this afternoon with another guy from Michigan. That guy got sick so they took him to the base hospital and an officer told the corporal to fill the bunk. Then he actually asked his fellow Alabamans who they would like to have added to the barracks and Red asked him to get them a New Yorker."

All of a sudden it became clear to Johnny. "I guess it *was* all a joke," sighed Johnny.

"A bad joke," answered Tom. "You were right to stand up to them. If you hadn't your life here would have been miserable. But I had to stop it. You were taking it a lot further than they thought you would. I think you surprised them by standing up to them. You've got balls, I'll give you that, but I think they would have kicked your ass and my corporal friend back there would probably have reported the brawl. Then we all would have been in deep dung."

Tom was right. Johnny knew it. He was outnumbered by a lot and would have taken a bad beating. "You're right, Tom," said Johnny. "How can I thank you?"

Tom grinned. "You can lend me five-bucks?"

"Really?" Johnny was surprised by the request.

Johnny remembered what Vinny Larini said to him about being a friend. Besides, Tom Swanson just got him out of a big jam. He reached into his wallet, fished out a five-dollar bill and handed it to Tom.

"Thanks. My family is wiring me some money. I'll pay you back."

The next few days went by swiftly. The army had the recruits running ragged all day, every day. First order of business the next morning was haircuts. Immediately after the haircuts, the recruits packaged their civilian clothes to be mailed home. The rabble began to look like they were actually in the army although most of the men wore ill-fitting fatigues. Next was a battery of written tests. More inoculations were given and then another medical exam.

By the time Johnny got back to his bunk at the end of the first full day, Tom was gone. His barracks bag was gone and his bedding had been removed. No one knew why and no one replaced him. Johnny kissed his five bucks good-bye.

The next day was more of the same. Forms upon forms were filled out. Insurance beneficiary forms, pay forms, forms for everything. After lunch the entire regiment was lined up in formation when the cadre asked all members of Barracks One to step forward. Johnny watched as all the Alabamans dutifully complied. He remained in formation. The cadre quickly picked out a dozen men for Kitchen Police (K.P.) and some other work detail. Red was one of them and Johnny caught his eye as he marched by. Johnny cocked his head with a look that said, *go ahead and open your mouth and I'll kick your ass.* Red said nothing and just kept marching.

The army was expanding rapidly and the growing pains showed in many different ways. "Hurry up and wait" became the bywords of the daily routine. Recruits would stand in lines for hours not knowing what they were waiting for before they would be shuttled off to another line, again to wait for hours. They were given work detail upon work detail including policing the area of trash and cigarette butts, painting (the army saying was if it moved, salute it, if not, paint it), K.P., cleaning latrines, digging ditches and on and on. Then they would be rushed to and through the mess hall for meals.

Finally, after days of this mass chaos and confusion the company received word they would ship out by bus the next morning for Camp Gordon, Georgia, for Basic Combat Training. Everyone had enough of this madness the army called a Reception Center. Now they would get down to the nitty-gritty of getting into shape and becoming soldiers.

On the last day Johnny was moving along the chow line having food ladled onto his tray by the servers. First the beef stew was slopped on, then the green beans, and in between the mashed potatoes server and the ice cream station a disembodied hand came through the soldiers serving the food and dropped a folded five-dollar bill onto the green beans. It was Tom Swanson who was on K.P. duty. "Thanks," Tom grinned.

"You're welcome," Johnny replied as he was swept down the line. "Where you been?"

"Infirmary. Sick call. I'll be leaving in a few days for Gordon." Tom was raising his voice as Johnny moved along the line.

"See you there. We're leaving tomorrow," he hollered back as he reached the end of the line and looked for a seat. There was something about what Tom did that made Johnny feel good and it wasn't just the money. The chances of running into Tom again were pretty small and Tom could have easily let Johnny pass by on the chow line without paying him back. It occurred to him that Tom was the sort of young man who always paid his debts. That gesture helped reinforce Johnny's rapidly depleting faith in human nature. *If you want to have a friend, you need to be a friend.*

Johnny had survived the Reception Center without being noticed. He managed to duck all of the work details and stay under the radar. With the help of Tom Swanson he dodged a bullet in the barracks and avoided a brawl that would have surely caused him great difficulty if not significant injury. The cadre didn't give him any trouble and he didn't give the cadre any trouble in return. He also earned the grudging respect of the Alabamans in his barracks although he was sure while respecting him, they surely didn't like him.

From time to time, over the days at Fort Jackson, some of them approached him about the "incident". They were mostly contrite about their part in the "joke". He accepted their grudging comments graciously. Thanks to the Alabamans, Johnny would be leaving for Camp Gordon with a nickname and a reputation. Behind his back they called him "Yank" and it was no secret they believed him to be one ballsy, crazy son of a bitch!

Chapter Nine

Georgetown – December 13, 1996

"Men in general are quick to believe that which they wish to be true."

Julius Caesar (100 BC - 44 BC)

There were two messages on his answering machine when he got home late from Christmas shopping. The stores were crowded even though he expected more people than normal to stay home. After all, it was Friday the thirteenth.

He hit the blinking play button and proceeded to pull off his tie and hang up his overcoat and sports jacket while he listened. Two messages within a few hours of each other from the same person indicated a matter of some urgency. Despite the late hour, J.P. decided to return the call, if only to leave a message. He was surprised when someone picked up the phone.

"Colonel Chase. May I help you?"

"Ah, yes, Colonel…this is J.P. Kilroy. I'm returning your calls." J.P. had his wireless telephone tucked between his ear and shoulder as he scurried around the kitchen to prepare his dinner, a nightly ritual that he became adept at since his divorce.

"Very good, Mister Kilroy, I was hoping it was you."

"How can I help you, Colonel?"

There was a slight pause and J.P. could hear the shuffling of papers in the background. "If you have a moment, this might take a bit of explaining." There was a tone of gravity in the colonel's voice.

"I have some time. I'm listening."

"I'm currently assigned to the Untied States Army Awards Branch here at the Pentagon. For the last six months my team has been researching the lack of Medals of Honor for African-Americans serving in World War II. We recently concluded our analysis and recommendations. There will be a ceremony in the East Room of the White House on January thirteenth for one living recipient and six posthumous awards. Here is where it gets a bit delicate. I would like to invite you to attend a…"

"Excuse me, Colonel," J.P. interrupted. "If you want that ceremony covered you should call the assignment editor at the *Times.*" There was silence on the other end of the line.

"I don't think you understand, Mister Kilroy," Chase began again but more slowly and deliberately. "We want to invite you to accept the Medal of Honor on behalf of your father. It would be a private ceremony but on the same day."

J.P. was utterly bewildered. He sat down at the kitchen table. "You're right, Colonel, I don't understand. My father is not African-American."

"True. However, your father participated in a combat action that resulted in the awarding of the Medal of Honor to both himself *and* an African-American named Lincoln Abraham."

This was all happening too fast for J.P. If he accepted the invitation, he would obviously have to meet with his father. He still was not ready for that confrontation. Perhaps he would never be. "Why can't my father accept the Medal himself?" he finally asked.

Again there was a pause on the other end of the line. "This is quite awkward for me, Mister Kilroy," Chase stammered. "Uh hum, didn't you know that your father recently passed away?"

J.P. let out an audible sigh. "No, I was not aware."

"My condolences, sir," Chase responded. "I'm sorry to break the news to you this way. I didn't know…"

"We weren't exactly close." J.P. realized how lame that sounded. "I mean…we weren't close at all. You could say that we've been estranged for some time." He took a deep breath. "We never stayed in touch."

"Once again, I sincerely regret having to break the news to you this way." Chase sounded sincere and contrite. "We have invited three of your father's wartime friends to attend the ceremony. If you choose not to attend, the Sergeant-Major-of-the-Army will accept the award."

J.P. considered what the colonel just said. All he had to do was decline and he would finally be done with his father. This news could conceivably put that chapter of his life behind him. He simply had to hang up the phone.

But he couldn't get his mother's words out of his head. He made a promise and hadn't kept it. His mother died knowing her last request went unfulfilled. And then there was the family secret he was supposed to uncover. It all seemed so damn important to her. Maybe if he accepted the Medal of Honor on behalf of his father, he would earn some level of redemption. It was the last possible act he might perform to partially honor his mother's last wishes.

But there was something else pulling him in the other direction, telling him not to go. Perhaps it was that other reason he never wanted to face his father again. Maybe his reluctance was the product of how quickly this all came to pass and the shocking news. Whatever the reason, he found himself suddenly adverse to the notion of attending any ceremony. Before he could distill the conflicting thoughts, the words began spilling out of his mouth.

"Thank you for the invitation, Colonel Chase, but I'm afraid I must decline."

Chapter Ten

Fort A.P. Hill, Virginia – June 4, 1942

"All that can be done with the soldier is to give him espirit de corps,
a higher opinion of his own regiment than all the other troops in the country."

Frederick the Great (1712 - 1786), *Military Testament*, 1768

"It's a damned suicide outfit, Jake," exclaimed Sergeant Harley Tidrick as they hurriedly walked across the parade ground toward the Regimental Day Room. "Everybody knows it. Those guys are all fucking crazy!"

"If you believe that Harley then why are you here? Why don't you go have a beer or something?" replied Jake.

"I'm trying to talk you out of this, kid. Why the hell would you want to join this outfit anyway?" Harley had seen this stubborn look on Jake's face before.

"Why the hell don't you mind your own business, Harley?" Jake blurted it out before he could catch himself. He was instantly sorry. Jake liked and respected his cousin. Harley had always looked out for him but especially since Jake joined the Stonewallers of the 29th "Blue and Gray" Division. Jake didn't make it easy for Harley. His frequent disregard for regulations resulted in numerous minor infractions, all of which were maddening to Harley.

After basic training, Jake was sent to Fort Meade, Maryland, halfway between Baltimore and Washington D.C. Discipline was lax. There were not enough weapons to issue a rifle to each infantryman so whatever little training they did, they did with broomsticks. Stovepipes served as mortars and baseballs as hand grenades. The morale of the once-proud division plummeted.

Then the draftees began arriving in April 1941. Their negative attitude was poisonous. They were already counting the days when their one-year term of service would be completed. Any unit cohesion that existed based on hometown friendships began to unravel. The War Department sent in regular army officers to "shape up" this former National Guard division. The resulting churn only served to further deteriorate morale.

Sergeant Harley Tidrick was a squad leader in the 2nd Platoon of Able Company of the Stonewallers. He arranged to have his cousin Jake assigned to his squad so he could keep an eye on him. All during the tumult and instability of 1941, Harley was a constant. He remained calm and focused and provided attentive leadership to his squad. They tried to stay out of trouble mostly because of their loyalty and friendship to him.

In September 1941 the 29th Division moved to Fort A.P. Hill, halfway between

Washington, D.C. and Richmond, Virginia. Jake continued to get home to Macie as often as he could.

Macie was tall at five feet eight inches and somewhat awkward and gangly. Most of the time she kept her long black hair in a ponytail. Her eyes were nearly as dark as her hair and the only minor imperfection to her otherwise flawless face was a small mole on her upper lip. Jake thought it gave her face character.

She found a job in a boarding house cleaning rooms and serving meals. It didn't pay much but she always had something to eat and a roof over her head. Nothing in the orphanage had prepared her for life on the outside. As a consequence, she remained shy and withdrawn. However, she was a hard worker and took pride in whatever she did. Jake was the center of her young life and she adored him. He would take a room at the boarding house whenever he got home. It was all very convenient and respectable. He realized before long that although he always loved her, he had fallen in love with her. She became the focus of his life. They would take long walks holding hands or go to the movie house or have a float at the soda fountain in Green's Drugstore. It was just understood that they would someday marry.

Throughout the fall of 1941, getting home made Jake's military life tolerable. He was not at all interested in the war in Europe or the brutal war the Japanese were waging in China. He rarely read the papers and was oblivious to American politics and the tension building between America and Japan. He was in the army only to stay out of jail and as long as he could get home to see Macie his military life remained bearable.

Then the Japanese attacked Pearl Harbor and everything changed. One could almost sense, if not envision, everyone in the young nation simultaneously wiping the milk-mustache of naiveté from their upper lip and setting their minds to the terribly fearful job ahead of them.

"I didn't mean that, Harley." Jake stopped and looked at his cousin. His remorse was sincere as it usually was once he regained his temper. "I have my reasons for doing this," Jake continued. "It's complicated."

Harley smiled. "Dames do have a way of complicating things." Jake ignored the comment and started walking again, this time faster. Harley trotted to catch up.

"I don't understand how joining the paratroopers can make things any better?"

"Well, it can't get any worse," Jake answered. "This goddamn War screwed everything up."

"For a lot of people, kid," Harley observed soberly.

Harley was alluding to the reality that America was in a virtual panic. Rumors were rampant the Japanese were about to invade the West Coast. There was barely a United States Navy left in the Pacific to stop them and everyone knew it. On

11 December, Germany and Italy declared war on the United States and within weeks German U-Boats began sinking ships right off the American coast. The shelling of an oil refinery in Santa Barbara, California by a Japanese submarine on 23 February served to emphasize how vulnerable America was.

On 1 April 1942, American soldiers began systematically rounding up Japanese-Americans. They were plucked from their homes and businesses on the West Coast and relocated to detention camps, complete with barbed-wire fences and armed sentries. The government was terrified at the prospect of a potential subversive element within the populace. A frightened and unprepared nation behaved desperately as it tried to shake off years of indifference and apathy and engage in global war.

Immediately after Pearl Harbor, the 29th Infantry Division received new orders. They deployed various units to a number of different places along the coast from New Jersey to Virginia to guard warehouses, rail lines and bridges to thwart any spies who might attempt sabotage.

Jake would never forget Christmas Eve, 1941. His platoon was assigned to patrol the beach area just south of Atlantic City, New Jersey. He walked his post alone on that freezing night as the surf pounded the shoreline and the biting wind whipped the beach sand into his face. He wore a long trench coat and a World War I style dish shaped helmet. He had his M1903 Springfield bolt-action rifle slung on his shoulder with the unsheathed bayonet fixed on his rifle and only one magazine of five rounds of ammunition. *What the hell was he doing here?* He shook his head in disgust, tugged on his rifle sling, lowered his head, leaned into the frigid wind and continued to walk his post. Merry Christmas to all and to all a good night!

The 29th Division finally reassembled at Fort Meade, Maryland in March of 1942 and the men were astounded by the changes that were announced. The division shed one of its four infantry regiments and got a new Commanding Officer (CO); Major General Leonard T. Gerow, a Virginian and graduate of the Virginia Military Institute. Jake watched these changes with a critical eye and concluded the division was preparing to ship out overseas. He decided it was time to transfer into another outfit.

"Jake," Harley interrupted his thoughts. "Ever hear that saying about jumping out of the frying pan and into the fire?"

As much as Jake didn't want to talk about it, he knew he owed Harley an explanation. "It's not just about getting out of the division before we ship out, Harley," Jake began. "Macie wants to leave Bedford and move to a place near Norfolk, called Newport News."

"Really?" Harley was genuinely surprised. He knew Macie and was shocked she would strike out on her own and out of her comfort zone.

"Yeah, really," Jake confirmed.

"To do what?"

"Build ships!" Before Harley could respond Jake continued to explain. "I know it sounds crazy, Harley, but a few weeks ago some people from the Newport News Shipyard stopped at Bedford. They've been recruiting workers and with the shortage of men they decided to hire women."

"No shit."

"No shit, Harley. The head guy was a shipyard construction foreman and the gal with him was a riveter or welder or something," Jake explained. "Macie said that the guy talked about how much the navy needed these ships and how great the pay was and the gal explained how she was trained, that there are a lot of women doing this and it wasn't so hard and they were really needed to finish building those damn ships." Jake paused to let it sink in. "Then they offered everyone a fifty-dollar sign-up bonus and a train ticket to Norfolk."

"And Macie signed up?" Harley continued, half asking.

"And Macie signed up," Jake stated emphatically.

"And you don't want her doing this, I figure. Right, kid?"

"Of course not," answered Jake. The thought of Macie alone in a big city scared the hell out of Jake. "So I need time to talk her out of it and it won't hurt if I can make more money so I could help her out more. Maybe she won't feel like she needs to take this job."

"And the training will keep you in the States a little longer," Harley finished the thought and he finally understood Jake's motives. "I get it. And if you don't mind my saying so, I think you're a perfect fit for the paratroopers because you're a section-eight too." Harley was smiling as he said it. Jake smiled back.

Just then Private Danny Peregory ran up alongside them. Peregory was from Kilo Company, 3rd Battalion, but he knew Jake from the regimental boxing team. Despite the fact that he was small and wiry, no taller than five feet six inches, nobody messed with Danny. He was a curious kid who was interested in everything that was none of his business. He also had an effusive personality. Born in Charlottesville, Virginia, most everyone called him Danny Boy. "You guys signing up?"

Harley answered first. "We're going to listen to what they have to say. Right, Jake?"

"Listen for what?" Danny asked. "This is the best outfit in the whole damn army and if I'm going into combat I want to go with the best."

"They're going to have to put lead weights in your pockets just to make sure your parachute opens, Danny Boy, " joked Harley.

"I hear the only size that matters in the paratroopers," Danny responded, "is the size of your heart."

Jake simply nodded. Danny was the featherweight champion of the 3rd Battalion.

As they neared the building that housed the day room, they converged with other small clusters of soldiers. They came together in groups of twos and threes from every direction, bunching together just prior to funneling through the single door. The soldiers knew the drill since Solicitation Boards were constantly visiting the post. Last week it was Army Intelligence and the week before it was the Signal Corps. Army specialties with critical skill needs were allowed to send teams of recruiters to any post to seek out uniquely qualified individuals. Today it was the United States Army Airborne Command looking for volunteers to join the paratroopers.

All the card tables were pushed against the walls in the day room and in their place were over fifty wooden folding chairs. The room still smelled of raw wood and fresh paint like so many of the newly constructed buildings on the post. In the center of the room a sergeant was threading a sixteen-millimeter projector. A captain was leaning over him offering assistance. Among other decorations they both wore airborne jump wings, which consisted of a silver metal badge in the shape of a fully deployed parachute with the shroud lines forming a V. Powerful eagle-like wings emanated from the base and curved upward to touch the sides of the canopy with their wingtips.

The projector was aimed at a sheet tacked to the wall over a makeshift stage. There was a poster on the wall, adjacent to the jury-rigged screen, of a tough looking young soldier holding a carbine with parachutes billowing in the sky-blue background behind him. Under the picture, it read:

Become A Paratrooper
Jump Into the Fight

As the men found their seats, the room filled with the background noise of voices and chairs scraping along the floor. Jake, Harley and Danny took seats in the front row. The unintelligible murmurs were punctuated by an occasional loud laugh and continued after all the chairs were taken. A few men, mostly officers, stood along the walls in the rear near the door. The sergeant walked to the rear to close the door as the captain stepped up on the stage.

"At ease, men," bellowed the officer and the room immediately fell silent. "My name is Captain Louis Wolff and I'm here to tell you men about the Army's newest and most elite unit, the paratroopers." He pointed to the poster and then paused to let his words sink in. "My assistant Sergeant Coleman and I will describe the particulars about the newest and finest outfit in the army. Then we have a short training film and finally we'll answer any questions at the end." The sergeant stood up briefly and nodded to the room. Wolff continued. "Smoke 'em if you got 'em!"

Captain Wolff was well over six feet tall and was in superb physical shape. He moved and spoke confidently. His overseas cap was tucked neatly into his belt with the paratrooper insignia facing outward. The insignia was an open white parachute on a circular patch of blue cloth. The nametag over his pocket was the first one Jake ever saw.

"First and most important of all, we're an elite outfit," Wolff began. "We only want the best so if you're not fearless, don't bother to volunteer." Danny nudged Jake and smiled.

"Like everything else in this man's army," continued Wolff, "there are pros and cons. Let me first talk about the benefits. If you qualify, enlisted men will receive an additional fifty dollars a month and officers will get an extra hundred dollars." There was an immediate subdued but affirmative buzz in the room.

"Everybody likes that part," Wolff went on. "And we have our own special equipment and uniform. A lot of our uniform accessories are necessary but I will confess that some of what we wear and what we do is for show. As I said before, we're an elite outfit and we want our men to feel that special espirit de corps which is so important to elite units." The captain reached down and picked up a helmet. "M-One helmet with chinstrap. The helmet is standard, the special chinstrap is strictly airborne." Then he picked up a battle dress uniform from the top of the table. "This is a brand new model M1942 battle jacket customized for airborne troopers." He held up the uniform. "Extra reinforced pockets on the sleeves and the shirt pockets cut on a slant so we can get to them with our chutes on." He explained the other special features of the jacket and the trousers before dropping the uniform back on the table.

"And these are Corcoran jump boots," he lifted his foot on the table so everyone could see his highly polished boots. "Steel toe, high cut and a beveled heel so we don't trip on the deck rings as we exit the plane. All necessary to our mission." He placed his foot back on the floor with a loud thud. "And we're the only unit in the entire army authorized to blouse our pants legs into the tops of our boots. Not necessary," he smiled, "but it sure looks sharp."

Jake really wasn't interested in all of this. He just needed to hear how difficult it might be to qualify. As if Captain Wolff read his mind, he began to discuss the training.

"The physical and mental pressure of jump school is enormous," continued Wolff, "and half of you that volunteer will wash out in the first week. The other half will wish they never volunteered." The room was silent as Captain Wolff took on a more serious tone. "You really have to want this badly, and I think you NCOs especially know what I mean."

"What *do* you mean?" asked a voice from the back.

"Everyone who enters jump school gives up his rank and enters as a private," answered Wolff. A negative murmur burst out in the room. Most of the NCOs were older men who had been Guardsmen through the lean inter-war years when promotions were difficult to come by. They were not inclined to voluntarily surrender their stripes after waiting so long to get them. About a dozen sergeants and corporals spontaneously got up and left the room.

"Not a problem for me," whispered Danny pointing to the single stripe on his sleeve, "or you, Jake," looking over at Jake's bare sleeve. Then he looked at Harley's three stripes and rolled his eyes. Harley didn't move as the other NCOs crowded toward the exit.

Captain Wolff expected this reaction. He had seen it many times before. "Let me just say that the rumors are strong that there will eventually be over a dozen new airborne regiments formed and prior NCOs will be given special consideration to fill out the open leadership positions." He was speaking to the backs of the NCOs walking out the door. It didn't change anyone's mind.

"How about officers?" a different voice called out.

"Officers keep their rank," answered Wolff, "but during jump school they will be subordinate to their instructors who are all NCOs and they will be extra hard on you."

"Why?" asked the same voice.

"It's the custom in the airborne that officers are last in the chow line and first out of the airplane door. Airborne officers lead from the front."

The officer who asked the questions got up and walked out along with some other officers.

"We have too many officers, anyway," joked Wolff after they exited. The remaining GIs laughed nervously.

Wolff sensed he was losing what little enthusiasm was left in the room. He decided to lay it on the line and challenge those remaining. "The rest of you can leave at any time. We only want men who want a challenge and want to prove they're good enough to hang with the best. Let me tell you why." He folded his arms and began pacing slowly back and forth.

"The airborne soldier drops behind enemy lines," he began. "We're always surrounded by the enemy. Being surrounded usually puts the fear of God into a normal soldier, but that situation is where our job begins. We need to be mentally and physically tough and we need to know the guys on our right and left are just as tough as we are. There are no re-supply depots behind enemy lines so we have to bring in everything we need. When we go in we expect to jump with well over a hundred pounds of supplies, weapons, ammo, food and whatever else we might need. Our troopers must be able to navigate, read maps, figure out where they are and where they need to be and act independently to complete their mission. If we have wounded we have to take care of our own. There are no aid stations or field hospitals. Because we're behind enemy lines, there is a good possibility that some of us might be captured although most of the paratroopers I know won't be taken alive. And we have to do all this after jumping out of a perfectly good airplane at night as well as in daylight." A few other soldiers got up and left the room.

"Jump school is very demanding. It's four weeks of pure hell," continued Wolff hardly noticing the men who got up to leave. "The first week, A-Stage, is all physical training. You'll run five miles before breakfast and then you'll get into some really intense physical training. You'll run everywhere! There's no walking in jump school. The instructors will be in your face all the time demanding pushups for the slightest mistakes!" Wolff hesitated for just a moment. "You all can do fifty pushups?" Some more men got up to leave.

"Rather than me talk about it," Wolff explained, "let me show you." He nodded to Sergeant Coleman who flicked on the projector. He motioned to the windows and some of the soldiers stood up and pulled down the shades. The room was dark except for the projector's shaft of light, which caught the swirls of cigarette smoke floating about the room. Almost immediately there was the scraping sound of chairs moving across the floor as some soldiers used the darkness to exit the room, which brightened for a few seconds as they opened and closed the door.

The picture was grainy and the sound scratchy and uneven as the film began. Wolff was silent as the narrator described the action in the film. A-Stage was depicted as Wolff had described it. Trainees in T-Shirts and shorts were running everywhere in formations or performing physical training such as jumping jacks, rope climbing, tumbling and pushups.

Danny watched intently and occasionally nudged Jake. He wasn't intimidated in the least and rather enjoyed that he was still there while so many others had already weaseled out.

"B-Stage begins the specialized training for paratroopers," the narrator went on. "Now you will learn the skills necessary to earn your jump wings." The screen showed men jumping from a mock-up of an airplane door into a sawdust pit. Instructors were showing the men the correct body position in the door. The picture then shifted to a tower that was thirty-five feet off the ground. Men were jumping out of the tower while their harnesses were connected to a guide wire. They slid down the wire a fairly long distance before they came to a sudden and rather violent stop in a sand pit. "Another technique called a Parachute Landing Fall," the narrator went on, "is practiced over and over until the trainee learns how to land properly." The noise of chairs scraping across the floor signaled some additional men had left the room.

"In C-Stage every trainee will learn to pack his own parachute." On the screen the trainees were folding the parachutes methodically into small bundles. First they folded the risers, then the shroud lines followed by the bottom of the silk chute and finally the apex. This package was then carefully packed into their canvas covered, metal-framed parachute pack tray.

The scene then shifted to men jumping from a 250-foot tower and perfecting the landing rolls and tumbles necessary to break their fall. The drill always ended with boys on the ground struggling to collapse their parachutes as a wind machine blew and billowed the parachute. Some men were dragged along the ground as the narrator warned how dangerous it could be if the parachute was not brought under control immediately upon landing. A shaft of light from the door announced that more men had left the room.

"And now the final exam," the narrator exclaimed. "Everyone who has made it this far will complete their qualifications by making five parachute jumps from heights starting at 1,200 feet to 800 feet with the final jump being a night jump from 1,000 feet." On the screen the men, all wearing their jump gear and football helmets, were filing out of a plane one at a time. The chutes popped opened in sequence as they descended slowly to earth.

The next clip had the trainees standing proudly at attention in formation, having their jump wings pinned on. The narration concluded. "This is the moment you have worked so hard for, when your instructors and your officers recognize your accomplishment and present your jump wings which acknowledge you as a paratrooper in the United States Army Airborne."

The music faded and the screen turned white as the training film ran off the feed reel with a loud snapping sound. Sergeant Coleman switched on the room lights.

There were only five soldiers left in the room.

Chapter Eleven

The White House East Room – January 13, 1997

"In valor there is hope."

Cornelius Tacitus (c. AD 56 - c. AD 120), *Annals*

When J.P. Kilroy entered the East Room of the White House there were already a sizeable number of dignitaries present. The room was more crowded than he expected. It was unusually full of energy as family members gathered in small groups and engaged in animated conversations with high-ranking military officers and politicians. At the west end of the room the television cameras were preparing for the broadcast. The media pool was managed by C-SPAN.

At almost 2,900 square feet, the East Room was the largest room in the White House. Its twenty-foot ceilings and huge windows gave the room a capacious feel. In addition, the room was generously adorned with beautiful art and furnishings. The floor was oak Fontainebleau parquetry and partially covered by two large oriental rugs. The drapes that covered the large windows were gold colored silk. There were three large Bohemian crystal chandeliers and four magnificent marble fireplaces. Bronze light standards and upholstered benches dotted the periphery of the eighty by thirty-seven foot room. The walls were paneled in light colored wood with classical fluted pilasters and relief insets. A full-length portrait of George Washington, painted by Gilbert Stuart in 1797, hung on the east wall.

J.P. Kilroy knew today would be a historic day as America endeavored to right the injustices of past generations. The East Room seemed like the perfect place to do just that. It had been used over its long history for both historic events as well as for some rather pedestrian purposes. When the White House was first built, Abigail Adams hung clothes on a rope line she strung in the East Room. Teddy Roosevelt's children used it as a roller skating rink and Woodrow Wilson employed it as a theatre. Over the years the large room had been the site of weddings, funerals, press conferences, receptions and receiving lines. Seven Presidents, including Lincoln and Kennedy, were laid in state in this room. It had a rich history.

In the center of the east wall, in front of a set of hanging silk gold drapes, was a temporary platform with seven chairs arranged next to a podium with the Presidential Seal. Further to the right, under the portrait of George Washington, was another podium. Behind this second podium was a table upon which the framed Medals of Honor were displayed.

The rest of the East Room was crammed with folding chairs save for the open aisle in the center. The extended families and friends along with military dignitaries, Congressmen and the press composed the rest of the audience. There was an electric buzz in the room.

J.P. meandered slowly through the crowd while looking for two people. One was Colonel Carlton Chase, whom he had spoken with just a few days before. After he refused the invitation back in December, J.P. was immediately filled with a healthy dose of guilt. When he reflected on the phone call, he really wasn't sure why he declined other than he simply didn't want anything to do with his father. After much agonizingly difficult reflection, he finally arrived at the conclusion that it no longer mattered. His father was dead. Gone! It was time he let go of the baggage. His mother's last wish was that he reconcile with his father and he blew it! Since he could no longer do that, perhaps he might uncover the secret his mother wanted him to know from his father's friends. It was a long shot but the colonel did mention that some of his father's wartime buddies would be at the ceremony. It certainly was worth a try. He had procrastinated until the last minute and then finally called Colonel Chase who advised J.P. he would be allowed to accept the Medal in a separate ceremony. The Chairman of the Joint Chiefs of Staff, General Aaron Clayton, would be more than happy to present his father's Medal of Honor to him immediately after the conclusion of the President's presentations.

As J.P. wandered through the crowded room he suddenly spied a group of men gathered under the portrait of Teddy Roosevelt in the far southeast corner of the room. They were engaged in a lively discussion. Among them, he assumed, was the second person he was looking for.

Chapter Twelve

Newport News, Virginia – June 28, 1942

"Whether they give or refuse, it delights women just
the same to have been asked."

Ovid, (Publius Ovidius Naso) (43 BC - 17 AD)

Macie Vance stepped off the bus and walked tentatively toward one of the access gates to the Newport News Shipyard and Dry Dock Company. The huge sign overhead read:

Gate 4 - Main Entrance

She followed the surge of shipyard workers flowing toward the gate and noticed an almost equal number emerging from the huge shipyard facility. People young and old, mostly men but some women, moved quickly with a sense of purpose. They were the shipwrights, welders, electricians, pipe fitters and machinists who toiled long and hard to give America a new navy to defend her shores and defeat her evil enemies.

As Macie approached the gate she stepped to the side and allowed others to pass so she could gather herself before approaching the guard shack. Her clothes were glaringly out of place compared to the jeans and coveralls the women workers were wearing. Most wore colorful bandanas rolled up and knotted in the front to keep their hair out of the way.

Macie, on the other hand, wore a pink flowered print dress and black high-heeled shoes with ankle straps. Her long black hair was neatly rolled up in a hairnet and she held her clutch bag in white-gloved hands. This was her best Sunday outfit and she decided to travel to Newport News dressed 'to the nines'. Compared to the men and women walking by, she felt conspicuous. She was too well dressed, too tall and too young.

Her first stop upon arrival was her assigned apartment in Hilton Village, three miles north of the shipyard in Warwick County. Hilton Village was the nation's first Federal War Housing project; a planned community sponsored by the U. S. Shipping Board and the Newport News Shipyard. Upon arrival at her apartment she met her roommate Nora Lee.

Nora was an ex-telephone operator and a sassy blond from Richmond. She was one of the first women employed at the shipyard. She was shorter and a year older than Macie. Her job in the Electricians Department was wiring instrument panels and switchboards. This complex work was done in the shops and the finished components installed on the ships as they were completed. Nora liked the work but was hoping to get promoted to the Joiners Department as a drill press operator with a higher rate of pay.

"This place isn't all that great but it's cozy and it's close to the yard," Nora explained as she walked a slightly nervous Macie quickly through the tiny apartment. "This whole complex was built by the shipyard during the first war for the workers and they're out of space already. That's why we have to share the place. Everyone's doubling up. I don't know where they're going to put all the workers they have to hire but that's not my problem." Nora walked through a doorway and pointed into a small room with a bed, chest of drawers, nightstand and a lamp. "This is your bedroom."

Macie nodded and put her suitcase on the bed. "I've seen worse," she said with a look that Nora realized was not an exaggeration.

"It's not that bad. We work ten-hour shifts, six days a week. We'll rarely see each other. And most people work the seventh day as overtime because there is nothing else to do," Nora explained. "The money is great but with rationing and shortages, there's not much to buy." Nora reflected for a second. "Except bonds. You have to buy war bonds. Everybody does."

"Okay," Macie smiled. Nora had a way of quickly making people like her.

"What did they hire you to do, Sweetie?" asked Nora.

Macie reached into her handbag and pulled out her offer letter. "I'm going to welding school." The letter assigned her to Welding School Number 2 with nineteen other young women.

"That's great," Nora commented. "You know, the men here haven't really accepted us yet. Some of them can be real bastards with their smart remarks. I don't take their shit. I just give it back to them in spades."

"Well, the men will just have to get used to us," Macie replied with just a touch of attitude. "We're here to stay until we win this war. The world is changing and people will just have to change with it." She immediately recalled her last conversation with Jake, which did not go that well. "Of course," she continued almost absent-mindedly, "that includes my boyfriend who's not at all too happy right now that I'm doing this."

"Where is he? What does he do?" asked Nora.

"He's in the army soon to be a paratrooper."

"Oh, I love their uniforms." Nora's mood suddenly turned glum as if she suddenly remembered something she wanted to forget. "My boyfriend is in the army too. He's in the Thirty-first Infantry Regiment in the Philippines. I haven't heard from him since the surrenders." She was referring to the surrender of the Bataan Peninsula to the Japanese on 9 April and the adjoining island of Corregidor on 10 May 1942. Those surrenders ended effective American resistance in the Philippines with almost 100,000 Filipino and American soldiers becoming prisoners-of-war. To make matters worse for Americans back home, there were rampant rumors of ruthless and cruel treatment and atrocities being committed by the Japanese. "I just pray every night that Butch is safe, wherever he is."

Macie was at a loss for words. She was instantly sorry she had brought up the subject. "The faster we build these ships, the faster we can get our boys back home," was the best she could think of.

"Right, girl!" Nora finally smiled again. "That's the spirit. Screw them all! The Japs, the Germans and those small-minded bastards who are scared we women are going to take their precious jobs." Nora seemed to recover. Macie could tell Nora was summoning up some inner reserve of strength to get herself past this awkward moment. Nora glanced at her wristwatch. "I'd love to chat, Sweetie, but I have to leave now. I'm working the swing shift this week."

Though it was Sunday and she was not to report until the following day, Macie decided she would take a dry run to the shipyard to be sure she would not get lost on her first day on the job. "Can I tag along?" she asked. " So I know my way tomorrow?"

"Sure, Macie. It looks like we'll be working different shifts anyway so we probably won't be seeing much of each other. That makes this small apartment a little more livable."

"That's too bad," answered Macie. "I think I'm going to like having you as a roommate, Nora."

Nora got off the bus at Gate 3 and explained to Macie where to go and what bus to take back. *The busses ran continuously so getting back should be easy*, Macie thought.

Macie took off her gloves and put them in her handbag. She took off her shoes and immediately felt less noticeable. Walking barefoot did not present a problem, as her feet were thick with calluses. With her offer letter in hand, she took a deep breath and approached the security shack.

Chapter Thirteen

The White House East Room – January 13, 1997

"A soldier will fight long and hard for a bit of colored ribbon."

Napoleon Bonaparte (1769 - 1821)

J.P. Kilroy threaded his way through and around the swarm of people crowding the East Room of the White House. He was working his way toward the southeast corner to a group of older men he presumed to be wartime friends of his late father. As he stood on his toes and inched his way toward the group he saw a black man dressed neatly in a dark blue suit talking with three elderly white men. The black man, he assumed, was Lincoln Abraham. He didn't know the other three but he certainly intended to meet them. He anxiously inched closer through the crowd.

"Excuse me, Mister Kilroy." The woman's voice took him by surprise as a beautiful brunette sidled up to him through the crowd and hooked her right arm tightly around his left arm. "My name is Cynthia Powers. I'm with the Army Public Affairs Office. Colonel Chase asked me to find you and take care of you." She smiled broadly as she spoke.

J.P. was momentarily taken off guard. She was in her early forties, he guessed, extremely attractive and well endowed. She was wearing a smart black business suit with a white silk blouse. She was nearly his height. He mustered a few words. "Well hello, Cynthia. How did you know it was me?"

"Ve have our methods," she replied in a thick mock Russian accent as she continued to smile at him. "Besides, your picture next to your newspaper column is a dead giveaway." She was referring to the political column he wrote twice weekly for the *Washington Times*.

"Where is the colonel?" he asked looking around. "We haven't actually met face-to-face and I'd really like to ..."

"Oh, he's getting ready for the ceremony," she interrupted. "That man is intense when it comes to preparation. He'll be reading the citations from that other podium," she nodded toward the second podium under the portrait of George Washington as they moved through the crowd. "I have reserved seats for us over there," she pointed toward the end seats of the first row on the far right directly opposite the portrait of Theodore Roosevelt.

"Good. There are some people right near there I'd like to talk to first," he gestured toward the group of men and noticed they were moving away toward the back of the room.

"No time right now. The ceremony starts in a minute." She pulled his arm tightly against the side of her breast and turned him toward their seats. "We'll find them after," she smiled again. He submissively let her guide him to their seats.

The muted strains of music slowly grew louder. It was classical music that he heard before but could not place. The people in the room took the cue to find their seats. The music became louder after all the guests had been seated and then changed to "God Bless America". All of the participants stood up and applauded as Lincoln was escorted onto the podium. The military escort was a sharp looking young soldier in dress blues, complete with full ribbons and a golden colored shoulder braid known as a *fourragere*. There were seven padded ornate chairs on the stage in front of the gold silk draperies. Lincoln remained standing with his hands crossed in front of him as the escort did an about face and retreated down the stairs.

The music continued and the clapping became progressively louder as two female escorts quickly brought two well-dressed older women up onto the platform and positioned them in front of their seats. The procession continued until the Sergeant-Major-of-the-Army was finally escorted to the last seat. All of them, with the exception of Lincoln and the sergeant major, were surviving relatives of the Medal honorees. They all stood respectfully with quiet pride, their faces etched with deep emotion. They were all African-American.

As soon as the clapping ceased, the sound of "Ruffles and Flourishes" filled the room. The voice over the loudspeaker said, "Ladies and Gentlemen, the President of the United States." The room was then filled with the familiar chords of "Hail to the Chief". The clapping began once again as the President entered. He strode down the aisle, took his position at the podium and raised his hands in a polite signal to stop the applause and then gestured for everyone to be seated.

The benediction followed. J.P. was impressed by the solemnity of the proceeding and the dignified grace of the people on the platform. He let his mind wander a bit and imagined himself sitting up there. There certainly was room for one more chair. Not that he felt any pressing obligation to accept the Medal of Honor for his late father, but he *could have*. Of course, his would have been the only white face up there beside the President's. He found that notion somehow trivially amusing. After the benediction the President rose to the podium.

"Secretary of the Army, Secretary of Defense, General Clayton and the members of the Joint Chiefs, Congressman Williams, families and friends of the Medal recipients and Mister Lincoln Abraham, I'd like to begin by thanking Colonel Carlton Chase of the Army Awards Branch and the members of his Process Team for the nomination of outstanding African-American soldiers for the Medal of Honor during World War II."

The President turned a page on his notes. "Today we recognize seven men as being among the bravest of the brave. Their names join other American heroes like Sergeant York, Jimmie Doolittle, Audie Murphy and only thirty-four hundred other Americans in the history of the United States." The President bit his lip and paused.

"For these men, heroism was a habit," he continued. J.P. turned slightly to see if he could locate the friends of his late father. Sitting at the end of the row, he had a good angle to scan the room without appearing to do so. He certainly did not want to disrespect the proceedings or the President by being inattentive or appearing uninterested. The President's words faded in and out as he turned his head slightly and sought out the three men.

"Reuben Rivers of Oklahoma was awarded a Silver Star while fighting in France with the Seven hundred sixty first Tank Battalion, was terribly wounded and refused an order to withdraw. He was killed on the battlefield," the President went on. As J.P. looked slightly over his shoulder, he became aware that Cynthia still had a firm grasp of his left his arm. He glanced at her and she simply smiled back at him squeezing his arm against her body a little tighter.

"Edward Carter," the President continued, "was wounded five times but still managed to kill six of the enemy and capture two prisoners."

J.P. noticed Congressman Williams among the other dignitaries. He was seated next to General Clayton. The general nodded knowingly to J.P. who nodded in return and turned his head back to the front.

"Lieutenant Charles Thomas was wounded numerous times while he helped others find cover but refused to be evacuated until he was sure his men were safe. Private First Class Wily James was pinned down for an hour while scouting a forward position. But he made his way back to his platoon, planned a counterattack, volunteered to lead the assault and then was killed going to the aid of his wounded platoon leader."

Despite being in the tender clutches of the charming Cynthia Powers, J.P. was determined to locate the three men. He peeked back over his shoulder again and spotted them seated together in the last row up against the wall near the entrance. The first man had a full head of bushy blonde-gray hair. His tweed sport jacket was ill fitted and his brown tie was askew on a blue shirt. It was as if he rarely wore those clothes and it was an effort to put them on for this occasion. His face was aged with lines and wrinkles, as all three of them were, but there was a youthful twinkle in his blue eyes. He reminded J.P. of an aging Beach Boy.

The President went on. "Private George Watson's ship was repeatedly attacked by enemy bombers. He helped others to the life rafts so that they might live, until he himself was so exhausted, he was pulled down by the tow of the sinking ship."

The second man, J.P. noticed, was not wearing a suit or sport coat. He had on an olive drab windbreaker zipped to the top, leaving just enough room to reveal the clasp of his string tie. J.P. had not seen a string tie in years and was curious about the emblem on the clasp. It was the same emblem that was on the front of the baseball cap the man was holding. It was a military insignia that he did not immediately recognize; a circle dissected by an S-shaped line on which the left side was blue and the right side gray. He was a big man, balding and had tears in his eyes. J.P. looked back to the podium as the President continued.

"When the enemy attacked a town in Italy and drove out our forces, Lieutenant John Fox volunteered to remain behind in an observation post. He directed artillery fire and insisted that the fire be aimed at his own position. The barrage he so bravely ordered killed him. When our forces recovered the position they found his body among one hundred dead German soldiers."

The third man, J.P. noticed, was dressed comfortably in a suit. Despite his age, he retained a full head of dark black hair. His suit was dark blue with a white shirt and yellow tie. His black horn rimmed glasses and slightly graying temples gave him a distinguished look.

"One of these heroes is here with us today," the President paused and looked at Lincoln. Cynthia leaned over and whispered, "This is the same action your father won his Medal for."

J.P. tried to focus on the President's words.

"On 20 December 1944, during the Battle of the Bulge, Private Lincoln Abraham along with another soldier, at great risk to their own personal safety and without orders, acting above and beyond the call of duty, provided needed cover and escort to a vulnerable column of wounded American soldiers. Although wounded twice, Private Abraham took out numerous enemy vehicles, infantry and a heavy tank. His aggressive actions saved the lives of over fifty wounded Americans and hundreds of other withdrawing soldiers. If he had not undertaken that brave and selfless action, the entire column would have been wiped out." The President paused and looked at Lincoln who was humbly staring at his folded hands in his lap.

"When that action was over," the President continued, "no officer who witnessed the deed considered recommending Mister Abraham for any commendation at the time, despite the protestations of the men he saved." The President paused and looked out at the audience to let the message sink in. "Why not?" he asked rhetorically. "Simply because he was a black man!"

J.P. shifted in his seat. Cynthia retained her death grip on his arm. He began to comprehend the significance of this ceremony. Black Americans who shed their blood and gave their lives had been denied recognition, not for lack of merit, but simply for the color of their skin. If ever there was a cry for basic fairness, it was for these men who fulfilled their oaths, performed their duties and made remarkable sacrifices only to have their deeds disregarded.

The President looked up from his notes. "Mister Abraham was asked how he handled the lack of respect and honor all these years? He replied with his creed in life 'Give respect before you expect it, treat all people the way you wish to be treated, lead by example, remember the mission and keep going.' These are words for all of us to live by."

The President looked down at his prepared notes. The men we honor today were denied their nation's highest honor, but their deeds could not long be denied. They helped America to become more worthy of them and more true to itself. To the families of the recipients who are gone," the President glanced over to the relatives seated in the rows of chairs on the platform, "may you take great comfort in the honor that has finally been accorded to them, and may God embrace their souls and God bless America."

The President glanced to his left and met the eyes of Colonel Carlton Chase who stood erect behind the other podium. "Colonel, post the orders!"

Chase began reading the orders in a firm, deep voice. "The President of the United States of America, authorized by act of Congress has awarded, in the name of Congress, the Medal of Honor to First Lieutenant Lincoln Abraham, United States Army for conspicuous gallantry..."

The words washed past J.P. Kilroy. He found himself unable to focus on them. There was something else nagging at him. As he watched the solemn dignity of the people on the platform about to receive recognition that was more than fifty years overdue, he realized how significant this event was to the people personally involved. And if doing the right thing and correcting past injustices were important to these people, it was also important to the conscience of the nation.

Before him were Lincoln Abraham and the relatives of the fighting men who had been systematically overlooked by this country, sitting humbly, proudly and patiently awaiting the reward that their loved ones had purchased with their lives so long ago. While the people on the podium embraced their past, he ignored his. Where they found the grace to forgive an ungrateful America, he could not forgive his father. In this realization of the important historical disclosures revealed before his eyes, he suddenly felt ashamed for both ignoring his mother's wishes and his father's past. It was pure curiosity that brought him to the ceremony and provoked him to seek out the few people who might shed some light on his father. But suddenly, witnessing history correct itself, it became more than just simple inquisitiveness. Watching these tearful and humble people, his curiosity morphed into a compelling desire to find out the truth about his own father. Here was a great place to start. He would track down the four old men as soon as the ceremony concluded.

Chase finished reading the order and J.P.'s attention snapped back to the platform. As the President placed the Medal of Honor around Lincoln's neck, an aide stepped behind him and quickly fastened the clasp. The President straightened the blue ribbon that held the Medal high on Lincoln's chest, almost as high and nearly as tight as a bow tie. The President took his hand and shook it. They exchanged quiet words that were inaudible beneath the clicks of the cameras. When the President stepped back, everyone in the room rose and gave a tearful Lincoln a two-minute standing ovation. Even Cynthia let go of his arm to applaud.

Chase asked the audience to remain seated for the remaining presentations. The colonel continued to read the orders and the President handed the remaining framed Medals to the nieces, sons, sisters and widows of the deceased recipients. J.P. feigned polite attention and applauded as each of the Medals was presented. He began to feel a newfound obligation and deeply felt compulsion to honor his own father's bravery just as the people here today were doing for their loved ones. And in his quest he may just find out the truth behind the secret.

After the final Medal was presented, the President concluded the ceremony by thanking everyone who worked so hard to make this day possible. The audience stood as the President exited the room, followed by the military aides and the recipients. People began to wander leisurely to the exits. Small groups gathered around the recipients as they left the stage to convey best wishes and admire the beautifully adorned Medals. J.P. could feel the room itself decompressing after such an intense atmosphere. From his vantage point he could see the crowd dwindle and watched Lincoln receive the handshakes and congratulations of the other three veterans. He noticed a young woman with Lincoln. If he didn't hurry, he would miss them all.

J.P. started to get up. Cynthia still had his arm and tugged on it. "Can you wait just a minute, Mister Kilroy? Colonel Chase wants to meet you."

"Well, I really..." He was thinking about the four men but when Colonel Chase began walking toward him, J.P. shifted gears. His attention was drawn to the colonel.

Cynthia stood up first. "Mister Kilroy, please meet Colonel Carlton Chase." She extended her arm toward the colonel.

"Mister Kilroy, my pleasure." The colonel extended his hand and J.P. stood up and shook it. "If you wouldn't mind just waiting here one moment, there is someone else who wants to meet you." The colonel headed into the crowd of spectators.

J.P. thought, *who would want to meet me?*

Chase returned with the Chairman of the Joint Chiefs. Before J.P. could say anything General Clayton extended his hand. "Mister Kilroy, it's very nice to meet you."

J.P. took the hand and shook it. "It's certainly my pleasure, General."

"I'm here to present you with your father's Medal and explain why you were not up on that platform today." General Clayton glanced over his shoulder to look at the room. It was about half empty as people were still filing out.

"I don't think you owe me an explanation, General," J.P. answered.

"But I do, Mister Kilroy, as a matter of courtesy and principle." Clayton cleared his throat. "Today was extremely important, not only to the recipients of the Medals but for African-Americans. It was a day for redemption, a day to set things right, for healing past wounds. The importance of this event extended far beyond this room."

"General, I'm not here as a reporter. I'm a columnist but you won't see this event in my column, ever. I'm here as the son of a soldier. Based on what I heard and saw today, nothing could diminish the honor of these men."

Clayton seemed to relax a bit. "That's very gracious of you, Mister Kilroy."

"General," J.P. replied. "It's all good. I originally declined the invitation anyway," he glanced over at Colonel Chase who nodded.

Clayton seemed to ignore the comment. "Without any disrespect to your father for the well deserved honor he earned," the general exhaled, "any white face on that platform, other than the President's, might have been interpreted by some as diminishing the honor." General Clayton paused. "We certainly didn't want to offend you or the memory of your father but today was envisioned by the President long ago as the day that America paid its long standing debt to deserved African-Americans who served with distinction and who were denied recognition. We didn't want to mar the event by anything that could be perceived by anyone as diminishing those achievements. That would include the ridiculous speculation that the only reason African-Americans were being recognized was because we missed the achievement of one white soldier. And in order to remedy that, we had to drag along his cohort and subsequently other African-Americans. In this instance, your father was the tail, not the dog, and we didn't want any speculation or misunderstanding that it was his missed award that dragged in the others."

J.P. smiled at that, considered it humorous. "That's absurd! Anyone can see these men deserved this honor."

"The absurd runs deep in this town and the President decided we would not fuel that speculative line of gossip. And so, we agreed that I would present your father's award to you in a separate meeting. Then you changed your mind and decided to come here today so we arranged to present it right here and now."

"I understand. Thank you, General."

General Clayton again glanced over his shoulder. The CSPAN lights and cameras were turned off and the equipment was being disassembled. The room was nearly empty. J.P. was happy to notice the four veterans still standing and chatting near the exit.

A thought occurred to J.P. and he looked at Cynthia. "And your role was?" he smiled.

"Colonel Chase asked me to keep an eye on you, make sure you were attended to, make sure you were comfortable until the ceremony was over," she smiled back. "I hope it wasn't too terrible for you?" She was smiling at him.

"It was delightful." He made a short bow to her and turned to the general. "What now?"

General Clayton looked behind him again. There were still a few people left in the room. He looked at Colonel Chase and said, "Colonel, post the orders."

J.P. raised his hand in mild protest. "No need to read them now. I'll read them later."

Colonel Chase looked at General Clayton who nodded. The colonel stepped up on the platform and pulled out a black cloth bag from beneath the empty table. The Medal of Honor was encased in a thick polished wooden frame covered in glass. It was suspended on a black velvet background by its blue ribbon in the form of a slightly angled V. Above the Medal was the accompanying blue ribbon adorned with white stars. The gold colored plaque read:

Corporal John Kilroy
United States Army

Chase handed it to J.P. who held the frame and began to choke up. After a solemn moment, Colonel Chase extended his hand.

"Congratulations and thank you," said the colonel. They all shook hands and he and Clayton hastily exited the East Room.

J.P. stared at the Medal of Honor; momentarily absorbed by the grave reality of what he had just experienced and was startled when Cynthia quickly hugged him. "I don't know about you, Mister Kilroy, but I enjoyed myself today."

He smiled back. He had to admit she played her part in an exceptional fashion. She was warm, gracious and sociable, almost too much so. "Me too," he replied. J.P. then looked to the back of the room and stopped smiling. The four men that he waited so patiently to speak to were gone.

Chapter Fourteen

Newport News, Virginia – June 28, 1942

"Remember upon the conduct of each depends the fate of all."

Alexander the Great (356 BC - 323 BC)

"Can I help you, ma'am?" The sentry at the gate was a white-haired older gentleman wearing a security guard's uniform. He was busy observing the credentials of the swarm of workers that were entering the facility. He deduced immediately, by her clothes and body language, Macie Vance was not a shipyard worker.

Macie handed him her job offer letter. He read it quickly. "Congratulations and welcome," he smiled. "But security administration and the welding school are closed today. They'll be open tomorrow."

"I know," she smiled back. "I was hoping to look around just a teeny bit, so I could find my way a little easier tomorrow?"

The security guard smiled. "I can give you a temporary visitor's pass but you'll probably be stopped by Navy SPs who patrol the yard." He was referring to the Shore Patrol, the navy's version of the army's Military Police. "Just show them your offer letter and this pass." He signed and handed her the pass. "The security building is on your right." He pointed to a building about a block away on the thoroughfare that led through the gate. "The welding school is a little further down on the same cross-street."

"Where are the big ships being built?" she asked.

"The dry-docks are straight ahead then left when you reach the river." He smiled. Everyone at the yard took pride in the construction of the big warships. "Follow the big cranes. You can't miss them."

She began to walk straight ahead, still self-conscious but mixing in with the throng of workers entering the yard. In a few minutes she was facing the security administration building. This would be her first stop tomorrow. She began to sense the excitement of embarking on this great, new personal adventure.

The shipyard was laid out like a miniature city with avenues and cross streets. She followed the directions, began walking down a cross street and easily found the white wooden building that housed Welding School Number 2. After she fixed the location in her mind, she backtracked to the main thoroughfare and proceeded toward the river.

The Newport News Shipyard was built on over 500 acres of a narrow strip of land flanking the James River. The river ran northwest to southeast into Hampton Roads Bay before finally spilling out into Chesapeake Bay and the Atlantic Ocean. On the south side of Hampton Roads Bay was the city of Norfolk.

It was nearly dusk and there was a slight chill in the air as she approached the river. Passing the many buildings, shops and warehouses, she could now see the huge cranes that pointed skyward over the wharves like giant sentinels. A light breeze whipped up as she neared the water and she could smell the salty air. As she cleared the last building before the James River, her eyes fell upon the most spectacular sight she had ever seen.

Before her were three enormous dry-docks stretching well out into the river. Within each dry-dock stood the unfinished skeleton of a ship towering well into the sky. One ship appeared nearly finished. Workers were everywhere, pouring over, inside and outside of the partially completed structures. They reminded her of bees building a honeycomb, each individual knowing exactly what to do and contributing unselfishly to the task at hand. The motion was constant and ceaseless. From the bowels of the three huge skeleton structures showered the sparks of the welding torches. The rhythmic clanging sounds of some unknown machinery, the harmonic beat of unseen motors and the pervasive hissing of the copious welding torches amplified the fantastic surreal sight before her. As the sun fell into the west and streaked the heavens in purples and pinks, the darkening sky silhouetted the streaming sparks into an incredible fireworks display. She stood there in awe of the incredible sight before her. It was no small comfort to realize this scene was being played out and repeated in every foundry, factory and shipyard across the vast breadth of the United States. The industrial giant that was America was awakening. Tomorrow she would take her first step in helping to build ships like the colossal hulks taking shape before her. This is why she came. This is what she had to be a part of. This is what Jake didn't understand. She stood there at the edge of the dock, exhilarated by the moment, and took it all in.

Before Pearl Harbor, Macie was mostly concerned about getting by. She was delighted Sheriff Abbott arranged for the job in Mrs. Gillaspie's boarding house but the job was menial and she soon tired of it. Nevertheless, she was grateful and continued to work hard. She spent her leisure time at the local movie house. Films such as *Citizen Kane*, *Sergeant York* and *The Grapes of Wrath* sparked her imagination.

She looked forward to Jake's frequent trips home. Those visits were the highlight of her existence and she awaited them with great anticipation. Jake would always leave her some money to be sure she had enough. She fastidiously banked it. They spoke of marriage and Jake was waiting to get his discharge from the army so they could start their lives in earnest, get married and raise a family. That all changed with the attack on Pearl Harbor.

Macie was just nineteen years old. She was not worldly but astute enough to know there was a lot about the world she didn't know. The Movietone Newsreel was updated weekly in the movie theatres and was the primary source of visual news for all Americans. The news, however, was heavily censored and the prevailing feeling among most Americans was the truth was always worse than what was reported. The Movietone News was usually tardy; the first films of a viciously devastated Pearl Harbor were not shown in theatres until February of 1942.

Macie often heard the names of places she had never known before. Places where America or its Allies had been badly defeated. Places like Wake Island, the Philippines, Malaya, Libya, Burma, Java, Bataan and others. She read the local newspaper, *The Bedford Bulletin*, much more thoroughly and listened to the nightly war news on the radio. She started visiting the local library to look up places in the atlas whose names were unfamiliar. Much of what was happening was still somewhat confusing to her, although she was learning more every day. The more she learned the more she realized that America was in grave danger of losing the War.

The first snippet of good news came in May when the newspapers excitedly proclaimed that American B-25 Mitchell Medium Bombers had bombed Tokyo on 18 April 1942. The reports electrified the American people who were starved for any morsel of good news. Macie listened to the stirring broadcast by Gabriel Heatter on the *Mutual Radio Network* on 10 May. It surprised her at how good the news made her feel. The United States had finally struck back and that was a great morale boost to a dispirited population. The details were top secret. It was not public knowledge that only sixteen bombers participated in the raid and the actual physical damage to Japan was negligible. "The Tokyo Raid" wouldn't signal the end of bad news but it was a long awaited and welcomed first bit of good news.

President Franklin D. Roosevelt was so elated that he joked to the newspapermen that the planes were flown from "Shangri-La", a mythical kingdom in the contemporary Hollywood film, *Lost Horizons*. But most Americans, as well as the Japanese, realized that the navy had figured out how to launch bombers from the deck of an aircraft carrier and after the planes dropped their payloads, they headed for China. That the bombers were launched from the aircraft carrier *Hornet (CV-8,)* escorted by the carrier *Enterprise (CV-6)*, was top-secret until well into the War.

While Macie was learning from the newsreels and newspapers, changes were taking place before her eyes that drove home the urgency. Ration books were issued to all civilians limiting the consumption of everyday items such as rubber, nylon, sugar, gasoline, meat, butter and shoes. Older men volunteered as air-raid wardens and could be clearly seen wearing their air-raid helmets and walking the streets of Bedford alongside busy school children collecting scrap. Schools conducted special drives to gather rubber, cooking fats, aluminum pots, tin cans and other scrap metal. Tin was particularly helpful in weapons manufacturing and the scrap drives provided half of all the tin required. The saying heard most was "Use it up, wear it out, make do or do without". The sign on the side of the scrap pickup truck read "Slap the Jap With Scrap." The country was slowly working its way out of the grip of a national panic.

America's population was 130,000,000, half of which lived on farms or in small towns. Many planted Victory Gardens to grow vegetables to ease shortages and make more food available for the troops. Gardens sprung up everywhere from the White House lawn to Alcatraz Island; from Copley Square in Boston to New York's Ellis Island. All manner of land was used including front yards, baseball fields, parks, vacant lots and unused commercial real estate. Rich and poor alike planted their seeds in fire escape flowerpots and country estate window boxes. The government hoped to encourage the citizens to plant 5,000,000 gardens. It got 20,000,000. By 1943 one third of the 30,000,000 pounds of produce consumed in the United States came from Victory Gardens.

With all of this working on her mind and psyche, Macie began to grow up. She was a witness to great events and they were changing her. That Jake hadn't noticed was hardly her fault. When she tried to explain how the movie film *Mrs. Miniver* affected her, Jake was barely listening. He had become angry with her when she traveled ninety miles to Charlottesville. Sheriff Abbott secured the round-trip bus ticket so Macie could attend a fundraiser sponsored by Greer Garson, the star of *Mrs. Miniver*. Macie got to meet her in person and even got an autograph.

This trip and all Macie discovered profoundly affected her. Lane High School, in Charlottesville, sold enough war bonds to buy nearly fifty jeeps and a bomber. She learned the government was financing half the cost of the War by borrowing money from American citizens. Nearly everyone bought bonds. They were designed not only to fund the War but also to soak up the excess money that would otherwise send inflation soaring in an economy fueled by growing wages and a shortage of consumer goods. Macie also learned other countries like Poland, England and France had suffered tremendous casualties among civilians and soldiers. If America hoped to avoid this devastation, she could not lose this War.

It was on the bus ride home that Macie, inspired by all that she had been exposed to, decided she needed to personally contribute more to the war effort. It seemed like everyone else was doing something. Even her favorite movie star, James Stewart, joined the Army Air Forces in March 1941 despite having just won an Oscar for Best Actor for his role in the 1940 film, *The Philadelphia Story*. If Jimmy could do it, so could she!

As if answering her prayer, the next morning there was a young couple sitting at a table at Mrs. Gillaspie's Boarding House. She poured them coffee and put some homemade cinnamon rolls on the table.

"Nice, steady hand," the young redhead said to the blonde man, commenting on Macie's pouring.

"That's hardly the acid-test, Roxie," the man answered. "But it's certainly a place to start." Then he looked directly at Macie. "How would you like to have a job in a shipyard, young lady?"

That's how Macie Vance met Roxanne Rawls and Derek Edson.

Macie was stunned but immediately slid a chair out from under the table, placed the coffee carafe down and sat. "Tell me more!"

The pair was on a recruiting drive through the east coast states in an effort to locate and hire shipyard workers. They were particularly looking for older men and young women since they were the only reliable sources of much needed labor left in America.

At first Macie was dubious about her own qualifications, especially her limited education. But apparently that was the reason Roxanne was part of the team. With neatly cut short red hair, green eyes and a cute round freckled face over high cheekbones, Roxanne's perpetual expression was a knowing grin. There was something about the way she looked right into Macie's eyes and carefully listened to every word that elicited a great deal of trust in a short period of time. The conversation between the two women became personal and comfortable with only an occasional glance toward Derek to seek validation of a comment or a point, to which he always dutifully nodded his agreement.

After speaking with Roxanne for a short while, Macie became convinced that not only could she be trained to become a welder, but that the shipyard and her country *needed her* to become a welder.

Her conversation with Roxanne relaxed her. The idea of being needed was new to Macie. She was always the needy one and now someone or something actually needed her. It was a good feeling and it inspired her. She glanced over at Derek. He was hunched forward, his hands on his lap beneath the table. She noticed he hadn't touched his coffee and said with a broad smile, "Are you going to drink that?"

He was caught off guard. "Uh, no. I...uh...don't drink coffee."

She glanced furtively around the room. There were no other guests and Mrs. Gillaspie was still in the kitchen. "Would you mind, then?" she asked as she slid the coffee over to her side of the table and took a long sip. "This stuff's in short supply," she joked.

"Not at all," he smiled back. She seemed like a bashful girl but was fighting through her shyness to engage in the conversation. He liked that.

"You've been pretty quiet all this time," she said as she placed her cup back into the saucer. "What do *you* think?"

Derek seemed surprised by the directness of the question. Everything about him looked young, in his early to mid-twenties, except the crow's feet in the corners of his green-gray eyes. Somehow, his eyes looked older than the rest of him. Macie thought him to be extremely handsome and assumed most other women agreed. Derek nervously brushed a wisp of blond hair from his forehead with his left hand and answered her while avoiding her direct gaze. "Roxie knows what she's talking about." He smiled feebly at Roxanne. "She took the welding course to prove it can be done by a woman." He was not speaking loudly but his baritone voice was convincing. "Together, me and Roxie have been touring the countryside speaking at high schools, colleges, churches, community groups...you name it." He glanced over at Roxanne again and she nodded. He continued. "I'm one of many foremen in the Fitters Department and I supervise a group of welders who are building my ship." Everyone in the shipyard referred to his or her work assignment as *my ship*. He hesitated for a few seconds. "And I have no problem with women working on my ship." He leaned back and looked at Macie. "Without knowing you I can tell that you are interested, passionate and more than willing. Pass the course at the welding school and you'll become a tack-welder. Fail the course and the worst that can happen to you is that you're right back here where you started." He waved his left hand around the room and shrugged his broad shoulders. "I don't think you'll fail but you have nothing to lose by trying."

Macie realized there would be one obstacle to all this. Jake! She would eventually have to deal with that. As if to signal her decision, she stood up, took off her apron and asked. "Where do I sign?" It was 15 May 1942.

The next time Jake came home in early June she had a difficult time broaching the conversation. It was not that she feared him; on the contrary, she adored him. But she also knew how fiercely protective he was. She couldn't recall how the discussion got started and subsequently tried as hard as she could not to remember the painful details. It was their first argument. She was surprised by the intensity of his anger. That he could not see or respect her point of view infuriated her as well. She could tell he was surprised by her forcefulness and stubbornness in defending her decision. The argument echoed in her ears. Words that she wanted to forget.

"Why are you doing this, Macie?"

"I need to do something Jake. We're in a war."

"It's those damn stupid movies," yelled Jake.

"Why don't you respect what I'm doing?"

"You didn't even talk it over with me. You just did it!"

"Because I knew this would be your reaction. You don't understand that I need to do this."

"You need to be here in Bedford where people can watch out for you. Where I know you're safe. You don't belong in a damn shipyard." Jake was angry but pleading.

"Jake, pretty soon you're not going to be able to get leave whenever you want to come home. You'll be shipped out sooner or later." She was grasping at straws, trying desperately to make him understand.

"All the more reason for you to stay here in Bedford where you have friends. And I can make more money. There's a volunteer outfit in the army, paratroopers, that pays more. And it will probably keep me in the States for a few more months, maybe even another year."

"Jake," she screamed. "Don't you do anything stupid or dangerous!"

Jake grabbed her arms as she burst into tears. "I need you to be safe. Just don't do anything yet. Let me handle this." He held her close to him as she sobbed.

What troubled Macie the most was the conversation ended without resolution. He didn't agree not to join the paratroopers and she didn't agree to cancel her plans to take the job. He walked her home while she was still sobbing and kissed her lightly on the cheek. The last thing he asked was that she not to do anything. That was four weeks ago and they had not spoken since.

For the weeks that followed that emotional argument, she replayed it in her mind. She relived it every day until it made her physically ill. Macie loved Jake and couldn't accept that he didn't respect her needs or wishes. Knowing how stubborn he was, Macie was sure he would volunteer for the paratroopers as soon as he could. They were both young and impulsive and were both doing exactly what the other one didn't want them to do. It frightened her. Handling conflict was never her strong point and now she was dealing with the biggest conflict of her young life.

As she stood near the James River at sunset she was proud of her own resolve and the courage it took for her to be standing where she was at that moment. Once she made up her mind, she discovered a newfound tenacity. Jake would probably call it stubborn, she mused. In spite of her determination, she knew she was risking a great deal. Learning new skills in a different world far from her comfort zone would challenge her to her absolute limits. A little voice inside her kept telling her that she and Jake would be all right. Jake would eventually come around if she just didn't give up on him. She had her work cut out for herself on both accounts.

Macie thought, *enough for today, time to go back.* As she began to turn around and take the long walk to the gate, she heard the deep voice behind her.

"Miss Macie Vance? Is that you?"

Chapter Fifteen

L'Enfant Plaza Hotel – January 13, 1997

"Desperate affairs require desperate measures."

Admiral Lord Nelson (1758 - 1805)

Cynthia Powers was relaxing in the lounge of the Café Pierre Bar, just where she said she would be. J.P. Kilroy immediately spotted her as he entered the wide, spacious lobby of the L'Enfant Plaza Hotel. Ignoring the concierge who stepped out to greet him, he turned toward the isolated but comfortable lounge tucked away in the far left corner of the lobby. There were just a few customers, businessmen he presumed, in the lounge.

She was smoking a cigarette while enjoying a Martini. She heard his footsteps echo off the white Marfil marble floor and looked up from her high-back quilted armchair to greet him. Cynthia was wearing the same business suit as earlier but changed the white blouse for a powder blue one with a neckline low enough to show ample cleavage. She quickly stabbed her cigarette into a crystal ashtray and glanced at her watch.

"Right on time, Mister Kilroy," she remained seated and extended her hand.

"Please, call me J.P." He took her hand, resisted a ridiculous urge to kiss it and shook it gently. "It's really nice of you to set this up." He sat in an identical armchair next to her with a view of the lobby entrance.

"Not at all. It was the least I could do, considering." She left the sentence unfinished but he knew what she was referring to. *Right, Cynthia. Considering that you and your boss kept me occupied for so long that the men I needed to speak to left by the time you finished with me!*

"Well, thank you just the same," he said sincerely. "You didn't have to do this."

"Oh, you'd be surprised what Public Affairs Officers are asked to do," she replied with an impish grin.

A waiter appeared and he ordered a glass of Cabernet Franc for himself as well as a refill for Cynthia. She reached for the pack of True Green Menthol Lights on the small glass-topped table between them. "Would you mind, terribly?"

"Go right ahead. I'm an ex-smoker myself."

"Isn't everybody?" She shook a cigarette from the pack and picked up the lighter. "Thanks. Sometimes ex-smokers are the worst…the most judgmental. I'm glad you're not."

He took the lighter and lit it. She surrounded his hand with both of hers, guided the flame to the tip of her cigarette, holding on to his hand just a little too long. He immediately got aroused. *She was coming on to him,* he thought. She was a sexy, sensual woman and he wondered how she would look naked. The heated metal on the lighter singed his thumb, shattered the fantasy growing in his mind and snapped him back to reality. He winced and the lighter fell to the floor.

"Too hot for you?" She had a broad mischievous smile.

"Uh…could you…I mean…could we…the dinner?" he stammered, changing the subject back to why they were there in the first place. She was certainly sending out strong vibes and he found himself increasingly more attracted to her. He would definitely have to see where this flirtatious mating-dance might lead, but only after he addressed the pressing matter at hand.

Her demeanor became slightly more businesslike after obviously embarrassing him. "Ah, yes, the dinner. The good news is they are all staying at this hotel, compliments of the DOD." She was referring to the Department of Defense. "That's why I arranged to have dinner here, in the American Grill Restaurant. The food's not all that great but it's convenient. By the way, dinner is on *you*."

"That's great. Is that the bad news?"

"No. Mister Abraham is not staying for dinner. He has a plane to catch."

"Shit! I really wanted to spend time with him most of all."

"Be good and maybe I can arrange something down the road," she flashed her impish grin again.

"Could we please focus here?" he asked calmly, exasperated.

He became rattled when she toyed with him and she was enjoying it. "Sorry," she smiled. "Sometimes I just can't help it." She composed herself. "Schuyler Johnson, Harley Tidrick and Frank West will be joining us. I believe they're all leaving tomorrow but I could be mistaken."

"Fantastic! I really do appreciate this."

"Actually, Colonel Chase…" she began but stopped when he suddenly stood up.

"There he is now, excuse me." J.P. hurried quickly to the main desk area of the lobby toward a distinguished looking black man and a beautiful, young woman. His short salt and pepper hair was heavily gray on the sides. A long cashmere overcoat covered his dark blue business suit but not his white shirt and gray tie. The white scarf around his neck made him look like a notable musical conductor. The young woman walking alongside him was wheeling a pull-suitcase toward the front door.

"Excuse me, Mister Abraham," said J.P. as he approached them and offered his hand. "My name is J.P. Kilroy, I mean John Kilroy."

Lincoln stopped and looked at J.P. a glint of recognition in his eyes. "Of course, you're John's son." Lincoln took his hand in both of his own and shook it warmly. "This is my granddaughter, Keisha."

J.P. nodded, smiled and shook her hand. She was polite but appeared hurried.

"I wonder if you have a minute to…" he began when she interrupted him.

"I'm sorry Mister Kilroy but we do have to go. We're late to the airport."

"She pretty much runs the show for me these days," Lincoln smiled at him and then at her. "I owe today to her persistence…and to your father, of course."

"Of course, today, I'm sorry." In his haste J.P. had completely neglected to mention the Medal. "Congratulations, sir," he apologized.

"Grandfather, we have to go," urged Keisha.

"Just one minute, dear." He turned to J.P. "I just wanted you to know, Mister Kilroy, that I asked the President, at lunch at the White House today, to include someone from…"

"It's all right," J.P. interrupted. He looked at Keisha. "I completely understand. It's not a problem." He turned his attention back to Lincoln. "I just was hoping that you could tell me something about my father, how you met him, what you knew about him, how you won that Medal together?"

Lincoln gave him a strange and quizzical look. "But, the President insisted." He continued as if not hearing what J.P. said.

"Please, Mister Kilroy, we do have to go," Keisha was getting impatient and tugged at Lincoln's arm, coaxing him toward the door.

"Perhaps I can call?" J.P. asked.

"Colonel Chase knows how to reach us," she called back over her shoulder. "Sorry, no time now." Lincoln had a look of resignation on his face as his granddaughter led him away. "Nice to meet you," were her last words as they exited the lobby.

J.P. became aware of Cynthia standing alongside him as Lincoln and his granddaughter entered a waiting taxi. "Well, that was a strange conversation," he remarked.

"The man is well into his seventies," she replied. "He seems lucid and articulate but I'm sure he has his senior moments. They probably all do."

"I'm sure," he sighed, still staring out the lobby door.

"I heard somewhere that they're dying at a rate of fifteen hundred a day."

"Who's dying?" he asked.

"The World War II veterans," she answered. "They're getting up there in years!"

"Dying," he muttered. "Yes, of course, just like my father." He mused on the thought for a moment as the taxi pulled away. He wondered if he would ever see or speak to Lincoln Abraham again. At that moment, he resolved not to let too much time go by before he contacted him. He turned to Cynthia, gently grabbed her elbow and guided her toward the hotel restaurant entrance.

"Well, if they're dying at such a rapid rate, we'd better hurry up and have dinner."

Chapter Sixteen

Newport News, Virginia – June 28, 1942

"There is a charm about the forbidden that makes it unspeakably desirable."

Mark Twain, (Samuel Clemens) (1835 - 1910)

Macie Vance assumed she was being challenged by the Shore Patrol but then recognized the deep baritone voice of Derek Edson. She was surprised and strangely delighted as she turned to face him.

"It *is* you," he smiled broadly. "I'm so glad to see you here." She reached to shake hands but instead of shaking hands, Derek held out his left hand and simply held her hand motionless. She automatically glanced down toward his right hand hanging by his side and was disturbed by what she saw. Derek didn't notice. He was avoiding her eyes, still that shy boy she met at the boarding house a few weeks ago.

"Hi, Derek," she answered weakly. "What a surprise to see you, too." She stumbled for words. "I came to check out the place so I could find my way tomorrow." She looked up and around and swept her arm in an arc. "It's huge."

"It certainly is, " he replied.

"I was just on my way back."

"So was I. I'll walk with you."

"What are you doing here?" Macie asked. "I thought you were out recruiting."

"All done with that," he answered. "Back to my regular day job now."

They walked toward the gate together. She sensed by his silence that he was also nervous. After a long minute he spoke. "So, you were looking at the carriers?"

"They're amazing," she answered. "I wandered over to the docks and saw those great big ships being built. It's so fantastic and exciting."

"We need those carriers badly," he volunteered. "We lost one in the Coral Sea last month and another at Midway just a few weeks ago," he whispered.

"Really? How do you know that?"

The newsreels were just showing accounts of the Battle of the Coral Sea but not that America lost an aircraft carrier and the censored accounts of the Battle of Midway, while claiming a great victory, were still shrouded in the utmost secrecy.

"Scuttlebutt," he answered.

She responded with a confused look on her face.

"I still have friends in the navy and they pass along the rumors to me. That's what they call rumors in the navy," he answered.

Macie nodded. She understood the concept of gossip all too well. "Is the… uh…scuttlebutt accurate?" she asked.

"Oh, yeah," he answered. "We lost the *Lexington* at Coral Sea and the *Yorktown* at Midway. They need to be replaced. These ships behind us are pretty far along in construction. One of them will be launched next month. They're desperately needed to replace those losses."

Macie nodded again. "So we have our work cut out for us. Right?"

Macie seemed genuinely interested so he just kept explaining. "These are all Essex-class fast-carriers, the most modern in the fleet. They displace twenty-seven thousand tons, can carry almost ninety planes and get up to nearly thirty-three knots."

"Displace? Knots?" she smiled back at him. "I'm sorry?"

"No, I'm sorry," he apologized. "I can get a bit carried away. These are terms you'll learn in time. But for now, just know they are big and fast and powerful." She nodded at the explanation and Derek continued. "The one almost done is named *Essex, CV-9*. That keel was laid down...uh...she was started...last April. She'll be launched next month, like I said."

"Then off to war?" Macie asked. She hoped she was not asking stupid questions.

"Not right away," he answered. "There's some more work to do once she's afloat to complete the construction. Then there are sea trials to make sure everything is ship-shape and some training cruises to work up the crew. Hopefully, she'll be commissioned by the end of the year. *Then* off to war."

"What about the other two?" she asked.

"The *Intrepid* and the *Bon Homme Richard*," he answered. "They were both laid down this past December. Hopefully we can get them launched in something between a year and fifteen months." Derek shook his head slightly as if in contemplation. "The problem is labor. Not just here but all over and not just numbers but skills. With most of the able bodied young men going into the services, we're left with older men, military rejects and women. And they all have to be trained."

"Well, thank the good Lord for the women," Macie quipped good-naturedly.

"I didn't mean it that way, Macie," Derek stammered. "It's just that it used to take three years to build an aircraft carrier and now we have to figure out how to do it in a year. It won't be easy but we just can't take three years to build a carrier any longer." He paused. "I'm afraid I'm boring you with all this ship talk," he finally said.

"Not at all," she sighed. "I have a lot to learn. It's my job now, too."

"Well okay," he smiled nervously. "My team is working on the *Bon Homme Richard* but I doubt she'll keep that name."

"Why?" Macie asked.

Derek glanced around to make sure no one was within earshot before he answered. "We just lost two carriers. The scuttlebutt is the carrier about to be launched from the Bethlehem Shipyard in Quincy, Massachusetts, will be renamed the *Lexington*, as sort of a memorial. I have it on good authority and also a strong feeling that my ship will be renamed the *Yorktown*."

"Maybe I'll get to work on the... *Yorktown*, too," she smiled.

"You never know," he smiled back hopefully.

The thoroughfare was lightly traveled between shift changes and only a few workers were walking to and from the gate. Macie grabbed for her arms as a crisp breeze blew by and sent a chill through her body. Derek noticed and immediately took off his jacket. She fought off the impulse to touch his hand as he placed his jacket over her shoulders. He saw her eyes focus quickly on his right hand and then look away.

"I'm one of those military rejects I spoke of." He held up his right arm so she could more clearly see the prosthesis on his hand. It was actually more of a flesh-colored glove. The thumb and first two fingers were his but the ring and pinky fingers belonged to the prosthesis. The apparatus was both awkward and ugly. "Compliments of the Japanese Imperial Navy."

"You were at Pearl Harbor?" she asked, astonished.

"Yes, I was."

"What happened to you?"

Derek hesitated. He hadn't spoken about what happened to him to anyone since he left the navy. Macie appeared to be a good listener and he was still trying to impress her, so he answered.

"I was a Machinist Mate aboard the seaplane tender USS *Tangier*. We were docked on the northwest side of Ford Island, the Pearl City side, at berth F-10. The target ship *Utah* was moored stern-to-stern with us. She was a big one, used to be a battleship but at the time she was a training ship. The newer battleships on Battleship Row were anchored on the other side of Ford Island. I was on my way to the mess hall for Sunday breakfast when General quarters sounded. I went right to my battle station, a fifty caliber anti-aircraft machine gun on the port quarter. If it wasn't for our captain...God bless him." Derek paused to gather his thoughts. The memories gripped him for a moment. Macie was captivated; afraid he would stop telling the story.

"What about the captain?"

"Well, the word came down that an Admiral's Inspection of all ships was to start on Monday. Captains were ordered to stow all the ammo from the ready boxes on all the deck guns, to below decks, in order to keep the gun tubs as neat as possible. They were also ordered to open up all bulkheads and watertight doors to air out the watertight compartments." Derek shook his head in disgust. "Imagine that? How many lives did we lose for a stupid inspection?" It was a rhetorical question. He continued. "Anyhow, our captain didn't buy any of that crap. He was a salty, tough son-of-a-gun and he ordered the gunners mates to keep our ammo with the guns. Because of that, and only because of that, we were the first ship in the fleet to open fire at the enemy planes."

"It must have been terrible," she prompted him again.

"It truly was. The *Tangier* is not a fighting ship but she fought like a lion that day. The Japanese sent three torpedoes into the *Utah* and she turned turtle. They bombed and torpedoed the ships on Battleship Row at will. They strafed and bombed the airplane hangars on Ford Island. They pretty much attacked wherever they wanted. Our ship was covered in smoke for most of the morning because other ships and the oil on the water were burning. The *Tangier* was undamaged, never took a hit. We were like a kid in a dark closet, peeking out but no one could see in. All of our guns were blazing away. The lowly seaplane tender taking on all those damned Jap planes. They never found us and they never hurt us. Then, after about forty-five minutes their planes just flew away."

"Was it over?" she asked.

"No, there was another wave. But we took advantage of the short lull to put some boats into the water to pick up survivors from the *Utah*. Then an officer, who knew I was a welder, told me there were men trapped in the *Utah,* which was capsized. That was some sight, that big ship almost upside down in the water. Anyway the captain wanted someone to go help them out so I took my acetylene torch and tanks over there and started banging on the hull. When I heard the banging back, I cut a hole. A couple of guys climbed out. I'll never forget the looks on their faces; sheer panic and pure happiness. But before I could cut any more holes the second wave hit and a bomb blast knocked me down. I slid off the hull into the water. My own guys from the *Tangier* pulled me out and I started helping them pull out other guys. I wasn't hurt that bad but I lost all my gear. Funny what you think of at a time like that." He paused again with a distant look in his eyes, as if he was able to see it all over again. "It was crazy out there in the water. Our ship was firing our three-inch guns at a Jap midget sub that somehow snuck into the harbor. Huge clouds of thick, black smoke billowed from the burning wrecks. Bullets were flying all over. You can hear them cracking past your ears and splashing in the water. I'm pulling this guy out and his skin comes off in my hands. I almost threw up! Everyone was yelling or screaming. Shrapnel was flying all over, singing through the air. Explosions so loud you could hardly hear yourself think. Then this guy yells 'look at your hand'. I look down and I'm bleeding like a pig and the last two fingers of my right hand are each dangling by a thread. Shrapnel must have sliced right through them. I didn't even feel a thing. So I tore my shirt and wrapped my hand to stop the bleeding. When we got back to the ship I was sent to sick bay and they cut off the fingers." He paused. By one in the afternoon it was all over. The navy doctor's treated my wounds, bandaged me up, shipped me out and before I knew it they discharged me from the navy and gave me this to wear." He picked up his right hand.

"I'm sorry," was all she could manage. His description of the attack left her breathless.

"It's okay," he answered. "I'd rather be out there with my shipmates, but right now I have an important job back here. And they didn't get any of the carriers. We caught a break there."

They walked along in silence for a few more minutes. She had the urge to comfort him. They passed through the gate and she returned her pass. As they walked across the road toward the bus stop in silence she turned to him and placed her arm on his shoulder.

"Stop for a second, please." She bent over slightly and with her free hand slipped a shoe on her foot. He instinctively grabbed her by the shoulders while she put the second shoe on. "Thanks," she smiled as she steadied herself. "I almost forgot I wasn't wearing them."

"My pleasure," he smiled back.

Macie hoped he didn't notice her blushing. Derek was handsome but there was something else about him that made her uncomfortable. She couldn't quite put her finger on it. Perhaps it was his boyish shyness or maybe because he had seen so much of the world already. Whatever it was, it confused her.

"Where's Roxanne?" she asked, changing the subject. "Are you still working together?"

"Oh, no. Roxie resigned. Got a better offer."

"We're you two...?" She let the question hang in the air.

"Involved? Oh no, certainly not," he answered. "We're good friends, but not that way."

They sat on the bench to wait for the bus and Macie asked, "Where did she go?"

"All these questions," he smiled at her. "Roxie Rawls has a degree in Aeronautical Engineering from Purdue and is a certified licensed pilot with over six hundred hours."

"I knew she was smart," Macie interrupted.

"She certainly is." Derek agreed. "Roxie went north to Washington D.C. to help her good friend and fellow pilot Nancy Harkness Love establish a ferry service using female pilots. They have to convince the Army Transport Command that the Women's Auxiliary Flying Service, that's what they call themselves, can fill the need for more ferry pilots to move planes from factories to air bases. She is lining up twenty-eight outstanding female pilots to start up this new unit once it's approved. Roxie was one of them and after she helps Nancy seal the deal, will be ferrying all kinds of planes, including combat planes."

"Wow! They're actually letting women fly military airplanes." Macie was impressed.

"I don't see why not," answered Derek. "The Brits have been doing that for years with their Air Transport Auxiliary. Besides, Amelia Earhart already paid the price to give women pilots credibility."

"Well, thank the good Lord for the women," Macie quipped again.

Derek smiled back at her. "I suppose so."

A GMC Yellow Coach bus turned the corner and he summoned up some courage. "Do you have a steady guy?"

"Yes, he's in the army." She stood up and walked toward the bus as it was pulling in.

"Serious?" he called out over the noise of the bus engine.

She wasn't sure if he heard the answer as she stepped onto the bus. Between the clamor of the motor and the swish of the pneumatic bus doors opening and closing, she could not be sure if he heard her mutter, "I hope so."

Chapter Seventeen

L'Enfant Plaza Hotel – January 13, 1997

"Things are not always as they seem; the first appearance deceives many."

Phaedrus (15 BC – 50 AD)

Cynthia Powers reserved a table in the small bar area of the American Grill Restaurant in the L'Enfant Plaza Hotel. It was the only area where smoking was still allowed. The country was becoming more and more paranoid about second-hand smoke and she was sure the day would come when smoking would be prohibited in every public place. She lit another cigarette and sipped her third Martini.

Cynthia and J.P. sat with their backs to the wall in a cushiony booth. Between them was the cardboard box he retrieved from his car. The strings were broken, the box was open and the envelope holding the letter was slit. While he waited, he hastily rummaged through the jumble of paraphernalia that included shoulder patches, medals, dog tags, letters, photographs and other military memorabilia. He would sort through the tangled mess as soon as he had the chance. On the opposite side of the table were three empty chairs and place settings that yawned at them.

"Are you sure they're coming?" he asked. She shrugged her shoulders in reply; afraid her words might betray she already had too much to drink. If only she could get some food in her before he noticed.

Three men appeared as the waitress escorted them to the table. J.P. stood and greeted them. "Gentlemen, thanks for coming, I'm J.P. Kilroy. I believe you all knew my father."

The man with the bushy gray hair and ill-fitting tweed sport jacket reached out first. He was no longer wearing a tie. "My name is Schuyler Johnson. My friends call me Sky. Yes, we all knew Johnny. That's what we called him, Johnny or Yank."

Before Sky sat down, J.P. motioned to Cynthia and said, "Cynthia Powers, Army Public Affairs. She set this dinner up." Cynthia remained seated and nodded silently.

As Sky took a seat, he made ample room for the gentleman with the black horn-rimmed glasses, dark hair and gray temples to introduce himself. "Frank West, I was his CO in the Hundred and first." They shook hands as Frank took his seat.

Waiting patiently behind the other two, the balding big-man extended his hand and J.P. took it. "Harley Tidrick. Very pleased to meet you and congratulations on the posthumous Medal of Honor for your father." He nodded toward Cynthia who nodded back. The other two men mumbled sounds of agreement as they sat and placed the white linen napkins on their laps.

"Thank you, gentlemen. I know the Medal is a huge honor but what's more important to me right now is to learn everything I can about my father. I was hoping you could help." J.P. didn't know if his father kept in touch with any of these men or if any of them knew he and his father were estranged. He didn't plan to burden them with questions about more recent news or happenings. That might come later. Better off to start them out from the beginning, knowing full well, as Cynthia mentioned, they might have failures of memory or faulty recollections.

J.P. continued. "I know many veterans are reluctant to talk about their own wartime experiences and if you want to keep that private I certainly respect that. But anything you might recall about my father, that you might be able to share with me, would be sincerely appreciated."

The three men looked at each other in a furtive manner. No one responded. There was an awkward silence while the waitress put some bread on the table. Cynthia took a slice and passed the dish.

"I know it was a long time ago," J.P. persisted. "But anything at all would be helpful to me." Again, silence. J.P. had an idea to break the ice. He reached into the open cardboard box and pulled out a four-inch by five-inch photograph, three army regulation shoulder patches and a pair of silver jump wings. J.P. placed the items on the table. Harley reached across and took the photo, studied it, turned it over and smiled. He handed it to Sky who nodded in recognition.

Harley finally broke the silence. "We would be glad to tell you anything we can about your father, as much as we can remember."

"Whose the other guy in the picture?" asked J.P.

"That was his best buddy, Jake." Harley pointed to the picture, looked at the other two and they nodded agreement.

"His best buddy, Jake?" J.P. repeated absent-mindedly.

"That's right, kid. His given name was John Kilroy, too. He was called by Jake."

"Really?" J.P. smiled. "I didn't know that. Please, go on."

"Well, Mister Kilroy, if you can keep the drinks coming, we can fill you in on what we remember," Sky laughed. The momentary tension of a few moments ago seemed to dissipate.

"Call me J.P. please." J.P. was more than willing to help loosen them up a bit. He signaled to the waitress for a round of drinks. Sky ordered a Vodka Collins, Harley a draft beer and Frank an iced-tea. Cynthia declined, still chewing on her bread. J.P. held up his empty glass containing the slight remnants of wine and the waitress nodded.

As the waitress left, J.P. pointed to the picture Sky was holding. "I know this question is going to sound ridiculous, but it's been a long time and I don't have many pictures of my father at that age and…well…with the shadows in their faces and all…I'm not sure which one is my dad and which one is his friend…Jake."

Harley took the photo from Sky and held it up facing J.P. "The one on the left with the M-One was your dad. The other one with the Browning Automatic Rifle is Jake. That weapon was more user friendly to left-handed shooters 'cause it had its bolt lever on the left side of the weapon." Harley handed the picture to Sky.

Sky studied the photograph for a moment. "It really is hard to tell with the shadows and all," he conceded. "But here," he pointed to the soldier on the right. "Jake is holding a cigarette. Your dad didn't smoke." He handed the photo back to J.P.

"That's funny. I remember he smoked cigarettes before switching to a pipe."

Harley turned to J.P. "He didn't smoke at that time. After combat, a lot of guys picked up the habit." J.P. accepted the explanation. He turned the picture toward Harley and pointed to Jake.

"Did Jake make it home?" J.P. asked. The question seemed to again unsettle the three of them. Sky looked down at the table and Frank coughed and shook his head slightly.

Harley answered. "No."

"That's a shame. I don't remember my father ever speaking about him. But then again Dad never really spoke about the War at all. Never." J.P. let the words hang in the air, realizing he had to be careful with his questions. He could sense these men were all on an emotional precipice, on the verge of conjuring up recollections they would rather not. He didn't want to disrupt the flow of the conversation with some unseemly memories. If he pushed any of them over the edge the whole meeting might go up in smoke. "And where's Oujda?" he asked, purposely changing the subject. He held up the picture again.

Sky answered. "Armpit of the freakin' world," he forced a laugh. "Morocco, North Africa. It was called French Morocco back then. Ten miles west of Algeria and forty miles south of the Med. The Eighty-second trained there for the jump on Sicily."

J.P. nodded and gently brought the conversation back to his father and said, "So, they were really close?"

"Thick as blood, thicker than thieves." Frank answered.

"Well I guess that explains some of the duplicate souvenirs in the box. There are two sets of wings and extra sleeve patches." J.P. gestured at the small pile in front of him as he spoke.

Something on the table caught Frank's eye. He reached over and picked up the two identical jump wings. They were striking in their silver appearance despite their age. They each were adorned with five small bronze stars, two on each wing and one on the apex of the parachute.

Frank showed the jump wings to Sky. "You have one of these, right Sky?"

Sky looked at the jump wings and nodded in the affirmative. "My original regiment, the Five-oh-five, made four combat jumps. We were the only regiment to do that in the War. I made all four with them and another with the Seventeenth Airborne Division." Sky seemed moved by the memories. The nostalgia was palpable.

Frank looked at J.P. "These are among the rarest jump wings you will ever find. There are only a handful of paratroopers in the history of the world who ever made five combat jumps!" Frank handed the wings back. J.P. had not realized how unique they were. He felt a chill when Frank dropped them into his hand.

Frank went on. "I only have two, and those were enough for two lifetimes. The 'Screaming Eagles'...the Hundred and first...only made two combat jumps, into Normandy and Holland. The Eighty-second had two combat jumps in Italy before D-Day and then Normandy and Holland. The Seventeenth Airborne made the last one when they jumped the Rhine near the end of the War in March of forty-five. Other smaller units like the independent Five-oh-nine battalion, jumped in North Africa, Italy and Southern France but no unit made more than four."

The facts and figures came rather easily to Frank. J.P. presumed he was a pretty smart guy and had his information right. Frank continued. The tiny few that survived long enough to make five combat jumps had a rare combination of luck and skill. Those wings represent men that were really, really special, son. The absolute best among the very best!"

The waitress came with the drink order and passed out menus.

"So, where do we begin?" J.P. asked.

Harley answered. "Well, Sky was with Johnny and Jake in the Eighty-second from jump school through Italy and then Frank was their CO when they transferred to the Hundred and first from D-Day through the Bulge. Then made a jump with the Seventeenth Airborne."

Sky interrupted, "That was really fun."

Frank continued. "Between us we should be able to cover most of your dad's wartime history and hopefully, if we didn't forget all that much, answer most of your questions."

"What about the Medal of Honor? What happened there outside Bastogne?" J.P. looked around the table.

The three aged men looked at each other. Sky slowly shook his head and raised his hands slightly in a sign of ignorance. Frank shrugged his shoulders. It was Harley who answered. "If the citation doesn't answer that question for you, I'm afraid Lincoln is the only one who can." Harley held his hands out. "None of us were there."

Cynthia looked up from her menu. "We can reach out and touch Mister Abraham. We have his contact information." *She comported herself rather well, J.P.*

thought, *considering how much she had been drinking*. He was actually surprised she was paying attention.

"That will have to do, I suppose. We'll ask Mister Abraham to fill in that piece," said J.P. He looked at Harley and smiled. "What about you, Mister Tidrick?"

"Call me Harley. I fade in and out of their wartime experiences. I was with both of them at different times. I met your father in England before D-Day and we ran into each other in Normandy. Jake started in the army in my National Guard outfit. You see…I'm Jake's cousin!"

"Wow," was all J.P. could manage in reply. He was really curious about how Jake died but it was too soon in the conversation to risk troublesome questions. He had to continually remind himself not to upset these men by conjuring up the nightmare memories of lost friends. J.P. would gently coax the information from them using all his learned interview skills as a lawyer and reporter. He ripped off a small piece of bread and nibbled on it.

"So, Sky, I guess it all starts with you."

Sky reached across the table. He slid the 82nd Airborne Division patch toward him. The tattered patch was a worn, faded red square with a blue circle centered within it. Inside the circle were two white letter A's in juxtaposition, the opposite legs of the letters conforming to the curve of the inner circle. The airborne tab was attached to one corner, held on with a few stitches. "Eighty-second Airborne Division," said Sky. "The best freakin' division in the world." He smiled and glanced over to Frank.

"In your dreams, Sky," Frank answered good-naturedly as he slid the patch of the 101st Airborne Division over to himself and examined it. It was crest-shaped with a mostly white, angry eagle's head on a black field, the gold colored beak breaking up the white eagle head feathers. "That distinguished honor goes to the Screaming Eagles, the Battling Bastards of Bastogne," Frank continued, smiling back.

"It started with me and almost ended with me," Sky continued, ignoring Frank's barb back at him. Sky reached for the 17th Airborne Division patch. It was a simple, circular shoulder flash, encircled by a gold ring with a golden claw of extended talons in the middle of the dark blue circle. He tapped the patch. "Their nickname was 'Thunder From Heaven'. Good outfit. Got pretty beat up at the Bulge as leg infantry. But that Rhine jump, Operation Varsity, was one jump that shoulda' never been made. War almost over, end of March of forty-five, Krauts ready to fold, pack it in, that Limey bastard Monty…General Montgomery… looking for more glory." Sky shook his head, began to choke up. "We lost a lot of good men in that one, for what? To pad Monty's reputation?" Sky was shaking his head, tears forming in the corners of his eyes.

J.P. sensed he had to change the focus before Sky brought the mood down. "I'm curious about that patch," he said pointing to Harley's windbreaker. Just then the waitress came over to the table. They each ordered. When she left, Harley continued.

"Twenty-ninth Infantry Division," he began, "also called the Blue and Gray Division since it was made up of boys from the South *and* the North." Harley leaned forward and continued. "That was a big deal in the first war, having a division made up of boys from different states. The Civil War was only fifty years in the past and the country was still divided, in culture, customs and attitudes. When this division was formed, they made the patch to show that the blue and the gray were fighting together against the Kaiser. The Eighty-second also fought in that war, had boys from all over the country and got the nickname 'All-Americans.'" He nodded to Sky who acknowledged the point with a grunt and a nod. "It was a really big deal back then, to have an army unit that represented the United States, and not just a region or a state."

"So, you weren't a paratrooper like my dad?" asked J.P.

"Nope," answered Harley. "My CO in the Twenty-ninth wouldn't approve my transfer when me and Jake volunteered. I almost became a Ranger, though. But that's another story, kid." Harley let the comment hang in the air. "But let's tell you what we remember about Johnny."

J.P. took a small audio recorder from his inside jacket pocket and checked the tape inside. "Before we really get started, does anyone mind?" He held the recorder up. The three men signaled they didn't mind. J.P. made a show of turning it on, placing it in the middle of the table toward Sky and waited for him to begin. Only J.P. knew the highly sensitive voice recorder in his pocket had been on since the three men sat down.

Chapter Eighteen

Fort Benning, Georgia – July 6, 1942

"Those who know how to win are much more numerous
than those who know how to make proper use of their victories."

Polybius (203 BC - 120 BC)

Two busses loaded with GIs rendezvoused at the Airborne Command Training Center at Fort Benning, Georgia. The instructors, who were to teach this class, were milling around. They all looked incredibly fit and wore white form fitting T-shirts with an image of a parachute on the front. Above the parachute was the word AIRBORNE. Their jump boots were highly spit-shined and they wore fatigue pants and baseball caps. No rank insignia was visible. When the doors opened the screaming began. The bus storage compartment contained the boys' barracks bags. The instructors yelled orders to grab the first bag they could reach, run it over to the nearby drill field and drop it in one huge pile. There were instructors all along the way who barked orders and pushed and nudged the troopers as they ran. The trip ended near an elevated wooden platform that was used to demonstrate calisthenics. The ragged line of soldiers staggered toward the platform under the continuing verbal and physical barrage of the instructors.

"Pile 'em up right here!!"

"Fall in right there!!"

The eighty soldiers swiftly fell into formation facing the platform, a group of freshly built barracks directly behind them. An officer stood facing them, hands on his hips. There was an air of confidence about him. It seemed everyone here, officers as well as NCOs, had that swagger.

"Welcome to Airborne Basic Jump School. My name is Lieutenant Colonel Reuben H. Tucker and I'm the XO of the Five-oh-four PIR. There are a few things you need to know before you begin here." Tucker paced slowly from one end of the platform to the other.

"First, half of you won't make it through the next four weeks. Hell, you might not even make it through the first four hours!" He stopped and looked directly at the middle of the formation. "You know who you are so why don't you save us all a lot of time and just quit right now." Johnny Kilroy believed the colonel was looking directly at him. No one moved.

"Fine! Then we'll do it your way, the hard way," Tucker continued while the instructors slowly circled the formation like sharks stalking prey. "At this school, we double-time everywhere. If you're not running it means you're seated or you're dead. Do not ever let anyone see you walking anywhere or leaning on anything or you will do enough pushups to slow the earth's rotation." Tucker began pacing again.

"If you're given an order or if you are asked a question in which you wish to respond in the affirmative, you will yell, 'Strike-Hold!' at the top of your lungs. Do you understand?" Two or three men yelled, "Strike-Hold!" Tucker shook his head. "This is not a good start, you can do better than that. DO YOU UNDERSTAND?"

The whole formation screamed, "STRIKE HOLD!"

"Better." Tucker stopped pacing again. "The last thing you need to know is that this is a cadre trained regiment. Most of the instructors will become part of the Five-oh-four or Five-oh-five after this class is trained. They may become your squad or platoon leaders. You'll go into combat with them." The subtle meaning was clear. Since they will likely be going to war with these instructors, they will not cut the students any slack.

"Captain Wolff, take over," Tucker descended the steps from the platform. Captain Louis Wolff ascended the steps at the same time, saluted, smiled and whispered as they passed each other, "Sir? Slow the earth's rotation, sir?"

"Right, Captain," he smiled back. "I need to come up with a better one than that." Colonel Tucker hopped into his jeep. His driver sped off quickly, spraying dirt and gravel.

Wolff looked out over the sweating and shaken group of trainees. "I'm Captain Louis Wolff. I'm the training officer for this class." Wolff scanned the faces of the men before him. "I think I recruited some of you." He paused. "What the hell was I thinking?" He shook his head in disgust. "Well, let's get this over with. When you hear your name, go find your bag and report to the barracks directly behind you. On the double!" He nodded to the instructor at the head of the formation.

"Adams!" yelled the instructor. A soldier broke out of the second rank, ran behind the formation, fished around for his bag with sharp, fast movements, found it and ran inside the barracks. Before Adams found his own bag the instructor had already yelled, "Brown!" That soldier did the same. The instructor continued down the alphabetical list as a group of searching soldiers milled about the pile, shoving, pushing, and trying to get close enough to read the names stenciled on the canvas bags. All the while another instructor was yelling at the group to hurry. The names were being called faster than the soldiers could find their bags. The crowd around the pile got larger and more unruly.

"Kilroy!" the instructor hollered. "Shit, we got two." He looked up at Captain Wolff, shrugged and yelled, "Kilroy, John! Fuck, we got two of *them*."

Two men broke out of the ranks from opposite sides of the formation. They both waded into the mass of scrambling GIs.

Johnny pushed his way in and started to turn the bags to see the names. Arms and bodies were struggling to do the same thing. It was chaos and the instructors continued yelling for the men to move faster. Johnny turned over a bag, heard a soldier yell behind him, "that's mine" and he tossed the bag back.

"Thanks, Mac."

He continued prowling the pile under the constant barrage of insults. The group began to thin out as more men found their own bags and fewer men looking at fewer bags sped up the process. Finally, there was one bag left. It was older and more worn than his. He turned it over, read the name. It was not his bag.

"What's the matter, little girl? Let's move, hubba-hubba," an instructor yelled.

"Not my bag, Sergeant," Johnny answered, his voice seething with anger and frustration. "I'm John P. Kilroy, this bag belongs to John No-Middle-Initial Kilroy."

"Well, pick it up sweetheart and we'll go find that dumb ass."

Johnny hoisted the bag on his shoulder and followed the instructor into the barracks. Double bunk beds lined the walls. Bunks were also set up in the center corridor. Instructors continued yelling and screaming. The barracks was bedlam.

"Attention!" the older instructor yelled and the barracks became silent, each man standing rigid at the foot of his bunk. Johnny dropped his bag and stood at attention in the middle of the corridor. "I'm Staff Sergeant Bancroft. I'll be running this platoon through this training cycle." Bancroft had thin lips and a hawk-like nose. His eyes scanned the room, black and piercing. "Don't worry about the crowding situation, by the end of the week there'll be plenty of room and we'll remove these extra bunks." He walked slowly up the corridor weaving between the soldiers. "Do you candy ass pussies really think you have what it takes to become paratroopers?" Before anyone could answer he continued in a louder voice. "Do you sorry pieces of dogshit think you have the physical toughness and intelligence to be paratroopers? I don't think so. Some of you can't even fucking read! Where's Kilroy?" he screamed.

"Right here Sergeant," a voice from the back answered.

"C'mon," Bancroft motioned to Johnny who picked up the bag and followed.

They moved quickly to the last bunk in the back. Jake Kilroy was standing there, at attention, the barracks bag he took unopened on the bunk.

Bancroft got right up in Jake's face; his fiery eyes boring into Jake's soul. "You took the wrong bag, lady. Can't you fucking read?"

"I realized it when I got in here..." Jake tried to explain. Bancroft was having none of it.

"You are John NMI Kilroy. That bag says John P. Kilroy. Belongs to this soldier here," he pointed his thumb over his shoulder. "If you can't even read your own name and serial number, how the hell are you supposed to identify landmarks, road signs, read maps?"

"I can read, Sergeant. It was a mistake."

"Oh, we rushed you too much? We made too much noise? Is that what you do under pressure, make mistakes?" Bancroft was nose to nose with Jake who realized answering his tirade was just getting Bancroft more agitated. Jake said nothing. Bancroft backed away.

"You're John NMI Kilroy. I can't just yell Kilroy when I want you because I got two of you ...so your name from now on is Enema. Get it...N-M-I... En-em-a? You better answer to that name. Know why, 'cause you're dumber than shit." Bancroft grabbed the bag on Jake's bunk and tossed it to Johnny, looked at him, said, "Take that bunk." He pointed to one a few feet away. He took Jake's bag from Johnny and tossed it on Jake's bunk. "I'll be watching you," turned to Johnny, "you too!" Bancroft stormed out of the barracks.

"That's great," Johnny complained out loud. "As if this wasn't going to be hard enough."

"Sorry, Mac. I'm Jake," Jake held out his hand.

Johnny looked at Jake's hand in disgust and backed away. "Fuck you. You're Enema. And it's an appropriate name for you too. If you didn't have your head up your ass, neither of us would be noticed. Now we're *both* on his shit list." Johnny felt his anger rising.

Jake clenched his fists and took a step forward. "I have to take his crap but I don't have to take yours."

Johnny didn't back down. He didn't know how. He dropped the barracks bag and took a step forward. "Why not? Let's go!"

Just then a blond haired, blue-eyed soldier stepped in between the two of them. "C'mon boys. This is not the time. You can settle this later. No reason to drag the rest of us into it." Some of the other soldiers murmured their agreement. Johnny stepped back.

Jake dropped his hands and pointed at Johnny. "This is not over."

Johnny replied, "Not by a long shot."

The soldier picked up Johnny's barracks bag and walked him over to his bunk. He put his hand on Johnny's shoulder. "It was an honest mistake. We can't be turning on each other. That's what *they* want."

Johnny exhaled, the stress of the moment leaving his body. "I know. It's just that I wanted to stay unnoticed." He managed a slight smirk. "So much for that. Thanks for stepping in. My name is Johnny Kilroy. Some of the boys call me Yank." He extended his hand.

The soldier shook it. "I'm Schuyler Johnson. My friends call me Sky."

Chapter Nineteen

L'Enfant Plaza Hotel – January 13, 1997

"Every man's memory is his private literature."

Aldous Huxley (1894 - 1963)

The waitress approached the table with five salad dishes balanced on her forearm. J.P. leaned back as she placed a plate before everyone. The restaurant was filling up and the din and clatter of utensils on plates and muted conversations became more noticeable. J.P. ordered another round of drinks and looked at Sky. "So, you knew them both pretty well from the beginning?"

Sky stabbed at a piece of lettuce. "It's funny, I can remember the most insignificant details way back then but I can't even remember what I had for breakfast yesterday."

"Amen." Frank added. Harley nodded.

"So how did Jake and dad become friends?" J.P. tried to jump-start Sky into continuing his story.

Sky chewed on some salad, put his fork down and picked up his Vodka Collins. "They really didn't like each other from the first time they met. There was a mix-up with their gear on the first day in jump school. Johnny blamed Jake for taking the wrong barracks bag and Jake blamed Johnny for ratting him out to Bancroft." Sky took a long pull on his drink. "For three weeks they eyed each other looking for an opportunity to settle it. They were always near each other because we did everything in alphabetical order, which meant I was near them, too. Then finally, they got the entire company in hot water."

"And they became friends after that?" asked J.P.

"From bitter enemies to the best of friends, closer than brothers."

"How did that happen?" J.P. asked.

"Before it got better, it got a whole lot worse. In A-Stage the instructors were brutal. They spent the entire first week weeding out the boys who couldn't keep up." Sky put down his drink and picked up his fork and poked at the air with it. "You see, anyone could sign up for the paratroopers. Some were curious, some were bored, others wanted the extra pay but not everybody was cut out for the airborne." Sky looked at Frank who was munching on his salad. "Did you find that to be true?"

Frank nodded. "The instructors in my jump school class could wash anyone out at any time but in reality, that was rare. They would rather push people to their limits and have them quit. They only kicked out the obvious psycho misfits who caused a lot of trouble."

"Same here," Sky agreed. "Problem was Bancroft labeled the Kilroys as eight-balls and rode them both the whole time, trying to get them to quit. Jake got the worst of it."

"How so?" asked J.P.

"Like I said, A-Stage was all about calisthenics. We double-timed everywhere. Then there were the long runs in the Georgia summer heat. Let me tell you, guys were passing out left and right. When they recovered, they would be given the chance to finish, a test of character and determination. Some did and stayed in. Most just quit right there." Sky glanced at Frank.

"Same thing," Frank agreed.

Sky paused to take a sip of his drink. "If you got caught wiping your sweat or scratching your nose you were ordered to drop and do pushups. Bancroft would drop Jake down for no reason. Jake was wiry and strong, not to mention stubborn, and he did the pushups every time, no problem. Johnny just got out of basic like me so we were in decent shape and able to keep up." Sky quickly chewed a mouthful of salad and continued. "We had four hours of calisthenics, an hour running, an hour of rope climbing, an hour tumbling and an hour of hand-to-hand combat. It was brutal." Sky looked over to Frank and smiled. "I can't believe I remember all this crap."

"You got it right," Frank confirmed.

Sky wiped his mouth and continued. "But old Bancroft was right about one thing. By the end of that first week the bunks down the center of the barracks were gone and in the bunks that were left, well most of the boys had the double rack all to themselves. We lost almost half the freakin' platoon that first week."

Frank put his fork on his empty salad plate, thought he'd give Sky a chance to finish his food. "In the summer of forty-two this airborne stuff was all new. The army was feeling their way along, trying different methods, looking for answers. What kind of equipment, training and command structure would be required? But in forty-two all this was still an experiment, a work in progress and there were growing pains. One thing we did know right from the start. A paratrooper had to be a unique and special breed. So we were trained, almost brainwashed, to believe we were an invincible force. We had to withstand the physical challenges of jumping from planes and landing hard, day or night, with over one hundred pounds on our backs and then come together with whoever was left standing and complete the mission. If you can find people who would do that, they also had to be smart enough to read maps, and landmarks and decide where they were and where to go." Frank stopped for a moment to gather his thoughts.

"If I recall correctly, your dad was very good at that. He had a photographic memory for maps and stuff, " Frank remembered. J.P. looked surprised but noticed Harley gave Frank a slight scowl. Frank continued without acknowledging either of their looks.

"If paratroopers were too far from their objective, they had to decide how to best disrupt the enemy in his rear areas. Cut phone lines, blow bridges, and hide road signs, anything to cause confusion. They had to decide whether to engage or evade the enemy they encountered. Use their initiative and judgment. If a corporal were the senior rank in a large group of troopers, he would be expected to take command at the platoon or company level. If a colonel found himself in command of a small group of troopers, he would be expected to lead them using squad tactics. They would have to be resourceful enough to use every weapon authorized for their regiment and enemy weapons as well. Finally, if you could find people who could do all that, they would also have to have balls of steel. They were expected to stand and fight regardless of the odds, to attack superior positions without hesitation, to accomplish their mission regardless of the obstacles, to be unstoppable." Frank leaned forward on the table, clasped his hands and looked directly at J.P. "It's not surprising we lost so many. It's a wonder so many volunteered."

They all leaned back slightly as the waitress removed their plates and placed appetizers before each of them. Frank continued. "That weeding out process and that severe training was supposed to flush out those who couldn't cut it. It wasn't perfect. We let some good ones get away. And we let some bad apples in, guys that belonged in a psych ward, you know, steal from other troopers, loot from civilians, shoot prisoners, that kinda' stuff. But, by and large, if you made it through the training and got your wings you had the right stuff to be a good paratrooper."

The table became momentarily quiet as they began eating. J.P. took advantage of the brief lull to change the tape in his recorder. He smiled at Cynthia who smiled back. She was regaining her composure. He was anxious to hear the rest of the story. After giving Sky a few minutes to work on his appetizer, J.P. flipped on the recorder and prompted Sky to get him speaking again.

"Why did you volunteer for the airborne, Sky?"

"Why?" Sky smiled and shook his head. "Why did we do the stupid things we did when we were nineteen?" He continued after a brief pause. "I was born in LA, flunked out of U.C.L.A. after a year and saw an article in *Life Magazine* so I joined, mostly for the adventure. Knowing what I know now, I would never do it again, but I wouldn't trade the experience for anything."

"Same here," Frank added.

"What did you do when you got out?" J.P. asked.

"Like a lot of guys, I went back to school on the G.I. Bill. Got my degree in engineering, went into the demolition business and retired a few years ago."

"Demolition?" asked J.P.

"Yeah, I really like to blow shit up." Sky smiled and reached for another clam.

Both Harley and Frank laughed. They understood how difficult it was for some to adjust from the adrenalin pumping high of constant combat to the relatively lethargic pace of civilian life.

"So, Sky, the tension between Jake and Dad, you say it got worse before it got better? They almost got the whole platoon in hot water?"

Sky scooped out the last clam into his mouth, chewed and swallowed and wiped his lips. "The whole damn company," he corrected. "On the last day of C-Stage. I would have bet they wouldn't have waited that long but somehow they managed to get that far before they finally threw down on each other." Sky waved his glass in the direction of the waitress and continued.

"With most of the misfits and pretenders washed out in A-Stage, the B-Stage training became all about learning the techniques for jumping out of planes and how to land. We prepared and trained by doing thousands of tumbles in the gym. We also jumped from platforms without gear over and over again. The jumps were called PLFs, parachute landing falls, and we did so many that we could do them in our sleep. Then we learned how to strap on the parachute and harness; not too tight, not too loose. We were taught how to check our equipment and how to exit the plane from a mock-up airplane door. They taught us the proper body position in the air. We went out of that mock-up probably five hundred times. Easier said than done with a hundred pounds on your back. Instructors would critique and correct us. Our goal was to jump a stick of eighteen paratroopers in less than ten seconds. We never quite made that in training but we got close."

The waitress brought Sky another Vodka Collins. "Every time Johnny and Jake checked each other's equipment or passed close by each other I held my breath. But other than looks that could kill, nothing happened. I don't think either of them wanted to screw themselves or their buddies out of making it through jump school." He took a sip and continued. The vodka was beginning to loosen him up. "Then we jumped from the thirty-four foot tower on a harness rigged to a cable that went from the tower to a pole a hundred feet away and eight feet off the ground. It was hairy and scary."

Frank finished eating his crab cakes and joined the conversation. "We had a lot of guys wash out on the thirty-four foot tower too. Once they got past that, they were likely to make it through jump school."

"Right," Sky agreed. "Most of the guys had never even been in a plane before they joined up." He leaned back in his chair. "Anyway, here we are in C-Stage and they take us to the two hundred and fifty foot towers. That's where they hook you up to a parachute, pull you all the way up and let you go." Sky was motioning with his hands. He had everyone's attention. "They trained us to guide the parachute using the risers, the straps that held the chute to your harness. Pull hard on one side, dump some air from the canopy and guide the chute in the direction you want to go. It was good to know and worked if the wind wasn't too strong. When you hit the ground they had these big fans blowing air into your chute. You had to learn to collapse it and muscle it down. A guy could really get busted up bad if he let himself be dragged along the freakin' ground. Suddenly, the pushups and rope climbing made sense. We were stronger and able to execute these difficult strength maneuvers."

J.P. was anxious to hear about what happened between his father and Jake and wanted Sky to get to the end of the story. However, he was reluctant to disrupt his train of thought. Sky seemed to enjoy reliving those days, which seemed seared indelibly into his memory. Harley and Frank seemed to be enjoying the reminiscence as well. J.P. decided to take a chance. "So, what happened on that last day of C-Stage?"

"Oh, yeah, sorry," Sky continued. "It started in the packing shed. We were learning how to pack parachutes. We were very closely supervised and everyone paid attention because our first jump would be with the chute we packed for ourselves. It was serious shit and we knew it. If you screwed it up you'd wind up with a streamer and they'd be scraping you up with a shovel. And you would have nobody to blame but yourself."

J.P. looked at Frank curiously. Frank responded. "A streamer was when you're lines get fouled up and keep the chute from opening. Usually happened when you didn't pack the chute right." J.P. nodded and looked at Sky who continued.

"I knew Johnny was feeling bad about how he acted but he wasn't about to apologize. Jake certainly wasn't going to offer Johnny his hand a second time. The situation was tense and it wouldn't take much to ignite it. So, we're next to each other in this hot packing shed, each of us with his chute laid out on this long, smooth table, listening to the instructors and flattening the silk panels and separating and clearing the shroud lines and carefully folding everything into the pack tray. Suddenly, Johnny notices that Jake left one of the shot bags under the folds of his chute and was just about to pack the chute into his tray and..."

"What's a shot bag?" J.P. interrupted.

Frank answered. "It's a cloth pouch about the size of a sausage with small round lead shot in it. They were used to hold down the silk while we straightened out the shroud lines. You know, so a breeze wouldn't blow your chute off the table. It's not a good thing if you pack them in with the chute."

J.P. nodded his understanding and looked back at Sky who continued. "So Johnny looks around, no one else sees it, he doesn't really want Jake to get killed so he innocently says, 'Hey Enema, you left a bag in the chute'. Johnny was trying to be helpful but unintentionally called him Enema. Jake went nuts, came flying around the table. Me and some other guys got between them again. Jake's friend, Danny Boy, was also trying to get at Johnny. It was a mess. The instructors jumped in, screamed at everyone and restored order. We finished packing the chutes and put our names on them. Johnny yelled over to Jake to remind him to make sure he picked out the right pack this time. They were seething at each other. So, Bancroft decided to punish the entire company with a forced march the

Friday night of C-Stage. If we all didn't finish on time there would be no passes for anybody. Now *everybody* was pissed at *both* of them."

"So you marched?" asked J.P.

Sky deliberated for a moment. "I'm not sure why Bancroft set people against each other. He seemed to particularly enjoy the conflict between Johnny and Jake, since he pretty much started it." Sky took a sip of his drink and then a deep breath. "Anyway, Bancroft did something that night of the march that I never saw an NCO do before or since."

Sky hesitated, enjoying a sense of the drama he was creating. J.P. prodded him. "And what was that?"

"Well, nobody actually witnessed it, but the story goes like this."

Chapter Twenty

Newport News, Virginia – July 22, 1942

"But for every man there exists a bait which he cannot resist swallowing."

Friedrich Nietzsche (1844 - 1900)

The cool breeze, hastened by an onshore gust from the James River, was refreshing as it swept the heat of the day from the sidewalks. The shadows of the buildings lengthened as the day wore to a close. Macie Vance and Nora Lee had just finished a double shift and chatted as they walked among the crowd headed toward the busses and home. Macie was wearing a pair of new coveralls over a man-tailored short-sleeved shirt. A red print bandana kept her hair in place. Nora was dressed the same, as were most of the other women, only Nora wore a white polo shirt under her coveralls. They both carried metal lunch boxes and Macie held a welder's helmet in her other hand. They sauntered with a casualness of having recently accomplished something worthwhile.

A group of men were walking in the other direction. They whistled the universally familiar two-note call in unison as they passed by. Macie became a bit self-conscious but Nora turned to face them as they looked back over their shoulders.

"Bring it on, boys," she smiled as she walked backwards and raised both of her arms as if to show off her entire body. "I just love the attention!" Then she turned and slapped her backside.

The young men quickly turned away. It was unusual for women to confront men who wolf-whistled at them. Nora surprised them.

She was a beautiful blonde who resembled a taller version of Veronica Lake. When Nora's shoulder length hair wasn't pinned under her bandana, it hung lazily over her right eye imitating the iconic peek-a-boo hairstyle of the popular actress. The men could have been whistling at either of the girls but it was Nora who instinctively responded. She simply would not be intimidated by any of the men in the dockyard.

"Don't ever let them get away with nothing," she whispered to Macie as they walked.

"You're something, Nora," was all Macie could say in reply.

"Gangway, ladies," an older heavy set man yelled as he pushed his way between them and walked quickly toward the gate. He knocked both of them off balance and Nora almost fell.

"Very nice, you old fart. What a gentleman *you* are!" Nora hollered as he made his way through the crowd.

"Listen sister," he yelled back over his shoulder. "Why don't you go to the tool crib and get the left-handed monkey wrench?" The older man guffawed at his joke.

"Try another one, fatso," Nora replied. "That stupid old prank won't work anymore."

"Why don't you go back to the kitchen where you ladies belong, barefoot and pregnant?" he yelled back. He got a chorus of catcalls and boos from the other women walking toward the gate. Nora flipped him her middle finger. A wide-eyed Macie stifled a giggle at the gesture.

"Oh my gosh, Nora. You're terrible," Macie laughed.

"He deserved it, the lazy fat bastard." She raised her head to look for him disappearing in the crowd and raised her voice toward him. "You heard me, you're a good-for-nothing lazy fat bastard and you can go to hell." The other women yelled sentiments of agreement.

Macie continued to laugh. None of the women behaved that way in Bedford. She was both amused and a little embarrassed.

"I've seen him around before," Nora continued. "He has a problem with women working in the yard and he doesn't care who knows it. He has a problem with niggers too. Next time he pushes me I'm going to crown him with this lunch bucket."

"Okay, me too. We'll both hit him," Macie smiled.

"I'm not kidding, Macie. It's bad enough some of these fat old men make almost twice as much as we do for the same jobs but then they run around treating us like we're shit. They make all that money while our guys are fighting this war. Bullshit! I'm not taking their crap." Nora became angrier at the thought of her boyfriend who was still missing in action in the Philippines.

"Really, they make more than we do?" Macie was genuinely surprised.

"More than the niggers, too," Nora confirmed. "I don't know how the shipyard gets away with it but that's the truth."

Macie shook her head in disbelief. She didn't doubt Nora but found it hard to understand. "There's probably a good reason. They probably have more experience than us," Macie rationalized. "Besides, I'm making more money than I ever did and more than I can spend."

"You'll see, Macie. When you start working rings around these guys and leaving them in the dust, you'll still be making less than all of them."

Before Macie could answer, she spotted Derek Edson coming out of the crowd and walking toward them. "Oh, there he is."

"That's the guy you told me about?" asked Nora. "Girl, he's a dreamboat!"

Derek approached them. "Congratulations, Macie. I heard you graduated and got assigned." He held out his left hand.

She took it. "Yes, over a week ago, thanks. They have me welding sub-assemblies in the big shed down by the wharf. I hear they're going into your ship, the *Bon*

Homme Richard." She let go of his hand and introduced him to Nora as the guy who recruited her to the shipyard. Nora didn't let on that she knew of him.

"Sub-assemblies. That's great. It won't be long before they have you right on the ship itself, joining iron, as they say, welding the hull and bulkheads and stuff. Maybe you'll even be on my crew," he speculated.

Macie smiled. Derek had a way of finding her despite the vastness of the shipyard. He bumped into her almost every day while she was in Welding School. Now, he *accidentally* ran into her again. She was flattered that he seemed to be making an effort to stumble upon her. Her question was not whether or not he was doing it on purpose; the question was *how* was he doing it on purpose.

"I'm glad I ran into you," he smiled back. "I hoped maybe we could go to a movie to celebrate your graduation."

Macie glanced at Nora and then back to Derek. "I don't think so. But thanks anyway, Derek." Macie averted Derek's eyes and looked back at Nora.

Derek recovered. "Oh, Nora, of course, please. You're welcome to come too. I have a buddy, nice guy..."

"I don't do blind dates," Nora interrupted. "Besides, we both have boyfriends."

Macie glanced quickly at Nora who gave her a quizzical look back.

Derek had to think fast. He appealed to Nora. "It's not a date, so it can't be a blind date." He shifted his gaze to Macie. "We'd be going in a group...just friends."

"As just friends, right?" Macie anxiously confirmed.

"Of course. There's a new Jimmy Cagney movie playing at the Palace, *Yankee Doodle Dandy.* Just released. I hear it's swell."

Macie looked over at Nora. She wanted to go but not alone. Nora picked up on the silent plea and answered for both of them. "Okay, Derek. Bring your buddy. We'll all go but just friends. No funny stuff, Derek. Got it?"

"No problem. I swear. As friends."

Chapter Twenty-One

Fort Benning, Georgia, July 24, 1942

"It is not so much our friends' help that helps us,
as the confidence of their help."

Epicurus (341 BC – 270 BC)

Johnny Kilroy was frozen at attention with the rest of his platoon. He was annoyed Bancroft had called the formation and surprised to see the other three platoons in their training company in formation with them.

Tradition held, and the rumors supported, the company would be granted a pass for post privileges for the weekend. But something else was in the wind and the sense was the company would not be double-timing over to the mess hall. If they were going to chow, they would not be in formation and straining under full field packs in the hot Georgia sun.

Johnny tried to occupy his mind. He had to be prepared to handle whatever Bancroft had in store for them. He gazed out over the landscape as he waited and just took in the vast expanse that was the Parachute School at Fort Benning.

Fort Benning was considered the home of the fledgling United States Army Airborne in the summer of 1942. Even though the Airborne Command staff under Colonel William C. Lee had moved to Fort Bragg, North Carolina, the action and the heartbeat of the airborne revolved around the Parachute School. The history of the airborne was short, less than two years old, but everywhere in the training area were signs of powerful and deeply held traditions. Paratroopers of legendary stature who circulated freely in the day rooms and beer gardens added to the mystical aura of this self-proclaimed invincible fighting force.

In early July of 1940, soon after the fall of France, the United States Army's Parachute Test Platoon began training. Formed from a pool of 200 volunteers from the 29th Infantry Regiment stationed at Fort Benning, the forty-eight enlisted men and one officer began the perilous process of experimentation and discovery into the feasibility of mass dropping heavily laden infantrymen into combat behind enemy lines.

The practicability of the theory had to be proven even though the idea was not entirely new. Leonardo da Vinci designed, drew and described a "tent of linen" parachute in the 1500s. In 1784 Benjamin Franklin pondered the idea of "ten thousand men descending from the clouds" to cause great mischief before a force could be brought together to repel them. In October 1918, Colonel William "Billy" Mitchell, chief of American Expeditionary Forces Air Units, wrote a memo to his superior, General John Pershing, suggesting that an armed force be dropped by parachute behind German lines to fortify and hold a position from where the enemy could be attacked from the rear. The War ended before the idea could be seriously considered but Mitchell has been credited with first suggesting the concept of "vertical envelopment" of an enemy force.

The concept of a Test Platoon had its genesis in an order from Chief of Staff General George C. Marshall in May of 1939. He had been receiving reports from U.S. consulates in Europe regarding the advanced development of foreign parachute and air-landing infantry units, particularly in Russia and Germany.

Marshall named Major William C. Lee, one of the brightest and most conscientious staff officers in the infantry, to lead the project. It received a boost from an unexpected source in May of 1940. The German *Wehrmacht* attacked France and the Low Countries. The *Fallschrimjager*, the German paratroopers, successfully spearheaded the attacks on Holland and Belgium by parachuting and seizing positions behind enemy lines. The Nazis had been training large-scale airborne forces in Stendal, Germany since 1935. The Americans were far behind and General Marshall hurriedly placed more emphasis on what he called the "air-infantry project".

Lee designed a grueling eight-week course covering all phases of parachute activities, a strenuous physical fitness program and rigorous infantry training. The Test Platoon double-timed everywhere. Even though future training cycles would be reduced to four weeks, the rigor and high standards established by the Test Platoon were never compromised.

Under the command of Lieutenant William T. Ryder, the Test Platoon moved into a tent city on the heights overlooking Lawson Field adjacent to Fort Benning. There they began their pioneering adventure into the unknown. Fundamental procedures were developed, such as the position of the head, eyes, hands and feet when standing in the door ready to jump, body position in the air and landing technique. After eight weeks they celebrated by performing a mass jump in front of a reviewing stand of VIPs including General Marshall.

By the end of September 1940, the War Department authorized the establishment of two parachute battalions, one army and one marine. The marine battalion of about 400 men would be named the 1st Parachute Battalion and to avoid confusion the army named its force the 501st Parachute Infantry Battalion (PIB).

The army sought out one of its finest young officers, Major William M. "Bud" Miley, to command its battalion. A West Point graduate of the class of 1918, he threw himself into the job with great passion. The first order of business was to find volunteers to flesh out his command. Initially, enlisted men had to be unmarried, between the ages of twenty-one and thirty-two, weigh under 185 pounds, and have at least one year in the army. In addition, the volunteer had to have a letter of recommendation from his CO and the necessary aptitude to enable him to learn map reading skills, demolitions and communications. While some of these restrictions were relaxed after the United States entered the War, the graduation standards were never compromised.

Fortified by key leaders from the Test Platoon, the 501st PIB finished training in mid January 1941. The battalion was jump-qualified and the officers and men were a fiercely proud group. However, there still was no insignia or distinctive uniform to distinguish them from ordinary soldiers.

Miley, realizing the morale implications of this shortcoming, issued orders authorizing his men to wear their jump boots with all uniforms and to tuck the trouser legs into the top of their boots so the entire boot could be seen. These visible boots, a unique source of great pride to paratroopers, always had a spectacular shine. He also authorized the distinctive circular patch of a white parachute on a field of infantry blue to be worn on the left side of the garrison cap.

Having no qualification badge for paratroopers, Miley enlisted the creative assistance of Lieutenant William P. Yarborough. Yarborough created a few designs from which they selected the paratrooper wings. He had the first set of 350 wings struck by the firm of Bailey, Banks and Biddle of Philadelphia and they were awarded to everyone in the battalion. Yarborough also designed a functional jump suit with slanted utility pockets so as not to be covered by the parachute harness. He redesigned the jump boots, making them more streamlined to prevent shroud lines from getting caught in the exterior buckle. His design reinforced the toe and cut the leading edge of the heel to a forty-five degree angle to prevent troopers from tripping on the metal tie down rings or structural ribs of a plane as they shuffled rearward to the door. While it was not against regulations for non-paratroopers to wear jump boots, the unwritten law was that only jump-qualified soldiers could wear these boots. Many a jaw was broken because a paratrooper caught a "straight-leg" soldier sporting unauthorized jump boots.

Having brought his command up to qualifying standards and developed training methods, equipment, customs and the insignia, Major Miley became an instant legend within the burgeoning airborne community. His battalion was the model for all that would follow. When the War Department authorized three additional parachute infantry battalions, Miley provided the cadre to lead them. He recommended a permanent jump school and the Army General Staff authorized the Provisional Parachute Group at Fort Benning in March 1941 to train and qualify paratroopers.

Beads of sweat were forming on Johnny's face. He resisted the urge to wipe them off and kept his eyes straight ahead. He concentrated on what he had been taught about the airborne since being in jump school.

The May 12, 1941 cover of *LIFE Magazine* sported a grim-faced army parachutist wearing a football helmet. While it sparked interest and encouraged recruitment among civilians, it did little to accelerate growth and development in the military. What did get the War Department's attention on 20 May 1941 was the German attack and capture of Crete.

Hitler authorized 25,000 troops for the mission, 13,000 of which were *Fallschrimjager*, parachute troops. Within two weeks they captured the island, which was heavily defended by 42,000 Allied troops. To the outside world it looked to be an impressive victory for Germany's airborne forces. Unbeknownst to all outside the German High Command, the casualties were appalling. The Germans suffered 3,000 killed and 8,000 wounded, a forty-four percent casualty rate. Over 170 planes had also been lost. German paratroopers would never again be deployed as parachutists on a large scale. Crete was the death knell for the German airborne forces while ironically the impetus for the rapid expansion of the American airborne forces.

Paratroopers were getting a reputation as "best of breed" throughout the American army. Ambitious and highly motivated officers and fierce individualists sought out the airborne. Phone calls were made, old debts cashed in and the best soldiers found a way to cut the red tape and finesse a transfer into the elite battalions. They attracted officers like Captain James M. Gavin, who completed jump school in August 1941 and eventually wrote the first manual of the army's airborne doctrine, entitled *The Employment of Airborne Forces*.

Then…Pearl Harbor!

With America at war, the old restrictions went by the wayside. While new equipment and more men would not appear overnight, there were no longer arbitrary limitations on what could be done. On 30 January 1942, the War Department authorized the immediate activation of four Parachute Infantry Regiments (PIR) from the battalions already formed. The Army Chief of Staff had also decided to transform two existing infantry divisions, the 82nd and the 101st, to airborne.

By war's end, Army Airborne Command eventually created fourteen Parachute Infantry Regiments, four independent Parachute Infantry Battalions, ten Glider Infantry Regiments, twelve Parachute Field Artillery Battalions and nine Glider Field Artillery Battalions. Most of these units along with jump-qualified medical and engineer formations were assigned to one of five full-strength airborne divisions.

Living up to the rich traditions of the elite airborne put great pressure on new trainees like Johnny and Jake Kilroy and Sky Johnson. They had great expectations to surmount. Names like Lee, Miley, Wolff, Yarborough, Ryder and Tucker had already achieved folklore status. Lieutenant Colonel James M. Gavin took command of the newly activated 505th on 6 July 1942 and their own instructors had already volunteered for combat in that outfit. It was up to the new leadership to infuse cohesion, teamwork and a strong fighting spirit into these new formations.

The extraordinarily high standards of the airborne weighed heavily on Johnny. Add to that the ongoing feud with Jake and the possibility of going into combat with the hated Sergeant Bancroft, it was a wonder he had made it through the first three weeks. But he had. And here he was, sweating profusely and standing at attention late on a Friday afternoon at the end of C-Stage, waiting to hear what that bastard Bancroft had in store for him and the rest of his company.

Chapter Twenty-Two

Carolina Maneuver Area, North Carolina, July 24, 1942

"The wise learn many things from their enemies."

Aristophanes (c. 446 BC - c. 386 BC)

Sergeant Harley Tidrick lay prone on his bedroll. He was looking out the front opening of his government issued pup tent. The view as far as he could see consisted of a desolate wasteland with sparse vegetation. The foliage was primarily mangled trees and clumps of scrub pine. Here and there he could see some of the other tents of his squad and platoon scattered in the dreary wilderness. The usually parched and barren land was laced with random dirt roads, paths no wider than a walking trail and the occasional streambed now swollen with rushing water. Although it was the dry season, it had rained mercilessly for the last few days turning the omnipresent red clay into thick gooey muck. Harley shared the tent with Corporal Wally Carter, his assistant squad leader for the 1st Squad, 2nd Platoon, Able Company, 116th Infantry Regiment of the 29th Infantry Division.

Harley eyed the rolling hills on the distant horizon that bounded this forlorn tract of land known to the United States Army as the Carolina Maneuver Area. The division had only been there for a few weeks but already the land was taking its toll. The brass was conducting large-scale maneuvers involving three army corps to prove the best way to combat the German *Panzers*, or armored tanks, was with mobile anti-tank units and not with other tanks. The Germans, on the other hand, had already discovered that the best anti-tank weapon was another tank. Unfortunately, the Soviet T-34, proved to be the best tank on the battlefield. The *Panzers* took horrific losses outside Moscow in December 1941 and in the subsequent Soviet winter counteroffensive in early 1942. The German High Command responded by producing an up-armored and up-gunned forty-five ton *Panzer* Mark V, with the long-barreled .75-millimeter high velocity gun. This was the weapon the Germans hoped could contend with the T-34. This was the tank the United States Army designed its "tank destroyer" tactics to defeat.

American tank designers in the United States Army Ordinance Department had nothing on the drawing boards to match either of the best Soviet or German tanks. The army was already committed to the M4 Sherman as its main battle tank and full-scale production began in February 1942. It was a medium tank of thirty tons and fielded a short-barreled .75-millimeter medium velocity gun. Though every expert agreed the Sherman would be at a tremendous disadvantage in a tank duel with any modern German tank, the decision to go into full-scale production was based on two major factors. The first and most important at the time was simply that every tank built had to be shipped overseas to fight. Shipping space was already at a premium and the German U-Boats were sending hulls to the bottom at alarming rates. A medium tank takes up much less shipping space than a heavy tank and therefore more of them could be transported. That led directly into the second reason. The Sherman could be mass-produced in great quantities on American production lines. What the M4 Sherman lacked in "tank-duel" quality would have to be made up in quantity. Since it was knowingly fielding an inferior battle tank, the army was compelled to consider other methods to engage and destroy enemy tanks. The mobile tank destroyer philosophy, which employed towed or mounted artillery and unarmored heavy caliber tank destroyers built on a tank chassis, were believed to be the answer to defeating heavy armor on the battlefield. The Carolina Maneuvers of the summer of 1942 were conducted to test that theory.

The 29th Infantry Division was part of the Blue Force in these massive maneuvers. In that role they chased the tanks of Red Force throughout the Maneuver Area with heavy caliber cannons mounted on halftracks and towed artillery. It was dirty and tiring work in the rain and the red muck of the Carolinas.

Harley was beat. He rested on his elbows looking out of the tent. The few weeks that the 29th Infantry Division had been deployed in this hellhole had already taken a toll on the men. The rain did little to mitigate the oppressive heat. The daily routine of executing the required tactics of Blue Force was brutal. He was sure whatever the war-ravaged lands of North Africa or Europe could bring upon them, nothing could be worse than this.

He had just finished the letter to Jake. The U.S.O. provided stationary had printed in bold red letters on each envelope and the top of each page, "IDLE GOSSIP SINKS SHIPS". He would read the letter once more by the fading light of the day just to make sure he didn't leave anything out.

Dear Jake,

You probably figured out by now I won't be joining you in that suicide outfit of yours. The old man didn't approve my transfer. So I'm stuck here with the Stonewallers. How's jump school? How's Danny Boy doing? We're not in AP Hill anymore. We're on maneuvers somewhere in the North Carolina boonies. Let me tell you, Jake, this is a hard place on humans.

We run around all day acting as "aggressor force" and try to knock out tanks with our mobile artillery. The trucks slip and slide in the mud, get stuck and we have to hump them out. This damn red clay gets all over everything and into every crack in your body, if you know what I mean.

The heat is terrible and these damn bugs, called chiggers, are all over everyone. Some of the guys got infections from the bites. And it's hot like hell. Even after only a few weeks, blisters, cracked lips and trench foot have sent a lot of the boys to the infirmary. Those of us who are left are just plain spent. If we actually had to fight in this condition, I don't know how we would do it. Sometimes I wonder what the brass is thinking when they expose us to this crap. Hard training is one thing but ignoring these hardships is entirely another matter. At this rate there won't be anyone left soon. The conditions are just too hard. Which is why I think they'll be moving us out soon. Rumor has it that we are pulling out, along with the 4th Motorized Division. Word is we're headed for Florida, a place called Camp Blanding. It can't happen fast enough for me. I really need a shower.

We're all issued the new M-1 Garand semi-automatic rifle. It's a beauty. Fires 8 rounds as fast as you can pull the trigger. Accurate too. I loved my Springfield but you can't beat this rifle for rate of fire. A lot of the guys are having trouble loading the magazine. They get their thumb caught by the bolt going forward because they're not inserting the dang magazine right. They call it M-1 thumb!

Hopefully, the next letter you get from me will be from Florida. Speaking of letters, I got one from Macie yesterday. She says that she wrote to you but that you haven't written her since you left for the paratroopers. I wrote to her that you were probably very busy in jump school. I hope nothing is wrong between you two? You might want to write her and tell her so.

Harley

Harley folded the letter and stuffed it into an envelope. His eyes again fell upon the warning. "IDLE GOSSIP SINKS SHIPS". He wondered if he had provided any sensitive information but he was too tired to reread it. *Let the censor worry about it!* He sealed the envelope, stuffed it in his field jacket pocket, put his head down and fell fast asleep.

Chapter Twenty-Three

Fort Benning, Georgia, August 1, 1942

"Body and spirit I surrendered whole, to harsh
instructors – and received a soul."

Rudyard Kipling (1865 - 1936), *Epitaphs*, 1919

Private John Patrick Kilroy stood at rigid attention in company formation on
the parade grounds of Fort Benning. He and the other boys of his training
company proudly endured the brutal midday heat. There was barely a breeze
to disturb the flags held upright by the Color Guard. The reviewing stand was
packed with dignitaries and relatives on this Saturday morning.

Lieutenant Colonel James M. Gavin walked smartly up and down the ranks of
the latest paratrooper class. He moved briskly from trooper to trooper, returned
a salute, pinned the wings, a handshake, spoke a few words and moved on. The
small jump wings represented a huge token to the select few who made it through
the grueling crucible of jump school.

As Gavin came closer, Johnny straightened up just a bit more, tightened his
shoulders back and puffed out his chest. Finally, Gavin approached Johnny,
pinned his jump wings on, shook his hand and moved on to the next trooper.
My god, he thought. *This colonel looks so damn young.* Immediately after that
observation his mind snapped back to the beginning. *Fuck you, Captain Wolff. I
made it!*

But there were moments, and more than just a few, over the last four weeks,
when Johnny was convinced the comment Captain Wolff made in New York City
months ago, was prescient. It certainly wasn't easy, he reflected, but he just earned
his jump wings and all he wanted to do was stick them in the captain's face. *Do
you remember me, sir? Whitehall Street? New York City? You said I wouldn't make
it in the paratroopers? Well, look who was so wrong!* He looked forward to that
encounter. Of course, he had to be careful not to be disrespectful but just rub the
captain's nose in it a little. The prospect had been a tremendous motivator for
him in his darkest and bleakest moments over the preceding weeks.

Johnny nudged Jake and glanced down at their jump wings. Both boys were
compressing huge smiles into small grins. They stood with their chests out and
their heads held high bursting with pride as Gavin continued down the line,
pinning jump wings on their equally ecstatic cohorts. Johnny couldn't help
thinking about that last detail when he finally came to peace with Jake.

Sergeant Bancroft bounded up the training platform and addressed the
formation. "We're going for a little march," he announced. "I'm tired of your belly-

aching and bitching," Bancroft continued. "I'm fed up with the petty squabbling that some of you seem to enjoy."

A few men glanced furtively in the direction of Jake and Johnny Kilroy. It was obvious Bancroft was referring to them after the commotion in the packing shed.

"And if everyone is not back by sundown, then all weekend passes will be cancelled for everybody." The groans became more audible.

"So ladies, let's get going," Bancroft hopped off the platform. The men shuffled slightly in position, tightening their grip on their rifle slings. Commands were shouted. The formation did a crisp left face and the detail moved out.

Baker Company of training class Number 22 stepped smartly out of the barracks area and marched in a column of four platoons into the wooded environs of Fort Benning. The platoons were now reduced to about thirty soldiers each from the original seventy. They kicked up the dust of the red Georgia clay as they labored under the load of full field packs and slung rifles. There was no cadence being called. Only the slight shuffling sounds of boots grinding into the clay as the company marched into the deep Georgia woods.

In mid-summer in Georgia, the sun set about nine in the evening leaving almost four hours of hard marching ahead. That it was at the end of the day, when the heat of the sun paled slightly, did not make the march any easier. The stubborn humidity persisted regardless of the time of day.

The formation eventually came upon a newly blacktopped road perpendicular to the line of march. At this crossroads deep in the woods one platoon turned left, another went right and the rear-most platoon did an about face and headed back. Bancroft led his platoon straight ahead for another few minutes before he called a halt to the formation.

"Attention," he ordered. The men snapped to attention. "Right face! Dress right, dress!" he bellowed. The platoon dressed up into perfect formation. "Enema, Yank, front and center." Jake and Johnny scrambled out to the front and stood at attention. Bancroft addressed his second in command, Sergeant Bruce Copping. "Sergeant, take the rest of the platoon back to the barracks and pick up the stragglers on your way. Everyone back by sundown or no passes!"

"Yes, Sergeant." Copping issued the orders. A few moments later the rest of the platoon, shrouded by a veil of rising dust, was rounding a bend in the wide trail and were soon out of sight.

Bancroft addressed the two soldiers. "I'm this far from washing you two duds out," he held his fingers about an inch apart. "You've been nothing but trouble since you got here. Every man in this company knows why they had to march tonight and they all hate your guts. Now, I'm going to make sure you don't get back by dark and they'll hate you even more. Probably beat the crap out of you so that you won't be able to make the jumps."

Bancroft looked at Johnny. "Yank, you're a fucking slacker," Bancroft got right up in his face. He had a crazed, wild look in his eyes. "You look for the easy way out every chance you get. You're a wise guy and a smart-ass and you think you're better than everyone else but I got you figured out. You can look down on all of us but you're just a gutless little college boy." Bancroft paused to let his words sink in. "And Enema here wants to kill you," Bancroft continued. "And I ought to let him do it. That would rid me of both of you."

Johnny refused the bait. He would not let Bancroft provoke him before jump week.

"Enema, you're a dumb fucker," Bancroft shifted his attention to Jake and got nose to nose with him. "You can't control your temper and you act without thinking. If I washed you out today I'd probably be saving your life since you're damn sure to get yourself killed dead on your first combat jump."

Jake also refused to respond although every fiber of his muscular being was a nerve pulse away from tearing into Bancroft.

Bancroft stepped back, and addressed both of them in an even tone. "My little problem is Captain Wolff is pleased with the company. He thinks we already washed out too many good ones and wants to go into jump week with what we got. He figures we'll lose even more next week when some of your little girlfriends chicken out at the door." Bancroft seemed to calm down a bit. But I'd rather you quit right now," Bancroft continued as his face screwed up in anger again. "If you quit, you see, I can't be blamed for washing you out. Quit right now and we can all go back and the rest of the boys will all get their weekend passes. What'll it be, girls?"

"I'm not quitting," Jake answered first and quickly.

"Me neither," Johnny said as fast as he could after Jake spoke.

"Okay, we'll do it your way." Bancroft reached into his pack and pulled out a large adjustable wrench and handed it to Johnny. "About a quarter mile up this trail is a running path to the right that goes up that small hill," Bancroft pointed as he spoke. "At the top of the path is a little clearing, a place to turn around. In the center of that clearing is a bell attached to a concrete post. Remove the nuts and bring me back the bell. And I want it and you two back before the sun sets or no passes. For anyone! Understand?"

"We understand," Johnny replied.

Bancroft spun on his heels and began jogging to catch up to the platoon that was by now out of sight. *That rat-bastard is in really good shape*, observed Johnny.

As soon as Bancroft was out of earshot Johnny turned to Jake and said, "Okay, Enema, let's go." He immediately realized his mistake.

Jake dropped his M-1 and took off his pack. "You and me need to settle this right now."

"I'm sorry Jake, it just slipped out. But don't be stupid. Look, this is what the bastard wants. If we're at each other's throats we'll never make it back in time."

"Then you need to mind your smart-ass mouth, college boy."

Johnny held up both his hands in a sign of surrender. "Okay, I'm sorry. How about a truce until we get this done?"

Jake just stared at Johnny, studying him, his face emotionless.

Johnny broke the silence. "And if you want to continue this later when it's just you and me and no one else is involved, I'd be happy to oblige."

A slight smile appeared on Jake's face. "Oh, so you'll give me a chance to defend my honor at a later time?" Jake asked in a mocking tone.

"Yeah, yes. Now can we get on with this?"

"Surely," replied Jake as he bent down to pick up his gear. "Let's get on with this."

Johnny dropped his pack and M-1 and pointed to Jake's. "Let's leave these here. We'll pick them up on the way back."

Jake nodded and took the lead as they started off down the dirt trail looking for the running path. Johnny, wrench in hand, noticed the low angle of the sun flittering through the trees. He estimated no more than two hours of daylight left, barely enough time to get back to the barracks assuming they retrieved the bell quickly and could find their way back.

Sweating profusely, the two men jogged for another few minutes when Jake abruptly took a sharp turn to the right. He found it! Johnny followed as they ascended a well-trodden path that led up a slight hill. Jake slowed and Johnny nearly bumped him as they came to a stop. Right before them, just as Bancroft had described, was a square concrete post standing about four feet out of the ground. On top of the post stood a brass-colored bell that hung from a cross piece so that it swung freely. The cross piece was attached to two upright stanchions that were welded to a flange that lay flat on the top of the concrete pillar. Four bolts came up from the post through the flange and attached it solidly to the pillar. Johnny looked at the area surrounding the bell and post. It was well trodden. He surmised the troops would run up the path and around the bell and probably slap it to signal that they had made it this far. There was something inscribed on the bell but before Johnny could read it, Jake snatched the wrench from his hand.

"Let's get to it," he breathed heavily as he adjusted the wrench around the first bolt.

Jake tugged mightily and the nut broke free. Repeating the same procedure for the remaining nuts, they lifted the bell off of the post. It weighed only about ten pounds but it was bulky and awkward to carry.

The two boys retraced their steps down the path and back onto the dirt trail. They finally reached their field packs and knelt down to strap them on.

"*Jake*, I don't know what the hell we're doing here with this bell," Johnny gasped, emphasizing the name, as he carefully placed the bell and the wrench on the ground and fished through his field pack, "but I'd bet were doing something we're not supposed to be doing." He wrapped the bell in his poncho and shoved it into his pack.

The two men worked quietly and quickly as they loaded up their gear and moved out toward the paved road, forgetting the wrench on the ground. In just a few minutes they were standing at the crossroads. Jake spoke first. "We came from that direction so we probably should go back that way," he pointed down the wide dirt trail they had come from.

Johnny deliberated for a moment. "He sent the other platoons off in three different directions so I figure there's more than one way to get back. We got about two hours of hard marching ahead of us and I think we'd be better off on the paved road." Johnny sensed a flicker of frustration in Jake's face, as if his original suggestion was inadequate. Johnny recovered quickly. "But if you really think that's the way to go, I'm with you."

Jake caught him off guard with his response. "You're right, Yank. The paved road should be faster."

"The problem is we didn't come that way so we'll have to find our way back to the barracks area somehow."

"This road curves off in the same general direction we came from," Jake answered. "We'll figure it out. With that, both men began to quickstep down the paved road. They traveled for a time in quiet until Jake broke the silence.

"You're not a slacker, Johnny," Jake surprised him again. "I've been in the army over a year and I never volunteer for anything either. That doesn't mean we can't do our job or we'd ever let our buddies down."

Johnny was impressed by Jake's overture. He had to admit that Jake was making an effort to resolve their differences, even if it was only for this challenge.

"Look, Jake, I'm sorry about the Enema thing. Slip of the tongue. And I was a jerk way back when you offered me your hand." Johnny felt better getting that off of his chest. He attributed his own bad behavior to the strain of jump school. "Besides," he continued, "Bancroft doesn't know us or what makes us tick. He's the idiot."

"I couldn't agree more," Jake replied as he extended his hand. Johnny grabbed the hand heartily, shook it and they continued their speed march down the paved highway.

They had gone a little while longer when Jake first heard the sound of the engine behind them. They turned to see a civilian pickup truck heading in their direction. They stopped and raised their hands to the driver of an old dilapidated Ford. Johnny assumed he was a civilian contractor working on some construction project. The truck stopped. Jake went to the window.

"Evening, sir. Could we get a ride with you down this road?"

The driver was a burly bald-headed man with a thick black beard. He seemed annoyed by the request and in a hurry to continue on his way. He spat some tobacco juice onto the pavement and looked at Jake. "We're not supposed to pick up any of you boys, so if I might be on my way."

"So, you won't give us a ride?" Johnny asked rhetorically.

"Can't do it," the burly man replied. He became indignant and surly. "Orders is orders!"

Jake swung the M-1 Garand from his shoulder. He leveled it at the driver. "In that case, we'll just have to borrow your truck, cousin. But don't you worry; you'll get it back, someday."

"Whoa, hold on there," the man replied. He raised his hands, began smiling and became more obliging. "Just get in back and I'll take you down the road. But duck down if you see any military vehicles pass by."

"That's more like it," Johnny answered. "We're going to the barracks in the Frying Pan."

"Yes, sir. It's just a few hundred yards off of this road a few miles up ahead."

"Well, let's get to it," Jake smiled. "And no funny stuff," he slapped his M-1 as if to remind the driver that the two young paratroopers were both armed and still dangerous.

The two soldiers hopped into the bed of the truck. The driver took his time and carefully navigated the paved road. In eight minutes they traveled the same distance they would have needed about an hour to travel on foot. The truck stopped and they scampered out. The driver pointed off to his left down a trail into the woods. "Right through there, a few hundred yards is the barracks area."

"Thank you, sir," Jake replied. "Have a nice day." The driver sped off, visibly pleased to have jettisoned his perilous cargo.

"You have ammo for that thing?" Johnny pointed to Jake's M-1.

"Nope." Jake laughed. "Now let's see if we can find our barracks."

The two men picked their way through the woods until they could see the trees thin out in the distance. When they reached the edge of the woods, they both recognized the area and were able to pick out their barracks. They had beaten the other platoons back by virtue of their fortuitous hijacking. They found a comfortable spot with good visibility. After a half hour of waiting, they observed the four platoons march back into the barracks area. Johnny looked out to the horizon. The full sun was just touching the mountains in the distance. It would be dark soon. He stood up and looked at Jake.

"Well buddy, I think it's time we deliver Bancroft's bell."

As they came running into view, the waiting soldiers erupted into a chorus of cheers.

"How the hell did you do that?" smiled Danny Peregory as they ran up the steps and into the barracks. Members of the platoon slapped them on their backs and continued cheering.

Sergeant Bancroft was sitting at his desk in his office. He yelled out the door. "What the hell is all that ruckus about, Sergeant Copping?"

"The Kilroys are back," Copping answered in amazement.

"No shit?" Bancroft was genuinely surprised. "Dismiss the rest of the company and send those two eight-balls into my office."

Copping complied and closed the door behind Jake and Johnny. They snapped to rigid attention.

"Reporting as ordered, Sergeant," Johnny managed to suppress the smile that was about to explode on his face.

"I don't know how you pukes managed to pull this off but I'm not nearly finished with you yet. You two are..." Bancroft stopped in mid sentence as Jake reached into Johnny's pack, unwrapped the bell and placed it on Bancroft's desk without saying a word.

"What's this?" Bancroft smiled.

"It's the bell you ordered us to bring back, Sergeant," Jake replied.

"Bell?" Bancroft said. "I have absolutely no idea what the fuck you're talking about."

Johnny thought Bancroft accepted the Kilroys victory too gracefully. He wasn't the type to be a good loser.

Jake looked puzzled. "You ordered us to get this bell."

"I did no such thing, Enema. Why would an NCO order his men to steal the property of another regiment?" Bancroft smiled again, a sinister sneer that chilled the small room. "You need to get that piece of shit out of here."

Suddenly Johnny realized it was a setup. "You're right Sergeant Bancroft, our mistake." He shot a hard stare at Jake that said *follow my lead*. He reached down and scooped up the bell and quickly wrapped it back in his poncho.

"We'll be on our way now, Sergeant," Johnny took a step backward.

"You'll leave when I dismiss you," Bancroft barked. The two men stiffened again. Bancroft paused, stood up and walked around and sat on the front of his desk. "Paratroopers are a rowdy bunch, as you know by now. Always pulling pranks and getting into trouble somehow." Jake and Johnny were not following Bancroft's drift. He sensed their confusion.

"How else could you explain why the hell two jump school students, not even paratroopers yet, would steal the bell that the Five-oh-four uses to mark the midpoint of their morning run?" Bancroft had a smug look on his face. "And when the NCOs from the Oh-four find it missing, they'll scour the barracks area looking for it. I imagine they'll punish the thieves pretty good once they find... *you*."

Johnny suddenly got the picture. Bancroft ordered them to take the bell but there were no witnesses. When the Five-oh-four finds their bell missing, Bancroft will rat them out, if he hadn't already done so. If the NCOs don't mangle the Kilroys there'll be severe discipline if not outright expulsion. *Pretty insidious way to get rid of us*, thought Johnny.

Bancroft stared hard at both of them. "I'm heading out to Phenix City so I won't be around to witness the slaughter." He paused at the door and put on his overseas cap. "*Now* you're dismissed," he said. "And confined to the barracks." He stepped smartly out the door.

Johnny and Jake walked to their bunks. Jake began stripping off his pack and gear. He looked at Johnny and extended his hand. "Let me have the bell and the wrench."

Johnny looked at the bell. The inscription said, *504th Parachute Infantry Regiment – Strike Hold.* "What are you doing?" he asked.

"I'm bringing it back. It's our only shot. I'm not waiting here for those goons to come in and kick our ass. Bancroft probably already snitched on us."

"I know," Johnny answered. "But how the hell are we going to find the place?"

"We? You coming with me?"

"Hell yeah, we're in this together." Johnny began shedding his heavy gear. "But how *are* we going to find that place?"

Jake nudged Johnny. "Hey, we're paratroopers. We're supposed to find strange places in the dark. If we can't do it on our own base, how the hell are we supposed to do it in some strange country with the enemy hunting us down and shooting at us?"

"Good point. But I doubt Copping is just going to stand around and let us go."

"We wait for lights out, for things to quiet down and then we go." Jake looked to Johnny for agreement. He nodded.

They used the few hours to recuperate in their bunks and waited for Copping to turn the lights out in the empty barracks. After another hour, the two men stuffed their gear under the blankets of their bunks. Johnny wrapped the bell in a towel and retrieved a flashlight from his footlocker. They dressed light, just their fatigues and a baseball cap. They slipped out a window and headed directly for the paved road. It was dark but the various lights in the barracks area made for decent visibility. They worked their way out of the barracks area unnoticed. The going got much slower through the woods but they were soon standing on the paved road. Thankfully, a full moon began rising in the direction they were traveling. Johnny knew they were doing the only thing they could to counteract Bancroft's plot but still wondered how they were going to find that one secluded spot in these vast woods.

Jake looked at his watch by the moonlight. "I figure between five and six miles based on how long it took the truck to get us back here."

"Right," Johnny agreed after a moment. "Since we speed-march about six miles an hour, we need to start looking for that crossroads in about an hour."

"That crossroads trail and the path will still be hard to find in the dark," Jake complained.

"I left the damn wrench where we dropped our packs. If we can find it, that will mark the trail for us."

Jake nodded. "Right, Yank, good idea." He reached for the bell. "Here, let me carry that thing for awhile."

Jake grabbed it by the clapper. There was no noise. They began their speed march back down the dark lonely road in silence.

Fatigue was straining to take over the two men but the adrenaline rush averted it. The moon continued to rise and illuminated the paved road enough for them to see each crossroad as they came upon it. The problem was that there were so many of them and they all looked alike in the dim light. After the prescribed time, they began to explore up the cross trails, one after the other in turn, far enough to satisfy themselves that the bell-path was not there.

Trail after trail yielded nothing as they worked through the night. They collaborated in silence through the darkness until they could see the faint glimmer of sunrise on the horizon.

"Sun is coming up," Johnny finally said. "Maybe we'll have better luck in the daylight."

Jake turned his head to one side, listening intently. "Hear that?" he asked.

Johnny perked up his ears. "No," he confessed.

"It's a cadence being called. Somebody is out there for a morning run and I'd bet they're headed for the bell."

"Shit," Johnny complained.

"Let's go, follow me," Jake ordered and took off back down the paved road. Johnny followed. Jake ran with an ear toward the sound, which now became slightly audible to Johnny. Assessing the angle of the sound as best he could, Jake tried to figure the direction of the runners and their likely course and destination. After passing a few crossroads they had already explored, Jake stopped. He looked directly across the paved road down the trail from which he believed the troop of runners was coming from, and then headed down the trail in the opposite direction.

"We were already here, Jake," Johnny observed.

"Yeah, we probably missed it." He kept running, still listening to the sounds now behind them and getting slightly louder. He scanned the ground ahead. Suddenly he saw the wrench, lying off to the side of the trail partially covered by some leaves. Jake stooped and picked it up. "Got it," he proclaimed.

Johnny slapped him on the back. "Well done, Jake."

"No congratulations yet, we still got to put it back." They quickly found the running path and clambered up the slope to the concrete post. Johnny quietly placed the bell stanchion back over the bolts while Jake dropped to his knees to find the nuts. He handed one to Johnny who spun it on a bolt and tightened it with the wrench. They repeated that twice more as the sounds became louder down below. They both scrambled on hands and knees as the first of the runners started up the path. Johnny found the last nut. He finished tightening it just as the first runner, head down and struggling up the incline came into view a few yards away. Both men slipped into the foliage as the runner came into the small clearing, ran around the concrete post, slapped the bell and started back down the incline. The ringing was sweet music to their ears as the two men edged their way back deeper into the woods.

The parade of runners continued in an unending stream. They wore white T-shirts with the AIRBORNE inscription on the front and back. Small groups of men would enter the clearing at the same time, each one slapping the bell, soon to be followed by single runners with gaps in between. Every so often a large gap would appear where no runners would be visible for a long period of time. Jake and Johnny remained concealed in the woods regaining their strength and contemplating their next move.

"Looks like the whole regiment is out this fine Saturday morning," Johnny observed.

"Yeah, just a little run before reveille," Jake added. "Now how do *we* get back before breakfast?"

"I got that figured if you got a three mile run left in you," Johnny answered.

Jake realized what he meant and nodded. They both shed their green fatigue shirts to expose their white T-shirts underneath. Johnny stuffed the wrench into his pocket. They waited for a large break in the line of runners and slipped out of the woods, slapped the bell as hard as they could, ran down the incline and merged in with the long line of runners.

They hid in plain sight in the flow of paratroopers streaming back toward the barracks area. No one noticed them. A running formation was usually tight on the way out but loosened up considerably on the way back as runners slowed and straggled. Johnny's calculation was right on target. Most morning runs were six miles and they joined at the halfway mark. They ran along the wide dirt trail at a six-minute mile pace, being careful to stay in a gap in the loose formation. When they came into the barracks area, they slipped out of the formation and made their way to their own barracks. The sun was up as they slipped through a back door and into their bunks.

At reveille they showered, shaved and joined their buddies for a jog down to the mess hall for breakfast. The weekend would be light duty as the men prepared for jump week. Most of the men had post privileges and could go to the Enlisted Man's Club, the Post Exchange or to the movies. Some stayed in the barracks.

Johnny and Jake stayed with Sky and Danny, both overjoyed that the Kilroys buried the hatchet. The four young men went to the mess hall together, checked their parachutes again and hung out for the weekend.

Monday morning broke sunny and promised to be another hot, humid summer day. The trucks were lined up outside the packing shed. No more macho running and screaming nonsensical musical ditties. This was now serious business. Men would be jumping from airplanes, risking life and limb to prove they were worthy of their selection to train for and become United States Army Paratroopers. Sergeant Copping was unusually quiet and businesslike that morning. He knew some of the men would be injured, a few seriously and others might die. The injured would be recycled to a following class. The seriously injured would likely be assigned to a leg outfit, a non-paratrooper infantry unit, after they recovered. Those who died might have a road or a movie theatre on the base named after them. Those who made it through would be awarded their coveted jump wings the following Saturday at graduation.

The men formed up after breakfast and ran down to the packing shed in formation. It was a mild jog by airborne standards. There they retrieved their parachutes. Jake and Johnny joked around as Johnny smiled and pointed to the "P" between the first and last names on his pack. Whatever tension existed between them was entirely gone.

The troopers loaded onto the two-and-a-half-ton trucks for the short drive to Lawson Field where the Douglas C-47 Skytrain aircraft awaited. The C-47 was the military version of the Douglas DC-3 commercial airliner. It was always easy to pick out from a crowd of airplanes because of its distinctive nose and cockpit configuration. The GIs affectionately nicknamed it the "Gooney Bird". It was powered by twin Pratt & Whitney Model R-1830-92 engines capable of generating 1,200 horsepower each. The C-47 could carry twenty fully loaded paratroopers over 3,600 miles at a top speed of 230 miles per hour. It was the mainstay of airborne transportation.

The training company was divided into twelve man sticks and assembled on the bleacher seats alongside the concrete runway. Johnny, Jake and Sky were in the same stick. A lone transport was sitting a hundred yards away, revving up its engines and belching out oily smoke.

There were some last minute instructions from Sergeant Copping. "Relax, men," Copping began. "Smoke 'em if you got 'em." Some troopers pulled out packs of Lucky Strike or Camel cigarettes. Copping continued. "Remember, if you stick in the door you're done. Sergeant Bancroft is your jumpmaster."

"Today you jump from fifteen hundred feet. Your T-4 parachute will deploy quickly but if you don't feel the pop in four or five seconds, pull the damn reserve chute," he demonstrated on a parachute resting on a small table. "You'll be in the air about a minute and remember the landing techniques we've been practicing for weeks. Knees slightly bent, hit and roll, recover and collapse your chute." The men nervously nodded their concurrence. "For the next three days we lower the height to six hundred feet and Friday we jump at night." He paused for a moment and scanned the group. Everyone was paying strict attention. "Okay, first stick up."

Twelve men jumped off the bleachers and marched to the waiting transport. The C-47 took off, circled the airfield and cruised over the drop zone. It only took a few minutes to reach the jump altitude before the troopers began counting the white parachutes out loud as they exited the plane. The first stick jumped all twelve men. They circled lazily above and came down to earth. The men collapsed their chutes and walked over to the trucks waiting to ferry them back to the packing sheds to repack their chutes for tomorrow.

This aerial dance was repeated over and over again as the plane dropped its anxious paratroopers and landed to pick up another load. By the fourth or fifth stick, a military ambulance, called a "meat wagon" by the troops, made its way out to the drop zone to pick up an injured paratrooper. A few sticks later the men counted only eleven chutes coming out of the plane. Someone had frozen in the door. Jake leaned over to Johnny, "After all we've gone through, how can anyone stick in the door? Not now! Not after all the shit we've put up with!"

"I don't know," Johnny replied. "I'm just hoping I don't freeze in the door."

"Don't worry. I'm right behind you. I'll get us both out," Jake smiled with that look of confidence Johnny was beginning to admire. He knew Jake was dead serious.

"Next twelve," shouted Copping. Jake, Johnny and Sky jumped off the bleachers with the rest of their stick, marched over to the C-47 and loaded up. Bancroft was at the rear of the plane directing the men in. After the boys had loaded, the plane taxied to the head of the runway. The pilots gunned the twin engines. As the transport plane picked up speed and raced down the runway, Jake began laughing.

"What's so funny?" Johnny asked above the roar of the straining engines.

Jake pointed his thumb at his chest. "Nothing. Just my first time in an airplane."

Johnny laughed. "Me too!"

The plane reached altitude quickly and approached the drop zone. The red light over the door blinked on. Bancroft went through the pre-jump drill with orders and hand signals. The hand signals were essential, as the men could not always hear the jumpmaster over the engines.

Bancroft put out two fists, raised his thumbs and jerked them upward. "Stand up!" The men stood erect on mostly trembling legs, their faces sweating and white with fear. The jumpmaster raised his right hand, crooked his index finger and made an up and down motion. "Hook up!" The men hooked their static line on to the wire cable strung down the centerline of the plane. The men stared down the cabin at Bancroft eagerly anticipating his next command.

Bancroft touched the reserve chute strapped to his chest with spread fingers on both hands. "Sound off for equipment check!" Each man checked the equipment of the soldier next to him, especially the gear that was strapped behind, to make sure there were no loose or missing straps.

Bancroft raised two fingers on his right hand, wagged them and yelled, "Count off!"

"Twelve Okay," came the barely audible shout from the end of the stick closest to the pilots.

"Eleven Okay," came next until each man in turn had counted down to one. Bancroft nodded, pulled his wind goggles over his eyes, took his position on his stomach and waited for the red light to turn green.

At this point in a combat jump the men would have closed the line and tightened the stick against the door. When the green light went on, the jumpmaster would have been the first out the door. A combat load of twenty fully laden paratroopers was expected to clear the door in less than twelve seconds. But speed was not the purpose of the qualifying jumps. Bancroft would control and monitor each man's exit for later critique.

"Stand in the door," Bancroft barked. The first man took his position in the door, facing outward with both hands on the outside of the door and feet on the threshold.

Both engines of the C-47 went nearly quiet as the pilot cut the throttles to reduce airspeed to ninety knots, the maximum jump speed decreed by airborne doctrine. Paratroopers learned quickly to anticipate the green light by the sound of the engines. Suddenly, the jump light turned green. Bancroft, lying on his stomach with his head out of the open door, tapped the first trooper on the leg and out he went. The next trooper stood in the door. "Hands outside!" Bancroft barked and the trooper quickly remedied the position of his hands. A tap on the leg and he too was gone.

Johnny was before Jake but after Sky. The line was moving toward the door at a slow but steady pace. No one had yet refused. Sky went out smoothly and Johnny stood in the door and observed the scene unfolding in front of him. The ground below didn't appear far away. Cars and trucks appeared rather large and the people on the ground looked bigger than the ants they were supposed to look like. Before Johnny could fully digest the notion that there may not be enough height for his chute to open, he felt the tap. Gritting his teeth, he closed his eyes tightly and stepped out of the plane, right leg first, into empty space. Johnny immediately swiveled to the left facing the tail of the plane. He was bent slightly at the waist in a semi-pike position. His knees were bent with his legs locked tightly together at the knees and feet. He tucked his chin, brought his elbows tight to his sides with his hands, fingers widespread, gripping his reserve chute. His position was textbook perfect. He was quickly caught by the slipstream and was propelled toward the tail of the plane. Before he could count or even focus his eyes, he felt the opening shock of the parachute deploying. It was gentler than he expected but it still jarred his teeth and he bit his lip. Blood trickled form the corner of his mouth. He opened his eyes revealing the most beautiful sight he had ever seen. The twenty-eight foot diameter parachute was fully deployed above his head and he swung gently beneath it.

The roar of the twin engines faded into the distance and he was struck by the peaceful silence. He looked around for Jake but could not tell who was in which chute as they all drifted leisurely toward the ground. He marveled at the sensation of floating in air, particularly after the anxiety preceding the jump. After a minute or so the ground came up fast and he assumed his landing crouch. He hit the ground, rolled once, bounced up and walked into his parachute to collapse it. He pulled in the shroud lines at the same time he was walking until he reached the silk chute. The ground wind was light so it was not difficult to gather his chute. Standing with both arms full of silk and a huge smile on his face, he turned to search for Jake and Sky.

Sky waddled over with his arms also full of parachute. "That was freakin' amazing."

"Unbelievable," Johnny replied.

"Everybody jump?" he asked Johnny.

"I'm not sure. You see Jake?"

They both turned to scan the drop zone. Most of the men were already heading for the trucks. The ambulance was speeding to the far side of the drop zone. One trooper was still down close by, his chute not yet collapsed and tugging at him.

"That's Jake," Sky declared. Both men ran over. Johnny reached him first. Sky ran to collapse Jake's chute.

"You okay?" Johnny asked.

Jake grimaced. "Got turned around. Landed backwards. Sprained my ankle pretty bad."

"Let's get you to the meat wagon," Sky offered, referring to the ambulance.

"No!" Jake demanded. "I'm not going to wash out now. Not after all this. No way."

Johnny looked into the determined face of his newfound friend. *If you want to have a friend, you need to be a friend.* The words called out to him. He lifted Jake up and threw his arm over his shoulder. "Don't worry buddy, we've got your back. We'll get you over to the trucks."

"Oh, shit," moaned Sky. "If we get caught…" He let the words hang in the air. "What about tomorrow's jump?"

"We'll worry about that tomorrow," Johnny replied. He looked at Jake. "Are you sure you're up for this?"

"Fucking A," Jake answered.

Sky grabbed Jake's chute and the other arm. They scurried back to the waiting truck, limping and hopping together, their ugly ballet hidden only by the fluttering loose folds of the silk parachutes they carried.

They all knew what they were about to do was against the rules. They would help Jake hide the injury, pack his chutes and do whatever else they could to get him through his jumps.

Back in the packing shed Jake tightened the laces on his boots. They fit him like a glove ever since they were issued and he, along with everyone else, stood in a tub of water to wet them down. Then they walked and ran in the wet boots to form-fit them. When the boots dried they conformed perfectly to each man's feet and ankles. With his perfectly fitted jump boots laced as tightly as he could stand it, he limped around the packing table as well as he could. In spite of the throbbing pain, he found if he could put his weight only on his heel, without flexing his ankle, he could shuffle around. With his limited mobility, Sky and Johnny did most of the work packing Jake's chute for the next day.

Back in the barracks Johnny secured some ice and Jake soaked his foot in a valiant effort to reduce the swelling. In the morning Jake taped his ankle, laced up his boot tightly and limped to the mess hall. Most of the men had aches and pains and many of them had bumps and bruises as well. A lame trooper drew no special notice and even less sympathy. Jake faked his way onto the trucks for the trip down to the packing shed. The instructors were too busy with other injured troopers and watching the sticks spill out of the planes to notice that Johnny was helping Jake move along to their C-47. Once in, Jake was able to sit again. The short trip to the door would be no problem. The rocking aircraft and the paratroopers would camouflage his limp. The problem would be the landing. Jake had to do it virtually on one foot. His injured ankle would not be able to withstand the stress of another hard landing.

Out they went, this time from 1,200 feet. The entire stick jumped again. It was rare to see a refusal after the first day.

Jake's jump went smoothly. He attained a good position in the air and his chute deployed quickly and gently. He immediately oriented himself and concentrated on the landing. He would have to take the brunt of the landing on his good leg and quickly roll over to take the rest of the stress on his side and shoulders. It wouldn't be easy but he was determined to pull it off, multiple times, in order to earn his jump wings.

The ground directly below him looked like a soft patch of high grass. He raised his injured foot to keep it from contacting the ground, bounced off his good foot and landed flush on his side before rolling over. He absorbed the hurt through the rest of his body but his injured foot remained protected.

Sky and Johnny were there in a flash. They both kept an eye out for him as they exited the plane. "That was the freakin' ugliest parachute landing in history," Sky laughed out loud.

"You looked like a ruptured duck coming in for a crash landing," Johnny agreed, also laughing. "Are you okay?"

Jake smiled. "Yep, I am. I think I'm going to be able to pull this off." He hesitated as they helped him up and collapsed his chute. "I mean I think *we'll* be able to pull this off."

The routine continued for the next two days. Jake beat up his body with his good leg absorbing the punishment from the next two daylight landings. On Friday afternoon, under threatening skies, the company picked up their chutes and prepared for the night jump. The men gathered in small groups inside the packing shed awaiting the arrival of the trucks.

Sky, Johnny and Jake stood near the large open door of the packing shed. They scanned the dark sky. Johnny pointed to Jake's heavily taped ankle. "Are you sure you can make it?"

"I made the last three, I've got one more in me."

The roar of a thunderclap shook the packing shed as the three men winced. "Those were daylight jumps," Sky reminded Jake. "You won't be able to see the ground coming up at night."

"I know," Jake confessed. "But by then I'll have landed and qualified. If I injure it more or even break it, I'll have plenty of time to get better *but* I'll already have my wings. I'll just curl up into a ball as soon as my chute pops."

"Ooh," Sky groaned. "That is *definitely* gonna' hurt."

"I know," Jake answered, the smile gone. "I'm not looking forward to it.." Jake looked up at the darkening sky. "I said a little prayer. Maybe the Big Guy can help me out."

"If there is a God," Johnny murmured.

Suddenly the wind whipped up and the trees bent over. The sky turned dark green and penny-sized hail came crashing onto the blacktop outside the packing shed. In less than twenty seconds the hail turned to a deep, heavy penetrating rain. The downpour splashed off the ground in mini-explosions, throwing sprays of water back up into the air almost a foot high. The three men backed up deeper into the shed. They watched the sky curiously for about five minutes as the weather worsened.

Captain Wolff strode into the shed from another door and hopped up on a table. He was soaking wet. One of the sergeants yelled, "Attention!"

"As you were, men," Wolff bellowed before the men could even snap to attention. He wiped his wet hair from his brow. "Gather around, men."

The company closed in on the captain. "I just got back from the drop zone. The ground is a mud pit and the winds are over forty-five knots. That's ten knots over the max for a jump." He paused and then smiled. "Tonight's jump is cancelled due to inclement weather."

A chorus of groans immediately emanated from the group. Wolff raised his hands in mock surrender. "You don't understand men. You all qualify for your jump wings by virtue of the jumps you've already made." The groans turned to cheers. Wolff continued. "With the scheduled parade tomorrow with dignitaries and families coming and all and a tight jump schedule next week for the next class, we simply can't delay or reschedule one jump. You'll have plenty of time to train in night jumps when you get back from your ten-day furlough." The cheers got even louder. "See you all tomorrow at the ceremony."

The next day Jake managed to march, more like limp, in the parade and received his jump wings right next to Johnny. Immediately after the parade, the company retreated to the Beer Garden to celebrate. The men guzzled 3.2 beer and were having a grand time celebrating their accomplishment. They told jokes and stories and toasted those who gave their all but didn't make it. They were all extremely proud and the universal ear-to-ear grins testified to their exhilaration.

Captain Wolff entered the Beer Garden and the men immediately stiffened to attention. "At ease men, as you were. I only need a minute." He hopped up on a table. "First off, congratulations, *paratroopers!* You are now part of the best fighting force in the army." A loud raucous cheer went up.

"I'm also very proud to say that this training company has been assigned to me, my company, Item Company, Third Battalion, Five-oh-five, the best damned regiment in the army." Another loud cheer went up. "So just relax. I'll be around to meet each of you."

Johnny was at the bar with Jake, Sky and Danny. He watched as Wolff went from table to table and met his men. He had heard the relationship between officers and enlisted men in the paratroopers was different, especially in the 505th under Jim Gavin. Despite that, or perhaps because of it, he could not wait to remind the captain of his unfulfilled prediction.

Finally, Wolff approached the small group at the bar. He shook hands and exchanged a few words with each one. "Where are you from? What did you do before the War?" Johnny was ready when Wolff got to him. He grasped the captain's hand and looked directly into his eyes. "Captain Wolff, some months ago back in New York, you recruited me. Do you remember?"

Wolff stared back at him, a faint glow of recognition in his eyes. "I was only in New York for a few days. Were you that guy who the Marine sergeant wanted so badly?"

Johnny smiled, "Yes, sir."

"Well congratulations, you made it," Wolff tried to move on but Johnny wouldn't let go of his hand while his three friends observed the scene with great amusement.

"Sir, you told me I wouldn't make it through jump school."

Wolff nodded his agreement.

"Well, here I am, sir," Johnny continued. "But what was it about me, what did you see, that made you say I wouldn't make it?" Johnny was enjoying his brief moment of redemption.

Wolff put his free hand on Johnny's shoulder, leaned in toward him and whispered in his ear. His smile disappeared as Wolff began to grin. Johnny let go and the captain moved on.

"What did he say?" Jake asked.

Johnny had a perplexed expression. "He said he told that exact same thing to everyone!"

Chapter Twenty-Four

Newport News, Virginia – August 7, 1942

"Learn from yesterday, live for today, hope for tomorrow."

Albert Einstein (1879 - 1955)

The Stage Door Canteen in downtown Newport News was packed with young servicemen, shipyard workers and local women as it usually was on Friday night. The crowd was larger than usual this warm and humid August evening because of the appearance of the Tommy Dorsey Band. The swing band alone would have been enough to fill the large ballroom but the addition of its newly famous lead singer guaranteed a packed house.

As Derek explained to Macie when he invited her, the rumors were strong that the band and the singer were soon to part ways. Derek predicted it would happen soon. The singer was a handsome young crooner with a sweet harmonious voice who was extremely popular among the "Bobby-Soxers". If they didn't take advantage of this stop on the band's latest tour, Derek reasoned, they would regret not being able to hear this famous crooner one last time. Macie again implored Nora and was surprised how easily she agreed to accompany them. She got along well with Derek's friend, Jonah Cash, during the group date at the movies but Macie suspected it might be difficult to get Nora out again. She was wrong. Nora actually liked Jonah and literally jumped at the chance.

Macie was sitting at a table with her friends, breathing heavily and enjoying a brief respite having just danced to an instrumental version of the fast-paced "Boogie Woogie Bugle Boy" made famous by the Andrews Sisters. The famous sisters, a musical icon for a war-obsessed America, introduced their trademark tune in the 1940 Abbott and Costello film, *Buck Privates*. The song was then nominated for an Academy Award in 1941, assuring the singers' popularity. Virtually everyone in America could sing, hum or whistle "Boogie Woogie Bugle Boy".

For someone tall and lanky, Macie was a good dancer. She was dressed in a simple and sporty outfit. With the great fashion designers of Paris sequestered under the German boot, along with wartime shortages, casual simplicity became the accepted style of the times. Her blouse was white cotton with slightly padded shoulders and she wore black culottes. Her shoes called "wedgies" were made of mesh with a cork sole and heel. The heels were one inch high as dictated by United States rationing rules. She was wearing her last pair of precious Nylon stockings. Fabrics of all kinds were in great demand for military needs. New clothes were rationed, hard to find and usually of poor quality. The popular saying regarding clothes was "Make do and mend". Macie did the best she could by frequenting flea markets, thrift shops and using her ration coupons to buy material when she could find some. It was her seamstress skills and creative flair that allowed her to dress in a stylish way for a fashion-starved America.

Macie looked out over the crowded dance floor. Nora and Jonah were doing the "Lindy Hop" with the ease of well-practiced dance partners. Macie enjoyed being with Derek even though her reaction to him still confused her. He was so laid back and mellow. He never put any pressure on her, never tried to kiss her and was always the gentleman. Some part of her liked that about him. Another part of her, her curious side, wondered what it would be like to hold him and to kiss him. Those two opposing forces struggled within her since she came to the shipyard.

Macie smiled widely and clapped to the beat as Jonah and Nora gyrated wildly across the dance floor. Something beyond them caught her eye. That was when she saw Jake standing at the entrance to the club with another GI. They were both in summer khakis with ties tucked into their shirts. Their trousers were bloused into spit-shined jump boots. There was no rank insignia on their sleeves and the only decorations on their chests were shiny new jump wings. They held their overseas caps, complete with airborne insignia, as they inquisitively scanned the room.

"Oh my gosh," she exclaimed. "Wait here," she instructed Derek as she stood and walked hurriedly to the door. About halfway there she began running across the dance floor, dodging "jitterbuggers", until she came to within a short distance of the two soldiers.

"Jake," she yelled as she ran to him and jumped up on him, hugging his neck and wrapping her legs around his waist.

Jake stumbled back, wobbled on his cane, barely kept his balance and grabbed her with one arm. She hugged him tightly, kissed him hard on the cheek and dropped down in front of him. Macie still had her arms around his neck as she spotted the cane. "Are you all right, Jake?"

"It's nothing," he quickly dismissed his injury and changed the subject. "Look at you," he smiled at her. "All grown up." He bent slightly to kiss her but she pulled away, still smiling.

"Not here." She was embarrassed as she turned her head in the direction of the dance floor. "Not in front of all these people." He pulled back and she continued. "And look at you," she pointed to the jump wings on his chest. "You went and did it anyway, didn't you?" She was still smiling and there was a tinge of pride in her voice.

"Seems we both *went and did it*," he answered as his eyes rolled around the room. She understood his meaning. Even though they were both still smiling, there was an uncomfortable interval of stillness as they stared at each other.

"Ahem!" Johnny coughed and broke the awkward moment.

Jake looked at Johnny appreciatively. "Excuse my poor manners. Macie, this is my good friend Johnny from jump school. We traveled up from Georgia together. We've got a ten-day 'delay in route' leave and he's on his way home to New York. He's okay, for a Yankee." Jake grinned at his own joke. "Johnny, meet Macie, my...girl." Jake looked to Macie for approval of his introduction but there was no acknowledgement as she let go of Jake and reached out to shake hands.

"Jake is always talking about you, Macie. You're even more beautiful than he described." He bowed slightly, and shook her hand gently. "I'm very pleased to finally meet you."

"My pleasure," she blushed. Macie thought Johnny was handsome, almost as handsome as Jake. "I'd love to say that I've heard about you too, Johnny," she turned her gaze on Jake, "but Jake hasn't been writing lately. Have you, Jake?"

"Ah, not that much," Jake responded lamely. "But I can explain. Can we go somewhere?"

"I'm sorry, but I'm with...people." She pointed to the table and allowed Jake a few seconds to draw the wrong conclusions. After she was satisfied he was uncomfortable enough, she continued. "They're my friends. Co-workers from the yard." The smiles on both of their faces were gone now. "Please come and join us."

Jake resisted the impulse to become angry and fought hard to remain calm. *Join us! Who are these damn people? What happened to just you and me?* He pointed to his cane, "I won't be much fun here, tonight." Jake held her gently by the shoulders. "I know I've been a jerk. I just want a little time with you alone to work things out. We're staying at the Y. We were lucky to get a room. Johnny is leaving tomorrow. I'll be staying for a few more days before I have to report back." His voice was steady and unemotional but his eyes were pleading. He seemed contrite and sincere in a way that surprised her. She rarely saw that side of him. It got her attention. "Maybe we can get together and work things out, get us back to where we were?"

Just then the bandleader announced a ladies choice dance. The crooner began to sing, "I'll Never Smile Again", and a pretty young woman rushed up and grabbed Johnny by the arm and dragged him onto the dance floor.

"Where we were?" she asked. "Maybe that wasn't such a good place." It was a poignant moment with the soulful ballad being sung in the background. Her eyes began to well up.

"Some of it was good, Macie. Maybe we can find that again and get rid of the bad." He paused. "I'm willing to try if you are. I'll call you tomorrow. There's nothing more important in my life and I have no place else to go." He looked deeply into her eyes and then turned to leave.

"Wait, Jake," she said. "Wait right here." She went back to her table and retrieved her purse and told Derek she was leaving. He didn't press the issue.

On her way back she passed Nora. Macie motioned to her and she left Jonah on the dance floor momentarily. "I'm leaving with Jake," she said. "We're going to talk."

Nora nodded and leaned over to whisper to Macie. "Would you mind staying out a bit later?" She cocked her head toward Jonah.

"You're kidding. You're not going to do that, are you? What about Butch?"

"Macie, please don't lecture me," Nora responded. "I still have a life and I don't know if Butch is dead or alive. Don't tell me you haven't been tempted."

Macie took a deep breath. She certainly was familiar with temptation. "I can't deal with this right now, Nora. It's none of my business. I'll be out late but I won't be out all night."

"Just a few hours, thanks, Sweetie."

Jake left Johnny at the dance and took Macie down the block to a diner where they drank coffee, talked and tried desperately to work out their issues. He was somehow different, less headstrong, and more open to different ideas. Macie concluded they were both growing up and she had to be more open-minded about Jake and how he might also be changing.

The next morning Jake said his good-byes to Johnny who boarded a crowded train for New York. Over the next few days Macie spent all her free hours with Jake together taking walks, going to the movies and ice cream parlors. They laughed a lot. Macie felt good when they could find something to laugh at together. Slowly she began to regain the feelings she had for him before their first lovers' spat. He seemed to finally understand she was living her own life and trying to find her niche in contributing to the war effort, like everyone else in the country. He was sincere when he apologized and promised not to try to run her life ever again. He just wanted them to be together and he wanted to come home to her.

It didn't take long for her to forgive him. This was the side of him she always adored. She loved that he was devoted to her. Finally, the day arrived when he had to leave.

"I promise I'll write as often as I can," he pledged while standing at the bus stop about to board the southbound interstate bus.

"Please be safe. Don't do anything foolish." She touched his jump wings. "Don't do anything *else* foolish."

"I won't. I promise." He tapped his heart. "You *will* wait for me, right?"

Macie thought of Nora and Butch and the uncertainty of the War. The idea that some strange men in some far off place will soon be trying to kill Jake disturbed her immensely. "I'll be here when you come home." She cried into his shoulder until he peeled her away, kissed her on the forehead and boarded the bus.

In the days and weeks that followed she found it difficult to decompress from the flood of emotions she felt when he left. She was doing her best to regain her equilibrium. The only times she saw Derek was in passing in the course of their job duties and he was cordial if not aloof. He was predictably giving her space to sort things out.

As she read the paper one evening, having almost put Derek into the back recesses of her mind, she noticed an article about the Tommy Dorsey Band. As she read the article, she thought, *how about that, Derek was so right!* On 28 August 1942, during the band tour stop at the Circle Theatre in Indianapolis, Indiana, Tommy Dorsey announced from the stage it would be the last performance with their hot young lead singer. They would heretofore be going their separate ways.

She couldn't wait to tell Derek and thank him for inviting her to the dance to see one of the last performances of that famous singer with the Tommy Dorsey Band; a young, handsome crooner by the name of Frank Sinatra.

Chapter Twenty-Five

L'Enfant Plaza Hotel – January 13, 1997

"It is only prudent never to place complete confidence
in that by which we have even once been deceived."

Rene Descartes (1596 – 1650)

"I can't tell you gentlemen how much I appreciate you telling me about my father," J.P. said as the waitress cleared the dishes.

"Our pleasure," said Sky.

"Hey kid, anything for a free meal," joked Harley.

"Seriously, I really do appreciate this very much," J.P. repeated. "It must be difficult for you to relive some of these memories."

They all nodded somewhat sheepishly. J.P. continued. "So they started out in the Five-oh-five PIR. How did the Eighty-second Airborne play into this?"

"The Oh-five was assigned to the Eighty-second," answered Sky. "But if you ask anyone in the Oh-five, it was the other way around. The Eighty-second joined us."

"Proud outfit, huh?" J.P. asked.

"Very," replied Sky. "Gavin trained us to a razor's edge. When we got back from leave the whole regiment moved to Camp Billy Mitchell on the Alabama side of the Chattahoochee River, known as the 'Alabama Area'. We trained there for six or seven months. Hard training. We learned hand-to-hand combat. Plenty of night jumps. Thirty-mile speed marches. If you dropped out, Gavin would have you transferred to another regiment by the next morning. Only the best of the best was good enough for him."

"Sounds like Gavin was running his own little army," J.P. quipped.

"He probably was," Sky answered. "But it was the best damn little army in the world." Sky sipped his drink. "He was the smartest SOB in the army when it came to anything airborne. He wrote the freakin' manual." Sky pondered the memory for a moment. "He was a damn good leader, an excellent fighter and an outstanding teacher. We were lucky to have him. Well anyway, your dad, Jake, Danny Boy and me became tight. We'd go into town on weekends. Cotton's Fish Camp in Phenix City was a real popular place. And there would be a brawl almost every weekend. Sometimes we fought the Five-oh-four or Second Armored guys but mostly we teamed up with the other army outfits and had it out with local civilians and police."

Cynthia slipped a cigarette from her pack. "Does anyone mind?" No one objected so she lit it. "You actually fought with the police?" she asked incredulously.

Sky shrugged his shoulders and nodded. "That's the way it was back then." He looked at J.P. "They were always looking to corner a few GIs and gang up on them. But the four of us always watched each other's backs. Gavin had a hell of a time keeping us out of jail." Sky chuckled. "But when you have that many tough hombres in one unit, each one trying to show the other how bad he is, all that fighting was inevitable."

"And that made Jake and my father even closer?" J.P. asked.

"It made us all closer." Sky took another sip of his drink and looked over his shoulder for the waitress.

Frank jumped into the lull in the conversation. "In August of forty-two, the War Department decided to form its airborne forces into division-sized elements, after the British and German models. So the General Staff named the Eighty-second Division as the first airborne division. At the same time, that division's cadre was split in two to form the other new airborne division, the Hundred and first. Problem was they had no paratroopers. The airborne regiments being formed were eventually assigned to one of those two divisions. I was with the Five-oh-six PIR and we went to the Hundred and first in June of forty-three."

J.P. was impressed by Frank's knowledge and recall. Still, something didn't feel quite right about what they were telling him. Or was it their body language? He couldn't put his finger on it but his reporter's instincts told him something was amiss. He still wasn't sure how Harley fit and decided to take a shot.

"What about you, Harley?" J.P. asked.

Harley studied his face for a moment and answered. "Like I said, I'm Jake's cousin. The Twenty-ninth shipped out to England in September on the *Queen Mary*. So while Jake and Johnny were stomping about the Alabama woods, my division was already in foggy old England. Later, I met your father there." Harley hesitated for a moment. "But Jake wrote regularly and talked about your father a lot. I may have some old letters and pictures somewhere back home. If I can find them, would you be interested?"

"Yes. That would be great," J.P. answered.

Cynthia stood up and placed her napkin on the table. "Excuse me, gentlemen, while I powder my nose." She walked toward the ladies room without wobbling.

That gave J.P. an idea. He reached across the table and picked up the recorder and made a show of turning it off. "I actually have to take a leak, too." He reached down into his lap with the recorder in his hand. He deftly switched it on and covered it with his napkin. As he rose, he casually dropped the napkin on the table with the recorder tucked into the folds.

After J.P. was out of earshot, Harley asked the other two, "Do you think he knows?"

Frank answered first, "He's pretty smart. If he doesn't know for sure I'm convinced he's at least suspicious."

Harley looked at Sky, "He hasn't said anything or asked any questions that would lead me to believe that he's suspicious. What do you think, Sky?"

"He may be playing it cool but I don't think he knows. Actually, I don't think he has a clue. He may find out if he keeps going down this road but right now I think he is absolutely clueless."

"I wouldn't be so sure," Frank warned.

"Well, in any case, we took an oath of silence," Harley reminded them.

"I know, but maybe we should reconsider since his mother is gone," Frank suggested. "If it were me, I would want to know."

Harley looked at Frank harshly. "It's not up to us to decide to change the rules. We just can't ignore the promise we made. You're not seriously considering telling him, are you?"

"Of course not," Frank answered. "I was just thinking out loud. I'll keep my word."

Harley looked at Sky. "Don't worry about me. I'll keep my word, too," Sky answered the un-asked question. "Funny thing is, the answer is right under his nose. But he'll probably find out anyway when he talks to Lincoln."

"I'm not so sure," Harley replied. "I don't think Lincoln will tell him anything either, but we can't worry about that now. I'll talk to Lincoln again before J.P. gets in touch with him. But we three are still solid, right?" Both Sky and Frank nodded. "Good, then just keep telling him what we truthfully remember right up until it happens and then let me finish the story. After all, I am Jake's cousin."

They sat in silence for a few minutes when the waitress came to their table. "Gentlemen, your dinners will be out momentarily." She scanned the table quickly for empty glasses and noticed the napkins on the table. She picked up Cynthia's napkin, refolded it and placed it neatly on the table. Then she walked to the far side of the table to refold the other loose napkin.

Chapter Twenty-Six

Newport News, Virginia – January 21, 1943

"In war, there is no substitute for victory."

General of the Army Douglas MacArthur (1880 - 1964),
Address to Congress, April 1951

It was a cold January day in Virginia and the multitude that gathered to view the ceremony pressed politely against each other to share their body heat and block the biting sea breeze.

Macie Vance stood with Nora and Derek. She had a good vantage point but still had to stand on her toes to get an unobstructed view of the platform erected near the stern of the floating city towering before them.

Today was the day the USS *Yorktown (CV-10)* would be christened and it was a particularly festive occasion for the thousands who built her. Macie was anxious to see the ship's sponsor, the person who would christen her.

Derek was right again, she thought. Back in September, this ship was originally to be named the *Bon Homme Richard*. But after the USS *Yorktown (CV-5)* was sunk at Midway in June, the Navy Department decided the ship under construction would be named the *Yorktown.* The huge ship's crew would be larger than the population of Bedford.

After two weeks in welding school, Macie was assigned to a sub-assembly building welding components. She did this for two months and watched as other young women were trained and brought online into the shipyard's workforce. Macie attained seniority quickly and was promoted to welding plates and bulkheads on the ship. She often felt like a worker bee in a busy hive as she, along with thousands of other workers and welders, showed up each day to add to this rapidly growing ship.

Derek treated her differently since Jake had come to Newport News back in the summer but there was no doubt in her mind that he still liked her. As a supervisor higher up on the management chain, he looked out for her and made sure she was treated fairly. Macie was still confused by her interest in Derek. Like a moth near a flame, she was attracted to the light but dared not get too close.

Her personal growth in 1942 mirrored that of the country. She bought an old but functional tabletop Philco radio at a flea market and listened to every Presidential "fireside chat" she could. She read the newspaper daily and was coming to grips with understanding the complex war news.

As 1942 came to a close, a year of transition for the United States, the American people were clearly more at ease than when the year began. For the most part, great victories still eluded the Allies but massive defeats no longer plagued them.

The unstoppable war machines of Germany and Japan had finally been slowed. During the course of the year there were many turning points upon which the American people could take encouragement.

Japan's thrust to outflank Australia was blunted in the Battle of the Coral Sea in May. In August the Americans took the initiative in the South Pacific by invading and occupying the islands of Guadalcanal and Tulagi at the southernmost tip of the Solomon Islands chain. The raid on Makin Island a few weeks later by a small group of Marine Raiders along with the United States Army's initiative in New Guinea, signaled that it would be the Americans who would dictate the time and place of every new battle in the Pacific.

The destruction of most of the Japanese Imperial Carrier Fleet at Midway in June demonstrated that U.S. aircraft carriers could hand the Japanese serious naval defeats. That Japan seized Attu and Kiska in the Aleutian chain, the first invasion of American soil in 128 years, did not panic anyone as it might have earlier in 1942. The Americans had even bombed Tokyo and other Japanese cities in April in the famous Doolittle Raid. The earlier setbacks in the Pacific, notably Pearl Harbor and the Philippines, had all but been eclipsed by the rising tide of better news. The American people began to sleep less anxiously.

Macie knew that all the news was not good. Precious American aircraft carriers had been lost in the Pacific staving off Japanese efforts to retake Guadalcanal. Along with the previously lost *Lexington (CV-2)* and *Yorktown (CV-5)*, the *Wasp (CV-7)* and *Hornet (CV-8)* were sunk supporting the Marines defending Guadalcanal. The *Enterprise (CV-6)* had also been damaged and the *Saratoga (CV-3)* crippled. This news gave additional urgency and energy to Macie's work at the shipyard.

In the Atlantic, the U-Boat attacks that had been an almost daily occurrence in early 1942, a period that German submarine commanders called the "Happy Time", were on the decline. The Americans had instituted a better convoy and escort system and more effective air patrols rendering the coastal waters of the eastern seaboard extremely dangerous for German submarines. American merchant ships were no longer easy pickings. In July, Admiral Donitz ordered all of his U-Boats back from their patrol zones near the American coast. The U-Boat menace had not been totally defeated but a small tactical victory had been achieved. Allied merchantmen could now navigate in and out of American ports in relative safety.

On the Russian front, the awesome power of the colossal German land and air forces were stopped in December. The German *Wehrmacht* and its partners, who once numbered over 166 combat divisions and over 4,300,000 men, had been whittled down by the brutal Russian winter of 1941-1942. The fierce counterattacks by suicidal yet effective Soviet forces finally dealt Hitler's supermen a severe defeat at Stalingrad. The German army was still dangerous but no longer able to mount large-scale offensive operations against the Soviet Union or anyone else.

Macie witnessed first hand the conversion of the American economy from peaceful to wartime production. Tanks and planes were coming off the assembly lines where automobiles had previously been built. Ships of all shapes and sizes were sliding off of the ways of newly constructed shipyards all over the country. Rifles and ammunition were being manufactured instead of refrigerators. Uniforms and equipment came out of the sewing shops instead of gowns and suits. Combat boots were being made in shoemaker shops instead of shoes. Meatless Tuesdays and ration books helped fill the small tin cans in the C-ration and K-ration kits carried by GIs. Small businesses all over the nation became subcontractors to the huge companies that were fashioning the implements of war in grander numbers than could have ever been imagined. Every facet of the American economy and production capacity was coming on line. They included small machine shops, manufacturing companies, coalmines, oil wells, transportation and mom and pop businesses of all shapes and sizes. Mothers, young and old, took in sewing and knitting and fabricated the sweaters, scarves and ski hats for the military and the sailors of the Merchant Marine. The industrial war machine reached down into every nook and cranny of everyday life and tapped into the unrelenting ability and ingenuity of the American people who were coming together like streams to rivers into oceans.

Most Americans realized by the end of that worrisome year it was merely the momentum of the War that had shifted in their favor. They were too frightened in early 1942 to become complacent too easily. There was much more to do and the price was already high. Thirty-five thousand husbands, sons and fathers would never come home again. Americans would be called upon to make many more sacrifices in the coming years. A great many more gold stars would be hung in a great many more windows across the vast landscape of America before victory. President Franklin D. Roosevelt had proclaimed the Allies would accept nothing less than unconditional surrender from the Axis Powers. There would be no peace negotiations or political settlements. The enemy could either submit or be destroyed. No one had any illusions about how difficult it would be to bring the Axis Powers to their knees. The end was still a long way off down a violent and bloody road.

Macie eyed the massive aircraft carrier rising up before her. It was the fourth Essex-class aircraft carrier to be launched after the *Essex (CV-9)*, *Lexington (CV-16)* and *Bunker Hill (CV-17)*. Her cheeks were red from the stinging wind and her eyes were tearing from the cold. She leaned closer to Nora Lee to block the wind.

Nora had also moved up the career ladder in the shipyard. She finally got her promotion to Mechanics Helper in the Joiners Department as a Drill Press Operator. She had become somewhat interested in Jonah Cash and then furious when he joined up. She didn't understand the stigma that young American men felt when they *weren't* in uniform. Jonah had to do his part and so he tore up his 2-B draft status slip, quit his draft-exempt job at the shipyard and joined up.

Nora finally heard from the War Department. The first telegram came in July, three months after the fall of Bataan. It said only that Corporal Gilbert "Butch" Blair was missing in action. Then Nora received a telegram just before Christmas that stated, based on a reliable report from the Swedish Red Cross, Corporal Blair was a prisoner of war, whereabouts unknown.

She was fully aware of the terrible stories of torture perpetrated by the Japanese during the Bataan Death March. She had almost accepted his death and was beginning to move on. But now, with this latest news, she had two men to worry about and not at all sure either one of them would ever come home again. The possibility of someday having to make a choice between them troubled her. It was all too much for her to deal with. She decided she would write both of them and free them from any obligation they may have felt to her. If either or both of them survived and decided to come home to her, she would deal with that situation then. In the meantime, she had to unburden herself from the emotional strangulation of being a "widow-in-waiting".

As Nora trolled the shipyard and USO Clubs for replacement companions, Macie warned her that she was one step away from becoming a "Victory Girl". V-Girls were known to be promiscuous with servicemen, particularly before overseas deployment. But Nora had reached a point where she simply did not care what people thought. She would never be alone again and would never again endure the broken heart she felt when she was advised that Butch was missing in action in the Philippines. Nora Lee would avoid romantic entanglements. She would seek out the comfort and companionship that only a man could give. And she would do it one man at a time.

In spite of Nora's moral failings, Macie loved her like a sister. She would never judge her and would be her best friend through thick and thin.

The ceremony was about to begin as the dignitaries climbed the steps to the platform. Macie finally saw who she was looking for. First Lady Eleanor Roosevelt was the sponsor for the *Yorktown* and would christen her. The assembled shipyard workers erupted in a hearty cheer as Mrs. Roosevelt slowly ascended the steps up to the platform.

The President's wife was known as the people's first lady. Wherever there was a just cause that needed a conspicuous leader, she was there. She was tireless in her support of women in the workforce and in the military. She was a major catalyst in getting women pilots engaged in the war effort by ferrying planes from factories to air bases. Black America respected her for her outgoing stand on the inclusion of Negroes into the armed forces in combat roles. Poor people everywhere believed she was the back channel to the President for the social programs of the thirties that helped sustain lower class Americans with public service jobs such as the Civilian Conservation Corps. While she was a lightning rod for criticism of her social positions, she was immensely popular with the working class people of the country, especially women.

Mrs. Roosevelt was dwarfed by the immensity of the ship's huge mass. Above her on the wide gray stern hung red, white and blue bunting from port to starboard. Under the bunting was a huge banner, which simply read, "*Newport News Shipyard presents The Yorktown.*"

Finally, the first lady stepped up to the microphone. "I christen thee, USS *Yorktown*. Long may you serve the great people of your country." She threw a magnum of champagne, which swung in a wide arc on a long ribbon suspended from the deck. The bottle smashed loudly into the steel stern of the great ship leaving a white foamy blanket dripping down the hull. The gathering erupted in a magnificent cheer, which lasted nearly a minute. During that time, the cheer was sustained by the slow passage of the great hull out of dry-dock and into the James River. It would be months before the *Yorktown* would be completed with her armament and crew and commissioned into the United States Navy but this was the day the USS *Yorktown (CV-10)* was born.

Nora looked at Macie and smiled proudly. "Look at that. Look at what we did!" There were emotional tears streaming down her face.

Wiping back her own tears, Macie kissed Nora on the cheek. She turned to Derek, leaned in and hugged him tightly. "We did it."

Chapter Twenty-Seven

Oujda, French Morocco, North Africa, June 5, 1943

"One man is much the same as another and he is best
who is trained in the severest school."

Thucydides (460 BC - 325 BC),
The History of the Peloponnesian War, c. 404 BC

The boys of 1st Squad, 2nd Platoon, Item Company, 3rd Battalion of the 505th PIR took shade under the wings of their C-47 transport. Johnny Kilroy sat on the hardscrabble ground leaning back on the front wheel of the landing gear. He was carrying a full combat load and wondered if he would be able to stand up when the time came to board the plane. Jake sat a few feet away, finishing a letter he started earlier in the day. "How do you spell Oujda?" Jake asked aloud.

"S-H-I-T-H-O-L-E," answered Private Danny Peregory.

"It doesn't matter," offered Private Sky Johnson. He was sitting back-to-back with Danny. "The censors will black it out, anyway."

"Maybe not," Johnny chimed in. "By the time that letter makes it all the way back home, according to the colonel, we'll be in Berlin."

The four boys laughed. Colonel James M. Gavin was indeed a brilliant motivator. There was a reason for the hard training, Gavin explained. It was to prepare them to endure the hardships of combat. If they survived that, they were clearly the toughest sons-of-bitches in the world and could easily crush anybody they faced.

"Yeah, he's a bit of a cheerleader," Sky answered. "But I'm sure glad I'm going into combat *with* him and not *against* him."

All the boys nodded their agreement but Gavin's popularity was not always so universal. When the men returned from leave after jump school, the entire regiment moved to the Alabama Area. They trained intensively for seven months. Gavin pushed his boys physically and mentally harder than they had ever been pushed before.

There were speed marches in full combat gear. Hand to hand combat and bayonet drills were stressed. The troopers were taught how to use their knives to kill quickly and silently in the dark. They were taught that they, and they alone, owned the night. Only the strongest survived and many were transferred for failing to measure up.

Night maneuvers were practiced regularly. Units would be trucked out to the Alabama boonies and would have to solve night navigation problems by the stars or, if clouds obscured the sky, by maps and road signs. The men also practiced nighttime jumps with an emphasis on exiting the plane as rapidly as possible.

Once on the ground, they practiced "rolling up the stick" and assembling as quickly and quietly as they could.

Every trooper was taught the fundamentals of small unit tactics. Men of all ranks were expected to proficiently lead a formation of any size on the attack or on the defense. And since Gavin wrote the book on airborne methods and tactics, when they found something did not work or something else worked better, Gavin simply rewrote the book.

His boys also trained with German, Japanese and Italian weapons until they were proficient enough to maintain, operate and fire every weapon in total darkness. They were taught to identify and disable enemy mines and learned a dozen words or phrases in each language that would help them communicate with the enemy. They were arguably the most well-trained and best-prepared unit in the entire army.

Time passed quickly. After months in the Alabama Area, the regiment moved north to Fort Bragg, North Carolina where it was officially assigned to the 82nd Airborne Division. On 30 March 1943 the regiment flew from Pope Airfield to Fort Jackson, South Carolina and made army history with the first mass jump of 2,000 paratroopers. What was supposed to be a routine training jump with high-ranking brass in attendance turned into a nightmare as one C-47 stalled and cut a swath through the descending paratroopers. Three men were killed. It was later determined the cause of the stall was the slow speed of the aircraft. Minimum jump speeds were increased. The price of lessons learned by the fledgling airborne was exceedingly costly.

On 20 April, the 82nd Airborne Division moved out of Fort Bragg for Camp Edwards in Massachusetts to stage for overseas deployment. The men were ordered to remove all patches and identifying insignia. They groused and complained about hiding their jump wings. Unit pride was becoming deeply ingrained in this elite group.

After a week at Camp Edwards, the division boarded trains for the New York Port of Embarkation. Once there, in the dark of night, three regiments boarded three transports in New York Harbor. The 504th PIR boarded the SS *George Washington*, the 505th went aboard the *SS Monterey* and the 325th Glider Infantry Regiment sailed aboard the SS *Santa Rosa*. Also aboard the *George Washington* were two additional battalions designated EGB 447 and EGB 448. The joke among the troops in these battalions was that EGB stood for "Excess Government Baggage". The paratroopers of the 82nd called them "Easy Going Bastards". It was a typical attempt at gallows humor, as everyone knew these battalions contained the replacements who would refill the ranks of the killed, wounded and captured.

It took twelve days to make the crossing in a massive convoy protected by nine destroyers, a small escort carrier and the battleship USS *Texas*. Twelve days of over-crowded conditions, two meals a day in continuous lines to the mess halls, boat drills, seasick soldiers and foul smelling overflowing heads, to finally get to their destination. On the way across the men were told their destination was North Africa. They were glad to finally sight landfall although Danny boasted he could smell Casablanca long before anyone could see it.

Despite the numerous orientations on culture and customs, the boys were not prepared to deal with the Arabs and the depraved conditions in which they lived. They particularly coveted mattress covers, which they fashioned into native garb for everyday wear. Failing to negotiate a proper price, the Arabs would try to steal whatever they could not barter for. The guards were more wary of them than the enemy.

It was a short-lived blessing that the 82nd only spent a few days bivouacked in Camp Don Passage on the outskirts of Casablanca. The two parachute infantry regiments and the 426th Parachute Field Artillery Battalion (PFAB) moved out to the small town of Oujda, French Morocco. Division Commander Major General Matthew B. Ridgway selected the location for its isolation, French-built airfield and expansive and barren surrounding areas for training. Before they left the Casablanca area, some of the boys heard a broadcast from Axis Sally, the English-speaking propagandist whose broadcasts were aimed at Allied forces. "Welcome to North Africa, Matt Ridgway and your bad boys."

So much for all the stupid precautions disguising themselves, Jake thought. *The German high command already knew they were there!*

The 82nd Airborne made the exhausting 400-mile journey in two-and-a-half-ton trucks as well as by rail in sweltering "forty and eight" boxcars, so named because they could carry either forty men or eight horses. They drew a desolate, dusty scrap of land for their bivouac area and laid out their tents in straight, neat company streets. That was the first day of six weeks of hell.

None of the rigors of the Frying Pan, the Alabama Area or the crossing could have prepared the men for what they encountered in Oujda. Nature and the army brass conspired to make conditions as unbearable as humanly possible.

First there was the unrelenting heat, which humbled the discomfort of Georgia and Alabama. Temperatures reached over 110 degrees regularly, draining the most determined men of their drive and energy. The fine gritty dust blew everywhere. It choked the throat, clogged the nostrils and burned the eyes. The equipment did not fare much better as fine sandy particles clogged mechanisms and rendered vehicles and weapons inoperable.

Water and rations were always scarce. The mess food was bland and sparse. The cooks were called "belly robbers". The boys barely ate enough to sustain themselves given their physical exertions. Their food was always covered in a fine layer of sand and immediately attracted large black flies. They couldn't help but ingest the insects along with their food.

Paratroopers were expected to practice water discipline. They would fill their helmet liners and canteens each morning from giant canvas Lister bags at the end of their company street. This was supposed to last them all day, for shaving, washing, cleaning their socks and for drinking. The water had a terrible, sickening taste, having been saturated with chlorine and hung all day in the heat of the sun. They also had to take their daily Atabrine tablets to ward off malaria.

It was not long before sickness and disease struck the division hard. Soldiers were coming down with malaria, yellow jaundice, dysentery and diarrhea. They carried toilet paper with them everywhere and often had to find a place to defecate on a moment's notice, a condition known as the "GI Trots". Sometimes they didn't quite make it, to their undying embarrassment. Paratroopers who had been in superb physical condition and in the peak of health just a few weeks before were being steadily worn down by undernourishment and disease. Oujda was grinding the finely honed paratroopers into powder.

Despite the impact of the heat and disease, Gavin continued to push his 505th PIR. Shortly after arriving at Oujda, he was summoned to division headquarters along with Colonel Reuben Tucker, CO of the 504th PIR. There, General Ridgway revealed their first combat mission. One reinforced regiment of the 82nd Airborne would jump into Sicily on the evening of 9 July 1943, spearheading the invasion by the Allies.

Operation Husky would land elements of the Seventh United States Army commanded by Lieutenant General George S. Patton alongside elements of the British Eighth Army under General Bernard Law Montgomery to seize the island. It would be the largest amphibious landing up to that time with 160,000 troops and 2,500 ships and landing craft. The sea borne landings would be preceded by airborne drops to seize vital road junctions and prevent enemy reinforcements from counterattacking the beaches. Since there were not enough transports to drop the entire division at one time, Ridgway gave the assignment to Gavin's 505th PIR. Ridgway reinforced the 505th with the 3rd Battalion of the 504th and the 456th PFAB, making up the newly structured 505th Regimental Combat Team (RCT).

Gavin trained his boys mostly at night. He held live fire exercises and practiced assembling his forces in total darkness. When the objectives were finally assigned, he looked for similar landscapes and built mock fortifications replicating the enemy bunkers and pillboxes. The paratroopers attacked these mock fortifications repeatedly until they could do so in their sleep.

By late May the additional airfields were completed. The 52nd Troop Carrier Wing (TCW) arrived under the command of Brigadier General Hal Clark. It quickly became apparent most of the pilots were young, green and never trained in close formation night flying. Their training would have to take place in North Africa.

General Clark devised the combat formation for the transports. The basic formation would be a flight of three planes, one in the lead and one trailing on each wing, forming an inverted V. Three flights would also fly in a rough V shape with two three-plane Vs trailing the lead three-plane V. These nine planes were called a V-of-Vs and could carry a full company of paratroopers. Four or five V-of-Vs, of nine planes each, would comprise a serial which could deliver a battalion of paratroopers. Serials would follow each other in ten-minute intervals. This became the basic combat formation for parachute drops for the rest of the War.

General Clark immediately tasked his five Troop Carrier Groups to begin training. They flew night navigation missions designed to familiarize them in close formation flying at low altitude with poor visibility. After a number of these missions, they were ready to train with the paratroopers. On 5 June, the 3rd Battalion, 505th PIR loaded up for a training drop with the 314th Troop Carrier Group (TCG).

"All right, boys. Saddle up!" Copping yelled as he looked under the wings of the C-47. "Let's load em' up!" When the cadre from jump school was assigned to Item Company, 3rd Battalion, Staff Sergeant Bancroft was designated platoon leader for 2nd Platoon. He selected Sergeant Bruce Copping as one of his squad leaders. The men liked him because he was not one of those NCOs who sold weekend passes to the enlisted men. They also respected him because he was an original member of the Test Platoon and had over seventy-five training jumps to his credit.

"Hey, Sarge. I gotta' take a crap," Danny laughed weakly.

"You're all geared up, Danny Boy. No time for that. Do it in your pants." The moans and groans from the men were raucous and loud.

"Aw, I was just screwing with you, Sarge." Danny laughed. "I don't gotta' go".

"Good thing, because we would have left you right here," Sky said as he grabbed Danny's forearm and pulled him from sitting to standing.

The men helped each other up and into the aircraft, squeezing each fully laden paratrooper through the door. Jake went in first. He was the "pusher" for this flight. It was his job to make sure everyone was moving quickly toward the door once the jump signal had been given.

The troopers filed in behind Jake, struggled up the inclined cabin and sat down on the folding wooden seats. As the last man was helped through the door, the right engines coughed thick black smoke and the prop turned slowly with a high-pitched whine. Suddenly the engine fired and caught and the prop began spinning faster as the oily smoke was blown rearward in a black swirling river of air. The pilot started the left engine and taxied the plane to the takeoff point. A brisk wind rocked the plane as it made its way toward the head of the runway.

Copping decided to leave the door open for the flight. It was to be a long one, the pilots practicing low-level flight and navigation before dropping the paratroopers. The open door would suck out the stagnant air. That would be helpful if anyone puked, or worse.

The plane started to turn from the taxiway onto the main runway. The runway was extremely wide allowing the planes to take-off three abreast with plenty of room to spare. Copping's plane was the middle plane, the leader of this three plane V. The pilot stood on the brakes and pushed the throttles forward. He ran the two 1,200 horsepower Pratt & Whitney engines to maximum RPMs. With both of the radial engines humming smoothly and the aircraft shaking violently in place, the pilot released the brakes and the plane lurched down the runway. In under a minute they were in the air. As the planes banked left, Jake could see the next flight of three racing down the runway. They would assemble into a V-of-Vs, then a serial and finally begin the long practice exercise.

"Hey Danny Boy," yelled Private Dominic Angelo. "How was that cathouse in Oujda?"

Danny was sitting halfway up the stick on the right side. Angelo was directly across from him. They got along well because they were the same size and both fun-loving pranksters. Angelo was first generation Italian-American from Providence, Rhode Island. He worked on the docks as a longshoreman before joining the paratroopers.

"If you mean La Rue 63, I was on guard duty." Danny had a big smile on his face. There was not much to do in the small dirty town of Oujda. At the French-American Soldiers Club, the paratroopers could drink wine and socialize with the troops of the French Foreign Legion and the American 509th PIB. That socialization usually wound up in a fracas of some kind. The boys eventually looked for other places to go. The brothels in Oujda were dirty and dangerous. Before the paratroopers wandered into the tougher Arab neighborhoods where they were likely to be robbed and even killed, airborne commanders quietly set up unofficial army-supervised brothels, complete with medical inspections and armed paratrooper guards. The armed troopers were there to keep the Arab hustlers and thieves away and to discourage the paratrooper clientele from fighting.

"Right," laughed Angelo. "You were guarding this," he grabbed his crotch. "Did you get any free samples?"

"Of course," Danny lied.

"Did you use a rubber?" Angelo asked.

"Nope. Hate them."

"Your gonna' get the clap," interjected Private Joseph Boothe who was sitting next to Private Angelo. "Don't you watch those god-awful training films?" Boothe was a former steelworker from Pittsburgh, barrel-chested with huge tattooed arms. His hazel eyes were large and round and made his face appear bug-like. He wore his blond hair short and had a large cleft on his chin. Boothe and Angelo were inseparable buddies and barely nineteen years old.

"Nazi propaganda," Danny laughed even louder.

The men settled back for the three-hour flight. They sensed a combat jump was imminent. They were exhausted and welcomed the respite of the long training flight to get some much-needed rest. If anyone got nature's call, there was a "honey-bucket" in the aisle. As disgusting as it was, there was no other choice.

The planes had been flying for a few hours in formation at an altitude of 400 feet. Occasionally there would be a sharp-banked turn, a course change at a predetermined waypoint, and then the C-47 would level out and drone on. They would ascend to 600 feet for the night drop when they reached their targeted drop zone. Johnny sat next to Jake, head back and eyes closed. "You sleeping, Yank?" whispered Jake.

"Not anymore," joked Johnny.

"I got this letter from Harley. Tell me what you think," Jake handed it to Johnny.

Johnny never met Harley but Jake talked about him often. Johnny unfolded the letter and struggled to read it in the dim light of the cabin.

> April 23, 1943
> Jake,
> As you know from my other letters, our division has been here in rainy and dreary old (blacked out) since last September. It's damp, foggy and rains almost every day. Not good for morale. We are the only American (blacked out) in this entire country. We've been here so long they're starting to call us the Queen's Own (blacked out). The entire defense of (blacked out) is just the Home Guard and us.

"He's in England," Johnny concluded. "And apparently his division is being called the Queen's Own 29th Infantry Division. That's pretty funny."

"I figured England but there is something else in the letter later on," Jake pointed at bottom of the letter. Johnny continued to read.

> In December, a call went out for volunteers to train for the (blacked out). Wally Carter, my assistant squad leader and me volunteered. I couldn't help myself. In February, about 175 of us, officers and enlisted, went to (blacked out) for training. It was the toughest training we ever had at the hands of the (blacked out) commandos who survived the (blacked out) raid. If I thought the weather was bad here, I sure was surprised to find out it was worse in (blacked out). I shouldn't have been surprised because (blacked out) is further north and it has its own rugged mountain country, moors and swamps.

We drill, practice and train even on our own time. The (blacked out)
instructors are really impressed with us. We hope to join the other three
(blacked out) battalions in (blacked out) soon so I hope to look you up.
   Harley
   P.S. *This is a really tough group of soldiers and we're even allowed to*
wear jump boots. Now I know how you feel.

Johnny handed the letter back to Jake. He deliberated for a moment. "He was in England for sure and trained in Scotland. I think he trained under British Commandos, veterans of the Dieppe raid and he expects to be here in North Africa soon."

"Right," answered Jake, "but to join three battalions of…who…what?"

"Rangers. Your cousin joined Darby's Rangers."

Jake smiled. "Well I'll be…"

Just then the red light went on and the twin radial engines strained to lift the Skytrain to jump altitude. Copping stood up and went through the hand signals and the men followed with practiced precision. When the equipment check was completed, Copping stood in the door. The stick crammed together tightly, supporting each other against the turbulence-rocked plane and awaited the green light.

The light turned green and Copping was immediately out the door. The rest of the eighteen-man stick shuffled quickly to the door and out. There was no hesitation. They spilled out into the night in less than twelve seconds.

Jake was the last man out. He held his breath and his parachute deployed and mushroomed open with a loud slap. The opening shock was hard and violent. For a moment it seemed to lift him upward and back toward the plane. Jake immediately knew something was wrong. He was swinging rapidly back and forth and out of control. His effort to pull on one riser and spill some air was in vain. The turbulent wind had him in its grip and tossed him wildly like a weight on a clock pendulum. He knew this would be a blind crash landing. Jake gritted his teeth and pulled hard on the risers with both hands. He hit the hard-baked dirt backwards and crashed hard into the sandy, rock-strewn desert. The wind kept his parachute inflated and dragged him along the ground. Pulling his safety knife from his right shoulder scabbard, he cut the right riser strap. Before he could cut the left riser, his chute dragged him struggling and twisting head first into a basketball-sized boulder. As he was being dragged he switched the safety knife into his right hand and cut the left riser. At last he was free from the deadly grip of his parachute.

Jake rose slowly to his feet while checking for broken bones and other injuries. Aside from the large scrape on his left arm, which tore a huge hole in his tunic sleeve, he seemed to be okay. Sky ran up to him.

"You all right, Jake?" he asked. "Where's your chute?"

Jake held up the cut strap. "Probably halfway to Egypt by now."

"I know," answered Sky. "Can you believe this freakin' wind?" Sky looked around the drop zone. "And look at this, big boulders all over the place. I don't think they were supposed to drop us here. They couldn't have found a worse place!"

Johnny limped over joining Jake and Sky. He too had been dragged along the ground. The three men looked out over the landscape and in the bright moonlight could clearly see the ghastly scene before them. All over the drop zone the boys were being hurled by the wicked surface winds and slammed into the ground. Troopers were wildly scattered as far as the eye could see. Many were struggling with their windblown parachutes while others were lying lifeless on the rubble-strewn ground. There was no effort to roll up the stick or to consolidate the force. The boys were too busy helping injured buddies. When the drone of the transport planes faded into the night, the cries and groans of the injured could be clearly heard from all directions.

Medics arrived on the scene. Ambulances soon began arriving to pick up the immobile soldiers and move them to the field hospital. Even those who could move on their own were badly battered and bruised. Oujda had not been kind to the 82nd Airborne ever since they arrived but the training drop on the night of 5 June was an unmitigated disaster for the 3rd Battalion of the 505th.

The trucks had brought the entire battalion back from the drop zone to the bivouac area. Sergeant Copping handed Johnny Kilroy a holstered .45-caliber pistol Model 1911A1 and the keys to a jeep parked outside his squad tent. "Take the captain to regiment, Johnny. I've got a mess to deal with here."

"Right, Sarge," Johnny strapped on the holster as he walked to the jeep. Sitting in the front seat was Captain Daniel B. McIlvoy Jr., the chief medical officer of the 3rd Battalion.

"Evening, Doc. We'll get you right there, hubba-hubba," Johnny drove the jeep slowly up the company street between the eight man pyramid tents. Doc said nothing, quietly staring out to the east and the sunrise. In less than five minutes, the jeep was pulling up outside Gavin's tent. Doc McIlvoy entered the tent while Johnny shut off the engine and waited.

"Doc, come in. Sit down," Gavin motioned to a folding chair. The tent was spartan with just a folding table in the center and a few chairs surrounding it.

McIlvoy sat down and pulled out a small pad from his breast pocket. He said nothing while Gavin slid some papers to the side and closed the maps he was studying.

"What's the damage from the Third Battalion drop?" asked Gavin. He had reports that high winds had scattered the drop resulting in injuries.

Doc McIlvoy hesitated. He had something to say and getting face time with the busy colonel was a rare opportunity. He decided to take advantage and get a load off his chest.

"Eleven hundred men jumped last night and the casualties were higher than they ought to have been. We've been here only four weeks and we won't last another three at this rate."

"Is that a medical opinion, Doc? Or a comment on the hard training?"

"Medical opinion only, sir. The boys have been coming down with malaria and dysentery at an alarming rate. It's almost an epidemic. Most of them have diarrhea and pretty soon every one will have it. They're not sleeping and not getting enough to eat or drink and can't hold down what little they do get to eat. They're dehydrated most of the time and they're all losing weight and strength. Soon they'll be just a shadow of the unit you trained and brought here. You should have seen the jump. The wind was pushing them around like rag dolls. They're losing their strength *and* their edge."

Gavin pondered the report. He had been driving the Oh-five hard since inception because he believed discipline and harsh training would harden his troops and provide them the best chance at defeating the enemy and surviving. "What would you have me do?" he asked.

"The conditions are not sanitary here," Doc McIlvoy continued as if he had not heard the colonel. "The heat is inhumanly oppressive, the men can't sleep or shower, the bugs are all over them, and in their food. This place is a cesspool. Who picked it anyway?"

Gavin smiled. "General Ridgway picked it because it's out of range of Italian and German bombers. Should we go tell him he screwed up?"

McIlvoy composed himself. "No, sir. But we have to take the conditions here into consideration or you won't have a regiment left that's fit for combat when you're ready to fight."

"I'm hearing pretty much the same from the other battalion surgeons. I'll ask again, Doc, what would you have me do?"

McIlvoy looked at his pad. He had previously jotted down some notes. "The men need to eat better, sir. You have to get more and better food to them. They also need to be hydrated more so I suggest you ease up on the water discipline. The officers need to make sure the men take their Atabrine tablets religiously." McIlvoy was referring to the medicine prescribed to prevent malaria that some of the men refused to take because of false rumors the medication rendered them sterile or impotent. "Finally, sir, if there is any way you can avoid mass night jumps like last night," McIlvoy hesitated, "well, sir, you can avoid the casualties."

"What *were* the casualties?" Gavin asked again.

"Two dead, sir. Fifty-three men with broken bones who won't be returning to duty anytime soon and hundreds more with various bumps and bruises who refuse to come to sick call."

Gavin stared at McIlvoy open mouthed. "Two dead?" He closed his eyes and shook his head. He would write those letters to the next of kin. He would always write the letters. It made every loss suffered under his command a personal loss. He never wanted his casualties to become impersonal statistics lest he lose his sense of value for human life. Two letters to write and he hadn't even led his men into combat yet.

Before McIlvoy could say anything else, Gavin focused himself, reached for a pad and started jotting down notes. "We'll only be here a few more weeks, Doc. I can do something about the food, water and medication. The pilots still need more training but we don't have to risk paratroopers in mass drops to do that." Gavin looked at McIlvoy. "Is there anything else?"

"No, sir. Thank you, sir." Gavin's tone signaled the end of the meeting. McIlvoy stood up, saluted and exited the tent.

Johnny was sitting in the driver's seat when Doc McIlvoy came out of the tent. The sky was cloudless, clear blue and the sun was up over the distant hills. It promised to be another scorching hot day.

"Take me to the field hospital, Private," he ordered. "I have a lot of patients to see."

Chapter Twenty-Eight

Kairouan, Tunisia, North Africa, July 9, 1943

"The more darkness in night attacks hinders and impedes the sight,
the more must one supply the place of actual vision by skill and care."

Scipio Africanus (236 BC - 184 BC)

The paratroopers of Jake's squad were lined up at the doorway of their dark green C-47 Skytrain preparing to load up. Their plane was one of 226 transports scattered among twelve new airfields recently gouged out of the Tunisian hardscrabble. The sun was low in the western sky as the boys began to climb up the narrow aluminum ladders that hung from the doors of the planes.

If all went according to plan, they would drop near midnight, by the waning light of the full moon, and attack their targets shortly after moonset. Wherever it was they were going, it could never be as dreadful as North Africa. Jake and Johnny were ready to jump into Hades itself while Danny kept repeating, "Where the hell are we going?"

General Matthew B. Ridgway moved his 82nd Airborne Division from Oujda to Kairouan in the beginning of July. Everyone sensed they were getting close to their first combat jump.

Upon arrival at Kairouan they pitched their tent city in the shade of pear and almond trees, which protected them from the brutal July desert sun that often pushed temperatures to 125 degrees. The trees also offered some concealment from the prying eyes of Axis reconnaissance planes. An occasional romp in the surf of the nearby Mediterranean substituted for showers and cooled them from the ever-present hot, dry desert siroccos.

Ridgway desperately wanted to deliver his entire division in one airlift. There simply weren't enough transports because General Dwight D. Eisenhower allocated some of the American C-47 Skytrains to the British. Ridgway was forced to cobble together a Regimental Combat Team under Colonel James M. Gavin. The 3,400 troopers in the 505th RCT would be the first Americans to take the fight to the continent of Europe. The jump was scheduled for the night of 9 July. The remaining battalions of the 504th PIR would be flown in the next night.

Gavin was true to his word to Doc McIlvoy. Immediately after their discussion, he increased the food and water rations and enforced the Atabrine tablet discipline. He still trained the men hard but mostly at night out of the scorching heat of the day. There were no more mass practice drops. Casualties from training accidents went to near zero. The 82nd Airborne was slowly recovering from the depths of depravity it suffered in Oujda and morale began to rise. The 505th was a proud unit with tremendous *espirit de corps*. They were once again becoming the physically and mentally tough fighting machine Gavin had envisioned.

A few days before the jump, each company was brought into a large tent to study their objectives. The Allies planned a sea borne landing along a one hundred mile stretch of the southern coast of Sicily. The British Eighth Army under General Montgomery - four divisions, an independent brigade and a commando force - would land on the southeast coast of Sicily on a forty-five mile front ending near the port city of Syracuse.

The Seventh Army, under General Patton, would land near the seacoast towns of Scoglitti and Gela. The first American amphibious wave of the 1st "Big Red One", 3rd "Rock of the Marne" and 45th "Thunderbird" Infantry Divisions and Lieutenant Colonel William O. Darby's 1st, 3rd and 4th Ranger Battalions would spearhead the sea borne invasion.

The airborne assault, codename Husky One for the American effort and Ladbroke for the British drop, was designed to buy the sea borne element sufficient time to build up adequate forces on the beachheads. The paratroopers would accomplish this by seizing the high ground inland above the town of Gela and controlling the roads inland from the beaches.

Gavin's greatest concern was the flight to the drop zones. In order to avoid flying over the invasion fleet, the planes would navigate a circuitous route looping around the convoy of ships. This lengthened the flight time to more than three hours. To avoid detection they would fly only a few hundred feet above the sea. These factors were daunting enough to the most experienced aircrews and Gavin knew the pilots who would ferry his troops were mostly green and inexperienced. Even though there were no alternatives, it still gave him sleepless nights.

Captain Louis Wolff's Item Company had been designated for a special mission. He gathered his troopers around a covered sand table. Behind the table, hanging on the wall was a large blurry blowup of a reconnaissance photo. In front of the photograph, standing on a low platform, was the unpopular CO of the 3rd Battalion, Major Edward C. Krause. He earned the nickname "Cannonball" for his gruff manner and fiery temper.

Wolff joined Major Krause in front of the aerial photo. Krause spoke first. "Before I let Captain Wolff brief you on your mission, I want to remind you this battalion is made up of the toughest bad asses in the army. You're going to go in amongst them and stack bodies!"

The boys listened in silence. Krause continued. "Intelligence tells us there are no German combat units and no heavy tanks." This information was important to the paratroopers. Being light infantry, they were particularly vulnerable to heavy armor. They did carry a rocket launcher, called a "bazooka", a light, portable anti-tank weapon, but the paratroopers never seemed to have enough rockets for it. Besides, they knew the bazooka could not stop the heaviest German tanks.

"We'll be landing and assembling after dark. The challenge is 'George', the response is 'Marshall'," Krause explained.

"Who's that?" Dom Angelo chuckled. The whole company broke up in laughter. Everyone knew that General George Marshall was the Chief of Staff, the highest-ranking officer in the military and President Roosevelt's right hand man on matters pertaining to the War.

Krause continued. "Very cute! Now pay attention! Item Company has been assigned a detached special mission. You men will be dropped on a different target than the rest of the battalion. I'll let your company commander brief you." With that, Krause stepped off of the platform and gave way to Captain Wolff.

Wolff snapped the tarp off of the sand table. He used a long wooden pointer to direct attention to locations carved into the sand. "We are tasked with the mission of reducing this pillbox complex at this road junction. Then we hold this road junction until relieved." He moved the pointer from the sand table to the blurred blowup of the photo and back. A murmur arose from the group as the troopers in front crowded closer. The targets were arranged exactly like the mock-ups they had repeatedly attacked in training.

Before Wolff could continue, Sky spoke up. "Captain, are those ridges on both sides of the drop zone to scale?" The drop area for the entire company was in a narrow valley between two high ridgelines at the western end of a large lake. The paratroopers looked around at one another. They instinctively understood this narrow drop zone would be difficult to find at night.

"Yes, everything is to scale," Wolff answered and continued. "Everyone except First Squad, Second Platoon will attack the pillbox complex and secure the road junction. Nothing gets by us to the beach. Nothing!" Wolff paused for affect and then continued. "Now this is important, First Squad under Lieutenant Clark will set a signal fire on this hill at exactly zero-two-hundred hours." Wolff rested the pointer on a bulge in the sand table. "We're lighting the way for the Sixteenth Infantry Regiment of the Big Red One," Wolff explained. "They'll land where they see the beacon, so this mission must be picture perfect."

"Sir," a voice called from the crowd. "Where is this place? Where are we going?"

"You'll find out soon enough. Right now I want each officer to bring his platoon up to the table one at a time and explain their exact mission down to the squad level. Your officers and sergeants have already been briefed."

"Sir," another voice called out. "That drop zone is pretty tight, isn't it?"

"I know, son," Wolff answered. "I'll talk to the pilots…see what we can do."

Wolff looked around at his company. "All right men, gather around the table." He turned to First Lieutenant George E. Clark Jr.

"George, pick two men and come with me," ordered Wolff.

"Yes sir. Where are we going?"

"To find my pilots."

Lieutenant Clark quickly scanned the group and pulled out Jake and Johnny. Wolff grabbed the smaller original reconnaissance photos and the four men exited the tent and climbed aboard a waiting jeep. Johnny jumped into the driver's seat.

Wolff tapped Johnny on the shoulder. "We're heading for the Three-fourteenth TCG area, this way." He pointed to a row of large tents in the distance. Johnny gunned the engine and the jeep kicked some dirt as it briefly spun out and headed toward a row of four-man tents. Johnny stopped directly in front of one of them.

"Wait here," Wolff ordered. Photos in hand, he pulled the tent flap back and entered. "Excuse me, I'm looking for Captain William R. Bommar."

A figure rose up from one of the bunks and swung his feet to the bare dirt floor. He was resting on his bunk, fully clothed with his boots on. "I'm Bill Bommar." The other officers in the tent grunted and rolled over in their bunks.

Wolff reached out and shook his hand. "I'm Captain Lou Wolff. Glad to meet you. I'm told you're the flight leader of the group that's taking my company on this mission."

"I am. I've been expecting you." Bommar tapped the bunk beside him. "Have a seat. I've been studying the problem." Bommar paused. "Do you have any ideas?"

Wolff was immediately impressed with Bommar's business-like manner and spirit of cooperation. Wolff pulled out the aerial photos and Bommar fished a flashlight from his musette bag along with a map. Together they studied the pictures alongside the map.

"Look here," Wolff pointed to the map. "When we hit the coast, we should be able to see this river coming out to the sea. The full moon should reflect off of it nicely. Then we can track the river up to this huge inland lake, follow the lake west until we spot this railroad track which should lead us to this major road and we should hit the mouth of the valley and drop zone right on target." Wolff traced the photo as he spoke and Bommar marked the map.

"The Acate River and Lake Bivieri," Bommar noted. "I agree on the lake." He pointed to the photo taken in daylight. "But the Acate River is dry. It shows up in this photo but it won't be easy to spot at night. The lake should be easy to find under a full moon once we hit the coast."

"Roger that." Wolff continued to be impressed by the young aviator. He certainly did his homework. Wolff had another request. "Can you be the last group of nine planes in the serial?"

"Why?"

"Because I'm going to ask you to approach the drop zone with your planes one behind the other and not spread out in echelon. The drop zone is far too narrow for the standard jump pattern. And if you're last, you won't get all tangled up with the rest of your group."

Bommar contemplated the request. "I can arrange that."

"Great, thanks." Wolff replied. "Now I know why they picked you for this mission. But I got one more request."

"Sure."

"The landmark for the drop, the point at which we can get all of our guys on the target, is this white house right here," Wolff pointed to a white dot along a road that was just a bit bigger than the white pillboxes near it. "As we come up the valley, this house is only visible from the right side of the plane. I'm asking if you would sit on the right side."

Bommar stiffened. The right seat was the co-pilot's seat. He looked directly at Wolff. "Sir, I don't sit on the right side."

"I know, I know," Wolff replied. "As the lead plane commander you sit in the left seat. I get that, but hear me out."

Bommar nodded but he was visibly uncomfortable. Wolff continued. "That landmark is hard to spot near all those pillboxes. If we drop on the right landmark we'll land where we're supposed to be. If we're late, we miss the DZ. If we're early, the tail end planes drop my boys into the lake. The whole mission depends on recognizing this one right spot. The guy who makes that decision and turns on the green light needs to be exceptional, on top of everything. I need that guy to be *you*. So, Captain, just this once, for me and my boys, would you *please* sit in the right seat and be that guy who decides when to drop us?"

Bommar deliberated on Wolff's logic. He could not let his ego get in the way of the mission's success. Sitting in the right seat for one mission was inconsequential when compared to the lives of the paratroopers that would be in his hands. "Yes, sir."

"Great! Thanks." Wolff shook his hand. "I'll be flying in the lead plane with you. See you on the flight line."

The fully burdened boys of 1st Squad pushed and shoved each other up the small steps and through the door onto their C-47. The plane rocked as they struggled forward and into their seats. Captain Wolff handed each man a piece of paper. Johnny began reading it.

> *Soldiers of the 505th Combat Team*
> *Tonight you embark upon a combat mission for which our people and the*
> *people of the free world have been waiting for two years.*
> *You will spearhead the landing of an American Force upon the island*
> *of SICILY. Every preparation has been made to eliminate the element of*
> *chance.*

"Sicily!" Johnny mumbled. He looked to the bottom to see it was signed by Gavin. Struck by the historical significance and the simple eloquence of the letter, he decided to save it. He folded it carefully and slid it into his jacket pocket after taking his seat. "So, it's Sicily, again."

Jake turned toward him. "Again?"

"Yeah, again. We're invading the most conquered island in history. Those poor people were invaded by the Greeks, Romans, Muslims, Vikings, Spanish, Franks, Italians, Normans." Johnny closed his eyes and looked up. "Let's see, did I leave anybody out?"

"Hmm," Jake mused. "Did they ever stop anybody? Defeat them, I mean?"

"Not one," Johnny answered without hesitation. "The stepping stone between Africa and Europe was always raped but never loved."

"You make that up?" Jake asked.

"Nah. I read it somewhere."

"Hey Dom," Private Danny Peregory shouted down the line of seated paratroopers. "You have people here? Maybe get us a homemade meal?"

"Nah," Private Angelo answered. "But wait till we get to Naples. My people are there. Teddy has people in Sicily." He pointed to Private Carmine Tedesco.

"Yeah, I got relatives in Palermo." Tedesco was from the Bronx. "They don't have no use for Mussolini. They're farmers, not Fascists. I just hope they're smart enough to keep their heads down when the shit hits the fan."

The men settled in, trying to find comfortable positions for the long plane ride. The same scene was repeated all over the small airfield as the forty-five planes were loading up.

Captain Wolff was the jumpmaster. Sergeant Copping was the pusher and was seated at the end of the stick, closest to the pilot's cabin. Bancroft was seated near Wolff by the exit door. The sergeant insisted on calling Jake "Enema" and Johnny knew Jake seethed every time he heard it so he sat between them. He would never let Jake get too close to Bancroft.

Abruptly, the familiar whine of the starter motors broke the calm. The sputtering, explosions of the fourteen cylinder engines produced loud coughing and jerking as the Hamilton Standard propellers picked up speed. The smell of smoke, gasoline and oil permeated the cabin. In a few moments both engines were running smoothly. The cabin vibrated with the familiar drone of the radial engines as the pilots ran them up to speed. Slowly, they began to move.

Their plane moved in line with other C-47s as they taxied toward the head of the runway. From the portholes the men could barely see other C-47s taking off in the opposite direction through the swirling clouds of dust being kicked up in every direction.

They were near the end of the line, among the last planes in the serial as Wolff and Bommar had agreed. Their plane began the slow 180-degree turn to line up with the runway. When the turn was completed, the pilots stood on the brakes and ran the engines to full speed. The cabin rocked violently as the torque of the engines tried in vain to twist the structural backbone of the heavily laden transport plane. The pilots released the brakes. Slowly, the fully loaded 25,000-pound aircraft heaved forward and headed, nearly blind, down the runway.

The transport lifted gently off the ground and into the heated desert air. Once the landing gear was up, the pilot banked the plane and smoothly fell into formation as the lead plane in the last nine plane V-of-Vs. They were on their way to Sicily.

The flight plan was a difficult one. The route almost doubled the straight-line distance from Kairouan to the drop zones in Sicily. In addition, they would have to keep formation in near total darkness. While the C-47 had a service ceiling of 24,000 feet, they would fly this leg at 300 feet above the waves for the entire 415 mile trip. It would require tremendous concentration.

The first leg would be easterly until the pilots sighted the special beacon on Malta. Then a sharp course change to due north would line up the flight with the southeastern tip of Sicily. Upon reaching that waypoint, the planes were to turn due west and run along the southern coast until reaching their landmarks. At that point they were to turn inland, ascend to jump level, find their drop zones and release their paratroopers. The challenge itself was daunting enough but nature had a surprise. Immediately upon leaving the ground and heading east, a stiff crosswind from the north began driving the entire air armada slowly but inexorably off course.

The cabin quieted as each man settled into his own personal routine. They camouflaged their fear and anxiety in different ways. Some would talk in hushed whispers. Others slept or pretended to sleep, heads bobbing to the rhythmic motion of the airplane. A few fingered Rosaries or had their Bibles out and were struggling to read in the darkened cabin. Specs of light glowing brighter then dimmer betrayed the handful that chain-smoked their way through the flight, illuminating their faces in an eerie glow.

All of them felt the buffeting as the crosswinds relentlessly pounded the planes further and further south of their intended flight path.

Johnny turned toward Jake whose head was leaning back against the bulkhead. A moment ago, Johnny thought he saw Jake reading but now he seemed to be sleeping. "Jake. You awake?"

"I am now," Jake smiled without opening his eyes.

"Seriously, we need to talk. I've been thinking."

"Oh, that's always dangerous." Jake's smile broadened even wider as he opened his eyes and looked at his friend. "What about?"

"About the jump." Johnny hesitated. For a moment he couldn't find the words. Finally, he blurted out, "If things get rough out there and we get in a tight spot…"

"What the hell are you talking about?" Jake interrupted. "We'll be fine. We're the most trained and best led infantry in the world. Nothing can happen to us. Krause said so!"

"That's not what I'm talking about. You and me, we've had each other's back since jump school. Remember the brawls in Phenix City, those survival night exercises at Camp Billy Mitchell, all of the shit we've been through? We always looked out for each other."

"And we always will," Jake interrupted again as he slipped a stick of gum into his mouth to relieve the pressure building in his ears. Over the long months of training they had bonded into inseparable friends, fond of and loyal to each other.

Johnny replied. "But this is combat and no one knows how they'll react. I don't want to let anyone down." Johnny let out a slight cough. "Ahem. If I freeze up or lose my nerve, just make sure you kick me in the ass or do something to shake me up and get me going again."

"Okay, Yank, I won't let you freeze." Johnny nodded his thanks. Jake's confidence always inspired him.

Jake sat back, closed his eyes and faced forward. "Me too. Don't let me freeze up either." And one more thing," Jake said without opening his eyes or turning toward Johnny. "I don't intend to be taken prisoner. I'll do whatever I have to do. If that's a problem, as much as I like you as a friend, you shouldn't hang close to me." Jake looked directly at Johnny for the answer.

"That's not a problem. They're not taking me, either."

Johnny reached a clenched fist out in front of Jake. Jake struck it with his own fist. With that simple gesture they entered into a blood pact. Because their personal honor meant everything, their word to each other was unbreakable.

As the formation soared on into a darkening sky, the young pilots struggled mightily against the wind to maintain formation. The cabin of the C-47 was silent yet filled with a palpable anxiety. Without warning the plane banked hard into a left hand turn and steadied on a course of due magnetic north. The crosswind now became a headwind and the buffeting turned into a disquieting turbulence as the twin radial engines clawed their way through the defying winds. Bommar sent word down the cabin for Captain Wolff. With the help of steadying hands and despite his gear load, Wolff made his way through the shuddering cabin to the cockpit.

The C-47 Skytrain had a seated position just aft of the pilots for the radioman-navigator. Since this flight would be made in complete radio silence and Bommar's flight was the last in the serial, they did not deploy the third crewman in order to save the precious weight. Wolff sat in the vacant chair and leaned forward between the pilots. True to his word, Bommar was seated in the right hand seat, the co-pilot's seat. He turned to Wolff.

"We missed the beacon on Malta," he shouted above the engine noise. "We should have seen it fifteen minutes ago," Bommar pointed to his aviator's watch. "The group leader turned the whole group north."

Wolff knew missing the waypoint was critical. They could not be sure where they were. If the formation came apart in the turbulence, most of the planes without navigators would be unable to find their way.

Wolff leaned forward, shook his head and hollered, "We can't go back."

"I know, I know," Bommar agreed. "We probably missed Malta on the south side based on the crosswinds. Turning north should get us somewhere in the vicinity of Sicily. Maybe even the toe of Italy…depending on how far we overshot the waypoint. Once we hit land, I can find our landmarks."

Wolff nodded emphatically in agreement. "Mind if I stay up here?"

"Suit yourself. We're still about an hour from landfall if I got this figured right," Bommar answered. "One more thing. I got word just before take-off that the ground winds in Sicily were over thirty-five miles an hour."

Wolff shook his head at the news. They would be jumping into winds much higher than they ever trained for. So be it!

Wolff looked out of the front windscreen. The moon was low in the sky and shimmering off of the water of the Mediterranean Sea. The moonlit waves flashing by gave the sensation of great speed. Up ahead, slightly above the horizon, the faint flicker of engine sparks from the planes ahead was the only visible object in an inky black sky.

The two pilots worked together, feeling each other's movements on the yoke and pedals. It was the only way they could manage the difficulties of the tricky buffeting and near-zero visibility. The same scene was likely playing out in every plane of the 52nd TCG.

One hour to go. Wolff looked back into the cabin. There was little motion. Only the slight rocking of heads with partially closed eyes on blackened faces broke the stillness as the C-47 bounced and swayed on the wind currents. The men all appeared relaxed, their special chinstraps loosened and dangling, while bodies jerked slightly with each shudder of the plane. He suspected that they were anything but relaxed.

Wolff closed his eyes and leaned his helmet back on the bulkhead. Just a little rest was all his burning eyes needed. His thoughts turned to home. *No, not that. Not now!* He replayed the mission plan in his mind. His thoughts drifted to contingencies and what to do if certain things went wrong. *Who could he trust? Who might be shaky?*

The whole purpose of the airborne drop was to keep the Italians from counterattacking the invasion beaches. Being mountainous, southern Sicily had only a few major roads leading inland from the sea. All the 505th RCT had to do was block these few roads. That's all!

The town of Niscemi was about ten miles from the coast. Wolff didn't know much about the 3rd Battalion of the 504th PIR but they got the job of dropping just south of Niscemi to block the main road to the seacoast town of Gela. *The 3rd Battalion, 504th must be a good one,* thought Wolff, *otherwise they wouldn't have been picked for the job.*

The 1st and 2nd Battalions of the 505th were to land further south on the Niscemi-Gela Road and block a major road junction called Objective "Y". This road junction also joined a major crossroad that ran parallel to the coast to the large city of Vittoria. Objective "Y" was the single most important blocking position to control both of these major roads.

The rest of 3rd Battalion, minus Item Company, would seize the high ground south of Objective "Y" and provide a firewall between the beach and the enemy. If the Italians blew through the rest of the 505th, Krause would be the last line of defense.

Wolff believed Major Krause to be a poor leader who caused problems wherever he went. Under their breaths his officers called him the "shitstorm artist". For this drop, however, Wolff and his company were thankfully detached from Major Krause.

Once dropped, Wolff and his 119 men and nine officers had their work cut out for them. Lieutenant Clark would take 1st Squad on a three-mile hike to light the signal fire. The rest of Item Company would block the road to the beach. But the priority of his mission, Wolff reasoned, was the signal fire. He had to make sure Clark successfully completed that mission.

If all went according to plan, the carpet the airborne would lay down along the key roadways would stop any enemy force from reinforcing the beaches. *But when does everything ever go according to plan? What was it that he learned at West Point? Was it von Moltke who said that the best plans never survive first contact with the enemy? How many men would be dropped on target and how many would be scattered all over the island?* The endless variations of potential pitfalls gripped his thoughts. The missions, orders, drop zones, objectives and combat leaders all swirled around in his head in an endless cacophony and he struggled to make sense of it. *I can't just think of everything that might go wrong. I have to stay positive.*

Suddenly, he was overcome by the strange sensation that he had forgotten something. He and all of his troopers were loaded down with all sorts of gear but the nagging feeling that something was left behind gnawed at his subconscious. Hard as he tried, he couldn't figure it out. Without intending to do so, he subliminally reviewed the standard paratrooper combat load.

Besides the main parachute and reserve, each man carried his weapon, usually an M-1 Garand Rifle with 150 rounds of .30-caliber ammunition. However, most of the men figured out how to scrounge an extra load of ammo. They also carried four fragmentation grenades, a smoke grenade, a Gammon grenade plus a ten-inch bayonet, trench knife and their Schrade-Walden switchblade knife. Some men carried an essential item for one of the crew-served weapons such as a mortar round or a bazooka round or a belt of .30-caliber machine gun ammunition.

In addition to their helmets, tunics and gloves, they were each issued two extra pair of socks and shorts, a handkerchief, silk escape map, wristwatch and compass. Each man carried a musette bag for personal hygiene items such as toothbrush, toothpowder, soap, safety razor and blades. The musette bag also held a mess kit, four "K" rations, ten packs of cigarettes, paper, pencil, matches, cigarette lighter, Halizone tablets for water purification, a thirty foot rope, blanket, a water filled canteen, shelter half, entrenching tool, two first aid kits and a gas mask. Officers and NCOs also carried a .45-caliber sidearm with extra ammunition. A Type B-4 inflatable life preserver, called a Mae West by the troops for the buxom-blessed movie star, rounded out the standard over water combat load.

For the life of him, Wolff couldn't figure out what he left behind. Or was it a person? *Did I leave Superman or Captain America behind? They would sure come in handy in this fight!*

"Land ho," Bommar shouted. Wolff's eyes snapped open. He had dozed off just slightly beneath consciousness. He was near that dream state on the thin edge of sleep where sense and nonsense coexist and the hour flashed by quickly. "We're going up to take a look. They already know we're here." Anti-aircraft "flak" and tracers were rising up from the shadows of the land. It was not yet heavy and it served to highlight the location of the landmass.

Bommar followed the engine sparks in front of him, as he pulled back on the yoke and rose up to 2,000 feet and leveled off. "There," Bommar pointed forward out the left window. "Southern coast of Sicily. We'll make our run along the beach like we planned."

Wolff nodded, keeping his eyes on the planes in front. They slowly banked left until the land was on the right side. They traveled west along the southern coast of Sicily for a few minutes. Suddenly the planes in front banked sharply left. Bommar found himself the lead pilot of his own little nine-plane serial.

"You're not going to follow them, are you?" Wolff asked.

"Nah, I know my way from here," Bommar answered as they both watched the entire group turn back south over the Mediterranean and away from Sicily.

"Where the hell are they going?" Wolff asked out loud. Before anyone could answer, Bommar pointed forward to the right. There, shimmering in the distant moonlight was the unmistaken outline of Lake Bivieri running parallel to the coast. Wolff looked toward the eastern end and found the faint outline of the dry bed of the Acate River, which he visually traced to the sea. Bommar nosed his plane over, banked slightly right and headed for the riverbed. The other eight planes in his V followed at 500 feet.

"That's it!" Wolff was excited. "There's the river and the lake. How long?"

"Hard to say. Strong winds up here. Ten minutes give or take," answered Bommar.

"Tell me when we're about five minutes out."

Bommar nodded. The anti-aircraft fire and multi-colored tracers were coming up from their right. It was not all aimed at them. Other flights of C-47s were also drawing their share of fire. Bommar maneuvered his plane up the riverbed and then across the lake. He picked up the railroad tracks and followed them to the southern section of the Niscemi-Gela Road. It would lead him right to the head of the valley.

"Let me line up my ducks," he said flashing his landing lights. On queue, the eight planes behind the leader moved from an echelon formation to a loose straight line and closed up on the leader. "Five minutes," he said over his shoulder.

Wolff took a deep breath and smiled. "There's a case of scotch with your name on it if you drop us on the mark."

"Johnny Walker Black," Bommar answered without interrupting his search for the landmarks. He reached a hand back over his left shoulder. "Good luck, sir," he said to Wolff.

"Thank *you*, sir," Wolff shook his hand and made his way to the back of the cabin.

"Five minutes," Wolff repeated as the seated troopers helped him clump back to the rear.

When he reached the rear of the cabin Wolff turned to look toward the cockpit. Bommar was looking over his shoulder flashing the thumbs up signal. He had spotted the key landmark. Wolff snapped off a sharp, respectful salute. *If we had more guys like Bommar*, Wolff thought, *we'd win this goddamn war in six months!*

The red light alongside the door flashed on. Wolff took his planeload of paratroopers through the equipment check sequence quickly. He then gave the order to stand in the door and took his position at the head of the stick. The rest of the troopers pressed together toward him like a coiled spring under tension, both ready and anxious to release.

The red light turned green. With a deep breath, Captain Louis Wolff pulled himself out of the door and into the darkness.

Chapter Twenty-Nine

L'Enfant Plaza Hotel – January 13, 1997

"Happy the man who has been able to learn the causes of things."

Virgil, (Publius Vergilius Maro) (70 BC - 19 BC)

The waitress reached for the unfolded napkin. A hand shot in from behind her and snatched it. "I got it." J.P. pulled the napkin into his lap as he sat down and smiled at the three elderly men.

Cynthia returned just as the waiters began to serve dinner. The conversation slowed as the group began the main course; the slight plinking of forks and knives on plates the only sound at the table.

J.P. reflected on what he had learned thus far. The secret apparently had something to do with the War. Since his father had spoken so little about it, almost everything he learned from the three men was news. He knew his father was a smart man. After all, he was a teacher. But he never realized his father had a photographic memory.

What exactly had he learned about the mysterious secret? Not much, he had to admit. He was sure if he had enough time with these men and with Lincoln, he would eventually figure it out. Unfortunately, the conversation was going more slowly than the dinner.

Sky had been doing most of the talking. He was a vintage version of the "surfer dude", with that distinctive west coast laid-back approach to life and an edgy attitude that continually challenged authority. J.P. concluded that Sky must have been a handful in his younger days. He knew Sky's involvement with his father was soon to end after Italy when his dad was transferred to another division.

J.P. had also determined Frank West was the *professor* of the group. He was intelligent, articulate and opinionated. Frank was fit and disciplined as further demonstrated by his dinner of Alaskan Halibut and baked potato without butter or sour cream. In addition to seeing the War first hand, Frank obviously studied the accounts of the War. He was a knowledgeable student of history. J.P. found himself anxious to hear Frank's recollections.

Harley Tidrick was a bit of a conundrum. He could easily be taken for a typical redneck, but J.P. knew that would be an oversimplification. Perhaps it was his attire or his flush face with large jowls that indicated simple good-old-boy backwoods folk but there were other clues in his demeanor that led J.P. to think otherwise.

Without saying much, Harley seemed to be controlling the conversation. The other two men seemed to defer to him and paid particular attention to his answers. When J.P. left the table for the men's room, Harley was doing most of the talking as he was earlier in the day in the White House. *Why was he the assertive one? Was he hiding something?* J.P. concluded there was more to Harley Tidrick than met the eye and he should not underestimate him. He would have to listen to his surreptitious tape recording at his earliest opportunity.

For the present, however, J.P. was surprisingly mesmerized at learning of his father's wartime exploits. And he did learn one important fact. His father's close friend, Jake Kilroy, never made it home.

Cynthia Powers sensed the discussion would not conclude before the end of dinner. She nudged J.P. "Do you want me to arrange another meeting with these gentlemen tomorrow?" She spoke loud enough for all to hear.

Sky answered first. "I have a flight back to L.A. in the morning. But there's not much more I can add. We went through Sicily together and after Sicily, Jake and Johnny literally disappeared. Next I hear they're in the Screaming Eagles." He jerked his thumb toward Frank. "I saw them briefly in England before D-Day and in Holland and Rheims…" Sky hesitated as he suddenly choked up. "And the parade in New York in forty-six."

Harley interrupted Sky. "Those two airborne divisions worked closely together so Frank can fill in all those blanks."

"Right, the parade, too," Frank offered. "I was there."

"That's not important," Harley barked but quickly regained his poise. "What I meant was you're done with Sky after Sicily anyway. If Frank can stay tomorrow he can fill in the rest."

"What about you?" J.P. asked.

"I'm driving back to Bedford tomorrow but I'll leave you my number in case you want to talk some more."

J.P. nodded. He made a mental note to look up the New York parade in forty-six. He briefly considered broaching the subject of the secret directly but thought better of it. If they were hiding something, confronting them would just shut down the discussion. He would glean as much information as gently as he could. It would be a slow process. If he deceived them into thinking he was only interested in getting to know his father better, perhaps one of them would slip and reveal something, if they even knew anything at all. It would be a risky, time-consuming game, particularly due to their ages, but J.P. decided it was the best course of action. He looked at Frank. "Can you and I meet tomorrow and talk further?"

"Sure."

"Thanks, Frank." J.P looked at all three. "In the meantime, can we continue tonight for as long as we can?"

The three elderly men smiled and nodded. Sky wiped his nose and composed himself. "I guess it's still me. Okay, where were we?" He squinted his eyes and set a pensive look on his face. "Right," he said to himself. "Sicily!"

Chapter Thirty

Sicily - July 10, 1943

"The soldier trade, if it is to mean anything at all,
has to be anchored in an unshakable code of honor."

Carl von Clausewitz (1780 – 1831), *On War*

Private Jake Kilroy knew he was right behind his buddy Johnny out the door. But now, on the ground, he couldn't see any other parachutes in the landing zone. He rolled up on his knees and slowly pulled his chute into his arms as quietly as possible. Still, he could not avoid the soft metallic sounds as his harness buckles and gear clinked together. The landing had been a decent one considering the high winds and broken terrain. He had just missed a stone wall and the weight of his load carried him violently into the hard baked ground. He shook off the cobwebs and strained to orient himself.

He tensed to listen to his surroundings but the drone of the planes and the distant crack of small arms and anti-aircraft fire made hearing nearby sounds impossible. His heart was pounding and he felt the familiar surge of adrenaline course through his body. Visibility was getting better as his eyes adjusted to the darkness and he could see the shadowy outlines of the high ridges both to the east and the west. Item Company was dropped right smack on the money.

After Jake cleared his parachute and gathered it into his arms he released the bellyband harness and the reserve chute. Still on his knees, he shoved the bundle of silk and canvas into a nearby hedge and slowly removed his gas-operated M1918A2 Browning Automatic Rifle from its Griswold case. He set the selector to "slow-auto" to conserve ammunition. *This was really stupid*, he thought. If he contacted the enemy, they would certainly not wait for him to unpack and load his weapon. He slammed a twenty round magazine of .30-caliber ammunition into his B-A-R and racked the bolt to chamber a round. It sounded louder than he expected.

"George," the voice in the dark whispered.

"Marshall," Jake replied.

A figure came out of the darkness. It was Sky Johnson. "You alone, Jake?"

"Yeah."

"Let's roll up," Sky said and began walking. Since they were at the beginning of the stick, they would walk in the direction the plane was heading. The troopers at the end of the stick would walk the opposite way in order to meet somewhere near the middle.

The two boys walked carefully, making as little noise as possible. They came upon a paved road in the direction of their line of advance and slowly proceeded in that direction. If it was the same road as on the maps, it would lead them to a junction that was their rally point.

"George, " said another voice from the darkness.

"Marshall," Sky replied. Joe Boothe, Dominic Angelo and Johnny Kilroy stepped out of the shadows. "It's Boots, Yank and Dom," said Angelo. "Who we got?"

"Jake and Sky," answered Jake as he tapped Johnny on the arm. They were both relieved to see each other.

The group moved out along the road with Jake and Johnny bringing up the rear. After a few moments Jake heard something on the other side of the wall. Johnny heard it too. It sounded like a whimpering animal. Until now, the group had not fired a shot and not been exposed. They could not take the chance of being discovered so Johnny leaned his M-1 on the wall and took out his bayonet. He peered over the wall slowly and made out a figure curled up in a fetal position with his face buried in his arms. He carefully hopped over the wall holding his bayonet in a striking position. Slowly, he disappeared below the wall.

"Jake," Johnny whispered as his head popped up. "You're never going to believe this. Come on over."

Jake propped his B-A-R against the wall and hopped over. There was a soldier uncontrollably whimpering while trying to stifle the sounds. Jake bent over to get a better look. It was Staff Sergeant Gene Bancroft. Jake stood up and looked at Johnny who shrugged his shoulders and shook his head. Lying at their feet was the toughest, meanest, nastiest bastard they had ever met in the army and he was crying like a newborn baby.

"C'mon Sarge, let's get you out of here, " Jake said feeling nothing more than pity for a man who had completely lost it on his first combat jump.

"Enema? Is that you?" Bancroft sobbed. Jake's pity immediately turned to anger.

Johnny kicked Bancroft in the rump and slapped him on the helmet. "Snap out of it you sorry piece of shit." Johnny pulled Bancroft to his feet. "Let's get the hell out of here," he whispered while wiping the dirt from Bancroft's tunic with hard slaps and rough hand brushes.

Bancroft struggled to gain his self-control. He took off his helmet, shook his head and wiped his tear-streaked face on his sleeve. "I don't know what happened," he sniveled. "I'm all right now. Don't tell the rest of the guys, okay?"

Jake was about to say something but Johnny stepped in front of him. "I'll tell you how it's going to be, Sarge." Though Johnny was speaking in low tones, the anger was hissing through his teeth. "The next time you call him Enema, the whole fucking battalion is going to know how we found you tonight. This is Jake. As long as he's not Enema, your secret is safe with us."

Bancroft took a deep breath. He was regaining his courage. He nodded and picked up his gear. "Fair enough."

"That way," Johnny pointed. All three hopped over the wall. Bancroft led the way.

"Whew," Jake whispered to Johnny. "Thanks!"

"You're welcome. That rat bastard deserved it. We'll have to watch our backs from now on. That scumbag just might try to get even."

"Fine. But somehow he doesn't intimidate me so much anymore."

The troopers moved up the road, gathering more boys as they went until they marched into the company at the rally point. The boys moved as quietly as they could but it was impossible to eliminate the rustling sound of shuffling feet and the noise of steel plinking on metal.

Under the light of the fading moon they could see the pillboxes a few hundred yards distant. So far they had not made contact with the enemy. When Bancroft and his small group arrived, they immediately sought out Lieutenant Clark. They found him sitting on a rock in a clearing just off the road surrounded by the other members of 1st Squad. His right boot was off and he was wrapping his ankle tightly in a thick bandage.

"Welcome, Sergeant. You report to Second Platoon. Leave Sergeant Copping and First Squad with me."

"Right." Bancroft went off looking for his platoon.

"Everyone here, Sergeant Copping?" Clark asked while slowly sliding his boot back on.

Copping looked around and quickly counted heads. "First Squad is all present. What happened to you, sir?"

"I think it's broken, Sergeant. I felt it snap when I landed," Clark said while sliding his bayonet down the inside of his boot on the interior side of his ankle. "Bad landing." He looked at Copping. "Can I borrow your sticker?"

"Yes sir. You plan on making this march?" Copping handed his bayonet to Clark.

"That's my mission, Sergeant." Clark took the bayonet and slid it inside his boot on the opposite side. He laced his boots as tightly as he could and then wrapped the entire lash-up with tape he scrounged from the engineers. A medic offered him a morphine Syrette but he refused.

"Gather around boys," Clark said. The twelve-man squad came in and knelt in a circle. "If I fall out, Sergeant Copping will lead the mission." He stood up to test his makeshift splint. "Make sure you each have a phosphorous grenade and plenty of ammo".

Copping turned to Clark. "Where's Captain Wolff, sir?"

Clark shook his head. "Not here yet," he said as he took a step to test his weight on the injured ankle. It was painful but tolerable. He looked to his troopers. "We got less than two hours to travel three miles, find the spot and light the fire. The moon will be down soon so stay in contact with the man in front of you. We need to all get there together." The boys murmured their acknowledgement. "Tedesco, take the point. You speak the lingo. I'd rather talk my way through than have to fight our way through. *Capice?*"

"Yes, sir. I got it."

Copping moved into the center of the group, "Dom, you go with him. Jake, Johnny, bring up the rear. Sky and Danny, stick close to the lieutenant. Okay, let's move out."

Just then there was a small commotion down the road. Clark strained to see in the waning moonlight. Some troopers were leading a mule into the temporary encampment. There was a soldier on the mule. It was Captain Wolff.

"Holy Christ," Clark exclaimed. "Jesus coming into Jerusalem." He immediately hobbled over to the captain along with the other platoon leaders.

"What happened, Captain?"

"I'll be fine. Gather close. We'll set up our CP right here." He was helped off the mule and onto a low wall in a small clearing that would contain his command post.

"He broke an ankle," somebody whispered.

Wolff summoned his platoon leaders closer. He looked at First Lieutenant Kurt Klee, 2nd Platoon leader. "What kind of shape are we in, Kurt?"

"Good to see you, sir," Klee answered. "We're in pretty good shape. Some jump injuries, a few boys still missing but it looks like most of the company is together and right on target."

"Outstanding, Kurt. Looks like I owe one ballsy smart-ass pilot a case of scotch."

"Sir?"

"Never mind, Kurt." Wolff motioned to the rest of the platoon leaders and their NCOs. "After we take the pillboxes, we need to take that large stone farmhouse behind them. Then move the entire force to blocking positions on this road. Dig in tight and hold the position. Nothing gets through to the beach. Not even a damned field mouse. Understand?"

"Yes, sir," Klee nodded and moved out to position his troops.

"George, are you and your boys ready?" whispered Wolff to Lieutenant Clark.

"Yes sir, we have the whole squad. We're just about to leave."

"Very well, George." Clark was about to turn away when Wolff continued. "George, your mission is the most important objective for Item Company tonight." Wolff paused. "So whatever happens, make sure you light that fire."

"Yes sir. We'll be back by morning to help out here."

The young boys of 1st Squad moved out into the darkness in single file. The group turned west onto a trail that would bring them to the heights overlooking the objective of the 1st Infantry Division; the coastal town of Gela.

Sporadic sounds of gunfire cracked through the night from all over the island. Small arms and machine gun fire, with an occasional explosion, echoed mostly from the north and east. There were small firefights and sharp clashes occurring in scattered locations. The sounds were disconcerting but the column silently continued.

The moon had set and they were now in complete darkness. All of the night training exercises and constant drills paid off as the small group successfully navigated the three-mile cross-country trek to their exact target location. As the column reached the final rise in the road, Clark looked to the south to discern the shimmering surface of the Mediterranean Sea about a mile away. The dim outline of the city Gela was also scarcely visible near the shoreline. Farther up the valley was a small stone farmhouse alongside a wooden barn. He assembled his boys.

"Teddy, make sure the house is empty. Take Dom and torch it."

As the two paratroopers approached the farmhouse, Clark found a rock to rest on. The pain in his leg, aggravated by miles of marching, tortured him in waves. He addressed the remaining men. "Set up a defensive perimeter and get good cover and concealment. This place will be like daylight in a few minutes." He looked at his watch. "It's almost oh-three-hundred. We're late so hubba-hubba!" The boys moved out. Jake set up his B-A-R near Clark's temporary CP to cover the road. Johnny covered Jake's position on one flank with his M-1.

Tedesco knocked on the farmhouse door. The old Sicilian couple was fully dressed when they answered the door. In the background behind them were three young girls cowering under the kitchen table. Tedesco began speaking to them in Sicilian while Angelo checked the barn. The old woman argued back with animated hand gestures. They argued for a minute before Tedesco and Angelo returned to Clark.

"They won't leave, sir," Tedesco informed Clark.

"Shit!" was all Clark could manage. "Tell them the United States Army will pay for the house." Clark was sweating. He looked toward the sea knowing the invasion fleet was just beyond the horizon. "If they still won't leave, light it up anyway."

"Sir," Tedesco protested. "There's little kids in the house."

Clark lost his patience. He was late getting to his objective. The pain in his leg was nearly unbearable. This was the only structure in the vicinity that could serve as a beacon and the occupants wouldn't leave. And now it seemed his boys were reluctant to burn it. He was about to dress down Tedesco and burn the house down himself when Angelo spoke up.

"Sir, that barn is made of wood. It's full of hay. It'll burn for hours and you'll see it for miles. Sir?"

Clark hesitated, glared at Angelo, absorbing what he had just been told. Tedesco and Angelo looked back at him with anxious, pleading puppy-dog eyes.

Jake overheard the exchange and spoke up. "Beg pardon, sir, but that farmhouse is stone. It won't burn so good."

Tedesco nodded.

Johnny joined in. "That barn looks like a tinderbox, sir. Should burn all night long."

Angelo agreed, nodded, "All night long, sir."

"All right, all right," Clark conceded wiping the sweat from his brow. "Burn the damn barn but get those people out of the house, just in case."

"Yes sir, thank you sir," Tedesco headed back up to the farmhouse as Angelo made his way to the barn.

The old couple continued to argue with Tedesco who had difficulty explaining they were not going to burn down the house. They were still arguing when Angelo tossed the first phosphorous grenade into the barn.

"Fire in the hole!" Angelo yelled as he tossed in another phosphorous grenade and ducked behind a tree. The grenades went off with a pop and a blinding flash of bright white. The intense heat generated by the grenades instantly ignited the hay, which in turn ignited the wooden frame. In a few minutes the conflagration engulfed the entire structure. The old couple took the children and sought cover in a nearby orchard as the fingers of flame reached out into the night.

Clark stood up and felt the heat of the fire on his face. "Time to go boys. This fire will attract every enemy soldier within miles." The squad pulled in from their makeshift perimeter and gathered around Clark who counted heads and looked at his watch in the light of the blaze. "Sunrise is at zero-five-fifty-hours. We have two hours to get back to the rest of the company. Dom, Teddy, point! Sky, Danny Boy, rear! Move out!"

Jake sidled up alongside Clark. He took the officer's arm placed it around his neck. Before Clark could protest, Johnny took the officer's carbine, slung it and took his other arm on his shoulder.

"We'll go faster this way, sir," Jake explained.

Clark offered a slight objection. "I don't think…"

Johnny interrupted. "It's all right, Lieutenant. Keep the weight off the leg. We'll go as long as we can and two others will take over. Otherwise, you'll slow us down, sir." Johnny smiled and Clark relented.

The small column moved quickly and without stopping as they retraced their path back. Every few minutes, Clark would look back toward the huge glow in the dark sky to affirm his signal fire was still effective. Far out at sea, the troop transports and landing craft of the 1st Infantry Division began to orient themselves toward the fiery signal beacon.

The sky became lighter but the sun had not quite broken the horizon when

Lieutenant Clark's unit arrived at the rally point. Jake and Johnny carried Clark all the way back. On the way, Johnny noticed Sicily looked eerily like North Africa except for its mountainous terrain. The ground here was also hard and crusty and the natural vegetation was sparse. The only differences he could see were the orchards of olive trees and grapevines separated by either stone walls or thick rows of cactus like bushes. At least these poor Sicilian farmers battled the angry land for sustenance and survival.

The distant rumble of the naval bombardment signaled the start of the amphibious invasion. Wolff had deployed his troops for an attack on the six small pillboxes protecting a large three story stone building that appeared to be a winery. First they would attack and seize the bunkers and then regroup and assault the large stone building behind them.

Wolff was listening on his 5.5-pound SCR-536 "handi-talkie" when Clark came up to the CP. "Mission accomplished, Captain." He grinned through the pain. "We lit up the sky. I'm sure they saw that blaze in Africa."

"Excellent, George," Wolff replied. "Stand fast right here with your squad and wait for orders. It's about to get dicey up ahead."

The mortars of the Heavy Weapons Platoon opened the attack with the familiar hollow thump of mortar rounds exiting their tubes. From 400 yards away they lobbed their three-pound explosive warheads right on top of the pillboxes. While the enemy ducked down under the firing slits to avoid the flying shrapnel, the paratroopers raced forward. When they were close enough, they lobbed smoke grenades, which was the signal for Klee to halt the mortar barrage. The .30-caliber machine guns took over having previously sighted on the pillbox firing slits. They poured fire at the openings, which kept the enemy down. Behind the curtain of smoke and suppressing fire, the paratroopers were virtually invisible as they rushed the bunkers and tossed grenades through the openings. There were numerous muffled explosions and then white flags appeared from the firing slits. It was a miracle anyone was left alive in the bunkers. The boys had moved quickly and executed the fire-and-maneuver tactics with great professionalism.

Paratrooper medics moved in to treat the wounded. They huddled beneath the shelter of the pillboxes attending to American and Italian casualties as Wolff waited impatiently for Klee to report in. Suddenly his handi-talkie squawked. "Home Plate, this is Second Base."

Wolff answered. "Go ahead, Second Base."

"We hit a home run, sir." All objectives were taken.

"Casualties?"

"A few wounded sir. We're treating them now."

Wolff closed his eyes in a solitary prayer of thanks. He was thankful he hadn't got half his command killed in his first combat. "I'm moving up with Lieutenant Clark's squad. Get the rest of the company in position for the next assault."

"Yes, sir. Out."

The command group and 1st Squad moved out. Captain Wolff was astride the captured mule; his broken ankle in makeshift splints, grimacing with every step the balky animal took. Lieutenant Clark sat on an M-1 Garand rifle suspended between two of his boys like a swing as they moved forward. His ankle had swollen tremendously inside the tightly wrapped boot. It could no longer bear any weight. Despite the excruciating pain, both officers refused morphine.

While the command group moved up and into the nearest pillbox, Lieutenant Klee was organizing the second attack. The basic plan was the same. Open with a mortar barrage, close in on the winery from three sides under the cover of the barrage and breach the stone house with rockets and grenades. The occupants of the house had seen what had happened to their comrades in the bunkers and were firing a steady but inaccurate stream of machine gun fire in the general direction of the paratroopers.

Klee met the group as they approached the captured pillbox and addressed Captain Wolff. "We have eight Italian prisoners, four more wounded and we pulled four dead out of the bunkers."

Wolff thought for a moment. He had not anticipated prisoners. Paratroopers operating behind enemy lines were ill equipped to handle Prisoners Of War (POWs). Wolff had an idea. "Kurt, give them a white flag and send them toward the beach. Let the infantry deal with them."

"With a guard, sir?"

"No, we can't afford to waste a man." Wolff looked at the ragged group of prisoners, some bandaged, others bleeding, uniforms disheveled and in tatters and all covered in a fine white chalky dust blasted loose inside the bunkers. "They don't look like they have any fight left in them. Make sure they're disarmed, point them to the beach and send them on their way."

Klee gave the orders and the shattered group of Italians headed down the road to the beach.

"Are you set for the attack?" Wolff asked.

"Just about." Klee looked at Clark. "But we could sure use your squad,"

"Take them," Clark replied through a grimace. "Bruce, you're in charge."

Copping stepped forward. "Where do you want us?"

"There," Klee pointed to a small ridge about a hundred yards from the southwest corner of the building. "From the ridge you'll have a good vantage point. We'll need supporting fire on the upper floors when First Platoon makes the assault."

Copping looked at the rise in the ground and nodded. He took the squad off toward the ridge and had them approach the crest in low crawl. He could clearly see the upper floors of the winery as he peered over the rise. Machine gun fire was emanating from the windows but it was sporadic and poorly aimed. He slid down the embankment to the waiting squad.

"It's right over the ridge about a hundred yards out," he pointed. "Jake, pick your spot for the Browning. Everyone else spread out and stay low. When I give the word, scramble to the top and let go with everything you got at the upper windows. Don't shoot low! Our guys will be rushing the place."

The young paratroopers nodded. Jake inched up to peek over the top of the rise and shuffled left until he found a spot with good visibility and a relatively flat surface for the bipod of his B-A-R. He slid down below the rise and nodded to Copping. Johnny dropped the musette bag he had been carrying that held the extra ammunition for the B-A-R. He took a position near Jake. The rest of the squad fanned out at five-yard intervals.

Copping gave a hand signal to Lieutenant Klee. In a few moments mortar rounds were dropping in and around the stone building. The enemy machine guns went silent as the gunners ducked to avoid the shrapnel. Flying debris and smoke obscured the front of the winery. The pop and hiss of smoke grenades could be heard as the paratroopers closed in on their objective.

"Now," yelled Copping and the squad crawled to the top of the rise. The riflemen fired at the upper windows in rapid succession until their eight rounds were exhausted. The last round was followed by the ejection of the empty "en bloc" clip punctuated by the telltale ping of the clip exiting the receiver. The boys quickly jammed another clip into the open breach of their M-1 rifle.

Jake moved the selector on his B-A-R to "fast auto". At that setting it would fire 650 rounds per minute. He knew he would run out of ammo quickly if he held the trigger so he fired three and four round bursts. He dug the bipod into the cement-hard dirt and muscled the nineteen-pound weapon steady during each burst. It only took about ten seconds to empty his twenty round box magazine, spraying all of the third story windows. When his magazine was exhausted, he rolled on his back and under the cover of the slope, yanked the empty magazine and slapped in another twenty rounds. He repeated this maneuver over and over until he reached to his ammo belt only to find he had used up all twelve magazines. Feeling for the musette bag, he fished out another magazine. As he slammed it home, he glanced at Johnny. His friend was doing his job, laying covering fire onto the openings in the house. So was everyone else.

The noise was deafening as nearly the entire company was firing at the windows of the winery from different vantage points. Stone chips and dust flew in all directions. Return fire became sparse but the enemy rounds crashing into the ground and smashing into the olive trees gave notice that death filled the air.

Under the cover of smoke and confusion, a bazooka team sprinted to the center of the action and fired a rocket at the main entrance of thick double wooden doors. The rocket exploded with a tremendous blast sending shrapnel and wooden splinters in all directions. The bazooka team reloaded and sent the next rocket through the open doorway to explode deep in the interior of the building. Fire, smoke and debris could be seen blowing out of the open first floor windows. Huge wooden casks inside were riddled with holes. Wine and blood flowed freely on the floor. Suddenly, a white flag was seen waving from a third story window.

"Cease fire, Cease fire!" someone yelled and as quickly as it began, it was over. The paratroopers came out from cover and gathered near the front door as enemy soldiers streamed out in a single file, hands over heads, some wiping eyes with elbows, others coughing, still others bleeding. The troopers guided them to the rear, continually motioning them to keep their hands in the air. A few Italian-American paratroopers barked orders in the native language. There were close to forty enemy soldiers in this parade of the vanquished. When the line stopped, some troopers entered the winery. They found six dead Italian soldiers and a dozen heavy machine guns with close to a million rounds of ammunition in the basement. Again the paratroopers suffered no fatalities. Some began to believe they were truly invincible.

"Bruce," yelled Klee as he raced over from the command post. "Take charge of these prisoners." Copping nodded.

The other paratroopers funneled the line of prisoners back to where 1st Squad had assembled. Copping lined them up and the men began searching them for concealed weapons, maps or orders. What they were really looking for was souvenirs.

Johnny noticed something strange about the last prisoner in line. His uniform was different. Although all of them were caked in white dust and debris, the cut of this uniform was unique. Danny was searching him, his netted helmet at a jaunty angle dangling his special chinstrap. He was smugly chewing a fresh piece of gum as he emptied the pockets of his captive. Boothe and Angelo held their rifles on the line of prisoners.

"Lookee here," Danny announced. He was holding a wallet and fingering some personal pictures of the prisoner's family. "What else do we have?" He removed a large watch and slid a ring from the prisoner's finger. The prisoner was tall with blond hair and blue eyes. He had an ugly scar on the right side of his face, which glared angrily at Danny as he went through the pockets of his tunic.

Johnny walked over and stared hard at the prisoner and his uniform. "Wait a second, Danny Boy." Then he asked the prisoner in Italian if he was Italian or German.

"*Fallschrimjager… Fallschrimjager,*" the prisoner answered motioning to himself with the thumbs of his raised hands. Then he pointed to Danny and Johnny. "*Fallschrimjager!*"

"Chrissake, he's a Kraut. There's not supposed to be any Krauts on the island."

Johnny brushed some dust from the prisoner's sleeve. "And a noncom." He turned to Danny. "And a paratrooper. We need to get this guy to Captain Wolff." Johnny looked at the booty in Danny's hands. "You gotta' give him back his stuff."

Danny stiffened. "No dice, Yank, this is mine. I liberated it. Fortunes of war. I ain't giving shit back!"

Johnny wasn't looking for a confrontation with Danny, especially in front of the rest of the guys who had stopped searching prisoners to stare at them. He tried a diplomatic approach.

"You're right Danny Boy, its a soldier's privilege to liberate souvenirs. Something to show our grandkids some day." He pointed to the watch and ring in Danny's hand. "But this is personal stuff. It has nothing to do with the War. It's personal. And it's not something you want to be caught with if *you're* captured."

Danny was listening but wasn't convinced. Jake stepped over to Danny. "Hear him out."

"If you want a real souvenir, take this." Johnny reached for the prisoner's collar and unlatched the pin behind a small metallic badge affixed to the upright collar. It was an oval shaped laurel wreath. The bird, a hawk or an eagle, was diving down from the upper right to the lower left, superimposed over the wreath. The wings were sharply swept back defining a bird of prey on the attack. In the claws was a swastika. On the reverse side was the manufacturer's stamp, G.H Osang-Dresden. "This is the German *Luftwaffe* paratrooper badge. Now, *this* is a war souvenir. You won't find many of these lying around." He handed the badge to Danny whose eyes went wide with delight.

"Now that's a real find," Jake added. "Almost as good as a Luger," Jake offered, referring to the German pistol that was the Holy Grail of war souvenirs for all GIs. "Give him back his personal stuff Danny Boy, please."

Danny looked at the badge in his hand, seemed to study it. He was pleased with this rare find and handed the wallet, photos, watch and ring back to the prisoner.

"What outfit are you with?" Johnny asked. The prisoner stared blankly at him while he put his family photos in his wallet and stuffed his watch and ring into his pocket.

"No English, huh?" Johnny asked the same question in Italian. No response. He tried again in German with the same few words taught to all paratroopers. Still, the same blank stare.

Copping walked over. "Yank, Jake, take this guy to the CP and turn him over. Find out where the lieutenant wants us and hurry back." He turned to his squad and pointed to the prisoners. "Give 'em a white flag and point them south."

Tedesco translated the orders to the gathered prisoners and sent them on their way. They were grateful to be alive and marched willingly down the road toward the sea.

Johnny and Jake escorted the German prisoner toward the CP.

Jake looked at Johnny. "There's not supposed to be any German combat troops on this island. What the hell is this guy doing here?"

"I wonder what outfit he's with. And a paratrooper too," Johnny replied.

"The brass is going to shit when they find out we're up against German paratroopers." Jake looked at the prisoner. "I wonder if this joker actually made any combat jumps or if he is just some rear-echelon pussy who stole that badge from a real fighter."

The prisoner's jaw tightened imperceptibly but he said nothing.

"This guy is probably a cook or something," Jake continued his insults. "He doesn't look tough enough to even be leg infantry. Forget about being a real paratrooper."

Both Jake and Johnny were startled when the prisoner answered in perfect English. "I have survived two combat jumps. One in Belgium and the other on Crete." He looked directly at Jake. "I am a paratrooper. A real fighter! I am not a cook and I am not a pussy cat."

"Son of a bitch," Johnny laughed as they walked toward the command post. "I guess you can't insult any paratrooper, no matter whose side he's on."

"And I would have made many more combat jumps if *Der Fuhrer* had not forbid it," the prisoner continued. He stared into the inquisitive eyes of both American paratroopers. "Our casualties were too great." He paused. "Something you will soon learn about."

"Your English is very good," remarked Johnny.

"I attended university in America," the prisoner explained. "And since I am prisoner, perhaps I shall be returning to America soon."

"That makes us even, bud. We're headed for Germany," Jake chuckled.

"So, what outfit are you with?" Johnny decided to try one more time.

The prisoner considered the question for a moment. "Oh well, you will find out anyway very soon. I am with the *Hermann Goering Fallschirm* Division. We are converting into a *Panzer* Division. You will soon be introduced to our newest Mark Six Tiger heavy tank and soon learn why paratroopers take so many casualties."

Johnny was stunned by the revelation. There were not supposed to be German combat units on Sicily and certainly not German tanks. He hid his surprise by tapping his airborne shoulder patch. "Eighty-second Airborne, Mac. Your people will soon learn why American paratroopers *give* so many casualties."

They continued walking toward the company CP in silence. When they arrived, Wolff was resting on a large, flat rock outside his captured bunker. He was dispatching runners and issuing orders for the defense of the road junction.

During the hike back to the command post the prisoner had at times been smug and argumentative. Now, at the last moment, he let down his hard façade and softened. He turned to Johnny and said, "Thank you for letting me keep these," he pointed to his watch and ring. "They are family heirlooms and cannot be replaced." He reached into his boot and pulled out an SS dagger and then unfastened his belt buckle. He handed both to Johnny. "Souvenirs." He then stiffened to attention. "I am fortunate to be captured by men like me. Men of honor." The prisoner snapped a salute, a small tear forming in the corner of his eye.

The two paratroopers answered with casual sloppy salutes as the prisoner was taken away. Johnny turned to Wolff. "He speaks damn good English as you can see Captain and get this…he's with the *Hermann Goering Panzer* Division, Tiger tanks and all."

Wolff's jaw dropped. He had seen a captured German Mark VI Tiger tank in North Africa and it was virtually unstoppable. Heavy German armor meant the American paratroopers would be woefully outgunned.

Wolff looked north up the road and imagined a brace of fifty-six ton Mark VI Tiger tanks rounding the bend in the road and pounding the winery into rubble with their dreaded .88-millimeter high velocity guns. He immediately issued new orders to deploy his soldiers behind the ridges, hills and ravines that surrounded the road junction. He didn't want to be caught in a static defensive position. Wolff spread his men out with orders to dig in but be ready to move on command. The small undersized airborne company had orders to hold, regardless of what the enemy sent against them. With the captured firepower and ammunition, they would be in a better position to do just that if they could use their superior mobility and not get caught in the bunkers.

There was a commotion down the road behind him and Wolff turned around to see. He could not believe what he saw and had to do a double take. Coming up the road from the beach, as if taking a Sunday stroll was General Matthew B. Ridgway, CO of the 82nd Airborne Division. His personal aide-de-camp, Captain Don Faith and two bodyguards from the 1st Infantry Division accompanied him. Ridgway walked right up to Wolff who was still sitting on a large rock. With Ridgway wearing his two-star helmet, Wolff didn't feel like he was giving anything away when he hopped off the wall on one foot and snapped a smart salute.

Ridgway spoke first. "Good morning, Captain. What unit is this?"

"Item Company, Third Battalion and a handful of strays, sir."

"What's your situation, Captain?" Ridgway asked.

"Well, sir, we have control of this strongpoint. We're spread out and dug in facing north. Anything coming down that road has to pass through us."

Ridgway nodded. "Very good, Captain. Have you been in contact with any other units?"

"No sir." Wolff looked up at the hills from the east to the west. "For all I know General, we're the only airborne troops on the island." Wolff was dog-tired and surprised himself by being somewhat cavalier with his commanding general.

Ridgway leaned in close to Wolff so only he could hear him. "For all I know Captain, you may be right." He had a concerned look on his face. "We came ashore this morning and General Allen had not yet made contact with any of my paratroopers," Ridgway said referring to the CO of the 1st Infantry Division, Brigadier General Terry Allen. "We've been walking for a few miles. Yours is the first unit I've been able to find besides a few stragglers that I sent back to our lines. And of course we passed by those prisoners you must have been sending down the road."

"Begging the General's pardon, sir, but I made a bad joke. The Eighty-second *is* on the island, in force. The other units may not be in the exact right place and they may not have reported in yet but we've been hearing gunfire and firefights all night. Our guys are raising hell."

"I get your meaning, son," sighed Ridgway. "But until I find Colonel Gavin and his battalion commanders we can't organize or concentrate our forces where we need to."

"Yes, sir."

Ridgway pointed up the road to the north. "What's out that way?"

"Objective Y, General. The major road junction leading to the beach from Niscemi and west to Vittoria." Captain Faith pulled out an unmarked map and pointed out the road junction to the general. Ridgway knew blocking this road network leading toward the sea was the primary mission for his paratroopers. Looking around he realized only one small company, with a seriously wounded company commander, seemed to have found their objective. *One company out of four battalions!* He feared that the rest of his force may have been captured or wiped out. If that were the case then the entire American beachhead was in danger of being surrounded and pushed back into the sea.

Wolff continued. "I have scouts out and an observation post up that way but so far no contact with the enemy."

"That won't last long," Ridgway concluded. "The Italians have to move their forces south and contest the beachhead."

"Which reminds me, sir." Wolff remembered. "We have a German prisoner who says he's from the *Hermann Goering Panzer* Division. The Germans are here and they have Tigers."

Ridgway's expression turned to stone. He was stunned and looked at his aide who seemed equally surprised. It was evident Ridgway was unaware of the presence of German armor.

Ridgway tried to mask his surprise. He turned to his aide. "How could we not know that?" He calmed himself and looked at Wolff. "We'll send you up some artillery spotters, Captain, either from the navy or from the First Division. If those tanks do show up we'll have a surprise for them." He nodded at his aide who wrote something in a small notebook. "Meanwhile, you take care of that leg. I'm going to take a little walk up this road."

"Sir," Wolff protested. "We don't know what's up that way. It's not safe."

Ridgway ignored the plea and began walking with his small entourage. He looked back over his shoulder. "Sorry Captain, but I have to find the rest of my boys."

Chapter Thirty-One

L'Enfant Plaza Hotel – January 13, 1997

"The God of War hates those who hesitate."

Euripides (480 BC - 406 BC)

The waitress circled the table and began collecting empty plates. She was assisted by two busboys who quickly replaced silverware, refilled water glasses and scraped the crumbs from the white linen tablecloth with hollow pencil-like devices. They moved efficiently and when they were done, the waitress placed dessert menus in front of everyone.

As each one decided, the waitress took the order. Frank was last and after he ordered he asked the waitress, "Can you make up a custom drink if I give you the ingredients?"

"I'm sure the bartender can," she replied. Everyone at the table became curious as Frank rattled off the ingredients.

"Two parts vodka and one part champagne and..."

"You're kidding," Sky interrupted with a wide grin on his face.

"Not at all," Frank continued. "And a touch of lemon juice and a little sugar."

"Of course," the waitress was writing the formula down as Frank explained.

"What is that?" Cynthia asked.

Sky answered before Frank could. "That's called a Prop Blast. The official favorite drink of all paratroopers."

"Actually, it was the favored drink of *officers,* but I'm sure the enlisted men joined in the tradition whenever they could."

"Agreed," Sky said and looked at the waitress. "Make that two."

"Why stop there?" Harley interjected. "I'll have one too."

J.P. looked at the waitress. "What the hell, we'll all have one. I'd like to find out what it tastes like."

"Right after dessert," Frank requested. The waitress nodded and took the order to the bar.

"So, Sicily was your baptism of fire," J.P. tried to jump-start the conversation again.

Sky answered. "That's right. It's funny I can still remember some of those details. I particularly remember how proud our squad was having come through that first action. No one froze up. We got through our first combat in good shape. It was a great feeling."

"What happened after General Ridgway passed through your lines?" Cynthia asked. J.P. believed she was trying to help him get more information about his father before the dinner ended.

Sky thought for a moment. "Ridgway came back pretty quick. It was mid morning and there was a big firefight at the Y Objective. So he went back to his headquarters near Gela."

Sky cleared the remaining objects off of the table. "Here, let me explain." He carved a crease in the white tablecloth with his finger and sprinkled some pepper along the mark that represented the coastline. It was a fairly straight line in front of J.P. "This is the south coast of Sicily." He placed a saltshaker on the line of pepper to the left of J.P. "Here is Gela on the coast. You're looking north. I'm doing this upside down, so bear with me."

J.P. touched the saltshaker with his left hand. "Gela. Got it."

"First Division landed here." He threw a pink sugar packet in front of the saltshaker. Sky then placed another saltshaker to the right of J.P. some distance from the first but inland from the coastline. "This is Vittoria, ten miles inland. I'm drawing a right triangle facing you, and this is the base." He traced a line in the air from Gela to Vittoria.

J.P. reached with his right hand and touched the second landmark. "Vittoria."

Sky dropped another sugar packet near the coastline trace. "Forty-fifth Division landed here." He then took a peppershaker and placed it above Gela, nearer to himself representing a town well inland. "This is Niscemi at the top of the leg. A little more than ten miles." He traced an imaginary line in the air from Niscemi to Vittoria. "I forget what this side of the right triangle is called."

"The hypotenuse," Cynthia chimed in as she lit a cigarette.

"Right," Sky continued. Then he took his two open hands and held them edge down and inches apart over the Gela-Niscemi leg. "This was our mission. All of our drop zones were in this corridor. This road complex from Niscemi to Gela had to be blocked to protect the beaches from counterattack. The Y Objective was halfway up this corridor. Thirty-four hundred men were supposed to drop right here and protect the landings at Gela." Sky paused. "We were lucky if we dropped four hundred in the right place."

Frank nodded. The inaccuracies of the Sicily drops were well chronicled.

"Third Battalion of the Oh-four was scattered mostly too far north and east to do any good. A lot of them became prisoners." Sky then placed a small pink sugar packet to the south of Vittoria. "The Second Battalion of the Oh-five made a nice, concentrated drop right here. Problem was, they were twenty-five miles away from their drop zone. They made the best of it and took on some of the Forty-fifth division's objectives."

J.P. wondered where this discussion was going but patiently listened to Sky as he became more and more animated as the story unfolded.

"Most of Third Battalion under Cannonball Krause scattered and dropped over ten miles southeast of their drop zone," Sky pointed to the middle of the triangle. "All except us. We hit our DZ dead on. That left First Battalion under

Lieutenant Colonel Gorham. Most of his battalion landed in the British sector," Sky pointed to his left over to the next table. "But "Hardnose" Gorham collected a few hundred paratroopers and stopped the Germans cold as they came down the corridor. Then he skillfully withdrew south, took Objective Y and held it until the First Division came up." Sky pointed to a spot halfway up the leg of the triangle. "Hardnose was a great leader who accomplished the mission of the entire regiment with a few hundred men. He bought it a few days later. Won the DSC posthumously."

"What about Colonel Gavin?" J.P. asked.

"He landed with a group of headquarter types over thirty miles away from where he was supposed to be." Sky motioned to the edge of their table. "Boy, was he pissed. Took him almost two days to get back in the fight."

"And my dad and your squad?"

"Captain Wolff sent our squad out with walkie-talkies to locate the rest of our battalion and report back to him. We had a pretty good idea where they were by then so our squad marched back to the beach and then east and headed for a town called Biscari about halfway between Niscemi and Vittoria on the… hypotenuse." Sky smiled at Cynthia as he placed a peppershaker at that point. "A road led south out of Biscari to where we were supposed to find our battalion."

"Did you find them?"

Sky reached for Cynthia's ashtray with a smoking cigarette still burning and placed it in the middle of the right triangle. "We never made it to Biscari but we sure found Cannonball and Third Battalion. And Gavin found them too. At a place called Biazza Ridge."

Chapter Thirty-Two

Biazza Ridge, Sicily, July 11, 1943

"To act in concert with a great man is the first of blessings."

Marquis de Lafayette (1757 - 1834)

"**F**ix bayonets!"

The order was unsettling and reverberated up and down the long thin skirmish line of kneeling soldiers. The men snapped their razor-sharp ten-inch bayonets onto their rifles with the audible clicks of metal on metal and waited for the order to charge up and over the crest of the ridge. *The Charge of the Light Brigade,* thought Johnny Kilroy.

This group was made up of paratrooper stragglers from various units and some infantrymen from the 45th Infantry Division. Colonel Gavin assembled this mixed bag of troops in one last desperate effort to hold Biazza Ridge. They awaited Gavin's order to attack.

A few days before, Gavin would have never predicted he'd be leading his men in a battle that would decide the fate of the entire invasion. He and a few of his staff had been dropped over thirty miles southeast of their drop zone. Without a radio they had no communications and no idea where they were. He and his small contingent headed west during that first night picking up small groups of similarly lost paratroopers along the way.

At daybreak on 10 July, while Captain Wolff's Item Company was taking the pillbox complex after lighting the signal fire above Gela, a frustrated Gavin was holed up in a grove of olive trees waiting for nightfall. It was too dangerous to move in daylight so the small group of rank-heavy paratroopers took turns sleeping and standing watch.

A disgusted Gavin contemplated his situation. Here he was, CO of a Regimental Combat Team whose mission was essential to the success of the invasion of Sicily, and all he could manage on his first day on the job was to avoid capture.

Somewhere to the northwest was a raging battle and all he could do was listen. For all he knew, the first mass combat drop of U.S. Army Paratroopers in history had been a total disaster. His mind worked overtime conjuring up all of the worst-case scenarios he could imagine. *Were all his men killed or captured? Were his troops scattered all over the island?* Not only was it personally appalling for him to be out of contact with his command but also reflected negatively on the airborne doctrine he had so passionately championed.

After sunset, he and his little entourage moved out, careful to avoid enemy positions while heading toward the sounds of the battle. After the first skirmish, his side-folding butt stock M1A1 Winchester Carbine jammed. So did the

Carbines of many of his staff officers. They moved through the night and by virtue of road signs and information from captured Italian prisoners, eventually located American lines. They were challenged by an outpost of the 45th Infantry Division and just before dawn slipped into the recently captured town of Vittoria. Gavin wasn't satisfied with simply finding American lines. He still sensed a battle developing ahead and he was determined to get into it. He commandeered a jeep and headed west toward Gela. A few miles down the road he ran into a large group of paratroopers bivouacked in a tomato field and just awakening. Major Krause had collected this force, mostly from his own 3rd Battalion, and was resting them. Whether it was from his own lack of sleep or the lack of aggressiveness displayed by the normally bellicose Krause, Gavin became enraged.

"What about your objective, Major?"

"We were dropped off target, sir." Krause stiffened at the rebuke he knew was coming.

"Apparently, so was everyone else," Gavin replied. "What the heck are you doing here?"

"We assisted the Forty-fifth in capturing the town." He was referring to Vittoria. "I've been collecting stray troopers and supply bundles. I rested my men overnight."

Gavin shook his head in disgust. "What's down that road?" He pointed west along the road to Gela where sporadic gunfire could be heard.

Krause cleared his throat. "I'm not exactly sure, Colonel, but I have scouts and an OP out that way. There's a German force down the road but I haven't been able to determine its size yet. There weren't supposed to be any Krauts on the island, sir."

Gavin ignored the news while glowering at Krause. "Get your men ready to move out, Major. I'm taking a patrol to scout the road west. Move up as soon as you can."

Gavin took a platoon of paratrooper engineers west on the Vittoria-Gela Road. Continuing toward the increasingly louder gunfire, the patrol soon rounded a bend and came upon a railroad crossing with a small stone gatehouse.

The ground rose gradually ahead for half a mile to a ridge about one hundred feet high. On both sides of the road were olive trees and beneath them tall burnt brown grass that provided some concealment but little cover. Through his field glasses Gavin could see Germans dug in on the ridge and firing in their direction. He reached into his map case and studied the map. Directly on the other side of the ridge was the north-south road from Biscari. If the Germans attacked down that road they would drive a wedge between the 1st and 45th Infantry Divisions and split the American forces. This was a golden opportunity for them to destroy the two American divisions and defeat the landings. Gavin knew intuitively he had to take and hold that ridge to interdict any German force heading toward the beach. Biazza Ridge suddenly became a commanding piece of terrain and critical to the success of the invasion. What he didn't know was that a potent German armored column was already attacking southward from Biscari toward the beaches. Gavin was about to unknowingly attack the flank of this powerful force with a handful of light infantry.

It was mid morning before the remaining paratroopers of the 3rd Battalion joined his small patrol of engineers and they assaulted the ridge with the fire and maneuver tactics they had so often practiced. A few hundred paratroopers attacked through the stands of olive trees across a broad front in the face of withering machine gun fire. The ripping sound of the German *Maschinengewehr 42* machine gun, called the MG-42 by the GIs, was as distinctive as it was deadly. The rate of fire was so high, 1,200 rounds per minute, that it was impossible to distinguish one shot from the next. The German machine-gunners spewed their deadly waves of bullets at the advancing paratroopers, shredding tree limbs and cutting leaves from their branches. Paratroopers eventually moved around the flanks forcing the Germans on the ridge to withdraw.

Although the enemy withdrew in good order, Gavin's small force gave chase. While he believed he was spoiling a German attack by pricking at the column's flanks, he actually ran head on into a frontal attack by a German battle group called a *Kampfgruppe*. The German commander had felt the pressure on his left flank and changed his attack plan. Instead of continuing toward the beach, he turned to face the new threat. This new plan of attack would aim his heavily armored tank column directly at the lightly armed paratroopers on Biazza Ridge.

Captain Wolff summoned Lieutenant Klee on the afternoon of 10 July. He ordered Klee to take a small patrol east to find Major Krause and the rest of the 3rd Battalion

Klee set out with Johnny and Jake Kilroy, Joe Boothe, Dominic Angelo, Danny Peregory, Sky Johnson and Sergeant Bruce Copping. The small patrol made it to a supply depot. There Jake replenished his B-A-R ammo with two twelve magazine belts. The extra thirty-six pounds on top of his eighteen-pound weapon convinced him he would have to rid himself of the B-A-R at his first opportunity. *Let someone else haul the squad automatic weapon around next time.*

The men stocked up on water and K-rations. Each K-ration box came with one day's supply of 3,000 calories broken into three meals. The main food for each meal was sealed in a small metal can. The variety was sparse and men quickly tired of meat and vegetables, meat and beans or meat and eggs. Canned cheese, a fruit bar and some candy were also included along with drink packets of lemonade or instant coffee. Some toilet paper, waterproof matches, a flat spoon, dried biscuits, cigarettes, gum, sugar and a can opener rounded out the package.

The patrol moved out along the railroad tracks in single file and in silence until nightfall. After they crossed the Acate River on the railroad bridge, Klee ordered the men to catch a few hours sleep in shifts. Most had been awake for over forty hours and were bone-tired. They continued their eastbound search before dawn on 11 July but were pushed south toward the coast by the sounds of a battle straight ahead. A German force heading south from Biscari was pressing the 45th Division. Klee found a company CP. The officers told him about a group of paratroopers assembling west of Vittoria on the east-west Vittoria-Gela road. Klee headed southeast toward Scoglitti and then turned northeast to intersect the road.

The patrol approached the road by mid-afternoon. The closer they got, the louder the sound of battle. They had stumbled upon a full-fledged firefight. They ran into Major William Hagan, 3rd Battalion XO, conferring with Colonel Gavin. They were summarily ordered to join the skirmish line. The men took positions just off of the Vittoria-Gela road that bisected the eastern and western slopes of Biazza Ridge. They would take part in the last desperate counterattack Gavin was planning to avoid losing the ridge and the beachhead.

All during the day, the force Gavin had sent over the ridge in the morning had been in a wild fight. Their initial charge had removed the Germans from the top of the ridge but as the paratroopers swept down the western side they were exposed to heavy mortar and artillery fire. They went to ground and tried to dig in but the hard shale was unforgiving and the earth surrendered only shallow holes. Despite these challenges, the paratroopers fought hard and kept pressing the Germans with fire and movement. It was a seesaw battle for most of the day, both sides giving and taking as circumstances created opportunities that were both seized and lost. Casualties began streaming back over the ridge to the hastily established aid station near the gatehouse. Minor wounds were quickly treated and the men were sent back into action. The more seriously wounded were hauled back to the field hospital in Vittoria.

On the western side of the ridge the battle began to go badly. German Mark VI Tiger tanks had arrived on the scene in force and were making their presence felt. The high-pitched supersonic fire from their .88-millimeter guns echoed across the battlefield. They shredded the stone walls of farmhouses and the trees in the olive groves and kept the infantrymen hugging the dirt in their shallow holes. Occasionally, small teams of men maneuvered their M1A1 Rocket Launchers into firing position only to see their 2.36-inch bazooka rockets bounce harmlessly off the frontal armor of the Tigers. Some bazooka teams maneuvered to the rear of the tanks to score effective hits but were vulnerable to German infantry when they did so. Other troopers disabled the tanks with hits on the treads or bogey wheels. But once they gave away their position with the bazooka's large back blast and smoke signature, German infantry and armor pounced on them. They became the most hunted men on the battlefield with Tigers firing both their machine guns and main guns at individual soldiers. It was raw flesh against cold steel and only the continued forceful attacks and fire and movement of the paratroopers kept the superior enemy force from overrunning their position. The aggressiveness of the paratroopers confused the superior German force. On more than one occasion during that hot day, the Tigers actually retreated to regroup and re-arm giving the besieged paratroopers a brief respite.

Casualties continued to mount. As more reinforcements trickled in, Gavin committed them to the battle. Two crews from the 456th PFAB, each with a .75-millimeter M1A1 Pack Howitzer, struggled to drag their cannons up the long sloping ridge. Gavin positioned them on the flanks of the ridge where they were able to lay direct fire on the Tiger tanks. The paratrooper artillery crews would disappear from the enemy's sight by pulling their guns below the crest of the ridge only to emerge in a different place. This grueling cat and mouse game went on for hours until a German .88 knocked out one of the guns. As the remaining artillery piece ran low on shells, the Germans began making grudging headway up the long western slope.

By late afternoon Gavin was in danger of losing the ridge. He called up an artillery spotter from the navy to secure gunfire support from the ships offshore. At the same time he assembled a force just beneath the crest of the ridge to counterattack the Germans if they made it to the top. The lone remaining towed .75-millimeter cannon was positioned in the center of the line. Gavin's small force was hanging on by a slim thread.

Klee and his squad came upon the scene just as Gavin was deploying his last-ditch counterattacking force and were immediately ordered to take positions in the ranks. The boys wished each other luck with pats on the backs and taps on the helmets and slipped into the line.

Gavin then called for his men on the western slope to withdraw in good order and called in naval gunfire. The five and six inch shells began landing on the western slope. The able-bodied did an about face and joined the skirmish line. There were perhaps a hundred paratroopers across a ninety-yard front preparing to charge. They were all that stood between victory and defeat.

Gavin paced up and down the center of the line, shouting at the top of his voice, hoping to be heard above the din of the battlefield. "If the tanks break through, we take on the infantry. We do not withdraw. We go in one direction only. Forward!"

His officers and NCOs repeated the order up and down the line of grim and determined troopers. For most of these reinforcements, this would be their first combat. Their strong desire to prove themselves and not let each other down overcame their fear. The adrenalin was flowing and their senses were in overdrive.

Most of these young boys would never again be as brave as they would be this day. Some would die. Others would suffer devastating injuries. The remaining, having witnessed the wanton and random destruction of their brothers around them, would forever see the world differently. They would become more thoughtful and more careful before they risked their lives again. But on this day they swallowed hard through dry mouths and gripped their rifles with sweaty palms. On this day they would stand tall, grit their teeth, lean into the fire and charge. On this day, boys would become men!

Johnny stood up with his rifle at port arms and awaited the order. "I didn't think wars were fought this way anymore," he shouted to Jake thinking of the long lines of British soldiers and American militiamen in the Revolution.

"Helluva' way to fight a war," Jake agreed as he loosened the sling on his B-A-R and looped it over his shoulder to take some of the weight. Without a bayonet he would move forward firing his B-A-R from the hip.

The noise was deafening as smoke and dust swirled everywhere near the ridge. Suddenly the artillery barrage stopped. Someone yelled, "Ready, men!"

The drone of a diesel tank engine and the clanking noise of tank treads could be heard just below the crown of the ridge. The long barrel of the .88-millimeter high velocity gun of a Mark VI Tiger poked its way menacingly over the crest. The airborne artillerymen quickly muscled their howitzer to bore-sight it at the emerging tank. Holding their ears, the crew fired at the vulnerable underbelly and scored a direct hit. The explosion was enormous. The men cheered as the turret flew off and flames and smoke belched from the view slits. The tank seemed to rise in the air a few inches and drop dead in its tracks at the pinnacle of the ridge. Thick black smoke and brilliant flames gushed from the mangled and lifeless vehicle like some slain dragon-monster.

The main gun of another Tiger appeared above the crest, moving slowly into view. The artillerymen repeated the dance with their artillery piece and took aim at the new threat. The tank stopped, refusing to expose its underbelly, its weaponry pointing uselessly to the sky.

Gavin sensed this was the moment. "Let's go," he yelled and the thin line surged forward as one organism up and over the crest of Biazza Ridge.

The German infantry advancing up the western slope were caught off guard, shocked at the sight of the charging paratroopers with flashing bayonets coming fast down the slope directly at them. The machine gunners were caught with their MG-42s on their shoulders as they hauled them up the slope to set up atop the ridge. The German rifleman were barely able to get off one or two shots with their bolt-action *Mauser Gewher 1898* rifles before the storming paratroopers were in their midst. The few tanks that remained functional on the western slope could not bring fire on the Americans intermixed with their own infantry and were forced to withdraw. Gavin had timed the charge perfectly.

The surge of the paratroopers carried into and through the surprised German infantry formations. The sight of the screaming horde with bayonet-tipped rifles panicked many Germans to flight. They retreated through the scattered smoking hulks of tanks and trucks knocked out by the artillery barrage. They ran headlong through the orchards and vineyards in fear-driven terror. The paratroopers surged forward into the olive groves pushing the retreating enemy before them. Some turned and fought. A flashing bayonet or a burst of rifle fire quickly cut them down. After a few moments the entire German force was in headlong retreat with the keyed up paratroopers in hot pursuit.

The scene on the western slope was grizzly. The carnage wrought by the artillery was devastating. Bodies were broken and strewn about the ground amid burnt and smoking human and mechanical wreckage. The stench was ungodly. Groans and screams of wounded and dying men were everywhere.

Jake and Johnny managed to stay side-by-side during the charge down the hill. Jake fired his B-A-R in short bursts and focused on avoiding spraying rounds into American paratroopers who had gotten ahead of him. That effort became difficult as soldiers of both sides swirled together in the wild melee.

Johnny avoided using his bayonet. The idea of sticking the ten-inch blade into someone repulsed him. He preferred shooting his M-1. The bayonet would be his last resort.

The flight of the enemy and the downward slope of the western side of the ridge gave the Americans great momentum. The rout was total and complete but the Americans were scattered all over the battlefield having chased their prey beyond visual sight. If it were a cavalry charge, the bugler would have blown *recall* on the trumpet.

Jake and Johnny, breathing heavily and separated from the group, pulled up by a low rock wall near a small stream that ran alongside a wide track to a vineyard. They stood hands-on-knees trying to catch their breath when Jake heard something between the sounds of their deep breaths. He peered around the wall. In a bend in the track stood a German Mark VI Tiger tank parked less than fifty yards away. Four crewmen, obviously unaware the battle had reached them, were standing casually outside their tank. Two of them were looking at a map while the other two were examining one of the bogey wheels on the tank tread. The tank's engine was idling. There were no German infantry in sight.

Jake nodded and raised his B-A-R. Johnny gently lowered the barrel with his free hand. "They're not armed. Let's take them prisoner."

Jake looked at Johnny intently. He said nothing but his eyes asked *why take chances?*

"They may have some intelligence," Johnny answered the unasked question. They were getting to know each other well enough to read the other's thoughts.

"All right, cover me," Jake said reluctantly as he replaced his twenty round box magazine having lost count of the rounds he expended. Johnny worked the bolt on his M-1 manually and ejected two live cartridges before the clip came flying out to land quietly in the long brown grass. He jammed in a fresh clip of eight, racked the bolt to chamber a round and nodded to Jake.

"I got this. It's my idea, it's on me," Johnny said as he brushed by Jake and stepped out into the open. He moved quickly toward the four Germans huddled around their tank. He raised his M-1 to his shoulder as he swiftly closed the open ground between them. "*Hande luften,*" he yelled in stilted German. "*Kommen sie hier, schnelle!*"

The four tank crewmen were shocked to be caught outside their vehicle by an American infantryman and quickly raised their hands. One of them began yelling, "*Kamerad, Kamerad.*"

"*Kommen sie hier, schnelle!*" Johnny repeated as he lowered his rifle. The German tankers started walking toward him. He motioned to them by pointing his rifle barrel up at their heads repeatedly. Then he tapped his free hand on his helmet. They quickly put their hands on their heads. One of them was wearing a sidearm in a shoulder holster so Johnny kept his M-1 pointing directly at him as they closed the distance to about ten yards.

Suddenly the turret of the tank started to turn the main gun toward the Americans. Johnny raised the M-1 to his shoulder and took aim at the armed prisoner. He would die first.

"*Nicht sheissen, nicht sheissen!*" yelled one of the prisoners as he waved his hands frantically at Johnny. The others were wide-eyed and pleading. They all dropped to their knees. One of them turned and began screaming orders in German toward the tank. The turret still turned slowly toward the paratroopers.

Jake jumped out from behind cover. "Yank, the hatch," he screamed. "I got these guys." Jake was running forward with his B-A-R at his shoulder.

Johnny saw the hatch in the commander's cupola was open. He dropped his M-1 and raced by the prisoners toward the tank. One of the prisoners was still screaming orders toward the tank but the gun continued to turn. The prisoners knew if their crewmate fired the gun, the Americans would kill them all. The turret continued to move gradually as the lone remaining crewman manually cranked it around.

Johnny pulled a grenade from his web belt. In one motion he slipped his razor-sharp Schrade-Walden switchblade knife from his shoulder scabbard and slit the electrical tape holding the spoon tight to the grenade. He hopped up on the tank chassis, pulled the safety pin and dropped the grenade into the open hatch as he jumped off the other side.

The turret was now pointing directly over the heads of the prisoners and the .88-millimeter main gun fired and split the air with a deafening supersonic roar. The shot was high and smashed into a twisted olive tree a few hundred yards behind Jake, turning it instantly into splinters. The shock wave knocked Jake to the ground. The crewman in the tank did not have time to depress the muzzle of the gun before the grenade went off. Bloody debris erupted from the open hatch.

Jake angrily retrieved his helmet and motioned to the prisoners to place hands on heads and begin walking. Johnny came around the tank, black smoke now curling from the hatch, and picked up his M-1. He joined Jake as they walked their shaken prisoners back toward their lines. They walked in silence for a few moments, decompressing from the frantic action.

Johnny took a deep breath. "Good thinking, Jake. Another few seconds and we'd have been dog shit."

Jake nodded. He was struggling to regain his hearing. "Hey, I didn't know you spoke German that well."

"I know six words, "Johnny lied. "And I used all of them." He was smiling the smile of a relieved survivor after a close call. "But you learn something every day."

"Really? Like what?" Jake asked.

"Like, a Tiger tank has five crewmen, not four."

The two men marched their prisoners back up the ridge. The counterattack had been a complete success. The Germans were weakened first by artillery and then routed by the paratrooper-led infantry. They would later ask if the Americans at Biazza Ridge had fought the Japanese in the Pacific because they fought so well.

The word came down that Colonel Gavin ordered all units to consolidate on the ridge for the night. The two paratroopers and their prisoners worked their way back up the slope. The hill was strewn with carnage. They saw dead and wounded men, material and body parts and smelled cordite mixed with the ubiquitous smell of burnt flesh. Army medics treated wounded soldiers of both sides all over the battlefield. Other troopers were helping injured buddies back over the ridge. The dead were left where they lay for the time being. Only their dog tags were collected. An upright rifle stuck by its bayonet into the rocky ground, some with a helmet on the butt stock, marked where they fell.

The two paratroopers came upon Major Hagan, 3rd Battalion XO, lying on a stretcher and conferring with Lieutenant Klee. Klee saw his two men first.

"Jake, Johnny, over here," Klee beckoned.

The two men herded their prisoners toward the officers. Johnny spoke first. "Tiger tank crew…minus one. The tank is in a clearing around that bend past the vineyard."

"You captured a Mark Six?" Major Hagan's thigh was wrapped with a thick bandage, which was bleeding through. Despite the pain he was ecstatic.

"Yes, sir, Major," Jake replied. "But it might not be functional. Yank here had to drop a frag grenade into it. I'm sure there are pieces of Kraut all over the inside."

"Excellent, men," Major Hagan complemented. He motioned to a nearby staff officer. "Take these prisoners to the command post at the gatehouse." Just before two brawny soldiers lifted his stretcher to cart him away, the major turned back to Jake and Johnny. "Well done, men."

The two paratroopers nodded, embarrassed by the attention. Johnny turned to Lieutenant Klee. "What about our other guys, sir?"

Klee shook his head and looked toward the ground. "Danny Boy was wounded bad. He's back at the aid station. Boots and Dom didn't make it."

Jake and Johnny were shocked. Soldiers were dying all around them and they accepted that outcome as the cold calculus of war. They certainly felt bad for all the fallen but losing a close friend was different. Just an hour ago they were laughing and joking with one another and now their friends were gone. It was a realization impossible to accept. It hit them both hard.

"What about Sky?" asked Johnny.

Klee pointed to a spot on the ridge near a small outcropping of rock. "He's fine. He's up there with Sergeant Copping. You guys need to join up with them. We're digging in for the night. The colonel expects the Krauts to make one more try at the ridge."

The two men nodded and made their way to the top of the ridge. Johnny stopped only to pick up bandoliers of .30-caliber ammo from some of the bodies they passed. The stony ground crunched under their feet as they navigated up the slope. Sky saw them coming and rushed down to meet them. They roughly hugged each other with great elation. Only the memory of their fallen buddies dampened their exhilaration.

"Glad to see you guys," Copping slapped both of them on the back. "We thought you were gone for sure." He walked them to the crest and pointed to a partially excavated foxhole. "Finish digging and you'll have a safe place to sleep."

Jake and Johnny set to work scraping out the hard shale and packed earth while Sky and Copping continued work on their holes. All up and down the line the men were digging furiously. Only the continuous sound of metal shovels striking earth broke the silence.

Some ammunition carriers from the 45th Infantry Division pulled up about fifty yards behind them. Soldiers from the trucks began distributing ammo and K-rations. Accompanying the ammo carriers was an M16 Gun Motor Carriage, called a halftrack. It had four M2 HB .50-caliber anti-aircraft machine guns in a synchronized gun mount on an electrically powered turret. The belt ammunition was fed from four attached canister drums. Another .50-caliber machine gun mounted behind the driver provided additional secondary protection. The quad-fifty mount was pointed skywards.

After an hour or so the holes were deep enough. The sun began to set and a cool breeze came up off the sea. Johnny settled down in his fighting hole while

Jake leaned back and pulled a small Bible from his pocket and began reading in the fading light.

There was a slight commotion behind them and Johnny turned to see what it was. He was flabbergasted to see Colonel Gavin kneeling alongside their hole. He was carrying an M-1.

"So," Gavin said, "you're the men who captured that Tiger tank! Outstanding!" He looked at Johnny. "What's your name, son? Where you from?"

"Private John Kilroy, sir. New York."

"I'm Brooklyn born," Gavin smiled. He turned to Jake. "And you, son?"

"Private Jake Kilroy."

"Oh…brothers?"

"No, Colonel, we're not related," Johnny answered.

"Hmm…" Gavin mused. "That's not so unusual in this regiment. There's a Sergeant Gavin in Second Battalion. I never met him personally. We're not related either but by now he's probably convinced everyone we are." Gavin chuckled. "Well, I just wanted to say thanks and see how you men were doing. Good work today!"

"Thank you, sir," said both in unison.

Gavin held Jake's shoulder as he stood up. "Something to tell the folks about back home."

"No folks to tell, sir. I'm an orphan," Jake answered.

Gavin knelt back down and looked at Jake. "Me too, son. So maybe someday we can tell our grandchildren what we did here today. It's a story worth telling."

"Yes, sir."

"Stay alert, men. I think the Krauts will attack again tonight. I know I would. And Colonel Tucker's regiment is dropping onto Farello Airfield tonight about ten miles west of here. Pass the word."

Gavin moved to the next foxhole. He said a few words of encouragement and moved down the line, no doubt advising the men reinforcements would be arriving by air. In fact, orders had gone out to the fleet and all ground units that paratrooper reinforcements were flying in.

Darkness fell and still no counterattack came. Unable to punch through Biazza Ridge with their armored spearhead, the Germans concluded the Americans were heavily armed and dug in strong defensive positions in great numbers. They decided to withdraw both *Kampfgruppe* during the night. The landings would no longer be contested. The Axis forces on Sicily would now be fighting to stave off annihilation.

Jake had dropped off into a semi-sleep while Johnny stood watch at the front of their hole. He was awakened by the familiar drone of the C-47 Pratt and Whitney engines as the V-formation of planes passed directly over their position heading for Farello Airfield. Serial after serial passed over at 700 feet in prefect formation.

It was a spectacular nocturnal aerial ballet. Tucker was bringing his remaining two infantry battalions, an artillery battalion and a company of engineers. About 2,300 men were planning to make nothing more than a routine training drop on conspicuously illuminated, soft, flat ground inside American lines. The weather was perfect, the visibility excellent and the winds were calm. The conditions were textbook. All of the men along the line were staring at the endless stream of C-47s ferrying in their brothers.

Suddenly, out on the water, an anti-aircraft gun from one of the ships opened fire. Soon another, then another opened fire. The firing quickly spread like a virus. The multicolored tracers reached up into the sky at the transports. The slow, low flying planes were easy targets and many were hit immediately. Land-based anti-aircraft batteries joined the slaughter and soon most of the ships at anchor had guns blazing at the formation of friendly planes.

Jake snapped awake. "What the fuck! No, you assholes!" The other paratroopers along the line were also yelling but their pleas were drowned out by the cacophony of noise made by the anti-aircraft artillery. The men along the ridgeline were helpless as they watched the low and slow flying planes being repeatedly hit. It was mass murder. In desperation, the planes turned on their lights to indicate they were friendly. That made them easier targets. Some of the planes, damaged and smoking, pushed through to drop their paratroopers on the airfield. Others aborted the mission and turned back out to sea. Still others jettisoned their paratroopers immediately after being hit but before they crashed.

Paratroopers standing hooked up and ready to jump were shredded as bullets tore through the thin-skinned fuselage of their plane. Some scrambled out only to come down too fast under torn chutes. Others were ripped apart by gunfire as they drifted down and dangled helplessly. Before the formation of 144 planes scattered out of danger, sixty of the aircraft would be hit.

Jake and Johnny stood by powerlessly. They were screaming to stop firing. It was butchery beyond comprehension and their fellow Americans were perpetrating it. Jake was screaming so loud and hard tears began streaming down his face. The sight of burning parachutes, ignited by anti aircraft tracers, with helpless men dangling beneath them was too much to bear.

All of a sudden the Quad-50 on the halftrack behind them opened up with a deafening roar. The crew was firing deadly armor-piercing rounds at the transports. Jake jumped up and ran to the vehicle yelling all the way. "They're ours! They're ours!" Johnny followed him.

A young-looking lieutenant was standing near the halftrack. He appeared to be in charge. Jake came up on him quickly and startled him. "Cease fire, sir. Those are our planes!"

The officer didn't hear due to the earsplitting noise of the guns. The Quad-50 kept pouring rounds into the over flying aircraft with devastating effect. Jake tried to climb onto the halftrack as he yelled but the officer, not understanding his intentions, pulled him down. Jake lost it. He shoved the officer to the ground and hopped up into the tracks and over the side into the rear of the M3 Halftrack. He pulled the gunner's hands off the triggers. "Stop firing, those are our planes!" He was still screaming.

The gunner looked at Jake stupidly. "I got orders, Mac."

Someone else said, "Who is this guy?"

The officer jumped to his feet, said, "Get down here right now, soldier."

The gunner made a move to re-grip the trigger and Jake punched him. While the gunner was still stunned Jake unhooked his harness and grabbed him. With strength only realized when adrenalin fuses with pure rage, Jake tossed the gunner from the rear compartment of the gun carriage. The gunner landed on the officer and they both hit the ground.

Jake looked out at the two of them. "Nobody is firing these guns any more tonight!"

The officer pulled out his .45-caliber sidearm and pointed it at Jake. "Get down right now, Private or I'll shoot."

"I believe you would, sir." Jake was enraged. "You've already killed some paratroopers tonight. Why not me too?" Jake stood defiantly in the vehicle.

The officer looked confused. He was certain he was firing at German bombers. He had no word American transports would be dropping paratroopers that night. He cocked the hammer of the .45 and pointed it directly at Jake's head. "If I don't kill you, you'll be court-martialed for sure. Now, get out of my vehicle, soldier."

"No fucking way, sir!"

Before the officer could react, he felt a cold steel rifle barrel poked under his ear. Johnny held his M-1 Garand with the stock under his armpit. "I would just slowly lower that forty-five if I were you…sir!"

Chapter Thirty-Three

L'Enfant Plaza Hotel - January 13, 1997

"Things that were hard to bear are sweet to remember."

Lucius Annaeus Seneca (4 BC - 65 AD)

"The main problem was, they just didn't know how to use us." Sky Johnson stabbed at a piece of apple pie on his plate. His mood slowly shifted from affable to morose. J.P. suspected many older veterans went through the same metamorphosis while discussing their war experiences. He decided to let Sky talk his way through this mood swing.

"*Who* didn't know?" J.P. asked.

"The brass, the big shots, the leaders who were supposed to know better. The made a lot of bad decisions that hurt us and got men killed."

J.P. didn't want to sound unsympathetic but he felt he had to draw out more information. "Well, it was an all volunteer outfit with highly spirited men. It stands to reason you would get the difficult missions."

"Sure." Sky put down his fork and clasped his hands under his chin. "That's not what I'm talking about. Take Sicily for example. First, they don't have enough planes to drop the whole division at one time. Ike gave too many of our planes to the Limeys. Then we take the long flight path to Sicily, get lost and drop us in thirty-five mile an hour winds when we never practiced in anything over fifteen. Then they scatter us all over the freakin' island and we find out later that only twelve percent of the guys actually dropped on target." Sky picked up his fork and poked another piece of pie into his mouth. "And then they shoot at our own planes. But the real killer was they knew the *Hermann Goering Panzer* Division was on the island with Tiger tanks but they told *us* there were no Germans and no tanks."

"They knew? Why didn't they tell you?" J.P. interrupted.

"It was Ultra," explained Frank. "The Allies broke the German High Command's code. The brass figured if they warned the airborne troops there were tanks on the island, and they were captured and talked, the Germans might figure out we were reading their mail. So they told the airborne there were *no tanks* on the island."

"That's ridiculous," commented J.P. "What the hell good is that kind of intelligence if you can't actually use it?"

"Exactly!" Sky agreed, pointing his fork at J.P. "They didn't need to tell us where they got the intel from. They could have told us they spotted the tanks from the air." Sky paused for a moment. "Another thing. When the Five-oh-four was sent in and got shot up, there were over three hundred casualties." Sky eyes clouded up. "We had eighty-one paratroopers and sixty aircrew killed. After all that hard work and training, to be shot down by your own guys…" Sky let the words hang in the air and just shook his head. The table fell into an awkward silence.

Sky continued after a few moments. "The men deserved better leadership than that." He paused. "The whole incident became top secret and not made public until the following spring."

"They kept it under wraps that long?" J.P. asked.

"If that happened today," Frank interjected, "It would be all over the *Nightly News!*"

Sky nodded in agreement. "What's the use in complaining now? Sorry, but it makes me feel better to get it out." He paused for a moment and resumed his narrative. "The day after Biazza Ridge we patrolled to the west and came to the Acate River. There were no Krauts. They all retreated. We crossed over a bridge named Ponte Dirillo. There is a marker there today, a memorial with the engraved names of the guys we lost. Angelo, Boothe, Lieutenant Klee and a whole bunch more." Sky shook his head in a gesture of deep regret. "They called the rest of the Sicilian Campaign a road march *but* we still took casualties." Sky collected the props from the table that he used to explain the airborne dispositions. "The Italians would fire a volley for *honor* and then surrender. We lost Lieutenant Klee on one of those *honorable surrenders.*"

Sky choked up again. Cynthia reached across the table and covered his hand with hers. She shook it gently.

Sky continued through the painful memories. "It took us only about five weeks to secure the entire island. Patton beat Montgomery to Messina but most of the Germans got away to the mainland. Another mistake! We would hear from the *Hermann Goering* Division again."

The waitress approached the table. "Here are your special order drinks." She placed one in front of each of them. No one reached for his or her drink right away.

"Let me see," Sky went on. "After that we flew back to Kairouan to take on replacements. Bob Hope and Francis Langford put on a USO show for the troops." Sky wiped his mouth and brushed away a small tear.

"God bless Bob Hope," Frank added. "The troops loved him."

Sky persevered. "After a few weeks we flew back to Sicily to a place called Castelvetrano. It had an airfield and we were preparing for a jump somewhere into Italy. That came close to being another disaster."

Harley joined the conversation. "There were plenty of 'cluster-fucks' made by the brass during the War." Harley glanced around to see if his words carried beyond their table. He looked at Cynthia. "Sorry, ma'am." He continued. "Omaha Beach was the worst, then there was the Huertgen Forest, the intelligence failure of the Bulge…the list goes on and on. Some generals had no damn clue." Harley tossed his napkin on the table and leaned back in his chair.

"Also, our own officers were reluctant to put us in for medals," Sky interrupted. "Since we were better than the rest we were expected to perform better than the rest."

"Right," agreed Frank. "And that stupid point system that allowed for rotation back to the States. And the dumb replacement system. Terrible mistakes!"

Harley gave Frank a curious stare. J.P. wasn't sure what Frank said to evoke such a reaction. He surmised it had something to do with the replacement system or the point system.

J.P. decided to provoke the men just a little to prolong the discussion. "What was this near-disaster jump into Italy?"

Sky put his head down and then looked up at J.P. "That was another one the brass came this close to screwing up royally." He held his thumb and forefinger about a quarter inch apart. "They were reckless with us and came that close to getting most of the division slaughtered. Just to drop us on Rome for political reasons. It would have been better if they just dropped us on Berlin and let us try to hunt down and kill that rat-bastard, son of a bitch, Hitler. Not one of us would have survived but maybe we could have ended the War a year earlier."

Sky's face softened. He coughed and wiped his nose on his napkin. He slowly composed himself. "Don't mind the ramblings of an old man," he said to J.P. "I'm set in my ways and happen to have strong opinions. It was the men, the grunts, the boots on the ground that won that damned War. And most of them were just boys. They made the difference. Not the damn generals! And if the generals were smarter and had listened and learned, we wouldn't have left so many of our guys over there in foreign cemeteries."

It was also clear to J.P. these men revered their fallen brothers as much as they resented many of their superiors. They also had great pride in what they accomplished and strong opinions about how it should have been done. *And what was this about Rome?* J.P asked himself.

J.P. looked directly at Harley. "So I guess my father's buddy Jake, your cousin, is buried somewhere over there?"

Harley returned his stare. As J.P. waited for a reply, he could see in his peripheral vision the other men were staring at Harley too.

"At the Henri-Chapelle Military Cemetery in Belgium with eight thousand of his brothers."

Everyone sat in stunned silence. J.P. knew many Americans were buried in foreign cemeteries in distant lands but the detailed reference to a specific place complete with that huge number took him completely off guard. He turned to Sky to get the conversation back on track. "So the Eighty-second went back to Sicily in," J.P. looked up at the ceiling, "had to be September by then, for a drop on Rome?"

"Early September," Sky agreed. "And just before we made our next jump, Jake and Johnny disappeared."

J.P. shook his head. "What?"

"They were pulled out of camp and sent off on a top-secret mission."

Top-secret mission? J.P. wondered. *Could this possibly be it?* "What was the mission?" he asked innocently.

"I couldn't tell you the details." Sky lied. "We didn't see much of each other after Sicily and the few times we did, we never got into it. I do know that it was classified…very hush-hush."

J.P. looked at Harley who shrugged his shoulders. Then he looked at Frank.

"I know some of the details and I can share them with you."

"Thanks Frank," J.P. replied. He looked around the dining room. It was nearly empty. Their waitress was standing near the kitchen with her eye on the table. She had the bill in her hand and would come as soon as he signaled. There certainly wouldn't be enough time for Frank to tell his story tonight. J.P. would have to make arrangements to speak to him soon. He also had to listen to his covert tape recording. This classified mission story may actually be the break he was waiting for. As much as he enjoyed the conversation, he knew time had run out.

He reached for his Prop-Blast and lifted the glass. "To the fallen."

Chapter Thirty-Four

Newport News, Virginia – August 15, 1943

"If we mean to have heroes, statesmen and philosophers,
we should have learned women."

Abigail Adams (1744 - 1818)

Macie Vance left the movie in conversation with Derek Edson. They had just seen the newly released film *Action in the North Atlantic* starring Humphrey Bogart with Raymond Massey, Alan Hale and Dane Clark. The movie, released to theatres in June, was primarily a tribute to the contribution made by the Merchant Marine. Bogart was her favorite actor ever since she saw him in the 1942 film *Casablanca* with Ingrid Bergman. That movie became her all-time favorite.

She was a bit disappointed there wasn't much romance in the film – Julie Bishop had a small part - but enjoyed watching Bogart just the same.

Besides, she thought, *not only was the movie exciting but the Movietone Newsreel contained some upbeat new developments as well.* In the Pacific the Americans had secured Guadalcanal and recaptured the Aleutian Island of Attu. Kiska would be next. In the Mediterranean, the news was also good. The Allies surrounded and defeated a large army in Tunisia. North Africa was finally free of Axis forces. Macie was glad the fighting ended there since that's where she believed Jake was.

Since the launching of the *Yorktown (CV-10)* in January, Macie worked on the USS *Intrepid (CV-11)* until her launching in April. After the *Intrepid* was launched on 26 April 1943, Macie went to work on the new USS *Hornet (CV-12)*. This aircraft carrier was originally named *Kearsarge*, but after the original *Hornet (CV-8)* was lost at the battle of Santa Cruz the prior October, the Navy Department decided to honor another lost ship with a namesake, just as they had done with *Yorktown*.

By this time there were five Essex-class aircraft carriers under construction at the busy Newport News Shipyard. Another five were being built in other shipyards around the country to add to the four that had already been commissioned since Pearl Harbor. The ranks of workers and laborers at Newport News had swelled to immense numbers. Macie was promoted to supervise a team of ten welders, mostly women her junior in experience although not necessarily in age. She was conscientious and was gaining more self-confidence each day, especially as others were showing respect for her. She wondered if Derek had anything to do with her promotion.

Macie and Derek, along with Nora and a sailor named Jesse, walked the crowded Saturday night streets of Norfolk to Harry's Drug Store and Fountain. Macie always enjoyed a chocolate malted or banana split after the movies. It reminded her of home. Derek always cheerfully deferred to her wishes.

Nora leaned over to Macie and said, "Will you be here for an hour or so?"

Macie smiled, "I'm sure we will. Have a good time."

"We're going for a walk, you kids enjoy your ice cream," Nora announced. She swung Jesse back in the other direction and waved goodbye.

Derek raised his eyebrows. Macie smiled, cocked her head and did the same in return. "She's a grown woman. She knows what she's doing."

"Personally, I think she's getting a little khaki-wacky," Derek used the popular term for women who went a bit overboard for men in uniform.

They walked into the drug store and took the only two empty stools at the end of the counter. Derek was his usual amiable self. He was hopelessly smitten with Macie but accepted that he was the *other guy*. The better he came to know her, the deeper in love he fell. He had been careful for more than a year, not risking any overt advances. As much as he wanted more out of their relationship, he was not willing to jeopardize their friendship by making his move.

She was an unusual young woman. He particularly liked the fact that she was beautiful despite not wearing makeup most of the time. The small mole on her lip punctuated her fine looks. At the same time, she was not vain. She didn't mind being seen in shabby work clothes or with her hair wet. He was also impressed that all of the women who knew her liked her. He watched her grow in her job and while she may not have always been confident, she was comfortable with herself and fearless when it came to trying new things. Macie was mature well beyond her years and Derek had to often remind himself that she was just twenty years old.

His best opportunity to be with her and make something more of their relationship was to bide his time, be ever-present and available. It may never work out, but he would rather be *just a friend* than not be anything at all.

Macie looked at his face as he leaned over to suck his malted through a straw. *How could someone so young look so much older?* Derek was only twenty-three but was aged by what he witnessed in life. He glanced sideways with his green-gray eyes and smiled.

"Did you have anything to do with my promotion?" she asked.

"Not one bit," he lied. "You earned it. You work hard and you're good at what you do."

That part was the truth. Macie was diligent. All Derek had to do was convince management that women would eventually have to be used in supervisory roles as the number of female shipyard workers increased so dramatically. The mathematics was undeniable. After that, it was easy to point Macie out as a candidate for supervisor.

She gave him a skeptical look. "I know I work hard but I just don't know if I can believe you had nothing to do with it. But if you did, thanks. You're a good friend." She stared at his face for a reaction.

"It was all you're doing," he countered without changing his expression. "You need to believe in yourself more, like Roxie."

Macie pondered that suggestion. "You're right, Derek. She *is* a very confident woman."

"Speaking of Roxie," he reached into his pocket. "I just got this letter today. You should read it." He handed the letter to Macie and she read it between bites of her banana split.

> Dear Derek,
>
> I hope and trust this letter finds you well. I'm doing fine. I love this job and I'm making a real difference in the war effort. My sister pilots and I have been part of the Women's Auxiliary Ferrying Squadron, the WAFS, since last year. In one month all women service pilots will become WASPs (Women's Air Force Service Pilots). Don't you just love the cute little names they create for us?
>
> I hope the women we recruited for the yard are working out. We need them so badly in the labor force. Just as we need women pilots to free up men for combat.
>
> I must say this job certainly has its moments. Last year I qualified to fly the B- (blacked out). They really need those planes in England so I volunteered to fly one over. Nancy sold it as part of the evaluation to see if women could do the job. I was the co-pilot. We were in a flight of 8 planes, with another B- (blacked out) and 6 P- (blacked out). We flew from Seattle to Long Island and on to Goose (blacked out).

Macie couldn't decipher the blacked out words. Derek knew from the reference to Seattle Roxie was flying a Boeing B-17 Flying Fortress. He also deduced she meant the huge new airbase at Goose Bay, Newfoundland.

> Those fighters are beautiful little airplanes with their twin booms and dual engines. I'm already checked out in that type and hope to be able to ferry them someday. That would be a rush!

Derek explained his interpretation each time Macie got stumped by the censor's deletions. Roxie was describing a Lockheed P-38 Lightning, a fast twin-engine pursuit plane. She was doing a good job communicating through the censor's erasures.

Our destination was (blacked out) using the northern ferry route. At the last minute, the brass found out that a woman pilot was involved and they pulled me from the mission, which was called Operation (blacked out).

"I've heard of Operation Bolero. It's a massive effort to get planes to England quickly."

I was really disappointed they wouldn't let me finish the mission. I was told they couldn't risk losing a woman. When will they ever let us decide what risks we're willing to take? Anyway, the flight ran into some serious weather and had to set down on the (blacked out) icecap. They all landed safely to ride out the storm. The army sent a rescue party. They had to leave the planes but saved all the pilots.

"It had to be the Greenland Icecap she was referring to," Derek concluded.

The thing I like most about this job, aside from actually flying the planes, is the look on the men's faces when they see a woman is flying it. That awesome look of wonder always brings a smile to my face. It's the best feeling in the world. Please write back. Tell me how the ships are progressing at the yard and how our lady recruits are doing. You too.
Your friend, Roxie

When Macie finished the letter, she handed it back. "Oh my gosh! She's amazing. She is one strong woman. I really do want to be more like her."

"You will...you are," Derek corrected himself. "When I write back, I'm going to tell her our lady recruits are doing just fine and that our prized recruit from Bedford, Virginia, just got promoted to supervisor." He had a huge smile on his face.

Macie blushed. "So, my good friend Derek. You didn't do anything to help me get this promotion. What kind of friend *are* you, anyway? Not helping your friend get ahead." She was toying with him, just having some fun.

Derek didn't realize she was joking. He got defensive. "I'm trying to be the best friend you ever had. I'd be more if I could but I'll settle for *friend* if that's all there is."

She turned on her stool to face him. He had broken the unspoken rule between them. Ever since she met him he intrigued her. She knew, as much as a woman's intuition could assure her, he liked her a lot. The fact that he was always a perfect gentleman was part of the reason she enjoyed his company. And he made her laugh. In fact, she not only liked to spend time with him but also felt safe with him. There were flirtations, of course, hugs and gentle kisses on the cheeks but he had never outwardly professed any love for her nor made any intimate advances. There were even times, she had to admit to herself, that she purposely tempted him with any number of playful, teasing gestures. He never bit. Derek, she concluded, would never make a serious sexual advance toward her. Nor would he speak of any. She was happy he never forced her to decide to accept or reject his advances.

"You want us to be more than friends?" Her candor shocked him. Derek became embarrassed and was not sure how to respond. He brushed back a wisp of blond hair from his forehead with his prosthetic hand.

"I know it's not possible," he replied slowly to her question. "You have Jake and I respect that. But in another time or in another life, I could easily see myself with you."

"And what about this life?" she probed.

"Yes," he confessed. "I want that all the time. But I'm not going to screw up our friendship. I'm not even sure you would choose me if things were different." He briefly waved his crippled hand.

"You're a good guy, Derek. You'll make some girl very happy someday and your handicap won't matter any more to her than it does to me. Nobody even notices any more."

"Thanks, Macie, but if it's all the same to you, I don't want to rock the boat. I'm perfectly happy to keep things between us just the way they are."

She too enjoyed the status quo. The last thing she wanted to do was to have this conversation. He didn't even date other women as far as she knew. "Maybe I shouldn't be taking advantage of you this way, Derek. I'm feeling a little selfish wanting to have both Jake and your company and friendship at the same time. You should be dating and not spending all your time with me."

"It's perfectly fine with me and besides," he stopped in mid sentence.

"What?"

He shook his head. "Never mind, this is coming out all wrong. There's no right way to say it."

"Go ahead. Say it. Let's get it all out in the open, once and for all."

Derek was struggling with this conversation. "I just want you to know, if anything happens to Jake…I'll be here for you." He took a deep breath. "There, I said it."

Macie just stared silently at him. There was no emotion on her face to betray her feelings.

"I'm sorry, Macie. I didn't mean to offend you. Please…"

She held up her hand to silence him. "You're right, Derek."

"About what?"

"There was no right way to say *that*."

Chapter Thirty-Five

Rome, Italy - September 7, 1943

"Secret operations are essential in war;
upon them the army relies to make its every move."

Sun Tzu (544 BC - 496 BC), *The Art of War*

Jake Kilroy peeked through a small clear spot in the translucent glass side-pane of the Italian military ambulance. The heavily armed German guard on the other side of the glass was speaking to the ambulance driver. Lying on a stretcher, Jake could see the long trains parked at the sidings in the rail yard. What he observed in the rail yard and from the soldier's collar insignia disturbed him even more than the proximity of the guard.

Johnny Kilroy lay on one of four stretchers secured to the interior sides of the ambulance, two on each side, stacked like bunk beds. Brigadier General Maxwell D. Taylor and Colonel William T. Gardiner occupied the last two stretchers. An Italian officer disguised as a medical orderly sat quietly on a small seat between them. Jake gently pressed the barrel of his M1911A1 .45-caliber sidearm to his lips in a gesture to silence the two officers on the other side of the vehicle. They nodded their understanding.

The German guard waved them through. This was the fourth and last checkpoint on their bumpy seventy-five mile trip to Rome along the historic Appian Way from the port city of Gaeta. Italian soldiers manned all the previous checkpoints and thus far no one had searched the ambulance. After a grueling nineteen-hour sea and land trip, the four soldiers were finally making their nocturnal entrance into the Eternal City.

Before the guns were silenced on Sicily, Allied strategic planners were already contemplating their next move. Against American objections, the British preference to invade the Italian boot prevailed.

On 23 July, while Allied forces were still fighting on Sicily, the Combined Chiefs of Staff ordered General Dwight D. Eisenhower to mount an invasion of Italy by 9 September. The ideal invasion objective would have been up the peninsula somewhere near Rome. Rome, however, was beyond the range of fighter cover. After their bloody experience in the waters off Sicily, Allied Commanders demanded continuous superior air cover for the invasion force. Thus, the choice was narrowed down to a wide bay just to the south of Naples called the Gulf of Salerno. The operation was codenamed Avalanche.

Just after Eisenhower received orders to plan Operation Avalanche, there was an astonishing political development. King Victor Emmanuel III of Italy arrested and deposed his Prime Minister of twenty-one years, Benito Mussolini, and exiled him. The king replaced *Il Duce* with the aging ex-military officer Marshall Pietro Badoglio. Hitler was furious. Although Badoglio publicly reaffirmed the "Pact of Steel" which bound Italy and Germany as partners, Hitler remained unconvinced and suspicious. He sent German troops to Italy under the guise of helping his ally defend their homeland.

King Victor Emmanuel, influenced by the first Allied bomber raid on Rome on 19 July, gave Badoglio secret orders to negotiate a separate peace with the Allies. Badoglio ordered Lieutenant General Guiseppe Castellano to make clandestine contact with the British and open direct negotiations.

Secret dispatches began flying immediately to Eisenhower's headquarters in Algiers from London and Washington. He was prodded to make an aggressive move to capitalize on this remarkable development. In response, Eisenhower busied General Ridgway to plan various airborne missions to take advantage of the possibility that a carefully placed airborne drop might facilitate Italy's surrender.

Eisenhower was then ordered to send representatives to the negotiations in neutral Lisbon, Portugal on 19 August. He sent American General Walter Bedell Smith, his Chief of Staff and British Brigadier General Kenneth D. Strong.

The Allied negotiators took a hard line with Castellano. They reiterated President Franklin D. Roosevelt's demand for "unconditional surrender" announced at the Casablanca Conference in January. They told Castellano if Italy wanted out of the War, they would have to sign an unconditional surrender agreement. Castellano was shocked. He came to negotiate but instead he was given an ultimatum and a deadline to accept or reject the Allied conditions.

Castellano returned to Italy, conferred with the Prime Minister and the king and radioed his governments' acceptance of the terms. However, when he showed up in Sicily on 31 August to sign the surrender documents, he had both reservations and conditions. After an angry exchange between he and General Smith, Castellano explained that the Germans were becoming stronger around Rome and that Castellano's first priority was to protect his government and the King. However, if the Allies would parachute troops into Rome, Italy would surrender on the morning of the invasion. If the Allies refused, Italy would not surrender until the Allies were in Italy in adequate strength to protect the King and the new government.

General Smith flew to Bizerte, North Africa with Castellano. Armed with the airborne idea, Castellano pleaded his case directly to Eisenhower. The opportunity to knock Italy out of the War with one stroke of the pen was too great to disregard. In addition to the forces on the Italian Peninsula, Italy fielded twenty-nine divisions in the Balkans and five in France. Eisenhower concurred and he and Castellano signed the surrender documents on 3 September. The

Americans agreed to drop the 82nd Airborne to secure Rome in synchronization with Operation Avalanche.

When Ridgway received these orders from Eisenhower he was beside himself. The plan called for parachute and air landing operations at five airports in Rome's northern suburbs. It was codenamed Giant Two but immediately took on the nickname, the "Rome Job".

Ridgway tried to convince his superiors that the operation was flawed. He explained to the supreme ground commander, General Sir Harold Alexander, he didn't have enough time to train for this operation. His division was scattered all over Sicily and North Africa, as were the planes of Troop Carrier Command. The mission required yet another long night flight over water for which no level of competence had yet been demonstrated and no training had been accomplished since Sicily. If that were not sufficient to cancel the operation, the flight was too far for fighter escort. That left the transports vulnerable to prowling *Luftwaffe* fighters. Even if these obstacles could be overcome, Ridgway had serious doubts the Italians could even hold the airfields for the drop and subsequent re-supply missions. If the Germans were around Rome in strength, and even Castellano admitted they were rushing in more troops, the division could get slaughtered. Ridgway desperately wanted Alexander to cancel the Rome Job.

The lure of knocking Italy completely out of the War was far too great. With Churchill and President Roosevelt solidly behind the endeavor, it would have taken a compelling reason to abort the mission. Besides, as Alexander pointed out, the Rome Job was already committed to the new Italian government and was a key component of the armistice they just signed.

Ridgway did manage to get an important concession. He was convinced the Italians could not deliver on their promises but he needed first hand evidence of his suspicions. General Alexander permitted Ridgway to smuggle two of his senior officers into Rome just before the planned drop to make a first hand assessment of the situation. If they suspected a trap or the inability of the Italians to guarantee their safety, they could call off the Rome Job.

General Taylor, Assistant Division Commander of the 82nd Airborne, volunteered to go. He was fluent in five languages and had Ridgway's complete confidence. Taylor was also highly respected by Eisenhower who was becoming more skeptical of the Rome Job as additional problems came to light. Taylor would bring Colonel Gardiner, an intelligence officer from the 51st Troop Carrier Group. Together, they would collaborate on the feasibility of success.

The wheels began to turn at 82nd Airborne Division Headquarters. Working with the British and Italians, transportation was arranged. It was determined that bodyguards would be needed. The division's Personnel Officer, the G-1, found three paratroopers with Italian and French language skills. One was an officer who had been wounded in Sicily and was in a hospital in Tunisia. Another was a sergeant killed in action in a place called Santa Croce Camerina. The third was a private in the 3rd Battalion of the 505th PIR that was currently bivouacked in the town of Castelvetrano. Immediate Priority AAA orders were cut for Private John P. Kilroy. The orders were sent over field telephone to 505th Regimental Headquarters (HQ).

High priority orders from Division HQ were not unusual but always a big deal. 505th HQ sent word down to 3rd Battalion HQ who bucked them over to Item Company. They were to detach and transport Private John Kilroy to Palermo for special assignment on the fastest available transport to be at the main warehouse on the wharf by 2330 hours, 6 September.

Staff Sergeant Gene Bancroft had only one question. *Which John Kilroy did they want?* When no one up the chain of command could answer that simple question quickly. Bancroft decided to cut orders for both. They could always send one back. Besides, this was the best way he could assure that his temporary lapse in courage would never be revealed. He had the company clerk type out the high priority orders and the officer of the day signed them for Colonel Gavin.

Both men were told to leave everything and were hustled onto a waiting C-47 that was officially "hijacked" from ferry duty between Sicily and North Africa. This bird had only one mission; fly two soldiers to Palermo.

Jake and Johnny were flabbergasted. At first they believed they were in trouble but then soon realized they were involved in a hush-hush operation. The flight was short and a waiting jeep sped them through town to the wharf and dropped them at a dilapidated warehouse. The armed guards outside checked their orders. Nobody along the way could tell them where they were going or why they were there. But here they were, in the dead of night, standing in the fog outside the doors of an old warehouse on the docks of Palermo.

The dark spacious warehouse smelled strongly of fish. In one corner under a bright lamp were two men. One was a sergeant and the other an officer, a tall, stout-looking colonel. The colonel was removing his rank insignia from his uniform. The two soldiers stepped briskly into the light and right up to the officer and were about to salute when Colonel Gardiner stopped them with a raised hand. "No saluting. From now on, I'm just Bill." He extended his hand.

"Johnny."

"Jake." They shook hands.

Gardiner didn't question the order for two escorts but was a bit surprised neither of them were officers. He continued. "I'm from Troop Carrier Command. Tonight we're taking a trip into Rome with General Taylor." He ignored the stunned looks on their faces. "You won't be saluting him either." The two soldiers nodded, unable to speak through gaping jaws.

"You're my language-skilled bodyguards, right?"

"That's right Bill," answered Johnny while he nudged Jake.

"Yup, that'd be us," Jake offered.

"Thanks for volunteering," Gardiner snickered.

Taylor was not at all keen on the idea of bodyguards but Gardiner convinced him otherwise, especially if they could find paratroopers who could speak the languages. The negotiations with the Italians were to be conducted in French. However, there would be collateral Italian spoken, hence the requirement for those two languages.

"Now empty your pockets of everything, especially personal items, tear off your unit and rank insignias and give everything to the sergeant here. Your belongings will be sent back to your units." The two troopers complied.

"Boots also," Gardiner pointed.

"Jeez, the boots too, Bill?" Jake complained.

"Boots too. You'll wear standard issue boots and bare basic uniforms under plain wool navy pea coats. If we're captured, hopefully that will prevent us from being shot as spies."

Captured? Jake looked hard at Johnny through squinted eyes. Johnny cocked his head slightly and flicked his eyebrows in response. They would talk about that later. Gardiner continued, "The sergeant here will arm you with forty-fives. Just in case."

Each trooper was given a .45-caliber semi-automatic pistol and an M36 belt with holster. The belt carried eight extra clips of ammunition. Both troopers worked the slides of their semi-automatic pistols, dry fired the weapons, eyed the sights, slapped in a clip and holstered the weapons. The pistols were nicely concealed once they donned their pea coats.

They waited patiently for an hour until Taylor entered the warehouse from a dockside entrance. "Bill, the PT boat will be here shortly. Everything is all set."

He turned to the two paratroopers. "I'm Max." He didn't extend his hand. "Remember that. No slipups."

"Johnny." He didn't extend his hand either.

"No problem, Max," Jake answered sarcastically. "I'm Jake."

Taylor came right back at Jake. "You've been told where we're going. Do your jobs and don't get in the way." He turned away and then turned back. "Can you handle a wireless?"

"We've been trained on lots of different radios, Max," Johnny answered.

"Yeah, Max, we're paratroopers. We got skills and can do a lot of stuff." Jake added. He was having difficulty with the General's dismissive attitude but was enjoying the repartee and took pleasure in tweaking him.

"Good, then take care of this," he slid a dark brown suitcase out from under a table. It looked like any other ordinary leather suitcase. Johnny took the handle from Taylor who walked outside and waited on the dock. It was rather heavy for its size. Johnny concluded it was a high-powered short-wave radio.

Gardiner broke the silence. "This trip has three legs. The first is a fast patrol boat. Then we transfer to an Italian corvette. That's the long leg. We'll slip into port disguised as rescued seamen. The ruse is that we'll appear to be under arrest from the boat to the vehicle. Then it's up to the Italians to drive us into Rome. That's all you need to know for now."

Both men nodded. Jake began pacing. Johnny and Gardiner sat in silence until they heard the deep-throated roar of high-powered gasoline engines outside. A Motor Torpedo Boat was nestling up to the pier. It was dark gray and flying the British Union Jack.

Some crewmen helped the four men onto the craft. The officers went immediately to the small bridge. Jake could see on the side of the open bridge the faint designation *MTB-102* peeking through dark paint. Someone tried to hide it. A crewman took Jake and Johnny below deck through a covered hatch to a crew space. Immediately, the lines were cast off and the small craft carefully picked its way out of Palermo Harbor. There would be no use for guards on this leg of the journey. However, they would have to be on their toes once they boarded the Italian vessel.

A Royal Navy crewman gave each of them a tin cup filled with rum and some hard biscuits. Johnny crunched down on the hard and tasteless biscuit. Jake soaked his in the rum before biting it. The rum warmed their insides. They sat in silence with the British crewman in the cramped area. The less said, the better.

The engines revved and suddenly there was a sensation of great speed. The front of the MTB lifted out of the water and a huge bow wave sprinkled seawater back onto the deck. The paratroopers finished their rum and biscuits and stepped up the stairs.

"You can sit on the top step, mates. No place to dally about on deck," the crewman explained. He stepped between them and took his position in a .20-millimeter Oerlikon gun tub near the stern and began scanning the horizon.

Johnny felt a little queasy. He had a penchant for getting seasick. The fact that he couldn't swim well contributed to his concern. The covered hatch offered some protection from the sea spray and he had a good view of the giant rooster tail wake being kicked up by the churning propellers. Johnny looked up at the starry night sky and found the Big Dipper and then the North Star. He estimated they were traveling over forty knots in a straight line directly north. They were in the Tyrrhenian Sea north of Sicily and he distracted himself with the notion he was riding the same waves that Roman triremes rode some 2,000 years before. The profoundness of that realization momentarily relieved him of any anxiety. He noted the location of the nearest lifejacket, held the suitcase tightly and decided to remain silent in deference to the growling roar of the three powerful engines.

They were only cruising at top speed for a little over an hour when they heard the engines gently cut back and felt the bow of the MTB glide smoothly back into the calm sea. They were approaching a landmass, a little island, and maneuvering into a small, protected bay. Another ship, a Gabbiano class corvette flying the Italian flag with the cross of Savoy, was waiting at anchor off the island of Ustica. The two ships exchanged recognition signals and the MTB pulled up alongside the larger craft's illuminated deck.

The captain of the MTB shook hands with Taylor and Gardiner as they climbed the short ladder to the deck of the corvette. Johnny and Jake followed. The crews of both boats moved quickly and silently as the sunrise was beginning to lighten the eastern sky.

"Welcome aboard the *Ibis*," the Italian captain said in reasonably good English. "Please follow my first officer to your quarters below."

The MTB separated from the corvette, circled slowly and departed in the direction from which it came. Jake looked at the speedy boat forlornly and realized their job of guardians just became a lot more serious. He watched the MTB gun her engines and disappear swiftly into the western darkness.

The Italian first officer showed Taylor and Gardiner into a small stateroom and the two paratroopers to an adjacent cabin. Johnny stowed the radio in their room.

Once the transfer of personnel was completed, the anchor was quickly raised and the idling engines came to life. The sleek ship jerked into motion as the propeller shafts engaged. She moved slowly and deliberately at first and gradually picked up speed until she eventually cleared the sheltered bay and was out into the open sea.

At 200 feet, the *Ibis* was over three times longer than *MTB-102*. She mounted a 4-inch gun on her foredeck and two eighteen inch torpedo tubes on her sides. For anti-aircraft defense she had seven .20-millimeter cannons. Her twin-shafts, powered by two diesel-electric engines, pushed out 2,500 horsepower and propelled her to speeds upwards of nineteen knots. She was a new ship with sleek lines and kept exceptionally clean by her one hundred-man crew.

This would be the longest leg of their journey, even though the Italian captain had obviously pushed the throttles to the wall. They each scouted a few yards up and down the corridor and took up positions on either side of the stateroom housing their officers.

Jake spoke first. "I don't know how we got into this but I still haven't changed my mind about becoming a prisoner. I won't be taken."

"I know how I got into this," Johnny answered. "Language skills. Had to be. I put down I'm fluent in Italian and French."

"Well I ain't," Jake countered. "Max will sure be pissed when he finds out."

"Jake, it's not on you if the army fouled up and sent you here by mistake." Johnny looked at him seriously. "I don't know why the hell they picked you, but I'm glad you're here."

Jake noticed how sincere his buddy was. "I know. But I'm still not being taken prisoner."

Jake reached into his pocket, took out a small Bible and began reading. Johnny noticed and said, "Jake, for as long as I know you, I never knew that you were a 'Bible Thumper.'"

"You mean this?" Jake pointed to his Bible. "It belonged to my daddy. It was the only thing left to me from my folks. I figured I must have held on to it for a reason. So I started reading it in North Africa."

"Does it help?"

Jake flashed his infectious smile. "Do you believe in God, Yank?"

Johnny pondered the question. "They say there are no atheists in foxholes. That everybody believes in God when they go to war. But I can't honestly say that I do."

"Well, maybe the War will change all that," Jake replied.

"Change that? For Chrissake Jake, I'm doing everything *not* to change. I liked my life before the War and I want to go back and pick right up where I left off. I liked who I was, so I'm trying my damnedest not to let anything I see or do in this fucking War change me. When it's over, I just want to be that guy I was before all this shit!"

"That's gonna' be hard, Johnny, even for you." Jake reflected a moment on the ghastly things he had seen since he became a soldier. "I'm hoping this War changes me a lot and for the better. I'm trying to turn everything I see into a lesson to make me a better person. I want to speak better, learn more about the world around me, become smarter, like you."

Johnny was unprepared for the compliment. It was the kind of thing one says to another when he expects not to see him again. "Thanks," Johnny replied. "But you've always had a more realistic grip on this War than me. And I think because you want to improve yourself so badly…well…you're probably the smarter one already."

The *Ibis* plowed relentlessly through the seas all through the night and into the next day. They came within distant sight of the Island of Ponza on the starboard beam in the Gulf of Naples. No one on the *Ibis* knew that Ponza was the island where their former *Il Duce*, Benito Mussolini, was currently living in exile. The Americans were now deep into the belly of the beast and clearly at the mercy of their one-time enemies. It wouldn't take much treachery for all of them to wind up in a Nazi prison camp or worse. Not that they could have done much on the ship outnumbered as they were. But they stayed alert.

During the voyage, the four Americans were fed and treated respectfully by the officers and crew. Late the following afternoon Johnny spotted land and a port city surrounded by ancient walls. A crewman told him it was the ancient port city of Gaeta. He remembered reading about the legend of the Trojan hero

Aeneas, son of Aphrodite, who, according to the poet Virgil, named the city after his wet nurse, Caieta.

They put in motion the deception they agreed upon; that the Americans were a group of sailors rescued from the sea. Just before the *Ibis* pulled into the dock, crewmen splashed buckets of water over the Americans wetting their hair and coats. As soon as the *Ibis* tied up at the dock, the four Americans were hustled roughly down the gangplank by armed Italian sailors. They were shoved brusquely into a waiting Italian navy vehicle and drove off. No one in the militarized port seemed to pay much attention. Once they reached the outskirts of Gaeta, they transferred to a military ambulance for the long trip to Rome.

Once inside the city, the ambulance took them to the Italian Supreme Headquarters in the Palazzo Caprara on the Via Firenze. The American officers had hoped to meet with Lieutenant General Giacomo Carboni, commander of the Italian corps assigned to defend Rome, and Prime Minister Badoglio. Instead they were greeted warmly by other lesser-ranking generals and were told Carboni and Badoglio were unavailable.

Jake and Johnny checked out the rooms adjacent to the large dining room and all appeared normal. The Italian generals seemed to have no sense of urgency. They began serving the American officers a sumptuous dinner. The two American bodyguards took up positions immediately outside the kitchen. When it was time to eat, they were served figs, grapes, and chunks of cheese with Parma ham. They ate standing up. Johnny asked for Espresso coffee. It was served thick, black and strong and helped the boys stay awake. The two bodyguards whispered quietly among themselves while they remained heedful of their surroundings. As they vigilantly moved about the dining vicinity and adjoining areas, they never let the two American officers out of their sight.

Johnny noticed General Taylor was becoming agitated. While the Italian generals were making a great show of enjoying their leisurely meal, the Americans were pressing them for details. Taylor kept telling them he needed to see the general in charge as well as the Prime Minister. Finally, at around ten in the evening, Generale di Corpo d'Armata Giacomo Carboni made an appearance in his highly polished cavalry boots and beribboned dress uniform.

Taylor pressed Carboni for answers. Carboni was immediately pessimistic about the ability of the three divisions of his corps to support the airborne landings. In addition, he seriously doubted the Prime Minister would announce the surrender on the evening of the eighth as previously committed. Carboni treated the entire issue with a casual disregard, further frustrating and infuriating Taylor. Johnny could tell by the snippets of conversation he picked up the discussion was not going well. Taylor did not seem the least bit impressed with General Carboni. With so much on the line and getting nowhere fast, Taylor insisted on seeing the Prime Minister immediately. Carboni was reluctant to disturb the Prime Minister at such a late hour. Pressed by Taylor and after some frantic phone calls, Prime Minister Pietro Badoglio agreed to see the Americans.

Carboni drove the Americans in his own car through a hot and humid blacked out city. The three golden stars on the car's flag guaranteed they would not be stopped at checkpoints or by roving patrols. Taylor observed that Italian soldiers, not Germans, manned the patrols and checkpoints. *Could it be that General Carboni was exaggerating the difficulty of supporting the American airborne forces?*

Prime Minister Badoglio received the Americans in his luxurious villa on the outskirts of the city, a gift from Il Duce for leading the invasion of Abyssinia. He was in his pajamas, looking particularly old and tired. They sat on facing couches. The discussion took place in French as Johnny Kilroy eavesdropped from his position inside the window overlooking the garden. Taylor didn't particularly like Badoglio and didn't enjoy having to negotiate with him. The rumors of atrocities committed under his command in East Africa were rampant. Nevertheless, Taylor apologized for inconveniencing the Prime Minister at such a late hour.

Badoglio essentially repeated what Carboni told the Americans. He embellished the details with accounts of German forces already disarming some Italian units, cutting off gasoline and ammunition supplies and moving reinforcements and armor into Rome. Badoglio rattled off some of the German units involved including the 3rd *Panzer* Grenadier Division and the 2nd Parachute Division. Taylor and Gardiner had seen no evidence of this. Badoglio did not want to antagonize the Germans. He would wait for the Allies to invade in sufficient force to be able to protect Rome before he announced an Italian surrender.

The discussion dragged on fruitlessly into the early morning hours of 8 September. Eisenhower planned to announce the surrender of Italy late that day just ahead of the invasion and expected the Italian government would make the same announcement to its own people. American paratroopers were at that precise moment gearing up in Sicily to depart at 1830 hours for the flight to Rome. The Italians were not privy to the exact time of the invasion and thus were not behaving with any sense of urgency. All of Taylor's efforts to move them to action were in vain. The Italians stubbornly stuck to their position. They could not support the airborne drop and would not announce their government's surrender to their people later that night.

Taylor reminded Badoglio the Allies already had the signed surrender agreement and General Eisenhower would not take kindly to this duplicity. All Badoglio could do was cite the changes in circumstances. Taylor offered to use his clandestine radio link to transmit any message Badoglio might want to send. While Badoglio went off into another room to compose his message, Taylor paced the floor. He was furious. The Allies had been suckered into signing an armistice agreement with the new Italian government at that government's initiative.

The Allies then based their operational plans and timetables on the agreed-to surrender. Now the Italians were backing out and leaving the Anglo-American forces high and dry. This was unacceptable to Taylor and infuriated him.

He spoke to Gardiner in English. "What do you think, Bill?"

"The Italians don't seem to want to piss off the Germans…but Ike will really be pissed." Gardiner reflected a moment. "Seems like they're more afraid of the Krauts than of us."

"Wouldn't you be?"

Gardiner nodded.

"Thing is," Taylor continued, "Ike may go ahead and announce the surrender anyway even if Badoglio doesn't. After all, he has the signed agreement. The real question is can we make Giant Two work without Italian support?"

"Hell, if they got no gas…" Gardiner began. The drop zones were over twenty miles north and west of Rome. The paratroopers were counting on Italian motor transport to get to the city.

"That's just it," Taylor interrupted. "We both agree these guys don't want to fight and are scared shit of the Germans. They want to sit tight and let us do all the dirty work until it's safe for them to surrender. Like, after we conquer the entire country." Taylor's words were dripping with sarcasm. "What if they're making up all this crap about reinforcements and armor to justify postponing the surrender? What if they're making it all up just to discourage us? Hell, I haven't seen a German soldier in Rome since that last checkpoint. I haven't seen any evidence to support what they're saying. And that's exactly why we're here. Not just to listen but to see first hand."

"Why would they make all that up?" Gardiner sounded exasperated.

"Because they don't want to fight, that's why. Because they're afraid of what will happen to them and their villas and their privileges if they get caught on the wrong side of the fight." Taylor paused to let his words sink in. "Because they got in over their heads in the first place and are trying to squirm out of it now. So they make shit up so we have to cancel the airborne drop."

Gardiner reflected for a moment. "You know Ike really wants Giant Two to go. He's under enormous pressure to get Italy out of the War. We could save a lot of lives if we can pull this off. But if the Italians are correct and are not just playing cutesy, it could be a slaughter."

Jake and Johnny had been listening carefully. They moved closer to the couch where the officers were speaking.

"I know," Taylor sighed heavily. "And my boss has been skeptical from the beginning," referring to General Ridgway. "But we need to have good reason to cancel it and all I have right now is the shaky word of a bunch of scared Italians."

Johnny edged a little closer. Taylor looked up at him, annoyed at the intrusion. "Yes, trooper?"

Johnny looked at Jake. "For Chrissake, tell him what you've been telling me, Jake."

Taylor looked at Jake. "Well, spit it out soldier."

"It may be nothing, sir, but when we went through that rail yard just outside the city, I saw some things looking out the window."

Taylor sat up. Jake had been the only one who had a clear view outside. "What did you see? Did you see any tanks?"

"Not exactly."

"C'mon, soldier what did you see?"

"Flatcars, sir. They were empty but there were only flatcars on all three trains."

"So, you saw flatcars? So what?" Taylor sounded abrupt.

Gardiner leaned forward, suddenly interested. "Wait a second. Flatcars move vehicles, right?" He aimed his question at Jake.

"In this case, heavy vehicles."

"How can you tell that?" Taylor asked, now also interested.

"Each train had three locomotives." Jake looked directly at Taylor, no longer hesitant. "I know railroads. You only chain that many together when you're pulling a very heavy train."

"Like one with tanks and heavy artillery," Taylor sighed.

"That's not all, sir," Johnny chimed in. He looked at Jake. "Tell him."

"What else did you see, son?" Taylor was not only now interested but also more receptive.

"That guard at the checkpoint was *Fallschrimjager*, a German paratrooper."

"And you know that, how?" Gardiner challenged.

"I was just inches away from him, sir. He was wearing a paratrooper badge on his collar."

"You sure, son?" Gardiner asked.

"Absolutely positive, sir. We captured a few in Sicily. Tough bastards," Jake added.

Taylor took a deep breath. He believed the Italians may have lost their nerve and their will to fight but they weren't lying about the Germans moving strong forces into Rome. "God help me, but I'm pulling the plug on Giant Two." He looked at Gardiner. "You agree, Bill?"

Taylor had the utmost respect for Gardiner. He had once been the governor of the state of Maine. He was intelligent and level headed. Taylor could not have hoped for a more competent officer to accompany him. "I agree, wholeheartedly."

"Begging the General's pardon, sir, but we had our fill of fighting Tigers on Sicily," Johnny recalled. "I know the boys would appreciate not having to fight tanks with their bare hands here in Rome."

Taylor didn't respond. In his heart he knew he was preventing a slaughter.

He also knew that by passing on this opportunity, he would subject himself to merciless second-guessing from the highest levels of government and maybe Ike too. However great the risk to his own career, he had made up his mind. *Now, to stop Giant Two before the planes got in the air.*

In the dead of night, Carboni drove back to the Palazzo Caprara where the Americans and Italians quickly coded and sent two messages to Eisenhower's headquarters. The first, from Badoglio, simply stated it was no longer possible for the Italian government to accept an armistice and the Italians could no longer guarantee the airfields. The second message from Taylor stated Giant Two was impossible based on the increased German presence around Rome.

Taylor waited for an acknowledgement. He received one for Badoglio's message and could only imagine the fury it caused at Ike's headquarters. Late that afternoon, coded instructions were sent to Taylor to return to Algiers immediately. The Americans took General Francesco Rossi of the Italian Supreme General Staff to explain the Italian position to Eisenhower. The small group was driven in the same military ambulance through enemy infested Rome to Centocelli Airfield on the outskirts of the Eternal City. Once there they boarded a Savoia-Marchetti tri-motor bomber for the two-hour flight.

Meanwhile, Eisenhower replied to Badoglio and advised the Prime Minister he had in his possession the surrender documents signed by Italy's duly authorized representative and planned to announce the surrender at 1830 hours that same evening. If Badoglio failed to also make his planned radio announcement to the Italian people and military, Eisenhower would expose Italy's duplicity to the whole world and Italy would "suffer the most serious consequences including the dissolution of the Italian government and nation." Ike was playing hardball with Badoglio.

In the meantime Ridgway's Pathfinders took off while the rest of the 504th PIR boarded their C-47s. When the cancellation orders finally arrived, Ridgway was delighted to recall the sixty planes that were already in the air heading for the Cerveteri and Fubara airfields north of Rome. He knew Taylor had made the right call and his division had avoided a massacre.

At 1830 hours Eisenhower made his announcement over Radio Algiers. He stated the Italian forces had surrendered unconditionally and were granted a military armistice. An hour later Prime Minister Badoglio came on the air and shocked the world by stating the same thing. Italy was officially out of War. Ike had forced Badoglio's hand.

Meanwhile, the Italian plane ferrying the American group delivered its human cargo safely to an airfield near Eisenhower's Headquarters. Two waiting jeeps with armed escorts drove the men to the immense white building that served as Allied Headquarters.

Taylor, Gardiner and Rossi were ushered in to see General Eisenhower. Jake and Johnny waited outside. After a few minutes, Gardiner came back out. He put his arms around Jake and Johnny and walked them to the side of the building out of earshot.

"You boys did a great job. I'd get you a medal if this wasn't so hush-hush."

"Thank you, sir," Jake smiled. "I guess we can't call you Bill, anymore."

"Did our guys get the word in time?" Johnny asked.

"They did. The drop was cancelled."

Both boys let out audible sighs of relief. Gardiner continued. "And Ike made the announcement anyway. Bullied Badoglio to do the same. Italy is out of the War."

"Wow, that's swell news, sir," Johnny smiled.

Gardiner looked at Jake. "Some in high places are not happy having to cancel the drop. General Taylor is in for some heat on this. But he's convinced he did the right thing and the critical observations you made convinced him the drop would be a slaughter."

Jake put his head down, speechless. Johnny put his hand on Jake's shoulder and shook it in a sign of congratulations.

"We'll be flying back to Sicily. You'll be back with your unit pretty soon. Needless to say, where you were and what you did the past two days is top secret. Nobody knows except General Taylor and me. You're to tell no one, ever." Gardiner was calm and matter of fact. What he said next shocked the boys. "If you do, you could be shot. So, please don't ever say a word about this mission to anyone."

The two paratroopers nodded solemnly.

"Your country owes you a great debt," Gardiner continued. "I'm sorry that my 'thank you' is all you're ever going to get." Gardiner shook their hands one at a time. "One more thing," he looked at Jake. "You can call me Bill, anytime."

At 0330 hours the next morning, 9 September 1943, 450 ships disembarked the Allied invasion force at Salerno. The troops stormed ashore buoyed by the knowledge that Italy was out of the fight.

Chapter Thirty-Six

L'Enfant Plaza Hotel - January 13, 1997

"Who naught suspects is easily deceived."

Petrarch (AD 1304 - 1374)

"We were really glad to see the boys show up after disappearing for those few days. They seemed happy to be back too. No one told us where they went. They wouldn't say anything either, not even to me." Sky sipped his Prop-Blast and held the glass up to the dim light and looked at it. "Brings back lots of memories."

"Did you ever find out where they were?" Cynthia asked.

Harley answered. "Not until much later, kid. They were on a top secret mission."

J.P. was intrigued by that answer but suppressed any reaction. The busboys came by again and cleared the last of the utensils. They even cleaned off the already clean white tablecloth with their little crumb-scrapers. The waitress remained by the kitchen door and held the dinner bill in a leather folder with hands clasped across her apron. J.P. knew he had run out of time. He signaled the waitress and she was over in a flash. He placed his American Express card on top of the folder without examining the bill. She disappeared toward the cash register.

"And you said they were transferred after that?" J.P. directed the question to Sky. He had a few more minutes before he had to sign the credit card slip and would squeeze every last drop of information possible. He sensed he would never see Sky in person again.

"Not immediately." Sky pursed his lips and squinted to help him remember. "The beachhead at Salerno was in trouble. The Germans counterattacked and punched this huge hole through American lines toward the beach. General Ridgway was ordered to send in reinforcements so we made what became know as the 'oil drum drop.'"

"Oil drum drop?" Cynthia asked. She seemed completely sober to J.P. now.

"We didn't drop oil drums," Sky chuckled. "The guys on the ground set up these sand filled fifty-five gallon drums and doused them with gasoline. They marked the drop zone, which was behind our own lines. When the planes hauling the Five-oh-four got close, the GIs on the ground lit fires in the drums. Guided them right in. Once the paratroopers hit the ground, they piled into British lorries... that's what the Limeys called trucks...and were ferried right to the front lines. They were crucial to holding the line the next day. The Five-oh-five dropped twenty-one hundred troopers on the DZ the second night. When we dropped we could hear the guys on the ground cheering. I remember it felt like the cavalry coming to the rescue. We held the beach and pushed the Krauts back. History says the Eighty-second saved the beachhead. I agree." Sky raised his glass and gulped down the last of his drink in a personal toast to that memory.

"Was that about the time they were transferred?" J.P. pressed for more even as the waitress returned his credit card and signature slip.

"Yeah, and even that was strange. Right after we loaded up on the trucks, Cannonball himself comes running to the back of each truck in a panic yelling out their names. When he found them in our truck, he pulled them out."

"What happened to them?" J.P. asked.

"They were flown back to Sicily right away. The next time I saw them was in London. They were with the Hundred and first, the Screaming Eagles. Imagine that! From an All-American to a Screaming Eagle just like that!"

"That's right, Frank said. They wound up in my company."

"I'd love to talk to you about that," J.P. said.

"My flight doesn't leave until tomorrow night. I'd be glad to meet you tomorrow." Frank seemed willing despite another stare from Harley.

"That would be great."

J.P. scrawled his signature on the credit card slip and turned to Harley. "I'd love to talk more with you."

"If I ever get back to D.C., kid, I'll be sure to look you up," Harley lied. "In the meantime, call me anytime. I'm only a four hour drive away and I'll be mostly busy with the D-Day Memorial…I'm on the committee…should break ground this year…so if you feel like taking a drive, you'd be welcomed."

"I guess I kind of dominated the conversation," Sky interjected. "Sorry, I got carried away. I hope I helped."

"You were a great help," J.P. exaggerated.

"Anyway, thanks for dinner." Talking about the War was cathartic for Sky.

The group moved slowly to the main lobby. J.P. gave his parking stub to the valet.

He turned to Cynthia. "Do you have a car?"

"I took a taxi."

"Can I give you a lift?"

She clutched his arm suggestively. "I thought you'd never ask."

Frank walked over to J.P and touched his arm. "About tomorrow, Mister Kilroy, how about noon at the Wall?"

Chapter Thirty-Seven

Vietnam Veterans Memorial - January 14, 1997

"We come, not to mourn our dead soldiers, but to praise them."

Francis A. Walker (1840 - 1897)

John Patrick Kilroy Junior walked briskly south on 23rd Street past George Washington University having just exited the Metro Station at Foggy Bottom. There was a bounce in his step. It had been a long time since he had been with a woman and Cynthia proved to be more than just another woman. She was spectacular.

It was a rather mild day for January with a moderate southerly breeze just strong enough to blow his thinning hair out of place. The sky was the kind of cloudless blue panorama often referred to as "severe clear". The street traffic and tourist crowds were normal for lunchtime on a weekday in Washington, D.C.

Soon after J.P. turned left on Constitution Avenue he crossed over and entered Constitution Gardens adjacent to the National Mall on Henry Bacon Drive. He had been to the Vietnam Veterans Memorial only once, shortly after it was dedicated in 1982, and had not been back since.

The Wall, with all of its inscribed names and bequeathed flowers and mementos at its base, was barely visible until standing at the top of the sloped paved walkway. The path declined gently to the apex of the V that divided the Wall into two distinct sections at an angle of 125 degrees, 12 minutes. The bright sun was low in the southern sky over the Potomac and glared brightly off the 144 black granite panels that comprised the structure. Kilroy started to walk, apprehensively at first, but soon steadier. He was looking for Frank West and as he walked down the path, the Wall rose on his left. Soon it was well above his head and the breeze stopped. The quiet stillness was overpowering. The hairs on the back of his neck stiffened and chills ran through his body. He looked at the endless sea of names and began to perspire uncontrollably. It was as if the souls of the 58,000 fallen were all crying out to him at once, *where were you?*

Kilroy recalled the controversy that surrounded the 246-foot wall when the design was first exhibited to the public. It was radically different than the figurative memorials most people had become accustomed to for thousands of years. In addition, a young undergraduate student from Yale University by the name of Maya Lin won the public design competition over more than 2,500 applicants. Yale was a hotbed of anti-war protest and this irked many veterans. However, it was the American people who were the final arbiters. They flocked to the Wall by the millions and were universally moved by the understated symbolism of the sacrifice of American youth. The acceptance by the people, and ultimately the living veterans, validated the selection of the peculiar and emotionally moving design.

As a concession to those who initially criticized the design as too unconventional, a more traditional bronze statue was erected in 1984. The Three Soldiers statue, depicting GIs easily identifiable as African-American, Hispanic and Caucasian in combat accoutrements, stood close enough to the Wall to appear as if paying silent tribute to their fallen comrades, yet far enough away so as not to interfere. It was next to the Three Soldiers monument that Kilroy spotted Frank wearing a windbreaker with a Screaming Eagles emblem on the back and a baseball cap. J.P. ambled over to him. Frank was examining a rubbing he had taken from the wall. *Probably a friend or relative*, thought J.P. *Hopefully, not a son.*

J.P. extended his hand. "Thanks for meeting me."

Frank accepted it. "You're welcome." He placed the rubbing in his wallet. "Thanks for meeting me here. I just needed to stop by to get this rubbing."

They both looked over toward the wall. Frank said, "This is an amazing place. I get goose bumps every time I'm here."

J.P. nodded in agreement. Frank looked at him. "Did you serve?"

J.P. shook his head in the negative and changed the subject. "Are you hungry? I know a great place for lunch." He was anxious to leave.

"I can eat," replied Frank.

They walked to Constitution Avenue where J.P. hailed a taxi. "Two thousand Pennsylvania Avenue," he instructed.

In a few minutes they were outside the door of Kinkeads Brasserie, a restaurant well frequented by Washington insiders. Frank took off his baseball cap as they waited to be seated. The room was large and already filling with the lunchtime rush. The long bar was heavily built from sturdy dark wood. A piano plinked out a soft tune in the far corner. Frank leaned over to J.P. as he smoothed back his black hair. "I don't think I'm dressed properly for this place."

"No problem, Frank. They know me here."

They were seated at a table for four in a far corner away from the piano. The table was behind an artificial floor plant. A young waiter approached with menus.

"Welcome Mister Kilroy," he addressed J.P. while placing the menus on the table.

"Hello Andrew. How's school?" J.P. answered. Andrew was a student at George Washington University.

"Graduating in June, sir. Everything is going well, thank you."

J.P. scanned the menu. "I'm ready. I'll have the Fish and Chips."

Frank looked at Andrew. "The Maine lobster roll looks good. I'll have that, please."

J.P. closed his menu and looked over to Frank. "How about a nice white wine? Unless you want to order another Prop-Blast," J.P. smiled.

"That was just for memories. I never really liked the drink. Wine will be fine."

J.P. looked at Andrew. "A nice Riesling then. Lingenfelder, if you have it."

"Of course, sir." Andrew picked up the menus and left the table.

Frank looked around, a bit self-conscious about his casual dress. He removed his windbreaker, folded it and placed it along with his baseball cap on the empty seat of an adjoining chair. "I know I agreed to meet you today, Mister Kilroy, but I'm not sure what I can tell you over lunch that would satisfy your curiosity. You had a lot of questions last night."

"Well, Frank. I took the day off so I have all afternoon. I really need to know everything you can tell me about my father. This is really important to me."

"I'll do my best."

J.P. started out slowly, hoping to lull Frank into a comfort zone that would loosen him up and permit him to speak more freely than he could last night. The absence of Harley should help in this regard. In addition, J.P. listened to the recording made at the dinner table the previous evening. He learned that there was something and it certainly didn't appear to be the Rome Job. On the recording Harley had asked both of them, "Do you think he knows?" *Knows what?*

They all agreed to keep their word and not reveal anything. The most important thing J.P. learned from the recording was that there was in fact a secret, they knew what it was and they swore never to reveal it! Armed with this insight, he would have to proceed carefully.

"First time at the Wall?" J.P. asked.

"No, but this time I came to get a rubbing for my sister," he tapped the pocket holding the tissue. "My nephew was killed during Tet in sixty-eight."

J.P. lowered his head. "I'm sorry. That was a lousy war to die for."

Frank stared directly at J.P. "Any war is a lousy war to die for."

"Well at least everyone in the country was behind your war. Not like Vietnam." J.P. had intended to start slowly but quickly triggered an emotional reaction in Frank.

"The whole country was involved in *my war*. Men, women and little kids. Everyone served in some capacity. Most people accepted the hardships and inconvenience. No one felt exempt. Very few tried to shirk their responsibility and get out of it. The social pressure was immense to contribute. Politicians and their sons served. Rich, poor, black and white…everyone was all in. It was the greatest feeling in the world to know so many Americans came together, took common cause and sacrificed to defeat our enemies. This nation was one hundred percent mobilized behind the war effort. It wasn't always all perfect but we didn't have any 'Hanoi Jane'. Hell, even Hollywood was on our side back then."

J.P. smiled. He wondered how fantastic it would be if the country were to ever come together the same way again. "I guess that's why they called it 'The Good War' "

Frank looked at him strangely. "I think I heard that phrase before but I don't know anyone who served in it who would agree. No war is a good war."

"I didn't mean to say any war is good…"

"I would rather call it a *just war*," Frank interrupted. "It was a war of survival for us. They started it; they made the rules and were hell bent on our annihilation. To be fighting for your survival, in both a personal and national sense, is a great motivator. It allows brutality to exist where it could never thrive before and brutality is necessary to wage total war. And total war is the only way you can win. Especially against the evil we were fighting."

J.P. had underestimated Frank. Not only was he once a proud warrior among warriors, he could articulate the conflict intellectually. J.P decided to protract the discussion as a way of loosening him up. "You're saying we had to hate before we could fight?"

"No. I'm saying that we had to be brutal to *win*." Frank let the words sink in. "And we will never again be allowed to be as ruthless as our enemies and wage total war. Consequently, our *instant gratification, touchy-feely* society will never win another war."

"Maybe that's a good thing," J.P. mused. "I mean to put wars behind us. Hitler was a horrendous man but we had our moments of brutality, too. Like the bomb."

Frank cocked his head and looked at J.P. in a peculiar manner. His voice softened as he raised a hand toward J.P. "Whoa, there."

Just then, Andrew returned with a bottle of Lingenfelder, two glasses and an ice bucket. He opened the wine, handed J.P. the cork and poured some wine into his glass. J.P. smelled the cork, sipped the wine and Andrew poured two glasses and slid the bottle into the ice bucket.

"I never know what to do first," J.P. lifted his glass. "Sip the wine or smell the cork?"

Frank didn't touch his glass. "Before I drink with you, there is something I have to get off of my chest."

J.P. put his glass back down. Perhaps Frank was ready to level with him. "Please do."

Frank cleared his throat. "I don't know what they taught you in school, Mister Kilroy, but I hear the same thing almost everywhere I go. That we were nearly as bad as they were. There is absolutely no damn truth to that! Germany and Japan were run by regimes of pure evil. America was good. Not perfect, by any means, but deep down we are a decent people. It was simply good versus evil. That's why it was a just war."

J.P. leaned back. He had touched a nerve and could see it in Frank's expression. "No offense, Frank. It's just that we had to be brutal too, you said so yourself."

"Brutal? Yes," Frank agreed. "Because we were fighting with the tactics the other guys started with. They callously bombed cities as a terror tactic to kill civilians and break our will to fight. We bombed Europe in daylight to try to hit only military targets. Our casualties were enormous. We lost a lot of our boys over daytime Europe trying to spare civilians. Japan was another story." Frank reflected on that for a moment then continued. "They relied on cottage industries for much of their war material manufacturing. Many were small shops in the middle of cities. It was a hard decision but we had to take them out."

J.P. stared blankly, unconvinced. Frank continued.

"Near the end of the conflict we were hardened to the horrors of war. Our enemies saw to that. Whatever we did, it was about ending the War quickly and going home. So we firebombed Tokyo on March nine of forty-five. Operation Meetinghouse. We created a huge firestorm. Probably killed over a hundred thousand Japanese and made a million more homeless. And we did it again and again to other cities and they still wouldn't surrender. Finally, the bomb did it."

"So, how were we better?" J.P. challenged.

"Look, Mister Kilroy, we had to learn some lessons the hard way. American boys are, and were, mostly about fair play and mercy. That's part of our culture, our way of life. It was hard to get them whipped up but when they saw their buddies get killed by Japs who were faking surrender, it got them really angry. Soon the word got out that the Japs weren't surrendering. They refused to be taken prisoner. They would rather die. So, we killed them. It's brutal but it was war by their rules. Meanwhile, when they captured Americans, they did things like cut off their heads with samurai swords and ate the organs of our dead soldiers like cannibals."

J.P. leaned back in his chair, shocked.

"The Japanese didn't even have field medics to take care of their wounded. If they cared so little for their own, how much contempt do you think they held for their enemy? Ever hear of the Bataan Death March or what they did in China? The Japs raped and killed civilians as a matter of course. It was not only accepted, their senior leaders expected it. Whole armies were sent into China without food supplies and were ordered to live off the population. So they stole whatever they needed and killed hundreds of thousands of civilian men, women and children in the Rape of Nanking. Over eleven million civilians in total." Frank paused to let that huge number sink in. "They performed medical experiments on captured civilians. The Germans did that too. And I saw the concentration camps we liberated…the way those poor bastards looked, barely alive, skin and bones, starving, filthy, scared out of their minds. And they were the lucky ones."

"I didn't mean to…" J.P. started to say.

"Nobody means any harm when they start talking about something they know nothing about." Frank was angry. "It's frustrating to me when people who were not there and don't know shit start rewriting history. That's a slap in the face to everyone in our country who fought in the War. Especially those who didn't come back." Frank paused. J.P. looked contrite.

Frank leaned forward. "My recollections of GIs, the images that stay with me, are young guys smiling and sharing their chocolate bars with little kids and exchanging cigarettes for fresh eggs with their parents. Young boys barely out of their teens would slip K-rations to civilians while their officers looked the other way. Our medics would treat injured civilians whenever they could." Frank paused, looked down at the table. "War de-sensitizes a man. Otherwise, men could never do the terrible things required to survive. These acts of kindness by American boys, that I witnessed so often, were their way of trying to retain their humanity. It was fairly common in our army, rare in the enemy." Frank looked up at J.P. "Sure, some of our guys went crazy and did bad stuff. I know some prisoners and civilians were shot and killed and there were rapes. But these were isolated incidents. They happened, but they were *not supposed* to happen. On the other hand, the concentration camps, medical experiments and the inhumane torture of people and prisoners by our enemies were *systemic*. They were policies from the highest levels of malicious, immoral governments. In Europe we had a madman hell bent on ethnic cleansing and was well on his way to doing just that. In Japan we had a brutal military regime practicing genocide in China led by an emperor who they believed was a divine God on earth."

Frank took a deep breath. "What we did was in self-defense. It wasn't for conquest or for treasure. We only wanted to end the War and go home. What they did was vile and vicious and a great sin against mankind. That is what the world would have been subjected to if the Japs and Nazis had won. But we stopped them cold!"

"I apologize if I gave the impression…" J.P. tried to calm Frank down.

"No need to apologize," Frank interrupted again. "But there's one thing you really need to understand. There was *no moral equivalence* between our enemies and us. They were malevolent as a matter of national policy. We were not. We weren't perfect but we were light years better than those savages."

Frank shook his head slowly as if not believing that all Americans didn't understand this. He went on. "The decision to drop the atomic bomb was made in the context of the alternatives. Our only other choices were to invade Japan or starve her out. If the Japanese people defended their homeland with the same fanaticism they fought with on Okinawa and Iwo Jima, millions more lives would have been lost, mostly Japanese. And I'm serious when I say *millions*. But I'm glad they ended the War when they did for the *American* lives it saved. We already had too many gold star mothers by then."

J.P. had stupidly stumbled through a tripwire and it blew up in his face. Frank had worked himself up and was breathing heavily. J.P. gave him time to recover.

After a moment, Frank continued. "Winning the War was the high point in our history and I'm very proud to have served in it." Frank began to tear up. "We'll never again be as united as a nation." He choked back a sniffle. "And you would never learn the truth by reading what is taught in school these days. They teach our grandchildren that America was the evil one. I'll never understand it. All I care about now is that we, all the living veterans, record our stories for posterity before the bastards wipe out our legacy and obliterate the truth." Frank leaned across the table, whispered, "So help me God, John, we were the good guys!"

J.P. lifted his wine glass. "To good and evil. May we always be good."

Frank lifted his glass a few inches off the table. "To the *difference* between good and evil. May we never confuse them again."

J.P. smiled and touched Frank's glass. "I can drink to that." Both men sipped their wine.

Satisfied he had weathered this near-meltdown, J.P. decided to confront Frank about the secret. There were just the two of them, no distractions and no Harley. The timing was perfect.

"So Frank, can you tell me about this hush-hush secret involving my dad and his buddy?"

Frank looked at him over the rim of his wine glass. "Sure, it's not a secret anymore."

J.P. felt a surge of energy through his body. He never expected it would be this easy and was surprised his excitement was so strong. He leaned forward anxiously.

Andrew suddenly appeared and placed some fresh bread and butter between the two men. Frank picked up a warm slice and buttered it as he spoke. "History tells us General Taylor and another officer snuck into Rome just before the Salerno landings. They met with the new Italian Prime Minister in secret to work out the details of an American airborne drop on Rome to secure the city and protect the new government."

"That's interesting." J.P. started buttering his own slice of bread. "I didn't know that."

"It's not well known." Frank took a small bite of his warm, buttered bread. "But when they got to Rome for the meeting, the Italians recanted and wouldn't support the drop. So, Taylor cancelled the mission and took a lot of crap from some higher ups and even a few historians after the War, but he was convinced our boys would have been slaughtered if they jumped."

"Was he right?" J.P. asked.

Frank nodded in the affirmative and took a sip of wine. "Ike announced the surrender over the radio anyway and Prime Minister Badoglio was compelled to do the same. Italy was out of the War so the aborted Rome drop was inconsequential and slipped into the margins of history."

"What does this have to do with my father?"

Frank took a deep breath, sipped his wine and put his glass down on the white tablecloth. He looked left and right elevating the suspense. "Taylor and the other officer didn't go into Rome alone. Your father and Jake were their bodyguards." Frank paused to let the words sink in.

"Go on," J.P. prodded.

"Don't you see? They were part of the secret mission but they were under strict orders to remain silent. When they got back with their unit, division staff panicked. They didn't want to risk the boys jumping back into Italy again."

"Why not?"

"After Badoglio made his surrender announcement, he had to flee Rome. He and his ministers snuck to a city called Pescara on the Adriatic coast. Otherwise the Germans might have killed him and the Allies needed him alive to try and hold his new government together. No one knew exactly how much your dad and Jake knew and paratroopers were always more susceptible to capture. No one wanted to risk that."

"I suppose that makes some sense."

"Problem was they were already on route to the Salerno drop zone when the brass finally figured out where they were. As soon as they landed they were whisked out of the drop zone and sent by boat back to Sicily. They received orders back to the States. They got a priority flight home and then were transferred to the Screaming Eagles."

"Sounds like a pretty good deal," J.P. smiled.

"The other problem was their records were altered to cover the time they were on that secret mission. Neither of them got credit for that combat jump or for participating in the Italian Campaign. It was as if they never made that jump or set foot on Italian soil. Their records were not corrected until after the War ended."

Andrew approached with their meals. He refilled their glasses from the chilled bottle.

J.P. grabbed a chip with his hand, blew on it and popped it into his mouth. Frank cut a slice from his lobster roll. He nodded in approval as he chewed vigorously.

"Go on, Frank, let's get to the secret." J.P. was anxious, his curiosity about to explode.

Frank looked at J.P. quizzically. "That was it. What I just explained to you. The top-secret, hush-hush mission the boys went on. They couldn't talk about it for a long time. I didn't find out about it until the end of the War."

J.P. exhaled, deflated by the letdown. While this story was fascinating, it could not possibly be what his mother had encouraged him to talk to his father about. It certainly didn't fit the context of the recording made the previous evening. Talk about being clever, he was just played by one cunning old man. There was only one approach left, the direct appeal.

"Frank, I'm convinced there is something else; something besides this Rome thing. You see, I accidentally left my recorder on when I left for the men's room last night." J.P. pulled the recorder out of his pocket. The tape was pre-positioned. He flicked the switch.

> *Harley: Do you think he knows?*
> *Frank: He's pretty smart. If he doesn't know for sure I'm convinced he's at least suspicious.*
> *Harley: He hasn't said anything or asked any questions that would lead me to believe that he's suspicious. What do you think, Sky?*
> *Sky: He may be playing it (inaudible) but I don't think he knows. Actually, I don't think he has a clue. He may find out if he (inaudible) but (inaudible) I think he is absolutely (inaudible).*
> *Frank: I wouldn't be so sure.*
> *Harley: Well, in any case, we made a pledge. An (inaudible).*
> *Frank: I know, but maybe we should reconsider since his (inaudible). If it were me, I would want to know.*

J.P. turned off the recording. Frank had a mouthful of lobster roll and was chewing slowly. "Even though some of the words were garbled, Frank, it's pretty obvious to me that the secret I'm looking for has nothing to do with the Rome Job."

Frank finished chewing. Took a sip of wine. He had the look of a kid caught with his hand in the proverbial cookie jar. "*Accidentally* left it on?" Frank smiled. "You seem to be a man on a mission, Mister Kilroy."

"I'm just trying to find out the truth." J.P. was exasperated. "Will you help me?"

Frank slowly shook his head in the negative.

J.P. lowered his head, disappointed. "So you won't help me?"

"Actually, I'm conflicted as you can probably tell. On one hand, I gave my word. On the other, I truly believe you have a right to know. But my word trumps my belief. As much as I would prefer to help you, I'm bound by my promise." Frank swallowed the last of his wine and looked J.P. in the eye. "I'm sorry."

J.P. nodded. He was extremely disappointed. His hopes were high for this meeting and now they were dashed by the scruples of this wise old man. "My mother wanted me to talk to my father about this secret and I didn't. Now, I feel as if I can't give up. I have to figure it out, somehow, before it dies with the people who know it. I'm working against time. So, please know I intend to pursue this." J.P. had a grin on his face. "So let's enjoy this excellent lunch and you can tell me more about my father. But I must warn you, I *will* try to trick you into revealing what you refuse to tell me." J.P. was deadly serious despite the congenial grin. It was *game on!*

Frank ignored the warning. "I would be honored to tell you about your father."

"Before you begin, can you answer this question?" J.P. asked. "When I find out this secret, and I will eventually find it out, will it have been worth the effort?"

Frank pursed his lips and considered the question. "Definitely!"

Chapter Thirty-Eight

New York City - September 17, 1943

"Women must try to do things as men have tried.
When they fail, their failure must be a challenge to others."

Amelia Earhart (1898 - 1937)

Jake Kilroy stood on the roof of the seven-story tenement building at 76 West 165th Street in the Washington Heights section of New York City. He marveled at the sights before him. To the northwest, the setting sun glinted off the massive structure and steel cables of the George Washington Bridge. It was a huge, relatively new span that connected New York City with New Jersey over the wide Hudson River. The cars looked like small toys as they traveled the length of the bridge. It was enormous and striking and he had never seen anything like it.

To the northeast was the largest stadium he had ever seen, the Polo Grounds. Across the Harlem River in the Bronx sat Yankee Stadium. To the east and west the East and Hudson Rivers were choked with bustling ship traffic transporting the men and goods of war to distant ports of call. Looking south the spire of the Empire State Building stood out among the many skyscrapers of the New York City skyline. Far away in the distance, at the lowest tip of Manhattan, stood the tall buildings that made up the financial center of the world. Beyond them, and not visible, he imagined the Statue of Liberty, her brilliant torch undoubtedly darkened by blackout regulations.

He shook his head in amazement, grateful for the opportunity to experience these sights yet still bewildered how he and Johnny got here. It all happened so fast.

The two men were plucked off the beach at Salerno and transported back to Sicily on a British Navy destroyer. They were driven overnight to their base camp at Castelvetrano where they picked up their personal gear. Every request for information about their destination was rebuffed. With travel orders that held AAA priority they bumped a captain and a major on a C-47 transport flight from Castelvetrano to Gibraltar, Spain. On the flight from Gibraltar to England they bumped a colonel and a brigadier general. They kept a low profile as they became the object of great attention from the other travelers, mostly senior British officers.

New travel orders awaited them at RAF Ridgewell Airfield outside London. As they walked from the plane to base headquarters, Johnny and Jake stared at the dozens of B-17 Flying Fortress heavy bombers squatting on new concrete hardstands as their ground crews worked feverishly on them. All of the tails were adorned with a large bright yellow L on a black triangle. They had apparently just returned from a bomb run and were being prepared for another.

The two paratroopers were the last passengers in a line that ended in a Quonset hut that served as headquarters. Above the door was a small sign that read: "Welcome to the Home of the 381st Bombardment Group (Heavy) – USAAF 8th Air Force".

The face of the technical sergeant behind the processing desk brightened instantly when he read the names on their orders. He had been expecting them and immediately summoned the Officer of the Day.

Jake and Johnny stiffened to attention as a young lieutenant entered the room. He was heavy set with dark curly hair and held a sheaf of papers.

"At ease, soldiers." The officer studied the two paratroopers. "Are you guys brothers?" he asked as he eyed the Kilroys curiously.

"No, sir," Johnny answered.

"Hmm," the officer grumbled. "Well I have new orders for both of you." He handed them each a manila envelope. "I'm to expedite you back to the States to your new outfit while they're still in Camp Shanks on the first available air transport."

"Yes, sir," both men answered.

New York, thought Johnny. *Maybe there would be time for a quick visit home?*

The officer continued. "I don't see many triple-A priority transit orders." He paused, hoping for an explanation. When none was forthcoming he went on. "My next regularly scheduled flight to Floyd Bennett is tomorrow but I figured that might not be good enough for Ike."

Jake and Johnny looked at each other in wide-eyed disbelief.

"Your orders came from Ike's headquarters," the officer explained. Still, there was no reply. "Anyway, I'm holding up a return ferry flight. It's not a transport. It's a war weary B-17 going back to the Boeing factory for an upgrade. Or maybe it's a 'Class 26' going to the bone yard, I'm actually not sure. But it's returning to the States with a group of ferry service pilots."

"Ferry service pilots, sir?" Jake asked.

"Yup. They ferried some new Model F Forts over to us." He was referring to the B-17F Flying Fortress. It was the latest version in a long line of modifications to the popular and sturdy workhorse bomber of the 8th Air Force.

"We're flying back on a shot up B-17, sir?" Johnny had a concerned look on his face.

"Don't worry, it flies just fine. We wouldn't risk the ferry pilots." The officer smiled. "We've patched up the bullet holes, buttoned up the open ports and threw in a bunch of sleeping bags. She'll stop to refuel in Goose Bay, Newfoundland, and you'll be in the States by tomorrow."

Johnny exhaled in relief. "Thank you, sir."

"Look men, I know you just had a long flight but I'm holding up this plane just for you two. So take a piss, grab some sandwiches and coffee and we'll get you a lift out to the plane."

"Yes, sir," Johnny answered.

"Oh, one more thing. You've both been promoted to corporal. Congratulations."

A jeep was warming up outside the hut and Jake and Johnny piled in. They were loaded down with their barracks bags, newly issued sleeping bags, a musette bag full of Spam and cheese sandwiches and a large thermos of hot coffee. The Army Air Forces ate well, Jake concluded.

The driver took only a few minutes to get to the end of one of the three 6,500 foot runways where a B-17E stood, engines warm and idling, ready for take off. As the jeep approached, the driver flashed his high beams at the cockpit. Johnny could make out the writing behind the Plexiglas nose. It said *Queen Bee*.

The jeep driver jumped out in the dark and unlatched the crew compartment door. The two paratroopers threw their gear in and followed. The driver slammed the door and banged on it twice. Within a few seconds the plane began to taxi.

The crew compartment had no seats. It was dark inside the cabin but Jake could make out the outlines of the ferry pilots sleeping on the floor. He muscled his baggage carefully forward until he found a small space between the last pilot and what looked to be the bomb bay. He dropped his barracks bag to function as a pillow, threw his sleeping blanket on the floor and sat down. Johnny followed him. There was barely enough room for the two of them on the floor. Jake leaned into the pilot beside him and gave a gentle shove.

"C'mon, Mac, shove it over a bit. Give us some room here."

The pilot, disturbed from a sound sleep, grumbled while shuffling over a few feet.

"Thanks Mac," Jake said.

Johnny plopped down in the open space as the plane maneuvered into takeoff position. The pilot goosed the throttles and the plane began moving faster. Then the pilot gunned the four 1,200 horsepower Wright R-1820-97 Cyclone supercharged engines and the plane lurched forward. In a minute they were airborne and heading west.

Jake and Johnny were dead tired. In the dark of the cabin they quietly grabbed a quick sandwich to ward off the hunger and shared some hot coffee. They curled up in their sleeping bags and fell quickly into a deep sleep to the drone of the engines.

The landing was as smooth as silk but the squeal of the tires shook Jake from his slumber. He looked at his watch. He'd been asleep for the fourteen hours it took *Queen Bee* to navigate the 2,500 miles to Newfoundland. It was light outside as he shook Johnny awake. *Queen Bee* taxied slowly to a hardstand where a fuel truck was waiting. The four engines shut down with a noticeable shudder. Johnny could hear the sounds from the cockpit of switches being thrown and the metallic snap of seatbelts being released. The group of sleeping pilots began to stir. There were six bodies rising slowly from the pile, groaning and complaining. Jake didn't take notice until he heard the women's voice from the cockpit over the intercom.

"Forty-five minutes, ladies. Clean up and get something to eat."

Jake grabbed Johnny's shoulder as they stood up. He nodded toward the pilots who were collecting their gear and moving toward the crew door behind the right waist gunner's position. They were all women and were wearing brown leather A-2 flight jackets over khaki coveralls. Each also wore a white silk flying scarf around her neck and a Ferry Division patch on her sleeve. Jake was speechless. The pilot he had shoved the night before turned to him and said, "You don't have to call me Mac. My name is Roxie Rawls." She held out her hand.

Jake shook her hand. "I'm Jake, this is Johnny." He jerked his thumb over his shoulder. She had a cute round face full of freckles and short red hair. Her green eyes were bloodshot.

She looked at his collar and then to his sleeve. "I figured you'd be at least a full bird colonel...the way they held up this flight for you. Maybe even a damn general." She grunted as she turned and headed toward the hatch.

It was cold and damp under overcast skies as the group exited the plane. The two paratroopers followed the line of female ferry pilots into the main base mess hall. The sign above the door read "Royal Canadian Air Force Station, Goose Bay, Newfoundland". From what Jake could see, the sprawling base was enormous and still undergoing expansion and construction. Goose Bay was already the largest airfield in the Western Hemisphere.

The mess hall was enormous, about the size of a small auditorium and with the same acoustical characteristics. Base ground crew personnel, soldiers and pilots filled the loud, busy chamber. There was a constant clatter of rattling plates and tin forks against stainless steel trays. The smell of warm food permeated the air and was both tempting and comforting. Along with the din of voices and noises from the aircraft engines outside, the mess hall was a fairly raucous place. The young women kept to themselves and stayed together within their own little group. Johnny could tell they were quite used to being a novelty, more like an oddity, wherever they went. They maintained a professional demeanor amid the various distractions and comments.

Jake and Johnny followed the pilots through the chow line. Once they had filled their trays, they walked over to join the women at a large rectangular table in a corner of the mess hall. The young ladies were all heads-down, quietly eating their food. Some ground crewmen at the next table were annoying them. As

Johnny sat down, Jake looked over at one mechanic, who was leaning in trying to get the name of one of the pilots. She was trying to ignore him.

"Give it a rest, Mac."

The mechanic started to stand up and Jake put his tray down and stepped over to him. Jake's glare was menacing and he flashed it at full intensity. The mechanic eyed Jake's jump wings and quickly sat back down. The ground crew table became quiet. Jake backed away and sat down between Roxie and Johnny. He spoke to her.

"I'm sorry about the *Mac* comment. I couldn't tell you were a dame in the dark."

Her mouth was full so she nodded her acceptance of his apology.

Jake was curious and felt a bit playful. "Aren't you going to introduce us?" He pointed to the other girls with his fork.

Roxie gulped down a mouthful of soup, tapped the table with her spoon to get the attention of the other women and gestured to the two paratroopers. "Ladies, meet *Private* Jake and *Private* Johnny…our high priority passengers. The very same ones we got held up for last night."

The women nodded, waved or grunted. They all quickly resumed eating…all but one. She was tall, pretty with large hazel-gray eyes over high cheekbones. Her face said she was about thirty but her dark brown hair already had sprinkles of gray. In addition, she had a shocking streak of solid gray hair flowing back from the right side of her forehead. As she stood up with her tray, she walked over and sat directly opposite the two paratroopers. Johnny guessed she was the leader of the group by the way she carried herself. She extended her slender hand.

"I'm Nancy. These are my pilots." The grip was a pilot's handshake, firm and confident.

"Pilots?" Jake was cynical. "All of them?" He shook her hand absent-mindedly.

"Yes, ferry service pilots. We take planes from the factories to their bases." There was a reserved shyness about her but also a disarming aura of authority.

"I didn't know there were any female pilots in the Air Corps," Jake confessed.

"Well, we're not in the military. Not yet," Nancy answered. "But we take our orders from U.S. Army Air Force's Air Transport Command."

Johnny studied her face, a glint of recognition in his eyes. "I think I read about you somewhere," he said. "You're that doctor's daughter. Aviatrix. Went to school at Vassar. Married a guy who owned an aviation company. Am I right?" He shook her hand.

She let out a deep sigh. "Wouldn't you know…I would run into the only grunt in the entire army who reads the society pages." She appeared annoyed at being recognized but continued. "That would be me, Nancy Harkness Love. I'm the Director of Flight Operations for the Women Airforce Service Pilots. We're also known as the WASPs." Then, almost as an afterthought, she added, "Pleased to meet you. I thought you'd be high ranking brass."

Johnny smiled. "We've been hearing that a lot lately, Miss Love."

"And just so you know, ma'am, we're actually *corporals* now." Jake chuckled as he brushed his sleeve where his new stripes would be placed.

"Well, that explains everything," Love chided. "But seriously, I need to ask you to stay away from my girls. We can't afford any gossip or rumors. Even the perception of impropriety could be extremely damaging to us so please, keep your distance."

Jake sensed Love was a classy lady who struggled a bit with the awkwardness of this conversation. Nevertheless, she was determined to get her message across.

"Our flight demands are hard enough on my girls. But in addition, we have to follow arcane rules of propriety to make sure there's not even a hint of a scandal. There are a lot of things we're not supposed to do. Fraternization is frowned upon. We make one mistake and we could be done for good. In fact, flying you two breaks all the rules and if the order didn't come from Ike himself, we wouldn't be doing it. Don't make it any harder on us than it already is."

"Not a problem, Miss Love," Johnny replied. "We're just hitching a ride. We don't intend to cause any trouble."

"That's good because we don't need any." She glanced over at the table where the loud mechanic was sitting. "And thanks for shutting those guys up but that still doesn't give you two any special consideration. This trip is our first mission outside the States. I fought like hell to get it. This flight is not even officially authorized because women are not allowed to fly the 'Snowball' yet." She was referring to the air route over the North Atlantic used to ferry bombers to England. "Some higher ups still think we shouldn't be doing this and a lot of them want us to fail. So we need to prove we *can* do this and the last thing we need right now is to be noticed."

"Well, forget about that, ma'am," Jake quipped. "You've already been noticed." He circled his index finger around the room.

"Look, boys," Love sighed looking both tired and exasperated. "These gals are part of my own handpicked group of original ferry pilots. Each one has logged over two thousand hours...more hours than most of our combat pilots. Every one of them is instrument rated on pursuit planes, the hottest and fastest we have. These gals fly the birds the men are scared to fly and they do it for two-thirds the pay and a pile of abuse."

The two paratroopers sat there in silence. Jake was impressed with their credentials.

She went on. "And it's my job to make sure they don't get screwed over for some stupid perception problem. So, give me a break guys and go sit someplace else."

The two young paratroopers picked up their trays. Johnny had a slight mischievous grin on his face. "Would you have banished us if we were generals?"

"Damn right!" she shot back. "*Especially* if you were generals."

Jake and Johnny finished their meals at another table in silence. When the group of ferry pilots left the mess hall, they followed. They all piled into the Flying Fortress which had been refueled and was ready for the next leg. Roxie and another pilot named Dora were making their way to the cockpit. They would fly the last leg of the trip. Roxie stopped to speak to the boys.

"Nothing personal, guys. We don't normally ferry passengers. We usually fly solo or in small groups. You didn't deserve that back there in the mess hall."

"No problem," Johnny offered.

Roxie continued. "We're needed right now. There's a severe shortage of service pilots. All we want is a chance to contribute to the war effort and be accepted. Nancy is a great leader who's just trying to protect her pilots and the ferry program."

Johnny spoke first. "I think you gals have a lot of moxie and what you're doing is great."

Jake added, "My girl works in a ship yard. A lot of women work there."

"Thanks, guys. But just so you know, what happened back there was nothing personal." She turned to Jake. "What shipyard does your girlfriend work in?"

"Newport News."

"Is that so?" Roxie's face lit up with a huge smile. "Last year I..."

"Roxie, let's get cranking!" Nancy Love interrupted with a barely audible but firm command from the back of the plane.

"Yes, ma'am," Roxie answered. "Excuse me. Time to go to work." She made her way past the bomb bay and into the cockpit. The other pilots spread their sleeping bags and took seats on the floor of the cabin. From the cockpit they heard the sounds of toggle switches being flipped and clicked, buttons pushed and dials turned. Flaps and ailerons were waggled. The radio barked garbled instructions between the noisy static. Suddenly each of the four engines whined, coughed, sputtered and started with a belch of sparks and thick black exhaust smoke. Roxie slowly ran up the engines to maximum revolutions and the plane began to vibrate under the harnessed force of the four powerful engines. She released the brakes and with a jerk the huge plane began to move. Slowly, she taxied the bomber to the head of the long runway for takeoff. In a few minutes they were airborne again, heading southwest.

With a brisk tailwind they managed the last 1,100 miles to Floyd Bennett Naval Air Station on Long Island in a little over six hours. When they finally landed, the two men were asked by Nancy Love to forget they had been ferried back by women pilots. She may have been a lot more paranoid than she needed to be but Jake had to admit her team was first-rate. He couldn't help but draw the obvious parallel between them and Macie. *He'd been such an ass!* He would have to be much more supportive of her job decision in his next letter. Maybe that would help convince her he finally understood.

Jake and Johnny boarded an army bus headed for Camp Shanks thirty miles up the Hudson River from New York City. After a brief stop at Fort Totten to discharge some military passengers, the bus arrived at Camp Shanks before heading off to West Point. Camp Shanks was an embarkation and staging area for units about to deploy to Europe. Its mission was to ensure each soldier had all of his required equipment and had been sufficiently inoculated against disease. The camp's confines extended to Piermont Pier which jutted out into the Hudson River from its west bank. From there, transport ships ferried fully laden combat troops to Manhattan docks for overseas transportation. Indigenous rail yards facilitated movement by train from many stateside origins as well as from Shanks directly to Hoboken and Weehawken, New Jersey. Camp Shanks was one of three main embarkation camps in the eastern United States and was an exceedingly hectic place. Its unofficial nickname was "Last Stop U.S.A.".

In short order, the two paratroopers found themselves yet again standing in front of the desk of a Duty Officer who was reading their orders. The officer began shaking his head.

"You guys brothers?"

"No sir," they answered in unison.

"Well I have bad news for you. The unit you're being transferred to, the Five-oh-six, shipped out a few days ago."

Jake looked at Johnny and rolled his eyes. Another army foul-up!

"We're going to have to cut new orders for you two. We'll catch you up to your division." He handed each of them a piece of paper. "In the meantime, here's a twenty-four hour pass."

"Thank you, sir." They both said surprised and delighted.

"Be back here tomorrow at the same time. We'll have your new travel orders for you." The officer continued. "Remember, no insignia, no jump boots when you ship out tomorrow. You can sew on your corporal stripes." He studied the two men for a second. "Stay out of trouble. Be back on time. Enjoy New York. Dismissed!"

"Thank you, sir." Johnny was fighting back an enormous smile. The men left the office grinning from ear to ear. They slapped each other's shoulders and headed straight for the bus station. Johnny stopped at a pay phone and called home. He told his shocked wife he was in New York and was coming home for a day and bringing his best buddy, Jake.

Rose was absolutely ecstatic and totally unprepared. As the boys traveled into the city, she gathered as many extra ration coupons as she could from her own small stash and from generous neighbors. She used the "red coupon stamps" from her War Ration Book and bought some steaks from the butcher. She would cook them a meal to remember. She would start them off with a tomato and onion salad, fresh from her Victory Garden. Along with the steaks smothered with onions, she would make mashed potatoes, gravy and peas; Johnny's favorite meal. The baker would provide the fresh bread and an apple pie. They would wash it all down with plenty of Rheingold beer, a local New York brew.

After scurrying around to secure all of the rare ingredients, she showered, powdered herself, put on her best floral print housedress and a fresh coat of makeup. A ponytail was the best she could do with her long jet-black hair but she knew Johnny loved that look on her. She finished just as the boys arrived at the apartment.

Johnny hugged her long and hard. She smelled sweet, clean and felt so soft. He could not help but notice her makeup was fresh and she was making an effort to be attractive, not that she needed to. Jake stood behind, a bit amused and waited to be introduced. Rose broke away from her husband; aware Jake had been standing there, and gave him a hug. She had tears in her eyes.

"You must be Jake. I'm so glad to meet you. Johnny has written so much about you. I can't tell you how happy I am that he found a friend like you."

"I'm pleased to meet you too, ma'am. Johnny can't stop talking about you." Jake looked at Johnny, wondering what he had written that had Rose so overjoyed. Johnny smiled and shrugged his shoulders. As if reading his mind, Rose provided some insight.

"Johnny doesn't make friends easily. He can be a bit standoffish…somewhat of a loner. And call me Rose, please."

"Yeah," Jake laughed out loud. "He's definitely a snob."

They all laughed at that. Rose sat them down at the kitchen table and they chatted over ice-cold beers as she cooked dinner. The boys shared the more humorous stories of jump school and North Africa being careful to leave out the hardships. They didn't speak about Sicily, the buddies they lost or their mission into Rome.

Rose joined the boys with a beer as she cooked and they chatted. Jake asked her about life in New York, her job at the hospital and the morale of the people on the Homefront. Rose was impressed he was such a good listener. He seemed genuinely interested in what she had to say. He was curious without being nosy and seemed anxious to learn and understand things of which he had no prior knowledge. She found humble people like him easy to like.

Jake spoke glowingly of Macie and how impressed he was with the ferry pilots. It seemed as if he just experienced an epiphany. Rose also liked the way he interacted with her husband. There was obvious mutual respect between them and an unspoken trust. They would sometimes finish each other's sentences and laughed easily with each other. There was a faith and a fondness that was palpable. She concluded Jake was good for Johnny.

The conversation slowed as the boys devoured the meal she had painstakingly prepared. Jake heaped praise upon the chef between mouthfuls. Johnny could not keep his eyes off of his wife. They ate eagerly, laughed and drank heartily and thoroughly enjoyed each other's company.

After dessert they all pitched in and cleared the table. Rose busied herself washing the dishes and Johnny sidled up next to her to dry them. They looked at each other playfully with endearing eyes. Jake got the message.

"Look, I'm stuffed. I'm going to take a walk," he announced.

"Where are you going?" Johnny asked. "You don't know this neighborhood."

"I'll be fine, I need the exercise after that enormous, delicious meal." Jake looked at Rose and nodded. She acknowledged the compliment but was already blushing.

"Wait, please." Rose reached into her closet and pulled out her Kodak Baby Brownie Special camera. "Just a minute, let's go to the roof. I want a snapshot and this camera has no flash."

Rose asked a neighbor, Mrs. Geelan, and they all went up to the roof. She was so happy to see Johnny she talked up a storm. Finally, Rose got her to take the last picture on the roll of film.

"I'll be back in a couple of hours," Jake winked at Johnny.

Jake walked down the stairs and into the street. It was late Friday afternoon and many people were walking along the sidewalks. A few were in uniform. Everyone seemed friendly. Despite the tall buildings and the heavily trafficked streets by Bedford standards, he did not feel terribly out of place. He was conscious of the admiring stares of the younger boys and the flirtatious glances of the young ladies. The rigors of the airborne, he concluded for the thousandth time, were well worth it.

He continued to walk south. As he approached 159th Street he saw a marquis for a movie theatre, The Loews Rio. He stepped into the lobby to look at the preview still pictures for the features that were playing. The double feature consisted of *Destination Tokyo* with Cary Grant and *Gung Ho* starring Randolph Scott. The army usually got to see movies fresh out of Hollywood. It wouldn't be the same without his buddies hooting and hollering at the screen for every exaggerated battle scene and every corny line. The guys always poked fun at the realism but appreciated the sentiment. Hollywood films of the time were inspirational, uplifting and patriotic. They did wonders for the morale and spirit on the Homefront. It would be a good way to kill a few hours. He bought a ticket for a dime and sat in an aisle seat in the back row.

When the films ended he walked back to the apartment. He listened at the door and when he heard nothing, he decided to go up on the roof and look at the view. He marveled at the sights. After soaking it all in and re-living the last hectic days, he was ready to rejoin Johnny and Rose.

They were both glad to see him when he knocked at the door though Rose still seemed to be blushing. They sat around the table talking and drinking beer. Rose graciously sewed the stripes onto their uniforms and carefully removed all of their airborne insignia. They would travel in those non-descript military clothes the next day.

Time passed quickly. Johnny fell into a deep sleep for a few hours. Jake and Rose stayed awake together all night and before long the sun was rising. Finally it was time to leave for Camp Shanks and Rose nudged Johnny awake. He apologized for falling asleep and the boys got dressed and collected their gear. Rose hugged Jake tightly again and kissed him hard on the cheek. "I want to see you back here when this is over. Johnny and you both need to come home."

"We will." He looked at Johnny. "Meet you downstairs."

Johnny nodded as Jake descended the stairs to the street. After a few minutes he dropped his barracks bag in the lobby and climbed back up the stairs. There, on the landing, stood Johnny and Rose. They were hugging and she was crying, neither of them wanting to be the first to let go.

"C'mon Yank, time to go," Jake prodded.

Johnny looked at Jake above Rose's shoulder, tears streaking his face. He still gripped her tightly, blinked his eyes, choked back a sniffle and said, "I can't go back."

Chapter Thirty-Nine

Newport News, Virginia - December 24, 1943

"It is true we have won all our wars, but we have paid for them.
We don't want victories anymore."

Golda Meir (1898 - 1978)

Macie Vance leaned closer to her Philco radio to listen to President Franklin D. Roosevelt's Fireside Chat. It was three o'clock in the afternoon on Christmas Eve. The President scheduled his address at the most suitable time for a worldwide audience. Macie found herself looking forward to hearing the calm, reassuring voice of the President. He had just returned from conferences with other world leaders and she was anxious to hear the outcome.

Gabriel Heatter of the Mutual Radio Network was speaking. He was a regular announcer of war news and an outspoken champion of the men and women engaged in the war effort. Macie listened intently to his distinctive, familiar voice as he provided a summary of the progress of the War in 1943 while waiting for the President.

Much of what was broadcast could have been considered propaganda but sustaining an enthusiastic and positive civilian population was an important part of the war effort. Nevertheless, 1943 did bring a marked increase in good news. The tide of the War was turning and one could sense the change.

The year started out with the Casablanca Conference in Morocco, North Africa in January. President Roosevelt and Prime Minister Churchill were the major participants. Charles de Gaulle and Henri Giraud co-represented the newly constituted Free French Forces. Josef Stalin declined the invitation. One significant outcome of that conference was an agreement on the direction of the Allied strategy in 1943. Sicily would be invaded in July and Italy proper by September.

The other major outcome was the declaration the Allies would only accept *unconditional surrender* from the Axis powers. Roosevelt insisted there would not be another negotiated armistice or fragile peace. This time, Germany, or Japan for that matter, would not be allowed to rearm in another twenty years. This global conflict would not be repeated.

The news from the Pacific was somewhat better than last year. American forces secured Guadalcanal in February after six months of brutal fighting. General MacArthur's forces were making substantial gains pushing the Japanese back in Papua, New Guinea. A huge sea battle took place in March in the Bismarck Sea. American planes viciously attacked Japanese ships attempting to reinforce their forces on New Guinea. There were few survivors.

On 18 April, American fighter planes shot down Japanese Admiral Isoroku Yamamoto while he was traveling to Bougainville Island. Sixteen P-38 Lightning fighters from the 339th Fighter Squadron were dispatched to shoot him down. The United States had broken the Japanese codes and knew Yamamoto's inspection itinerary. Since he was the master planner behind the Pearl Harbor attack, Americans felt a strong measure of justified retribution in killing him.

Macie recognized names of places that were once captured by the Japanese. In May the Americans recaptured the Alaskan island of Attu and reoccupied Kiska in August. The Aleutian Islands were back in American hands.

Macie pulled her chair closer to the radio as Heatter continued. In June, American forces assaulted Munda in the New Georgia Island group. The island of Bougainville was invaded in November. In all cases the Japanese forces were defeated and pushed back.

In the Central Pacific, United States Marines attacked the island atolls of Tarawa and Betio in November and defeated the Japanese after savage fighting. While much of the detailed information was heavily censored, there was no hiding that casualties were high. The Japanese remained stubborn fighters even in defeat.

In the Mediterranean, even though the Italian government had surrendered to the Allies, the Germans occupied the peninsula and put up a tenacious defense. The end of the year found the Allies stalled before the Gustov Line by determined German forces.

On the Continent, the Soviets were battering German armies on all fronts. In February, the German Sixth Army under Field Marshal Friedrich von Paulus surrendered 93,000 troops to Soviet forces who surrounded them in the city of Stalingrad. The Soviets chased the other German field armies eastward until a brilliant counterstroke by Field Marshal Erich von Manstein recaptured Kharkov from the Russians and stabilized the front.

That set the stage for the German offensive in July against a well-defended salient near the city of Kursk. In the largest tank battle ever fought, the Germans were soundly defeated.

At home, American industry was hitting full stride. As Gabriel Heatter spoke, Macie confirmed the report by her own experiences. In the Newport News Shipyard, they had just launched the USS *Franklin (CV-13)* in October. She was the fourth Essex-class aircraft carrier built and launched from Newport News in 1943 and there were still four more under construction. A fifth carrier was launched from the Bethlehem Steel Yards. That total of five fast carriers compared to only three launched in 1942. More importantly there were nine hulls under construction in all four carrier-capable shipyards in the United States. All were scheduled to launch the following year. American mass production was beginning to gain traction and would eventually build twenty-four Essex-class carriers.

As recently as 8 September, in his Third War Loan appeal, President Roosevelt challenged the American people to continue to buy more war bonds. He appealed to them so their brothers, husbands, fathers and sons would have the best quality and highest quantity of essential war equipment. He emphasized the urgent need to end the War as quickly as possible to save innocent lives. While always gracious to thank the American people, he continually raised the bar. And Americans responded. The Third War Loan raised the staggering sum of 19,000,000,000 dollars.

Macie was gratified she actually understood most of the war news. She'd grown a great deal in the past year and a half.

Gabriel Heatter was winding down. It was time for the President to speak. She edged closer and turned the volume up just a bit.

> *My Friends:*
> *I have recently returned from extensive journeying in the region of the Mediterranean and as far as the borders of Russia. I have conferred with the leaders of Britain and Russia and China on military matters of the present, especially on plans for stepping-up our successful attack on our enemies as quickly as possible and from many different points of the compass.*
> *On this Christmas Eve there are over 10,000,000 men in the armed forces of the United States alone. One year ago 1,700,000 were serving overseas. Today, this figure has been more than doubled to 3,800,000 on duty overseas. By July that number overseas will rise to over 5,000,000 men and women.*

President Roosevelt acknowledged the global War had dampened the Christmas spirit but that free people everywhere still cling to the noble notion of "peace on earth, goodwill toward men". He recognized that great progress was purchased at great sacrifice. His last Christmas address consisted of a message of hope. This year he was confident of the eventual victory.

With a poised and confident voice, the President reported on his recent meetings in Cairo on 22 November with Chiang Kai-shek and in Tehran on 28 November with Josef Stalin and Prime Minister Churchill. He assured the American people that all of these distinguished world leaders were cooperating fully on wartime strategy and structuring a peaceful post-War world.

The President then reminded the American people the War was far from won, that victory was far in the future and as we closed in on our enemies' homelands, we should anticipate long casualty lists of dead, wounded and missing. Macie shuddered at the thought. He ended his Fireside Chat by sending out a Christmas message to all American soldiers around the world.

*On behalf of the American people — your own people — I send this
Christmas message to you, who are in our armed forces:
In our hearts are prayers for you and for all your comrades in arms who
fight to rid the world of evil.
We ask God's blessing upon you — upon your fathers and mothers
and wives and children — all your loved ones at home. We ask that
the comfort of God's grace shall be granted to those who are sick and
wounded, and to those who are prisoners of war in the hands of the
enemy, waiting for the day when they will again be free.
And we ask that God receive and cherish those who have given their lives,
and that He keep them in honor and in the grateful memory of their
countrymen forever. God bless all of you who fight our battles on this
Christmas Eve.
God bless us all. Keep us strong in our faith that we fight for a better day
for human kind — here and everywhere.*

Macie began to tear up. She always found the President's words both
comforting and brutally honest. While predicting a victorious outcome, he tried
to inure the citizens of America to the terrible toll it would require. Americans
needed to prepare for the toughest part of the long road ahead. She wiped her
tears with a tissue and prayed Jake would not be among those who would pay the
ultimate price for freedom.

The door to the apartment swung open with a rush. Nora Lee stormed in
and slammed the door behind her. She was crying as she sat down at the kitchen
table. She put her face in her hands to muffle the sobs and catch her tears.

Macie rushed to her quickly and sat down beside her. "Nora, what's the
matter?"

Nora embraced Macie. "Jonah was killed on Tarawa."

"Oh my gosh!" Macie hugged her close. "Hold me honey. Hold me tight. I'm
right here for you. It'll be all right. Just let it out."

Nora sobbed uncontrollably for some time. Macie brought her a glass of water.
Nora gained control of herself. She took a deep breath and looked at Macie.

"You would think I would be better at this by now," she chided herself. "First
Butch, now Jonah." She paused. "I mean, I really loved Butch and I really liked
Jonah…a lot." Nora began sobbing gently again.

Macie held her as she continued.

"I mean, why did he have to join up, anyway? He was safe here, had a good job
so why?" She sniffled and wiped a tear.

Macie chose not to answer. She just held Nora and rocked her gently.

"I went with Jonah to help me forget about Butch and wound up getting my
heart broken twice," Nora complained. "It doesn't pay to wait for someone."

"We don't know about Butch, Nora. Maybe…" Macie tried to console her.

"I know," Nora interrupted. "I know what those fucking Japs do to prisoners over there. Butch is as good as dead. And if he were not, he'd be better off dead. In any case, he's not coming back to me."

"You don't know that, Nora. You're just upset."

"I tried not to care. I went with a lot of guys. I tried to protect myself from this heartache…but I can't do it anymore." Nora suddenly controlled herself, straightened up in the chair and raised her head high. "Would you like some tea?"

Macie had seen this before, the rapid mood change. It was as if Nora commanded herself to regain control of her mind and body.

"I'd love some," Macie replied. "Let me do it." Macie got up to fill the teapot.

"I'm not raising my hopes that Butch will come back. The odds are against it. They're against anyone coming back." Nora was calm and now speaking matter-of-factly.

Macie lit the stove and sat back down. "If hope is all we have, why just throw it away?"

Nora suddenly realized what she had said. "I'm so sorry, Macie. What was I thinking? Selfish me! I didn't mean Jake. I didn't mean to…"

Macie raised her hand and Nora stopped. "I understand, Nora. Believe me, I get it!"

"You're like a sister to me, Macie," Nora continued. "I don't want to see you hurt. Derek is a great guy and he's here and he's not going anywhere near a battlefield."

Macie just nodded. Derek had been her struggle since she met him.

"If you don't nail him down now, plenty of other girls will." Nora got up and retrieved two large coffee mugs and four teabags from the pantry.

"Do you know what he actually said to me?" Macie didn't wait for an answer. "If anything happened to Jake he would be there for me." She paused. "Imagine that? I worry about Jake all the time. What am I supposed to do with that information?"

"Nothing Macie. He's just telling you how much he cares for you right now but you can't keep him on a string forever."

"I'm not trying to, Nora. At least I don't think I am. He just won't go away."

"All I'm saying Macie is that Derek is a catch and if I were you, I'd reel him in before he gets away. Derek's a sure thing and losing Jake would rip your heart out."

"I understand you, Nora, but it's not that easy."

"Sure it is! Which one do you love right this minute, Sweetie?"

"In some ways I think I love them both."

Chapter Forty

Devonshire, England – December 24, 1943

"The pen is the tongue of the mind."

Horace, (Quintus Horatius Flaccus) (65 BC - 8 BC)

Sergeant Harley Tidrik sat on his bunk in a Quonset hut in the town of Ivybridge, Devonshire, England. He had just returned to his former unit, Able Company, 116th Infantry Regiment, 29th Infantry Division.

Unexpectedly and even more unexplainably, the United States Army disbanded the 29th Ranger Battalion (Provisional) after eleven months of training. The order came through on 18 October 1943 and Harley recently arrived back to his old unit. It was Christmas Eve and he decided to write Jake. He was angry and upset as he chain-smoked his way through the letter. He reread it for the third time.

> *December 24, 1943*
> *Jake,*
>
> *First let me say Merry Christmas to you, kid. I hope this letter finds you in good health. I know you're in England somewhere and we have to get together on leave sometime and whoop it up. Maybe we can meet in London for a weekend.*
>
> *I've never been so down in all my time in the army. They just disbanded the 29th Rangers. They sent us all back to our outfits. What a waste of all that training. I can't believe the army is so fucked up. Unbelievable.*
>
> *We started last December with a call for volunteers. About 170 men and 10 officers volunteered. I wrote you about that. Our cadre was made up of British Commandos, tough bastards.*
>
> *Our CO was Major Milholland. I didn't know him because he came from the 115th Regiment but he turned out to be a swell CO. They sent us to Tidworth Barracks for training. We trained hard for two months. At least we thought it was hard. Then we went north to Scotland to the British Commando Depot at Achnacarry House. This was a rugged desolate place that God made just to break men. A combat veteran Scottish Black Watch officer named Captain Hoar of Number 4 Commando trained us. They worked us hard. We did speed marches, PT, hand-to-hand combat, we climbed mountains, ran courses and were thrown to the wolves and had to find our way back. Some of the boys dropped out but most stuck it out. The Stonewallers were well represented. The British instructors were impressed and they're hard to*

impress. We were so into it we would run the obstacle course for fun.

We trained in seven or eight different places. Then finally in September we went to Scotland to Dorlin House Commando Training Depot. By then we were hard as steel and in great shape. There were calluses where there used to be blisters and we could speed-march for hours on end without rest. We could climb anything with or without ropes. We were ready!

Then a mission came up. It was a hit and run raid to destroy a radar station on the Ile d'Ouessant. This small island in the Atlantic just off the Brittany Peninsula is also called Ushant on British maps. Lieutenant Gene Dance (you remember him) led a team of eighteen Rangers on the raid. I was one of them. Some British Commandos also came along. Our orders were to destroy the radar station and bring home 2 prisoners. We were also supposed to leave some sign that American Rangers were there so we left Major Milholland's helmet and pistol belt. We demolished the radar station but the boys got too excited and killed all the Germans. No prisoners! Who can blame them?

Then we moved to Dover to prepare for another raid, this time on France. We had a hundred men ready to go but were turned back by the weather.

Then we got word in October that the War Department pencil pushers had dissolved the 29th Rangers. Major Milholland went to bat for us along with General Cota, the Division G-3, but they couldn't stop this. I'm sure we're all better off for the training but if we could have fought as a unit, I think we would have been a special fighting force. We turned in our jump boots. We kept the shoulder tab and decided to sew it on our combat blouse. We earned it. Fuck them all if they don't like it.

I was proud to be a Ranger with my boys from the 29th. This will take a long time to get over. Have to go now. Wally is playing Father Christmas at a local town party. That's what they call Santa here in England. Merry Christmas. Write soon.

Harley

Harley finished reading the letter. Having written it all down, he already felt slightly better. The censors, he imagined, would have a field day. There would be barely anything left to read once they got through with it. He lit a match, touched it to the lower corner of the letter and let it burn in the ashtray.

Chapter Forty-One

Cookstown, Northern Ireland - December 24, 1943

"Be slow to fall into friendship but when thou art in,
continue firm and constant."

Socrates (469 BC - 399 BC)

December 24, 1943
Dear Yank,

Thanks for your letter. I was surprised at the return address. I never thought that's where you would wind up. Anyway, at least I have your APO address.

After you and Jake disappeared from Sicily, we kept asking about you guys. Nobody knew. Other guys have been transferred but at least we were able to have a party and say goodbye. But you guys disappeared off the face of the earth. Even that freaking heel Bancroft didn't know.

Anyhow, after you left, we moved into the line defending the right flank of the 504. The Krauts backed off and retreated north. We marched north along the coastline. We passed Castellalmare, Pompeii and Mount Vesuvius before marching into Naples. We were first into the city. This was early October. The Germans pretty much destroyed the place and the harbor on their way out.

Old Cannonball is still our CO. He raised his American flag over the post office. The same one he raised in Gela on Sicily. He carries it around with him all the time and intends to raise it over the first town in France that we liberate. He's still the same asshole he's always been.

We spent some time in Naples. Teddy came through for us. He looked up Dom's relatives. They took him in like family and they fed us real good. These are remarkable people. They hardly had enough for themselves but they shared everything with us. We left them whatever we could, some C and K rations, D bars and cigarettes, which are like money here.

The Third Battalion was ordered to guard Naples while the rest of the regiment pushed on north with the Limeys. All we had to do in Naples was keep the peace and beat the shit out of any rear echelon mother fuckers we caught wearing jump boots. We caught a bunch of them. That's why the replacement boots hadn't been making it through to us. Those REMF bastards were pilfering the boots for themselves. All of a sudden, after we kicked some ass, that problem went away. Paratrooper ingenuity!

Colonel Gavin got promoted to Assistant Division Commander. We're all happy for him. He still looks too young.

Danny Boy and Teddy are doing fine. We all pal out together. Danny spent two months in the hospital but came through OK. We took on replacements after Sicily. It's hard for those new guys to fit in.

By early November we got orders to ship out. Nobody would say where, but the rumors were flying. We sailed on the SS Fredrick Funston, a true troop carrier ship. It was still crowded but there were enough showers and working latrines for all the guys and the food was great compared to our first trip over. We left the 504. I don't understand why Ridgway let that happen. They're being used up in the mountains like straight-leg infantry. Sure, they're great soldiers but what a waste and now our division is split up.

After 21 days at sea with a brief stop in Oran, where we spent Thanksgiving, the rumors kept flying. Finally, we pulled into Belfast. Then we came here to Cookstown by train. We're in a camp once occupied by British troops. The land is mostly farmland. We can't do maneuvers so we train on all types of weapons.

The people here are great although some of the Catholics in our company get a rough time from the Protestant locals. I can't believe how important religion is over here. It's freaking ridiculous. Not like back in the States where nobody cares. At least these people speak English, they're clean and they're not begging all the time. It's a pleasant relief from the places we've been. It's still a lousy place to spend Christmas! Rumor has it we'll be heading for (blacked out) in a few months. When we get there, I'll contact you and Jake and maybe we can all meet in London. That would be great to get together before the big one. Say hi to Jake. Merry Christmas.

Your Buddy, Sky

Johnny assumed the censor wasn't paying strict attention to let so much information through. Or maybe he never read past the first few sentences. Whatever the reason, Johnny was glad to hear from Sky after so many months and looked forward to getting together in London.

He handed the letter to Jake.

Chapter Forty-Two

Washington, D.C. - January 14, 1997

"Lord, Lord, how subject we old men are to the vice of lying."

William Shakespeare (1564 - 1616)

"They arrived in Liverpool on the SS *John Ericson* at the end of October with some other Hundred and first artillery and engineer units," Frank West explained between bites of his lunch. "All that bullshit about removing patches and jump boots…as soon as we got to England we hear Axis Sally on Radio Berlin welcome Max Taylor and his convicts of the Hundred and first Airborne." Frank reflected a moment. "Sky tells me she did the same thing when the Eighty-second arrived in Africa, only that time it was 'Matt Ridgway and his bad boys.'"

"Really? Security was that bad?"

"I suppose so. The Jerries had a daily broadcast called *Home Sweet Home* where Axis Sally played American music and tried to discourage the GIs with anti-Semitic and anti-FDR stuff. No one took it seriously but everyone liked the music." Frank paused. "I can't remember her real name." Frank took another bite. "Anyway, when the boys got to England they joined us in Littlecote, Wiltshire. I was an officer in the Second Battalion, Headquarters Company of the Five-oh-six and they reported to me."

J.P. had finished his lunch while Frank was talking and poured himself more wine. "Do you remember what kind of soldiers they were?"

"They were both good, smart soldiers. Jake was more intuitive, Johnny more analytical. I remember when they first came to my unit it was unusual. Two paratroopers with combat jumps, both corporals and nobody asked for them? We had no open billets, and one day they just showed up with orders. It was very unusual. We made them jeep drivers and they shuttled brass back and forth to the nearby villages. Our division was pretty spread out."

Andrew came by and picked up the empty plates. Both men declined a dessert menu and J.P. broke the brief silence as he emptied the wine bottle into their glasses.

"Nothing notable or unusual up until D-Day?" J.P. asked.

"Jake and Yank were good troopers until that bar fight in London. Then they both got busted back to private. It was a month or so before D-Day. I found out much later what it was all about but they wouldn't talk about it at the time. Quite frankly, troopers were getting busted left and right for brawling. Everyone was on edge for so long, pent up on that island and ready to explode, it didn't take much to start a fracas."

J.P. noticed Frank was getting melancholy. His memories were flooding back both strong and emotional. The whole D-Day experience was resurfacing in his mind and not all the recollections were pleasant ones.

"Sky was right last night when he said there were screw-ups," Frank added. "In Normandy they dropped us all over the place. Instead of cutting engines to jump speed, most of the pilots sped up to avoid the flak. Men went out the door at over two hundred miles an hour from less than five hundred feet. The shock ripped equipment off their bodies and in some cases broke bones. Some of the landings were deadly, in swamps and lakes and even into the sea. Some of the chutes never deployed they were dropped so low. But those who landed all over the place killed Germans and eventually seized their objectives."

J.P. decided to gently provoke Frank. "You were all trained for that, right?"

"Right. We *were* trained to anticipate the unexpected, to take the initiative and think for ourselves. The men who found themselves on the ground that night in Normandy did just that." Frank was less emotional than Sky had been the night before but was also fighting off old ghosts. "But General Taylor told our men to give him three days of hard fighting and we'd be relieved to plan for 'bigger and better missions', as Taylor called them." Frank took a sip of wine. "*Thirty days* later we were relieved and shipped back to England." Frank hesitated. "Thirty days! They used us as regular infantry for a month with no consideration of our limitations. What a huge waste. They had landed plenty of regular straight-leg infantry by then but they exhausted us instead. Our unique knowledge and training were shot to shit in line combat. They bled us white."

"Why do you suppose they did that?" asked J.P. He was planning to order another bottle of wine.

Frank poked his near empty wine glass up in the air. "I suppose it was because we were aggressive, reliable and tough soldiers. But we were light infantry and poorly equipped for long campaigns. We were highly trained troops with a unique specialty. It took two years to train most of us. There had to be other airborne operations we could have been saved for. Instead, they wasted us as regular infantry when so many others could have done that job." He gulped the last of the wine in his glass. "This wine *is* good."

J.P. nodded and took a long sip from his glass.

Frank wiped his mouth and continued. "And of course there was the Bulge when the Germans counterattacked through the Ardennes and punched a huge hole through our lines. Both American airborne divisions were sent in as regular infantry to stop the Krauts."

"Bad idea?" asked J.P. He signaled to Andrew for another bottle of wine. If Frank intended to relive the entire War then J.P. would furnish him with plenty of wine and patiently wait for him to slip up.

Frank thought a moment and answered. "In Ike's defense we were getting our butts kicked. He had no choice but to use us to plug the hole. But after the Bulge we were just a shadow of what we once were. The replacements weren't as good as the original guys, not nearly as well trained and never fully accepted."

"What about that *other* airborne division?" J.P. asked.

"That was the last combat jump for Sky and the boys. He *borrowed* your father and Jake, called in a few favors, to help train some of his green paratroopers and somehow they wound up making that jump too. I never quite understood how they got involved with Operation Varsity and the Seventeenth Airborne but that made five combat jumps for the three of them. After the surrender Sky transferred back to the All-Americans."

J.P. considered what Frank had just told him. "I had a feeling Sky had more to tell."

"Call him," Frank suggested. "He gave you his number. I know they met in London before D-Day and Jake ran into Sky on D-Day and in Holland. They both saw Sky again at the Bulge and..." Frank hesitated.

"And?" J.P. asked.

"And Sky saw your dad at the victory parade through Manhattan's 'Canyon of Heroes'. The entire Eighty-second marched. That was back in forty-six when America was still fiercely proud of its heroes and honored them."

J.P. reflected a moment. "I have to call him. He definitely has more to tell and I'm pretty sure he'll talk to me some more."

"He won't tell you anything about what you want to know," Frank warned.

Andrew came over, uncorked the bottle and poured wine into both glasses. J.P. took a sip and looked over the rim of his glass. "It's just a matter of time before I figure it out." J.P. smiled. "In the meantime, these are great stories and I'm learning a lot about my father."

"You may not have as much time as you think." Frank smiled back. "But I will confess there are two reasons that many of us are talking about our experiences."

"And they are?"

"Well, first, we're dying. About a thousand a day, I'm told. We were too humble to talk about the War when we were younger but now I think we fear dying without telling our story. That would dishonor our fallen brothers."

"That's a good reason. The other?"

"I fear we're not teaching our young people enough about the War. They don't seem to know that much and what they do know appears to be distorted." Frank took a long pull on his wine and continued. "There is too much revisionist history circulating out there. That's why I volunteer to visit schools, make speeches, contributed my oral history to the Library of Congress Project." Frank leaned back in his chair. "I do anything I can so people will remember."

"Remember the victory?" J.P. asked.

"No, remember the *struggle*. Remember the *price* of victory. Remember what our generation had to sacrifice and how we endured it in order to claim victory. Otherwise, without that knowledge and the blueprint for winning, we will collapse as a nation."

"Isn't that a bit of an exaggeration?" J.P. asked.

"I fear for my country, Mister Kilroy."

"Why is that?"

"We're losing our greatness. We're turning to mush. We are going to fall."

"Really? I don't agree."

Frank took a deep breath and sighed. "Throughout history, after a nation rises up to defeat a great threat posed by a powerful enemy, they lose that sense of community sacrifice for the common good. They get selfish and greedy. When the people of a nation demand more from their country than they are willing to give, the nation crumbles."

"I'm not sure I follow. I don't think this country will ever fall."

"I'm sure the Athenians thought the same after they defeated the Persians. They were free, enlightened, contributed much to mankind in government and the arts and sciences. And they fell in less than a hundred years. It took Rome a bit more time to lose their Republic after they defeated the Carthaginians in the Punic Wars. They held on as an empire for many more years but there was little benefit to the people as emperor after emperor drained the treasury trying to placate the masses with public works and entertainment. It took Rome a long time to rot from the inside but they got corrupt and went broke. Other great nations have fallen after their people abandoned the notion of service for the common good and started looking for handouts instead. The Egyptians, Persians, Chinese and most recently the British who at the beginning of this century effectively ruled the world. Today they are just another second rate, socialist country. All the greatness in all these great nations was squeezed out by a sense of greed and entitlement."

"But those were different times," J.P. objected although impressed by Frank's command of history.

"The times were different, Mister Kilroy, but human nature remains the same." Frank reflected for a moment. "The greatness comes from the giving, from the service, from the sacrifice. It never comes from the taking. Today we are an impatient nation of takers. 'What can the government do for me?' We no longer have the stomach for sacrifice and we look down on those who serve." Frank choked up a little bit. "No, Mister Kilroy, our greatest days are behind us. I'm afraid my generation reached that pinnacle of greatness for this country during the War. We just bought America a little more time. It won't be long before we fall, less than fifty years. I'm just happy I won't be around to see it happen."

"Whew," J.P. breathed out loud. "That's still pretty cynical."

"Look around and pay attention. We've kicked God out of our schools and replaced him with feel-good teachers and bullshit history. We've become a permissive society without discipline. Personal accountability is gone and we find blame with everyone else for our misfortune. Everything has to be *politically correct*. Heaven help us if we offend anyone."

J.P. stared at Frank without responding. There was more than just a little truth in what he was saying. However, in order to learn what he wanted to know, J.P. would have to keep Frank talking in the hope he might get careless and let something slip. That would be the plan for today. He would figure out how to approach Lincoln, Sky and Harley tomorrow.

"How about a nice hot pot of Espresso coffee? We'll order Sambuca and some biscotti and chat a little while longer?" J.P. had a warm smile on his face. He made the offer sound tempting and inviting.

Frank looked at his watch. "That sounds good to me."

J.P. signaled Andrew and ordered. The second white wine bottle was still half full. Andrew placed it back into the ice bucket and brought two clean wine glasses. Frank had calmed down by then and seemed a bit less anxious. He was deep in thought. Then his eyes opened wide.

"Mildred Gillars," he said.

J.P. looked at Frank curiously. "Who?"

"Mildred Gillars. She was Axis Sally. American born. Arrested after the War and convicted of treason. Served twelve years in prison if I remember right." Frank seemed pleased with himself for digging that name out of his deep memory. "If that happened today we'd give her a Hollywood contract...if she didn't already have one."

"All right then, Frank," J.P. began, getting back on point. "Tell me some more about dad and his buddy. Let's start with that bar fight in London that got them both busted."

Chapter Forty-Three

London, England – May 2, 1944

"The antidote for fifty enemies is one friend."

Aristotle (384 BC - 322 BC)

The official name of the pub was The Queen's Bazaar but it didn't take long for the cocky young Americans to corrupt the name to the Queen's Brassiere. It was a popular watering hole on Archer Street for GIs in London, due to its proximity to Piccadilly Circus. It was just one of the dozens of pubs within walking distance of the famous London Underground.

Nighttime in blacked-out London was always a busy and vibrant place with reckless young people continuously seeking fun and comfort. If they looked to dance the night away, there were favorites such as the Bow and Arrow, Charring Cross, The Cove and Gardens and the huge USO Club. If it was a special meal and ice-cold beer they sought, The American Bar in the Savoy Hotel was the best place in town.

Piccadilly Circus, the Times Square of London's West End, was not a circus in the conventional sense and the name confused many GIs. Rather, having been derived from the Latin word for circle, it represented a large circular open space at a multiple road junction. The many roads that led into Piccadilly Circus made it one of the busiest intersections in the world. It was a main center for commerce, shopping, sightseeing, pubs and prostitution. The girls of the night were called Piccadilly Lilies or Piccadilly Commandos, depending on one's experience with them.

With four tube entrances from the London Underground nearby, it was an easy place to get to. It regularly attracted the troops of many nations for the entertainment and distractions it provided. Troops who were massing for the invasion of Europe and who generally behaved as if there were no tomorrow, regularly swarmed Piccadilly Circus. The Queen's Bazaar, along with the Windsor Dive, were paratrooper favorites.

Jake and Johnny hopped on a two-and-a-half-ton truck, called a "deuce-and-a-half ", for the nine-mile trip from Aldbourne to the nearest rail station in Swindon. From there it was a reasonably comfortable eighty-mile train ride on the Great Western Railway through the English countryside. When they reached London, they saw uniforms from many nations prowling the streets looking for fun or trouble, whichever came first. There were servicemen from the Allied navies of the world, infantry soldiers, tankers, rear echelon clerks, pilots and crewmen from the air forces and stevedores and drivers from the Service of Supply. Almost every branch from every Allied nation was suitably represented in the masses.

The two young paratroopers found the Queen's Bazaar without difficulty. It was a large pub, crowded with mostly American GIs. Johnny saw shoulder patches from the 1st, 4th and 29th Infantry Divisions as well as the 82nd and 101st. Young English women carted warm pints of Guinness ale in and around the tables through the smoke-filled, loud and boisterous pub. The smell of cigarette smoke and beer made Jake instantly thirsty.

"Hey, Kilroys!" The loud voice from the back of the pub was distinctively Schuyler Johnson. He was standing on a chair waving his arms. The two men picked their way through the crowd and reached the table in a corner near the entrance to the kitchen. Danny Peregory was standing next to Sky. All four men grabbed each other by the shoulders in turn. There were handshakes, bear hugs and gentle slaps. They greeted one another warmly through broad smiles as they examined each other.

"Wow, you're a sergeant now," Johnny touched Sky's new stripes.

"And corporals, you two," Sky replied. "Just like Danny Boy here." Sky pointed to Danny's chevrons. "We must really be getting hard up in this man's army." They all laughed and took seats around the table. There were four air crewmen from the 8th Air Force at the next table and two colored soldiers at a small table beyond that one. The colored soldiers were wearing square blue shoulder flashes containing two white interlocking squares that identified them as part of the 2nd Service Command.

Jake sat next to Danny and slapped him again on the shoulder. His memory of sitting next to an enthusiastic Danny Peregory at Fort A.P. Hill evoked a nostalgic feeling of a time before he knew death. It seemed like so long ago.

Jake grabbed Danny by the scruff of the neck and shook him good-naturedly. "It's great to see you, Danny Boy. How the hell are you?"

Before he could answer a big soldier walked up to the table and put Danny in a light headlock. The soldier looked at Jake and said, "He looks great, don't he, kid?"

"Harley!" Jake yelled.

Harley let go and Danny popped up out of his seat to hug him. "I thought I recognized you sitting here," Harley chided Danny. "I wasn't sure. You looked bigger, older. But when I saw Jake come over, I knew it was you."

Sky and Johnny watched in amusement as the cousins and friends reunited. Jake introduced Harley and he shook hands all around as they sat down. A fat middle-aged English waitress in a dirty white apron took their orders for pints of ale and fish and chips and the five young men engaged in conversation.

"What do you hear?" Johnny whispered to Sky.

"Same as you. Normandy or Calais. It doesn't matter because we've been really practicing hard with the Fifty-second Troop Carrier Wing and with our Pathfinders for months. So wherever we drop, we'll definitely have a tight drop."

Sky cocked his head toward Danny. "Our Danny Boy is a Pathfinder now."

Everyone at the table looked at Danny. He shrugged his shoulders, a bit embarrassed. "Somebody has to be the first one in." He leaned forward and whispered, "We have this great equipment, a Krypton light and a Rebecca-Eureka radar transponder system. We set up the Eureka beacon in the drop zone and it tells the Rebecca receiver in the cockpit which way to go. That guides the planes right to the drop zone. Easy peasy. Piece of cake."

"Right. Assuming they drop *you* in the right place," Jake joked.

"We get the best pilots," Danny responded. "If *we* can't find the right drop zone then nobody can and we're all screwed anyway."

"How are the boys?" Jake looked at Sky referring to the members of their original squad.

"Well, you know Dom and Boots didn't make it. Lieutenant Klee got it too. Teddy is doing fine. He was promoted and transferred to Dog Company I think." Sky was squinting, thinking. "Oh, and Captain Wolff is back from the hospital and is leading Golf Company now. Came back in February." Sky paused. "We got two new green regiments, Five-oh-seven and Five-oh-eight. The Five-oh-four just got in from Italy. They're pretty worn down and beat up. The word is they'll probably sit the big one out. They're really pissed about that. Looks like the Oh-five will be the only veteran combat regiment to make the big jump."

Sky paused. A thought seemed to pop into his head. "Say, what the hell happened to you guys in Italy?"

The two men shook their heads. Johnny was the first to speak. "Can't talk about it, sorry."

"And you should have two combat stars on your wings, like us." Sky pointed to Danny and himself. "What's going on?" Sky was persistent.

"Just another Mickey Mouse army foul-up, Sky," Jake answered this time. "Someday I'm sure we'll tell you. But for now, just let it go, please?"

Sky cuffed Jake on the forearm. "So, you guys got nothing to tell us? I guess I can live with that."

"Well, that's not exactly true," answered Johnny. "I have some news. Rose is in family way. I'm gonna' be a father."

"When is she due?" Harley asked.

"June."

Sky thought for a moment. "So, you guys got home after Italy?"

"We did, Sky," Jake answered. "And that's all you need to know right now."

Sky flashed a devilish smile. "I can wait to hear the story *someday*. I'm sure it's good."

Just then the waitress brought their pints. Sky picked up a mug and held it high. "Congratulations. Johnny's gonna' be a freakin' father. Here's to you."

The boys clinked their mugs and each took a huge gulp.

Harley looked to Jake. "How's your new outfit? The Five-oh…what?"

"The Five-oh-six." Jake paused. "You know how it is, Cuz, they've all been together for nearly two years. Same CO. They took basic and jump school together. They call themselves "Toccoa Men", after the place they trained at. They're like one huge family. It's rough for outsiders to break in. We'll never be as close to them as they are to each other, but that's all right by us." Jake looked at Johnny and nodded. "We're doing all right."

"What *are* you doing?" Harley asked.

"Right now we're jeep drivers. We ferry the brass around since we're spread out all over Wiltshire County."

"Jeep drivers?" Harley was surprised.

"Yeah, it's crazy," Johnny acknowledged. "But we figure we'll be plain old infantry when we jump since there won't be any jeeps waiting for us." Johnny chuckled at his sarcasm.

Danny touched Harley's sleeve. "How are the Stonewallers doing?"

"Lotta' changes," Harley confessed. "Especially the officers. We got a new commanding general last year. General Gerhardt. Put old Gerow out to pasture somewhere."

"We got a new CO too." Jake interjected. "We had a General Lee, which made *me* feel good," Jake smiled at Johnny. "Then he gets a heart attack and now we got General Taylor, used to be Eighty-second. He's got combat experience in Sicily but I'd still rather have a *Lee*."

Johnny looked at Sky. He had a big grin on his face. "I keep telling him we're better off. Robert E. Lee lost the war for the South. If Lee kept his army intact like George Washington did, instead of pissing it away at Antietam and Gettysburg, the South might have outlasted the North."

Harley rolled his eyes while Danny gave a dismissive wave at the criticism of one of Virginia's most fondly held legends. Jake shook his head and smiled. "For a smart guy, sometimes you are so full of shit, Yank."

Johnny was laughing. He took a long pull on his beer, shook his head and shrugged his shoulders at Sky. They were all laughing and having a good time.

Sky looked at Jake. "The Oh-five got a new CO last month too. His name is Lieutenant Colonel Ekman. Gavin was promoted to assistant division commander."

"No shit," Johnny exclaimed.

"No shit. Gavin's a freakin' general and he's still in his thirties."

After a few moments, Jake noticed the Ranger tab on Harley's right sleeve. The Ranger tab was diamond shaped. The gold border and gold letters were arrayed on a blue field. The letters spelled RANGERS. Harley had his Blue and Gray "S-patch" for the 29th Infantry Division on the regulation left sleeve.

Jake touched the Ranger patch. "I'm really sorry about that, Harley."

"Thanks Jake. The guys and me were really pissed off at the time. It was a raw deal but we got over it. What else you gonna' do?" Harley didn't wait for an answer. "They don't like us wearing the patch but fuck 'em, we earned it. Besides, we're too busy now gearing up for the invasion. We've been practicing amphibious landings for months at a place called Slapton Sands. The word is we're in the first wave."

"No shit, Harley."

Just then there was a commotion a few feet away. The five men at the table turned to see. A group of about a dozen soldiers were walking slowly toward the two colored service troops seated at a table. Most of them were paratroopers. They were chanting, "Nott-ing-ham, Nott-ing-ham, Nott-ing-ham!" The air crewmen at the next table got up quickly, slid their chairs back and hastily scrambled from the area.

"Oh, shit," whispered Sky. "This is not good."

"What's going on?" Johnny asked.

"There's been friction between the colored troops and the paratroopers in the Leicester-Nottingham area. A paratrooper was knifed in a brawl and rumored to be killed. This looks like payback."

"Jeez, guys, it's not our fight!" Jake concluded and turned around.

"Problem is the rumor's not true. The paratrooper didn't die," Sky explained.

"They don't seem to know that." Johnny noticed some of the paratroopers with their switchblade knives down by their sides. The two black soldiers stood up and backed against the wall. They were wide-eyed with faces painted in pure terror.

"It's not our fight!" Jake repeated.

The apparent leader of the paratroopers was a brawny, bald young man with close-set eyes and a scar on his forehead. He led the chanting group deliberately and purposefully, closing the distance between them.

Suddenly, Johnny jumped up. He positioned himself between the paratroopers and the service soldiers. The distance between Johnny and the group was only about six feet. Surprised by this lone paratrooper, the group stopped.

Jake took a deep breath. "Shit!" He jumped up to stand with his friend.

"That's enough, boys. This isn't happening. Turn around and walk out the door." Johnny was holding up his hand like a traffic cop. Despite the odds, he seemed calm and confident.

One of the young airborne troopers noticed the Screaming Eagles patch and yelled out, "Hey guys, what do Eagles scream?" A few others yelled out with a high pitch, "Help!" It was a rehearsed ditty that members of the 82nd Airborne sang loudly to antagonize members of the 101st Airborne.

Sky rose to stand beside Johnny and Jake. "I'm Eighty-second. Five-oh-five. If you want them, you got me too! What unit are you?"

"Five-oh-seven," someone said from the back. "Five-oh-eight, Red Devils," said another voice. Danny got up and flexed his fists.

"Shit, look at the combat stars," someone else whispered loudly. The group appeared to lose some of its enthusiasm at the sight of four resolute paratroopers with six combat jumps and an Army Ranger ready to join them.

The bald sergeant wasn't intimidated. He looked directly at Johnny. "This is none of your goddamn business. These niggers knifed a fellow paratrooper. You're a paratrooper. Why the hell are you defending them?"

"Because you don't know these are the guys who cut your friend." Johnny stood defiantly in front of the sergeant.

"Killed him!"

"He didn't die."

"You don't know shit, get out of the way!" Sergeant Scar ordered.

"I know for a fact he didn't die," Sky bellowed back.

"No matter, we're gonna' kill these niggers and set an example. Nobody fucks with the airborne."

Harley got up and stood beside Danny. "Any Twenty-niners in this group had better leave right now. If you don't, I'll find out who you are and make your life a living hell, especially if you're a Stonewaller."

A few soldiers slipped out the back door. Harley wasn't surprised some of them had joined the group. There had been some racial trouble in the small town of Ivybridge, where the 29th Infantry Division was based. There were a number of fights between the black service troops and the white infantrymen. While it was not that common, it was not altogether unexpected in a segregated army.

Sky continued. "They'll be enough fighting and dying to go around in a few weeks. Save your attitude for the Krauts." A few more left but the seven or eight paratroopers remaining seemed determined.

"Out of the way," Sergeant Scar repeated. "You're not going to stop us."

Johnny turned to look at the black soldiers. They were backed against the wall. One was a huge man, well over six feet tall and about 250 pounds. His eyes were wide with desperation but he looked willing to fight. The other soldier was wiry and rangy, a lot smaller by comparison and had the look of a cornered wild animal.

"Have it your way, Sarge," Johnny turned back to Scar. "Put those blades away. If you get by us, then you can have them."

Scar smiled at the challenge. He looked down and began folding his safety knife. That's when Johnny hit him with a roundhouse right that splattered his nose. Blood gushed everywhere and a stunned Sergeant Scar staggered back and fell to the floor. Everyone jumped in and the mêlée began. While the rest of Johnny's friends kept Scar's group at bay, Johnny grabbed the smaller black soldier by the arm.

"Follow me." He pulled the soldier through the kitchen door. His friend followed. Johnny pointed toward the back of the kitchen. "Out that door."

"I want to fight them," the smaller man answered.

"For Chrissake, stupid! They're not here to fight you. They're here to kill you! Now get the hell out of here."

The smaller soldier became indignant. "Now I owe a white man something. I don't like to owe a white man nothing!"

Johnny shook his head in disgust. "Now that's thanks for you." He pushed the smaller soldier toward his friend. "You don't owe me shit." Then he spoke directly at the bigger soldier. "Get him out of here!"

"Yassuh," the larger soldier grabbed his friend's arm in his mammoth fist. He pulled him toward the back door.

Johnny already regretted his decision to stand up for the two black soldiers. The raucous sounds of the brawl he started beckoned to him. In a few short moments he would join his buddies but his curiosity got the best of him and he yelled at the backs of the fleeing soldiers. "Hey, who the hell are you guys, anyway?"

The small one, still in the clutches of his larger friend, stopped and turned. He still had a defiant look on his face. "He's Chauncy Gibbons and my name is Lincoln Abraham!"

Chapter Forty-Four

East Lake, Upper Peninsula, Michigan – *January 15, 1997*

"I will permit no man to narrow and degrade my soul by making me hate him."

Booker T. Washington (1856 - 1915)

Lincoln Abraham tightened his blanket against the cold as he snuggled in his rocking chair on the porch of his Michigan lakeside cabin. He loved this place and was happy to be back as he gazed out over East Lake. The other lakeside cabins were hundreds of yards away and tucked into the woods. Even with the leaves off the trees, he could barely see them. He reveled in the isolation and came to the Upper Peninsula every chance he could. The strong north wind had blown the loose snow off of the frozen lake, which glimmered in the sunlight like a mirror. He was comfortably bundled up, the blanket just another layer against the chill.

He bought this refuge immediately after returning from the War. It was relatively cheap because the Upper Peninsula was difficult to reach before the Mackinac Bridge opened in 1957. The cabin was perfect for a hunter and fisherman like Lincoln. Whenever he could get away, he would drive the 300 miles from Flint, where he worked in an auto plant. The log cabin was easy to maintain. The pristine drinking water came from an artesian well. A huge fireplace supplied the heat and a gasoline generator provided electricity when required. No telephone, no television. After the horrors of war, he appreciated the peacefulness and cherished the solitude. He hoped he would die right here marveling at a luminescent sunset or a spectacular sunrise.

The events of the past few days were still spinning in his mind. The Medal of Honor, the ceremony and lunch with the President were all so overwhelming. He was delighted to see some of his old friends and wished he could have spent more time with them. He was immensely gratified someone made the effort to correct mistakes made so long ago. His only regret was that some "so-called" civil rights leaders had tried to score political points with the African-American community over his experience. He wanted no part of that. Lincoln remained humble and God-fearing and refused to be a puppet in their manipulative hands. He could not have gotten out of Washington D.C. any faster and left them with mouths wide open and nothing to say.

Had they gotten him to speak he would have likely said some things that were not particularly popular. Instead of playing the race victim, he would have told his own black community to take responsibility for their own lives and take advantage of the immense opportunities available to them. *Stay married. Keep the family unit together. Reject the culture of violence that is popularized by gangster rap and treat your black sisters with dignity and respect. Stop children from having children. Turn in the murderers and drug dealers who are killing your babies. Show the world you can stand proudly on your own merits, with high self-esteem, righteous lives and love for each other, and what's left of racism will crumble before your eyes. Trust in God. You are great in His eyes. Live up to your promise!*

He smiled to himself. That wouldn't have gone over very well with those black leaders whose only method of keeping power was to convince the black community they were perpetual victims and to keep them cynical and suspicious of the society around them. It was a good business for black demagogues, from preachers of Black Liberation Theology to ambitious politicians, to keep the tensions high. It assured they remained in power. *What ever happened to the content of character instead of the color of the skin?*

It was different in his day. Racism and segregation were rampant, especially in the Jim Crow South. It wasn't easy for him. He had to overcome the scary stories his father told him about his ancestors hiding in cellars to escape lynch mobs of Klansmen. He was taught the only way a black man could ever attain respect was to fight for it. And even that didn't guarantee he would get any. It was certainly wrong that he was denied equality in the *land of the free*. But Lincoln would not surrender to the stereotype or accept being a victim. World War II became an opportunity for him to prove himself and fight the prejudice. It was his way of challenging the status quo and representing his race with action, not just with hollow words. Surely, there were enough men of good will who would change things if they saw how dedicated and competent American Negro soldiers were and how valuable they were to the war effort. But it certainly didn't start off well, having been assigned to the Service of Supply as a truck driver. That immediately caused him to develop a huge chip on his shoulder. He was an angry young man but one of great determination and faith and could not be long denied. He bided his time.

Lincoln worked tirelessly and drove relentlessly as part of the historic "Red Ball Express". For the first time in the army he saw the appreciation and felt the gratitude of white soldiers. He worked even harder, matured and awaited the next opportunity to prove himself. Then, finally, there were those thirty minutes on the fog-filled road between Noville and Foy in Belgium, with his newfound companion. Thirty minutes of sheer terror on that cold December day outside Bastogne in which he not only found himself, but also found what he was looking for in another human being. Thirty minutes that he should have been doing something else, someplace else, had events unfolded in the usual, normal way. Thirty minutes he believed were eradicated from the memory of mankind by racist officers who observed the action but refused to bear witness. Thirty minutes that changed his entire life and ultimately justified his faith and steadfast belief in God and in the innate goodness of his country.

"Hot tea, Grandfather?" His granddaughter Keisha intruded into his thoughts as she walked out on the back porch holding two steaming cups. She was beautiful with short black hair and large brown animated eyes.

"Thank you, dear," he smiled broadly at her. She was the light of his life and he was so happy she was between semesters at the Johns Hopkins School of Medicine so she could attend the Medal ceremony and spend a few days with him.

She handed him the cup and he cradled it in both gloved hands and drew the warmth from it. He motioned to the chair beside him and she sat down. "Only for a few minutes," she warned. "It's cold out here."

He reached out and held her hand. "I'm happy you came."

"I know, Grandfather. I'm happy to spend my break with you but you should be back in Baltimore with us so we can take care of you. This is not a place for someone in your condition."

"We've been over that ground, Keisha. This is my home now. This is my sanctuary. Out here I'm most comfortable with nature and with God. I can still chop wood, drive to town, do what I have to. When I die, it will be right here."

"Don't talk like that, Grandfather," she admonished. "I will call you every day." She held up the cell phone she planned to leave with him. The new cell tower near Interstate 75 covered the cabin and made up for the lack of landlines. "All the same, I would rather have you where I can take care of you, but I know I won't change your mind," she conceded. "Anyway, we could have stayed in D.C. a few more days."

"No, we could not," he disagreed. "Those charlatans were hell bent on making political points from my Medal. Instead of celebrating with me, there would have been endless damnations of the military for overlooking my deeds and more recriminations for my country. They would have cursed the darkness after a candle had been lit." He looked at the dubious expression on her face. "I know you don't agree," he confessed, "but these guys are in it for themselves. Have no illusion about that. When racism disappears, they lose power."

She sipped her tea carefully. It was still hot. She could not bring herself to believe racism would ever disappear in America. She could not imagine how difficult it had been in the forties. "How did you possibly handle all of that discrimination back then? And still love your country? It must have been awful."

He reflected for a moment. "Segregation was lawful back then in many states. It was also lawful in the military. Equality *should have* been ours, but it wasn't to be." He spoke slowly, thoughtfully. "The white enlisted men in the army just followed orders and obeyed policy but I knew that many of them resented us for *not* being allowed to fight." He sipped his tea, which was cooling off a bit. "Their resentment towards us, as well as ours towards them, was misplaced because the senior leaders in the military and the government made the policy. Everyone else in between was just doing what they were told to do. In spite of that, I could see it in their eyes; most of the guys knew that we blacks were getting a dirty deal. We were being denied the freedom that America was fighting for, it was wrong and everybody knew it. Many white people I knew were embarrassed by it but could do nothing about it."

"It must have been so hard," she surmised. "My country 'tis of thee, sweet land of bigotry."

Lincoln disregarded the comment. "It would have been harder if there was never any hope, but I witnessed many isolated acts of acceptance and inclusion. I saw with my own eyes the dead bodies of black men and white men, side by side, their red blood flowing together, fighting for the same thing. Nazi bullets didn't discriminate. In spite of the segregation in the military, well meaning men and women of both races fought to change the status quo while at the same time fighting a national war of survival. Where else but in America could that have happened?"

Keisha didn't answer, the words left drifting in the cold gray air. She stood up and fixed the blanket wrapped around her grandfather.

Lincoln continued. "We heard about Mrs. Roosevelt championing the Tuskegee Airmen and General George C. Marshall's order to form the Triple Nickels." He was referring to all-Negro combat units that were formed during the War. "It wasn't exactly integration, but it was a huge step in the right direction. People in high places were defying the racial stereotypes and giving us a chance to prove ourselves. And in life, the most precious things are a level playing field and freedom of opportunity. And opportunities should never be squandered."

She looked at him wondering if there was a message in there for her. "Don't worry, Grandfather. I plan to complete Med School."

He loosened the blanket around his shoulders, the hot tea warming his insides sufficiently. "I know you will young lady. You are the pride of my life and I believe in you so much." He turned in his chair to face her. "I know I dance to the beat of a different drummer than most black men. I'm proud of that. I'm very proud that I'm defined by my actions and my beliefs and not by the color of my skin. I'm proud that in some small way I helped to advance opportunities for black people and seeing you in Med School is the culmination of my life's accomplishments."

"Thank you, Grandfather," she choked back a tear. "But I'm so proud of you, too. For all you did and the Medal you won."

Lincoln overlooked the compliment. "Grab life, young lady. There is nothing you can't do. There are no obstacles that you cannot overcome. You are a child of God, live up to your promise." He felt funny lecturing her. She had her feet solidly on the ground but he sensed she was conflicted about the state of racial discourse in the nation.

"America is far from perfect," he changed the subject to what he thought she was concerned about. "Political correctness and hidden agendas will always be a way of life. Hell, we even left Kilroy's Medal out of the ceremony. If it wasn't for him, not only would there be no Medal of Honor for your grandfather, but there would be no grandfather," he snickered at his little joke. "But America eventually gets it right. We're a nation with a deep and relentless conscience. We're the world's last best hope…an imperfect union striving for perfection." He let the words drift away, finished, nothing else to say on the matter. He hoped his explanation was compelling enough to span the generations, overcome the distortions and convince her she alone was accountable for her own success.

"He seemed like a nice man, although a little bit hyper." Her words snapped him out of a momentary lapse in thought.

"Who?"

She laughed. "That old white guy they left out of the ceremony."

"Oh, yes. Mister John Patrick Kilroy Jr." Lincoln pursed his lips and nodded his head. "That young man is on a quest and I'm pretty sure he will wind up here some day."

"Really?" she asked. "Are you going to tell him the truth about his father?"

"I'd like to but I don't think so," he answered and then deliberated for a moment. "I did swear an oath." Lincoln coughed and leaned back. "Of course, it's all a moot point if I die before he gets here."

Chapter Forty-Five

Normandy, France - June 6, 1944

"Perish yourself but rescue your comrade."

Field Marshall Prince Aleksandr V. Suvorov (1729-1800)

The dark object came up quickly and Jake couldn't avoid it. He smashed into it violently, his chute collapsed and he fell hard to the ground. The landing on his side was vicious and he lost his breath. *Did he hit the side of a barn or building? Whatever it was, he was still alive!*

The sky was lit up like a fireworks display. Colored tracers reached into the night like wiggling fingers of death. The noise was deafening. The rattling gunfire was continuous and the drone of the C-47s only a few hundred feet above him was thunderous. The rhythmic clatter of a distant church bell sliced through the cacophony of sounds. It quickly occurred to Jake that he could move and make some noise without revealing his position so he dragged himself to the base of a hedgerow. His senses were acute and his eyes were wide but the shadowy shapes on the ground were still indistinguishable.

He realized he wasn't breathing. The crash had knocked the wind out of him and he gasped for air. When his breath finally came it was heavy and labored. He cut away his parachute with his switchblade while he lay on the cold, wet ground. A brisk breeze grabbed the empty chute and blew it away. The confused crack of gunfire was sporadic but continuous. Jake struggled to breathe and strained to see while kneeling at the base of the hedge.

First he had to find Johnny. Before he could do that he had to orient himself and take inventory of his equipment. His leg bag was gone; a frayed, broken rope the only clue something had once been attached to him. His padded Griswold bag that contained his M-1 Garand rifle was nowhere to be found. It must have slipped clean out of his bellyband during the opening shock of his bone jarring parachute deployment. It nearly tore him apart. He needed a few minutes to clear his head and he nestled more closely into the hedge.

At the end of May, the 101st Airborne Division left their enclaves and bivouacs in Wiltshire and Berkshire for their marshaling areas. The 506th PIR said good-bye to Aldbourne. They marched through the narrow streets of the small hamlet to the silent tears and muted waves of the villagers who had come to adopt and love them for the past nine months. The waiting trucks and trains transported the regiment southwest to an encampment near Exeter in Devonshire. It was made up of long, lines of large pyramidal tents. This enclosed area was adjacent to the airfield at Uppottery and was completely sealed off from the outside. Wire fences and British guards in German uniforms, to acclimate the paratroopers to the silhouette of armed Nazi soldiers, ensured no one slipped out after being sequestered.

By 3 June the officers of the 506th had been briefed and began briefing their companies and platoons. The paratroopers of 2nd Battalion were herded, a company at a time, into large tents with huge sand tables representing the topography of the drop zones and the essence of their missions.

They were told the 4th Infantry Division would land at Utah Beach at dawn. Four causeways were the only exits from the beach because the Germans had flooded the tidal marshlands. They all had to be secured from the land side. Failure to do so would leave the 4th Infantry Division stranded on the beach and jeopardize the landings.

The 506th was also briefed on the missions of the other regiments so they had a more comprehensive picture of the overall battle plan. Wherever they landed, they would know where to go and what to do. The radical theory that properly trained light infantry, stranded behind enemy lines, would take the initiative to carry out any mission was about to be tested.

Along with constant briefings and unit discussions, the paratroopers were issued ammo and grenades. They were each given a silk escape map of France, an American flag to sew on their right jacket sleeve and a compass. It would be another night jump so identification was essential. Each man received a small metal clicker that was supposed to sound like a cricket. One click was to be answered by two clicks. If this non-verbal means of identification didn't work, then the challenge "Flash" was to be answered by the password "Thunder".

The boys were kept busy cleaning weapons and sharpening knives. Some opted for Mohawk haircuts. Officers removed their rank insignia. The helmets of the four regiments were painted with the white symbols from a deck of cards. The 506th was spades. The 501st used diamonds. The 502nd took hearts and the 327th Glider Infantry Regiment became clubs.

On the evening of 4 June, the paratroopers were issued their parachutes and the rest of their gear. They would be going that night. The evening meal consisted of steak, peas, mashed potatoes, white bread and ice cream for dessert. Of all the meals, this one was by far the best. Just before they were to board the planes, they were ordered to stand down. Ike postponed Operation Overlord, the codename for the invasion, for twenty-four hours.

England had been in the grip of a spring storm for a number of days. The evening of 4 June was one of the worst. The wind-driven rain soaked everything in sight. Streams flooded, small bridges washed out and roads turned to mud. The visibility was poor and the conditions were brutal. The high waves and churning tides of the English Channel were not at all conducive to releasing the armada of 5,000 ships and 150,000 men to storm the shores of France. All along the southeastern English coast, in the great seaports of Southampton, Plymouth, Portland, Dartmouth, Portsmouth and others, ships and barges laden with men and material bobbed in the churning waters like corks in a raging river. All the scheduling, all of the planning, all the movement to the staging areas had come down to the moment when these massive forces were to be let loose on the enemy. But the unstoppable power of nature compelled General Dwight D. Eisenhower, Supreme Commander of the Allied Expeditionary Forces, to reluctantly delay the greatest invasion armada the world had ever seen.

The next day broke clearer and drier. Visibility had improved and the winds subsided. Late in the afternoon, the paratroopers of HQ Company, 2nd Battalion were trucked to the large hangar to collect their gear. Lieutenant Frank West pulled his 2nd Platoon around a large sand table. He was a quiet officer his men had come to like. He was easy to embarrass and the boys always seemed to have some fun at his expense. He didn't drink, smoke or curse. His glasses, soft-spoken manner and shy demeanor played into the stereotype. Even though he was tall and muscular, the general opinion was he was soft by paratrooper standards. The only aspect of this officer that the men didn't understand was his obsession for bayonet drills. 2nd Platoon would drill with the bayonet more than any other unit in the Screaming Eagles. In spite of this contradiction, they gave him the nickname "Casper", after the timid comic strip character Casper Milquetoast.

"Gather around men, get closer," ordered West. He pointed to a spot on the sand table. "Let me repeat for the hundredth time. This is our objective. DZ Charlie. We're being dropped by the 439th Troop Carrier Group of the 50th Troop Carrier Wing." The young lieutenant paused, "Just in case anyone gets lost out on the tarmac." A few laughed lightly.

"Our mission is to take Sainte-Marie-du-Mont, about six miles south of the larger town of Sainte-Mere-Eglise, and secure the exit to Causeway Two. We also have to secure the exit to Causeway Number One, near the town of Pouppeville. Exits three and four belong to the Five-oh-two." He pulled back the pointer and waved his arm across the sand table. "If you get miss-dropped anywhere in Normandy, join up with anyone headed for the causeways. If we don't secure those roads, the Utah Beach invasion will bog down and fail."

The hangar was silent. West was speaking louder than he normally spoke. There was a determined look in his eyes. "They gave us this mission because we're paratroopers. And we've been given the right flank of the invasion. *The right of the line*, the position of honor for the best soldiers throughout history." He thought the notion was inspirational.

"Why?" he continued. "Because we're tougher than any troops on the battlefield. That's why! We are better motivated than our enemy." His voice seemed to get louder. "Remember *this* if you remember anything. You're fighting for the guy on your left and the guy on your right. They trust you so don't let *them* down!" He paused to let them all contemplate that. "If you're separated and too far away from your objective, whether alone or in small groups, you *will* engage the enemy. Cut their communication wires. Ambush their vehicles. Attack gun positions and otherwise raise holy hell." West paced back and forth for a moment. "Use your bayonets at night. Don't give yourself away. That's why we practiced so long and hard with those stickers."

There was some shuffling of feet. Most of the troopers didn't like to use the bayonet. It wasn't easy to get up close and pierce a man's body with it. The idea repulsed even the most hardened soldier. However, since they were so adept at it, they could do it if they had to.

"Try not to hurt any civilians," West lowered his voice again. "But don't take any unnecessary chances. Bringing you back alive is more important to me than some French farmer." There was an affirmative murmur in the crowd. "Questions?"

"What about the diamonds?" someone asked.

"The Five-oh-one will drop southeast of us and secure the locks over the Douve River so Jerry can't flood the whole damn peninsula." West thought for a moment. "And one more thing. You don't need to take any prisoners unless you need intelligence. There's no way you can guard prisoners in the dark behind enemy lines and still complete your mission. And there's no way you can let them go to kill more Americans." He left the obvious alternative unspoken. "I'll say the words if I have to, but you need to know I won't be asking any questions or second-guessing anyone when you get back. Believe me, I don't think they'll take you prisoner either. They'll probably shoot you in your chutes on the way down if they get the chance! I trust you men. What each of you decide to do is good enough for me." One could hear a pin drop. Most became true believers right then and there. They decided on the spot that he would look out for them and do his best to get them home alive. That's all a soldier ever needed to know. They would follow him once that irrevocable bond of trust had been forged. They would still refer to him as Casper behind his back but it became a respectful epithet rather than one of derision.

Jake and Johnny carried their gear to the two-and-a-half-ton truck that would ferry them to their C-47. They followed their squad leader, Sergeant Clint Stockett, an amiable man with a wide friendly face and thin wispy blond hair. His eyes squinted when he laughed. Stockett was a truck driver in Cincinnati before the War. On this day he wore a cardboard placard around his neck with the number seventy-nine scrawled on it. The two young men threw their gear up onto the truck bed along with the rest of their squad-mates.

The heavily laden vehicle drove toward an air fleet of nearly ninety dark green C-47s poised in revetments lining the runways. This same scene was repeated in eighteen airdromes across southwest England. Places with colorful names such as

Cottesmore, Merryfield, Folkingham, Saltby, Spanhoe, Ramsbury, Nottingham, Membury, Welford, Greenham Common and Exeter. Before the sun would rise on the following day, more than 800 airplanes would drop over 13,000 American paratroopers into occupied France.

After a few minutes the truck pulled up near one of the planes and unloaded the troopers. The plane had a large number seventy-nine stenciled in chalk on the nose just below its name, *Buzz Buggy*. In addition, it had three broad white stripes painted around the fuselage and around each wing. They were called "invasion stripes" and they would identify every Allied plane in the air on D-Day. Rumor had it that there was not a single bucket of white paint left in all of England.

The paratroopers dropped their gear on the ground under a wing and gathered around the tail section. There would be sixteen troopers in this stick along with two A-5 para-pack equipment bundles slung underneath the wings. Their new jump suits were impregnated with a treatment to protect the men against a chemical attack of mustard or lewisite blister gas. It made the cloth stiff and trapped body heat and moisture. It was a dreadfully uncomfortable combination as the cuffs and collars chafed on the sweaty skin of the uneasy troopers.

Stockett was giving last minute instructions. "Listen up! Come and get your airsick pills." He held up a small glass jar of tiny white tablets.

"What the hell is that for, Sarge? We ain't never used no airsick pills before," complained Private Billy Christian, a miner from Coalwood, West Virginia.

"Orders are orders." Stockett picked up a bag attached to a long rope. "Also, everyone come and get one of these. The Brits invented these leg bags. You fill them full of stuff, tie them to your leg and go out of the plane with them."

"Jesus, Sarge," questioned Private Homer Smith, a steelworker from Pittsburgh. "Don't you think we got enough shit to carry?" Smith had a simple face with close-set eyes and an eager expression that said he was anxious to please.

"Stop bellyaching, Homo. Just take a bag and fill it before you saddle up."

They lined up and collected their pills and bags. In addition, many troopers were blackening their faces with burnt cork or greasepaint. Some were shaving their heads while others were applying war paint in the tradition of the great American Indian warriors.

Johnny was blackening Jake's face when Jake asked, "What about these pills and the bag?"

"Not for me. We didn't train with them, I'm not using them."

"Screw the pills, I agree," Jake nodded. "I think I'll try the bag, though."

"Suit yourself, buddy." Johnny finished applying the face-black and gave the stick to Jake. When both their faces were blackened, they started cutting strips of burlap with their razor sharp switchblades to weave into the netting of their helmets. The camouflage was designed to break the stark outline of their steel pots and make them harder to distinguish in the dark. Despite the lack of war paint they both looked ferocious.

The two men reacted quickly to a commotion behind them. They turned to see three military sedans pull up along side their group. One of them had a stiff flag with four stars attached to the front fender. General Eisenhower stepped out of the back seat. A British major stepped out of another sedan and beckoned to the troops to gather around.

Eisenhower and his entourage joined in with the group of stunned paratroopers. They didn't know whether to stand at attention or at ease. The general broke the silence.

"As you were, men." He waved his arms in the air. "Gather around." The paratroopers closed in a rough circle.

"Where are you from soldier?" He addressed a paratrooper with a blackened face. He was holding his battle helmet under his arm.

"West Virginia, sir."

"What's your name?"

"Private Billy Christian, sir."

"Good luck, Private." The general shook his hand and moved to the next soldier. It was another private and he was wearing his helmet and had his musette bag hanging over his chest. His pockets were bulging with equipment. "What's your name, son?"

Private Homer Smith was so flustered by the presence of Eisenhower he froze. After an awkward moment of silence, he answered with what he could remember.

"Pittsburgh, Pennsylvania, sir."

"They make good steel in Pittsburgh. Keep up the good work, son."

"Yes, sir. Thank you, sir."

At the appearance of the staff cars West hurried over from his plane, number twenty-three, which was parked in the next revetment. He stepped into the circle now surrounding Eisenhower and extended his hand.

"Lieutenant Frank West, sir. Headquarters Company, Five-oh-six."

The general shook his hand. "Your men look ready and eager, Lieutenant." Eisenhower seemed strangely uneasy.

"They've trained hard, General. They'll do their jobs."

West noticed the general's gloomy demeanor. It was almost as if he came to say good-bye rather than to inspire them. What West didn't know was Eisenhower had been given dire casualty projections for the airborne operation, codenamed Operation Neptune. His senior officer in charge of all air operations, Air Marshal Sir Trafford Leigh-Mallory of the British Royal Air Force had projected casualty figures as high as seventy percent. The year before, after the 82nd Airborne suffered twenty-seven percent casualties in Sicily, Eisenhower became convinced the airborne divisional formation was too large and the risk of losses outweighed any benefits gained. His subordinates eventually convinced him otherwise and he reluctantly agreed to an airborne component to Operation Overlord. All of this weighed heavily on his mind in the hours before the invasion and compelled him to visit some airdromes and meet and encourage as many of the young paratroopers as he could. He went on to the next soldier.

Before the general could say anything, the soldier spoke. "Private Robert Goldbacher, New York City, sir."

Eisenhower shook his hand and moved on to the next paratrooper. After a few more minutes of exchanging pleasantries with the men, he stepped back into the center of the circle. By now more paratroopers had joined the group and surrounded him. They strained to see and hear the general over the heads of their comrades.

"Men, you have a most important mission on D-Day…secure the causeways behind Utah Beach. The Hun is a tough soldier but you're tougher, better trained and better equipped. The only thing they have over you is combat experience and that advantage will disappear within minutes of your landing. I know you will you do your duty. Good luck and God bless you all."

As the general turned to walk away, Jake Kilroy stepped into the circle. "General Ike, sir. Jake Kilroy, Virginia. Are we going tonight or do you think it will be postponed again?"

Johnny rolled his eyes as Lieutenant West covered a feigned cough. Jake was determined to get an answer from the only person in the world who knew for sure.

Eisenhower looked Jake straight in the eyes and said with a grim smile, "We go tonight!"

The group erupted in a cheer as the general and his staff retreated back to his sedan and made off in a hurry.

"You love screwing with generals, don't you? You can't help yourself." Johnny smiled.

Jake had a big grin on his face. He really liked flaunting authority and immensely enjoyed tweaking the Supreme Commander. "At least I got an answer."

Just before sunset, the planes began loading. Sergeant Stockett assigned Johnny as the pusher because he had already made a combat jump.

Johnny was first into the transport. Privates Billy Christian, Homer Smith, Robert Goldbacher, Stanley Zebrosky, Leland Brewer, the platoon medic, and Corporal Manuel Sosa, the assistant squad leader, climbed in after Jake. The rest of the stick followed. They struggled through the door with their heavy loads, getting pulled from within and pushed from behind. Each man was given a piece of paper as he boarded. Johnny read it as he worked his way up forward to the pusher position immediately behind the flight cabin.

Soldiers, Sailors, Airmen of the Allied Expeditionary Force.
You are about to embark upon the Great Crusade, toward which we have
striven these many months. The eyes of the world are upon you.

It was a long note signed by General Dwight D. Eisenhower. He had seen this kind of note before, in Sicily, so he tucked it into his tunic pocket. He would save it and read it later.

When all of the C-47s were fully loaded, the engines began firing up. As more and more planes revved up their twin engines, a mechanical symphony began to play out. In a few minutes every plane had its engines humming smoothly and they began to taxi into position. The vibration was so strong that the ground beneath them began to throb and shudder as the massive armada positioned itself for take-off. It was at once both terrifying and beautiful.

Jake tilted his helmet back, his chinstrap dangling and his eyes closed. Johnny leaned forward, resting his chin on his reserve chute. Each man sought out his own personal place of comfort both in his seated position and in his personal thoughts. The trooper across from Johnny spoke above the engine noise.

"Hey, Yank."

"What, Goldbrick?" Private Robert Goldbacher was one of the hardest working soldiers in the platoon. Some nicknames had nothing to do with attributes or flaws but rather simply a corruption of a name.

"What's it like to be in combat?"

Ever since the Kilroys joined the Screaming Eagles and it became common knowledge they had jumped in Sicily, they had been asked this on numerous occasions. There simply was no answer to that question. It was a different experience for each individual. Regardless of how many times they were asked both Jake and Johnny agreed it was impossible to put into words.

Goldbacher was a smart Jewish kid from the Lower East Side of Manhattan and a hard-nosed soldier. Johnny gave him the most introspective answer he could muster. "Put it this way, Goldbrick. Combat is when you first find out that you can't live up to your own expectations."

Goldbacher nodded vigorously as a confused look gathered on his face.

Christian looked across the aisle at Smith. "Hey Homo," he hollered over the engine noise. "In case another general asks, your name is Private Homer Smith."

The nearby paratroopers laughed heartily at the barb...anything to break the mounting tension. Smith cocked his head to the side. "Yeah, yeah. I got nervous in the service."

Buzz Buggy taxied to the start point and took off in sequence. It maneuvered gracefully into a precisely choreographed formation designed to place 800 planes over their drop zones, on time, on target, in the dark. Although it would take barely an hour to make the 136-mile trip, it would take nearly five hours for all of the planes to deliver their loads. They were in the eleventh of twenty serials. Each serial was comprised of forty or more aircraft.

As their plane lifted into the darkened sky, Jake shoved a stick of gum into his mouth and leaned toward Johnny. "We need to be careful...stay together. Anything can happen tonight."

Johnny nodded. Jake looked more apprehensive than normal. They both felt invincible on their first two jumps but this time Jake appeared to feel vulnerable. It was a product of what they had both been through in Sicily. Sometimes a soldier felt strong and other times he felt his nerve slipping away. It happened to Johnny in New York when he couldn't bring himself to leave Rose. Both Jake and Rose convinced Johnny to gather himself and report back for duty. The two friends never spoke about that incident again.

Johnny turned to look out the oval window. The plane was banking sharply and on his side he could see the murky shadows of some of the farms in the English countryside by the faint light of dusk. He began to murmur softly. "We few, we happy few, we band of brothers, for he today that sheds his blood with me shall be my brother." Johnny shifted in his bucket seat and looked directly at the dim outline of one of the larger blacked out farmhouses and spoke louder. "And gentlemen in England now abed shall think themselves accursed they were not here, and hold their manhood cheap whiles any speaks that fought with us on..." he hesitated, looked at Jake and changed the quote. "On D-Day."

"What's that?" Jake asked.

"Shakespeare...from *Henry the Fifth*. At least the part I can remember."

Jake shook his head and chuckled. "You're something buddy. Quoting Shakespeare on our way to hell."

Johnny snorted a dismissive chuckle. "It seemed like a good idea at the time."

The C-47 clawed for its cruising altitude of 1,500 feet and settled into a staggered position in one of many V-of-Vs. The stream of planes took a southwest heading out of England over a spit of land called Portland Bill. From there they skirted the right side of the invasion fleet heading south in the English Channel toward the beaches of Normandy. The plan was for the air contingent to skirt the German occupied Channel Islands of Guernsey and Jersey and make a left hook onto the west side of the Contentin Peninsula. The Contentin was twenty-three miles wide at its base with all six of the drop zones within the last five miles. Once they released their loads, the planes would fly straight north, out over the English Channel and return to England flying directly over the invasion fleet but in the opposite direction.

After some time, Jake nudged Johnny to look out the oval window. Below them was the most spectacular sight they would ever see. From horizon to horizon, visible by virtue of the reflected moonlight, was an unending and countless mass of ships of all shapes and sizes. The invasion force was enormous and was relentlessly plowing the choppy seas toward its destination. The immensity of the flotilla was a great comfort to him. They shouldn't be behind enemy lines for too long before link up.

Jake spoke first over the engine noise. "General Lee once said this division would have a rendezvous with destiny." He shook his thumb at the scene in the window. "He was right. This is bigger than anything we'll ever see again."

They sat in silence for a few more minutes. The cabin was dark and each trooper was occupied in his own pre-jump ritual. There were smokers, sleepers, daydreamers and those who simply prayed. Each one lost in his thoughts and reflections and most making some sort of deal with his God for a safe return.

Johnny leaned to Jake. "Jake, I need to ask you something."

"Sure."

"Me and Rose want you and Macie to be the godparents for our kid."

Jake was caught off guard. "Are you sure? Me? And you don't even know Macie."

"Hey, we talked about it in our letters and we want the godparents to be a couple. You and I are closer than brothers. Besides, if you hadn't taken in that movie back in New York, the kid would have never been born." Johnny laughed.

"That's true," Jake joked back, "But you two looked like you were ready to do it right there on the kitchen table!"

Johnny laughed again. "I think you're right." He paused to look at Jake. "Well?"

"It would be an honor. I accept."

Johnny slapped Jake on the knee to seal the deal. "Great. That settles it. Now don't you go and get yourself killed on me."

"I won't. You neither."

The C-47 bucked and banked and skidded to the right. The view outside the window became cloud shrouded. They had flown into a low-lying fog bank as they crossed the coast and were flying blind. In an effort to avoid mid-air collisions, the pilots began to veer away from each other. The tightly packed formation began drifting apart and was irrevocably broken. All unit cohesion was immediately lost.

It seemed longer than the few minutes it was, but when the plane cleared the fog bank it was already well inland and heading into a steady stream of ground fire. The plane rocked and twisted as the pilots tried to evade the flak. Paratroopers were being thrown about the cabin. The shrapnel from the flak banged against the skin of *Buzz Buggy* like stones on a tin roof. Suddenly a salvo of bullets came up through the floor of the plane and exited the roof. The pilots continued to jerk the plane around while at the same time trying to join up with the few other planes around them. They may not be from the same serial but if they could match speed and altitude, the troopers would be dropped in some semblance of a group.

Sergeant Stockett was looking at Johnny with an anxious expression. He appeared to be asking Johnny why there was no light signaling four minutes from the drop zone. It was getting dicey and the plane continued to take hits and bounce around the sky. It didn't seem likely they would survive for four more minutes. If the C-47 took a fatal hit while the troopers were still seated, they would never get out.

Johnny looked into the flight deck. The crew was panicked. He answered Stockett's query with a firm thumbs up gesture. The sergeant nodded back and yelled, "Stand Up!"

The entire plane stood and Stockett gave the hand sign for hook up and the paratroopers hooked their static lines to the overhead cable. "Count off," hollered Stockett. It was the fastest equipment check Johnny had ever seen and before it worked its way completely to the door, he was already pushing in and compressing the stick. The boys leaned heavily against each other and were being held up by one another as the plane bounced and rocked and twisted in a fruitless effort to evade the flak. *Buzz Buggy* was still absorbing a great deal of punishment.

Johnny looked back into the cockpit to see the pilots struggling to find the drop zone. Another brace of .20-millimeter anti-aircraft shells stitched the cabin behind the cockpit. The muscular wide-eyed navigator was looking back at Johnny with stark terror in his eyes.

"Let's go!" some were yelling. "We gotta' get out!" The plane continued to bounce and shudder wildly. Johnny looked back into the cockpit. "Let's go," he yelled.

Suddenly the plane sped up and pitched up slightly. The red warning light went on and turned quickly to green. Johnny yelled, "Go, go, go," and leaned on Jake's back, literally pushing the frightened stick out of the plane.

The paratroopers, some with injuries, shuffled quickly along the blood-soaked deck and sprang out of the door in one continuous stream. *We must be setting some kind of record for getting sixteen guys out of a plane,* Johnny thought. *No one wants to be left behind, including the wounded.* As Johnny neared the door he pushed hard on Jake's back. As Jake went through the door, there was a loud explosion from the front of the plane. The C-47 shook violently and twisted as the nose dropped. Johnny was thrown back inside the plane and stumbled forward, off balance and out of control. He stopped rolling halfway down the cabin and looked up toward the cockpit. The plane's windshield was shattered. Blood and gore was splattered all over the instrument panel. The navigator was struggling to his feet. Both pilots appeared lifeless and the plane was diving out of control. The navigator reached forward over the slumped body of his co-pilot, grabbed the yolk and yanked back with all his might leveling the plane and then pitching it up. He turned to see Johnny struggling to stand up, get untangled and regain his balance.

"Get out, now," the navigator yelled as the plane pitched up further. Johnny scrambled back to the door, aided by gravity and the transport plane's nose-up attitude but struggling under his heavy load. He crawled to the door and looked back only to see the navigator straining to keep the damaged plane's nose up. Johnny nodded, a weak but heartfelt *thank you* as he rolled out of the door into the tracer-streaked sky.

Jake got to his feet when he had recovered sufficiently and strained to hear what was around him. But the constant droning of the continuous stream of C-47s, punctuated by the torrent of anti-aircraft fire, drowned out all other sounds save for that piercing church bell. He stripped his yellow Mae West life preserver and shoved it into the hedge. Next came his harness and his reserve chute. The .45-caliber pistol was still in its shoulder holster and he silently thanked Colonel Gardiner for not taking it back after the Rome Job. Besides a few grenades, it was his only weapon. He racked the slide, chambered a round and started walking.

Jake moved carefully in the shadows of the shrubbery. He came upon a road and moved along it. Up ahead on a slight crest he saw and heard a German "flakwagon" firing skyward at the planes. The rapid-fire .20-millimeter anti-aircraft guns were tearing the bellies out of the transports. He felt for a grenade, cut the safety tape and crept into throwing range.

All of a sudden there was an explosion and the gun went silent. The blast was followed by rifle fire as two paratroopers jumped up on the flakwagon and emptied their M-1 Garands into the Germans manning the gun. Jake let a few minutes go by and edged closer to the smoking vehicle. Then he heard the ominous single click of the cricket device. He groped for his but couldn't locate it in his pocket. The challenger repeated the click and Jake knew if he didn't answer quickly he would be shot. "Flash," he whispered as loud as he could through a dry throat.

"Thunder," came the reply. "Jesus, Jake, is that you?" Two men stepped out of the shadows. "Where the fuck is your clicker?" It was Private Billy Christian breathing hard and trying to remain quiet. "Me and Homo here almost shot your ass."

"It's in here somewhere, I think. Shit, I lost everything on the jump. Too low and way too fast," Jake was groping in his pockets. "You guys take out that AA gun?"

"Yeah, that was us," Private Homer Smith answered, also excited and breathing heavily. "And Goldbrick here." Private Goldbacher walked over to the group.

"Good job," Suddenly Jake remembered he hung the cricket device around his neck. His was issued with a small lanyard. He felt for it, found it and breathed a sigh of relief. He looked at Christian. "You guys figure out where we are yet?"

"No idea!" Christian was an outdoorsman, comfortable in the woods and always did well in night navigation exercises. If he had no idea, it would not be easy to find out where they were.

"Anybody see Johnny?"

The three heads shook negatively.

Jake looked around. He was a private like the rest of them but with three combat jumps he figured he outranked them all. "Okay, let's get to some high ground, take a look around and figure out where the hell we are." Before anyone could object he started walking. "Follow me."

They did.

Chapter Forty-Six

Pointe-du-Hoc, France - June 6, 1944

"One man with courage makes a majority."

Andrew Jackson (1767 - 1845)

Johnny Kilroy dove out of the plane at a bad angle and knew he was in imminent danger of fouling his shroud lines. The snapping impact of his parachute opening jarred him breathless. He groaned as his lungs expelled his air. Despite the shock and pain, he looked up thankfully to a full canopy. Before he could feel relief he looked down to see only the wide, angry moonlit ocean. He was about to experience a paratrooper's worst nightmare, a night water landing.

He had to work fast. He only had moments before plunging into the roiling sea with his 130-pound load. Under this extreme burden, it would only take seconds to sink like a rock.

First came the reserve chute since it was easy to unbuckle. With it went the M-1 Garand in its Griswold case. Next he slid his Schrade-Walden switchblade knife from his breast pocket, snapped out the razor sharp blade and cut one riser. The other one would be cut just above the water so his parachute wouldn't settle on top of him and keep him submerged. He began to spin wildly, suspended by one riser, and saw the spit of ground he had nearly landed on. It was jutting out into the ocean like the pointed prow of a ship. It was a steep and high cliff with an escarpment that ran back into the Normandy countryside and he cursed his bad luck for just missing it.

No time for recrimination! He quickly cut the straps on his ammo bandoliers and they dropped into the sea. With his left hand he began pulling the heavy Gammon grenades from his pants side pockets and dropping them into the water hoping they would not somehow detonate. With his right hand he fumbled to find the pull-ring on his Mae West life jacket, careful not to pierce it with his knife. When he found the ring and jerked it the vest inflated with a controlled explosion of air. He cut loose his musette bag as he neared the water and saw *Buzz Buggy* crash and cartwheel into the dark ocean. He took a deep gulp of air just before cutting the second riser.

The icy cold water was yet another shock to his system and in spite of the inflated life vest, he sank to the bottom quickly under the remaining weight of his load. He knew he only had thirty or forty seconds to find the surface. He desperately looked for something else to cut off of his body, only to realize that in the shock of the water landing he dropped his safety knife. By kicking his feet he would barely leave the bottom. He had neutral buoyancy at best and had to lose more weight quickly if he was to reach the surface. The water was dark and murky and he couldn't see much. He began to work by touch.

Keep your head. Think. He willed himself to take action as he fought off the panic that was an impulse away from taking over. *Grenades!* He pulled and dropped six fragmentation grenades from his harness where they were hooked in by their spoons. *Gas Mask!* It was attached to his web belt but would not come free. *Trench knife!* He reached down to his boot and pulled out his razor sharp trench knife. He had no difficulty slicing off his web belt, which took the gas mask and his water-filled steel canteen with it. His .45 was in a shoulder holster under his life vest so he slipped his hand beneath the vest and dropped his pistol. All the while he was kicking his feet slowly and he began to rise slightly. At least he thought he was rising. It was hard to determine his orientation in the dark waters. He felt his pockets and pulled out and dropped some K-rations as he slowly breathed out the bubbles from the deep breath he had taken before he hit the water. He only had a few seconds before the unstoppable urge to breathe would take over and he would suck water into his lungs and drown. Hoping he was at least oriented upward, he dropped the trench knife and began to kick and pull his arms violently toward the surface. He pulled and kicked relentlessly and just before he was about to suck in a lung full of deadly seawater, he broke the surface and gasped hungrily for air.

He lay there, buoyed by his life jacket, sucking in mouthfuls of life-giving oxygen. His silk parachute had blessedly drifted away and did not obstruct his emergence. *Buzz Buggy* was nowhere to be seen having disappeared into the swirling waves without a trace. His thoughts went to that brave navigator who kept the plane in the air long enough to give him a fighting chance. Johnny didn't even know his name. Someday he would find out. His family had a right to know how he died.

When he finally caught his breath he turned toward the shore. The cliffs towered above him to the height of a ten-story building and blocked out a good piece of the night sky. Looking left and right, the cliffs extended for thousands of yards in both directions from the point. The night sky was full of planes still dropping parachutists inland and returning to England over the English Channel. The gunfire could still be heard and the tracers and floodlights continued to spray the inky night sky.

He wasn't that far off shore and with the help of his Mae West and his lightened load, he would make it in. Despite his relief, he had to remind himself he was disembarking on a fortified enemy shore and if not careful, he could be killed or taken prisoner. He had no weapon and no plan. *What a way to invade Europe,* he thought.

The tide was out and he crawled up onto the sandy part of the beach on the east side of the promontory. He continued to crawl on his belly until the sand turned to shale at which time he stood up in a low crouch and skulked to the base of the cliff. The huge craters on the shale part of the beach looked deep enough to devour a man so he carefully avoided them until he came to the base of the vertical cliff. There was no cover or concealment so he worked his way eastward until he came upon a hollow cleft in the steep bluff partially covered by some wild growth of shrubbery. It wasn't exactly the cover he would have liked but it was nevertheless some concealment. Johnny stepped inside the cleft and sat down on the hard ground. His teeth were chattering and his body was shivering as he held himself and tried to draw some heat from the stone cliff face. He pushed his wet hair back off of his forehead, tried to wipe his face with his still wet hands and braced against the chilling breeze. The seawater dripped slowly from his stiff clothes as he waited helplessly for the Allied invasion from the sea. *At least he was still alive.*

The C-47 transports droned overhead for two more hours as the empty planes made their way home. Shortly after the last one passed above at no more than 500 feet, he began to hear a more distant, deeper drone of engines, higher, obscured by the clouds. The rumble of bombs dropped from invisible bombers shook the landscape. Loose stones and small rocks tumbled down the side of the cliff and peppered him with sandy debris. He looked for a safer place and scrambled higher up to an outcropping loosened from the side of the bluff by previous bombings. He climbed twenty or thirty feet up and while no longer being covered by the shrubbery, he was not easily visible to anyone on the heights or the beach because of the overhang directly above him. The bombing continued but Johnny wondered why they were targeting so far inland. He knew Omaha Beach lay just a few miles to his right as he looked out toward the sea. On his left, blocked by the high escarpment, was Utah Beach a few miles in the opposite direction. Thus far, none of the bombs had come close to either of the beaches or the heights overlooking them. The inaccurate bombing went on for what seemed like hours. Then there was near silence, just the sound of the angry surf slapping against the peaceful shore.

Johnny looked out toward the east. The sky was just beginning to brighten. Out over the northern horizon there were bright orange flashes of light. At first he thought it might be lightning but a few moments later the shells roared overhead and exploded inland. Then he heard the sound of the booming naval guns. Each salvo, sounding like a huge thump, sent 2,000 pound artillery shells onto the headland above. He could feel the pressure waves on his face. More bright lights lit the horizon as more ships joined the fusillade against the shoreline. The far horizon glowed red as more ships added to the barrage. Low clouds reflected the flashes in a kaleidoscope of colors. Many of the artillery shells landed well inland beyond both Utah and Omaha Beaches. The sky was filled with the screeching sounds of shellfire. Each salvo sounded like a runaway freight train crashing into a mountainside. The ground shook repeatedly and violently under the enormous barrage.

From his perch up the side of the cliff he could see the small dots on the horizon become slightly larger as the vast invasion fleet became more visible. It sent a chill up his already frigid spine. Before long, the sea between the horizon and the shoreline filled up with all types of small craft bringing soldiers to establish the beachhead. There were more than he could count. The great invasion from the sea had begun.

Johnny glanced at his watch. It was 0610 hours. Bombers appeared, came in low and began dropping bombs on the plateau above. They were American B-26 Marauders, and they were dropping their bombs from low altitudes. Meanwhile the large shells continued to pour in from over the horizon and two destroyers ventured closer to the shoreline, adding to the firepower pounding the cliffs. Smoke and dust swirled everywhere partially obscuring the massive fireworks display of rockets, tracers and gun flashes.

Johnny became aware he was in danger and scrambled down the rubble pile to the beach as shells continued to whistle overhead and bombs cratered the land above the cliffs. He found his former hiding spot and, determining it was not safe enough, moved farther west to the base of the steep cliff. He came upon a small cave and hid in it. At 0625 hours the bombers abruptly stopped. Five minutes later the sea bombardment ceased. Small arms and cannon fire could still be heard coming from the east. Flares, rockets and bursting shells lit up the sea around Omaha Beach but it became eerily quiet where he was. He stepped out of the cave and looked out to sea. Normally, when a barrage stopped a landing was close behind. No ships were visible off the beach. He strained his eyes to scan the horizon and then he saw them. A small flotilla of nine landing craft was running parallel to the beach. He recognized them as British Landing Craft Assault vessels, called LCAs. He watched them for a time as they slowly closed the distance to the small narrow spit of land he was standing on. They were running westward and fighting the tide until they were only a few hundred yards away from the beach. The fingers of the tracer rounds from high above on the cliff probed at the defenseless line of small boats. Machine gun fire opened up, rippled the water and peppered the landing craft. They were under heavy and accurate fire and taking casualties as they struggled westward through a rip tide and an angry, pounding surf.

Time seemed to stand still as the men on the small ships returned fire. Clearly, they were late to their target. Their destination appeared to be the narrow shale shelf under the high cliffs. *But where would they go from there?* The sheer vertical walls were at least a hundred feet high and appeared unassailable.

Finally, the nine landing craft turned toward the beach. They came in roughly abreast and slightly staggered. Johnny noticed four more craft hovering out to sea seemingly waiting for the initial nine to clear the beach. Some of them looked to be American DUKW amphibious vehicles. This ingenious design married a boat hull to the standard General Motors deuce-and-a-half truck to create a unique vehicle that could bring men and supplies from the water to anyplace on land.

The first LCA of the nine neared the beach and fired a rocket-propelled rope up toward the cliff. It fell short and the rope came crashing down on the sand. The ramp dropped from the front of the landing craft and men came pouring out. Johnny glanced at his watch. It was 0710 hours.

The same LCA moved in closer and fired another rocket-propelled rope ladder and this one held. Immediately, soldiers were scaling the rope and heading up toward the heights.

As more landing craft neared the shore, they too fired ropes up to the top of the cliff. Some landed to his left and others to his right. They covered a stretch of beach nearly 400 yards wide. Scruffy looking soldiers stormed out of the boats, avoided the water-filled shell craters and began to climb. Others added to the ropes already dangling from the cliff by firing hand-held rockets with attached ropes tipped by grapple hooks. Still others were assembling scaling ladders as they ascended the cliff face. Johnny couldn't believe his eyes. They were scaling the precipitous cliff walls like spiders.

The Germans on the top of the cliff fired on the climbers. They also dropped concussion grenades into the mass of men at the base of the cliff. The soldiers returned fire. This counterfire, along with a barrage from two destroyers, maneuvering in close, gave the first climbers a chance to get over the top and establish a small bridgehead. The covering fire, however, did not prevent some of the soldiers from being killed or wounded by sporadic German fire. More than just a few bodies crashed back down to the narrow beach from their ropes and ladders.

Johnny stepped out of the small cave. A soldier, a grimy looking staff sergeant, carrying a machine gun immediately challenged him. He was wearing a Ranger tab on his sleeve. Johnny instinctively raised his hands over his head. The soldier shouldered his weapon and took aim at Johnny's chest.

"I'm an American," Johnny yelled over the din of gunfire and began to drop his hands.

The Ranger looked confused and motioned for Johnny to keep his hands up.

"I'm an American paratrooper," Johnny yelled again.

"This way," the Ranger motioned with his weapon. "Keep those hands up."

Johnny locked his hands on his head and walked in the direction the staff sergeant had indicated. The soldier fell in step behind him. In a few moments they came to a group of officers huddled under the base of the cliff giving orders while other Rangers continued to send ropes up and over the cliff and began to climb them.

"Look what I found, Colonel," the soldier prodded Johnny in the back and pushed him toward the officer. He was a large man with a map case and binoculars hung around his neck. He stared at Johnny for a moment and before Johnny could speak, said, "Why Sergeant, can't you tell one of our own men from the Krauts?" He studied Johnny for a moment. "What outfit are you with, son?"

"Private John Kilroy, Five-oh-six," Johnny snapped a quick salute and pointed to the Screaming Eagle shoulder flash on his left sleeve.

"Lieutenant Colonel James E. Rudder, Second Rangers," the officer casually returned the salute. He seemed calm and very much in control despite the chaos around him. "What the hell happened to you, soldier? Where's your gear?"

"Bottom of the Channel, sir. I got dropped into the water."

Rudder shook his head and laughed. "You airborne guys are crazy. Stay right here and we'll get you onto one of those LCAs taking our wounded back to the ship."

Johnny interjected. "Sir, if it's all the same to you, I'd like to rejoin my outfit."

Rudder paused and turned back to Johnny. "Fine, Private." Then he looked at the sergeant. "Sergeant, let's get this soldier a weapon and some gear. He's going to be our guest. Take him up the ladder after we secure the cliff. See that he gets back to his unit." He turned back to Johnny. "Like I said, you guys are crazy."

Johnny snickered. He pointed up toward the hundreds of Army Rangers scaling the steep cliffs like ants on thin slippery ropes under enemy fire. "Sir, you think *we're* crazy?"

Rudder's mission was to silence six large 155-millimeter captured French artillery pieces deployed on Pointe-du-Hoc. From this vantage point, the large guns, with a range of ten miles, could interdict Utah and Omaha Beaches as well as the ships and landing craft off shore. It was the highest Allied priority to destroy these guns. Since the landside of the Pointe was heavily defended with bunkers and minefields, a sea borne attack was planned. The 2nd Rangers had been practicing this assault in England for months. After destroying the artillery pieces, they were to take up positions astride the coastal road between Grandcamp and Vierville, and deny its use to the Germans. Here they would remain until relieved by the 116th Infantry Regiment coming in from Omaha Beach.

The Rangers had 200 men up and over the cliff within fifteen minutes of landing. Thirty more lay dead or wounded at the base of the cliff. It was a marvelous tactical feat carried out under the most extreme and difficult circumstances. Once atop the cliffs the Rangers spread out quickly. The entire plateau was pockmarked with bomb craters and eerily resembled a moonscape. Rangers moved quickly and silently, without verbal orders. They were experts at fire and maneuver and were trained to use speed and stealth to make up for their lack of firepower.

The first order of business was to eliminate resistance against the Rangers still climbing so the Rangers on the Pointe cleared the cliff sides and overhangs of all opposition. The Germans grudgingly retreated toward the landside of Pointe-du-

Hoc using the single exit road. Rangers pursued until they reached the casemates that held the long guns and detoured to destroy them. Much to their surprise, the guns were not there. They found only long telephone poles under camouflage netting used as decoys. At this news, the Rangers were ordered to move inland and continue to look for the guns.

The Germans never expected an assault from the sea and didn't have enough soldiers to thwart the attack. As they withdrew toward the landside of the Pointe, they took up positions in bunkers and craters and harassed the Rangers moving inland. Ambushes flared up and had to be dealt with. Pockets of resistance formed and had to be cleaned out. The random isolation of these battles further delayed the advance southward toward the Normandy countryside.

The sergeant who had *captured* Johnny now took a personal interest in him. He retrieved an M-1 Garand rifle, ammo and a helmet from a dead Ranger and gave them to Johnny. They both then climbed to the top of the cliff on a tubular steel ladder. The action was still going strong when they reached the top. Johnny and the sergeant jumped in a crater from which they both began firing at German soldiers and snipers.

Another soldier, a first sergeant, jumped into the crater and addressed the staff sergeant. "Zack, we gotta' take Second Platoon inland and block the road. What are you doing here?" He nodded toward Johnny.

"Sorry Len, but Big Jim got me baby-sitting this airborne guy. He wants back to his unit."

Johnny answered quickly. "I don't need a damned baby-sitter. Just show me the way out of here." He was not about to be intimidated by these shabby looking Rangers.

"Calm down, son," Len said. "Our mission comes first. We're headed out that way so just tag along with us for now. We'll get you on your way." Len turned to his friend. "Zack, the guns ain't here…just some long black poles. We gotta' find them guns."

With that Len jumped out of the crater and headed down the exit road followed by Zack and Johnny. They dodged and weaved through sporadic enemy fire until Len pulled up next to a bunker and called out for his platoon. Slowly and deliberately, Rangers began to appear on the sheltered side of the bunker. When he had about twenty men, Len took half and Zack took the other half and they made their way down both sides of the road, heading south toward the countryside. They used skillful covering fire and maneuver all the way down the road.

By the time the group reached the paved highway that ran perpendicular to the exit road, they had lost almost half their men to skirmishes along the way. Len deployed his remaining men to block the highway and decided to scout further south for the guns.

"Zack, follow me. Bring your friend," Len ordered. "Let's find out what we got up here."

They moved quietly west along the paved road until they came across a sunken lane, with hedgerows on both sides, heading south and inland. Len led them a short distance down the lane and spoke to Johnny. "If your buddies are anywhere, they're inland. Just keep heading south and you should run into them sooner or later. We're going to scout a little further down this lane."

Johnny was no longer keen on crossing Normandy in broad daylight but he nodded. The three men proceeded cautiously down the sunken lane until Len noticed some camouflage netting hung high on the other side of the hedgerow. He raised his index finger to his lips and crawled up the hedgerow to peek through. He could not believe what he saw.

"Zack, here they are! We found them. Here are those goddamn guns!" Len whispered loudly. Zack and Johnny climbed the hedgerow. Straight ahead were the five large artillery pieces they had been looking for on the Pointe. The guns sat silently in an orchard under camouflage with no artillerymen near them. Their deadly ammunition was stacked neatly in piles well behind the guns. At the other end of the field, well over 200 hundred yards away, were about a hundred German soldiers listening to an officer addressing them from atop a vehicle. It was a golden opportunity the fortunate Rangers needed to seize.

"Zack, you cover me. I'm going to take care of those guns. Watch the Krauts across the field. Open up on them if they make a move toward the guns." Len handed Zack his Thompson and fished two thermite grenades from his pockets. "I only have two. There are five guns."

Len needed Zack to cover him and Johnny quickly figured out he was the one that had to fetch the needed grenades. It was too long a trip back to the command post at the edge of Pointe-du-Hoc but Johnny had an idea.

"Do all you guys carry these grenades?"

Zack shook his head. "They only issued about ten per company."

Johnny slid his M-1 rifle over to Zack. "Then some of your guys should have one. I'm going back to the roadblock." He looked at Len. "Will three do?"

Len smiled. "Three is perfect. Hurry back. I'm not sure how long those Krauts will stay away from the guns."

Johnny slipped out of the hedgerow and ran back up the sunken lane. An adrenalin rush from finding the guns fueled him. He reached the roadblock out of breath.

"Thermite grenades. We found the guns. I need three," he gasped.

A few of the Rangers pulled grenades from their packs and Johnny stuffed three of them into his slash pockets.

"Hey, where did you come from?" Two soldiers stepped up to him wearing a Screaming Eagles patch.

Johnny was surprised to see other paratroopers. "Five-oh-six," he answered.

"Five-oh-two," one of them answered for both. "We dropped south of here last night. Got separated. Saw the Rangers and decided to join them. It's crawling with Krauts south of here."

"Good to know, thanks." He slapped one of them on the shoulder. "We'll catch up when I get back." With that he took off down the highway.

When he got back to the hedgerow he handed the grenades to Len.

"I got two of them," Len said. "These will take care of the other three."

Johnny and Zack covered Len as he slipped down the other side of the hedgerow. The Germans were still on the opposite side of the orchard. The smell of melted steel was perceptible even over the smell of cordite that permeated the air. Len picked a big gun and slipped a thermite grenade into the traversing mechanism. He pulled the pin and the chemical reaction was instant. The extreme heat melted the metal, which began to flow in a molten stream fusing the gears irreparably. Len took care of the last two guns in turn and retreated back undiscovered.

"Hurry up, Len. Get out of there!" The three soldiers slid down the other side of the hedgerow smiling like kids who just got away with playing hooky from school.

"Didn't you want to find your unit?" Zack asked when they returned to the roadblock.

"Changed my mind," Johnny answered. "I think I'll hang with you guys for awhile."

"Glad to have you," said Zack and Len at the same time.

Chapter Forty-Seven

Omaha Beach, Normandy, France - June 6, 1944

"Fear is the beginning of wisdom."

General William Tecumseh Sherman (1829 - 1891)

Sergeant Harley Tidrick peered out over the port side of his British LCA at the small armada heading toward the Dog Green Sector of Omaha Beach. The gusty breeze whipped the briny salt spray into his face and he wiped the sting from his eyes to get a better look at the other five Able Company landing craft in his boat section. They were lined up in formation when one was hit by enemy shellfire. Another was foundering in the rough surf. Beyond them, further to the east, the six landing craft of Golf Company, American made LCVP Higgins Boats, were headed for neighboring Dog White Beach. They were farther away than planned and continued on a course that further opened the distance between them.

His group of LCAs was ordered to use the steeple of the church in Vierville-sur-Mer as their aiming point as they fought the rip tide driving them eastward. Although the church steeple was easily visible from afar, there had been some doubt as to whether the steeple would still be standing after the B-17s got through bombing the town.

Able and Golf Companies' mission was to capture the town of Vierville. However, Golf Company drifted eastward with the winds and strong tide and eventually lost contact with Able's left flank. Without Golf, Able Company would be isolated and absorb much more direct enemy fire. Harley knew this was not a good beginning for him and his men. He wiped the salty film from the face of his watch and noted they would hit the beach exactly on time at 0630 hours.

The first assault wave in the Dog Beach Sector was made up of the 116th Infantry Regiment of the 29th Infantry Division. Four companies abreast of Stonewallers would hit the hostile shores of Hitler's Atlantic Wall at the same time. Eight more companies of Stonewallers would follow. On the starboard side of Harley's LCA, lagging a few minutes behind, were two LCAs carrying Charlie Company of the 2nd Ranger Battalion. They were headed for Charlie Beach, the western-most designated beach sector on Omaha Beach. Harley could barely make out the white painted numerals on the side of the nearest LCA as it fought through the swells and waves. *LCA 1038*. He absent mindedly wondered if there was actually that many. Salt spray from a near miss mortar round snapped him back to the moment.

Beyond LCA 1038, Harley spotted the group of twenty-nine amphibious Dual-Drive tanks of the 741st Tank Battalion that were to provide fire support once the infantry hit the beach. They were specially designed M4A1 Sherman Medium Tanks with dual propellers, a rudder and an inflatable flotation collar. The thirty-five ton monster DD tanks were released from their ships three miles out and were now struggling to maintain their course in the rough waters and against the driving tide. A brisk northwest wind of eighteen knots whipped up the water into four foot swells that pushed against all the tanks. As the three-knot tide slanted their vessels easterly, the drivers tried to compensate by turning their vehicles back toward the church steeple. Eventually, as they turned to a more acute angle to the wind, the following seas began to hit them broadside. That was when they got swamped and began to sink. Harley was horrified as he watched the tankers scramble out of their steel death traps and into the frigid waters. One after the other, twenty-seven of the twenty-nine DD tanks foundered and disappeared into a watery grave. Most of the tanks that were to support the infantry on the beach were now at the bottom of the channel.

Harley yelled to his assistant squad leader, Corporal Wally Carter, who was bailing. "Wally, the tanks are gone!"

Carter stopped bailing and looked out over the stern of the LCA. He stared wide-eyed at the grizzly sight. "Holy Mother-of-God!"

Harley looked forward at the serene green bluffs rising above Omaha Beach. They were not supposed to be lush with green foliage but brown with the burnt remnants of hours of aerial bombing and naval shelling. There were no craters on the beach or bluffs either. Those were promised in the pre-invasion briefings. Everything he had been told to expect thus far had been wrong. *The Krauts are probably more than a single battalion and not the fat, old, third-rate unit that they predicted, either,* he thought. *The brass got everything wrong!*

Harley took off his steel pot helmet. "We're gonna' catch hell, Wally." He bent over and began bailing.

The booming thunder behind them was followed by the screeching roar of artillery shells screaming overhead as the Allied armada continued the ineffectual barrage. The sky overhead was overcast and the low hanging haze clung to the sea as if to escape the storm of projectiles hurtling through the air. The clouds eerily reflected the brilliant reddish orange flashes of the bombardments. Explosions on the shore could be heard loudly along with the concussive pressure wave on the faces of the soldiers. But the shell-fall was too far inland. Rockets being fired from barges let out a loud whooshing sound as they ignited. They arched colorfully in the air and fell uselessly short of the bluffs.

The engine of their landing craft roared loudly as the flat-bottom boat plowed its way through the angry waters. The thrum of the bilge pumps added to the overall loud and continuous din. Fountains of white water plumed skyward as enemy artillery fire found the range. Waves broke over the gunwales and threatened to swamp every landing craft. Despite being issued Dramamine tablets, boys vomited from seasickness. Having long ago exhausted the brown paper vomit bags they were issued, the soldiers were forced to bail the vomit-laden seawater from the bottom of their boats with their steel helmets. Nearing the end of the ten-mile run, nearly every soldier was shivering wet, soaked to the skin, nauseous from the sea and the putrid smells of vomit, urine and the oily engine smoke. The young men were racked with anxiety and fear and exhausted from both the weight of their gear and the gravity of their mission. Suddenly the naval bombardment stopped. They were but five minutes from hitting the beach. The young soldiers were already on the brink of despair and the worst was yet to come.

The plan for Operation Overlord underwent years of detailed preparation, training and innumerable modifications as the day drew nearer. The code names for the two forces that comprised the largest sea borne invasion in history were the Western and Eastern Task Forces. The Western Task Force, on the right flank, was made up of the United States First Army divided into the U.S. V and U.S. VII Corps. The former would assault Omaha Beach and the latter would attack the westernmost beach of the invasion, Utah Beach. This attack was added late in the planning and caused considerable consternation because it was twelve miles as the crow flies from Omaha Beach to Utah Beach. In addition, the wide mouth of the Vire River estuary separated the two beaches. In order to assist the isolated 4th Infantry Division, American airborne forces were targeted to drop behind Utah Beach.

The British and Canadian Forces of the Eastern Task Force would invade across three beaches covering a twenty-one mile front. Gold, Juno and Sword Beaches would be the targets for the British Second Army comprised of the British XXX and I Corps. These forces included British and Canadian Divisions supported by three Royal Marine Commando Battalions.

German General Erwin Rommel, Commander of Army Group B, had been given command of the defenses of the Atlantic Wall and worked diligently to improve them in the months preceding the invasion. However, a fractured command structure and Hitler's constant meddling made a cogent defensive strategy virtually impossible. Rommel, arguably Germany's best general, was frustrated by his inability to apply his experience and leadership. He left Normandy for Berlin on 5 June to celebrate his wife's birthday on 6 June. The weather was poor, he reasoned, and the Allies had never mounted an invasion in bad weather.

It was 0200 hours when the alarm bells of the HMS *Empire Javelin* sounded general quarters and jolted the men of the 1st Battalion, 116th Infantry Regiment awake. Harley wolfed down a breakfast of mutton and white gravy even though he had no appetite. Eating was something to do to pass the time and he wasn't sure when he might get his next meal.

By 0400 hours the men of Able Company, sixty percent of which came from the same small town of Bedford, Virginia, started loading into British LCAs hanging from the davits of the ship. It was a slow process. Once launched, they would circle until all six boats had been assembled and then depart for the long trip to shore. The men were weighed down with nearly seventy pounds of gear, much of which was stored in special canvas assault vests with multiple pockets for extra rations and ammo. Each Stonewaller carried enough supplies to sustain himself for three days. This load made them heavy and hampered their movement. Despite the encumbrances, they all had to bail with their helmets as soon as the boats were launched into the choppy waters of the English Channel.

From horizon to horizon the Channel was filled with ships of all shapes and sizes. There were heavy battleships and cruisers providing bombardment support. Smaller destroyers would range in close to shore to provide direct fire support to the troops. Thousands of vehicles were also aboard hundreds of supply ships, which carried the other necessary victuals of war. Small craft darted in and out of numerous transport ships bringing the troops to the beaches; soon to be returning with the dead and wounded. This carefully orchestrated waltz of ships seemed haphazard and chaotic but the small pieces meshed with the larger ones and the timing, with some exceptions, was conducted with the precision of a masterpiece.

The commander of the LCA yelled, "Ready, mates!"

The men braced for the shock of the boat grounding on the shore.

"Remember," yelled Harley. "Disburse. Go right and left off the boat and keep moving."

The Allied plan was to invade at low tide so the beach obstacles would be visible. The Germans had erected a wide array of obstructions to sink or damage the landing craft. Some were as simple as sturdy wooden posts built at a forty-degree angle designed to pierce the bottom of the boats or capsize an incoming craft. Others, called "Belgian Gates", were made of steel and were taller than a man and wider than a vehicle. Finally, three iron beams welded together formed a tetrahedron called a "hedgehog". These were often mined and placed randomly below the high water mark. It would become impossible to negotiate these obstacles when covered by high tide.

The men of Able Company had over 300 yards of firm golden colored sandy beach to cross before they could get to the smooth round stone shingles near the seawall. The LCA grounded with a loud scraping sound, the ramp dropped and the men filed out, spreading out as ordered. The entire shoreline erupted in fire as the first man stepped off of the launch. Two men on the right disappeared into a water filled crater and struggled against their load to climb out. A machine gun stitched a trail of bullets into the soft sand with a zipping sound. The unseen gunner walked the bullets right up into the LCA and more men were hit. The soldiers behind pushed their way over their dead and wounded comrades and made their way to the front of the boat and onto the spit of sand they had grounded on. A few men went over the side to avoid the blistering fire coming directly at them. Some men were running, others found their way behind steel beach obstacles. Yet others, who were killed instantly, dropped to the smooth blood soaked sand. No one was fighting back at the unseen enemy. The wounded were screaming in agony. The medics tried to attend to them and they too came under fire. Other wounded were crawling, vainly trying to find cover or get to the meager protection of the distant seawall. The ground shook with the vibrations of enemy artillery and the air cracked with the sound of flying bullets. The entire coastline was infested with German machine guns and they were all firing at the few remaining LCAs of Able Company.

Harley and Wally worked their way to the front of the boat as bullets ricocheted off of the steel sides. Once out they headed for one of the obstacles. Machine gun bullets traced a stripe in the sand next to Harley. Wally was hit and went down. Harley scrambled behind one of the wooden obstacles. There was a dead Stonewaller clinging to it. Harley hid behind the body. He was in the grip of the greatest fear he had ever known. Nothing in his life could have prepared him for this moment. Absolute terror rose up from deep within him and froze his body. It was the strongest emotion he had ever experienced. He hugged the base of the obstacle, paralyzed.

"Hey Mac, you gotta' move. I gotta' blow this son of a bitch!"

Harley turned. It was one of the beach demolition team who was blowing up obstacles before the tide covered them. Harley looked at the demolition soldier, or was he a sailor? *How in the hell is this guy getting around the beach without getting killed?* The demolition expert was wrapping some C-4 explosive around the long pole near its own explosive charge. The combination of the two would turn the wooden obstruction into splinters.

"You and your buddy gotta' move, Mac. This is a fifteen second fuse."

"He's dead," Harley answered.

"Then move out! I can't stand here all day."

Harley hesitated. The soldier pulled on the fuse and it sparked and started to burn. Harley got up and sprinted to the right while the demolition man took off left. "Fire in the hole!"

Harley's helmet came off as he ran but he didn't dare stop to retrieve it. He found another steel obstacle and jumped behind it. He hit the ground while the charge blew the first obstacle sky high along with dismembered body parts of the dead soldier. Harley crouched behind the steel obstacle as bullets continued to hammer the sand, the boats and the men.

It appeared the Stonewallers would never be able to accomplish their mission. There were five exits from the beach, called *draws*. They were the only egress from the seashore to the tableland above in the entire Normandy area. Some of these exits were simple dirt roads and some were merely footpaths. The only wide paved road was at Vierville. The Allies were well aware of this so they made the opening of the Vierville draw a D-Day priority. The only way to accomplish this was to defeat the defenses with a frontal assault. The DD tanks, that were supposed to provide some cover and firepower, never made it in. The naval and aerial bombardments missed their mark and were useless. The infantrymen were left defenseless and paid the price.

The Germans were equally aware of the high-value objectives and built an incredible series of fortified strong points to defend the exits and deny their use to the Allies. They called their strong points *Widerstandnest; Resistance Nests.* There were mortar pits inland with pre-sighted target areas on the beaches. The dreaded .88-millimeter and .75-millimeter artillery were sighted in hardened bunkers to shoot down the beach at an angle so as not to expose them to frontal fire. Numerous machine gun positions featuring the deadly MG-42 were sighted for plunging, grazing and enfilade fire. All five of the draws from Omaha Beach were similarly fortified but the Vierville exit was by far the most heavily defended. Able Company landed directly into the teeth of this formidable array of defensive weaponry and were being systematically slaughtered.

As Harley peered over the obstacle, which stuck out of the sand like a three-legged iron X, he watched the men of his company struggle to reach the tenuous shelter of the seawall to the left of the draw. It was flesh against steel as they scrambled forward or, like him, hunkered down in a precious protected spot on the beach. Some men played dead and others hid behind the dead. But Harley knew that was only a temporary respite as the tide would soon sweep in and cover everything on the beach to within a few meters of the seawall.

Smoke began to swirl across the beach from the burning wreckage of landing craft. Harley willed himself to move but his body wouldn't respond. Bullets ricocheted off the obstacle with loud pings and clangs. Lying prone and fighting unsuccessfully within himself to get off the beach, he soiled himself and began to cry.

A wave washed in and temporarily covered his lower body in foamy seawater before it drained back out to sea. The relentless tide was coming in. Harley was still frozen and in an utterly hopeless state when he felt the presence of another soldier kneeling beside him. The soldier was holding a helmet in his hand.

"C'mon, Ranger," the soldier said in a loud but calm voice. "We don't want to die out here among strangers. Let's get off this damn beach." He dropped the helmet. It had camouflage netting and an orange diamond on the back. As the soldier moved away toward the right, Harley noticed he was an officer and he wore a similar helmet.

The officer ran low for about twenty yards, dropped down and looked back. Harley nodded to him and put on the helmet and strapped it tight. He decided if he were going to make a run for it, he would have to shed some of the overload he was carrying. Another wave washed up on him and receded. He ripped off his invasion vest and stripped down to a just a few bandoliers of .30-caliber ammo and his M-1. The rations he carried would not be necessary if he was dead and if he made it, he would certainly be able to find more gear than he had to throw away.

The Ranger officer motioned to him. Harley nodded again and got up to one knee. Still hugging the obstacle he willed himself to move but his body remained frozen in place. Another wave came up, higher and stronger this time and something bumped him from behind. He looked down to see the body of Wally Carter, face up with a bullet hole clear through his right eye. It was as if Wally was nudging him off the beach. He sprung up with a muffled scream and ran low, right past the officer. Harley zigzagged and headed for the bluff while falling repeatedly over the dead and dying. The bullets raked the sand around him with a zip-zip-zip sound. He kept his eyes closed and kept running. After what seemed like an eternity, he fell at the base of the escarpment totally out of breath but safe from enemy fire. The officer came in behind him and huddled next to him. He didn't recognize Harley but then noticed the 29th Division patch on his other sleeve.

"What outfit are you with, soldier?" the lieutenant panted.

"Hundred and sixteenth Regiment, sir." Harley took a few quick breaths. "Thanks for getting me off the beach, sir." Harley was embarrassed but appreciated the encouragement. He was beginning to regain control of himself.

The lieutenant smiled. "I thought you were a Ranger." He pointed to the Ranger tab on Harley's other shoulder.

"Oh, that," Harley smiled back. "Twenty-ninth Rangers."

The lieutenant nodded knowingly. "We tried to get you guys but the brass wouldn't let us." He cuffed Harley lightly on his shoulder. "You're where you belong now. Welcome back!"

There was no seawall here so the Rangers gathered at the base of the escarpment and hugged the cliffside, which looked to be about fifty feet high. There were more men straggling in every few minutes. They were out of the direct line of German fire, which focused on the landing craft coming ashore near the Vierville exit. The wounded were being dragged under the cover of the cliff whenever possible. Medics were working furiously on them. Harley could see there were only about thirty men left in this Ranger Company able to fight. At first he felt simple gratitude to be alive but now the anger began to swell up inside him.

"Lieutenant Moody!" a voice barked out at the officer who had helped Harley get off the beach.

"Yes, Captain."

"Lieutenant, Plan A is no dice! We'll never get through that draw. Take a few men and find another way up."

The mission of Charlie Company, 2nd Rangers was to proceed through the Vierville draw, through the town of Vierville and head west to Pointe-et-Raz-de-la-Percee. After cleaning out any enemy emplacements, they were to proceed further west to link up with Colonel Rudder's Ranger Force A on Pointe-du-Hoc and complete that mission if they failed to scale the cliffs. The entire plan depended upon the successful landing of the DD tanks, which were to support the opening of the draw. With the tanks at the bottom of the English Channel and Able Company all but wiped out, Charlie Company had to find another route to complete their mission.

"Yes, sir."

With that, Lieutenant Moody took some men and worked his way westward, away from the draw, and searched for a place to climb the bluff. Harley went with them. After a few hundred yards they came across a crevice in the bluff and Moody began to free climb. Using his trench knife to carve out handholds and footholds, he reached the top of the bluff unseen. Once there, he attached a toggle rope to the base of a sturdy stake, which held a sign warning of mines. The remainder of Charlie Company made its way up the toggle rope. It was 0730 hours.

From the top of the bluff, Harley had a bird's eye view of the Dog Green sector of Omaha Beach. Subsequent waves had landed and the carnage continued. Along the seawall, dead, wounded and frightened soldiers of the 116th Infantry Regiment were stacked up like cordwood. No one was firing back at the enemy. The onrushing tide was collecting dead bodies from the sandy beach and floating them toward the seawall. The water was red with blood and the Germans kept firing their MG-42s until their barrels glowed red. His friends and neighbors in Able Company were being massacred with brutal efficiency just as their namesake, the Stonewall Brigade, might have been savaged in the Civil War. Harley shook his head in disbelief. The horrendous sight was fueling his rising anger.

Captain Ralph E. Goranson was the CO of Charlie Company, 2nd Rangers. The temptation to strike out to the west and complete his mission was great. However, he could not ignore the bloodbath that was taking place right before his eyes. His small unit had managed to breach the defenses undetected and he was in a position to suppress the killing fire by taking out some enemy positions. He called Lieutenant Moody over and changed his mission.

"Lieutenant, change of plans."

"Sir?" Moody queried.

"We're going to stay here and take out as many of those damned machine guns as we can."

"Yes, sir!" Moody acknowledged enthusiastically.

"Get some teams together to take out those Kraut positions. It's payback time!"

An angry and superbly trained killing force was about to be unleashed. There was a stone farmhouse to their east overlooking the Vierville draw that was pouring murderous fire onto the beaches. That would be their first target.

Harley joined Moody and a sergeant named Julius Belcher as they worked their way closer to the stone building. There was an elaborate trench system around the farmhouse that concealed the Rangers' movements. The Germans were too busy spitting out death to notice them approaching. Moody kicked in a door and tossed a white phosphorous grenade into the room. The MG-42 stopped firing and the Germans burst out of the door screaming from the burns. The Americans mercilessly gunned them down as they ran out. There would be no prisoners this day.

The Rangers didn't have enough men to hold the farmhouse. They were also afraid the navy might decide to bombard it so they took the MG-42 and all the ammo they could carry and retreated back to their temporary CP. If the Germans reoccupied it, the Rangers would do it all over again. The three men then set out to destroy another firing position. They located what the Allies called a "Tobruk", an open-top circular slit trench lined with concrete from which a machine-gun or mortar could be deployed. This particular one was firing mortar rounds onto the beach. The telltale thump of the rounds leaving the hollow tube gave the position away. The three soldiers crept up on it from behind. They lobbed fragmentation grenades into the open pit and it went up in a blazing sheet of flame. The Ranger force atop the bluff was just getting started.

Moody, Belcher and Harley returned to the CP and occupied a shallow shell hole overlooking Omaha Beach. Harley was astounded by the continuing butchery. No troops were advancing beyond the seawall; the beach was littered with bodies and clogged with the twisted wreckage of vehicles and sunken craft. Landing craft were no longer approaching the beach. The invasion at Omaha Beach had been halted!

Captain Goranson was scanning the beach with his binoculars. He spotted a single LCA well off course and headed for the shoreline directly under their cliff. He looked to Harley.

"Sergeant, that looks like some of your boys. Get them over here and up the rope before they run into a wall of lead. We could use the help!"

"Yes, sir." Harley scrambled down the rope and ran out and signaled the LCA. The LCA pulled in closer to the bluff as the tide was rising and Stonewallers from Baker Company scrambled out of the craft. Harley directed them to the toggle rope. Twenty thankful soldiers made it up the bluff. The rest of the men on that LCA, as well as the rest of Baker Company, were slaughtered just as their Able Company brothers were earlier in the morning.

Harley climbed back up to the top of the bluff and returned to the shell hole. He was anxious to exact more revenge. Belcher was climbing out of the hole. Harley found Moody lying dead, a bullet through his forehead. In a day filled with indescribable emotions of fear, anger and regret, Sergeant Harley Tidrick found himself welling up at the death of the stranger who had helped him off the killing sands of Omaha Beach.

"Sniper," answered Belcher to the unasked question.

Harley reached down and closed Lieutenant Moody's eyes. "Are you ready to get some?"

"Let's go."

Having become aware of an American force on the bluffs, the Germans began to counterattack. Their communication trenches fed back beyond the beaches. The defenders were able to funnel in far more reinforcements than the Rangers could muster. Mixed squads of Rangers and Stonewallers clashed with Germans all morning as the Americans fought to eliminate the killing fire and the Germans sought to replace their losses.

Harley and Belcher worked their way inland. They were planning to interdict the communication trench that led to the stone farmhouse and intercept any reinforcements. The further inland they got, the more separated they became from the main force.

They stumbled upon a branch in the trench that seemed to lead nearly all the way back to Vierville. They took covered positions on each side of the north-south trench and waited patiently. Soon, a dozen German soldiers carrying boxes of ammo came down the trench. Harley tossed two grenades into the trench. After they exploded, he and Belcher finished off the squad with small arms fire. No one was left alive. Suddenly, the two soldiers came under fire. Another squad of Germans was coming their way. They split up, Belcher heading back north to the beach and Harley starting west. He soon had to turn south as German infantry slipped in behind him. They were in hot pursuit. He came upon a paved road. If he remembered his map study, this coastal road ran from Collevile through Vierville-sur-Mer to Grandcamps Les Bains. The road was only one-quarter mile from the beach. He decided to continue further south.

The noise from Omaha Beach faded as he moved inland. As soon as he lost his pursuers he would retrace his steps back to the beach. He crossed bordered fields in the shadows of the hedgerows that surrounded them and kept to the countryside, avoiding trails and lanes. The distinctive ripping sound of a German MG-42 broke the silence and he became aware of it before he could see it. He could either skirt the position or scope it out. The chugging 500 round per minute rat-tat-tat sound of a Browning M1919A6 .30-caliber air-cooled machine gun indicated Americans were returning fire. He decided to investigate.

Crawling through one hedgerow he came to an open orchard. The sound was further south still. He crossed the orchard quickly and peeked through another hedgerow. About a hundred yards away was a German MG-42 machine gun crew. They had their backs to him and were spitting 7.92-millimeter rounds at Americans. There was the gunner, a loader on his left feeding the belt into the twenty-five pound weapon and two riflemen guarding each flank. The flankers were about twenty yards to each side and carried the standard German Mauser bolt-action rifle. They were spotting for the MG-42.

Harley had one grenade and could not get all six Germans with it. They were too spread out. He had to devise a plan that would allow him to take out all of them without giving them a chance to return fire. But first he would have to get closer.

There were four rounds left in his clip and he ejected them. The metal clip popped out with an audible ping and he caught it in the air. He collected the rounds from the grass before inserting a fresh eight round clip. He hooked the grenade's spoon into a high buttonhole on his battle blouse and slipped out of the hedgerow.

Harley crawled slowly and deliberately. The Germans were focused on their targets. He had to get close enough to use the grenade, perhaps thirty yards. No further if he was to make an accurate throw. But he needed an edge, something to keep some of them busy while he took out the others. If he threw the grenade at one target and fired at another, the third pair would get him. No matter which sequence he played out in his mind, the third pair would get a shot at him.

He continued to crawl. If they discovered him at this distance, they would get him for sure. He had to get closer. When he was about thirty yards behind his targets lying flat in the grass, it came to him. In order for his idea to work he had to be patient. The German machine gun continued to fire while the four riflemen held their fire. *What was it he learned in Ranger school? The German infantry squad was built around the machine gun. The rest of the men were there to carry ammo and support and protect the machine gunner. They needed all of these ammo carriers since the superbly designed weapon could fire an astounding twelve hundred rounds per minute at a muzzle velocity of twenty four hundred eighty feet per second. It had a voracious appetite for ammo.* But it had one weakness and Harley relied on that flaw to execute his plan. He slid his M-1 out in front of him and slipped the fragmentation grenade from his buttonhole. He pulled the pin and held the spoon tightly and waited.

Then it happened. The machine gunner yelled something in German to the four riflemen on his flanks. They began firing at the Americans. The assistant machine gunner came up on his knees with a large rag in his hand. He grabbed the barrel of the MG-42 and twisted if off. Harley was up in a flash and hurled the grenade at the pair on his right. Before it exploded, he put two shots into each flanker on the left. He ducked down as the grenade went off. When the smoke cleared, the assistant machine gunner was still holding the replacement barrel in his hands. Harley had caught them in a barrel change, a process the Germans were trained to execute in under seven seconds after 250 rounds were fired through the gun.

"*Kamerad!*" The loader yelled holding the barrel above his head. The gunner had a stunned look on his face but was helpless without a barrel in his MG-42. If Harley had not waited for that precise moment, the gunner would have turned the MG-42 on him and cut him in half.

Harley moved in and from the hip fired two shots in each chest. The empty clip hit the ground with a ping and Harley jammed another full clip into his M-1. All six of the Germans were dead. It didn't make up for what he witnessed that morning but it was a start.

"American GI," he yelled. "I got the bastards!"

The Americans approached cautiously, fearing German treachery. They came through a cut in the hedgerow. When the point man saw Harley, he waved his officer up to the front.

"Nice work, Sergeant," the lieutenant said. He was a young, boyish looking lieutenant, but then again they all seemed so young. He was wearing a Ranger tab. "What outfit?"

"Hundred and sixteenth regiment, sir, Twenty-ninth Division," Harley answered. "What outfit is this?" There seemed to be a little over twenty men coming through the hedgerow.

"I'm Lieutenant Charles H. Parker Jr., Able Company, First Platoon, Fifth Rangers. What are you doing here, Sergeant? Where's your outfit?"

"They're all dead on the beach. I hooked up with the Second Rangers. We were fighting on the bluffs above the Vierville draw when I got separated."

Parker pulled out a map. "Show me!"

Harley pointed. "They're here." Then he pointed to the beach area directly in front of the draw. "My company was wiped out here on Dog Green. Most of the second wave, too." Harley looked at the lieutenant. "They stopped sending landing craft in. Did the invasion fail?"

"No," Parker answered. "We came across the beach near the border of Dog White and Easy Red right between two strong points." Parker was fingering the map as he spoke. "Between the Vierville and the Les Moulins exits. We took some fire but we made the seawall, crossed the road and came up the bluffs." Parker paused. "Seems like the Krauts fortified the beach exits up the ass but not so much in between them. Took us a while to find the soft spots. Things are kind of fouled up down there and it's rough in places but the landings are still on."

Harley exhaled loudly. Parker continued. "Rangers from the Second and Fifth Battalions and soldiers from the Twenty-ninth made it up the bluffs and got behind the beach defenses." Parker looked to the north toward the beach. "What's over there?"

"Charlie Beach and plenty of Krauts between here and there. Where are you headed, sir?"

Parker pointed. "We're headed west for Pointe-du-Hoc. We missed the rest of the battalion at the assembly area. They're probably way ahead of us by now." Parker took a sip from his canteen. "We'll probably catch hell for being late. We got three or four more miles to go. Our guys may need our help taking out those big guns up there. Care to join us, Sergeant?"

Harley looked around. *What choice do I have? It's a miracle I'm still alive and hanging with the Rangers has been good for me so far.* He slung his rifle. "Count me in, sir."

Chapter Forty-Eight

Neuville-au-Plain, France – June 6, 1944

"We fight, get beat, rise, and fight again."

Major General Nathaniel Green (1742 – 1786)

Armed only with his .45, Jake Kilroy led his small band of paratroopers through a sunken lane between two immense hedgerows. They moved quietly and stayed in the moon shadows of the overhanging shrubbery. Planes were still flying overhead and tracers and flares were still sprinkling the sky with deadly colors. The incessant noise masked their movement.

Jake asked Christian to bring up the rear as they sandwiched Goldbacher and Smith between them. At the end of the sunken lane they came upon a paved road. In the intermittent light of the anti-aircraft artillery reflecting off the low clouds, Jake saw a square stone pillar astride the road with brass plaques affixed to the side.

"Stay here," he ordered Goldbacher and Smith. He waved at Christian. "Billy, on me."

They looked up and down the road and crossed over to the base of the stone pillar. Jake read the plaque in the moonlight. "This is Route Nationale Thirteen."

"Yeah, but where on N-13?" Billy whispered.

Jake looked at the second plaque. "Monteberg. Fifteen kilometers." He deliberated for a moment trying to envision the sand tables. "We're northwest of Sainte-Mere-Eglise."

Christian nodded and they scampered back to the shadows of the sunken lane. Jake gathered the small group in a circle and knelt down. Jake looked into the faces of the young men not sure what to expect and saw a look of determined confidence on each man.

"We're way off the mark. The drop was screwed." They all knelt down with him. "There's a village called Neuville-au-Plain about a mile north of Sainte-Mere-Eglise right here on N-13. If we take this main road we'll have to pass through that village. Or we can go cross-country. Either way we're staying together."

Christian spoke first. "I feel a lot better staying off the roads and going cross-country."

Goldbacher and Smith indicated agreement. In the midst of their conversation the planes suddenly stopped flying overhead. The guns fell silent and their whispers seemed unusually loud. They froze in silence and strained to hear anything at all. Only the dim sounds of small nighttime creatures and the distant sounds of gunfire could be heard. Jake nodded his agreement, got up and began moving down the sunken lane away from the road. The three men followed. They had only traveled a hundred yards when they heard the sound of hobnail boots back on the paved road. The Germans were patrolling Highway N-13. Jake was relieved they made the right decision.

The eerie silence of the night was disturbed by an occasional crack of small arms fire, emanating from every direction. The sporadic bursts of gunfire signaled small engagements and firefights, confrontations and withdrawals, unexpected encounters and clashes in the night as opposing forces of varying sizes stumbled upon one another. Jake knew they would have to get to their objective by daylight when German counterattacks were bound to come in organized units and with considerable force. Christian took the lead. They continued to work their way through hedgerows, across open fields and down sunken lanes. Progress was slow as they zigzagged across the countryside, unable to move in a straight line because of the patchwork of hedgerow protected fields. Christian kept his easterly direction by using the North Star. They moved quietly and alertly, weapons at the ready.

They came to another paved road running northeast to southwest. Christian halted them and signaled for Jake to come to the front. Jake looked up and down the road and tried to envision it in his mind's eye.

"Wait here," he instructed Christian and slipped away to find a road marker. A few minutes later he returned. The group gathered around in a small circle and took a knee.

"Ravenoville," he pointed northeast up the road. "Sainte-Mere-Eglise," he pointed in the opposite direction down the road. Then he made a chopping motion with the knife-edge of his left hand toward the southeast, perpendicular to the road. "Sainte-Marie-du-Mont. I remember this road on the sand table. We're about ten miles away from our objective, cross-country as the crow flies. Through more hedgerows and swamps. Maybe a small river or two."

Goldbacher observed, "We'll never make it before daylight."

Jake looked at his watch. "It's oh-four-hundred. I think we should head up this road to Ravenoville and try to find a causeway exit near the coast."

"The Krauts are bound to be watching the roads," Christian warned.

"Yeah, maybe we could hold up here and wait it out?" Smith suggested.

"We have to keep moving," Jake stood up. "We can't be out here alone when the sun comes up. If it's between the coast road or cross-country, I say let's make for the coast."

They all stood up. "Ravenoville it is," concluded Christian and he stepped out onto the paved road to lead the way. The group moved along the roadside in single file. A distant drone could be heard that became increasingly louder. After a few minutes the familiar sound of C-47 engines filled the sky. The men looked skyward. The C-47 Skytrains were towing small American CG-4A Waco gliders. Jake quickly counted six nine-plane V-of-Vs. Shortly the drone of the engines faded into the north as the tow planes slipped their cables and released their gliders onto silent currents of air. It took a moment for Jake to grasp that the distant sound of splintering wood was from gliders crash landing violently into hedgerows, trees and man-made obstacles called "Rommel's Asparagus".

In short order the tiny group was once again engulfed in the scattered but muted sounds of the night. Insects and critters chirped, small arms fire erupted and cracked in the distance. Allied bombers barely audible at high altitudes dropped their bomb loads on railroad yards and marshalling areas well inland. Christian hugged the side of the road as he stepped quietly and carefully. The three other troopers followed, eyes and ears searching the darkness.

"FLASH!"

They all heard the challenge from the shadows and froze in their tracks.

"THUNDER," Christian answered. Three other paratroopers stepped out from the hedgerow alongside the road. The relief in their voices was all too obvious.

"Jesus, we glad to see you guys. What outfit?" whispered a corporal with his arm in a makeshift sling. He was also carrying a .45.

Jake stepped forward. "Hundred and first, Five-oh-six. What about you?" They spoke in hushed tones.

The corporal tapped his arm. "Dislocated my shoulder on landing. We're Eighty-second, Five-oh-five."

Jake's old outfit! He didn't recognize the trooper in the dim moonlight. Jake's instincts told him the entire airborne drop had been a complete fiasco and this encounter proved it. Troops seemed to be scattered all over the countryside and nowhere near their objectives and now even the two American airborne divisions were intermixed. "Where are you headed?" Jake asked.

"Our rally point. Sainte-Mere-Eglise. What about you?"

Jake looked up the road toward the coast. "Sainte-Marie-du-Mont."

"It's crawling with Krauts up the road," Corporal Sling answered pointing over his shoulder with his pistol. "We just came from up that way." One of Sling's men nudged him and jerked his head toward the brush. "Oh yeah, shit, you gotta' see what we found."

The corporal moved up the road a few yards and pulled back the shrubbery. Lying on the ground, barely visible in the moonlight, were two dead paratroopers. They were stripped naked of clothes and equipment except for a musette bag with some orange panel markers used to identify friendly troops during air strikes. Each soldier had a large hole that almost obscured their faces, the exit wounds from a shot to the back of their head. Both of them had their genitals removed and stuffed into their mouths. It was a horrendous sight. Goldbacher threw up.

Jake recognized the thin wispy blond hair of Sergeant Stockett. He fought off his own revulsion and stepped closer to identify the other trooper. The Mohawk haircut told him it wasn't Johnny. That was all he wanted to know. He turned to

Christian. "Billy, we need to find out what Kraut unit was stationed around here. There *will* be payback!"

"Fucking-A," whispered an equally furious Christian. "Who was that with the Sarge?"

Smith answered. "It was Manny. I could tell by the tattoo on his arm." He recognized assistant squad leader Manuel Sosa.

Jake stepped back from the gruesome scene, tried to contain his outrage and turned to the corporal from the 82nd. "We'll join your group and head toward Sainte-Mere-Eglise with you. It's almost sunrise and we'll never make it to our objective in time anyway."

The corporal nodded nervously. He seemed more than willing to defer to Jake.

"Okay, then. I'll take the point. Billy, you bring up the rear. Everyone stay alert!"

Jake led the group back down the road from where they came. Their pace quickened as the sun brightened the eastern sky. Soon they came across the smaller outer buildings of a village. The steeple of a church was visible through the morning haze on the southern horizon.

"FLASH!" Jake heard the loud challenge clearly, even though he could not see anyone.

"THUNDER," he answered and a dozen fierce looking paratroopers came out of hiding with their weapons trained on the small group. A second lieutenant approached the group and noticed Jake's Eagle patch. "We got a bunch of your guys in the center of town. Head for the church. Watch out for snipers."

Jake looked up at the spire of an old stone Norman church some distance away. He led his small detachment toward it as the 82nd members of his small party broke off to find their own units. Corporal Sling nodded a brief farewell, which Jake acknowledged with a thumbs up.

The group picked their way cautiously along a street leading into the town square. Jake noticed the street sign said Rue du Cap de Lain. The shops were boarded up and closed on both sides of the street. There was no sign of civilians as they made their way deeper into the town.

A few hundred yards farther they came across a large two-story building with a sign that read Hotel de Ville. As they neared the building, an American flag shot up the large flagpole in front. It was a nine by twelve foot, tattered, forty-eight star banner. A colonel had personally run the flag up. There were some muted cheers from nearby paratroopers. The colonel then jogged toward the center of town. Jake knew him immediately. It was Lieutenant Colonel Edward. C. "Cannonball" Krause, CO of the 3rd Battalion, 505th PIR. That exact same flag had flown over Gela, Sicily and the main post office in Naples, Italy. Jake quickened his pace to keep up.

The courtyard of the old stone church faced the wide town square of Sainte-Mere-Eglise. Jake led his group toward the square. As they walked past the church they saw the bodies of dead paratroopers lining the road. They were wrapped in their parachutes and laid carefully. Jake's companions stiffened at the sight. The smell of human blood mixed with cordite was palpable. Jake had smelled the wicked brew and seen the dead before. He simply lowered his head.

They continued to walk. Parachute canopies were still hanging from the trees, a few with dead paratroopers in grotesque positions still in their harnesses. Some of the paratroopers were in the process of cutting them down. It was a grizzly scene. The cold dark gray stone blocks of the old church were flecked with slashes of light gray shrapnel marks and bullet gashes. An empty dappled green parachute still fluttered from the church steeple. *Must have been some damn fight for this town,* Jake thought to himself.

Krause jogged over to a group of American officers in the square. Another colonel was sitting in a jeep. Jake walked over to report in.

"First town liberated in France, Ben," Krause smiled to the other colonel. Jake noticed the colonel had his left leg splinted and it was dangling out of the side of the jeep. He was injured on the jump and the jeep had come in by glider. Jake recognized the colonel. It was Lieutenant Colonel Benjamin H. Vandervoort, CO of the 2nd Battalion of the 505th PIR. He wasn't happy.

"Right, Ed. Now all we have to do is hold the damn town!" Vandervoort grimly replied. He felt Krause was showboating with the flag stunt. Their personalities could not have been more different. Krause was fiery and loud while Vandervoort was reserved and soft spoken.

"We'll hold it just fine, Ben, now that your Second Battalion is here."

Krause's 3rd Battalion seized the town at 0400 hours after a concentrated drop. The German troops had unexpectedly abandoned the town after they defeated a small group of Screaming Eagles who had been miss-dropped into the center of the town while the townspeople were fighting a fire at 0100 hours. Those paratroopers were slaughtered in their parachutes as they descended into the lighted square.

Colonel William E. Ekman, who succeeded Gavin as the CO of the 505th PIR, was unaware Krause had already captured the town so he ordered Vandervoort to seize it. Now, there was the better part of two battalions defending Sainte-Mere-Eglise.

A small group of paratroopers entered the town from the southwest. Jake could tell by their equipment they were Pathfinders. The men sat down under the shade of a tree while their leader walked toward the command group. Jake recognized him. It was Corporal Danny Peregory. Danny paused slightly to look at the dead paratroopers still hung up in the trees. Just as Jake was about to holler out, Krause noticed the men sitting and immediately challenged them.

"What the hell are you men doing?" Krause screamed.

Danny stepped up to the colonel. He had been in the 3rd Battalion as long as anyone and absolutely despised Krause and his obnoxious behavior and abusive ways.

"This isn't a rest camp, Corporal," Krause continued hollering before Danny could say a word. "Turn those men around and set up a blocking position on that road."

"Yes, sir," Danny answered and turned to his team who had heard the whole exchange. They started to get off the ground slowly and began laughing at Krause's behavior. They found it amusing that Danny got chewed out. Their laughter sent Krause into a rage.

"You men, there! What the hell do you think is so goddamn funny? Get your asses in gear you bunch of stupid, yellow bastards!" Krause turned to Danny. "Your men are not taking this seriously, Corporal. See that they get moving and pronto."

Danny was furious. His men had just successfully completed a dangerous mission and instead of praising them; he was chewing them out. Danny and his team had hauled their lights, signal panels and Eureka sets from the original drop zone south of Sainte-Mere-Eglise, to another drop zone northwest of the town. It was backbreaking work, at night under combat conditions but his Pathfinders had pulled it off. They guided the glider force in exactly where they had been ordered to land them. That the second drop zone was too small and somewhat obstructed was not their fault. The field became a junkyard of smashed gliders and the glider men suffered dreadful casualties. But the much-needed supplies made it in.

Danny stood toe to toe with Krause and had had enough. He did something a paratrooper never did in combat and something that stunned everyone present. Danny stiffened to attention and snapped off a perfect salute. "Yes, sir." He held the rigid salute awaiting a return.

Krause instantly understood. He was immediately at risk that an enemy sniper would target him. Everyone in the square held their breath expecting the report from a sniper's rifle. It seemed like an eternity before Krause returned Danny's salute with a half-hearted flip of the hand. Danny held his salute a few more seconds as if to emphasize the point and then dropped his arm. Krause pretended to be oblivious to the danger and continued to bark out orders.

Jake stepped into the area and was immediately challenged by a major. "Where are you going, soldier?"

"Sainte-Marie-du-Mont." Jake replied.

"Impossible," the major replied. "Road south is crawling with Krauts."

"I have my orders, sir. We'll try cross-country."

"You're not even armed properly, soldier," the major noticed. "Pick up a weapon and stay with us. We can use you men right here. Better than getting killed or captured."

Krause and a captain stepped forward. They had been listening to the exchange. The captain spoke first. "Do I know you, soldier?"

Jake took off his steel pot. He recognized Captain Louis Wolff. "Yes, sir. I was in the Five-oh-five, Item Company…in Sicily. We lit the bonfire. Gela-Niscemi Road. Biazza Ridge."

"Of course," Wolff acknowledged. "I thought I recognized you. You're an Eagle now!"

"Got transferred, sir. I'm glad to see the Captain has recovered." Jake continued.

"More like a stupid injury than a wound," Wolff answered referring to the broken ankle he sustained on the jump. "But I appreciate the sentiment, son." Wolff put his arm on Jake's shoulder. "We can sure use you. Get yourself a weapon. We've built a pretty big stockpile from our dead." Wolff pointed to a pile of scavenged weapons.

"Yes, sir. Thank you, sir." Jake didn't salute. He walked over to the weapons pile. His three cohorts followed him.

The pile contained a few dozen weapons. There were M-1 Garands, M1A1 .30-caliber Carbines with folding stocks, a few BARs and a single Thompson submachine gun.

Jake reached down and picked up the Thompson. It was an original M1928A1 variant. He could tell by the Lyman sight, the Cutts compensator and the charging handle on the top of the receiver. It was stronger and more rugged than the later M1A1 version, which was redesigned to be manufactured faster and cheaper. The stock, pistol grip and forward barrel grip consisted of smooth, highly polished wood. Someone had taken meticulous care of this weapon; a weapon usually reserved for sergeants and above. However, Jake shot expert with the Thompson in training and there was no one here to tell him not to use it. He picked up an ammo sling, with five long thirty round box magazines, and slipped it over his shoulder.

"There's more ammo in the gliders," the familiar voice said over his shoulder. "They should be bringing in more any minute."

Jake turned. It was Sky Johnson wearing a huge grin. They grabbed each other's shoulders warmly and shook each other in elation. Sky spoke first. "Glad to see you made it, buddy. But aren't you in the wrong place?"

"We're definitely in the wrong place. We're supposed to be in Sainte-Marie-du-Mont." Jake introduced his three buddies to Sky. They all shook hands.

Sky looked at Jake. "Johnny?"

Jake shook his head. "We got separated on the jump."

Sky put his arm around Jake's shoulder. "He'll turn up. He's a good trooper.

Right now you got to say hello to some old friends." Sky motioned to Jake's companions and they all made their way toward the church where Item Company was gathering.

"I saw Danny Boy a few minutes ago. He had a run in with Colonel Krause," said Jake.

"I need to kiss him when I see him," answered Sky. "The Pathfinders did a great job. We were right smack on our freakin' drop zone. Just like I told you we would be. We had this town captured before breakfast!"

When the group reached the church, a number of the men in Item Company who knew Jake greeted him warmly. There was much backslapping and friendly pushing and shoving. When the small commotion died down, Sky pulled Jake aside.

"What are you going to do? You going to stay here or try for Sainte-Marie-du-Mont?"

Jake looked around. "I don't know. We probably should hook up with you guys and stay right here. We'd be sitting ducks trying to make our way in daylight." Jake looked over at Christian, Smith and Goldbacher. "We're staying here, okay?" They all nodded.

"Who with?" Smith asked.

"Whoever needs us, Homo," Jake answered. He turned to Sky. "Bancroft still first sergeant of Item Company?"

Sky shook his head. "No. He transferred over to Second Battalion, Easy Company."

Jake nodded and changed the subject. "Do you know what Kraut outfits are in this area?"

"Not yet, why?"

"Because we came across a pretty gruesome sight. Paratroopers executed, stripped and their bodies mutilated." Jake leaned in closer to Sky. "The Krauts cut their balls off and shoved them in their mouths."

Sky nodded. "We've been hearing rumors about that but we don't have any prisoners yet."

"We need to get some and figure out who did this." Jake looked over his shoulder and spotted something. "Sure as shit we won't get any prisoners standing around here."

A platoon-sized unit was forming up in the square. A staff sergeant was yelling, "Second Platoon, Dog Company, shape up here." Paratroopers were running into a loose formation. The lieutenant in charge was talking to Vandervoort. They were both reading a map and the colonel was issuing directives. The lieutenant was nodding vigorously as he received his orders.

Jake looked at his small contingent of Screaming Eagles. "Let's go with them, what d'ya say?" He pointed to the platoon forming up.

"Where they going?" asked Goldbacher.

"I have no idea but they look like they mean business and could use some help," Jake noted. "Maybe we can bag some prisoners."

The four men walked over to the sergeant. Jake spoke first. "We're kind of separated from our outfit. Can you use some help?"

The sergeant called to the officer. "Lieutenant Turnbull, sir. Do we need any help, sir?"

"We'll take all the help we can get, Sergeant."

The sergeant smiled. "Fall in, troopers."

"Jesus Christ almighty. Is that you Jake?" The voice came from the formation.

"Teddy!" Jake shouted back. Private First Class (PFC) Carmine Tedesco broke out of formation and grabbed Jake by the shoulders.

"How the hell are you? We thought you died or something," said an excited Teddy. He looked at the amused sergeant. "We know each other from Sicily. He used to be Eighty-second."

"What is this? Old home week?" said Christian sarcastically. "Do you know *everybody* in this god-forsaken town?"

"Is Johnny with you?" Teddy looked around.

"Not yet. We got separated."

The platoon fell in and marched north along both sides of Highway N-13 in combat separation. Jake and his small party were on this same paved highway, but further north beyond Neuville-au-Plain, earlier in the morning. This was Vandervoort's initial objective. He decided to send a platoon north to secure the town and serve as a tripwire for any German advance from the north toward Sainte-Mere-Eglise. Vandervoort chose Lieutenant Turner B. Turnbull and his platoon of forty-three men to capture and hold a town originally assigned to an entire battalion.

As the platoon headed northwest along N-13, the stone buildings of Neuville-au-Plain shortly came into view. The road was as straight as a rod and the two towns were only a mile apart. Patches of farmland separated by pastures bordered by thick hedgerows flanked the road. With scouts forward and flankers out, they spread out and marched off the side of the elevated road in a drainage ditch. They moved quickly with the precision of experienced, combat-hardened veterans. No orders were given. None were necessary. Every man knew his job and what to do when they encountered side trails, small walls, undergrowth and other obstacles.

Jake cradled his newly found Thompson submachine gun in the crook of his right arm with his left hand on the pistol grip. Scattered thoughts raced through his mind as he scanned the roadside for movement. So much had happened in the last twenty-four hours. From the safety of his bivouac in England to the maelstrom of liberating occupied France were the most contrasting of emotional extremes. The jump was harrowing and excruciatingly disorienting. One moment he was lost and the next he was in the company of friends, although the one that counted most was still missing. Jake was tired and hungry but most of all he was angry with the Germans for the desecrated bodies of men he trained with, ate with, laughed with. Finding out which German outfit perpetrated that atrocity became a personal obsession and there would be a measure of violent revenge. He was also annoyed at not being dropped where he was supposed to be. Nevertheless, if he couldn't fight with the Five-oh-six, he would fight with his old friends in the Oh-five. At least he wouldn't die among strangers.

Turnbull was gratified to find the town unoccupied by the Germans. He knew his small force would not be capable of holding the town against a determined German attack with artillery and armor. But he would put up a delaying fight and provide the alarm to his superiors in Sainte-Mere-Eglise. He was confident he would at least be able to hold back the enemy for a little while.

As the American force moved cautiously into the town, Turnbull deployed most of his men on the far side where some slightly elevated ground gave them clear sight lines and good fields of fire. They could see out in three directions to a distance of about 600 yards. Two of his squads dug in to the right of the road behind a small hedgerow and one squad was deployed to the left of the road behind a low wall.

Turnbull set up his CP in a small château just north of the old stone church at the crossroads of the town. He had a good vantage point from the upper floor. The church steeple would have provided better visibility but the lieutenant was sure it would be the first structure shelled when the Germans attacked. The small group of Screaming Eagles was assigned to CP security and Jake and his buddies manned the north side second floor windows. The first thing Jake did was to break the glass completely out. The other Eagles followed his lead. Veterans knew the shock wave from the first artillery rounds would shatter the windows and send deadly shards of flying glass in all directions.

Jake pulled a small couch up to the window and set himself in a comfortable position with a good field of vision. Turnbull's communications section had strung wire from Sainte-Mere-Eglise as they marched to Neuville-au-Plain. He established contact with headquarters and reported his status. His men were in position and dug in. It was 0900 hours on D-Day.

As Turnbull's force awaited the inevitable counterattack, some of the paratroopers spotted supply bundles that were scattered over the fields to their rear. They retrieved the bundles and were rewarded with extra ammo for their machine guns, rations and bazooka rounds. The troopers immediately began to dispense the supplies among their squads. A few hours went by and still no sign of the Germans.

PFC Tedesco came up the stairs with his arms loaded down. He dropped a pile of K-rations on the floor. "Come and get it! Breakfast is served."

Most of the men hadn't eaten since the afternoon before and many of them lost their rations when their leg bags were ripped off during the night jump. The K-rations, for all their monotony, were greatly appreciated.

Teddy walked over to Jake. He dropped two canvas cartridge belts with five box magazines each on the floor next to Jake. "I noticed you were carrying the Thompson. Three hundred rounds...all I could find."

Jake smiled. "Hey, thanks Teddy."

"I wouldn't want you telling everybody that the All-Americans didn't treat you well on your little visit here." Teddy handed Jake a K-ration box. "Mind if I join you?" He took off his helmet and sat down.

"The hospitality's been great, Teddy! Sit down." Jake took the wax-wrapped carton and broke it open. It was the size of a Cracker Jack box. That same company manufactured the K-rations for the military.

They ate in silence for a few minutes, looking out the window up the highway. Teddy broke the silence. "Remember that night in Sicily when we almost burned down that farm?"

Jake nodded.

"That family was scared shitless. I still dream about them...the fear in their faces."

Jake nodded again. He wondered why Teddy was bringing this up.

"Dom and I talked about it a lot before he bought it. We agreed that civilians are the ones who get the shaft in a war."

"That they do," agreed Jake.

"If it wasn't for you and Johnny that night, I think the lieutenant might have burned their home down and shot them if they got in the way," Teddy confessed. He was staring down the road, shaking his head ever so slightly and looking further than he could possibly see.

Jake studied his face. Some of what happened in the past was bothering Teddy. That was the problem with combat veterans. While they were physically proficient at the craft of killing, they were emotionally vulnerable to the memories of the waste and carnage they had already seen. They were somewhat diminished as human beings by what they had already been exposed to.

"I don't remember it that way, Teddy," Jake replied. "You and Dom decided not to burn that family out. You stood up for them. You gave the lieutenant another option. Johnny and me just stuck up for you and it all worked out. But it was you guys who saved that family."

Teddy reflected for a moment. "I'm not so sure we could have pulled it off without you...and I just wanted to say...thanks."

Jake laughed. "Sure, no problem." He looked down the road. "It's funny the things that stick in our minds. I almost forgot about that family."

"They remind me of my grandparents back in the Bronx. It's hard for me to forget them."

Teddy tossed an empty food tin out the window. "Whatever happened to you guys? You two just disappeared."

"We got transferred. Simple as that."

"Nothing that happens that fast is simple," Teddy commented. Suddenly he jumped up. "What the hell…"

Jake stood up too. In the distance a column of German soldiers was marching down the center of the road. They had their hands on their heads. Walking alongside them were two paratroopers guarding them, one on each side of the column. One paratrooper was holding an orange cloth identification panel.

"Where's the lieutenant?" Jake shouted.

"Down in the street. He's meeting with the colonel," someone in the room answered.

Jake slung his Thompson over his shoulder and flew down the stairs and into the road. He found Turnbull staring down the road with his binoculars. Vandervoort was sitting in his jeep doing the same. The colonel had just delivered a .57-millimeter antitank gun that came in by glider. He drove out to get a first-hand look at the tactical situation and provide more firepower. While the paratroopers were unhooking the artillery piece from the jeep, a French civilian rode up on a bicycle and told the officers a large collection of German prisoners were coming down the road from the north. The two officers were scanning the road as Jake came out the door.

"What do you make of it, Lieutenant?" Vandervoort asked.

"Looks like our guys bagged some prisoners, Colonel."

"I make it a few hundred or more. More than a company," observed Vandervoort.

"At least," agreed Turnbull.

"But what's that at the end of the column?"

Turnbull strained to see. "Looks like two vehicles of some kind. Can't make them out."

Vandervoort turned quickly toward the French civilian who reported the column. "What are those vehicles?" The civilian was gone.

Jake stepped in between the officers. He addressed Turnbull directly. "It's a trick, Lieutenant. They're just trying to get closer to our positions."

"What makes you so sure, son?" Vandervoort asked.

"Well sir, we were up that way this morning. We found some of our guys stripped down naked. They were carrying those orange panels." Jake paused. "The bodies were mutilated, sir."

Vandervoort nodded knowingly. He raised his binoculars. "Sure seems like a pretty small guard for such a huge captured force, Lieutenant."

"Those guards are Krauts, sir. They're wearing the uniforms they took off our guys," Jake persisted.

"Tell you what, Lieutenant. Fire some machine gun rounds off to the side of the road. Let's see what we shake out."

Turnbull gave the order and the .30-caliber light machine gun opened up. Suddenly the column of prisoners pulled their rifles from their backs and scattered to both sides of the road. They took cover in the natural folds in the terrain and began firing on the American positions.

Turnbull turned to the antitank crew. "Take out those vehicles on the road," he yelled.

The crew aimed, fired and scored a direct hit on the first vehicle. They were obviously some type of self-propelled artillery as the armor on the heavy German *Panzers* was not susceptible to the .57-millimeter antitank rounds. Before they could target the second vehicle, it began to fire smoke rounds onto the battlefield. This shielded the movements of the German infantry and defeated the visibility of the sole American antitank gun.

"Good job, son," Vandervoort slapped Jake on the shoulder. He turned to Turnbull. "It's show time, Lieutenant." There was concern and urgency in his voice but no panic. "Hold on here as long as you can and then fall back to help defend Sainte-Mere-Eglise. I'm not interested in another Custer's Last Stand!"

"Yes, sir!"

The driver started the jeep and turned it around heading back south down N-13. "Watch your flanks, son. They'll try to outflank you," Vandervoort yelled over the noise of shellfire as his jeep sped away. It was 1300 hours on D-Day.

Turnbull turned his attention to his positions. He knew he was outnumbered and immediately began issuing orders to keep his force compact and mobile. He ordered the men in the CP out of the building and into the streets where he would set up a mobile CP. No sooner had they left than a towed .88-millimeter artillery piece began shelling the chateau and the church. The unique high-pitched sound of a German .88 high velocity round was easily identifiable on the battlefield. The noise was deafening as stone splinters showered down onto the street.

German mortars started laying down a barrage making movement difficult. Turnbull knew he had to put up a mobile defense and try to suck the advancing Germans into favorable fields of fire before withdrawing further. He was concerned about his right flank where the woods came right up to the town. If the attackers got in among the buildings they could easily cut off his escape route. He pulled back the two squads defending along the low stone wall on his right, the east side of the highway, and deployed them facing east toward the woods. Turnbull took a huge risk by abandoning the defense of his center along the axis of N-13 in order to keep most of his force deployed to the flanks. *Perhaps the*

Germans didn't have adequate forces to try to envelop him and attack his center at the same time, he wished more than reasoned.

Casualties began to mount as the small force executed a textbook fighting retreat through the town. Turnbull could tell the axis of attack by the direction of the sounds of the gunfire and the unique sounds of the various weapons. The heavy ripping sound of the German MG-42 on his left flank indicated the squad defending that area was under intense pressure. The rapid-fire sounds of M-1 Garands and Browning Automatic Rifles along with the melodic chugging sound of the .30-caliber Browning Light Machine Gun told him his right flank protecting force had ambushed some Germans trying to work their way around his position.

This cat and mouse game played out for a few hours as the paratroopers fired and maneuvered toward the rear of the town. The Germans fired their mortars as they moved their circling forces around the flanks. All the while, Turnbull was pulling his CP back while staying in touch with Vandervoort's headquarters on the field telephone. The Screaming Eagles and a few All-Americans provided security and kept an eye on the open center down N-13.

"Let's pull the CP back to the next street," yelled Turnbull.

"Ready?" One of the sergeants yelled. "Now!"

Every paratrooper in the small group fired their weapons as the lieutenant and a few men pulled back to the next cross street. It was the last cross street in the town.

There was a low stone wall just off the road outside the rear of the town. A nearby drainage ditch provided additional cover. Turnbull eyed it as his last stand position from which he might gather his men and hold out while still having the option of withdrawing. He was already gathering his wounded there; Goldbacher and Smith being among those being treated. As he considered his options, his telephone went dead. Now he was isolated as well as nearly surrounded.

"Trooper," he called to Teddy. "I need a runner to get word back to the CO."

Teddy hesitated. Jake saw the frightened look in his eyes. Teddy wasn't a coward. He'd been through some rough combat and acquitted himself well. But every so often an otherwise brave man would lapse into a paralysis of fear. Teddy could stand at the corner of the stone house and fire his weapon all day long but he could not step out in the open and expose himself.

"I'll do it, sir," Jake slung his Thompson on his shoulder and stepped forward. "Just take care of my boys." He nodded toward the wall where the wounded were being gathered.

Turnbull looked at Teddy and back to Jake. He sensed what was going on. "Very well, Private. Tell the colonel we have six dead, a dozen wounded and we're being enveloped on both flanks." Turnbull cleared his throat. "Unless we get some help it'll be difficult to disengage. In that case, we'll just hold on here as long as our ammo holds out."

"Yes, sir." Jake began to move out.

"One more thing. Trace the wire. If you find the break, see if you can repair it."

"Yes, sir," Jake acknowledged.

"Get ready." Turnbull ordered. "Wait for our covering fire."

Jake nodded and Turnbull gave the order to open fire. Everyone in the CP security detail aimed their weapons at suspected enemy positions in the town and let loose a fusillade of small arms fire. Jake slipped out and ran down the road in a low crouch until he reached the drainage ditch alongside N-13. His Thompson at the ready, he picked up the field telephone phone wire and resumed running in a low crouch as he let the wire slide through the fingers of his empty hand. He had almost a mile to go and had to pace himself.

After a few minutes and a few hundred yards, the wire slipped from his fingers. It was broken clean. Jake stopped in his tracks. Usually when an explosion tore a wire, the ends were frayed. Not only was this end clean, the other broken end was ten feet away and also cut clean. Someone had snipped the wire in two places and removed the middle piece so it could not be easily spliced back together. *Krauts!* He thought. *But so far in the rear?*

He heard the crackle of the brush in the hedgerow behind him at the same instant the shadow flickered across the ground in front of him. His reaction was instinctive. He fell off to the left and spun around quickly depressing the trigger of his Thompson. The bullets started flying in an arc before he completed his turn. By the time he spun fully around, the .45-caliber slugs had nearly torn the German scout in half. The German fell with a surprised look on his face and was dead before he hit the ground. Jake pulled a grenade and flipped it over the hedgerow. He didn't wait to see if his grenade took out any more Germans.

So, the Krauts already had some forces between Neuville-au-Plain and Sainte-Mere-Eglise. He would have to be extremely alert in case that German soldier was not alone.

Jake alternately jogged and walked as he made his way back to Sainte-Mere-Eglise. The drainage ditch offered some protection but he had to leave it at times when it became too shallow. He darted from one concealed position to another, resting only briefly, but not long enough to fully catch his breath. The adrenalin was flowing, his heart rate was up and he was sweating profusely. His encounter with the German scout had pumped him up.

He finally saw the buildings of Sainte-Mere-Eglise and was challenged at an outpost and passed through to Vandervoort's headquarters. Jake gave his report. Vandervoort put his hand on Jake's shoulder. "I've got one platoon that I can send. Can you show them the way back?"

Jake nodded. "Yes, sir."

Vandervoort turned to his aide. "Get Lieutenant Peterson and First Platoon up here pronto. Get those Pathfinders, too!"

Orders were shouted and repeated down the line and paratroopers began to assemble on the double. Jake stared down the length of N-13 towards Neuville-au-Plain. He could barely hear the gunfire nearly a mile away. That there was still firing was encouraging. The terrain to the left and west of N-13 was fractured and broken by hedgerows and fields. It would take longer to reach Turnbull by this off-road route. However, they would not be as easily observed moving through the bocage country.

"Well. I'll be damned," Jake heard the familiar voice behind him. "If it isn't my old friend, Enema."

Jake turned slowly. It was Sergeant Gene Bancroft and he seemed as surly as ever. Jake walked up to him and whispered through gritted teeth. "I should have killed you where I found you in Sicily, crying like a little baby in the night."

Bancroft didn't react. He just stared at Jake. "I surely thought I was rid of you, boy. You and your friend, Yank. And here you are, like a bad penny."

Suddenly a paratrooper wedged himself in between the two soldiers. It was Danny Peregory. He looked at Bancroft. "Leave him the fuck alone, you sadistic bastard!"

Bancroft took a step back, surprised at the aggressive move from Danny. "We'll finish this another time," he said to Jake. "If you make it through the day." He turned to Danny. "You too, you little bitch."

Danny grabbed Jake's arm and pulled him away. "Jesus, Jake, I thought that was you. What the hell are you doing here?"

"Long story," Jake replied as he hugged Danny playfully around the neck. "I saw your little flare-up with Cannonball this morning. What are *you* doing here?"

"Me and my team are in this relief force."

Lieutenant Peterson approached Jake. Bancroft backed off as if nothing was wrong. "What's the situation up there, Private?"

Jake explained the tactical situation of the remnants of the 3rd Platoon and how Turnbull, against orders, was intent on making a stand rather than abandon his wounded. He described the terrain to the west of the highway as best he could and suggested that approach to get to Turnbull. They would be easy targets for the Krauts if they took the road back.

"The Krauts seem to be making a wide swing around Lieutenant Turnbull's left flank, sir."

Peterson nodded. "They may be so intent on encircling *him* they won't be looking for us. We may be able to surprise them." He handed Bancroft a handi-talkie radio and addressed them. "You three scout up ahead. Let us know if you run into anything. I'll take my platoon on an end run to the left and try to intercept the Krauts. If you see anything I ought to know, use the radio."

Bancroft replied, "Yes, sir." The three men headed out down the highway for a few hundred yards before they slipped into the hedgerows to the left of the road.

Peterson moved his platoon into the bocage country. They navigated through the hedgerows quickly and ready to fight. The radio remained silent; a good sign the scouts had not run into a German formation.

Nearly an hour went by when Peterson finally found what he was looking for. In a large open field to his front, a force of about one hundred Germans were gathering to attack the unsuspecting rear of Turnbull's small force. Peterson brought up his mortar crew. When all the preparations had been made, he gave the order. His mortar crew opened up with a barrage that caught the Germans in an open field with no cover. The paratroopers opened up with everything they had. Bits of vegetation flew in all directions and dirt kicked up from the ground as the troopers mowed down any Germans who survived the mortar barrage. It was all over in a few minutes. The small victory had been overwhelming. Peterson suffered no casualties. With this enveloping force out of the way, he struck out for the road to get to Turnbull faster.

Turnbull was being pressed hard on all sides. He had less than twenty men left and was about to be surrounded. When Jake and Danny miraculously came out of the hedgerow to his rear, they advised Turnbull a relief force of paratroopers was on the way. It was not large enough to stop the Germans but was powerful enough to disrupt them so he could disengage and withdraw.

"Well done, trooper." Turnbull knew this would be his last chance to withdraw his men.

Twenty yards behind, Peterson's platoon crashed through the hedgerow onto the highway.

"Time to go, sir," Jake pleaded when he heard the commotion. "Those are our guys."

"All right," he yelled. "Covering fire on my command. Everyone who can walk head back down the road." Then he yelled, "Fire!"

Every gun let loose with a high volume of accurate fire. Under the cover of the small barrage, Turnbull led his remaining force on the quickstep back down N-13 firing as they retreated. The relief force added their volume of fire and successfully extricated the remnants of Turnbull's platoon from Neuville-au-Plain.

As the combined force worked their way toward Sainte-Mere-Eglise, the lone body of a paratrooper lay off to the side of the road. Lieutenant Peterson recognized the stripes and flipped the body over using his foot. It was Sergeant Gene Bancroft. He was dead, a neat hole between his eyes. Peterson looked at Jake and Danny. Danny spoke. "Sniper," he curtly explained. Peterson nodded and the men continued back toward Sainte-Mere-Eglise.

Turnbull had held off a much superior force of the German 1058th Regiment of the 91st Airlanding Division. He staggered back into Sainte-Mere-Eglise with only sixteen men of his original force of forty-three. But they held all day and now dug in along with the rest of their paratrooper and glidermen brothers to hold Sainte-Mere-Eglise.

Jake finally learned what German unit was in the area that day and he would never forget it. It was 1900 hours on D-Day.

Chapter Forty-Nine

Newport News, Virginia - June 6, 1944

"The oaths of a woman I inscribe on water."

Sophocles (496 BC – 406 BC)

June 6, 1944
Dear Jake,

We just got the news that the invasion has started. The radio played Ike's order of the day. We were told it was the same order piped into the ships waiting to invade France. I got goose bumps just listening to him.

They stopped the yard for a few minutes and blew all the whistles on all the ships at the same time. Everyone was crying, even the men. The tears were more from hope that our boys come through this day safely and with victory. Almost everyone I know has someone who is serving. Most people have either lost a loved one or know someone who has. The Western Union delivery boy is the most hated person in the country. We hate to see him riding his bicycle because he only brings bad news. But I'm afraid the news will probably get worse before it gets better. There is comfort knowing the whole country is standing together with a single goal to win the war and bring our boys home. We're all in this together and we lift each other up when a lift is needed.

The spirit here in America is unbelievable. We heard on the radio that church bells have been ringing all over the land all day. The Liberty Bell was even struck once today for the first time in over a hundred years and it was broadcast live on the radio. Volunteers are crowding into Red Cross shelters and rolling bandages and packing first aid kits and doing something, anything, to contribute. The lines for giving blood are around the block. Everyone is buying war bonds. It's almost as if we're right there beside you. I know that sounds silly but I feel so close to you today. I pray that you are safe.

We launched the Intrepid a few months ago and right now there are 5 big aircraft carriers under construction. I'm training other young women now and I supervise a crew of 20 welders. That's a lot of responsibility for someone my age but I'm sure there are a lot of 21 year olds getting shot at. This war is making us all grow up faster!

Let's pray that today is the turning point and that the planes and ships and tanks we're building and the men and women that are serving can finally end this ugly War once and for all time. Please know that all of us back home are working and praying for all of our boys to return home soon.

I know our future has been kind of up in the air and a little unsettled, Jake. I'm no longer willing to leave it that way. If you still want to get married when you get home, I would be proud to be your wife.

Love, Macie

Chapter Fifty

Pointe-du-Hoc, France - June 6, 1944

"Mercy to the guilty is cruelty to the innocent."

Adam Smith (1732 - 1790)

Having scaled the heights of Pointe-du-Hoc, the U.S. Army Rangers patrolled vigorously inland beyond the shell pocked and bunker laden area adjacent to the cliffs above the sea. The Ranger command post was located cliffside, behind one of the concrete casemates near a knocked-out bunker on the east side of the Pointe. By late morning, neither the Pointe area nor the inland roads and fields had been fully secured. German snipers used the trench network to pop up and take shots at the CP before disappearing into the maze. They became increasingly more aggressive as the day wore on. There were simply not enough Rangers to secure the area. Movement was dangerous and the Rangers guarding Colonel Rudder's CP remained vigilant.

Further inland, south of the CP, the bulk of the Ranger force was probing the German positions. It didn't take long to discover a superior German force located nearby. It was massing with the intention of counterattacking and dislodging the Rangers from the escarpment. The Americans had stirred up a hornet's nest and had no choice but to go on the defensive. Three depleted Ranger Companies, sixty men, dug in and set up blocking positions along the hedgerows to deny the Germans use of the paved Vierville-Grandcamp Highway.

Their position formed a right angle facing southwest as dictated by the hedgerows. Each side of the angle was nearly 300 yards long. Easy and Fox Companies had dug in facing south. They had good open fields of fire in front and the paved road was behind them. Dog Company dug in facing west along a lane covered by another hedgerow. The right flank of their north-south line ended at the paved highway. The left end of Dog Company's line touched the right flank of Easy Company's line facing south, forming the apex.

There were inadequate numbers of men to fortify a continuous line further to the east. This gap in Rudder's left flank was the weak link in his defense. An outpost was established and a captured machine gun was assigned to that sector. It would prevent the Germans from flanking the roadblock defensive lines. The Americans made good use of the existing barbed wire and minefields the Germans had previously set up to defend the Pointe from an inland Allied attack.

Rudder was concerned his meager force was so stretched out. Despite his doubts, he decided it was more important to maintain control of the highway. There was no mobile reserve. If the Germans broke through, Rudder planned to make his stand around the bunker complex that comprised his aid station and CP. It wasn't an ideal defensive setup but it would have to do.

The Germans probed the American defenses during the day, mounting two attacks from the southwest. The Americans doggedly held on. They even took some prisoners. But Ranger casualties were mounting. Without reinforcements, the Ranger foothold on Pointe-du-Hoc remained tenuous at best. The officers expected a determined attack after dark.

The preparations to repulse the night attack were undertaken with desperation. All the wounded who could not fight were lowered to the beach from the escarpment. The wounded would wait for evacuation in the relative safety of the caves at the base of the cliff.

About forty German prisoners were placed in foxholes inside the apex of the angle of the defensive line. Although the Americans were running out of ammo, there were plenty of German supplies in the captured bunkers. NCOs passed out German "potato-masher" grenades to the less-than-enthusiastic Rangers who had the greatest disdain for that weapon. However, the German MG-42 machine guns were welcomed with their abundant supply of ammunition. Rangers, like paratroopers, were trained extensively in enemy weaponry.

Johnny Kilroy was at the CP bunker, having just helped bring some wounded Rangers back from the roadblock position along with Staff Sergeant Zack. Suddenly he heard gunfire. The MG-42 manned by Rangers at the outpost fired off a string of 7.92-millimeter rounds. The intruders answered with the unmistaken sound of M-1 Garands. It became obvious to the Rangers it was an American patrol once they heard their weapons. Johnny could hear the shouting.

"Hey Pal," someone in the outpost position yelled. "We're Rangers… Americans. Come on in." The rifle firing stopped but no one moved.

"Fuck you, you Kraut rat-bastard," came the distant reply from the undergrowth. "We know what a lousy Kraut MG-42 sounds like."

"Fuck you too, you stupid asshole. We captured this MG."

Rudder ran to the outpost. A few Rangers followed him. Johnny joined the group. The firing had stopped but the conversation continued.

"What outfit you with, Mac?" came the voice from the outpost.

"Yeah! What outfit *you* with, dumb ass?"

The banter went back and forth until Rudder came up behind the outpost. He knelt down and addressed the NCO manning the captured MG-42.

"What do we have here, Sergeant?"

"I think they're Americans but they won't identify themselves," replied the sergeant.

"What makes you think they're Americans?"

"Well, Colonel, they're firing M-Ones and they sure curse like GIs."

Rudder nodded. He decided to take a chance. "This is Colonel Rudder,

Second Rangers. Identify yourself!" His voice was loud and dripping with authority.

"Holy shit," the hidden voice exhaled. "Wait one, Colonel."

After a few moments another voice was heard. "Colonel Rudder, this is Lieutenant Parker, Fifth Rangers. I'm coming out, sir."

With that, the young lieutenant stepped out into the clearing from the thick vegetation.

Rudder rushed forward with a big grin on his face. "Charlie! Am I glad to see you! Where's Colonel Schneider?" Rudder was referring to the CO of the 5th Ranger Battalion.

Parker looked baffled. "I'm glad to see you too, sir. Are we the first to arrive?"

"You are and damned well in the nick of time. Where's the rest of the battalion?"

Parker paused. "When we missed them at the rendezvous I figured they already left, so we left too, sir. I thought for sure they were ahead of us."

"No Lieutenant. You're the first to arrive." The grin disappeared from Rudder's face. "How many men are with you?"

"Just my platoon, sir. And a straggler we picked up along the way. Twenty-three men, sir." Parker turned and made a hand signal and his men began filing out of the brush, past the outpost and into the CP area.

Rudder's face betrayed his disappointment. There were so few reinforcements. Parker sensed his frustration.

"Sir, I'm sure the rest of the Fifth will be along any time now. It was dicey for a while but our forces are moving inland from Omaha Beach. We're in France to stay."

Rudder shook off his somber look and smiled slightly. He clapped Parker on the shoulder. "I'm sure you're right, Charlie." Rudder perked up a bit. "We're sure glad you and your platoon made it through." He put his arm around Parker's shoulder. "Most of what's left of my three companies are dug in around the Vierville-Grandcamp Highway about a mile from here. I know you've come a long way but I need your men up there right away."

"Yes, sir. Wherever you need us, sir!"

Rudder pointed to Johnny and Zack. "These men are on their way back and will show you the way." Rudder clapped Johnny on the back and smiled. "We picked up some stragglers, too."

"I see," Parker said noticing the Eagle patch on Johnny's sleeve.

Zack looked at Johnny. "I'll take the front and you bring up the rear. We go back the same way we came in. Okay, sky boy?"

Johnny nodded and Zack took off for the front of the column with Parker. Johnny waited as the rest of the platoon filed by. He wasn't paying attention to each man but rather looking for the end of the column. He didn't notice the infantryman from the 29th Infantry Division with the Ranger tab who stopped in front of him looking him squarely in the face.

"Well I'll be…" the soldier exclaimed. "If it isn't Jake's buddy, Yank."

Johnny focused on the grimy face under bloodshot eyes. It took a split second before he recognized the soldier. "Harley? Goddamn it! How the hell are you? What the hell are you doing here?" Even though they met only once, Johnny embraced his best friend's cousin as if he knew him for a lifetime.

"I could ask you the same question," Harley smiled.

"Hell, Harley, I got dropped in the damn drink," Johnny flipped a thumb over his shoulder toward the English Channel. "I hooked up with these guys until I can get back to my outfit."

Harley nodded. "Jake?"

"We got separated on the jump. I'm pretty sure he got out over land. What a goat rodeo!" Johnny winced at the memory of the night jump. Harley nodded in agreement.

"What about you, Harley? How did you hook up with these guys?"

"We came into Omaha Beach side by side. It was a slaughterhouse, Johnny. The Krauts had every inch of the beach zeroed. MG-forty-twos, eighty-eights…they threw everything they had at us. Our guys…" Harley choked up momentarily. "Our guys…didn't stand a chance."

Johnny reached out and grabbed Harley's shoulder. Harley continued. "Somehow I got across the beach and hooked up with a Ranger unit. We climbed up the bluff and took out some positions. Then I got separated and met up with these guys and here I am."

"Well I'm glad you made it." Johnny looked over as the last man in the Ranger column filed by. "I have to bring up the rear. C'mon. Stay with me." Harley nodded and they set out trailing the snaking column.

Sergeant Zack led the Rangers back along the same rock strewn trail they came in on. They weaved around bomb craters and empty bunkers as they navigated the pock marked area near the exit road to the Pointe. Rangers were known for their speed and they moved silently and quickly as they made their way toward the intersection of the exit road and the highway.

Thirty minutes later the front of the column reached the paved highway. Parker met with the Ranger officers in charge. The officers interspersed 5th Ranger men into the line of 2nd Ranger troops. The critically needed reinforcements were heartily welcomed. As darkness closed in, roughly eighty American troops manned the forward defensive line of Pointe-du-Hoc.

Harley and Johnny brought up the rear of the column and were the last men placed into position. They started digging a fighting hole deep within the double hedgerow. The digging was rough, as they had to tear out large roots with a borrowed entrenching tool and their bayonets. After an hour of sweat-laden work, satisfied the hole was deep enough, they settled into their firing positions angled toward the highway. The hole provided cover and the hedgerow good concealment. Their orders were to take out any enemy that came down the highway.

"Hungry?" asked Johnny as he fished into his pocket and pulled out a scrounged D-bar.

"Starving! I haven't eaten since yesterday. Lost all my stuff on the beach."

"Yeah, me too." Johnny placed the D-bar on the lip of their fighting hole, cut it in half and gave half to Harley. D-bars were four inches long, an inch and a quarter wide and an inch thick. They were made of a sweet chocolate compound that defied all but the strongest teeth. It was a high-protein, high calorie virtually indestructible shot of pure energy that could sustain soldiers if they couldn't get anything else to eat.

"Thanks." Harley peeled off the heavy coating of wax paper and took a small bite. "I never thought it would be like this. Not in my wildest dreams."

"Like what?" Johnny asked, also looking straight ahead along the highway.

"All those guys...my friends...cut down like that...never had a prayer of a chance."

Johnny just listened. Harley needed to get some of what he saw off his chest.

"And they just kept going in, one after the other, getting shot up, blown up... yelling for their mothers...screaming for help... and there was no help!"

Johnny remained silent, chewing his D-bar while straining to keep his eyes on the highway in the fading daylight.

"I grew up with most of those guys...there won't be anyone left to go home to Bedford. They're mostly all gone...their poor mothers."

There was nothing Johnny could say. He knew from Jake most of Able Company came from Bedford. And now they were all butchered on a foreign beach in a distant land thousands of miles from home.

"Tell me, Yank. Why do some guys live and others die? Is it just dumb luck or is God's hand at work?" Harley was fatigued and weakening.

"I don't think God, if there is one, has anything to do with who lives and who dies. It's random. All pure luck." Johnny hesitated a moment. "The real problem is the survivors will be haunted by that question for the rest of their lives."

"You don't believe in God, kid?"

"No. How can a decent God let all this happen? Everything I've seen of the War, the killing, the maiming, the misery and heartache just confirms to me that there can't be a God."

Harley shook his head in disagreement. "Most guys wouldn't admit that, Yank. Not out loud sitting in a foxhole, anyway."

They sat in silence as the sky continued to blacken. Harley finally said, "I'm not that brave or foolish. I'll say a prayer now and again. Right now I just want God to give me the strength and enough time to get even…to get my revenge. Maybe even get me home but if not, at least let me avenge my friends." Harley paused, still looking out over the darkened field. "I wasn't the bravest guy out there on Omaha Beach today, kid. But I'll do better from now on." Harley popped the last morsel of his D-bar into his mouth.

Johnny chuckled, still looking forward. "I didn't see any fearless guys today or back in Sicily. All I remember is a bunch of scared kids trying like hell to fight their fears, do their jobs and not let their buddies down." Johnny paused. "Bravery isn't the absence of fear. It's action in the face of fear."

"You guys okay?" The loud whisper came from behind them. It was Dog Company's CO First Lieutenant George F. Kerchner.

"We're fine, sir," Harley answered.

"Here," Kerchner pushed a burlap sack through the undergrowth. Johnny grabbed it.

"On your toes, men. Jerry will be attacking tonight."

"Yes, sir. Thank you, sir," Johnny replied as he unwrapped the bundle. In it were a few German potato-masher grenades and a loaf of black bread. It felt hard and stale but Johnny cut it in two and began chewing on it.

"So, Harley," Johnny began after chewing a few mouthfuls of hard bread. "You finally got to fight with the Rangers. Funny how things work out."

Harley considered that for a moment. "You're right, kid. I wanted to be a Ranger so bad and fight with them more than anything else before today. But now…I'm as happy as I can be just being a Stonewaller in the Twenty-ninth Infantry Division." He coughed and choked back another tear. "Just as damned proud as I can ever be to have known and served with those boys!"

Johnny nodded his understanding. Harley could no longer see Johnny's face in the shadows of the hedgerow.

"Yup. I'm proud of my Bedford boys…and I'm thankful that I won't die among strangers if my time is up tonight." Harley reached out and gently slapped Johnny on the back.

Before Johnny could respond, an earsplitting whistle broke through the darkness. It came from the apex of the angle and was followed by flares and men shouting in German.

The unmistakable sound of a thundering American B-A-R shattered the night and immediately all hell broke loose. The distinctive sounds of the weapons of both sides could be clearly heard. All of the firing was taking place at or near the angle. Even though there was a full moon, the shadows and blackness of the trees in the surrounding orchards and hedgerows made visibility nearly impossible. The sounds, gun flashes and exploding grenades were all coming from their left, at the point of the angle. Tracer rounds flashed through their position and both men ducked lower into their holes. The rounds were high and rip-sawed the leaves and branches above their heads. The noise was deafening.

Johnny fingered the trigger guard of his M-1 Garand. He didn't have much ammo for the weapon, just a few eight-round clips, so he would choose his targets carefully. Harley sighted down his barrel and scanned the field in front of him. Nothing! They held their positions amid the chaos and confusion and waited for the enemy.

Suddenly, someone pushed through the shrubbery. It was Lieutenant Kerchner. "Make some room, men," he ordered as he slipped into the hole. Johnny and Harley moved to the sides of the now cramped foxhole.

The lieutenant seemed dazed. He was breathing heavily.

"What's going on, sir?" Johnny asked first.

Kerchner tried to respond between gasps. "Krauts broke through…at the angle…between us and Easy. If Easy retreats, we'll be cut off!"

The Germans now occupied the angle position and set up an MG-42 to provide enfilade fire down the Easy Company line. The sound of the battle drifted in a different direction away from Dog Company whose men turned to face east but still maintained their fire discipline.

Shortly, the deafening noise and firing stopped. The Germans pushed through the angle but could not further exploit their breakthrough in the dark. They could be clearly heard barking orders and moving about in the field behind the apex to the rear of the Ranger lines.

One nearby voice in particular stood out. It was both high pitched and gravelly and had the authority and gruffness of an NCO. Johnny listened carefully to the distinctive voice, which could be heard above all others.

"That's a prisoner, sir," Johnny whispered to Kerchner. "He's telling his comrades where our lines are." Johnny continued to listen. "He's telling them that they're already behind us."

"Bastard," growled Harley.

"He doesn't know we're here, sir. He's pointing his pals to where E and F are."

"I knew we should have sent those prisoners back to the Pointe," Kerchner lamented.

"Or shot 'em," Harley added.

The three American soldiers could hear the Germans moving about in the field to their rear. They were organizing for another attack to roll up the flank of the Easy-Fox Company line. Kerchner had no choice but to hold his fire. If he opened up, he was just as likely to hit Rangers as Germans. He passed the word down the line.

At 0300 hours the Germans attacked again. They came right at Easy Company's line along the open flank. The attack was furious and again was accompanied by shouts, screams and whistles. The tracers ripped through the air and the German mortars plastered the ground. Then, silence. The distant shouts of *Kamerad* in a deeply American accent told Kerchner some soldiers had just surrendered. After a few minutes, the sound of a B-A-R from a slightly different direction indicated other Rangers were still fighting. Kerchner recognized it immediately for what it was; *Covering fire for a withdrawal. E and F Companies had retreated. Dog Company was now alone.*

When the Germans pressed with another attack, Fox Company and what was left of Easy Company withdrew to the exit road and the bluffs above the sea. The forty men who were able to extricate themselves withdrew to Rudder's CP to form the nucleus of the Rangers' last stand.

At sunrise Kerchner realized they were surrounded. The Germans had not discovered them burrowed deep into the double hedgerow. The Dog Company Rangers had not eaten or slept for nearly forty-eight hours when the sun set on 7 June. Kerchner had decided he would fight his way out at dawn.

Sunrise on 8 June brought Kerchner a welcome surprise. The German force had abandoned the field. He strode up and down the hedgerow and rousted his men out. The men who survived the German attacks and Allied strafing unfolded their cramped and aching bodies from their overcrowded holes and stretched their way out into the open. The Rangers greeted each other silently but warmly having shared a survival experience as fortuitous as it was unbelievable. Some lit cigarettes and others swigged the last drops from empty canteens as they formed up on Lieutenant Kerchner. The small group cautiously worked their way to the paved coastal highway.

"Lieutenant!" a scout pointed east. Far off in the distance was a group of men and vehicles proceeding warily along the road from the village of Auguay. "Looks like our guys, sir."

"Spread out. Take cover." Kerchner was not taking any chances. He waited alongside the road as the column approached. He could hardly contain his elation at meeting another larger American force. He stepped out and revealed himself.

The scouts at the head of the column approached Kerchner. Right behind them was a colonel. He stepped forward and extended his hand. "Colonel Charles Canham, Hundred and sixteenth Regiment, Twenty-ninth Division."

"Are we glad to see you, Colonel!" Kerchner replied as he shook Canham's hand and whipped off a smart salute. "Lieutenant George Kerchner, Second Rangers."

Canham looked around and saw only a handful of men coming out from behind cover. "Where are the Krauts? Where's the rest of Ranger Force A? Colonel Rudder?"

"Krauts are gone, sir. Pulled out overnight. As far as Colonel Rudder, I don't know for sure, sir. We've been isolated out here for two days now. If any are left, they're on the Pointe." Kerchner pointed to the exit road that led to Pointe-du-Hoc. "We were on our way to find out."

Canham looked at the ragged remnants of Dog Company. "Let's get your men some food and water. I'll bring up medics to treat your wounded. We'll take ten right here."

"Thank you, sir."

Canham issued the orders and the Stonewallers brought up rations, water and ammunition. Canham then pulled a map from his case and he and Kerchner discussed their dispositions.

The sight of soldiers from his regiment buoyed Harley. Some of them had persevered across Omaha Beach and came up through the bluffs to relieve the Ranger Force. He was about to join them when he heard a commotion behind him.

"Look what we got here!" One of the Rangers was escorting a single German prisoner at the point of his M-1. "Found him hiding out in the weeds."

The soldier pushed the prisoner down to the ground in a sitting position. He aimed his M-1 at the prisoner's genitals and started asking him questions in English.

Harley and Johnny walked over to the prisoner near to where a medic was treating a nearby wounded GI. The German looked defiantly at his captor. He pointed to his genitals at the end of barrel of the rifle and shouted loudly in a high-pitched gravel-like voice, "*Nicht hier, nicht hier.*" He then pointed to his own forehead. "*Hier!*"

Harley and Johnny looked at each other. It was the same voice that had betrayed the Ranger positions the night before last. It was just as arrogant and defiant as it had sounded in the blackness of the night.

The medic spoke. "Jesus Mac, don't wound him. I don't have enough supplies to treat them all. If you're gonna' shoot him, kill the bastard!" The medic turned to treat his casualty.

The German continued to stare defiantly at the soldier, pointing to his forehead. His steel-blue eyes were piercing and insolent. The soldier lowered his M-1. Just then Harley stepped in and nudged the soldier aside. He pointed his own M-1 at the prisoner and shot him through the forehead, exactly where he was pointing. The prisoner's eyes held the insolent glare until the instant the back of his head exploded in a bloody gore of bone and red fleshy pulp.

The medic was shocked! "Holy shit, Mac. I wasn't serious. I was just fucking with you."

Lieutenant Kerchner and Colonel Canham came running over. Kerchner saw the dead German and spoke first. "What happened here?" The Ranger who captured the prisoner had already walked away and the medic, busy dressing a leg wound, never looked up.

"What happened here, men?" Canham asked again. There was a moment of cold silence before Johnny spoke up. "The prisoner made a move, sir. We thought he was armed."

Canham looked at Johnny suspiciously, then to Harley and back to Johnny before staring at the wide-eyed prisoner lying on his back. "All right, men, just calm down. We need prisoners."

Abusing prisoners was not condoned and soldiers were constantly reminded to adhere to the Geneva Convention. Officers, however, were aware of the strain mortal combat placed on a human being. Some GIs momentarily lost control in a frightful moment of intense anger. The stress of seeing one's buddies torn up by enemy fire and the anxiety of surviving a firefight placed a huge emotional burden on young boys barely out of their teens. Sleep deprivation and combat fatigue also contributed to a loss of composure. Those factors contributed mightily to a normally disciplined soldier committing a rare repugnant act against a helpless enemy prisoner. The trauma and chaos of D-Day saw an unusual rash of such incidents. American officers used scrupulous discretion and prudent judgment when adjudicating cases of prisoner abuse that came before them.

Canham chose to accept the explanation of the airborne paratrooper and ignore the incident. He also noticed the Blue and Gray patch of the 29th Division on Harley's shoulder.

"Twenty-niner? What regiment, son?"

"Your regiment, sir. Stonewallers. Sergeant Tidrik, Able Company." Harley snapped a proud salute.

Canham raised his eyebrows. He knew Able Company had been nearly wiped out on Dog Green Beach. He placed his arm around Harley's shoulder. "First Battalion is down the line." Canham pointed to the rear of the column. "Go join them. You're home now, son."

Canham turned to Kerchner. "Lieutenant, you take your Rangers to the Pointe. I'm going inland to hunt Krauts."

"Yes, sir," Kerchner replied. He marched his ragtag unit toward the exit road

Harley walked over to Johnny. "Thanks for covering for me."

"No problem, Harley, but if you don't mind my saying so, you need to get under control."

"That bastard gave away our positions last night when he was a prisoner the first time."

Johnny took a deep breath and looked away. "I just don't want to see you get into hot water because of scum like that."

Harley nodded and touched Johnny's shoulder. "Thanks. Where are you headed?"

"I'll stay with the Rangers for now until I can locate my outfit."

"Good luck!"

They parted. Johnny slung his M-1 over his shoulder and marched away with the Rangers toward the Pointe.

History would record that of the 230 Rangers who assaulted the cliffs of

Pointe-du-Hoc, plus the twenty-three reinforcements from Lieutenant Parker's platoon, barely fifty men survived unscathed. Despite heavy casualties, the Rangers had accomplished their mission. The big guns were never fired onto Utah or Omaha Beaches. They cut the paved Vierville-Grandcamp Highway for a time and denied its use to the Germans for all of D-Day. They drew German forces into mortal combat that would have otherwise been sent to either of the two invasion beaches.

In spite of heavy casualties, they never surrendered Pointe-du-Hoc to the enemy. The Rangers of the relief force would eventually make their way to the enclave at Pointe-du-Hoc that was doggedly guarded by the paltry survivors of Rudder's Rangers. There they would relieve the desperate men who held on stubbornly for two days and nights without much hope or reinforcement. But the history of Pointe-du-Hoc would be written at some future time. For the present, the young boys who kicked open the door to occupied Europe were still in grave danger.

After a few minutes Johnny turned to see Harley marching away. From a great distance their eyes met. Harley nodded his understanding of a bond forged and of a debt owed. Johnny nodded back.

Suddenly a single shot broke the morning silence. Johnny Kilroy spun around from the impact and crumpled to the ground.

Chapter Fifty-One

New York City - June 6, 1944

"There should be weeping at a man's birth, not at his death."

Charles Louis de Secondat Montesquieu (1689 - 1755)

June 6, 1944
Dear Johnny,

Earlier today we got the news that the invasion of Europe had begun. I can't help but worry about you and pray that you're okay. Everything here at the hospital stopped as nurses and doctors gathered around the radio to listen to Ike. He announced the invasion had begun. The only thing he said was "the French Coast". There was no word on casualties or the units involved. This is what everyone wants to know, as we all worry about our loved ones.

The feeling in the country is unbelievable. It's hard to describe in words but even though this is a troubled time of great worry and fear, that burden seems easier to bear because everyone is sharing it. It's also a time of great hope. We all hope that this invasion is the beginning of the end to this War.

Just to give you an idea of what's going on in New York, people were standing around the electric news bulletin sign in Times Square all day just reading the latest. Broadway plays have shut down for the day. The actors are going to USO Clubs and canteens to perform parts of their plays for servicemen for free. All of baseball and horse racing cancelled their games. In the late edition of the Daily News, the paper printed the Lord's Prayer instead of its headline articles. Big name stores like Lord and Taylor stayed closed. Macy's closed at noon. Small shops turned to selling war bonds instead of their regular goods.

All of the churches and synagogues are holding special services and their pews are packed with folks praying for relatives or friends or just for the country. Tonight President Roosevelt came on the radio and prayed. The words of his prayer were reported in the newspapers and America joined him late tonight as he prayed over the radio. Imagine a President on his knees praying to God along with millions of Americans for the safety of their sons. I know you have your doubts about the existence of God but if you were here and saw what I saw and felt what I feel, the emotions would overwhelm you, too. It would be hard to deny God in the face of all the prayer and faith that is happening all over America today.

One last thing before I turn off the lights and end this hectic and wonderful day with some sorely needed sleep.

You have a son. Or should I say we have a son?

He was born today. I named him John Patrick Kilroy, Jr. as we discussed. He is 7 pounds, 11 ounces and looks so much like you. We're both doing fine and we can't wait for you to come home and put your arms around both of us. Until that wonderful day, may God take you in his hands and hold you and protect you. (Just because you have your doubts doesn't mean I can't throw a prayer or two in there every once in a while – smile).

Please take care and write back soon.

With All My Love,

Rose

Chapter Fifty-Two

Washington, D.C - January 14, 1997

"Duty is the sublimest word in the English language."

Robert E. Lee. (1807-1870)

The dining room at Kinkeads Brasserie was nearly empty during the lull hours between lunch and dinner. Andrew stood alone near the entrance to the kitchen. He was within eyesight of J.P. Kilroy in the event his sole remaining lunch customer required additional service.

A few waiters were rearranging tables for the dinner reservations under the faint, soft room lighting. The gentle chink of silverware and the brush of busy feet were the only background sounds to the muted voices of J.P. and Frank.

Frank was dipping a biscotti into his black espresso coffee. He had long ago emptied the snifter of black Sambuca into his cup. The brew tasted warm and sweet. The coffee was getting cold so he warmed it up from the steaming pot Andrew left on the table. Frank chomped on the softened biscotti as he spoke.

"D-Day was an ungodly mess. Our guys were dropped all over France. Some planes went down in the channel. Some troopers landed in the swamps and were swallowed up. Landing craft were sunk in the English Channel. Bodies were blown to bits." Frank paused. "All this on a huge scale. Remains unidentifiable. People missing. It was impossible to know exactly what happened to everybody that day and the days that followed."

J.P. nodded and Frank continued. "Your father and his buddy Jake were separated on D-Day. Jake wound up in Sainte-Mere-Eglise with the All-Americans. He didn't rejoin us until Carentan a few days later. Your father landed on Pointe-du-Hoc and fought with the Second Rangers. He never rejoined our outfit in Normandy. He was wounded and evacuated. There was tremendous confusion. Many telegrams were sent out to next of kin by the War Department that were flat out mistakes."

"He obviously didn't die," J.P. smiled. "He raised me."

"No, of course he didn't die in Normandy. But he was severely wounded and evacuated to the First Army Hospital in St. Albans just outside of London."

"Funny, Dad never mentioned or spoke about his wounds," J.P. answered.

Frank smiled. "He was shot in the ass. One bullet, four holes. Two on the outside, two in the crack. Missed the spine by an inch or so. Not exactly the kind of war wound one would talk about or show off."

J.P. smiled. "It's just that he never spoke about that or much of anything else."

Frank took a sip of his coffee. "When we got home, nobody wanted to talk. It was over, we won and that was good enough. The most rehab I got was a smile from the Red Cross doughnut honey and a hug from my wife. That was the drill for everyone else, too. We didn't have the time for therapy back in the day. We had a country to rebuild."

J.P. nodded. "I guess today's society seems pretty soft to you guys. You had it much tougher back then."

Frank stared hard at J.P. "I'm not judging this generation. All I know is when it counted, we had the grit to deal with the Depression and a World War one after the other. Not just the guys who fought, but the whole damn country." Frank waved an unconscious finger at J.P. "We played the cards we were dealt without whining, took our lumps, mourned our dead, came home, went to school and went back to work." Frank paused. "And we didn't want to talk about it."

"I get that part. Dad was a prime example."

"But then we got older. A lot of us started to die off, their memories and stories lost forever. So we started talking. People began putting tape recorders in our faces and we talked some more. More and more of us attended reunions and there was always some local reporter or aspiring author to tell our story to." Frank wiped his mouth with his napkin. "Most of us who survived came back with a heavy dose of survivor's guilt. And, as I got older, I realized I was not so much afraid of dying as I was of not being remembered. So, we owed it to those guys who never came back to tell their stories and make sure they were never forgotten."

J.P. reached slowly for the coffee pot. Frank reached across the table and grabbed his hand. "Please understand. We can never break faith with those who didn't come back. Never!"

J.P. didn't understand the point. Before he could pursue it, Andrew came over to the table. "Is there anything else, Mister Kilroy?"

They had overstayed the lunch hour by a considerable amount of time. "Check, please."

Frank drained the last drops from his demitasse cup. "A history professor from the University of New Orleans wrote a book in ninety-three about Easy Company called *Easy Does It*. It recounts the history of the company from training to the end of the War. You should read it."

"Anything in there about my dad?" J.P. asked.

"No," Frank answered quickly. "There were about a hundred and fifty men in the company and many of them are not mentioned. Your dad and Jake joined that company later, just before the Bulge at the same time I got transferred to Easy."

"What's the point in reading it?"

"Well, for one thing, it may help you understand your father better. More importantly, it will help you understand the strong bonds of loyalty that tie all of *us* together and the solidarity we share about this secret." Frank nervously clinked his empty cup on its saucer. "There. I said it!"

J.P. nodded. What Frank was telling him was J.P. would never learn the secret from any of his father's friends. No matter how hard he cajoled or pleaded, no one would willingly tell him. J.P. had already come to that conclusion. If he were going to find out, it would have to be by trickery or deception.

Andrew brought the check and J.P. began to sign it.

"Thank you for lunch, Mister Kilroy. I'm sorry it was not very productive for you."

"It was my pleasure, Frank. And be assured that I have not given up my quest." J.P. handed the leather check-holder back to Andrew who thanked him and slipped quietly away.

"I suggest you read some books, especially the one I recommended. Also, attend the reunions and meet the men who knew your father best. Get to know them, to understand them. Listen to their stories and let them introduce you to the ghosts that haunt them and the memories of those friends they left behind. Maybe then you'll come to understand."

J.P. was about to rise from the table but the gravity of what Frank was saying along with how he was saying it froze him in his seat. It was as if Frank was trying to tell him, without actually telling him.

Frank continued. "You may not ever learn the specific secret you seek, Mister Kilroy, but you might come to understand the greater meaning of the special connection between warriors …which is stronger than steel or family. It's all about the binding promises and sacred oaths that supercede everything else in life."

J.P. Kilroy gave Frank a quizzical look.

"And that, my son, may be as close as you will ever get to unraveling the secret."

Chapter Fifty-Three

Chilton Foliat, England - August 28, 1944

"My wounded are behind me and I will never pass them (in retreat) alive."

Major General Zachary Taylor (1784 – 1850) *at Buena Vista*, 22 Feb 1847

The paratrooper standing at parade-rest in front of Corporal Jake Kilroy fainted. The medics quickly bore him out of the regimental formation on a litter. They did so unobtrusively so as not to disrupt the speaker facing the men of the 506th PIR. General Eisenhower didn't seem to notice.

It was Sunday, a customary day off for American soldiers not in combat. The morning broke with a typical misty rain from a cloud-shrouded sky. Some of the men complained when they were ordered to attend a service in Class-A uniform. The men who did most of the grousing were replacements. They were young, wet-behind-the-ears, green nobodies who the veterans disdained from the moment they arrived. They had not tasted blood and didn't count for much. Besides, the veterans had their own problems and their own nightmares to deal with.

Sergeant Bill Christian woke the men early enough to be on time. He was bumped to three stripes after he rejoined the Screaming Eagles at Sainte-Marie-du-Mont. The 2nd Platoon was decimated and the just-promoted First Lieutenant Frank West went about the gruesome task of assessing his losses. Stockett and Sosa were confirmed dead. Goldbacher and Smith were in a field hospital recovering from wounds received at Neuville-au-Plain and Zebrosky was still missing. There would be many letters to write once the confusion had been sorted out but for the moment West had to focus on the task at hand. He had to rebuild his command structure.

The 2,000 men of the 506th were herded onto freshly cleaned trucks and busses in Aldebourne for the short trip to regimental headquarters outside of Chilton Foliat. Christian gathered his squad and loaded them up. When the trucks arrived, the troops stepped off and formed up. The foggy mist gave way to an unusually bright sun, which soon poured blinding heat onto the overdressed soldiers from a bright blue cloudless sky. They marched crisply but slowly to the subdued melancholy strains of the "Death March" played by an army band. *What were the words, again?* Jake thought to himself. *Once in the dear, dead, days beyond recall.*

The 506th formed up smartly, dressed the lines and stood at parade rest. They were assembled on the wide green lawn facing a temporary raised reviewing stand. A slight breeze whispered through the surrounding trees but offered little relief to the sweltering troopers.

Jake took in the scene. The grandiose sixteenth century estate of Lord Wills, with its colorful ivy covered brick walls, stood in stark contrast to the somber message to be delivered that day. Jake was surprised when someone mentioned that Littlecote, the name of the estate, was the site of an ancient Roman villa. He didn't even know the Romans expanded this far to the island of Britain. But he figured he should not have been surprised. After all, they were the mighty Romans who could have gone anywhere they damn well pleased and besides, there was a lot he didn't know. Something he was determined to fix after the War if he ever made it back home.

Jake looked up at the reviewing stand. He recognized regimental commander Colonel Robert F. Sink. And there was the unmistakable profile of General Eisenhower. Jake also recognized the Chaplain of the 506th PIR. He saw another general mount the platform and recognized him immediately. It was the CO of the 101st Airborne Division, Major General Maxwell D. Taylor. Jake knew him from the Rome Job and didn't like him from back then. He disliked him even more when the general broke his word about the Normandy jump.

Taylor told his men, "Give me three days of hard fighting and you will be relieved." Thirty-one days later, the wretched remnants of the once superbly trained and highly motivated division were pulled off the line and limped back to England. Jake held that lie against him. Taylor was a general. If he didn't have the authority to make that promise good, he should never have made it! *If only Jim Gavin had been given the 101st. Things might have been different.* The word was Gavin had been promoted to CO of the 82nd Airborne Division the previous day.

After the initial chaos of the night drop, members of different units began to assemble. Like raindrops forming into rivulets pooling into small streams and then rivers, the paratroopers coalesced to complete their missions. Along the way they cut phone wires, destroyed bridges, mined roads, ambushed convoys and captured and held the four causeway exits from Utah Beach. They owned the night. Acting on their own, these isolated units acquitted themselves admirably.

Once the 101st had assembled a formidable critical mass, they were ordered to attack and hold the strategic town of Carentan. This town stood at a vital road junction that would facilitate the link up of American forces from Utah and Omaha Beaches. The 101st took the town at great cost. They also took the towns of Sainte-Marie-du-Mont, Sainte-Come-du-Mont, occupied the town of Sainte-Sauver-Le-Vicomte and assisted in securing the Cherbourg Peninsula. They returned to England on 13 July. Fighting as regular infantry for thirty-one days, they were bled of many of their best troopers and left the flower of their great division in shallow dirt graves hastily dug throughout the bocage country of Normandy.

Casualty figures were still top secret but it was evident that every other bunk was empty and nearly every other man in the division was a replacement. Jake would eventually learn the division suffered 868 men killed, more than 2,300 wounded and nearly 700 missing. Many of the wounded would eventually return but the unit cohesion and high standards of training that weaves the fabric of an elite group was ripped asunder at Normandy.

Another formation of men began marching into the field. Jake peered over to see a group of Army Air Forces pilots who formed up alongside and to the left of the paratroopers. Jake realized these were pilots from the 15th Troop Carrier Wing, the unit that dropped the paratroopers on D-Day. *What in the hell are they doing here?*

Chaplin McGee stepped up to the microphone and tapped it. The thumping sound immediately got everyone's attention. Any chaplain who would drop into German occupied France at night armed with nothing but Rosary beads and a Communion kit easily won over the rough and tough paratroopers. They perked up as he stepped to the microphone.

Jake couldn't take his eyes off the pilots. They looked nervous and uncomfortable standing alongside the men they miss-dropped in Normandy. As Chaplain McGee was saying some fine words about the sacrifice of their paratrooper comrades not being in vain, Jake wondered how these men became transport pilots. *Didn't they possess the right stuff to be fighter pilots? Did they not have the requisite skills to be bomber pilots? Were they volunteers? Or did the paratroopers get the pilot rejects and washouts from all of those other schools?*

Chaplain McGee droned on. *What could anyone possibly say to ease the pain of those who lost friends and brothers? That they did not die in vain and should inspire us? Hell, what difference does it make? They're dead. They're never going home!*

Chaplain McGee stepped back from the podium, as if he read the disapproving mind of Jake Kilroy. A lieutenant stepped up and unfolded a paper. He began to read.

"Almighty God, we kneel to thee and ask to be the instrument of Thy fury in smiting the evil forces that have visited death, misery and debasement on the people of the earth."

What the hell does smite mean? Jake asked himself. *I don't want to smite them. I want to kill every last fucking one of them!*

"Be with us, God, when we leap from our planes into the dark abyss as we descend in parachutes into the midst of enemy fire…"

A paratrooper must have written this especially for this memorial service, Jake concluded. *I need to listen to this.*

"Give us iron will and stark courage as we spring from the harnesses of our parachutes to seize arms for battle. The legions of evil are many, Father. Grace our arms to meet and defeat them in thy name and in the name of the freedom and dignity of man."

Now Jake hung on every word. This was no 'turn the other cheek' prayer. This prayer asked God for help in dealing out revenge and retribution. *I wonder if God is listening?*

"Let our enemies who live by the sword turn from their violence lest they perish by it." *Fat chance! They're going down swinging and I can't wait to help them perish by my Thompson!*

"Help us to serve Thee gallantly and be humble in victory."

The young lieutenant stepped away from the microphone to make way for Taylor whose words were drowned out by a flyover of C-47 transports in formation. The flight only lasted a few minutes but it was enough to drown out most of Taylor's remarks. *Nothing lost,* thought Jake.

Eisenhower replaced Taylor at the microphone and scanned the assembled ranks before him. The men waited in eager silence to hear from their Supreme Commander.

"Men of the Screaming Eagles," he began. The man in front of Jake wobbled, leaned and toppled over onto the grassy field. The medics scurried there immediately to ferry him off on a stretcher. Jake missed a few words but picked back up on Ike's comments.

"... and met every single one of your objectives. Men, you exceeded my most optimistic expectations and I want to personally congratulate you and thank you for a difficult job well done. Your countrymen owe you a great debt of gratitude." Eisenhower paused.

"Paratroopers, attention! Left face!" The troopers turned in unison to face the pilots.

"Air Transport Command, attention! Right face!" The pilots turned to the right and were now facing the paratroopers.

"You pilots need to look into the eyes and faces of the men you dropped in the wrong places at lower altitudes and faster speeds than you were ordered to." There was undisguised anger in his voice. Eisenhower went on.

"A lot of their buddies will not be coming back because of the way they were dropped."

Most of the pilots knew Ike spoke the truth. There were silent gulps and lowered eyes from the most guilty. At the same time, those that performed well and knew it stood upright and defiantly glared back at the paratroopers.

Ike cleared his throat. "We're going in again and perhaps again after that. I have to know that every pilot will be able to look me square in the eye and tell me you dropped your men where, and when they were supposed to be dropped." Eisenhower glared at the pilots for a moment and stepped back from the microphone. It was the largest mass ass chewing Jake had ever seen.

Another lieutenant stepped up to the microphone and gave the orders for the men to face the reviewing stand. He began reading the names of the men killed in action, alphabetically. The impact on the assembled paratroopers was stunning. It was as if they had been collectively hit with a sledgehammer. Men gasped and struggled to maintain their self-control when they heard the name of a close friend. This group of rough and rugged warriors was reduced to a weeping mob of mourners by the time all 231 names of the dead in their regiment were read. At the completion of the memorial, taps was played and the men marched back to the trucks to the playing of "Onward Christian Soldiers". The powerful service moved Jake more than he realized. He knew too many of the names.

In combat, things move quickly. It's about survival and those who dally, think and mourn will not long avoid injury or escape death. Instincts and training take over. No time to think. No time to grieve. But now, back in garrison, there was too much time to think. *Why was it that some came home while others did not? Was it luck? What was it that pushed some men toward danger while others would shrink and cower?* The questions raced through his mind on the ride back.

Jake often considered courage or bravery to be a fixed but diminishable commodity. Each man had his own unique quantity. Each man depleted it at his own personal rate. It was a finite amount and if used too quickly, would be completely expended. When totally drained, only time away from combat could replenish it. Regardless of how many times the cycle occurred, the replacement supply of this intangible commodity never quite reached the prior level. He saw that on Tedesco's face in Neuville-au-Plain.

During the attack on Carentan, he felt his own resolve weakening. The vessel of his own courage was nearly drained. His nerves were shot. There was no audacity left. Perhaps it was because Johnny, his soul brother and one-man support system, was not there beside him. Or maybe it was because he had used so much of his courage so quickly and completely in Normandy already. Whatever the reason, he instinctively knew he desperately needed the cherished time away from combat to recharge his batteries. It was a mixed blessing to be re-staged in England after the Normandy drop. The time away from combat was a necessity. Jake wondered how infantrymen like Harley stayed on the line for so long.

It was almost three months since D-Day and two months since both airborne divisions returned to their respective bivouacs in England. Assimilating the replacements was a slow and tedious process, as most of the airborne veterans really wanted no part of the FNGs, the "fucking new guys". Some of the wounded began to trickle back to the 506th PIR. Training was stepped up and the entire division was re-equipped. Planned jumps were cancelled with frightening regularity as Allied spearheads overran drop zones in France and nerves began to fray.

During this time, the Glider Troops were finally recognized with their own distinctive insignia and the same hazardous duty pay as their paratrooper brethren. After seeing the carnage of wrecked gliders all over Normandy and having fought side by side with the glidermen, every paratrooper firmly believed the belated acknowledgement was well deserved and long overdue.

In their spare time, what little of it they had, most of the paratroopers went to London. They partied and celebrated with much more recklessness than they did before Normandy. Fights were commonplace. Drunken paratroopers were thrown into jail with regularity and officers like Lieutenant West spent a fair amount of time extricating his bruised and battered warriors.

The men of the 506th knew to confine their wildest celebrations to places far away from Aldebourne. When they frequented the local pubs, they behaved like choirboys and spent their leisure time playing darts and learning local dance steps like the "Bump-A-Daisy" and the "Lambeth-Walk". The paratroopers had become well known to the local people who cared for them as they would care for their own sons. The men respected the many sacrifices of their hosts and accepted their collective embrace. It was just a matter of time before they would depart on another mission and the next time they left they would not return to England.

Administratively, the status of numerous paratroopers was in a constant state of flux and confusion. There were thousands missing after the first few days. Some men drowned in the muck of the flooded Merderet River or landed in the angry English Channel and were never to be heard from again. Others joined different units, fought, died and were left on the battlefield for mostly colored troops of the Graves Registration details to sort out. Still other men who were erroneously reported missing or killed in action strolled into Aldebourne weeks after D-Day to the astonishment of grieving friends. Paratrooper units suffered the most confusion and uncertainty in the weeks following D-Day. They were also the victims of the most grievous administrative errors. In some cases, no details were available to console the next of kin. Worse yet, in spite of the onerous precautions and careful attention to detail, some of the notifications of killed or missing in action were sent out prematurely or were in error.

Finding Johnny after a harrowing few weeks was miraculous. He was in the First Army Hospital in St. Albans. It took a long time to determine his whereabouts because he was evacuated with the wounded from the 2nd Ranger Battalion. He was unconscious from blood loss and was near death, his buttocks ripped nearly to shreds. His wound was severe and there were many jokes. Even he could not help but chuckle when he thought about it. *How do you tell people with a straight face you were shot in the ass?*

The sniper's bullet entered the side of his right buttocks with a neat round hole. The bullet tumbled slightly in his flesh and exited in his crack with a larger more irregular bullet hole. The bullet then penetrated the left buttocks on the opposite side of the crack with an even more expansive penetration wound. By the time the round exited the left buttocks, the final exit wound was sizeable and jagged. Johnny began losing blood rapidly. He was semi-conscious when the medic rolled him over to treat the wounds. The shot of morphine relieved the pain and Johnny fell asleep under the sedation. He awoke briefly on a stretcher aboard the ship ferrying wounded soldiers back to England. A bottle of plasma was hanging from an extension on his stretcher. The smells of dried blood, burnt flesh and antiseptic were everywhere. The navy corpsman gave him another shot of morphine and said something about a new miracle drug invented by some Limey, called Penicillin. Before Johnny could grasp what was happening, he was unconscious again.

The next time he awoke, he was in the hospital and lying on his stomach among a large contingent of seriously wounded men from the 2nd and 5th Ranger Battalions. The army nurse explained his wounds were severe but no longer life threatening. However, they required an extensive period of time to fully heal. He was told he was being rotated back to the States. He had received the proverbial "million-dollar wound" along with the Purple Heart.

Johnny asked his nurse to contact his unit. She sent the information, which was delayed in transit. For over two months Private John P. Kilroy was carried on the regimental rolls as "missing in action".

Weeks rolled by and Johnny heard nothing as he remained bed bound, eating on his stomach. He was down to 150 pounds when Jake showed up one Sunday; having finally gotten word from regiment that Johnny was recuperating from wounds in a hospital outside of London.

The reunion was emotional. Both had been through a brutal time in the days following the invasion. They exchanged stories about their ordeals and what each of them had witnessed. They felt close enough to share their innermost fears.

Jake was interested in Johnny's chance meeting with his cousin. Johnny related all of the details but omitted the shooting of the prisoner. If Harley wanted Jake to know that, he would tell him himself. Johnny made a point to tell Jake that Harley ended up fighting with the 2nd Rangers on D-Day. However, he also told him that Harley was more proud of his Stonewallers and their courage on Omaha Beach than he could ever have imagined.

Jake found out that Johnny was scheduled to fly back to the States for further recuperation. Jake was happy for his friend but he didn't discuss it. While others might have celebrated, Jake knew his buddy well enough to know he would feel guilty about being sent home. So the subject never came up. But Jake had one thing to do before Johnny shipped out and he made sure to ask Johnny to be the best man at his wedding when they got back home. Johnny happily accepted.

On 25 August, Jake visited Johnny for what he believed to be the last time in England. The week before, on 19 August, a planned airborne drop on Chartres, France, was cancelled at the last minute. The paratroopers were geared up and loaded down when they got the word. General Patton had overrun the drop zone to the delight of the veteran paratroopers. Operation Transfigure was the sixteenth drop that had been scrubbed.

The trucks pulled up outside of Aldebourne and Jake and his squad mates jumped off and entered the converted horse stable that was their quarters. Standing in front of his bunk was a sight he never thought he would see.

"Johnny! What the hell are *you* doing here? I thought you'd be back in the States by now!" The two men gripped each other's shoulders and exchanged a brief bear hug.

"I'm really not bad enough to go home." Johnny pointed to an empty bunk next to Jake's. "Is that mine?"

The rest of the squad gathered around. Christian slapped Johnny on the back. "Boy, you're nuts but we're glad to have you back."

Johnny winced and dropped his gear on the bunk. "The guys they're sending home are in really bad shape. Some had an arm or a leg missing or part of their skull was gone or they were badly burned. I just couldn't go home with them." Johnny waved his hand at the assembled group of paratroopers. "Any of you would have done the same thing."

"I don't know about that!" The voice belonged to Lieutenant Frank West as he entered the stable after hearing the commotion. "But I'm certainly glad to have you back."

"Thank you, sir. But I'm afraid I might have made of mess of things."

"How's that, son?" West was barely older than most of his men but often used that term.

"Well, sir, technically I'm AWOL. I just packed up my stuff, and walked out of the hospital last night. Hitched a ride here. Heard rumors you were about to leave this beautiful island and make another jump. I didn't want to be left behind. I'd rather be with the fellas."

There was no official policy to return soldiers to their original units after they recovered from wounds. They were sent to a replacement depot, called a "repple depple" by the GIs. Once there, they would be assigned to any outfit that had a need. This misguided policy was a huge morale-killer. It irritated and aggravated every soldier who wanted to rejoin his old outfit. The instances of paratroopers going AWOL from army hospitals to rejoin their units were epidemic in the weeks immediately following the invasion.

"I'll take care of it," West smiled. There were other cases and he had orders from Colonel Sink to protect those paratroopers who went AWOL to return to their unit and *make it right* with the army. "No firing squad for you, Johnny. You'll just have to face Jerry like the rest of us."

"Thank you, sir," Johnny replied with sincere appreciation.

The group dispersed, West heading immediately to the company headquarters to administratively rescue yet another faux deserter from the clutches of the Provost Marshal.

Johnny carefully lay down on the bunk on his stomach.

Johnny looked at Jake. "I saw Sky. He came to visit in the hospital."

"How's he doing? I ran into him and the old outfit at Sainte-Mere-Eglise on D-Day."

"He's doing fine. They want to make him an officer."

"Good for him. He'll make a great officer." Jake reflected for a moment. "Remember back in jump school when he jumped in between us and saved your life?" Jake joked.

"Yeah, took a lot of guts. He could have gotten you *and* him killed." Johnny smiled at the exaggeration. "Good man. Wish he was with us."

They sat quietly for a few moments, Jake arranging his gear and Johnny trying to get comfortable on the cot. Jake broke the silence.

"Jeez, Yank! Why'd you come back? You had a ticket home."

Johnny took a deep breath. "Couldn't do it, brother. Not with you and the rest of the boys still fighting here." Johnny put his head down. "I wanted to, believe me. My biggest fear is dying before I see my son and not being able to raise him and take care of him." Johnny lifted his head. There were tears in his eyes. "But I couldn't live with myself knowing that I left you and the boys. Besides, I have to make sure my son's godfather gets home," Johnny smiled.

"Well, you don't look like you're in such good shape to me," Jake chided.

Johnny jerked his thumb over his prone shoulder. "I'll be fine. I just need a little time to heal." He broke into a big grin. "It's painful to sit down."

Jake laughed. "Well, I guess if I want to make sure I have a best man when we get home, I'll just have to take care of your sorry ass."

"No pun intended," Johnny added.

Chapter Fifty-Four

Newport News, Virginia - September 1, 1944

"The heart has its reason of which the mind knows nothing."

Blaise Pascal (1623 - 1662)

Nora Lee stepped off the bus and into the inky black fumes that spewed from its exhaust as it pulled away. *No need to be annoyed,* she thought. She was coming home from work, after a double shift on the drill press and was wearing her scrubby denims and wrinkled shirt. It was only when she was all decked out and perfumed up for a date that those bus fumes really drove her crazy. She began to walk toward the apartment.

Nora Lee loved Hilton Village and always enjoyed the walk from the bus stop. The village was built in World War I to provide housing for the shipbuilders and their families. It was modeled after a typical early-English village. The houses were styled after the Jacobethan and Colonial revival designs of the time. There were over a dozen variations of size, color and style randomly scattered. Some of the houses were sheathed with stucco and others with shingles or clapboards. The steeply pitched slate roofs were styled in both gambrel and gable. It never ceased to amaze Nora that she would notice something new about the houses of the quaint village each time she walked to and from the bus stop. She was thoroughly enjoying her stroll home on this cool, brisk late summer afternoon.

The Western Union bike rider broke her daydream. He was coming in her direction. The other women on the steps of the houses were familiar with him. They kept shouting as he passed by. "Keep on going!" "Don't stop here you little shit!" "Move along!" The solemn rider always had a grim look on his face as he peddled his bike, head down with the brim of his policeman-style cap pulled low over his eyes. The basket attached to the handlebars was full of dark yellow envelopes. His brownish tan uniform lent some official bearing to his rather undesirable job of delivering bad news to the families of fighting men. As he drew nearer to her, peddling furiously to the negative chants of angry citizens, Nora added her insults to the chorus.

"Keep on going that way, bastard!" Nora threw her thumb over her shoulder in a hitchhiker gesture.

He lifted his head ever so slightly to look at her as he churned his legs faster. His shoulders were hunched as if he expected to be hit with flying debris. There was a look of dread in his eyes. The volume of telegrams had increased considerably since D-Day. The paper torrent of heartbreak had hardly let up since the casualty reports started pouring in and the young delivery boy had been busy and stressed.

Nora immediately felt guilty and somewhat ashamed for adding to his anxiety. *Poor Boy. He's only doing his job.* But there was something else about the look in his eyes. It was more than just anxiety. She studied the mental picture of his face and suddenly realized the look he gave her was dread mixed with recognition. He knew where she lived!

She immediately started running. *The little bastard delivered a damn telegram to my apartment.* She turned the corner, came to her apartment and bounded up the steps, tripping in her haste. She pushed through the outer door and up the stairs. The apartment door was ajar and she saw Macie sitting on a kitchen chair, her face in one hand and a tear stained crunch of telegram paper squashed in the other.

"Oh, no…Sweetie," Nora moaned softly. "No!"

Nora dropped to her knees and embraced Macie who reached out and hugged her tight. Macie was shaking and trying to catch her breath. They sobbed together silently for a few minutes until Macie finally stopped shaking. Nora pulled up a chair and put her arm around Macie's neck in a soft embrace. She held her face cheek to cheek with Macie's and tasted her bitter, salty tears.

After a few minutes Nora asked, "What's it say?"

Macie held up her fist and Nora gently peeled back the fingers that had compacted the telegram. With one hand she struggled to flatten the crumpled paper on her knee while still holding Macie in her other arm. She finally spread it out enough to be able to read it. She blinked through her own tear filled eyes in an effort to focus.

The bold letters at the top read **WESTERN UNION**. Directly beneath the oversized letters read A. N. Williams, President. *What am I reading?* She scolded herself silently and ignored the instruction blocks on either side of the top of the telegram as well as the coding strip across the center of the page.

MISS MACIE VANCE
819 PALEN AVENUE HAMPTION, VA
THE SECRETARY OF WAR DESIRES ME TO INFORM YOU
THAT PRIVATE JOHN KILROY WAS REPORTED MISSING
IN ACTION ON OR ABOUT 6 JUNE 1944 IN THE EUROPEAN
THEATRE OF OPERATIONS. WHEN FURTHER INFORMATION
IS RECEIVED YOU WILL BE INFORMED.
L MCNAIR COMMANDING GENERAL
ARMY GROUND FORCES

"Oh, God," Nora murmured softly. She threw the telegram on the kitchen table and sniffled. "Macie, this is awful. I'm so sorry!"

"He's gone, Nora. I know it." Macie dried her tears with a soaked handkerchief.

She was breathing better now, still labored but without the violent involuntary shakes and shudders.

Nora gathered herself. "I'd love to give you some hope, Sweetie, but this is not good." She waved the telegram. "Take it from me. False hope is the worst punishment you can put yourself through. I wish I would have moved on sooner."

Macie nodded. She understood. Slowly, her breathing steadied and a strange calm settled over her. "I got a letter the other day from Mrs. Gillaspie in Bedford. She wrote that on a Sunday in July, the Western Union operator in Green's Drug Store signed on and got a message from the regional office in Roanoke simply saying 'We have casualties'. She then started receiving the telegrams addressed to the boys' next of kin. Day after day more telegrams would come in with more names of the dead. Over twenty of our hometown boys killed on D-Day. She wrote me some of the names. I knew so many of them. Too many killed. D-Day was a nightmare for our small town." She sniffled and wiped her nose. "I haven't received a letter from Jake since before the invasion. I know Jake didn't survive. I just know it."

"You're probably right and I'm so sorry for you." Nora hesitated. "This may sound cold, and I don't mean it to be, but you have to be practical." Nora paused, searching for the right words. "You still have Derek and I wouldn't let him get away if I were you. Now let's wash your face and clean you up. You've cried enough for one day."

Macie had been in a confused state of panic until Nora came home. Nora's advice made sense and pushed Macie over the edge. She called Derek and he arrived just as Macie finished cleaning herself up.

"We're going for a walk," Macie declared to both of them as she grabbed Derek's arm and hustled him out the door.

They walked down to the street toward the waterfront in silence. All Derek knew was Macie had received bad news about Jake. He didn't want to press her for information and judging by the grip she held on his arm, she needed someone to lean on at that moment. That was fine with him. He would gladly be there for her. Derek had long ago fallen hopelessly in love with Macie and would do whatever she needed him to do.

They walked quietly through Riverfront Park and along the waterfront. The sun was low and the sea breeze was soft and cool. The only sounds were the lapping of the waves, the caw of the seagulls and the distant warning gongs of the buoys.

She stopped at the railing and looked out over the busy river traffic. "Derek, I need to ask you something."

"Sure, Macie."

"Remember when you told me you would be there for me if anything happened to Jake?"

Derek stiffened. He certainly remembered that awkward conversation. For over a year he had buried that embarrassing moment in the deep recesses of his memory. He recalled feeling like a vulture circling over dead remains. She had given him a look of deep disappointment. Or maybe he just imagined it because he was so ashamed of himself. He never mentioned that conversation again and was delighted she never did either. And now it was she who brought it up again.

"Yes, I remember, Macie."

"Did you mean it?" She turned from gazing out over the water and looked directly into his eyes. "I mean do you still feel that way?"

Derek nodded. "Yes, I meant it. And I still do."

She tightened her grip on his arm. "Thanks, Derek. That's all I needed to know."

Chapter Fifty-Five

Zon, Holland - September 17, 1944

"The object of war is not to die for your country,
but to make the other bastard die for his."

Lieutenant General George S. Patton (1885 - 1945)

"There it is!" First Lieutenant Frank West, CO of 2nd Platoon, Headquarters Company, held the binoculars to his eyes and aimed them along the Wilhelmina Canal toward the 150 foot highway bridge that spanned it. He was in a concealed position along the north bank and had a good view of the span. Jake was lying beside him in the shrubbery and Johnny was slightly behind both of them. The woods were silent save for the chirping of birds and the hum of insects and there was no enemy activity on or around the bridge. They just may have caught the Germans by surprise.

The main objective of the airborne invasion of Holland was to outflank the Siegfried Line and sneak into Germany through the back door. This opportunity presented itself during the latter stages of the battle of Normandy.

While the airborne forces were withdrawn to England to rest and refit, German resistance on the Continent stiffened. On 25 July, Lieutenant General Omar N. Bradley's United States Twelfth Army Group had finally succeeded in breaking out of the lodgment and cutting off the Cotentin Peninsula at Avranches. The Allies were finally moving after weeks of stalemate in hedgerow country. General Patton's Third United States Army was activated on 1 August and he exploited the wide, flat plain to attack and push back German forces.

On 7 August, the Germans initiated an ill-advised counterattack intended to drive a wedge between the American and British armies. The assault was halted near the town of Mortain. This German force of twenty-one divisions, thrust deeply into Allied lines like a probing finger, was now vulnerable on both flanks. Bradley proposed an aggressive plan to surround them.

Patton's Third Army attacked northward and the Canadian First Army attacked southward. They planned to meet near the town of Argentan. Patton reached his objective on 12 August but heavy resistance held up the Canadians near the town of Falaise. The Germans fought tenaciously to keep a small gap open at the eastern end of the Falaise Pocket, the name the Allies gave to the area of nearly encircled Germans. The Germans called it the *Kessel*, the Cauldron.

It was 20 August before the Falaise Gap was finally sealed shut. An estimated 50,000 German troops were captured and over 10,000 were killed in the pocket.

In spite of the overwhelming victory, 30,000 German soldiers escaped to fight another day. They abandoned most of their equipment and made their way back to Germany using horses, carts, bicycles or on foot. Anyone seeing this raggedy column of dirty, dusty beaten soldiers might have concluded the War was over. They would have been wrong. This defeated rabble of an army would reconstitute into a stubborn fighting force. The Allies considered their escape from the Falaise Pocket a lost opportunity. The Germans called it the "Miracle of the West".

As summer unfolded, the Allies experienced more remarkable victories. On 15 August, Operation Dragoon, the invasion of southern France on the Mediterranean coast, was successfully launched. On 25 August, Paris was liberated. On 3 September, Montgomery's Twenty-first Army Group liberated Brussels, Belgium and Antwerp the next day. The successes were continuous and equally dizzying. The German army had lost over 500,000 men and 2,200 tanks and was on the verge of collapse. In all of this success, Eisenhower still had a significant problem. He had forty-nine divisions on the Continent organized into four Allied Armies and they had all out-distanced their supply lines. Feeding, fueling and arming a fighting force of this size would have been an extraordinary challenge under the best of circumstances. But the Allies had yet to capture a deep-water port and were forced to supply these armies primarily over the Normandy Beach more than 400 miles from the front lines. Despite the Herculean efforts of the Red Ball drivers, who operated their trucks around the clock, there simply was not enough transport to feed and fuel all of the armies. Eisenhower had to prioritize his offensive or it would stall along the entire front.

General Montgomery, promoted to Field Marshall on 1 September, presented an idea to Ike to end the War quickly. When they met on 10 September in Brussels, Monty explained his audacious plan to lay an airborne carpet of three divisions over Holland and seize five major river crossings. The British Second Army would thrust up this corridor and advance rapidly over the captured bridges. They would breach the lower Rhine at the city of Arnhem sixty-five miles away. Once over the last bridge, they would strike into the industrial Ruhr region of the Third Reich.

Eisenhower was intrigued. He thought it might be the perfect time for such a bold and daring gamble. Allied forces were chasing the disorganized and dispirited remnants of the German army across France. The *Wehrmacht* chain of command seemed to be in chaos. Ike was also under pressure from Prime Minister Churchill to take out the launch sites for the new V-2 terror weapon. The Germans started launching the rockets at London on 8 September from western Holland and civilian casualties were high. General Marshall was also pressing Ike to use the newly formed First Allied Airborne Army.

Eisenhower approved the plan and gave Montgomery operational control of the First Allied Airborne Army. He shut down all the other offensives and diverted all air support and supplies to Montgomery. Operation Market-Garden was scheduled for Sunday, 17 September.

The Allies assigned 1,400 bombers to take out anti-aircraft sites along the route, 2,023 transports to haul 20,000 paratroopers and 1,500 fighters to protect them from Nazi interceptors.

The British 1st Airborne Division would be dropped at the end of the line at Arnhem. The "Red Devils" would be supported by the Polish 1st Parachute Brigade to be dropped a day later. Their assignment was to seize the road bridge at Arnhem.

Eleven miles further south the 82nd Airborne Division would seize two huge bridges near Nijmegan. The nine-span 1,500-foot bridge over the Maas River at the city of Grave was assigned to the veteran 504th PIR. The 508th PIR was responsible for capturing the highway and rail bridges over the Waal River. The All-Americans also had to secure a ten mile corridor for the single highway. This was particularly worrisome to Major General James M. Gavin as the road bordered on the *Reichswald* Forest in Germany proper. The forest was close to his flank and could hide menacing German forces. Gavin had to secure that flank near the town of Groesbeek on a high ridgeline known as Groesbeek Heights. If the Germans succeeded in gaining these heights, their artillery would stop the flow of traffic on the highway. The 505th PIR, Gavin's most experienced regiment, was assigned the task of seizing and defending Groesbeek Heights.

A yawning gap of fourteen miles separated the southern boundary of the 82nd Airborne and the northernmost objective of the 101st Airborne at Veghel. Major General Maxwell D. Taylor assigned the 501st PIR to capture the four bridges over the river Aa and the Willems Vaart Canal. In the center of his sector, Taylor tasked the 502nd PIR with capturing the bridges at St. Oedenrode and Best. He ordered the 506th PIR to capture the roadway bridge over the Wilhelmina Canal near the village of Zon and four bridges over the Dommel River in Eindhoven four miles further south.

Sitting at the start line thirteen miles further south was XXX Corps of the British Second Army. It was their job to attack north and charge up the corridor over the captured bridges.

The men of HQ Company, 506th PIR, were gathered around a hastily constructed sand table in a large briefing tent. They were told the Brits were going to make a run at entering Germany. All the airborne needed to do was to capture and hold the bridges leading north to Arnhem.

It would be a daylight drop. Some men groaned. They would be easy targets. The Normandy veterans silently approved. Jumping into a night sky full of tracers, too fast and too low, in the wrong place and unable to see where they were landing was by far the scariest moment in most of their young lives. They would take their chances in the daylight.

Unlike Normandy, there would be no clickers, no gas masks, no impregnated clothing and no password. They would have to get off of the drop zone immediately since the DZ had to be cleared for the next serial. Small groups of paratroopers would be dispatched to their objectives as soon as they had an officer. There was no time to wait for the coalescing of larger formations. Enemy resistance was expected to be light. Old men and young boys were guarding the bridges. But the Germans would react quickly so rapid deployment was essential. After securing the bridges, the single highway had to be kept open until the British armor arrived.

"We're jumping from a thousand feet and we land here, on DZ Charlie, with the rest of the Five-oh-six." First Lieutenant Frank West held a pointer on the sand table. It was aimed at a spot north of the Wilhelmina Canal and west of the village of Zon. "We're in the first serial so you'd better get off the damn DZ hubba-hubba or shit from the sky will be raining down on you."

There was some nervous laughter. The veterans held a new respect for Casper. West had proven in combat he had a spine of steel. He continued in his trademark soft-spoken demeanor.

"I'm not kidding, guys. The next serial will be only four minutes behind us. When they drop their para-packs you'd better not be standing there." West was referring to the equipment bundles loaded with weapons and ammo that fell much faster and hit the ground much harder than a paratrooper. "Drop your chute, gather your gear and get the hell off the DZ fast. Got it?"

"Yes, sir," replied a weak chorus of voices.

"Good." West cleared his throat. "Head south out of the DZ to this forest." He moved the pointer. "It's called the *Zonsche* Forest. That should give us the cover we need to reach the Wilhelmina Canal undetected. Then we turn east and take the bridge at Zon." He moved the pointer again to the bridge. "Questions?"

"What about these damn patches, sir?" Private Homer Smith asked the question and the murmur around him indicated he was speaking for more men than just himself. "What the hell is this First Allied Airborne Army crap anyway? We're Americans, sir."

West nodded. They were ordered to sew on the new patches by the high command of the newly formed First Allied Airborne Army. It was a crest-shaped gray patch with a gold winged white numeral one above crossed swords. Across the top was the legend "Allied Airborne". The men of the 101st universally disdained the patch because they had to cover the American flag on their right sleeve to accommodate it. They would have reacted the same way if they were ordered to cover the Screaming Eagle patch on their left shoulder. Unit pride grew stronger as the casualty lists grew longer.

West responded. "All right men. If you haven't had time to sew on the new patch, just forget about it." Muted whoops and hollers followed. "We have more important things to do today than worrying about patches." West looked cautiously around the tent. "If anyone asks, just tell them you never got the darn patches." With that, the few men who had sewn them over their American flag patch unceremoniously ripped them off to the delight of their comrades.

"Any other questions?"

"Who's up ahead of us, sir?" someone from the back asked.

"Eighty-second. They have two large bridges to capture at Nijmegan and Grave."

"And the last bridge, sir?" asked PFC Leland Brewer, the platoon medic.

"The Brits have that one, Beerman. The bridge at Arnhem."

"Are we under British command?" asked Brewer.

"We are. Monty's running the show."

"Aw, fuck," someone mumbled out from the crowd.

West reacted. "What was that?"

"Aw fuck, *sir*," the same voice repeated. It was Sergeant Christian. The men laughed.

Christian explained. "Their rations are shit, sir. Pardon my language Lieutenant but we can't eat that bully beef, pudding pie and tea and the rest of the crap they eat. It ain't human food." The company broke out in agreeable laughter.

West replied to all the men. "I understand. Hopefully, it won't be for that long."

"Right, give me three days of hard fighting…" someone in the back yelled out in satirical mimicry of Taylor's D-Day promise. The men laughed again.

West continued after the noise subsided. "After we take the bridge, we go four miles south to Eindhoven and capture that town and the four bridges over the Dommel River. We secure the highway and wait for the Brits there. They'll be starting off sixteen miles from Eindhoven at the Meuse-Escaut Canal. They should be linking up with us by the end of the day."

West looked around the tent trying to make eye contact with each man while waiting for the next question. After a few moments when no one spoke, he did. "The Screaming Eagles have a fifteen mile stretch of highway to keep open and a bunch of bridges to seize and hold until the Brits arrive. That's our mission, open the road and keep it open! Any questions?" No one responded. "All right! The trucks are outside. Saddle up. I'll see you on the flight line."

The 120 men of HQ Company filed out of the tent and piled onto three two-and-a-half-ton trucks. It was a typical misty, damp, fog-shrouded morning in England. The men were advised the weather was better over Holland.

After a few minutes they were delivered beside one of the ninety C-47

Skytrain transport planes lined up neatly alongside the main runway at Membury Airdrome. The men dismounted and gathered beside their assigned C-47 with a huge J7 painted behind the cockpit. This was the unit designation for the 303rd Troop Carrier Squadron, one of four in the 442nd Troop Carrier Group. On the nose of the plane was a painting of a beautiful woman in a sitting position wearing a bathing suit. Under the nose art was the legend, *Tallahassee Lassie*.

The veterans of D-Day tended to stay together in small groups. They considered themselves living on borrowed time; fugitives from the law of averages. Some of the men were loading a mortar, bazooka and ammo into A-5 para-packs to be fastened under the wings and released when the squad jumped. Jake and Johnny were in a group with Smith, Goldbacher and Brewer. They were loading up on ammo and K-rations when Lieutenant West walked over.

"Everything okay here?" The men nodded. West looked at Johnny and shook his head. "You shouldn't be here, Johnny. You're not right just yet."

"Lieutenant West, sir. I'll be fine. I won't let you down."

West nodded. He looked at Jake. "Keep an eye on him. Watch out for him."

Jake flashed his trademark smile. "I always do, sir." Johnny gave Jake an affectionate shove on the shoulder.

Many men carried non-issue personal weapons such as brass knuckles, hunting knives and revolvers or pistols bought or sent from home. Jake still had his .45 from the Rome Job. Johnny had lost his .45 in the waters off Normandy but traded a Nazi belt buckle to a rear-echelon officer for a pistol. Jake picked up magazines for his Thompson and shoved them into his pockets.

"Don't worry about the standard combat load. Take what you need." It was West. He was telling his men to ignore the rules regulating the amount of ammunition each man was to jump with. That was another reason they loved him.

Another pile contained the main and reserve parachutes and they began to strap them on.

"What the hell is this?" Goldbacher asked holding up one of the parachutes. It was different and distinctive by virtue of the white straps leading into a central round buckle.

"Relax, Goldbrick. It's one of the new harnesses the British are using," Christian answered. "Quick release!"

Goldbacher gave Christian a skeptical look.

"It's sort of late in the game to introduce new equipment, Sarge," Smith chimed in.

"No, look Homo, there's nothing to it. It's a standard T5 chute with a new harness." Christian strapped on a parachute and adjusted it to his body. "Look, here." The men gathered around as he snapped the straps of the harness into the buckle. "Now watch." Christian rotated the large button in the center and punched it with the side of his fist. All the straps simultaneously released with a loud metallic click and the parachute and harness dropped to the ground.

"Quick release. Pull the pin, turn the button and whack it. Bingo, the chute's gone."

"Clever, but I don't trust anything the Brits invented," Jake joined the conversation.

West was observing this scene. "If it makes you feel any better, these gizmos were invented by an American company called the Switlik Parachute Company." West looked around to see the impact of his pronouncement. Most of the men seemed assured by that information.

"Well in *that* case..." Goldbacher reached into the pile and strapped on a parachute. The rest of the men followed.

Strapping on his chute, Jake turned to Johnny. "Yank, what kind of soldiers were those Rangers you fought with?"

Johnny pondered the question for a moment. "Besides being a scraggly-looking bunch, they were damn good soldiers. Kind of like us."

"In what way?"

"Too light to fight, too stupid to run!"

Jake nodded. While the paratroopers were among the toughest, most highly motivated and intelligent combat soldiers in the field, they lacked the firepower to be successful in all situations. The airborne planners developed a parachute artillery element but delivering the .75-millimeter howitzer and ammo using gliders was always an iffy proposition. Even when they successfully deployed this artillery, re-supply was always a challenge for men fighting behind enemy lines.

More often than not, paratroopers would find themselves up against tanks and artillery without sufficient firepower to answer back. In the battle of flesh against steel, it was only the courage and determination of the individual paratrooper that turned a would-be rout into a contestable skirmish. They won battles they should have lost by dint of their amazing unit loyalty and cohesion. These accomplishments were all the more remarkable because they were designed to be light-infantry; quick hitting, fast moving and swiftly withdrawn. They proved to be hard-hitting and fast moving but never rapidly withdrawn. Despite their lack of organic support elements, the paratroopers were always kept on the line much longer than they should have been.

Jake knew exactly what Johnny meant by his short answer. The Rangers were designed and trained to be the same fast moving, hard-hitting shock force as the paratroopers. The longer they stayed in one place, the more their weakness in firepower was exposed. But the longer they held on and made a fight of it, the more reluctant the brass was to relieve them.

As the paratroopers filled every available space in their uniforms, an American Red Cross coffee van drove up the flight line. Two young ladies moved from plane to plane, serving coffee and doughnuts to the waiting paratroopers.

"Who likes it black?" asked the young redheaded volunteer with a thick British accent.

"Here," said Christian, Jake and Brewer in unison.

She handed out three cups of black coffee from her van.

"Milk and sugar," Johnny asked. "Me too," Goldbacher announced.

"Milk's in it, love. Sugar's right there," she pointed to the packets of sugar.

The replacements lapped up the coffee and doughnuts. Most veterans ate the doughnuts and sipped the coffee since there was no place to take a piss in a crowded C-47 at 2,000 feet.

An army ambulance, olive drab with a huge red cross on a white square on the roof and sides, made its way down the flight line. It was the familiar three-quarter ton, four-by-four Dodge truck-ambulance designated WC-54. As the paratroopers geared up, the army nurses moved from group to group making sure they had adequate medical supplies, morphine Syrettes and attending to any latent injuries. The nurses treated wounds that were not completely healed or scars that were tender and painful. They also provided blank V-Mail forms to any paratrooper who requested one and then tucked the hastily written letters into a pouch slung over their shoulders.

Jake took a V-mail form and a pencil. He leaned on the back of Johnny's parachute and began writing in big block letters. He spoke as he was writing. "I need to send another letter to Macie. She always says I don't write enough."

"When did you write last?" Johnny asked.

"Well, I sent a V-Mail a week after we got back from France and started writing a long letter. We got busy with replacements and then finding out you were in the hospital, I didn't finish that letter for a couple of weeks."

"Don't blame me," Johnny chided. "You didn't write that much before I got wounded."

"I know…I'm trying," Jake confessed. "But I love this V-Mail."

The United States military copied the idea from the British. There was usually insufficient space aboard transports to haul the tons of mail passing between the Homefront and the troops. In order to save space, V-Mails were photographed to microfilm at the point of origination. The Eastman Kodak Company provided the high tech equipment to both compress and expand them at their destination. A normal letter size form would be shrunk to the size of a postage stamp and filed on a roll of microfilm. A single reel of microfilm, about the size of a deck of cards and weighing only twelve ounces, carried more than 1,600 letters. A musette bag of V-Mail microfilm replaced over sixty sacks of conventional mail.

V-Mail forms could be obtained at post offices back in the States and were readily available to GIs overseas. When completed, the originator folded the letter so the destination address was visible. All of the V-mails were routed to the few centrally located photographic stations where the letter would be censored and photographed onto microfilm at 2,500 letters an hour. The original letters were kept until verification was received that the microfilm had reached its destination. If there were difficulties, the batch was re-photographed and resent.

It cost three cents to mail a V-Mail from the States and about twelve days to get to Britain. It took a few more days to reprint the letter from the microfilm before it entered the standard paper mail delivery system at its destination. The average time for a regular letter was about a month.

When the form was folded, they were easily recognizable by the red border on top and the legend, *V dot-dot-dot-dash MAIL*; the dots and dash being Morse Code for the letter V. The restrictions on V-mail did not deter its popularity. Since the reproduction was half the size of the original, it was important to write in large, dark, clear letters to assure legibility on the receiving end. With practice, most people adjusted to the restrictions.

Jake finished his V-Mail. "You writing one?" he asked Johnny.

"Already done and mailed," Johnny smiled back.

Jake folded his and handed it to the nurse. He had no way of knowing his V-Mail of a few weeks ago had to be reprocessed because the PBY-5 Catalina carrying the original microfilm had crashed. His regular letter was still winding its way through the bureaucratic maze of bulk paper mail. As of that day Macie had not yet received either of his letters.

Almost without notice, the fog burned off and the morning sun began peeking through the clouds. As the time for loading came nearer, it became eerily quiet on the flight line. The only audible sounds were those of truck engines and the click and clatter of equipment as the men helped each other gear up. Individual paratroopers took on the grotesque shape of a hunchback as the heavy burden weighed them down and they struggled, zombie-like, to hobble around.

The flight crew of the *Lassie* arrived and boarded the plane and the men followed. Pushing and pulling each other through the door, the paratroopers painstakingly squeezed aboard. Jake was first in as he was the designated pusher. The smell of leather, hydraulic fluid and oil permeated the plane. It brought back memories of the other jumps. Johnny was right next to him. He would kneel for the take off and stand right behind the flight deck for the rest of the flight.

When all the C-47s were loaded, the planes taxied into takeoff position. At ten second intervals it took only fifteen minutes to launch all ninety planes. Off the English coast over Bradwell Bay, this serial rendezvoused with others from various airfields. The elaborate plan lined up the 424 C-47 transports that would haul more than 6,700 paratroopers and seventy gliders of the Screaming Eagles to Holland. The line of transports on this southern route would be one hundred miles long and ten miles wide. *Tallahassee Lassie* was in the first serial.

Planes and gliders transporting the 1st British Airborne and American 82nd

Airborne Divisions would fly the northern air route. Before it was over, Operation Market-Garden would land 20,000 airborne troops and 500 vehicles supported by over 4,700 planes. The most powerful airborne force ever launched was winging its way to seize the vital bridges of Holland.

Jake looked out the window. As predicted, the weather had cleared considerably over the Continent. The sky became azure blue with just a whisper of white, puffy clouds. What began as a relatively serene ride soon became intense. Jake could see the American P-47 Thunderbolt fighters diving down and strafing suspected enemy anti-aircraft batteries with devastating firepower. Despite the efforts at flak suppression, some of the enemy guns began scoring hits.

The crew chief removed the door, a sure sign they were nearing the drop zone. The sounds of gunfire were more clearly audible to the anxious paratroopers. The flak became more intense as the *Lassie* neared the drop zone. One C-47 Skytrain in their serial was hit and started a slow rollover. Troopers were still spilling out as the plane crashed into the countryside.

Lieutenant West sensed the uneasiness in his men. The red light had not yet gone on but he decided to prep his men for the jump anyway. He stood up near the door and faced the cabin. All eyes were on him.

"Get ready!" West yelled over the roar of the engines.

The men shuffled in their seats and tensed.

"Stand up!" West jerked his thumbs upward while the men struggled to their feet.

"Hook up!" West crooked his forefinger and jerked it up and down. The troopers snapped their static line fasteners onto the cable that ran over their heads down the center of the cabin.

"Equipment check!" West pulled on his harness with his thumbs. Each man began to check the equipment of the man in front of him. Johnny turned around and ran his fingers up and down Jake's harness. He visually verified Jake had hooked up his static line. As the paratrooper jumped, the line would play out and rip the cover off the pack tray exposing the canopy. The canopy would be pulled loose by a thinner cord, which would break when the canopy inflated. Johnny made sure Jake's Thompson was secured to his equipment. He tapped Jake on the shoulder with the bottom of his fist and turned around. "Sixteen Okay!"

Jake did the same to Johnny. He patted Johnny's helmet. "Fifteen Okay!"

Johnny proceeded to check the trooper directly in front of him. It was Homer Smith. Johnny tugged slightly on the harness, visually checked the fifteen-foot static line that was coiled up on Smith's shoulder and tied off with a rubber band. The end of the coil snaked up to attach to the overhead cable. "Fourteen Okay!"

Smith patted Private Robert Goldbacher's harness. Goldbacher's M-1 was inside his bellyband, without the Griswold case, sticking straight up and down. Smith grabbed the butt over Goldbacher's shoulder and shifted the angle of the weapon so it would not slip out during the opening shock. "Thirteen Okay!"

Goldbacher fingered the harness of PFC Leland Brewer's parachute. Brewer didn't carry a rifle; just a .38-caliber revolver his father had sent him. He was otherwise weighed down with musette bags filled with medical supplies. Goldbacher tugged on all the straps to make sure Brewer's heavy load was secure and would not rip away during the five G force of the opening shock. After he pulled Brewer's chinstrap tighter he yelled, "Twelve Okay!"

Brewer visually inspected Christian's static line and pulled on his harness. He turned Christian's shoulder slightly to make sure his reserve chute was fastened securely to his main parachute harness. He checked the safety pin of the quick-release buckle. Brewer clapped Christian on the shoulder to signal everything was in order. "Eleven Okay!"

The countdown reached West just as the indicator light turned red. He took his position in the door looking for landmarks and watching for the green light. The men crowded together behind him, ready to spring out in one continuous stream. The plane rocked and bounced as the flak increased but the course remained true. The engines throttled back to jump speed.

Suddenly, the cabin floor erupted in a succession of explosions. A series of .20-millimeter anti-aircraft rounds smashed through the thin aluminum skin and floorboards. Jake pushed hard against Johnny. "I think I'm hit!"

Johnny wheeled around and quickly scanned his friend. "Where?"

"My back!"

Johnny turned him around. There was a large hole in the top of Jake's parachute cover. A camouflage colored silk plume fluffed out from the perforation. The round had gone straight up through Jake's parachute and out the top of the airplane. Jake's chute was shredded and useless.

"You can't jump!" screamed Johnny over noise. "Your main chute is blown out!"

Jake looked toward the door. Lieutenant West was looking outside the plane and focused on the drop zone. Suddenly the light turned green and out he went. The stick started moving.

"I'm not staying back," Jake pointed toward the door and the fast disappearing stick of paratroopers exiting the plane.

Johnny began moving backwards toward the door. He thought Jake didn't understand him. "You can't jump. No parachute!"

Jake nodded and grabbed the D-Ring of his reserve chute and pointed to it. Johnny understood but immediately recognized the danger. If Jake's main chute deployed, it might foul the shroud lines of his reserve parachute but there was no time for Jake to remove it. Johnny pulled out his switchblade and cut Jake's static line just before he turned and went out the door.

When Jake reached the door he leaped out and quickly pulled the D-Ring on his reserve parachute. He heard the zip of the shroud lines playing out and the welcome snap of the opening shock. His main chute was still safely tucked away in his pack although a small stream of silk was billowing out through the crack on top.

Jake looked around. The scene was incredible. The stream of planes seemed to stretch back beyond the horizon. Camouflage parachutes filled the bright sky as far back as he could see. There were red colored chutes on the para-packs indicating weapons and ammo and blue colored chutes signifying rations and medical supplies. It was a spectacular once-in-a-lifetime scene.

At this height a normal drop would take about sixty seconds but he and the para-packs were falling faster. Jake came down hard. All around him troopers and supply packs were hitting the landing zone. The sky remained full of parachutes in a jump that reminded him of the demonstration jumps they made back in the States.

Jake took inventory of his body and his equipment. Shaking the anxiety from his mind, he cut loose the reserve parachute and knelt down on one knee to orient himself. His weapon was still secured by its sling over one shoulder and under the other and all the equipment and supplies he was carrying survived the hard landing. It was the most frightening two minutes of his life.

Johnny came rushing over. "Holy shit, that was close!" He pulled the safety pin behind Jake's parachute harness buckle, rotated it and slammed it with his fist. Jake's useless main chute dropped off of his back. Johnny helped Jake to his feet and pulled him toward the woods. Supply packs, parachutists and debris were raining down all over the drop zone.

"We've got to get off of the DZ," Johnny yelled as they scrambled for the shelter of the tree line.

As they entered the pine forest Johnny saw Colonel Sink in consultation with Major James L. LaPrade, CO of the 1st Battalion. They were organizing small parties and sending some through the woods along a forest trail and others down the main highway toward the bridge over the Wilhelmina Canal. When Lieutenant West came off the drop zone, they ordered him to take a squad of paratroopers. Jake, Johnny, Brewer, Christian and Goldbacher were in that group.

"Follow me," West whispered as he took the lead.

"Jake," West called back and Jake was instantly at his side. "Point!"

"Roger that," Jake whispered and took off in front of the group. He moved silently through the pines for a few hundred meters before he stopped and raised his Thompson over his head parallel to the ground. *Enemy sighted.* Jake took cover as the group cautiously closed up on him. West pulled out binoculars and searched along the canal.

The unmistakable shriek of a German .88 broke the calm. The shock wave could be felt as the flat trajectory shell smashed into the trees along the main highway hurling sharp steel splinters and deadly wooden shards in all directions. The Germans had spotted the main body coming down the highway but not this little group on its flank just yet. It fired again, then quickly again. There was more than one gun guarding the bridge.

The small group edged closer, still undetected. The .88s kept firing down the road and the main body of paratroopers returned fire with small arms. West was upright now, standing next to a tree. He imagined the paratroopers under fire were setting up their mortars and maneuvering closer to get a shot at the guns. He spotted the .88 gun flashes. There were three of them along the canal on this side in sandbagged revetments. Dug in infantry with machine guns were guarding the positions.

He held up three fingers without taking his eyes from his binoculars. "I count three." Immediately a 2.36-inch bazooka rocket found an opening in the far sandbag emplacement and blew up a gun. "Make that two!"

The two remaining .88s continued to fire flat trajectory rounds into the trees sending deadly slivers in all directions. As West's undetected group crept closer, the men could feel the muzzle blasts of orange fire and the hot pressure waves hitting them with tremendous force.

West moved out in a trot to get within striking distance before his team could be discovered. The men followed. An MG-42 machine gun opened up with a ripping sound, firing blindly into the woods. Goldbacher absorbed the full brunt of the salvo. He flew backward and went down like a rag doll. Brewer was on top of him before he could yell for a medic. A few other men fell under the hailstorm of bullets and shrapnel.

Johnny went forward and fell into a trench in front of a high mound at the base of the sandbag emplacement. The .88 traversed in their direction and fired again but was unable to depress the muzzle sufficiently to hit anyone in West's group. The blast knocked West and Johnny down as the round crashed into a warehouse along the canal well behind them.

Some German soldiers appeared on the crest of the mound. Jake emptied his Thompson and they fell back wounded or dead. Johnny fired off eight rounds and reached for another clip. Jake dropped his empty magazine and reached for a full one. He fumbled trying to get the magazine out of its canvas case and when he finally yanked it free, it fell to the ground. He reached for it and couldn't find it in the swirling dust. He pulled another magazine from the case and saw two more Germans reemerge on the crest as he slammed the magazine home.

It was too late. The Germans had him.

"CRACK! CRACK!!" Johnny fired two quick rounds into their center mass and the Germans fell dead into the trench. Johnny stepped over them and out of the trench.

"Thanks, buddy!" Jake hollered.

"A bit slow on the draw, hey partner?" Johnny joked.

Jake nodded; a little too embarrassed to respond with one of his sarcastic quips.

"Grenades," ordered West and the men each tossed a grenade into the gun pit. In a loud, blinding flash, the second gun was destroyed. They moved past that position to the final .88 alongside the canal. It was still firing down the main highway north of the canal. They were out of the woods now and maneuvering among some structures. There was a water tower, a brickyard, a warehouse and some small buildings. What was left of West's small group approached the .88-millimeter gun from its flank and took the emplacement under fire. The Germans were in crossfire from the road and from West's group on their flank.

West looked back. All that was left were Jake, Johnny and Christian. They were spread out among the structures. Jake was crouched at the base of the water tower, Johnny peered out from behind a pallet of bricks and Christian was at the corner of the warehouse.

The main group of paratroopers launched an attack up the main road. With the defenders distracted, West yelled, "Follow me!" The group took off toward the emplacement firing and hurling grenades. The .88 belched out one more round before it was silenced. The Germans in the position raised their hands and came out under a torn and tattered white flag. The paratroopers took the dusty and dirt-caked defenders prisoner.

Jake took a seat on the shady ground, his back up against a small brick building. Johnny stood alongside him. They both were breathing heavily as West and Christian approached. They sat on the ground in the shade as the main force of paratroopers continued toward the bridge.

"Good work, men. I'm surprised that..." A blinding flash and a tremendous explosion interrupted him. The shock wave knocked Johnny to the ground and tore the helmets off of the other soldiers. An enormous dust cloud was kicked up and fragments began falling all over. Chunks of concrete and huge pieces of wood rained down on them. The four men squeezed against the wall of the building while scrambling to retrieve their helmets. The debris shower continued as the lighter stones, smaller pieces of wood and clumps of dirt descended to earth.

In a few moments the dust cleared and everyone could see the bridge over the Wilhelmina Canal was gone. West began to pull his Company together. Johnny saw Brewer treating some troopers with superficial wounds and he and Jake walked over.

"How's Goldbrick doing, Beerman?" Johnny asked. "Is he gonna' make it?"

Brewer just shook his head. "He nearly had his leg severed at the hip. Nothing left of his crotch as far as I could see. He was alive when I shot him up with Morphine and sent him back to the aid station." Brewer worked on another paratrooper as he talked. "He was a mess."

"Thanks." The two men walked away to rejoin what was left of their squad.

Jake spoke first. "If that ever happened to me, I need you to kill me."

"What? What are you talking about?"

"If I ever get my balls shot off or lose a leg I want you to finish me. Right here on the battlefield. I'm not going home like that." Jake looked solemnly at Johnny waiting for an answer.

"You're nuts, Jake. You know that?" was all he could think of saying.

"Well, I couldn't ask just anyone. I wouldn't trust anyone else. But if *you* promise me, I know you'll do it."

"You're still a fruit cake, Jake. Who else thinks of this shit?"

"I'd do the same for you," Jake persisted.

"Well, that makes me feel a whole lot better."

"C'mon Yank. Do you want to go home with your dick shot off or without your legs? Is that something you want to put her through? Are you that selfish? Could you even handle it if she left you because of that?"

Johnny pondered that for a moment. "She wouldn't leave me because of that but I get your point about putting *her* through it. Still, I have a son to take care of."

"Well if it came to that, I'd make sure your son was taken care of but at least promise to finish me off if it happened to me. I don't have a son to worry about and I'm not about to put Macie through that and I know I couldn't handle it if she left me because of that. Besides," Jake smiled his impish grin. "What good is a godfather with no balls, right?"

Johnny pulled Jake off to the side behind a pine tree. "Just to make sure I get this, you want me to kill you if you get shot up really bad, right?"

"I'm *begging* you to kill me. Otherwise I'll have to do it myself and I'm not sure I can. I'm not going home half a man," Jake answered.

Johnny looked around. No one was within earshot. "All right, all right. We'll do each other if it comes to that."

Jake reached out his hand. Johnny took it and shook it once vigorously and said, "So, we have *this* pact and we have the other one about not being taken prisoner." Jake nodded.

Johnny continued with a wry smile. "Hanging out with you is starting to get very dangerous. And I'll need to start a damn journal to keep all these pacts straight!"

West walked over. "Good job today, men."

"Thanks," Jake answered.

"I have a job for you two. Division lost a glider with some jeep drivers in it. Go back to the DZ and pick up a jeep each. You'll be driving division staff to visit the regiments."

"General Taylor?" Johnny asked wondering how he would manage to sit all that time but not wanting to complain.

"Probably," answered West. "Heck, I don't know. Whatever the heck they want you to do. Now go!"

Chapter Fifty-Six

Washington, D.C. - March 30, 1997

"In war there is never a chance for a second mistake."

Lamarchus (465 BC - 414 BC), quoted in Plutarch, *Apothegms*

"Hello, this is Sky."

J.P. Kilroy froze in his steps. He was whisking a small bowl of eggs and was about to pour them into the sizzling pan when Sky Johnson unexpectedly answered the phone. He looked at Cynthia Powers who was sitting at his kitchen table in a borrowed man-tailored shirt holding a hot cup of coffee and reading the Sunday newspaper. The article describing former President George H.W. Bush's parachute jump near Yuma, Arizona, at the age of seventy-two had her complete attention. She was reading aloud to J.P. when the phone call was answered.

J.P. had asked her to hit the speed dial for Sky's telephone number and set the phone on speaker. He had done that numerous times in the last few weeks. But unlike those other occasions, Sky answered this time. J.P. set the bowl down and moved toward the phone.

"Mister Johnson, this is J.P. Kilroy. How are you today, sir?"

"I know who this is. You've left me enough freakin' messages."

"I'm sorry about that, sir. I just have a few more questions for you. We really never finished our conversation back in January and you did give me your number."

"I've been out of town...on one of those battlefield tours in Europe. I like going back from time to time. Nobody is shooting at me anymore." J.P. heard Sky chuckle on the other end.

"Well, thanks for answering my call, Sky."

J.P. motioned to Cynthia to get his recorder. Sky was undeniably a part of the conspiracy of old soldiers dedicated to keeping the secret.

"I'll be quite blunt, Sky. I had lunch with Frank West and he all but confessed there was something you men were hiding from me. Some sort of secret you all agreed to keep." J.P. paused and waited for some reaction. There was none. "I couldn't help but wonder if I could perhaps bribe you into telling me," J.P. jokingly probed.

After a moment of silence, Sky responded. "Ah, that Frank always had a big mouth."

"In all fairness to him, I sort of figured it out for myself. You guys were, well, acting kind of suspicious at dinner." Cynthia clicked on the pocket recorder and placed it near the phone.

"Really? I thought we just acted hungry." Sky chuckled again. "I'm sorry,

Mister Kilroy, but I'm really not sure what you're talking about. Frank may have been involved in something with the boys but I didn't spend as much freakin' time with them as he did."

This was the opening J.P. hoped he would get. "But Sky, you never mentioned you ran into Jake at Sainte-Mere-Eglise, either. Or anything after D-Day."

There was another pause. "I think we actually ran out of time back there at dinner." Another pause. "But sure, I remember. Jake straggled into that town with some guys from the One-oh-one." Sky seemed to be dredging up the old memories. "Yeah, I remember and boy we were glad to see each other after one helluva scary night. Then Jake went off on a rescue patrol, I think, with Danny Boy and Sergeant Bancroft."

"Is that all you remember of that day? Did you run into my father, too?"

"Oh, no. They were separated on the jump." Sky coughed. "It's pretty hard to remember everything that happened that day but I know Jake wasn't with your father when he went out on patrol and Bancroft never made it back from that patrol."

"What happened to him?"

"Killed. Danny Boy told me a sniper shot him. Hole clean through his head."

"Isn't he the one who hated Jake and my dad?"

"And vice-versa."

J.P. glanced at Cynthia and nodded. This might be what he was looking for. "Are you sure my dad wasn't there? That Bancroft was killed by enemy fire?"

There was another hesitation, and the sound of ice tinkling in a glass. Sky was drinking. *Good.* "Are you absolutely sure, Sky?"

"I'm sure."

"Which one? That my dad wasn't there or how Bancroft was killed?"

"That Johnny wasn't there. Who could be sure of what happens on the battlefield?"

J.P. believed he was on to something and perhaps he would learn more if he kept Sky talking. "Isn't it unusual for you guys to run into each other like that? I mean friends from different divisions bumping into one another all the time like that?"

"Not really. The Eighty-second and the One-oh-one were deployed together a lot from D-Day on. We worked together in combat and fought each other like crazy while on furlough. I ran into the boys in Holland, and again in Rheims and one more time when we made our last jump in Operation Varsity in March of forty-five. I asked for their help in the last one."

J.P. reached for a napkin, wrote something down and gave it to Cynthia. She went into the bedroom. "I did some reading on the Holland jump. Operation Garden-Market?"

"Market-Garden," Sky corrected. "Dumbest airborne plan ever invented and the worst execution of an armored advance in the history of tank warfare."

"How so?" J.P. recalled how Sky cleared the table and used ashtrays and saltshakers to describe the Sicilian campaign when they had dinner. He prepared himself for a long explanation.

"Well, there were these three groups of bridges that Monty had to have so he could push his armor up this highway and into Germany. He only had to go sixty miles and he would be over the Rhine. The Screaming Eagles had the first group of bridges near Eindhoven, the Eighty-second was assigned the second group of bridges at Grave and Nijmegan and the first Limey airborne division had the last bridge at Arnhem. We were supposed to surprise the Krauts and push through to the Rhine in two days and sneak into Germany before they knew what was up."

Cynthia returned with a book. It was *A Bridge Too Far* by Cornelius Ryan. It was considered the definitive work on Operation Market-Garden when it was published twenty-three years prior. J.P. opened to a marked page with the map of the battlefield. "So what went wrong?"

"Depends on who you ask. In my opinion we surprised them all right but the Krauts reacted faster than we did. We had the initiative on day one and maybe day two. Jerry took it from us and had it the rest of the way. Of course, it didn't help that we dropped the Limeys on top of two SS *Panzer* Divisions that weren't supposed to be there…but we could have overcome that if we had a better plan and moved faster."

J.P. settled back on the couch. "By a better plan you mean that the First British Airborne Division dropped too far from the Arnhem Bridge?"

"Mister Kilroy, I'm impressed. You *have* been doing your homework!"

"I've been doing some reading," J.P. replied as he sat back.

"Of course you're right. It took nearly seven hours for one British battalion to seize the northern side of the great Arnhem Highway Bridge. Before they got there, a recon battalion of the Ninth SS *Panzer* Division crossed the bridge and went south. It was those guys who made up the bulk of the defenders on the north side of the Nijmegan Bridge eleven miles south of Arnhem. If the Limeys closed off their bridge an hour sooner, those Krauts would never have gotten out of Arnhem and we could have walked over the Nijmegan Bridge on day one. As it turned out, they got a strong force to the bridge before we did."

"And the British drive north moved too slow," J.P. encouraged.

"As slow as shit," Sky agreed. "They were supposed to be in Arnhem in two days but they just reached the outskirts of Nijmegan by that time and we hadn't taken that last bridge before Arnhem yet. We were too freakin' slow. And our Air Transport Command decided it was too risky to make two drops on the first day. Hell, we still had them by the freakin' balls on the first day. We could have brought in more men and ammo while the weather was still good. It turned out by the next afternoon, the Krauts had moved up more anti-aircraft guns and brought in more planes from the *Luftwaffe* and they were ready for us. Chopped up our re-supply flights pretty good. After that the weather was never good enough to allow enough flights to supply us."

Another clinking sound of ice on glass. It was pretty early on the west coast and J.P. wondered what Sky was drinking so early in the morning.

"Bloody Mary," said Sky over the speakerphone as if reading his mind. "Breakfast of champions!" J.P. couldn't hold back a smile. Sky continued. "Where was I? Oh, yeah. So, by day two, the Krauts were all over us like roaches. They came out of the *Reichswald* Forest and cut the highway in a couple of places. We had to beat them back time and time again. It was like cowboys and Indians. The road quickly got the nickname "Hell's Highway". We lost a lot of guys trying to keep it open. And by the third day we still didn't have the main Nijmegan Bridge and that single Limey battalion that made it to the bridge couldn't be reinforced because it was surrounded and getting the living shit kicked out of it."

"Is that when the Eighty-second crossed the river?" J.P. asked. Cynthia quietly brought him a cup of coffee and nestled up next to him on the soft suede couch.

"Yup, the Eighty-second had to make a river crossing of the Waal River in canvas boats to attack the bridge from both sides. H and I Companies of the Oh-four made the assault. It was pure hell!" Sky paused. J.P. could imagine him choking up. "We lost a lot of guys that day."

J.P. sipped his coffee. He decided to let Sky tell the story without interruption.

"The Limeys brought up twenty-six canvas boats. They were about nineteen feet long and had these plywood floors and canvas sides. Paratroopers weren't ever trained in amphibious river crossings but we were the only ones there. So, two hundred and sixty guys jumped into those crummy boats and paddled across this four hundred yard wide river, the Waal. The Krauts opened up on us with everything they had. Mortars, machine guns, eighty-eights, the kitchen sink. They were helpless out there paddling with oars and rifle butts and the tide pushing them around like little rubber ducks in a bathtub. Men were getting hit and falling overboard and they sank like stones. Boats were blown out of the water by direct hits and they still paddled their hearts out. The noise was deafening, the river looked like it was raining there was so much small arms fire. I watched from the shore as one GI in a boat just disappeared, blown away by an eighty-eight shell, I think. The smell of gunpowder and burning flesh was everywhere. The river ran red with blood. The screaming and yelling of the wounded could be heard above the din of the battle." Sky paused. "I couldn't get that day out of my system until I went back fifty years later." He paused again. J.P. envisioned a tortured old man on the other end of the line.

"After what seemed like an eternity, they finally made it to the other side, about half the boats made it. The engineers rowed the boats back to bring over the rest of Third Battalion while the first wave attacked the Kraut positions on the shore. I don't know why any of them even tried to surrender. After slaughtering our guys who were helpless in those boats they thought they could just put up their hands and say 'Kamerad'? I don't think we took many prisoners that day. The men were on an adrenalin rush and a fierce rage that was almost uncontrollable. We were up against soldiers from the Ninth SS *Panzer* Division. They were brutal soldiers and our guys knew it. After we took them out, we still had to capture the north side of the bridge."

Cynthia and J.P. exchanged troubled glances. Sky was struggling with these memories.

"To make a long story short, we captured the bridge. The Germans failed to blow it for some reason. Some think the Dutch sabotaged the wires. I wouldn't be surprised. They're great people. They love their freedom and they never forget. Every day the schoolchildren still put fresh flowers near the granite slab monument in memory of the Waal River crossing. Wherever an American GI is buried in Holland, someone puts fresh flowers on his grave every day." Sky hesitated. "Every freakin' day for over fifty years! Imagine that. And our kids never even learn squat in school about what Americans did during the War." Sky hesitated. "Tell me, Mister Kilroy, what's wrong with that picture?"

Cynthia got up and took their coffee cups to the sink. She picked up making the scrambled eggs where J.P. left off.

"And the plan still failed," said J.P. in a matter of fact manner.

"Of course it did," Sky answered. "Because after we spilled all that blood and lost all those guys taking the freakin' bridge, the Limeys refused to push on to Arnhem. They crossed the bridge, pulled over and had tea! We were furious. If we knew they were going to wait until the next day, we would have made a night river crossing. But the main thing is they hung their own paratroopers out to dry in Arnhem. If it was Patton, that son of a bitch would have been in the first tank charging up that highway, balls to the wall, and he would have broke through and relieved those poor guys. Anyway, it was already the fourth day by the time the Limeys finished their tea and got ready to go. By then the Krauts in Arnhem took back the bridge and reinforced their positions. The Limeys couldn't push through any more. They evacuated around two thousand of their paratroopers from Arnhem across the Rhine at night, lost over seventy-five hundred Brits and Poles, and it became a stalemate. We couldn't advance any further north and they couldn't push us further south. We end up with a fifty-mile salient to nowhere. All that for nothing!"

"History records it as the airborne liberation of Holland," J.P. suggested.

"History is the fable most believed, Mister Kilroy," Sky retorted. "Spin it any way you want, it was a waste of the best troops the Allies had. In addition, the two American airborne divisions were kept at that front for another two months in stinking cold and wet conditions and getting bled again. Mud all over. Couldn't find a dry place to sleep. Hadn't had a freakin' bath for two months. It was like World War I trench warfare all over again. Anyone caught out in the open could expect to draw artillery fire. We were still eating lousy British rations because Monty wouldn't give us back. Imagine the brass balls on that guy. He begs Ike for paratroopers for his masterstroke to end the War by Christmas. Then Ike gives him an airborne army *and* priority on supplies. He hatches this half-ass plan and then his own freakin' armored forces drag their feet to execute it. It falls on its face! Then he has the gall to refuse to give back two airborne divisions so he can waste us as leg infantry. For two months. I tell you, if that Limey son of a bitch wasn't getting paid by the Krauts, he should have been!"

"That's a bit harsh, Sky."

"Yeah, yeah, I know. If he wasn't such a pompous ass I might cut him some slack but Patton would have made better use of the supplies and the airborne divisions." There was a moment of silence before Sky continued. "Hell, I always get upset when I talk about Monty." J.P. allowed a few seconds for Sky to recover before asking his next question. "You said you ran into my father in Holland," J.P. reminded Sky.

"Right. I think it was day two or three. We were still near Grave. We just took the bridge over the Maas River. We were under pressure from the Germans who started to probe our flanks. We're up near Groesbeek Heights near Gavin's CP, guarding the road and bridges. We were waiting for a resupply drop that was late coming because of the damn weather in England. Around noon, a jeep convoy comes up from the south. Four jeeps, three had a general each and the forth full of armed troops for security. All the jeeps had thirty-cal machine guns mounted in the rear. The jeeps pulled up and they all got out and started talking to our battalion commander, Major Julian Cook. Generals Brereton, Ridgway and Taylor are all in this small convoy. I never saw so many generals in one place at one time. So anyway, Taylor, Ridgway and Brereton, he's the CO of the First Allied Airborne Army, spread this map on the hood of Ridgway's jeep and Major Cook starts pointing at stuff and doing all the talking. That's when I recognized two of the drivers, your dad and Jake. So I scoot over. We're really glad to see each other. We're catching up on what we missed. I remember your dad was injured and had a real hard time sitting down. I scrounged a few cans of .30-caliber ammo for my light machine gun. We were running low. Mooched some grenades, too. After a few minutes the briefing was over. Ridgway stayed and other two came back to their jeeps. So I leave. My outfit is ordered to head for the Nijmegan Bridge. Taylor notices something and he pulls the boys over to the side. I don't know what he was talking about but he seemed to know them and it looked like he was bawling them out. At the time I thought they were being chewed out for giving me the ammo. Generals usually don't take the time to speak to privates but he spent a good few minutes with them and he was doing most of the talking. Then we heard the distant sound of thunder in the skies. We look up and see this huge air armada heading north. There were miles and miles of transports, towing gliders and carrying supplies. At first I think it's for us but they just keep going. They're headed for Arnhem. The roar was deafening. Everyone stopped to look up. German flak batteries opened up from the *Reichswald* and planes start falling out of the sky. German fighters jumped a bunch more. A full-scale aerial battle erupted overhead. With that, I took my platoon to the bridge and Taylor and Brereton mount up and head back south to the Hundred and first sector."

J.P. asked a question as Sky paused. "Any idea what Taylor said to my father and Jake?"

"I asked them when I saw them next on leave in Rheims. They said he was pissed about them possibly being captured. Seems they were on some sort of hush-hush mission with him."

J.P. deliberated for a moment. He already knew about the Rome Job. *That makes no sense. Why would he care?* J.P. nodded toward Cynthia. This episode also sounded suspicious and he wanted to discuss it with her after the call.

"Made no sense to me either. Especially since when we met in Rheims, they'd been transferred to Easy Company, Five–oh–six."

"Interesting." There was a long silence. J.P. sensed Sky was done talking. He took a shot. "Can you tell me how Jake died?"

There was another pause. "I wish I could but I can't. And I really have to go. It's time for my morning walk on the beach."

"Well thanks for..." The phone clicked dead before J.P. could finish.

Cynthia brought a steaming plate of scrambled eggs to the table. She spooned some in a dish for each of them. J.P. joined her and poured two cups of hot coffee.

"What do you make of that?"

"Sky is sort of a character," she answered. "He's definitely hiding something." She paused. "But then again, they all are. We know that much."

J.P. nodded. "He knew Jake and my dad well. Even though they spent a lot of time in different units, they started together, met whenever they could and spent lots of time together. It wouldn't surprise me at all if he kept in touch with my dad after the War."

They ate in silence for a few moments, J.P. contemplating his options.

"I'm convinced this secret has something to do with Jake. We know now they were in Rome with General Taylor so the discussion in Holland may be important. We also know they both hated Bancroft so his death may be more than meets the eye. I know I sound like I'm reaching but some of these stories we've been hearing have too many discrepancies."

Cynthia put her cup down. "Don't drive yourself crazy. You're a trained interviewer. Keep talking to them. Eventually one of them will slip and reveal something relevant."

He contemplated her advice. "You're right, Cynthia. I know what I have to do."

"Besides jumping back into the bed with me, what would that be?"

J.P. smiled. Her aggressiveness turned him on. And he could see the outline of her erect nipples through her shirt. "After finishing these great scrambled eggs and spending more time with you..." he reached across the table and held her hand. "I have to arrange a visit with Lincoln Abraham. Can you get an address for me?"

Chapter Fifty-Seven

East Lake, Upper Peninsula, Michigan – August 31, 1997

"It is never too late to give up our prejudices."

Henry David Thoreau (1817 - 1862)

The rental car pulled slowly into the gravel driveway to the twisting sound of the tires crunching the small stones. Keisha opened the door to the back porch where her grandfather was sitting in his rocking chair.

"He's here," she announced while wiping her hands on a dishtowel. "Don't get up, Grandfather, I'll bring him back."

"Thank you, dear," Lincoln smiled at his only grandchild.

J.P. Kilroy got out of the car and reflexively yawned and stretched. It was late morning and promised to be a warm and humid day. There was a light, crisp breeze coming off the lake and it felt soothing in the shade of the huge oak trees that covered the driveway. He reached into the back seat of his rental car and pulled out a small briefcase. Keisha stepped out the door in time to greet him as he climbed the front steps. "Welcome, Mister Kilroy," she extended her hand. "I'm Keisha, Lincoln's granddaughter."

J.P. shook her hand gently. "Very pleased to see you again. I remember you from the hotel lobby. Please call me J.P."

"Please, follow me." She walked him around the covered porch, which encircled three sides of the cabin. "What a beautiful place. In the middle of nowhere, I might add," he smiled.

"That's the whole point. Part of the beauty is in the isolation." She didn't say *visitors were both rare and unwelcome* but her tone and expression exposed that sentiment.

They reached the rear porch in time to see Lincoln rising from his rocking chair. "Please Grandfather," she pleaded. "Sit back down."

Lincoln strained to stand up straight and proud and he extended his hand. J.P. took it and Lincoln gripped his hand firmly. "Welcome to my home. Please sit."

Lincoln was wearing faded jeans and a plain white t-shirt. He had on a black baseball cap with a set of white jump wings embroidered on the crown. At the apex of the parachute was a single five pointed star surrounded by a wreath. Under the wings in white bold capital letters was the word "AIRBORNE". It was also written on the side of the bill and back strap of the cap. J.P. recognized the symbol from his recent research. The laurel wreath around the star signified a

Master Parachutist. He couldn't remember all of the criteria but did recall at least sixty-five jumps were required to qualify.

Lincoln unconsciously tugged at the cap as he sat back down. There was a small round wooden table in the middle of the porch. Lincoln's rocking chair was alongside it. Two other chairs were next to the table as well. Lincoln motioned to one of the chairs as he sat down. Keisha walked over to a plain metal barbecue and began spraying lighter fluid on the charcoal briquettes. She threw a lit match into the coals and they ignited with a small puff of explosion.

"We're about to have lunch," Lincoln commented. "Burgers and ribs and of course you'll join us." It was more of a statement than a question.

"Of course," J.P. agreed.

"In the meantime it's hot enough to be an ice cold beer day." Lincoln reached into an ice chest near his feet and pulled out three Michelob Light beers and popped the tops.

"Grandpa only likes cold beers on hot days," Keisha added as she brought out a covered tray of meats. She set the tray aside and sat at the table.

"Thanks for agreeing to see me. We had a hard time tracking you down. Nice place you have here," J.P. commented as he gazed out over the serene lake.

"It's served its purpose over the years and I am quite fond of it," Lincoln answered. "So, Mister Kilroy, what brings you all the way up here? Are you doing an article on World War II veterans, Medal of Honor winners or just black soldiers?" Lincoln took a slug of beer. "Or is this personal?"

J.P. smiled. Lincoln was still sharp. "It's primarily personal. I'm trying to find out as much as I can about my father."

Lincoln hardened his eyes and J.P. noticed the subtle defensive reaction. "And of course, I'm curious about your story. How was it to be a black soldier in World War II?"

Lincoln nodded. He looked skeptical.

"Mister Abraham…"

"Call me Lincoln, please."

"Lincoln. I could have made up some story about doing this for my newspaper and come here under false pretenses but I respect you too much to trick you. I am curious about your story but I'm primarily here to find out about my father. I'm sure there's an intersection between your personal story and my father's story somewhere in the past."

"I really didn't know your father that well. But I know you've been talking to people that did. Like Harley, Sky and Frank."

"I have," confessed J.P. "However, they all have little or no recall of some events." J.P. had decided to slow play Lincoln and not immediately challenge him with the suspected conspiracy. "And how did you know all of them?" J.P. took a pull on his beer and placed his recorder on the table. "Do you mind?"

Lincoln laughed. "Of course not. I've been interviewed so many times about what I did in the War. I'm not afraid of that," he pointed to the recorder.

"And you knew them, how?"

"Well first, when I was a truck driver in the Service of Supply, we were assigned to the Three Hundred and ninety seventh Quartermaster Truck Company attached to the One Hundred and first Airborne Division. They called us the 'airborne niggers.'"

"Grandfather!" Keisha mildly admonished.

"I can say it," Lincoln smiled. "Sorry, but that's what they called us back then." The recollection seemed to disturb him slightly but he continued. "I first laid eyes on Johnny and Jake Kilroy in a pub in England."

"Yes, I heard that story from Frank," J.P. acknowledged.

"Then I saw them again in Rheims and at Bastogne. I never really got to know them all that well."

"And the others? You all seemed pretty tight at the White House."

"There are so few of us left, Mister Kilroy. You remain close to the ones that are still alive. The older you get and the fewer are left, the closer you become."

"He hasn't missed a reunion in years until recently when..." Keisha began until a glare from her grandfather stopped her. She placed the burgers and ribs on the barbecue and the rolls on the upper rack to warm them. Ears of sweet corn were cooking in a pot of water on the side grill.

"I met Frank West at Bastogne too. He changed my life. Turned my whole military career around. We also met in New York City on the day of the big parade."

"What parade? Who met?"

"We all met just before the victory parade. January of forty-six. That was the first time I met Harley. He came to New York for the parade. And I met your mother. I already knew Sky."

There's Sky again, J.P. thought. *He never said anything about a meeting with all the guys and my mother.*

"Why was my mother there?"

"Your parents lived in New York City and the Eighty-second was marching in a homecoming parade up Fifth Avenue so Sky reached out to pull everyone together. A homecoming reunion, of sorts."

"I never heard of black paratroopers in the Eighty-second Airborne division. How did that happen?"

Lincoln straightened up in his chair. "You know the military was segregated in the War and many black people were very angry about that...you know...fighting for freedom around the world and not having it back home for ourselves."

J.P. nodded. He was familiar with the military policy of segregation.

"And some people are still angry about that even today," he looked at Keisha who was busy turning the ribs and burgers. "But we shouldn't be angry at everyone who was white. Sure, some were complicit in this racial tragedy and others stood by and didn't object but there was always a ray of hope in the seeds of change. I didn't see many of them at the time. I was too angry to see anything good back then. Then I found Jesus Christ and he opened my eyes to the truth. I realized that some white people back in the day were taking great risks to make great changes."

"Besides Eleanor Roosevelt?" J.P. asked. He wanted to show Lincoln that he also knew something about the history of segregation in the War. The First Lady personally championed the training and deployment of the Tuskegee Airmen, in part by making a demonstration flight for the press in a plane flown by a black pilot.

Lincoln nodded. "Her story is pretty well known but have you ever heard of Lieutenant General John C. H. Lee?"

"Another Lee?" J.P. chuckled. "Can't say that I have."

"Well," continued Lincoln, "he was second in command to Ike in SHAEF... Supreme Headquarters Allied Expeditionary Forces. He also was commander of the Service of Supply in Europe. Great man! He organized the Red Ball Express. Ever hear of that?"

J.P. nodded. "Sure. The trucks that kept the front lines supplied after the breakout."

"That's just the tip of the iceberg. Lee pulled in trucks and drivers from all over. Most of them were black, or as we said back then, colored troops."

"African-Americans, Grandfather," Keisha corrected as she painted barbecue sauce on the ribs.

"Yes, dear," he smiled at her with glowing eyes. Lincoln turned to J.P. "So for three months, six thousand vehicles delivered twelve tons of supplies to the front lines every day. We did it despite the weather, accidents and the Krauts. They were the most important three months of the War in Europe, from August to November, when we kicked Jerry's ass all the way back to the German border. General Lee planned all that and I drove the Red Ball and darn proud of it!"

"As well you should be, sir," J.P. conceded. Lincoln Abraham was no different from the other veterans he spoke with. They were reluctant at first but with a little prodding, they began to speak more freely. Once they got going, the flood of emotions and memories usually came out in a torrent. J.P. didn't wait for Lincoln to continue. "What did you do, specifically?"

"Mister Kilroy," Lincoln answered quickly. "I never talk about what I personally did in the War. I believe that bragging dishonors the fallen. I'll talk about my shared experiences with the outfits I served with, but I won't brag on myself. But I can attest to others who made great contributions."

"Who else?" J.P. prodded.

"I'm not finished with General Lee. He did more for the black soldier besides the Red Ball. After the Battle of the Bulge, when Ike was short of infantrymen, Lee offered to train..." he looked over to Keisha, "African-American volunteers to fight as infantrymen to be used as replacements. He was bucking the army policy of segregation and his offer to provide individual replacements was denied. He did however create and train self-contained rifle platoons to be assigned to rifle companies as needed at the front. Over four thousand Negro soldiers volunteered and over two thousand were trained and assigned to fifty-three rifle platoons and attached to combat rifle companies in action."

"They weren't integrated into the existing platoons?" J.P. asked.

"No," Lincoln answered. "They were attached as a complete unit and were called the Fifth Platoons. Those men performed very well. Sergeant Ed Carter Jr. from the 12th Armored won a Distinguished Service Cross, which was upgraded to the Medal of Honor. His people collected the medal at the ceremony we were at." Lincoln paused. He looked over to see if Keisha was there but she had slipped into the small kitchen area. "Those volunteers for combat traded blood for dignity and respect and General John Lee, a white man, made that all possible."

Keisha came out to the porch and placed a bowl of potato salad and a large dish of condiments in the center of the table, including hefty slices of tomato, onion and leaves of crisp lettuce. She went back to the grill to turn the meat whose delectable aroma now filled the porch.

Lincoln continued. "Then there was General George Catlett Marshall Junior, Chief of Staff and America's top military man."

J.P. was curious about General Marshall's contribution since the military remained segregated during the War. It wasn't until President Harry Truman signed Executive Order 9981, more than two years after the War, that the military became integrated. "How did he help black men in the service?"

"He paved the way at a time when it was pretty unpopular to change racial policy in the middle of a war. But he had guts and he did a lot...but one of the most important decisions he made was to order the formation of an all-black parachute company, including black officers. That company eventually became the Five-hundred and fifty-fifth Parachute Infantry Battalion. The Triple Nickels."

"Were you part of that outfit?"

"I was. I volunteered after I returned from Europe in early forty-five. They had it really rough getting started. It's hard enough becoming a paratrooper with the high acceptance standards and brutal physical and mental challenges. You can only imagine how hard it was to become a black paratrooper!"

"But they had to meet the same standards as white paratroopers, correct?" J.P. was genuinely curious about this little-known battalion.

"True. We were elite troops, the best of the best with an average IQ of over one hundred and ten. And we had the same dropout rate but that's where the fairness ended. We were segregated to our own section of Fort Benning. We were not allowed to enter the PX, enlisted man's club or movie theatres on base. Eventually they had facilities built just for black soldiers but they were separate and hardly equal. We rode in the backs of the busses and eventually had to ride in a colored-only bus. When we went into town we were subjected to the same insults and discrimination as every black person was. It was the Jim Crow South and that treatment was legal. The fact we wore the uniform of the United States military meant nothing and we were treated just hideously." Lincoln paused. "Our superior officers warned us confrontations had to be avoided. Only black pride, before it became a popular expression, got most of us through. We weren't going to give anyone an excuse or reason to disband the unit or disparage the black paratroopers."

"That's awful," was all J.P. could reply. "It's amazing that you're so forgiving and gracious considering what you went through back then."

"My grandfather is a saint," Keisha interjected, obviously not in total agreement with his outlook on life. "My country tis of thee, sweet land of bigotry," she mocked. He simply smiled at her, not wanting to disagree.

"Well," Lincoln said after reflecting for a moment. "One thing really did disturb me more than anything else. Over time I was able to rationalize and forgive everything but that one thing. But those were different times; I keep trying to explain that to my lovely granddaughter. Every chance black people were given to prove themselves was both an opportunity and a trap. Many good people wanted us to succeed while others wanted us to fail. It was the defining moment of truth in turning the corner on racial attitudes in this country. So, we were told to hold our tempers and our tongues when provoked and try harder and do better and not retaliate when harassed. It was hard, especially for those of us from the North who had no idea what the South was like, but we did it. We shouldered that burden with as much dignity as we could and went about proving we could do everything in the military that anyone else could do. We knew we were pioneers, guinea pigs, lab rats, whatever. We knew we could make it easier or harder for those who came after us. We chose to do whatever it took to plow the road ahead for the sake of those behind."

"Sort of like Jackie Robinson?" J.P. suggested.

"Very much so, with the same quiet dignity, determination and perseverance," Lincoln agreed. "And because of what my generation sacrificed and accomplished in part, people will be calling my wonderful granddaughter doctor by next May."

"Well, congratulations young lady," J.P. held up his beer bottle. "Doctor of medicine?"

"Yes, medicine. But after Med school there's so much more work to do. Internship. Residency. All that."

J.P. looked over at Lincoln. There were tears of pride in his eyes as he said, "She is what we did the heavy lifting for...her future...and it was all worth it."

Keisha brought the burgers and ribs to the table in a covered dish. The hamburger rolls were slightly toasted and still warm. Keisha quickly made hamburgers and buttered an ear of corn for her grandfather and herself. J.P. fashioned his own burger. Lincoln opened three more ice-cold beers and they continued talking between bites of lunch.

"Did the Triple Nickels ever see combat?" J.P. finally asked. He found himself enjoying his conversation with Lincoln so he decided to wait until later to question him about the secret the others were so ardently protecting.

"No, Mister Kilroy, but did you ever hear of Operation Firefly?" Lincoln answered. J.P. shook his head negatively. Lincoln continued.

"Shortly after I finished jump school in April of forty–five, the Nickels were transferred to Pendleton Air Base, Oregon, for a top secret, highly classified mission."

"Operation Firefly?" J.P. asked.

"Operation Firefly," Lincoln confirmed. "It seemed the Japanese developed these high flying hydrogen balloons made of paper and silk and released them into the jet stream over the Pacific. The Japs hung incendiary bombs and booby traps on them. They came across the ocean and flew over the Pacific Northwest and released these anti-personal and incendiary bombs. They were meant to cripple our war industry by starting massive forest fires in California, Washington and Oregon. After the War we figured out they released over nine-thousand of these suckers and over two-hundred and fifty actually reached America."

J.P. was surprised. "I never heard about that."

"Most people haven't. It was classified Top-Secret. After a camp counselor and five children on a picnic were killed by one of the bombs, the local authorities asked for help from the military. The Triple Nickels got the job. We were trained as smokejumpers and in ordinance disposal. Eventually we made thirty-six jumps into forest fires in the summer and fall of forty-five. We were the first and only military smoke jumping, bomb disposal outfit in the world."

They ate in silence for a few minutes. J.P. was impressed with Lincoln's knowledge and recall. The ribs were great too and he had been famished after his long ride that morning. After a brief time, Lincoln picked up the story again.

"After Operation Firefly, we were assigned to Fort Bragg, North Carolina. We continued smoke jumping after the War. In late 1945, we were assigned to the Eighty-second Airborne Division who was returning to the States after occupation duty in Berlin. There was a big victory parade scheduled for New York City. General Gavin insisted the Nickels march up Fifth Avenue with the rest of his division."

"That was a very nice gesture," added Keisha. "When I wrote the letter to

Congressman Williams, I described my grandfather as a member of that division because that was the unit he was discharged from. I had no idea he earned the Medal before he became a part of the Eighty-second. I was told it caused a bit of confusion in the research," she smiled innocently.

"It was a wonderful gesture of inclusion," Lincoln continued. "General Gavin was truly colorblind. We were part of his division and he welcomed us in every respect. Even though we never set foot in Europe, he insisted that our uniforms include every battlefield decoration and citation his division had earned. The Nickels were assigned as the Third Battalion of the Five-oh-five." Lincoln choked up a bit. "It was men like him that gave me hope and the strength to carry on." He made eye contact with Keisha. She knew he made many sacrifices and suffered untold indignities for her to achieve her dreams of equality and equal opportunity.

Lincoln continued. "So, we marched better that day than we ever marched before. So straight, so proud. The drums were beating, the bands were playing and confetti filled the air all the way up Fifth Avenue through the arch at Washington Square. Black people in the crowd were cheering and crying, running out into the streets to cheer us on and touch us. The look in their eyes was priceless. Chills ran up my spine! It was a cold day but nobody noticed. It was a day to remember. A day to make all the sacrifices and all the struggles worthwhile."

"That's a wonderful story. I'd like to hear more about the reunion before the parade but may I use your bathroom first?" J.P. asked.

"Right through there," Keisha pointed.

J.P. got up and went through the doorway. He left his recorder running. No one noticed.

"Are you going to tell him about his father?" Keisha asked.

"I don't think I'll need to. He's smart enough to figure it out for himself."

"Are you going to tell him anything at all?"

"I might tell him something but I'm not breaking my promise."

In a few minutes J.P. came back out to the porch. "That was a lovely lunch, Keisha. Thank you very much."

"That was the least we could do since you've come so far for nothing."

J.P. was taken back by her sudden frankness. "I'm not sure it's for nothing. I've learned a lot and I really haven't asked any questions yet." He smiled, tried to be friendly, as he sat back down. J.P. knew he had to start probing Lincoln but decided to start off slowly.

"A while ago you said only one thing really disturbed you back then. What was that?"

Lincoln reflected for a moment and appeared to recoil at the memory. "I could put up with a lot but when I saw German prisoners getting better treatment than black American soldiers…well that enraged me. These prisoners probably killed

Americans. So, to treat them better than black soldiers made absolutely no sense. I could never get my mind around that! They could go places we could not, ride in the front of the bus and sit in the white section of the movie theatre. They got more respect and decent treatment from the townspeople than we did. That infuriated me more than anything else and still does!"

"I can understand that," J.P. acknowledged.

"A little anger is okay, Grandfather," Keisha contributed.

"As long as I live I will never understand that. For all the bad behavior and indignities I was exposed to, that is by far the absolute worst."

J.P. decided to change the subject. "I was curious about the reunion before the parade?" He let the question hang in the air.

Lincoln looked to be thinking, trying to remember. "Like I said, not much to tell. Sky was a captain by then. He came back to the States ahead of the division as liaison to the Triple Nickels. I was a lieutenant assigned to work with him to coordinate the transfer and assimilation of the Nickels into the Eighty-second. We became friendly. We found out we had common friends in Jake and Johnny. Like I said, your parents were there and Harley, who knew Sky and your father. And Frank, who was your dad's CO for most of his time in paratroopers."

J.P. was having a hard time reconciling all of the friendships and relationships and decided to wait until he got home when he could listen to the recording and draw a diagram. He was a visual person and often solved problems by writing them down. He decided to move on to another subject.

"Can you tell me anything about how you and my dad won the Medal of Honor?"

Lincoln took a deep breath and shook his head. "As I said, I won't brag about what I did. But I will tell you, Mister Kilroy, all that you need to know about that day is written on the citation for the Medal of Honor. Have you read the entire citation yet?"

"Not really. Not all of it."

"Well you should," Lincoln advised.

J.P. noticed Lincoln seemed to be getting tired and Keisha was beginning to lose her patience. He decided to go for broke before he ran out of time.

"Mister Abraham, before my mother passed on, she made me aware of a family mystery which she pleaded with me to find out about from my father. He died before I could do that and I've been trying to find out about it ever since. I've spent a lot of time talking to Sky, Frank and Harley. They have all but admitted they know something about this secret but refuse to reveal it. It's like they entered into some sort of agreement never to talk about it."

Lincoln sat silently, listening carefully to every word, nodding his head slightly.

J.P. continued. "I've listened to a lot of stories. In those stories a number of unusual or suspicious events have occurred. But as of yet I still can't conclusively put my finger on anything specific. So, I ask you, sir. Do you know what I am talking about? Do you know anything about this oath of silence? Are you part of it?"

Lincoln caught Keisha's eyes. He glanced back at J.P. with a look of resignation on his face. "Yes, I know all about it. I'm part of it!"

J.P. stiffened up in his chair. Lincoln's admission was unexpected. It surprised him. "Then what can you tell me, sir?"

"Not a thing, I'm afraid. You see, Mister Kilroy, I took an oath as well as the others. I'm not about to break my word and I'm happy to hear none of my brothers did either."

J.P. slumped back in his chair. He had run into another brick wall. There was no way, he concluded, that any of them would voluntarily break ranks. Lincoln was his last hope. He suddenly became extremely discouraged.

"Well," J.P. sighed, "I suppose there's no one left who knows or is willing to come clean."

Lincoln had long ago decided he would not break his promise under any circumstance. However, he did sympathize with J.P. and decided to point him in the right direction without breaking his word. "I can give you two pieces of advice."

"Yes, I'm listening."

"The first is you already have everything you need in your possession, right now, to uncover the secret. Letters, papers, memorabilia, citations…all you need to figure it out."

J.P. pondered Lincoln's words. He had been through all of that dozens of times in the last months and discovered nothing. He and Cynthia examined all of the memorabilia and nothing jumped out at them. *Maybe they had been looking at them the wrong way?*

"And the second piece of advice?"

"There is someone living in Bedford, Virginia, who knows everything, more than the rest of us, and you need to talk to him face to face."

"Who? Harley? I plan to visit him next."

"No. Not Harley. Your father! He's not dead but rather very much alive."

Chapter Fifty-Eight

Newport News, Virginia - October 31, 1944

"Whoever has trusted a woman has trusted deceivers."

Hesiod (c. 800 BC – c. 720 BC)

Frightened, overwhelmed and encouraged by Nora Lee, Macie Vance reached out for Derek Edson in desperation and from fear of losing him also. When she received the delayed letters from Jake in one bundle, and noted the dates, she was shocked and horrified. A week later a telegram arrived from the Secretary of War, verifying Jake was not missing in action. It was all a cruel mistake but now she could not unravel the tryst she created.

A part of her was relieved and happy Jake was alive. Another part of her was extremely angry. She was furious with herself for having bailed out so quickly and for seamlessly moving into another relationship. That angry side of her had forgotten what it felt like to be terrified and to face the world alone. After coming so far in personal responsibility, independence and self-confidence, she crumbled and panicked when she believed she had lost Jake. She dealt with the sudden insecurity by grasping at the first available lifeline, Derek. Ever since then she had been at war with herself. Her hasty action had made a mess of her life and now she struggled to rebuild the torn and twisted remnants of what was left. She couldn't tell Derek she no longer needed him. Not after he accepted her so openly and easily. It would be impossible to dial back their relationship to where it was before. If she tried she would lose him. Her other choice was to send Jake the dreaded "Dear John" letter. For days she agonized between the two alternatives.

Nora's advice was influential on Macie. Nora had already suffered great personal loss with Butch being a prisoner and Jonah Cash being killed on Tarawa. Macie saw how those tragedies changed Nora, made her a fast and loose woman, and she didn't want to follow that example. Macie was not judging Nora. She just didn't want to emulate her.

Macie finally made a decision and it was based primarily on the heartbreak she had already suffered when she believed Jake was dead. The pain was unbearable and she knew she could never survive that torture and torment a second time. Jake was always in harms way and the reality was he was more likely to become a casualty than return home unscathed. Besides, she had a wonderful guy in Derek who adored her and was right here safely tucked away from the ravages and risks of war. She made the safe though agonizing choice to break up with Jake.

It was a simple letter without detailed explanation. She wrote it so there was no ambiguity and no hope for reconciliation or negotiation. The ink on the letter ran from her tears. It took four tries to create a dry V-mail whose space limitation lent itself well to the brevity she was trying to achieve. Her large, bold print strokes left no doubt their relationship was over. She mailed it that morning.

It was Halloween and the doorbell rang. It was probably the neighborhood kids. She grabbed the candy bucket and opened the door. It was Derek dressed up as a sailor.

"Well, Derek, that didn't take much imagination." She pointed to his sailor outfit. "I thought you'd be more bold, my pretty!"

She was dressed as the Wicked Witch of the West from the 1939 motion picture, *The Wizard of Oz*. Her face was covered in green grease paint and she wore the black robes and spindly black hat of the infamous witch. A large false nose and a few well-placed large black moles completed the masquerade.

"You slay me, Macie." Derek laughed. "Your costume is swell! Watch out Margaret Hamilton!" He was referring to the actress who played the part in the popular movie. "We're late. We have to go. Is Nora ready?"

"I'm coming. I'm coming." Her voice came from the bedroom. "Where is this party, anyway?" Nora emerged dressed as Cleopatra and performed a quick twirl. "How about this?"

"You look great. We're going to the Officer's Club at the Naval Base," Derek answered her question. "And Julius Caesar is in the car." Nora giggled as she went down the steps.

"Ready to go?" he asked Macie.

She nodded and they headed toward the door.

Derek locked the door to the apartment and walked down the stairs. "What made you decide on that costume?" Among the many attributes he admired in Macie was her lack of vanity. She rarely wore makeup, was not preoccupied with her hair and had the nerve to dress up as the homeliest character in Hollywood. She had a humility rarely found in beautiful women.

"I just felt like a witch today, Derek."

Derek knew Macie struggled with her decision. When he found out Jake was alive, he expected the worst. He was somewhat surprised but delighted when Macie chose him.

"Don't punish yourself, Macie. If you've changed your mind…"

"I mailed the letter today, God forgive me," she interrupted. She realized Derek might mistake her uncertainty for animosity toward him. "It's not you, Derek. It's me."

He flashed his disarming smile and reached for her hand. She took it and forced a smile in return. He knew it would take some time for her to fully accept her own decision. He would give her all the time she needed.

Chapter Fifty-Nine

Rheims, France - December 17, 1944

"Nothing but heaven itself is better than a friend who is really a friend."

Titus Maccius Plautus (254 BC - 184 BC)

The major sat on the cold cobblestones in the dark alley. He moved his short chubby legs slowly in a bicycle motion as his feet pushed him backward into the wall. His nose was crushed crooked and bleeding profusely. The major tried in vain to stem the bleeding with his forearm as he continued to push his body against the wall. He wore the dragonhead shoulder flash of the XVIII Airborne Corps but there were no combat decorations or jump wings on his chest. He was what combat troops called a REMF – a Rear-Echelon Mother-Fucker!

"I'll ask you again, sir. Take off the goddamn boots." Corporal Jake Kilroy stood over the major with curled fists.

"Shit! Shit!" Johnny shut his eyes tightly and grabbed his temples with his palms immediately after Jake threw the left hook squarely into the major's face. "What the hell are you doing, Jake?" Johnny whispered through his teeth as he walked to the street to stand lookout.

"I'm tired of these rear area bastards taking all of our equipment," Jake leaned closer to the major who was unlacing a boot with one hand. "We spend two months in that mud hole and our uniforms are rotting off our bodies and our jump boots are falling apart and we can't get replacement gear. And these *legs* intercept all our special gear just so they can look good? Bullshit!" He looked at the major. "C'mon, hurry up, *sir*."

The major loosened the first Corcoran jump boot and Jake pulled it off. "They take everything first," Jake rambled on. "They take the Lucky Strikes and the Camels and we get the Raleighs. We never see the ice cream or the canned peaches. Isn't that right, sir?"

Jake pulled off his worn out boots and tossed them at the major's feet as he cowered under the verbal onslaught and silently loosened his second boot. Jake shoved his foot into the new boot. "Pretty good fit," he commented. "Besides, ain't there some unwritten law that if a paratrooper catches a straight-leg with jump boots he can kick his ass and take the boots?"

Johnny was looking from side to side down the street. "Yeah, but I don't think that rule applies to majors, Jake," he said without turning around.

"Screw that. It does now. What the hell are they going to do to me? Hang me? Put me in the stockade? Like I really give a shit anymore?"

Johnny had been worried about Jake ever since he got the Dear John letter from Macie. Jake hid his heartbreak behind his anger. His already quick temper was on a hair trigger. He wasn't the first or only paratrooper who received such a letter but it hit him harder than most. Johnny was determined to help his friend through this difficult time, but this latest incident spun out of control too quickly.

When the 101st Airborne Division left Holland in late November, they were a tired and battered outfit. After the slashing mobile tactics of the first week of Market-Garden, in which the Germans frequently cut Hell's Highway and the paratroopers repeatedly reopened it, the battle settled into static trench warfare. The Screaming Eagles, along with the All-Americans, were deployed in defensive positions on "The Island", so called because it was bounded by the Waal and Lower Rhine Rivers. The unrelenting and incessant mud and dampness gave way to an early winter chill and it became uncomfortably cold and wet. A dry farmhouse was considered heaven until the Germans started shelling everything over two stories high. The paratroopers were forced to scrounge sleeping spots in the rubble or in the cellars. Sleep quickly became a rare luxury and lacking cold or wet weather gear, many suffered from trench foot in the quagmire.

Both sides patrolled aggressively day and night. Local skirmishes and firefights were the norm and the casualties began to mount. It all seemed so fruitless as the static lines rarely moved in one direction or the other. Seizing ground was not the objective. Killing the enemy was.

The food was atrocious. Johnny particularly hated it. The British rations were called "fourteen-in-one" and were designed to feed one man for fourteen days or fourteen men for a single day. The items were all canned and included such servings as kidney pie, kippered herring, plum pudding, scrambled eggs, mutton stew and bully beef. The meat items had a wretched smell and tasted rank and spoiled. Nearly every American GI became sick at one time or another. In addition, there was no coffee, which irked many American soldiers. The British issued tea instead. Even the British troops unanimously preferred any type of American rations to their own.

The paratroopers scavenged in order to survive. They pilfered food from the farmhouses though they would argue anything found in an abandoned house was fair game. They milked cows found roaming the polder and Jake even shot a yearling heifer for food.

Thanksgiving came and went and the American ten-in-one rations promised to the front line troopers never arrived. It was generally believed among the paratroopers that the rear area officers and staff confiscated and consumed them. Thanksgiving was only salvaged by the rumor that they were soon to be relieved and rotated to the rear for rest and recuperation.

At the end of November orders were issued and the 101st Airborne Division pulled out. Most of the airborne units were at half strength or less and many of the men had lost ten to twenty percent of their body weight. The Screaming Eagles suffered over 1,600 casualties during this defensive operation. The All-Americans lost over 1,900 killed, wounded or missing.

On the roads leaving Holland for the fourteen hour trip to a place called Mourmelon-le-Grand in France, Dutch civilians lined the streets and roads to salute the Screaming Eagles. They acknowledged the paratroopers were the first to liberate their homeland by yelling *"September Seventeen"* as the trucks rolled by. Hardened men like Sergeant Bill Christian were brought to tears by the show of respect and appreciation. Seventy-one days after Operation Market-Garden started, the last of the paratroopers were withdrawn.

Camp Mourmelon, just outside Mourmelon-le-Grand, was once a French garrison. The Germans used it as a tank depot during their occupation and it was in terrible shape when the Screaming Eagles arrived. Their first order of business was to clean up and repair the low stucco buildings in order to make them habitable. The young men set to work with a purpose. Weapons and vehicles were overhauled and repaired. The regiments requisitioned equipment and clothing, which began to arrive from the supply depots in Rheims. There was a noticeable shortfall of jump boots and the venerable and much desired .45-caliber sidearm. Rheims was the Headquarters for SHAEF and the XVIII Airborne Corps. The rear-echelon brass and their minions continued to intercept supplies intended for the frontline troops despite complaints from their commanders.

Red Cross clubs were opened and men started receiving passes to Rheims and Paris. A bit of normalcy began to set in as a large backlog of mail arrived and rumors abounded about a jump on Berlin in the spring. All these rugged men needed to regain their bravado was a few nights of good sleep, a few weeks of rest, hot meals and showers. They needed time away from the smell of blood and death and the horrible scenes of gaping wounds and limbs lying on the battlefield. Many had trench foot, trench mouth or lice. Some had all three. The new wonder drug penicillin would perform miracles in curing these afflictions. Rest and care would bring the men back closer to their normal selves. After a few weeks the paratroopers were beginning to regain their swagger.

Replacement paratroopers were received straight from jump school in Chilton Foliat and were feathered into the various units. They walked around wide-eyed and in awe of the veterans who strutted around camp with grenades and knives hanging from their web belts. Most of the combat veterans were stoic and withdrawn though many did their best to prepare their younger charges for the rigors of battle.

Jake took twelve magazines for his Thompson to the motor pool. He traded an SS dagger he "liberated" in Carentan for a welding job. He had the mechanic spot weld two magazines back to back and upside down to each other. They were offset lengthwise by a fraction of an inch more than the magazine needed to seat firmly into the receiver. He tested each set of two magazines by inserting one end into his vintage Thompson, ejecting it, flipping it over and inserting the other end. When the mechanic was done, Jake had a dozen thirty-round magazines welded into six. He then took his canvas ammunition sling into town and for a few packs of cigarettes had a French tailor cut, expand and sew the five pockets to accommodate the slightly enlarged magazines. Jake then topped off his magazines with .45-caliber ammo and sealed the open ends with condoms. He would take three hundred sixty rounds into combat the next time he jumped.

Johnny was impressed with the creativity Jake employed to implement his idea. It started at the bridge at Zon, when Jake fumbled while swapping out a magazine. Then he came up with a fairly simple and ingenious solution. Johnny had already figured out that Jake had great intuitive intelligence. That was one of the many things Johnny liked about him. *If only he had a chance to get an education.*

At first, many three-day passes were issued for the cathedral city of Rheims in the Champagne region of France. It was only a short nineteen miles from Mourmelon. The All-Americans of the 82nd Airborne Division were also camped a short distance away at Camp Suippes and Camp Sissonne. Both divisions sent men to Rheims on weekend passes. It was a bad mixture. The two divisions were fierce competitors in the never-ending battle to prove who was the toughest dog in the junkyard. After a week of bar-wrecking brawls and numerous apologies made to the mayor, passes were severely curtailed. The men were off to Paris instead, much to the delight of the troopers of both divisions. Rheims quieted down, as did the entire western front as the Allies halted strategic offensive operations and dug in for the winter. No major hostilities were expected. Lieutenant General Matthew B. Ridgway, CO of the XVIII Airborne Corps sent Major General Maxwell D. Taylor, CO of the 101st Airborne Division, back to the States on 5 December for a series of conferences on the organizational makeup of the airborne divisions.

Five days later Ridgway sent five top unit commanders of the 101st back to England to present a series of lectures on the division's experience during Operation Market-Garden. Ridgway himself remained in his rear area command post in England. It was not lost on the paratroopers that the regular COs of the 101st Airborne and XVIII Airborne Corps were absent. Brigadier General Anthony C. McAuliffe and Major General James M. Gavin were in temporary command. With so many of the top commanders out of theatre, the troopers reasoned, they were unlikely to be deployed in combat operations in the near future.

Sky Johnson got word to Jake and Johnny to meet him in a small out-of-the-way bar in Rheims on Sunday, 17 December. The two boys wangled a pass from Captain West, the newly promoted CO of Easy Company. West warned them to keep out of trouble as he signed the passes.

Sky was sitting alone at a table in the corner when the boys walked in. They saw him, sat down and greeted each other with slaps, pats and handshakes.

They ordered some beers and Sky spoke first. "Jake, I'm so sorry to hear about…"

Jake held up his hand, "Thanks Sky, we don't talk about it."

Sky nodded. He heard about the Dear John letter and could see Jake was still seething inside. He turned to Johnny. "How are Rose and the boy?"

Johnny pursed his lips and shook his head ever so slightly. He didn't want to talk about them either in front of Jake. "Fine." Johnny changed the subject. "What's new with you, Sky?"

Sky got the message and went along. "The word is I'm getting a battlefield commission. I'll get to go to 'ninety-day wonder' school." Sky was referring to the three-month course for new officer candidates and what they were called by the troops after completing the course.

Johnny cuffed Sky on his forearm. "Congratulations, *sir!*"

"Not just yet," Sky smiled.

"I'm happy for you, too," Jake added. "If that's what you want."

"I can use the dough," Sky reasoned. "And what the freakin' hell, I haven't made much of my life so far and someone seems to think I'm a pretty good soldier." Sky became uncomfortable with the topic of conversation. "What's new with you guys?"

Jake answered first with his impish grin. "Well, Yank here took us on a tour today."

Johnny rolled his eyes and looked at the ceiling, "You're something, Jake."

"Where?" Sky was interested.

Johnny answered. "We scrounged a jeep and went to see some World War I battlefields."

"Where'd you go?"

"We went up to Château Thierry, Belleau Wood and the Argonne Forest. Took most of the day."

"What's to see in those places?" Sky continued.

"Exactly my point," Jake interjected as the waitress placed three pints of beer on the table.

Johnny smiled. "There were a few memorials and the earth was still not healed after all these years. You could still see the outline of the trenches and the shell holes in the fields." He paused. "And Julius Caesar camped his Roman legions on those same fields outside Mourmelon in fifty-four BC." He took a slug of beer. "Imagine that? It's not what you can see. It's what you *feel*. The hairs on the back of my neck stand up when I'm standing on top of history."

Just then five soldiers from the 82nd Airborne came into the bar and sat at a large table on the other side of the room. The three men took notice and resumed their conversation.

Sky looked at Jake. "You're not too happy about the historical tour?" he chided.

"I'm just busting balls," Jake smiled. "I'm always amazed at how much shit he knows," he nodded in Johnny's direction. Jake got serious for a moment. "Hanging out with him is like hanging out with an encyclopedia. When I get home, I'm going to school on this new GI Bill."

Johnny looked a bit surprised. "Really? That's fantastic!"

"Absolutely!" Jake answered. "I always told you, as much as you didn't want this war to change you, that's how much I want it to change me." Jake looked at Sky. "I'm tired of being the only guy who doesn't know stuff. I'm going back to school and get an education and Uncle Sam is going to pay for it. I'm going to make something of myself, if I get back!"

"You'll get back," Sky assured. "We'll all get back!" He held up his glass and the three men clinked glasses, drained them dry and ordered another round.

Sky looked across the bar at the other paratroopers. They seemed young and fresh, probably replacements. He had heard the stories of the bar-fights in Rheims. "I heard that Taylor had to apologize to the mayor of Rheims in person for all the brawls since he's the only senior general who speaks French. He had to apologize for *both divisions*."

"Good for him. He deserves it. He speaks Japanese too and I'm hoping he winds up in the Pacific pretty soon," Johnny commented.

"Speaking of Taylor, what was that all about with him back in Holland when you guys drove him up in the jeep?" Sky had been meaning to ask them since they got there. "Was he pissed that you passed over the thirty-cal ammo?"

"Oh, what the fuck," Jake said.

"No, no, no," Johnny pleaded.

Jake looked at Johnny. "It doesn't matter anymore." He looked at Sky. "When we went missing back in Sicily for those few days we were assigned to General Taylor."

Sky had a puzzled look on his face. Johnny had his head in his hands looking at the table. Jake was about to spill the beans on the Rome Job.

"Taylor went to Rome to meet with the Italians to work out a plan to drop the Eighty-second on Rome. We were his bodyguards. Taylor did a good thing canceling the drop even though I still think he's an asshole. We were sworn to secrecy."

"Now you're sworn to secrecy, too, Sky," Johnny added. "If this gets out we're dead."

Sky sat there in shock. "There were rumors about Taylor being in Rome but nobody believed them." Sky whistled through his teeth. "How about that!"

"Well anyway," Jake continued, "the bastard recognized us and started to grill us to make sure we hadn't told anyone. We told him we hadn't. Then he said maybe we shouldn't be allowed in combat anymore since we could get captured. Then Johnny told him we were paratroopers and wanted to stay paratroopers.

When he left we were sure he was going to transfer us to some rear area outfit. But we wound up in a line company, Easy Company, Five-oh-six."

"He was throwing his weight around," Johnny joined in the storytelling. "He seemed pissed off about General Brereton, ordering him to visit the units up and down the road. So he takes it out on us. As they say, shit rolls down hill. I just didn't want to give him the satisfaction of bullying us. Besides, we kept his damn secret!" Johnny looked at Jake and smiled. "Until now."

"But we'll never be captured anyway. We have a pact."

"What pact?" Sky asked.

"Never to be taken alive," Jake answered. "Come to think of it, we need another one."

"Oh, no. Not another pact," Johnny moaned.

"Yeah, one more," Jake answered. He placed his hand in the middle of the table. "If any of us should die, the survivors have to promise to keep his last wishes."

Sky put his hand on Jake's. "Sounds reasonable to me."

Johnny smiled and said, "I can't keep track of all these blood pacts."

"Sure you can, Yank. One, we'll never be taken prisoner, two, we don't go home with a missing body part and three, we keep the last wishes of anyone not making it back. Simple."

Sky laughed. "Okay, sign me up for all three."

"I know, simple." Johnny stuck his hand on top of Sky and Jake's hands. Jake placed his other empty hand on top of the pile and shook it slightly. "It's done."

The three men sat quietly and talked. The beers kept coming as Sky related the story of the Waal River crossing. The boys hung on every word and could only imagine the fright and horror felt by men, never trained in boats, crossing a wide river under enemy fire. When the men of the 82nd boasted they would follow Gavin into hell, they had no idea what hell was really like.

Sky's tone became quieter and more somber as he described the casualties and named some of the men he thought they might know. Then his voice rose a bit in anger when he explained that after they took the bridge at Nijmegan, the British failed to race up the highway to rescue their own besieged paratroopers. Sky had absolutely no use for the British. He despised their leadership, planning, tactics and general attitude. He only had respect for the foot soldier, the "Tommy", who had to serve and fight under these incompetent commanders.

Soon they were talking about different subjects. Their relationship went all the way back to jump school and the bond between them was strong. They remembered their lost buddies and toasted them. They sat for some time, joked and enjoyed their reunion. When they were done, they paid the check and left. They were standing outside in the gathering evening darkness, bidding farewell and didn't notice the five paratroopers who came out the door behind them.

"What do Eagles scream?" howled one in a high-pitched voice.

The three men turned. Sky had his right shoulder facing them so they could not see his sleeve patch. Jake and Johnny had their Eagle shoulder flash facing the five young paratroopers.

"Help," squealed another in a mocking girlish tone. It was the same old chant used by All-American paratroopers to provoke a fight with the Screaming Eagles. It always worked. The Eagles would usually respond by loudly asking what the AA stood for on the 82nd patch. Others would derisively holler "almost airborne" and the knockdown drag out brawl would begin.

The five soldiers stepped forward a few paces but stopped when Sky turned his sleeve patch in their direction. "How many combat jumps do you girls have?" He turned to face them.

"None Sarge, we're replacements," said one.

"Sorry Sarge, we didn't see you were Eighty-second. We just want those Hundred and first guys," said another.

"You want them, you get me too!" Sky gave the come-here sign with both hands. "Just so you know, we each have four combat jumps so we're not just going to beat you to a pulp, we're gonna' kill you and eat you and bury your bones behind that cathedral over there."

Johnny attempted to be the peacemaker. "Why don't you kids save it for the Krauts?" When they didn't respond he said, "We used to be Eighty-second, just like you." The young paratroopers appeared less aggressive and seemed to have changed their minds but no one would make the first move to back down.

"Fuck all this talk," Jake started toward the group of five. "If these bitches want action we'll settle it right here." He moved aggressively until Sky and Johnny each grabbed an arm.

Finally, one of the troopers spoke up. "Sorry, Sarge. This is all a big misunderstanding." He turned to the group. "Let's go." They followed him back into the bar.

Jake, Johnny and Sky stood out on the dark street and breathed a sigh of relief. Sky bid farewell and headed toward the south side of town to pick up his bus back to Camp Suippes. Jake and Johnny headed north and walked quickly up the street. After walking some distance, they saw a figure of a soldier walking toward them. They could tell from a distance it was an officer. He appeared short and a bit on the plump side. Both recognized the rank insignia as the officer walked past and they each snapped off a smart salute. As the major returned the salute Jake noticed the boots and the empty chest. He stopped and immediately became enraged. He already had an adrenalin headache from the near brawl.

"Major," he called out. "There's something in this alley you need to see."

"What, soldier?"

"Come and see for yourself, sir."

"What are you doing, Jake?" Johnny whispered.

"Shush," Jake hissed.

The major followed Jake into the cobblestone alley. When he was about ten feet in, Jake turned to the major.

"Are you airborne qualified, sir?" Jake asked politely.

"What's the meaning of this, soldier?" the officer demanded.

"I'll take that as a *no*, sir. You're not authorized to wear these boots, sir, so I'm going to relieve you of them." Jake moved closer.

"How dare you? What's your outfit?"

"I'll take that as a *no*, too." Jake then threw a crisp, short left hook squarely into the major's nose. The officer staggered back, stunned and nearly unconscious hit the wall with his back and slid to the ground.

After Jake laced up his new boots he and Johnny continued walking up the dark street toward the bus depot. They left the major sitting in the alley holding his bleeding nose and trying to lace up Jake's old boots.

"Crap," Johnny complained. "We're in for it now. I hope he didn't recognize us."

"If he recognized anyone, it's me," Jake shot back. "You're not *in* for anything."

Johnny looked at him and smiled. "When are you going to get it, brother? What happens to you happens to me. When you're in shit, I'm in shit, too."

Jake contemplated that thought for a moment. "You're right. I should know that by now." He shook his head. "You're right!" Then he smiled broadly. "*We're* in deep shit."

They both laughed. "I get your point," Jake finally said.

They continued walking in step with long, quick strides anxious to get to the bus depot and out of Rheims. It was about a mile to their destination and they were nearly halfway there when they heard the unmistakable engine sound of an American jeep behind them. The vehicle stopped to the loud screech of its brakes. There were two MPs in the jeep.

"Hey, Mac. Are you two airborne?" the Military Policeman growled as he tapped his white nightstick on the side of the windshield.

Johnny was sure the major had called out the MPs and reported the assault. He was equally sure they would be thrown into the stockade and probably be shot at sunrise.

Jake answered. "Hundred and first." The driver shined a flashlight at Jake's face and then the patch. Jake winced at the bright light. He had been identified. The MPs surely had them now.

"Your outfit's been alerted for movement. All leaves are cancelled. You've got to get your butts back to camp immediately," the MP ordered.

"We're headed to the bus depot now," Johnny explained.

"Hop in, we'll give you a lift. We've been rounding up paratroopers all night."

Jake and Johnny could not believe their luck. They had amused looks on their faces as they piled into the back seat. The driver pulled away.

"What's going on?" Johnny finally thought to ask.

The driver responded. "Krauts launched an offensive. Attacked through the Ardennes. Punched a pretty big hole in the First Army lines. You airborne guys are supposed to plug it up!"

Chapter Sixty

Bedford, Virginia - November 11, 1997

"A man is his own easiest dupe,
for what he wishes to be true he generally believes to be true."

Demosthenes (384 BC - 322 BC)

J.P. Kilroy made a left turn at the small school that served as his landmark. He drove slowly up the gravel road, which elevated as it proceeded toward the eighty-eight acre tract of land that would contain the National D-Day Memorial on Bedford's highest hill. The small Blue Ridge town lost twenty-one of its sons on Omaha Beach. It was the highest per capita loss in the nation. Only twelve of thirty-five members of its Able Company survived the War. They could not have picked a better day, Veterans Day, to break ground for the ten-acre memorial to be built there. It was a symbolic day for this most solemn yet uplifting event.

Senator John Warner and Governor George F. Allen were speaking at the dedication. Senator Warner had pushed the bill through Congress resulting in the selection of Bedford as the site of the National D-Day Memorial. The bill was signed into law on Veterans Day, 1994.

As J.P. traveled south on Interstate 95 that morning his mind mused over the events that had brought him to this point. He reflected back to the beginning as the milepost signs of I-95 whispered by. It all started with his mother asking him to reconcile with his father who had abandoned the family nearly thirty years before. She told him about a family secret and that his father should be the one to reveal it. To his everlasting regret, he dismissed the idea and procrastinated long enough to see his mother pass on without ever fulfilling her last request. Time passed, life took over and the entire matter was about to be shoveled into the deepest recess of his mind when Colonel Chase called out of the blue. *Would he receive his father's Medal of Honor?* Was this a coincidence or was the spirit of his saintly mother working overtime to compel him to face the consequences of his negligence? But then Colonel Chase perplexed him with the news that his father had passed away. That revelation, coming as a complete shock from a stranger, spooked him.

Once he agreed to attend the ceremony, his conscience and curiosity coerced him into a simple plan to seek out Lincoln Abraham and determine if there was anything between the two men that might help him get to the bottom of the mystery. It might require a bit of amateur detective work and some research but since he would be there anyway, he had nothing to lose by trying. When he spotted

Lincoln speaking cordially with three other veterans, he became confident that if they knew anything at all, he ought to be able to get them to reveal it.

J.P. also met Cynthia Powers, a colleague of Colonel Chase. Her assignment for the day was to keep him occupied so she latched onto him so tightly that he missed his chance to speak to the four veterans. With her help he invited them to dinner that evening. Sky Johnson, Frank West and Harley Tidrick accepted but Lincoln couldn't attend. The men seemed to enjoy talking about their experiences during the War but were somewhat evasive when J.P. probed about his father. He wasn't even sure they knew anything at all until he left his recorder running while he went to the rest room. When he played it back later, he discovered there was something they all knew. While he didn't learn of any specific secret, he understood the men were engaged in a conspiracy to withhold information they swore never to reveal.

J.P. continued probing at Frank, Sky and finally with a visit to Lincoln's cabin in Michigan. Initially Lincoln was no more forthcoming than his buddies. However, one thing became clear. The old men knew J.P. was aware of their collusion but remained persistent despite their alliance of silence. But then Lincoln stunned him when he told J.P. his father was alive. His initial reaction was to drive directly to Bedford but then the same old familiar fear paralyzed him into inaction. He returned to D.C. to mull over his next move.

J.P. took I-95 straight through Richmond as he looked carefully for his exit in the maze of intersecting roads. He finally found State Highway 360 and took it west.

After he left Lincoln's cabin in July he called Cynthia. He wanted her to find out how Colonel Chase knew his father had passed on and how Chase knew to contact J.P. After a few hours she called him back while he was driving home from Dulles Airport. Cynthia told him Chase found out about his father's passing from Harley, who also told of the existence of a surviving son.

When the Pentagon began reaching out to the survivors and family members of the Medal of Honor awardees, they sought out military service records indicating next of kin. That otherwise simple task was more complicated than it should have been. The service records of more than 16,000,000 veterans, many from the Second World War, were destroyed in a fire at the National Personnel Records Center in St. Louis, Missouri on 12 July 1973. The army lost eighty percent of the records for personnel discharged between 1912 and 1960. Colonel Chase had to employ alternate sources such as reaching out to veteran's organizations and associations. It was the only way he was able to locate the family members of the honorees.

It didn't make sense to J.P. that Harley would have been the one to pass information on to Colonel Chase. Either Frank West or Sky Johnson was more likely to have contact information for his father. So why was it that Harley provided the information to Colonel Chase? Besides that little ambiguity, Harley also lied about his father's death. He sat across the dinner table, never said a word and seemed determined to keep the others silent as well. What was he hiding?

J.P. knew Harley lived in Bedford because his mother once told him his father had moved there but this still didn't explain why Harley would be playing such a prominent role in his father's affairs. J.P. would soon confront Harley and his father about all these nagging questions.

J.P. also asked Cynthia to check up on one other thing. Was a John Kilroy buried in the Henri Chapelle Cemetery in Belgium? Nobody wanted to tell J.P. how Jake died in the War so he wanted confirmation. Cynthia checked with the American Battle Monuments Commission (ABMC) who administers, operates and maintains twenty-four American burial grounds on foreign soil. She received verification from senior executives of the ABMC who consulted their official records. At least this piece of information was accurate.

J.P. navigated the turnoff to State Highway 307 bypassing the village of Farmville. The countryside was a beautiful scene of rolling hills dotted by small farms and old wood frame barns. It would be a straight shot into Bedford.

Following Lincoln's advice, J.P. decided to search through what possessions he already had. Sitting on the living room floor of his condominium, he and Cynthia turned over the small box of memorabilia for yet another time. They carefully poured out the precious cargo of the shoebox on the rug and sat around the contents as if sitting around a campfire. Every article had a history or its own little story. They went over the items one by one, held them, shared them, treated them with reverence and speculated about their origin and purpose.

They quickly discussed and dismissed some of the more routine items they were familiar with. J.P. picked up and held the two sets of jump wings. Obviously, his father had saved some of Jake's memorabilia as well as his own.

"Frank said these are very rare," he commented as he handed them to Cynthia. She gently wiped them clean with a small cloth before placing them on a fresh white towel. The towel would go back into the shoebox when all the contents had been inspected.

Next were the patches for the three different airborne divisions in which the boys served. J.P. handed them to Cynthia. Before placing them on the towel, she turned over the Golden Talon patch of the 17th Airborne and scraped off a sticky substance. "Chewing gum, I'll bet."

J.P. reached into the shoebox and handed her the photo of Jake and Johnny in Oujda. The two boys looked dangerous with grim shadow-covered faces as they held their deadly weapons. "It's hard to imagine those nice old men in their youth when they were all full of piss and vinegar," she muttered as she placed the picture aside.

The other photograph was more interesting. His mother, father and Jake were posing on the roof of their apartment building in Washington Heights. They were all smiling. One of the towers of the George Washington Bridge could be clearly seen in the background. On the back of the picture was written, *Johnny, Rose and Jake, September 1943*. J.P. didn't realize his father had brought Jake home with him until he saw that picture.

"He was only home for about a day," J. P. handed Cynthia the picture. "The day I was conceived," he added wryly.

She looked at the picture and studied it for a moment. "It's kind of weird to know that," she smiled. "I mean…to know the specific day you were actually conceived."

"I suppose," he acknowledged.

He picked through the small pile and handed her two medals. One was a Bronze Star and the other was a Silver Star. The Bronze Star was a five-pointed star, deep bronze in color and attached to a ribbon that was mostly red with a white-bordered blue stripe down the center. The Silver Star was actually gold in color with a red, white and blue ribbon. He handed her the two medals and the lapel ribbon bars that matched them. "I don't know about these," he confessed. "I'll have to remember to ask the next time I talk to one of the guys."

Cynthia nodded, took the medals, wiped them, held them for a moment and placed them on the towel. "You don't get these for just showing up for work!"

Next he handed her two sets of dog tags. The tags had name, serial number, religion and blood type. There was a set for John NMI Kilroy and John P. Kilroy. The information on the tags was not a surprise. Jake was Protestant and Johnny was Catholic. Both were blood type "O".

She straightened out the long link chains used to hang the tags around the neck and said, "It seems like your father took back a lot of stuff that belonged to Jake."

"It certainly seems so," he answered. "But I guess you would do that if your best friend was killed. Perhaps he couldn't get Jake's personal belongings back to his family though I'm not sure Jake had any family besides Harley. Who knows why he kept most of this stuff?"

He handed her one Combat Infantryman's Badge. It was a silver musket on a rectangular blue field superimposed over a laurel wreath. The musket was awarded to any soldier completing Advanced Infantry Training. The laurel wreath was added after the soldier saw combat.

"Now these are really special," he picked up three Purple Heart Medals along with the bar ribbons and handed them to Cynthia. The medal was a heart-shaped device of deep purple trimmed in gold. A brilliant raised white cameo profile of George Washington was inscribed in the center. The ribbon was deep purple with slender light blue stripes down both side edges. "My father never talked about any of these. But I think one or two belonged to his friend."

"Probably. There is so much other stuff from Jake in here." She reached in to retrieve the next item, which was a pocket bible in the King James Version. It was stained, dog-eared and the back cover was torn in half. It obviously had been through a lot. On the inside cover was the name Clyde Kilroy. She thumbed through the pages and a marker fell out of Luke Chapter 20. She carefully placed it back and closed the Bible.

J.P. took out the last items. They were the Medal of Honor and the citation. He opened the citation. "Lincoln told me I already had what I needed to figure out the secret. I've read this citation a dozen times and it really doesn't provide any insight."

She took it from him. "Let me try. I'll read it aloud."

The citation was written on a piece of letter-sized paper. The top of the letter had a color picture of the Medal of Honor. Directly under the picture, centered in the middle of the page, was his father's name in big bold letters. JOHN KILROY. Then there was a paragraph for Rank and Organization administrative information and then the actual citation. Cynthia began.

"Rank and Organization: Corporal, Unites States Army, Company E, 506th Parachute Infantry Regiment. Place and Date: Near Noville and Foy, Belgium, 19-20 December 1944. Yada, yada, yada." Anxious to get on to the actual body of the citation, she skipped the rest of the prologue.

"Citation: He displayed conspicuous gallantry and intrepidity in action against the enemy near Noville and Foy, Belgium on 19 and 20 December 1944. Volunteering to secure arms and ammunition for his regiment, he commandeered a truck and requisitioned supplies from the 10th Armored Division near the town of Noville making numerous trips to supply his airborne comrades in Bastogne. On the last trip, superior encircling German Panzer forces cut him and another soldier off from friendly lines. Mounting a halftrack, he used the weapons aboard the vehicle to hold off the enemy forces and, knocking out a .20-millimeter enemy flakwagon, allowing his comrades to escape encirclement. Still surrounded himself, he drove the vehicle through the enemy force and escaped into a thick blanket of fog. He took refuge in an abandoned farmhouse with enemy patrols all around his position. He then killed four Nazi soldiers masquerading as Americans. Had they not been discovered, they would have been exceedingly disruptive to retreating American forces. Some time later he heard the sound of engines. The American force at Noville was conducting a fighting withdrawal to the village of Foy and back to Bastogne. There were dozens of wounded men on this evacuation convoy and it came under enemy attack. Without regard to his own personal safety, he attacked a superior enemy force with his vehicle and drew fire allowing the convoy to proceed. Undaunted by this enemy fire, he closed with the enemy and knocked out two scout cars. He also caught a company of infantrymen in the open and drove them back inflicting heavy casualties although wounded himself. While the enemy infantry retreated, the convoy continued toward Foy with its wounded. Finally, using the fog for concealment, he knocked out a Mark V Panther tank, as it was about to attack the column approaching Foy. Had the tank attacked the column, hundreds more soldiers would have become casualties. Corporal Kilroy's intrepid courage and superb daring while vastly outnumbered during his all day action of engaging and distracting enemy forces at grave risk to himself enabled the successful evacuation of over fifty wounded and more than 500 soldiers safely to friendly lines."

She looked up at him. "This is remarkable. But I don't see anything revealing in here."

"Like I said, I've read the citation over and over and I can't derive anything from it. Except that my father was a crazy son of a bitch who never talked about anything that happened in the War. Not with me, anyway."

Cynthia Powers gently lifted the towel and placed it and all of the contents back into the shoebox. "What makes you think there are any clues in here?"

J.P. pulled his recorder from his pocket and hit the play button.

Keisha: Are you going to tell him about his father?

Lincoln: I don't think I'll need to. He's smart enough to figure it out for himself.

Keisha: Are you going to tell him anything at all?

Lincoln: I might tell him something but I'm not breaking my promise.

J.P. pushed fast-forward on the recorder. He stopped it and hit play again.

Lincoln: The first is that you already have everything you need in your possession, right now, to uncover the secret. Letters, papers, memorabilia, citations…all the information you need to figure it out.

J.P.: And the second piece of advice?

Lincoln: There is someone living in Bedford, Virginia, who knows everything, more than the rest of us, and you need to talk to him face to face.

J.P.: Who? Harley Tidrick? I plan to visit him next.

Lincoln: No. Not Harley. Your father! He's not dead but rather very much alive."

Cynthia placed the cover on the box. "Okay. Let's go over it again when you get back from Bedford."

There was a large group of cars parked on the grass and two volunteer firemen directing traffic. He parked next to a Ford pickup and walked toward the large tent and temporary platform. From this vantage point the background of the Blue Ridge Mountains was breathtaking. It was a wonderful, reflective and inspiring location to honor the fallen.

Inside the tent was an artist's conception of the finished memorial. He spent a few minutes studying it. It was both compelling and unique. A large drawing of a thermometer on an easel marked the level of funds raised for the memorial. The red line was filled in up to the four and a quarter million dollar mark and the thermometer topped out at fourteen million. The table next to the easel contained a pile of programs and a large glass jar filled with green bills. J.P. added a twenty-dollar bill. He picked up a program and meandered toward the stage.

The crowd numbered about 1,000 and he mingled freely among them looking for familiar faces. There were some dignitaries on the stage and a number of older veterans. J.P. recognized Harley. He was wearing his Stonewaller windbreaker and a dark blue overseas cap with the American Legion Post 54 designation on it. The other older veterans wore an assortment of uniforms, brightly decorated caps and medals.

After a time, Governor Allen was introduced. He made a short but heart-rending speech. He ended it by saying, "Time has washed away the blood of our fallen heroes from the beaches of Omaha and the cliffs of Normandy, but time has not washed away, and must not dim, our memories of those horrific and heroic events. By breaking ground for this National D-Day Memorial, each of us is doing our duty to help insure that the eternal flame of freedom will never be extinguished by force from without or neglect from within."

J.P. recognized Charles M. Shultz, the creator of the popular comic strip Peanuts. He was sitting on the platform. The program said Shultz, a World War II veteran, was to head up national fundraising efforts for the memorial. It also said he personally donated one million dollars.

Finally, Senator Warner took the microphone. He was the second ranking Republican on the Senate Armed Services Committee and a veteran of World War II and the Korean War. His speech was a little longer. "This event marks a milestone in what has become a final campaign for the surviving veterans of the greatest military operation of all time," concluded Senator Warner. "The National D-Day Memorial will insure that the lessons of that historic event will never be forgotten by future generations."

When the speeches were concluded, the dignitaries took turns being photographed pushing a silver shovel into the soft earth. After the symbolic groundbreaking, the crowd began to disburse. J.P. stood in the field, taking in the moment when he saw Harley heading his way. As frustrated as he might become, J.P. promised himself to always treat these men with respect. All the cards were on the table now. They pledged to keep a secret he was determined to uncover and he would engage them politely though firmly in an effort to trip them up.

He had to remind himself these were fine men and whatever their reason to keep their oath, it must be a good one.

J.P. extended his hand as Harley approached. Harley shook it vigorously. "Well, kid, we're finally going to get the memorial we deserve." There were tears in his eyes.

"Congratulations," J.P. smiled. "This is a wonderful spot."

Harley took a deep breath and seemed to compose himself. He leaned over toward J.P. "I know why you're here. I got a call from Lincoln. I expected you sooner."

"I had to decide if I really wanted to do this," J.P. confided. "My life is a bit more complicated than I'd like and my job keeps me hopping. I had to figure out if I really wanted to jump into this right now." J.P. was unconsciously making excuses for not coming sooner.

"No need to explain, kid. We haven't exactly welcomed you with open arms."

J.P. nodded in affirmation. "Tell me one thing, Harley. Why did you tell Colonel Chase my father was dead and then tell him about me?"

Harley looked around and whispered, "That's the way your father wanted it. He didn't want the notoriety or the publicity and he wanted you to have the Medal."

"I get that. I got the Medal. But why was it you? As far as I can tell you only met my father a few times."

"Let me explain, kid. Your dad's records were lost in the big fire. Colonel Chase contacted all of the veterans' associations for units your father served in. The colonel was asking if anyone had any information about his whereabouts. Sky is on the Board of Trustees of the Eighty-second Airborne Association and got the request. He called your father who asked me to call Colonel Chase and tell him what I told him."

J.P. nodded. "I hear what you're telling me but faking being dead is kind of extreme. It makes no sense to me. Why would he do that?"

"Well, kid, you probably came all this way to ask him that question." With that Harley raised his arm and looked at J.P. "Are you ready for this?"

J.P. sighed. "Ready as I'll ever be." He felt like a kid again, about to be spanked.

Harley waved and a man came out from behind the platform. At the sight of his father, his knees buckled slightly. J.P. touched Harley's sleeve for balance.

His father walked slowly with a slight limp. He had an unlit pipe in his tightly clenched jaw. His hair was all gray and short cropped. He wore no unit insignia or association cap, his collar was upturned against the breeze and his hands were stuffed deeply into his coat pockets. There was no discernable expression on his face as he averted his son's eyes. J.P. would have recognized him anywhere even though his features had aged considerably after thirty years.

J.P. swallowed hard. What was it about the relationship between a father and son that drove a son to seek his father's approval? *It was more than seek*, J.P. thought. *More like a psychological imperative.* J.P. dreaded this moment and had often prayed he would be fortunate to pass from this earth without ever having to see or confront his father again.

His father stopped a few feet away and stared blankly at him. J.P. simply looked at him. It was an awkward moment.

Harley coughed, "I'll leave you two alone," and walked away.

The two men looked at each other for a time, neither wanting to break the silence. Finally, his father said, "You come all this way just to stand there and stare at me. I knew this was a bad idea." He turned to walk away.

"No, please wait," J.P. pleaded. "It's just…well, it's just hard after all these years."

"On both of us."

"Of course. Can we walk and talk a little?"

His father nodded and they began walking slowly, aimlessly toward the open field where the cars were parked. J.P. broke the silence. "You look well."

"I've been better. How are you doing, Son?"

"It's all good." J.P. suddenly stopped. "I have a million questions."

"A million, huh?" the old man smiled. "Okay. Let's take them one at a time."

J.P. began walking again. "I know why you left. You left because I disappointed you."

"That's not a question."

"Is that why you left? Because I took off for Canada rather than be drafted and go to Vietnam?" He turned to look directly into his father's eyes. He finally summoned the courage to confront his nightmare and needed to know the truth.

"You've got it all wrong!" His father took out a package of nicotine gum and popped two chiclets into his mouth. "Trying to quit," he muttered by way of explanation.

"C'mon Dad, you being a war hero and all. I'm sure you were angry and disappointed that I chose not to serve."

"I didn't agree with your decision, Son, but I fought for your right to make it." He was looking directly into his son's eyes. His gaze was firm and truthful. "I served with wonderful, honorable guys. In our darkest hours when we had no hope and we despaired for our lives, we all agreed it would be worth every drop of our blood if our children didn't have to fight in another war." He paused. "If there be trouble, let it be in our time, so that our children will have peace."

"Thomas Paine." J.P. remembered the paraphrased quote.

"So you see, I fought so you wouldn't have to. So why would I be angry?"

J.P. considered the logic. "It's hard to believe you're not holding me accountable."

He smiled again. "It would have been better for you if you felt the obligation to serve your country. But you have to deal with that within yourself. President Carter gave you amnesty. I long ago forgave you if there was ever anything to forgive. Like I said, I fought so you wouldn't have to. It's time you let it go!"

They walked on a bit further. J.P. felt the weight of the past gently lifting from his shoulders. This brief conversation expunged demons that he rarely acknowledged. "So, if not because of me, why did you leave?" he found himself asking.

His father seemed to struggle for words. "I'm not going to make any excuses. It's way past that point. What's done is done. But I will say this. I made sure you got your education and that your mother was taken care of financially. I sent her money regularly until she told me she didn't need it anymore."

"She never remarried," J.P. volunteered.

"I know. We stayed in touch."

"And I still don't know how you paid all that tuition on a teacher's salary," J.P. said referring to college and law school.

The old man smiled. "I just finished paying off the loans a few years ago."

J.P. was stunned. He always thought of his father as a selfish man who just decided one day that he didn't like his life and quit. His assumptions about his father were totally wrong.

"Why did you leave?" The question was serious and direct.

"Does it matter?"

"Of course it matters. Please, I really need to know."

His father stopped, shoved his hands deeper into his pockets and shuffled his feet. "When a man gives his word, makes a promise, he has to keep it…even if it's hard…especially if it's hard. You can only become free of a pledge once you've kept it."

J.P. shook his head. It wasn't making sense to him. His father continued.

"When you take on obligations, you have to fulfill them. It doesn't matter how long it takes or even if others get hurt. A man is only as good as his word."

J.P. tried to finish the thought. "So you left us and came here to fulfill a promise you made involving who…Harley? Macie? Did it have anything to do with this memorial?"

"I've said all I'm going to say about that. Just know it was nothing you or your mom did. That's all you really need to know." The old man started walking again.

J.P. took a deep breath. It was exasperating trying to get these old veterans to give him a straight answer. He would have to get more creative to try to figure out this mystery. No matter how much his father skirted the issue, his gut told him to keep pushing. He caught up to his father and steered him toward a mobile canteen truck parked at the edge of the parking lot.

"How about a cup of coffee, Dad?"

"Sure, Son," he agreed.

J.P. looked up into the side window of the truck. "Two coffees, please." He looked at his father. "Still black?"

"Black. No sugar."

"One black, one regular with milk and sugar."

After a moment J.P. handed his father the coffee in a cardboard cup. It was hot and steaming. They walked along together, sipping their coffee.

"Mom sent me all your old war mementos before she passed," J.P. broke the silence.

"Keep them. They're supposed to be passed on." He paused. "Any more questions?"

"I believed you were dead. What was *that* all about?"

His father stopped again, spit out his gum and took a sip of coffee. It was cooling off a little and he took longer slugs. "I didn't ask for the Medal, I didn't want the Medal and I felt foolish accepting the Medal in a ceremony for African-Americans who got screwed during the War. I got the Silver Star for that day and Lincoln got shit. The only reason I got the Medal of Honor after all these years was because they gave one to Lincoln...after all these years." There was an edge in his voice. "I thought it was best not to rain on Lincoln's parade and let him have his day in the sun. He damn well earned it! The only way I could think of to do that gracefully was to be dead. So I told Harley to tell them I passed away."

J.P. nodded. "I understand now." They walked a little further, almost to where J.P. had parked his car. "And this secret that mom wanted me to find out from you? She pleaded with me to work things out with you and find out about a family secret you were supposed to tell me."

His father stared at him blankly, shrugged his shoulders and shook his head.

"Come on, Dad. Mom told me to seek you out. I've been speaking to all of your old buddies. They already admitted to me they're hiding something."

His father averted his eyes and then looked squarely at him. "If your mother thought I knew something that you should know, she never told me about it. It went with her to her grave. Perhaps it was her devious little plan to get you and I together." He shook his head. "I'm really sorry, Son, but you've come a long way for nothing."

J.P. let out a huge sigh. *His father was part of the conspiracy!* But there was one more thing he had to do so he decided to play along. "I wouldn't call it a wasted trip, Dad. If you and I are speaking again then mom's last wish *would* be fulfilled."

"That's fine with me. I always wanted to remain close to you. I followed your career and read all the stuff you published." He drained the coffee cup and looked around for a garbage can.

"I'll take it," J.P. extended his hand. "I have a trash bag in my car."

"Then we'll stay in touch?" he asked as he handed J.P. his empty cup.

"Of course." They hugged briefly and J.P. got into his car, started it, strapped on his seat belt and drove slowly down the road. He left his father standing alone at the top of the hill. Through his rearview mirror he noticed Harley walk up alongside him. J.P. could barely make out the Cheshire cat-like grins on their faces as they faded into the distance. Soon, only the animation of their gestures was visible.

J.P. pulled up to a stoplight, opened his glove compartment and pulled out a plastic bag. He carefully slipped his father's cup into the bag and gently placed it back into the glove box.

Chapter Sixty-One

Bastogne, Belgium - December 18, 1944

"I always make it a rule to get there first with the most men."

Lieutenant General Nathan Bedford Forrest (1821-1877)

"Tailgate jump! Currahee!" one of the paratroopers yelled as another lifted the four-by-four foot gate from the straw-covered trailer bed from which the men began jumping. It was dark, damp and chilly as the troopers scurried off the flatbed and onto the roadside.

"Shush," admonished Captain Frank West in a loud whisper as he walked up and down the line of troopers forming alongside the truck. "Why not just yell out your regiment and division while you're at it? The Krauts would love to know who you are."

West lent a hand to the last few men off the flatbed. They complained, stretched and relieved themselves on the side of the road. When the trailer was empty, West walked to the cab and banged on the door. The truck pulled the tandem cattle-trailer a few yards up the road, made a wide u-turn and headed back the way it came.

The men of Easy Company gathered up in a loose formation on the side of the road. They were a ragged looking bunch. Some had overcoats while others wore jumpsuits and field jackets. There were even some men in dress uniforms having been plucked from leave with no time to change into combat gear. Most had some sort of weapon but some had none. Not a single soldier had sufficient ammo or grenades. Their pockets were stuffed with K-rations and D-bars, the only commodities that were in plentiful supply in their encampment.

The headgear ran the gamut from standard issue GI steel helmets to woolen under caps. If they were on a jump mission they would have all been wearing jump boots but in their haste to depart Mourmelon, many had still been wearing dress shoes or tennis shoes. They came with whatever they were wearing and looked like a rag tag collection of itinerant hobos.

It was just before midnight. The troopers watched with great interest all along the horizon as the flashing lights were followed by deep rumbles of distant thunder. Somewhere over the horizon a huge battle was raging. They were marching to the sound and fury of a thousand guns.

"Move out, hubba-hubba, one time, follow me," West whispered and the men began shuffling their feet and marching. The captain marched his company toward the town of Bastogne. This is where the Screaming Eagles would make their stand.

On 16 December 1944 at 0530 hours, the Germans launched a surprisingly powerful attack across an eighty-five mile front through the Ardennes Forest on the border of Belgium and Germany. A force of nearly 300,000 men, 2,000 artillery pieces and 1,000 tanks attacked the weakest section of the American line whose troops were outnumbered by ten to one in places.

This section of the American front line came under the command of the United States First Army and was thinly manned by only three infantry and one armored division. Major General Troy H. Middleton's VIII Corps consisted of the 9th "Phantom" Armored Division, the 106th "Golden Lion" Infantry Division just recently arrived from the States and the 4th "Ivy" and 28th "Keystone" Infantry Divisions. The latter two veteran divisions had been recently chewed up and worn out in the Hurtgen Forest campaign. They were assigned to a "quiet" sector to rest, refit and absorb replacements. The northern boundary of VIII Corps linked up with the southern edge of V Corps within which both the 99th "Checkerboard" and 2nd "Indian Head" Infantry Divisions manned positions in the Ardennes.

In the preceding weeks Middleton complained to his boss, General Bradley, that his defensive line was too thinly held. He had only half the forces required to defend his front. Due to a severe shortage of American infantry divisions, Bradley decided to take a "calculated risk" since he believed the enemy was also weak in the same area. He was dead wrong.

The reason the attack of 16 December was so powerful and such a surprise was due mainly to the determination and paranoia of Adolf Hitler. Operation Watch on the Rhine, the codename given to this counteroffensive, was a concoction entirely of his brewing.

With his armies in full retreat before the Allies in the west and being systematically pushed back by the Russians in the east, Hitler felt the noose tightening around the Third Reich. The Russians were on the Vistula River near Poland and the Allies were approaching the Rhine.

On 16 September, Hitler listened patiently to General Alfred Jodl, Chief of the Armed Forces High Command (Oberkommando der Wehrmacht or OKW). At the mention of the Ardennes Forest, Hitler perked up and stood over the map. "I have made a momentous decision. I will go over to the offensive, here from the Ardennes." He pounded the map. "With the objective, Antwerp!" he pointed to the seaport approximately one hundred miles from the Ardennes.

His senior military staff was stunned. They began to raise questions about the source of this new attack force. Hitler was prepared. He had been nursing this idea for months.

The Wehrmacht (all of the German Armed Forces) was ordered to eliminate all rear-area non-combatant jobs. The administrative troops would be assigned to these new divisions. In addition, the draft age was increased from the range of eighteen to fifty years to sixteen to sixty years of age. Light duty personnel recovering from wounds would go into fortress battalions to free up more capable men to serve in the attack force. Hitler would then cherry-pick the best divisions on the western and eastern fronts, secretly withdraw them from the line, re-equip them and let them spearhead the attack. He planned to raise twenty-five new divisions he called *Volksgrenadiers*, or People's Infantry, and supplement them with ten new or rejuvenated *Panzer* brigades and three revitalized veteran infantry divisions. This new force would be given priority on all new tanks and artillery coming off the assembly lines.

Germany's losses had been severe in five years of war. They had lost 3,250,000 men. But Hitler had reason to be optimistic since there were still 10,000,000 men in uniform, including 7,500,000 in *De Heer* (The Army). Surely, *OKW* could carve out 300,000 men for this counteroffensive from all of these units!

The *Luftwaffe* promised to throw 1,500 planes into the battle, including one hundred of the new ME-262 jet fighters. Newly built medium Mark V Panther and heavy Royal Tiger tanks would be provided and self-propelled assault guns would make up any shortfall in armor.

Hitler reasoned if he could drive a wedge between the American and British forces and seize Antwerp, he might achieve a negotiated cessation of hostilities or even a separate peace. Then he could turn his forces to the east to face the Russian horde.

His generals argued the Ardennes was virtually impassible to large formations. It was mountainous country with few roads and deep snows in winter when biting cold and harsh winds swept the few plateaus. The heaviest rains came in November and December and the foggy mists were frequent, heavy and unpredictable. The Germans had proven it possible on two previous occasions, in 1914 and 1940, but those offensives were not undertaken in the winter months. The generals pointed out the soil permitted heavy vehicle movement only when the ground was dry or frozen. Snowfall often attained a depth of ten inches in a twenty-four hour period and lingered for a long time in the Ardennes. The winter conditions would not favor an attack based on speed.

Hitler brushed aside all of these objections. It was for all those reasons the Allies would not anticipate an offensive from the Ardennes. Besides, the thick forests on the German side of the Ardennes, known as the *Eifel*, would provide adequate cover from the prying eyes of the Allied air forces and allow the buildup to proceed undetected. In no other place could Germany secretly collect such a massive force close enough to Antwerp.

Hitler then explained the extraordinary security measures he was prepared to implement. First, no communications for this operation were to be made by wireless or telephone lines. All dispatches and orders were to be sent and acknowledged by courier. Second, the officers selected to lead the attack would not be notified until weeks before the operation. Ever since the failed bomb plot to assassinate him on 20 July, Hitler held a considerable mistrust of his army. He would wait until the last moment to pull in some of his finest generals to lead this offensive.

To augment the plan and improve its chances of success, Hitler issued some rather extreme and unconventional orders. He ordered Lieutenant Colonel Otto Skorzeny to organize a force of English-speaking German soldiers. Dressed in American uniforms, the members of the 150 Brigade, as it was named, would infiltrate the American rear and disrupt communications and pass along false and misleading orders. Skorzeny recruited a few hundred German military personnel to mount Operation *Greif* ("Griffin" in English) in captured American vehicles.

Hitler dispatched orders reminding his commanders the upcoming battle would be a life or death struggle and must be fought with brutality and all resistance must be broken in a wave of terror. Many took these orders to mean no prisoners would be taken. For the SS troops who were veterans of the Russian front, prisoners were rarely taken anyway.

On the night of 15 December, the Germans had twenty divisions, and nine in reserve, poised and ready to roll out of the cover of the *Eifel* and smash into the thinly held line in the Ardennes. Hitler's paranoid security precautions had worked beyond his wildest expectations. The Americans were not remotely expecting any trouble.

The German plan called for three Armies to attack abreast. In the north, the Sixth SS *Panzer* Army, the main attack force, would break out for the Meuse River. In the center, the German Fifth *Panzer* Army would surround the Americans on the *Schnee Eifel*, a heavily forested plateau on the American side, and charge for the road hubs of St. Vith and Bastogne. They would guard the left flank of the main attack force. The German Seventh Army, made up of mostly *Panzergrenadier* Divisions, had only one job; secure the southern flank of the penetration and protect the flank of the other two mobile Armies.

The artillery barrage began at 0530 hours. With the low clouds bathed in the harsh glow of huge German searchlights, nine divisions of surging *Panzers* and infantry troops attacked! Fierce battles were fought under the eerie glow of this artificial moonlight. The Germans smashed against the American outposts like white water rapids crashing down a raging river, bypassing rocks and sweeping everything before it.

Hitler gave the Sixth SS *Panzer* Army the main task of seizing Antwerp. He only trusted the SS whose loyalty was unshakable. As a result, he placed half of his striking force strength under his old friend and crony, *Oberstgruppenfuhrer der Waffen-SS* Josef "Sepp" Dietrich.

Elements of the Sixth Panzer Army poured through the Losheim Gap, the six-mile wide flat plain that served as a historic invasion route into the heavily wooded Ardennes. It was their mission to brush by resistance and make haste for the Meuse River. What the Americans called a "line" was in many places nothing more than a series of widely spaced outposts anchored in small hamlets or villages. The thin defenses in the Gap were badly battered and gave ground. The tide was overwhelming and units that stood firm were either swallowed up or bypassed. By nightfall of 16 December, the first of the *Panzer* elements, *Kampfgruppe Pieper*, the 1st SS *Panzer* Regiment of the 1st SS *Panzer* Division, was behind American lines.

The Fifth *Panzer* Army in the center, commanded by *General der Panzertruppen Hasso von Manteuffel*, attacked alongside the left flank of the Sixth SS *Panzer* Army. It was not easy country for tanks to negotiate and Manteuffel had to clear the *Schnee Eifel* of Americans before he could capture the two key road-towns. Elevated plateaus and high gorges cut by fast flowing rivers and twisting, winding roads were the norm in this part of the Ardennes. The elevation of the land changed quickly further inhibiting mobility. The topography would become more suitable for mobile operations once Manteuffel breached the thin crust of the American defenses and broke into more hospitable tank country. His force of four *Panzer* Divisions, one *Panzer* Brigade and five *Volksgrenadier* Divisions was a formidable one and he was anxious to get his forces out into open country to keep up with the Sixth SS *Panzer* Army on his right flank.

These simultaneous attacks took the Americans completely by surprise. Communications immediately broke down all along the thin front. Telephone lines connecting front-line outposts with their headquarters were severed by the enemy artillery barrages. Many small groups were left to fend for themselves without orders. Units became confusingly intermixed and effective command and control impossible. The weather precluded air support and long range artillery was useless without communications. In isolated villages and outposts all along the front there were more than a few repetitions of Custer's Last Stand. Many junior officers made the decision to stand and fight until they ran out of ammunition and disbanded into small groups to work their way back to friendly lines. Some men simply bugged out and still others naively surrendered. The situation was one of overall chaos in which small pockets of courageous troops, cooks, signalmen, bandsmen, drivers and engineers skillfully resisted the enemy to the last round while at the same time long lines of retreating soldiers choked the roads west.

Some isolated American units had enough towed artilley or tank destroyers to make the Germans pay dearly in blood and time for every inch of ground. They lowered their muzzles and fired anti-personnel cannister rounds into the charging infantry. Though lightly armored, the high velocity guns of the M10 and M18 Tank Destroyers wreaked havoc on the *Panzers* as they approached. There were so many targets that shells were expended at a rapid rate. But eventually the

Americans had to withdraw. There were simply too many of the enemy and they kept coming.

The GIs on the front line positions killed thousands and still more came. They came with tanks and self-propelled artillery. Endless streams of German soldiers marched across the woods and fields or rode on the turrets of their *Panzers*. On their shoulders they muscled mortars and *Panzerfausts,* the self-contained infantryman's anti-tank weapon. They gripped their sub-machineguns, called a *Sturmgewehr 44,* with suicidal determination. And they kept coming.

The American GIs distinguished themselves in the cold, foggy mist. Despite being placed in indefensible locations and assigned untenable positions with insufficient numbers they disrupted, delayed and otherwise frustrated the timetable of the surging German forces.

Back at VIII Corps Headquarters in Bastogne, the first few scattered reports started coming in. The front line divisions had thrown all of their local reserves into the breach to stabilize their situation. They had nothing left! Two regiments of the 106th Division on the *Schnee Eifel* were in jeopardy of being cut off and surrounded.

All across the front lines, small units were fed into the battle piecemeal. It was like throwing pebbles into the huge grinding gears of powerful machinery. They might slow the gears down for a moment but eventually they would be crushed. By nightfall of the first day the American forces on the front line were spent. Powerful reinforcements were needed to stop the German onslaught. It would take days to bring additional reserves to bear. The only question was how long could the outnumbered and embattled American foot soldiers keep their finger in the dike while reinforcements in sufficient quantities could be brought up?

Sunday, 17 December, dawned murky and cloudy with the smattering of a cold, chilling rain. SHAEF became aware of a captured enemy document distributed to the German forces by Field Marshal von Rundstedt. The message exhorted the troops to "give everything" in the offensive to protect the Fatherland. It proclaimed "large attacking armies" have begun pressuring the Anglo-Americans and "we gamble everything" on this bold stroke.

All during the day, reports filtered back to SHAEF. Captured enemy documents not only revealed the German orders but also plans for Operation *Greif.* English-speaking German soldiers in American uniforms infiltrating behind the lines was alarming news.

The most disturbing news, however, came from the northern front. *Kampfgruppe Peiper,* a German *Panzer* unit of the Sixth SS *Panzer* Army had succeeded in breaking through American lines and was massacring civilians and American prisoners. They had already moved into the rear supply area. The Americans were in serious trouble in the north.

In the center, the veteran 28th Infantry Division and the 9th Armored Division provided stiff opposition. As a consequence of this dogged resistance, the Fifth *Panzer* Army fell behind schedule almost immediately. The Germans still had a number of rivers to cross and harsh terrain to deal with. The few twisting roads in the deep cut gorges and river valleys were not conducive to tank warfare and massive traffic jams materialized almost immediately. Bastogne was only twenty miles from the jump-off point and Fifth *Panzer* had planned to capture that strategic town on day two. They were already late.

The situation all along the front quickly became desperate at the end of the second day. Isolated American forces were running low on food, medical supplies and ammunition. The weather remained bad enough to ground Allied air forces and the German *Panzers* roamed the fields and roads without fear of attack from the air.

As desperate as the situation was for the Americans, Hitler's aggressive schedule was falling apart. The Sixth SS *Panzer* Army still had only two of the five roads they needed to support a push to the Meuse. The Fifth *Panzer* Army had not breached the formidable Clerf River valley in their front due to difficult geography and tenacious résistance.

Middleton was fully aware that his front was crumbling. He was staring down the barrel of the Nazi juggernaut. The roads were choked with the rabble and refuse of defeated American formations and frightened civilians. So great was the retreating exodus that relief forces, meager as they were, had great difficulty getting up to the front lines. As the reinforcements were being directed to Bastogne and St. Vith, the remaining American formations in the path of the *Panzer* steamroller were ordered to hold their positions "at all costs".

On Sunday, 17 December, Eisenhower placed a call to the headquarters of the XVIII Airborne Corps. The situation was so desperate he needed to call on his only strategic reserve; both of his beat up, battle weary, under supplied and unprepared airborne divisions; the All-Americans and the Screaming Eagles.

Major General James M. Gavin was standing in for Lieutenant General Matthew B. Ridgway as the acting CO of the XVIII Airborne Corps. He received orders to immediately move the two airborne divisions toward the Ardennes. His own division, the 82nd Airborne, had been out of the line longer than the 101st and was better positioned to move out first. He sent out orders to cancel leaves, revoke all passes and prepare the divisions for immediate movement. He led a team to the SHAEF motor pool in Rheims to commandeer the required motor transport. The 101st would follow in whatever transport could be scrounged and head for the town of Werbomont. After issuing the orders, Gavin, his operations officer and his temporary aide and driver, Second Lieutenant Schuyler Johnson, hopped in a jeep and set out for the long drive to Spa, Belgium. But first he would stop off at the SHAEF main motor pool in Rheims.

As Jake and Johnny Kilroy stepped off the bus from Rheims, Camp Mourmelon was a beehive of activity. MPs were directing traffic as jeeps and small trucks shuttled between the barracks and the supply sheds. The streetlights and vehicle running lights were shining vividly. The inside barracks' lights were burning brightly throughout the camp. Men were moving about with a sense of urgency. The excitement was palpable. Captain West was standing near the exit door of the bus, hands on hips.

"You two," West pointed at Jake and Johnny.

"Crap," whispered Johnny. "We're busted for sure! That major must have identified us."

"Yes, sir," Jake answered.

"Get in those jeeps over there. You're driving me to Rheims. SHAEF motor pool." He pointed to a pair of parked jeeps. In the rear seat of each jeep were two armed paratroopers.

Johnny breathed a sigh of relief. "Yes, sir," he echoed.

West jumped into the jeep with Johnny. The two jeeps headed out of the camp toward Rheims. The road was filled with traffic in both directions.

"What's going on, sir?"

"Big breakthrough. We've been ordered to move out. Some place up north called Werbomont. I've got to secure some transport." West spoke loudly to be heard over the noise of the engine and the blast of wind over the open jeep.

Johnny turned his head toward the captain and jerked it toward the armed troopers in the rear. West nodded knowingly, smiled and said, "Most of our officers are still not in camp. General McAuliffe sent me. I don't have any written orders."

Johnny smiled again. Captain West was about to seize some army transport by force. *Casper never ceases to amaze me!*

The jeeps navigated the country roads carefully until they reached Rheims and approached the motor pool. As they neared the entrance, West stood up in his seat. A steady stream of two-and-a-half-ton trucks were exiting the main parking lot and turning south on the main road out of town. The motorcade seemed endless. The two jeeps waited for a break in the column, scooted into the motor pool and parked outside the main garage next to another jeep with a large SCR-300 radio set in the back seat. West led his men through the doorway and stopped suddenly.

The motor pool officer, a young lieutenant, along with a rotund master sergeant and five MPs were standing facing the wall with their hands over their heads. Behind them, brandishing all manner of weapons, were four paratroopers from the 82nd Airborne. One of them was Sky Johnson. Standing next to the paratroopers was General Gavin. A small group of black truck drivers were sitting on a bench directly outside the small office. They stood up and saluted as Captain West went into the office. West was surprised to see General Gavin.

"Good evening, Captain," Gavin smiled. "Seems like you had the same idea we did." Trucks continued to drive out of the motor pool as they spoke.

"Yes, sir. However, it seems we're a bit late."

Gavin nodded. "The Eighty-second is moving out first, Captain. We've been in camp the longest. I'm taking five hundred trucks. It's a mess up there. We don't have time to wait for written orders in triplicate." Gavin pointed to the motor pool personnel he had under guard. "Our master sergeant here insisted on having those written orders before he let us have any trucks."

The sergeant overheard the conversation. "General, sir. I'm sorry but I got my orders, sir. Nothing leaves here without written orders from SHAEF. My ass is grass now, sir!"

Sky answered. "You must be hallucinating, Sergeant. There's no general here. Just me and these boys got the drop on you." He winked at Gavin. His men would go to their graves swearing General Gavin was not present and had nothing to do with hijacking five hundred military transport vehicles.

Gavin smiled and looked at West. "Your division will follow the Eighty-second at fourteen hundred hours tomorrow. By then there should be enough transport for you. After we're done here you can take what's left in the depot. Ike has ordered every truck in the theatre to drop their loads wherever they are and drive here. By morning this place will be crawling with transport. I just can't wait until then."

"Yes, sir."

Gavin looked at Sky. "We have to leave now, Lieutenant. You'll drive. We have enough reinforcements now to keep them under guard." He looked toward the motor pool contingent. "I'm sure those written orders will show up here any time now, Master Sergeant."

As Gavin stepped toward the doorway, Jake caught his eye. Gavin stopped. "Do I know you, trooper?"

Jake flashed a big grin. "Biazza Ridge, sir." He pointed to Johnny and then Sky. "With Johnny and Sergeant Johnson." Sky was still wearing his sergeant stripes even though Gavin had accelerated his promotion due to the crisis.

Gavin smiled and looked around. "I thought so." He tapped Jake on the shoulder. "Looks like we'll have another story to tell our grandkids. This will be a big one. Good luck, troopers!"

"Thank you, sir," Jake replied as Gavin stepped out and into his jeep. Jake and Johnny exchanged a few words with Sky before he joined Gavin.

The jeep feathered into the line of trucks leaving the motor pool and began the long overnight road trip to the First Army Headquarters in Spa, Belgium. The trucks would turn off to Camp Suisse and Sissonne and load up the 82nd Airborne Division before proceeding to Bastogne.

As Johnny, Jake and West exited the motor pool, Johnny lagged behind. He recognized a large Negro soldier among the small group of drivers sitting on the bench. He couldn't remember the big guy's name, or if he ever knew it, but he did recall the name of the scrawny young kid sitting beside him.

"Well if it isn't Abraham Lincoln," he held out his hand. He knew the name was Lincoln Abraham but Johnny chose to screw around with the young black soldier.

Lincoln Abraham looked up at him through disinterested eyes. "I know you?"

"Queen's Bazaar Pub, London. I saved that huge mob from getting killed by you."

A flicker of a smile crossed Lincoln's face. "It's Lincoln Abraham...and you probably did save all those guys...from him," Lincoln jerked a thumb at his perpetual sidekick, Chauncy Gibbons. Lincoln looked at Johnny's name stenciled over the breast pocket on his combat jacket. "And you're Kilroy?"

"That would be me."

Chauncy grabbed the outstretched hand and almost swallowed it up while shaking it. "I'm Chauncy and excuse Lincoln here. He ain't got no manners that he was born with."

Lincoln took Johnny's hand and shook it unenthusiastically. "Kilroy, like in … 'Kilroy was here'?"

"I've got nothing to do with that though we get blamed for that crap all the time." It became sort of a mysterious happening in the army that the first troops into a town or city would scrawl the words "Kilroy Was Here" in chalk or paint on anything and everything. The words were found on buildings, bridge abutments, knocked out tanks, road signs and even staff cars and command vehicles. Nothing was sacred. It was a universal prank every GI reveled in and many participated in. No one actually believed there was a single mythical "Kilroy" who got to every place first and left his unique calling card.

Johnny paused and looked around. "So what are you guys doing hanging around here?"

"Relief drivers," explained Chauncy. "We'll bring you boys to wherever you be heading."

Johnny nodded. "We're heading for trouble, for sure. See ya' around." Johnny turned to head back out to the jeeps.

Chauncy stopped him. "Like I said, my friend here sometimes forgets his manners, so let me say thanks for getting us out alive from that bar in London."

"You're welcome. I just didn't like the odds. I think my buddies are still pissed at me for getting them into it. Some of us lost stripes because of it." Johnny looked at Lincoln for some reaction. There was just an angry expression of defiance.

Finally, he spoke. "See ya' around Kilroy."

"No good deed goes unpunished." Johnny slipped out the door into the waiting jeep.

Back in Mourmelon the camp was still bustling with activity. Troopers were showing up from cancelled passes and leaves. More showed up as each hour passed. Few slept as every man tried to scrounge weapons, ammo and rations. Armorers worked through the night repairing broken or malfunctioning weapons. Foot lockers belonging to men on extended leave or in the hospital were opened in an effort to find a coat, wool cap or boots that were better than what some of the men had. The divisional mess hall opened early and began serving a huge breakfast of eggs, ham, rolls and butter. It was another one of those "condemned man" meals that the paratroopers had become accustomed to. The men ate their fill.

The officers ordered the troopers to cover their shoulder patches. Many didn't bother. The Germans always seemed to know whenever they showed up. Not that it made any difference to the men. They were going to "stack bodies" and who cared if the Krauts knew they were coming!

Dawn broke gently under a damp cloudy sky and the trucks began to arrive. A few at first and then some more and finally by noon a flood of transport descended on the camp. MPs stacked the trucks in an orderly manner so they were lined up to embark their human cargo expeditiously. There were the ubiquitous two-and-a-half-ton trucks that hauled everything on the battlefield, and tandem trailers normally used to ferry cattle. The trucks had come from all over the vicinity in response to Eisenhower's emergency order. The Germans had no such volume of transport and could never have imagined the Allies could command such mobility during a crisis. Before the first truck left Mourmelon, 380 of them were fueled, warmed up and queued to move over 11,800 anxious men of the 101st Airborne to the heart of the crisis.

By mid-afternoon the division was ready to leave. Truck engines growled to a start and the troopers helped each other mount up. Crew-served weapons and ammo were loaded first followed by the paratroopers helping one another with a hand up, the distinction between veteran and replacement slowly diminishing. They were becoming 'comrades in arms' heading into a vicious battle. They would rely upon one another, protect each other and die for any one of their brothers.

With the grinding of gears and the whining of transmissions, the first trucks pulled out for the one hundred mile trip. The caravan twisted its way out of Camp Mourmelon and headed east toward the city of Verdun. From there it would turn north toward Belgium and the Ardennes.

Drivers kept their regulation separation but there was still some bunching up as the convoy made its way up and down the inclines in the road. In the fading light of day, all trucks were running with full headlights and taillights. From the air it must have looked like some giant fiery, slithering snake.

Onward they traveled through the damp, misty night. The stream of vehicles turned north at Verdun and passed through the city of Sedan. Before they reached the city of Bouillon, the front of the 101st convoy caught up with the tail of the 82nd column. At that point the column of nearly 900 trucks stretched out for twenty miles.

Just before midnight, after passing through a village called Neufchateau, the convoy stopped at a small crossroads in the tiny hamlet town of Sprimont. There was an MP on the side of the rode talking to a senior officer of the 101st. The MP pointed, the officer nodded, they saluted and parted. Jake and Johnny watched as the last of the 82nd Division trucks drove off to the left. There was immediate trouble in the north and the 82nd Airborne was rerouted to Werbomont in a desperate effort to defend the road hub at St. Vith.

Jake and Johnny could see way up ahead in their own column as the trucks began making a hard turn to the right. As truck after truck turned right, they watched the red taillights head off into the distance marking the road they would soon follow. But the word on their destination was out and it was already being passed from truck to truck like wildfire.

The Screaming Eagles would make a stand in a small Ardennes town to deny its precious road hub to the advancing enemy. The Germans pushed west while the Americans hurried east. The race for Bastogne was on.

Chapter Sixty-Two

Spa, Belgium - December 18, 1944

"The nature of the ground is often of more consequence than courage."

Publius Flavius Vegetius Renatus, *Military Institutions of the Romans*, c. AD 378

More than any other ground campaign in the War, the Battle of the Bulge was a battle for roads. It was about securing and moving rapidly along the few usable roads and denying them to the enemy. Whoever controlled the roads controlled the fight. In this fluid struggle for force mobility, the crossroad villages and road hub cities became the most important real estate in the Ardennes Forest.

Bastogne was a small market town serving the surrounding farming villages as both a commercial center and the major road hub. With a population of 4,000, Bastogne stood on a high plateau 1,600 feet above sea level. Its surrounding grazing land and rolling hills were a stark departure from the densely forested river-cut ravines and violently undulating terrain that characterized most of the Ardennes. While there were occasional patches of thick pine trees to break up the pastures, Bastogne had no natural defensive features. The Americans would occupy the sturdy stone farmhouses surrounding the town and use them as fortified strong points. Their defensive line would encircle the town to protect the nexus of five major and three minor roads.

St. Vith, less than fifteen miles from the *Schnee Eifel*, was closest to the front line. The 7th Armored Division was directed to St. Vith in a failed attempt to extricate the 106th Infantry Division from their predicament on the *Schnee Eifel*. They arrived too late but provided the backbone for the defense of St. Vith. In addition, the village became a collecting place where retreating American formations coalesced, rearmed and turned back to the fight.

Bastogne was further south and farther away from the breakthrough. It was the headquarters of VIII Corps, which watched stunned and helpless as its front collapsed and the Germans raced westward. General Troy Middleton received scant reinforcements in the form of Combat Command B of the 10th Armored Division. That was all the help available until the two divisions of paratroopers were alerted and sent in to put out the fire.

Major General James M. Gavin walked into the Grand Hotel Britannique, Headquarters of the United States First Army, in Spa, Belgium. It was 0900 hours on 18 December and he had been on the fog-shrouded roads all night under a cold, driving rain. A twist of fate had made the thirty-seven year old general responsible for executing orders that were vague and required clarification.

The best way to do that, he reasoned, was to visit General Courtney Hodges, commanding general of the First Army.

"Welcome, Jim," Hodges extended his hand. He breathed a slight sigh of relief.

Gavin took the hand warmly, shook it and looked around the room. It was relatively quiet but he could sense the chaos. Staff officers were moving about hastily. Some were writing on a clear plastic overlay of a map of the Ardennes. Others were on telephones or radios. Typewriters were clicking and coding machines were whirring. A small group of NCOs were packing up files. To anyone else Hodges might have looked gaunt and haggard but Gavin had previously served under him in the Philippines and knew that was how he always looked.

"Thank you, sir. I got here as fast as I could. What's the situation?"

"Well Jim, the Krauts have ripped open a pretty big hole in our lines." He walked Gavin over to the large wall map, which was marked with danger points in red grease pencil. The map looked like it had the measles. "They caught us with our pants down. We've identified twelve new divisions." Hodges shook his head. "Where the heck did they get all these new divisions?"

Gavin studied the map. The situation looked bleak. Hodges pointed to the bottom of the map. "They're pretty much having their way with us right now but I think we can hold this southern shoulder."

Gavin nodded but his attention was drawn to the center. Hodges continued. "They caved our center, ripped it to pieces. Chewed up the Twenty-eighth and they have two regiments of the Hundred and sixth surrounded." Hodges was pointing to the *Schnee Eifel*. "I don't think we can get them out, Jim."

Gavin nodded again. Courtney Hodges was highly regarded in army circles. After washing out of West Point for academic reasons, he joined the army as a private, earned a commission and won the Distinguished Service Cross in World War I. He was a protégé of General George Marshall and advanced quietly through the officer ranks to command of the Infantry School. Although widely revered, the Georgia-born gentleman was humble and modest and never sought headlines. He was simply an extremely competent and compassionate commander. Gavin knew the loss of so many men was wearing on him.

Hodges then pointed to an egg-shaped blue grease pencil marking around the town of St. Vith. "We're going to make a stand around St. Vith. It's an important road junction and I've already sent the Seventh Armored there along with one Combat Command of the Ninth Armored."

"How long can we hold?"

"We have to hold until we can organize a counterattack. The Krauts took Clervaux late last night and are almost out of the river valleys and into open tank country. We have to deny them the roads. We're still not sure what they're up to or where they think they're going."

"Is that where you want us, sir?"

"No, Jim. It's the northern boundary that has me worried. Their First SS *Panzer* Division is running wild along this stretch." Hodges made an east west tracing with his finger from the villages of Losheim to Werbomont and back. "Twelfth SS *Panzer* is right behind them. If your boys can hold them up, it'll take pressure off of St. Vith." Hodges paused. "There are more *Panzer* Divisions attacking in the center. Regular *Wehrmacht*. Not SS. They'll probably flow around St. Vith and isolate it but we can't let them have the roads through the town. We have to force them onto fewer roads, create bottlenecks and congestion in their supply trains, and slow down their advance by virtue of its own weight and volume." Hodges paused. "We're going to hold at the shoulders and squeeze his attack into the narrowest possible front. When we have ample forces on his flanks, we'll counterattack and cut him off at the knees!"

Gavin was elated Hodges had not abandoned his aggressive spirit. Other generals in his position might have collapsed under the pressure and went on the defensive but his approach was textbook. Strengthen the shoulders, reinforce the flanks, and let the penetration overextend itself.

"But we're not at that point yet," Hodges explained. "We're still moving blocking forces into position. Right now we have to slow the Krauts down and buy some time." He went back to the map and put his finger on the northern boundary. "These SS *Panzer* Divisions are still a threat to break out to the north to the cities of Liege or Huy on the Meuse River. The main roads to these two towns cross at the village of Werbomont. I need one of your divisions to defend that city and deny those roads to the Krauts. Who's first in your column?"

"Eighty-second, sir," Gavin answered.

"Eighty-second it is. I have another job for the Hundred and first."

Gavin frowned ever so slightly and Hodges picked up on the facial gesture. "What is it?"

"Nothing, sir. I was hoping to deploy our two airborne divisions side by side. They're the two best infantry divisions in the world and with some armor and artillery help they could crush anything the Krauts could throw at us."

"That would be something to see, Jim. But right now I have to deal with another *Panzer* Corps breaking out to the south of St. Vith. They're headed for Bastogne. We have to block those roads too. That's where I need the Hundred and first."

"Of course, sir. I understand." Gavin nodded to his G-1 Operations Officer, Lieutenant Colonel Al Ireland, who began issuing the orders using the powerful headquarters radio.

"When will your two divisions arrive?"

"They're on the road now, sir. They'll arrive tonight and should be deployed and dug in by tomorrow morning."

"Excellent, Jim. I don't know many generals who could move two divisions on 'R and R' a hundred miles and be ready for combat in a single day."

Gavin smiled. "It's *come as you are*, sir. We'll need everything, clothes, guns, ammo, and medical supplies. We were virtually in our pajamas when we got the fire call."

Hodges allowed himself a small chuckle. "Don't worry, we'll take care of supplies."

"Thank you, sir. With your permission, I'd like to recon the positions around Werbomont before my division gets here. General Ridgway should be here late tonight to assume command of his corps and I'd like to start being a division commander again." Gavin thought for a moment. "Then I'll personally carry your written orders to Bastogne to make sure there is no misunderstanding. I'll be back tonight."

"We won't be here," Hodges glanced at the soldiers packing the equipment. "We're moving headquarters to the Hotel Des Bains in Chaudfontaine." Hodges touched his protégé on the shoulder. "Be careful, Jim. We don't need to have you captured on top of everything else."

Hodges was about to let Gavin leave when he remembered one last thing. "Jim, this northern spearhead, the SS units…we have reports of them shooting American prisoners."

Gavin stared back at Hodges, absorbing the gravity of his words. He snapped a salute. "That's good to know, *sir*."

Colonel Ireland joined Gavin as they returned to the jeep. Waiting for them was Gavin's driver, Lieutenant Sky Johnson. They mapped a course for Werbomont eleven miles to the southwest and took off down the crowded road.

It was "Hitler weather" as the Germans called it; low clouds, deep gray sky with a heavy overcast. Nothing could fly in these conditions. The Germans counted on the bad weather since the Allies owned the skies and the *Luftwaffe* could not stop the Allied fighter-bombers from ravishing the German columns. So the *Panzers* prowled through the twisting valleys of the Ardennes protected by a blanket of thick fog and zero-visibility skies.

The roads were heavy with traffic in both directions. The little jeep darted in and out of the flow. At one brief stop, Gavin observed a group of Negro soldiers loading supply trucks. He stared hard at the scene with a look of deep concern carved on his face. There was something in what he saw that deeply disturbed him.

The jeep traveled on through light rain and cold sleet as Gavin observed the terrain with the trained eye of a master tactician. The rolling hills and patches of forests made for decent tank country. If the Nazis could claw their way out of the twisting Ambleve River valley onto this plateau, they would become a much more formidable foe. Hodges was right. They had to be stopped before they could get here.

It was early afternoon on 18 December when Sky rolled the jeep up to a two story stone farmhouse, the only building in the crossroads village of Werbomont. Army combat engineers manned the single sandbagged roadblock. It was set up to check traffic heading north and was surprised by the lone jeep traveling south. Two men in a sandbagged position leveled a .30-caliber light machine gun at the jeep while a single soldier, a private, turned to face it. His M-1 Garand was tucked under his armpit and a cigarette dangled lazily from his mouth.

"Password," he demanded with anxious eyes.

Sky stepped out from behind the driver's seat. "We're not from this command, soldier. We're about to take over this section of the front. We don't know you're freakin' password."

The lone sentry hesitated for a second. "Okay, then. Who's married to Betty Grable?"

"Harry James," answered a relieved Sky Johnson.

"Wrong," the soldier raised his M-1 into firing position and leveled it at the jeep. "Hands up!" Sky was wide-eyed.

A lieutenant stepped out from the farmhouse. "At ease, Hatfield. That's the right answer."

"Really? Shucks!" was all the surprised soldier could say. He lowered his rifle, disappointed. The two soldiers behind the machine gun stifled a chuckle with their glove-covered hands. Gavin couldn't help but allow himself a slight smile. *Just like typical American GIs,* he thought. *Playing pranks and finding a little black humor in the worst of places.*

"If you're going to ask those kinds of questions, Hatfield, you damn well better know the right answer." The lieutenant saw Colonel Ireland and saluted. "Sorry, sir. We've had reports of Krauts in American uniforms driving American vehicles all along this sector."

When Gavin exited the jeep, the lieutenant saw the two muted stars on his helmet and stiffened and saluted again. "General, sir. My apologies, *sir!*"

"At ease, Lieutenant. I'm Jim Gavin, Eighty-Second Airborne. What outfit is this?"

"Two-ninety first engineers. Able Company. I'm First Lieutenant Al Edelstein."

The Combat Engineers had been almost single-handedly holding off the *Panzers* by blowing bridges and offering resistance at different choke points. Edelstein's dirty face and sleep-deprived expression testified to the lonely, desperate struggle they had been waging. "My division is taking over the defense of this area and Werbomont. We should be dug in by tonight."

Edelstein studied the shoulder patch. *Eighty-Second Airborne,* he thought. *The paratroopers are coming. Those lousy Krauts are in for it now!*

Gavin continued. "I need to do a recon of our forward positions and the terrain. Would you accompany us and give me the lowdown?"

"I'd be glad to, sir." Edelstein hopped into the back seat of the jeep and directed them south out of Werbomont. He was familiar with the area and pointed out the various terrain features and American positions while Colonel Ireland made markings on a map. Gavin and Ireland agreed the ridgeline just outside of town made for a good defensive position. The jeep continued south as Edelstein provided more information.

"We're headed for a hamlet called Habiemont near Lienne Creek."

"What's there?" Gavin asked.

"Another bridge. We blew the bridges at Trois Ponts this morning but the Krauts got over the Ambleve River at Cheneux. If they plan to go north through Werbomont, they've got to get past this creek and cross this bridge."

"Is it still up?"

"Yes, sir. My orders were to prepare it for demo but don't blow it until we see the Krauts approaching. The creek is not wide or deep but the banks are too steep for tanks. Infantry can make it so if the Krauts want to come across here, they'll have to do it without their armor."

The jeep rolled slowly into the hamlet of Habiemont. A staff sergeant rushed out from behind an ancient gray stone building waving his arms. Edelstein knew him.

"Lieutenant Edelstein. Pull the jeep behind this building, sir." Sky stopped the jeep as directed and the sergeant froze when he saw General Gavin step out. The other officers dismounted as well but it was the sight of a two-star general with an M-1 that startled the sergeant.

Edelstein spoke first. "Sergeant Pigg, what the hell is going on?"

"Follow me, sir. The Krauts are approaching the far side of the bridge." The sergeant led the small group around the house and they knelt behind a sturdy low rock wall. There were more buildings between their position and the bridge but the vantage point offered a clear view between the structures. Gavin took out his binoculars and scanned the bridge and the far bank. The sound of squeaking bogey wheels led Gavin to look up the steep mountainside. In the fading light, between the thick pine trees, he could see the shadows of German tanks and scout cars proceeding slowly down the mountain road. One more switchback and they would come around the last curve and be level with the bridge.

"Sergeant, is that bridge wired?" Sky asked.

"We have enough TNT under that bridge to blow it twice."

The tanks prowled closer, creeping cautiously.

Colonel Ireland coughed nervously. "Any time now, Lieutenant. What do you think?"

Edelstein looked at his sergeant with an inquisitive stare. "Sir," the sergeant began. "Those damn Krauts have been beating the crap out of our guys for two days now. I was hoping we could wait long enough to get some of them on the bridge before we blew it to shit."

"Sounds like a damn good idea to me, Sergeant," said Gavin without taking his eyes from his binoculars.

They all turned their attention to the creeping column as it wound its way around the last bend in the road. German paratroopers, pressed into infantry duty, accompanied the first vehicle as it motored toward the bridge at walking pace. It was a captured American M4 armored car whose white star markings had been marked over with the Iron Cross.

"Aw, shit," Pigg commented. "I was hoping to get us a Tiger."

The column suddenly stopped. The third vehicle was a Panther mounting a high-velocity long barrel .75-millimeter gun. It fired one round with a loud concussive shriek. It hit the first building in the tiny hamlet and sent rock splinters flying through the air. The four men ducked behind the cover of the low wall.

"They don't know we're here," Pigg suggested. "My platoon has orders not to fire back and give away their positions."

"All you have here is a platoon?" asked Sky incredulously.

"That's right. Just one pissed off platoon of combat engineers sick and tired of these Krauts having everything go their way!" He waved his hand as the dust cleared and got the attention of another GI who was behind a different building across the narrow street. "Besides, no armor is getting to this side of the creek. If the infantry wants to make a try for it, we've got the entire bank zeroed in a crossfire."

The first few vehicles began to move again. They crept toward the bridge. The infantry was walking ahead now. The vehicles followed and cautiously crawled onto the bridge. When they were halfway across the bridge, Pigg raised his right hand and made a circular motion.

He looked over at the officers. "Gentlemen, it's time to hug some dirt."

Pigg watched as everyone hit the ground at the base of the wall. He saw the brilliant flashes of the string of igniters along the length of the bridge, followed immediately by a huge explosion. Men and vehicles were hurled wildly into the air. The earth trembled with the shock wave as the bridge disintegrated into fractured pieces soaring randomly in all directions. Debris rained down from everywhere. When the smoke finally cleared, there was a yawning gap where the small sturdy bridge once stood. The Americans waited to see if the infantry would make a try for the small town without their armor. But there was no point in attacking the village if they couldn't get their tanks across. After a few minutes, the column began to backtrack up the winding road. The *Panzers* would have to find another way to Werbomont.

"Good work, men," Gavin complimented and looked to Sky. "We have to go."

The four officers piled back into the jeep and sped back to Werbomont. Gavin left Colonel Ireland with Lieutenant Edelstein to prepare for the arrival of the 82nd. He and Sky found the N-15 Highway and started heading south for Bastogne.

Gavin reached into his pocket and pulled out a pair of gold-colored second lieutenant's bars. "I'm sorry we couldn't do this the *right way* with a ceremony." Gavin fastened the gold bars to Sky's collars as he was driving. "These were mine. Now they're yours. Charm school will have to wait until we're finished with this business." Gavin then took out his bayonet and carefully removed Sky's stripes.

"Thank you, sir. It's a great honor. This is much better than the *right way.*"

"Well we can't have a general being driven around by a mere sergeant, Can we?" Gavin let out a hearty laugh.

It was already dark but still foggy and the jeep ran with its headlights blazing. They intermixed with a convoy of various units heading for the battlefield. At ten miles out from Werbomont, most of the southbound military traffic on the highway turned east toward Vielsalm on the road to St. Vith. There was no sign of the enemy as the two officers continued another ten miles into the town of Houffalize. Bastogne was eleven miles away. The fog thickened and Sky slowed the jeep down considerably. The sounds of artillery could be heard not far to the east. They drove slowly through the small village of Noville. They passed some houses, a few barns, a church and what looked like a schoolhouse and a beer hall. The wind picked up and swept debris across the street like a ghost town of the old west. The small village appeared deserted. There were still some abandoned American vehicles parked on the narrow side streets and fresh but empty foxholes dug along the main road. Someone had left in a hurry.

They picked up speed and rode the straight highway through the small village of Foy. They passed several ragged formations of confused and defeated soldiers retreating westward. The ragtag groups hardly paid them any attention as the jeep sped by. The steady stream of troops retreating from the battlefield appalled Gavin. He assumed they were following orders, if only to assuage his own personal disgust at the sight of retreating American soldiers.

After more challenges from nervous MPs, they made their way into Bastogne. Sky parked their jeep in front of the Heintz Barracks, the CP for the VIII Corps, at 1730 hours. They made the dangerous trip in under an hour. The street outside headquarters was filled with trucks, tanks and armored cars all with engines running. It was a welcome sight.

Gavin stepped quietly into the large war room. The scene was reminiscent of the evacuation routine he had just witnessed in First Army Headquarters. The staff was piling papers and equipment into boxes. One of the corps staff officers acknowledged Gavin and signaled him to queue up along with other officers waiting to speak to General Middleton.

In the center of the room, in front of a large wall map, stood Middleton. Gavin knew him to be a bright man, a reserve infantry officer, World War I veteran and a previous dean of admissions at Louisiana State University. He was cleaning his thick glasses as he spoke to a colonel from the 10th Armored Division. Gavin slid silently along the wall to get within earshot. When he was close enough he un-slung his M-1 and he leaned against the cold brick wall.

"Colonel, how many teams can you make up from your command?" Middleton asked Colonel William L. Roberts in his thick southern drawl. Roberts commanded Combat Command B (CCB), which comprised approximately one third of the 10th Armored Division.

"Three, sir, but…"

"I know, Bill," Middleton interrupted. "Armored warfare doctrine frowns on committing forces piecemeal. I get that. My problem is there are three roads from the east that the Krauts already have columns on. I need to stop, or at least delay, all three until we can fortify the town."

Roberts nodded. He empathized with the general's predicament and didn't want to become an irritant over doctrine. "Which roads, sir?"

Middleton went to the map. "My biggest threat this minute is Longvilly out four or five miles to the east. Combat Command R of the 9th Armored is involved out there with some Kraut forward units. The situation is unclear. Send one team out there and stiffen their spine."

Roberts turned to an aide. "Advise Colonel Cherry. Call sign, Team Cherry." Roberts was referring to Lieutenant Colonel Henry T. Cherry, commander of the 3rd Tank Battalion. He turned back to face the general.

"Send the next team south along this road," Middleton was back at the map fingering the road southeast to the town of Ettelbruk.

"Lieutenant Colonel James O'Hara," whispered Roberts to his aide. "Team O'Hara."

"Send your third team to the northeast, to Noville. And Colonel, you need to hold these outposts until relieved."

"We'll hold, sir. May I ask one thing, sir?"

"What is it?" asked an impatient Middleton.

"I would like your permission to stop all of these units retreating through town. I'm seeing artillery battalions with full ammo trains, tanks and tank destroyers in good condition, supply trucks and troops who seem fit to fight. If we're going to make a stand here, we could use all the help we can get."

Middleton nodded. "I agree. I'll issue the orders. You'll have that authority."

"Thank you, sir." Roberts headed for the door when a tall, lanky major stepped into the room. Roberts pulled him over to the side. "Bill, I was just looking for you. We have orders. I need to send your team northeast to a village called…" Roberts looked at his map, "Noville."

Major William Robertson Desobry nodded and also looked at the map. "Up this road, past Foy? Yes, sir, of course."

Gavin observed the exchange between the superior and the subordinate. It was more like a father-son discussion. He stepped up to the two men.

Colonel Roberts had his hand on Major Desobry's shoulder. "We don't know what's up there. You need to take the town and hold it, whatever happens."

The young major nodded vigorously. "We'll leave right away, sir."

The major turned to leave when Roberts grabbed his arm. "Bill, don't withdraw until I order you to do so." There was an ominous look on Roberts' face.

"Don't worry, sir. I'll obey my orders."

Gavin edged closer to the two men. "I just came through Noville not more than thirty minutes ago. It's deserted."

"Thank you, General Gavin." Roberts recognized him. It wasn't difficult to recognize the youngest divisional commander in the army, especially since he was universally known to tote an M-1 Garand around with him everywhere he went.

"How big is your combat team?" Gavin asked.

"One armored infantry battalion, about four hundred men, twelve Shermans and some engineers."

Gavin looked at Roberts. It was a pathetically small force to confront the potent *Panzer* Divisions bearing down on Bastogne. Roberts just shook his head and looked at the floor. He wasn't at all happy about sending his men to sure annihilation.

"Well, Major," Gavin looked at Desobry and spoke in an upbeat voice. "As soon as I'm done here I'm heading back to Werbomont. I'd be happy to accompany your column as far as you're going but then I have to continue on through Houffalize and beyond."

"Glad to have your company, General."

As Roberts and Desobry left the war room, another general stepped in through the door. It was General McAuliffe, acting CO of the 101st Airborne Division. Being far ahead of his convoy, he decided to stop by VIII Corps HQ to get the latest news. He ran right into Gavin at the door.

"Jim, am I glad to see you." McAuliffe shook his hand. They had not spoken since the day before when Gavin issued the orders to move both airborne divisions to the Ardennes.

"Likewise, Tony. I've got your orders from First Army."

"Gentlemen," interrupted Middleton as he waved them closer to the big map. "It's great to see the airborne here. How far behind are your troops?"

"Sir, I have orders from General Hodges," Gavin began. "Hundred and first is temporarily attached to VIII Corps and ordered to defend Bastogne. Eighty-second is on its way to Werbomont to be attached to V Corps." Gavin handed the written orders to Middleton.

"You mean we're not fighting the two airborne divisions together?" asked McAuliffe.

Gavin shook his head in the negative.

"Nuts," declared McAuliffe.

Middleton scanned the orders quickly then turned to the map. "We've identified three German divisions bearing down on Bastogne." He waved his hand up and down the map in the general direction east of the city. "The Second *Panzer*, *Panzer Lehr* and the Twenty-sixth *Volksgrenadier* Division make up the Forty-seventh *Panzer* Corps under Manteuffel and are closing in on the city. I'm pushing out armored columns along these three roads to hold them back until we can fortify the town." Middleton ran his index finger along the roads to Noville, Longvilly and Ettelbruk.

"Is that all you have to stop them?" asked McAuliffe. "What happened to the Twenty-eighth Infantry Division?"

"They were overrun." Middleton rubbed the bridge of his nose between his thumb and forefinger. "Two regiments of the Hundred and sixth Division are surrounded and cut off on the *Schnee Eifel*. Both these divisions held up the Krauts while outnumbered at least five to one. They blew up Jerry's timetable and bought us the two precious days we needed to fortify Bastogne." Middleton shook off the bad news and straightened up. "They paid a hefty price. Let's not waste it." Then he looked at McAuliffe. "So, where is your column?"

McAuliffe answered by pointing at the map just to the west of Bastogne. "Right about here, sir. We'll be in the city in strength by the morning."

Middleton nodded. "Good, because I'm pulling corps headquarters out of the city tomorrow. We're re-establishing in Neufchateau about twenty miles southwest of here." He placed his hand on McAuliffe's shoulder. "The city is all yours to defend and I have to say there is nothing to stop Jerry from flowing behind Bastogne and cutting you off. You'll be surrounded in short order. No doubt about it."

McAuliffe chuckled. "We're always surrounded, sir. That's how we make our living."

Middleton continued. "Your orders are to deny the Krauts use of the road network that flows through this city."

"Yes, sir!"

"And, one more thing, the Seven-oh-five tank destroyer battalion is on its way here. That's all I can give you, Tony. Everyone in Bastogne will be under your command."

"Yes, sir."

"Very well, gentlemen," Middleton concluded the impromptu conference. "Good luck."

The two generals walked toward the door. McAuliffe spoke first. "It appears I'm going to have to hold Bastogne with the second string." He was referring to the fact that the division's regular commander and many of the line officers were out of theatre and not present.

"Second string for the airborne is still enough to beat the crap out of the Krauts." He patted McAuliffe on the shoulder. "You'll do just fine here, Tony. Maybe even make history."

Gavin took his M-1 from against the wall and clamped the sling onto his shoulder. His jeep was waiting outside, engine running and ready to go.

"Where to, boss?" asked Sky.

"Back to Werbomont. The way we came is the fastest."

The jeep pulled out and made its way through the center of town. The main road was lined with trucks and tanks from Combat Command B. The jeep veered left at a fork onto Highway N-15. They observed an armored column bearing right at the same fork on the way to Longvilly. *Team Cherry*, Gavin remembered. N-15 was a straight, hard packed macadam highway and in thirty quick miles Gavin would be back with his division.

As they proceeded north they began to pass a row of trucks and Sherman tanks pulled over to the side. Gavin concluded it was Team Desobry. When he saw the command jeep, the one with multiple high whip antennae, he asked Sky to pull over. Major Desobry was in the front seat. He snapped a salute as Gavin startled him.

"What's the holdup, Major?"

"We're waiting on our supply train, General Gavin. It's overloaded with everything we need and I don't want those trucks traveling up this road without the protection of my armor."

"It's your call, Major, but getting to Noville first, before the Krauts, is more important."

"I've sent a recon team up ahead. Scouts out on the flanks. If they see or hear any Krauts we'll haul ass up there. It's only about five miles."

Gavin nodded. "Good. I'd love to wait around and drive up with you but I'm in a bit of a hurry. So we'll be on our way. Good luck, Major."

Gavin's jeep jerked into motion and disappeared into the swirling fog.

"And good luck to you, sir," Desobry mumbled at the mist shrouded road.

Chapter Sixty-Three

Wichita, Kansas - December 19, 1944

"I am not afraid. I was born to do this."

Joan of Arc (1412 - 1431)

December 19, 1944
Dear Derek,

I hope this letter finds you well. I must confess I find myself missing you. I'm writing from Wichita, Kansas, which has been home for the past few months. Boeing has a plant here that builds the new B-29 Superfortress. Dora and I are members of the Engineering Flight Test Unit for Boeing. We've also been learning how to fly this monster. My God, Derek, it is such a beautiful airplane. It's twitchy because it has some teething problems, little things like engines that are prone to catch fire, but it's a dream to fly.

It's funny how it all worked out. This officer, Colonel Paul W. Tibbets, was in charge of training up a special bombing unit but his men were hesitant about the B-29. It had a bad reputation as a widow-maker when it first came out and the men were nervous. So Colonel Tibbets contrived a plan and checked out Dora and me on the plane. After much patient and exacting instruction and encouragement from the colonel, we ferried a brand new B-29 from the Wichita plant to Wendover Field, Utah, where the colonel had his training unit. You should have seen the looks on the faces of those pilots when Dora and I popped out of the crew hatch. Their jaws dropped when they saw that we were just two little old girls who could barely reach the pedals. The colonel had no more trouble convincing his men the plane was "safe and reliable" after that. No more complaints. I don't know what his mission is but he seemed desperate and his ploy worked! When the Air Staff found out about his little trick, they forbade any more WASPs from flying the Superfortress. But we continued to fly them on occasion anyway under the covers. In fact I'm scheduled to ferry one out to Fairmont Army Air Base, Nebraska, this afternoon.

Derek, this is the best job I ever had. I even got to fly a Jap Zero and an early-version Bf-109 Messerschmitt. Who else could ever get a chance to do that? Right now we fly three-quarters of the planes ferried in the States with a lower accident rate than the men. We also do other jobs the guys won't do. Our gals tow target planes and get shot at. The ladies are also test pilots in repair depots to make sure repairs were done properly.

Others were assigned to Training Command as flying cadet navigators and instrument instructors. Some fly experimental planes for evaluation because the more senior of us have nearly 3,000 hours in the cockpit and know damn well what the hell we're doing!

But it's all going to end soon. The WASPs will be officially deactivated tomorrow – that's why I have to ferry this plane out today. It seems we're no longer needed like we once were. Combat pilots coming home want the ferry jobs to help them get the hours they need each month to make flight pay. And there are higher-ups who never accepted women pilots from the beginning. So, the WASPs will officially cease to exist tomorrow. It's a sad day for me. But maybe we advanced the cause of women's aviation by our contribution in the War. Just maybe they'll be aviation jobs for us after it's over. If not for us, then for our daughters and granddaughters because they can never deny what we did for our country when she needed us most.

I'm not complaining. It will be the same for all the women who joined the WACs or WAVEs or picked up a welding torch or a rivet gun and did a man's job while their men were off fighting. We'll all be expected to go back to the kitchen, to raise our families while the jobs go to the returning veterans. It may not be fair but that's the way it will be. Some women will do it happily. Others, like myself, would rather still be flying. I think we've earned that opportunity.

Nancy Love is my inspiration and my idol. Along with Amelia Earhart, who as you know I met when she was an aviation advisor at Purdue. I'm proud to have been among the 28 pilots Nancy recruited to demonstrate women could contribute to the war effort. She calls us her "Originals", a nickname I accept proudly. She also has been trying to get all us women pilots into military status so we can enjoy the same benefits as servicemen. So far she has been unsuccessful but she is determined never to quit. Not many people know what we have been doing so Nancy gathered some startling statistics and shared them with us. In our 28-month life, the WASP organization attracted over 25,000 applicants; 1,830 were accepted, 1,074 won their wings, and 38 were killed in their duties, 11 in training and 27 on active duty. We ferried more than 12,000 aircraft of 78 different types more than 60 million miles, served without military benefits, and were paid two-thirds as much as the male civilian ferry pilots who we replaced.

I know first hand that we frequently endured the worst kind of discrimination, yet I also know many of the girls would gladly continue ferrying aircraft for no salary at all. So would I. We would do it just for the love of it and the opportunity to be respected for what we can do.

Perhaps someday we'll even be treated as equals. Where do we find such strong and loyal women?

But no one will be able to deny the contributions of American gals to this war effort. They can make us go back home to the kitchen but they can never take away what we did. Things will never be the same in this country, ever again, thanks to these brave women. I'm so proud of all my sisters in America, especially the WASPs. We 'dames' proved we could get the job done; make guns and ammo, build ships and tanks and planes and fly them too! It will make a big difference to all the women in this country, if not today, then someday in the future.

I'm not sure what I'm going to do. Boeing has offered me a job and…

Roxie Rawls looked up from her letter as Dora Dougherty stuck her head in the door of the small bedroom. "Gotta' go, Roxie. You're gonna' be late, dearie."

Roxie screwed the top back on her fountain pen and gently placed it on the incomplete letter still attached to the writing pad. She softly closed the cover of the pad. "Thanks Dora, I'll finish it when I get back."

Chapter Sixty-Four

Bastogne, Belgium - December 19, 1944

"The merit of the action lies in finishing it to the end."

Genghis Khan (AD 1162 - 1227)

D awn broke nearly invisible on the morning of 19 December. Only the shift of color to a paler gray gave a hint the sun had risen beyond the impenetrable blanket of fog enveloping the eastern sky. The overnight trip from Mourmelon took place under a misty rain with the temperature hovering at forty degrees. The Screaming Eagles were transported packed tightly together in open trailers. If they slept at all, it was standing upright.

After dismounting, the paratroopers formed up in a bivouac area immediately outside of Bastogne as their senior officers rushed into VIII Corps Headquarters to receive orders. The unexpected warmth of the previous evening gave way to a crisp northwest breeze that blew steadily through the low man-made canyons of the town. The wind foretold the return to colder temperatures with a subtle promise of snow. When the officers returned, the entire division was rousted from snatches of fitful sleep and formed up on the main road into town. Thundering cannon fire testified that battles were still raging and men were still dying east of the city.

The long lines of Screaming Eagles, exhausted from the long trip and their short naps, began streaming into town on both sides of the main road. Despite being cold, wet and hungry, they walked with a confidence and a swagger that bordered on arrogance. Each face sported a mean and ugly disposition. The unspoken message seemed to be *the paratroopers have arrived and the situation would soon be under control.* They had won the race to the obscure farming town of Bastogne by the slimmest of margins.

The 506th PIR followed the 501st into Bastogne. They marched past the buildings, small storefronts and an occasional church that lined the main road. The morning wore on and the sky brightened slightly. Out of the misty fog, like ghosts coming to life, troops and vehicles began moving in the opposite direction between the two files of paratroopers. The Screaming Eagles strutted taller as these soldiers retreated toward the rear. But this group was not the expected ragtag wounded and dispirited gaggle of men retreating from a lost battle. They were cleanly dressed, well armed and traveling in good order. Abruptly, the paratrooper column came to a halt.

"What outfit?" Jake asked a GI as he walked past.

"Corps Headquarters," the embarrassed soldier answered. "We got orders to set up our HQ in the rear." The young soldier, probably a clerk, seemed uncomfortable as he watched other men head into the firestorm he was walking away from.

"Got any extra ammo?" Johnny asked as he walked up.

The soldier slipped off a bandolier of .30-caliber ammo and tossed it to Johnny.

"Thanks, Mac," Johnny waved. The soldier lowered his head and kept walking.

All along the line paratroopers were scrounging weapons and ammo from the withdrawing soldiers. The men with the white on blue VIII Corps shoulder patches had been ordered to the rear. Some 10th Armored Division HQ personnel were mixed in and they all willingly parted with ammo or medical supplies as they passed.

"I could sure use some forty-five ammo," Jake intoned.

"Don't worry, we'll get some," Johnny assured.

"I'm not worried," Jake answered staring into the eastern sky.

"You know, Jake," Johnny spoke to the back of his head. "This is a suicide mission."

Jake turned around. "Johnny, every mission we go on is a suicide mission. It never bothered you before."

Johnny nodded and pulled an envelope from his pocket. "If anything happens to me, you need to give this letter to Rose. Promise me!"

Jake turned his back on his friend. "Nothing is going to happen to you."

"Jake!"

"No, I'm not taking it."

"Look, Jake, I've sworn into all your blood pacts and you know you can count on me. I know I can count on you, too. That's why I'm giving this to *you*. So, take it."

Jake turned around and faced Johnny. "All right. But I'm giving it back once we get out of this shit." He reached for the crumbled envelope but Johnny pulled it back.

"No, you need to hold it. This goes to Rose if anything happens to me no matter when. And you have to do it in person!"

Jake nodded impatiently and took the envelope from Johnny's hand. "Sure... sure thing!"

Jake stuffed the letter into his battle blouse pocket and buttoned it.

"And don't read it," Johnny pointedly admonished.

They heard the distinctive sound of a deuce-and-a-half before they saw it. It crawled forward between the files of paratroopers. When it passed, Johnny pointed to the officers hanging out the back. They were wearing "pinks and greens", their dress uniforms. They were nabbed from leave and were being rushed up to their unit. The truck proceeded eastward until it disappeared into the fog. They had not seen any transport come this far into town and assumed the officers were of sufficiently high rank to warrant risking the vehicle.

They marched through town for ten or fifteen more minutes and were ordered to stop. Suddenly, through the fog, came a ghostly procession of soldiers in various states of disarray. Some were without helmets or without jackets or overcoats. Others wore bloody bandages and were being helped along by a buddy. Some ambled along slowly, dragging their feet zombie-like. There was the "thousand yard stare" from the hollowed out eyes of blank expressions. Some faces showed abject fear, while others appeared shocked and vacant of any emotion. A few were murmuring sentiments of despair -"they got tanks", "we can't stop them" "we're all gonna' die". This small army of the damned appeared hopeless beyond redemption.

Johnny noticed the red keystone patch of the 28th Infantry Division. That Pennsylvania National Guard unit had been involved in some of the most brutal fighting of the War, which had earned their patch the nickname "Bloody Bucket". Mixed in with them were GIs from the 106th Infantry Division with their distinctive Golden Lion patches along with the Checkerboard patches of the 99th Infantry Division. Other patches from various tank destroyer units, artillery units and armored formations were too numerous to count. It was a slovenly, dispirited group that straggled through the two lines of paratroopers who continued to beg for weapons and ammo with mixed results. Some retreating soldiers gave up their rifles easily and therefore felt relieved from their obligation to fight. Others hung on with stubborn determination, refusing to give up any supplies.

Johnny stepped in front of a technical sergeant from the 28th Division who was carrying a Thompson. He was hoping to scavenge some ammo for Jake.

"Tell me Sarge, what's going on up there?"

The sergeant was a big man with a course beard and bushy eyebrows. His field jacket was ripped and tattered and dirt and grime covered his clothes and smeared his face. His expression was more of exhaustion than fear. "Got any water?"

Johnny handed over his canteen. "Here, Sarge."

The sergeant splashed a little on his face and poured some into his mouth without putting his lips on the canteen. "Thanks, Mac."

"Will you be needing that weapon and ammo?" Jake asked

The sergeant clutched his sling tighter. "I got no ammo but damn fucking right I'm keeping my weapon! Right now I'm going for a hot and a cot and then join Operation Snafu."

"What's that?" Johnny asked.

"Some colonel, I think his name is Roberts, is forming a company of us guys who got separated or got our asses kicked and came back through the lines. We're going to stay here in Bastogne and help defend the place."

"Glad to have you," Jake quipped. "Join the party."

"So what's going on out there?" Johnny asked.

The sergeant paused and took a deep breath. "They caught us with our pants down, is what's going on." He leaned in closer so as not to be overheard. "The fucking geniuses who put us in front of three German divisions ought to be shot. We were here to rest after getting chopped up in the Hurtgen Forest and before we could absorb our replacements, the Krauts mauled us."

"Where were you?" Johnny was curious.

"My outfit, Headquarters Company of the Hundred and tenth Infantry, were surrounded in a château in Clervaux about fifteen miles from here. It was like the Alamo. We were inside this old stone fortress, with a drawbridge and all, and the Krauts were outside trying to get in. We made them pay. They brought in Tigers and pounded the crap out of the place. That's when my CO decided to surrender, yesterday around noon. Fuck that! I wasn't about to surrender. I slipped out into the woods with some guys and we made our way back here."

"Good for you, Sarge," Jake added.

"So don't get the wrong idea. The only reason you guys beat the Krauts to Bastogne was because my boys fought like hell against those bastards. We bought you the time. We killed a lot of Krauts and we held them up in the Clerf River valley for two days until we ran out of damn ammo. We made them pay for every inch of ground. It was only after they killed most of us that they got past us. We didn't bug out!" Tears of exhaustion began to form in the sergeant's eyes.

"No one said you did, Sarge," Johnny answered him.

The burly sergeant nodded and with a grunt continued on his way. He could be heard repeating, "We didn't bug out!"

"Chrissake, Jake. I figured all these guys retreating were cowards. I couldn't have been more wrong! Most of these guys are damn heroes!"

Jake nodded and reached out to the next infantryman walking by, a private. He had a handsome face except for his harelip. His uniform was still clean and tidy, making him appear woefully out of place.

"Got any spare ammo or grenades?" Jake asked.

The soldier stopped. "No. I'm staying in Bastogne."

"Operation Snafu?" Johnny asked.

"Right, I'm Tom English," he held out his hand. Both boys shook it.

"Going to a dance," Jake pointed to the tie.

"I'm with the Four hundred twenty-third Regiment, Hundred and sixth Division. General Jones makes us wear these damn ties. Division regs," English explained. He didn't look particularly fatigued and didn't appear wounded. He just looked scared.

"Good luck." Johnny attempted to speed him on his way so they could accost the next soldier for supplies.

"I'm gonna' be a paratrooper, too," he said nervously. "I volunteered."

"Good for you, Tom," Johnny was humoring him. He couldn't have cared less.

"I mean it. I'm serious. I volunteered. Got accepted. Just have to make my three jumps."

The demand for replacements was so severe the airborne had recently relaxed its standards for qualification. The jump schools in the States were not producing enough trained paratroopers to replace the enormous losses the airborne divisions were suffering. To remedy this deficit, the airborne brass decided to qualify parachutists in theatre. They would learn the ropes in an accelerated class and make three jumps in one day. Since the airborne had priority on transfer requests and many young men saw this as an easier back door to becoming a paratrooper, with its extra pay and glory, there was no scarcity of volunteers. This whole new replacement program did not sit well with the majority of veteran paratroopers.

"Yeah," Jake agreed. "We just can't wait for you one-day wonders to join up with us veterans. How could we ever survive without you?"

English sensed the sarcasm and reacted to the slight. "You guys think you're so damn tough? Big, bad paratroopers! I can do what you do! You're not so tough!"

Jake's temper was about to kick in when Johnny stepped between them. "Good luck, Tom." Johnny gently moved him toward the rear and Tom resumed walking. Suddenly, the column of paratroopers started to move.

After some time, they stopped again. The fog lifted and Johnny could see the sign for the Hotel Lebrun on the Rue de Marche just off the main square. Along the side of the street was a conference of officers. Johnny recognized Colonel Sink, CO of the 506th PIR and Colonel Robert L. Strayer, CO of the 2nd Battalion of the 506th. There was also a colonel from the 10th Armored Division. The high-ranking officers were leaning over a map draped on the hood of a staff car. Captain West was within earshot and listened intently.

When the conference broke up, West addressed his company. "First Battalion is moving up to Noville to reinforce some of our guys up there. They've been fighting a Kraut armored spearhead most of the night and need infantry support. The rest of us will be moving up to Foy."

While West was speaking, a jeep drove up from the direction they were headed. It had wooden boxes stacked up on the rear seats with ammo of all kinds. Upon seeing the paratroopers, the young second lieutenant pulled up between the columns and began unloading the boxes onto the roadway. A few paratroopers helped him unload the cases of .30-caliber ammunition and fragmentation grenades. Captain West walked over. The officer spoke first.

"I'm Lieutenant George Rice, Tenth Armored, Supply Officer for Team Desobry."

"Thanks for the supplies, Lieutenant. Any more where that came from?"

"Plenty," Rice answered. "I have all my supply trucks on the road to Noville and we're passing out ammo to the paratroopers heading up that way. If I had more transport I could really help you out." Rice looked mockingly at his jeep.

Just then the deuce-and-a half that brought the airborne officers forward was coming back on the return trip. West stepped out on the road and stopped the empty truck.

"Driver! We need this truck to make a few supply runs for us." West tried to sound as authoritative as possible.

"Can't do it, sir," the black driver answered.

"We only need this truck for a short time, soldier," West insisted. Hearing the exchange, Colonels Sink and Strayer approached.

"I got my orders from Ike." The driver pulled out a piece of paper from his pocket. The colonels didn't need to see it. They knew what it said. All transport was dedicated to moving troops into the Ardennes and no one had authority to change those standing orders. They were about to let the truck go when Johnny stepped forward.

"Let me try, sir," he asked permission from West.

West shrugged his shoulders. Johnny jumped up on the running board. "Remember me?"

Lincoln looked at Johnny, a glint of recognition in his eyes. "Yeah, I remember you, 'Kilroy was here'. I remember you but I still got my orders."

"Look Lincoln, we're going to make a stand here but the army forgot to give us enough ammo! A few miles up the road is all the stuff we need. It'll only take a few minutes to scoot up there, load up and drop the supplies right back here. Two trips at most. Who's to know? Half an hour and then you'll be on your way. What d'ya say?"

Lincoln stared straight ahead without answering

Johnny looked past Lincoln to Chauncy Gibbons. His eyes were pleading for help. Chauncy slapped Lincoln's arm with the back of his left hand and startled him. "Just a few trips, Linc. Right up the road and back. We can do this and nobody needs to know."

"Goddamn it," Lincoln shook his head. "All right." He looked at Johnny, agitated. "Get us some help." He turned to Chauncy. "I hated that I owed this white boy a favor. This cleans the slate." Chauncy just smiled back at him. Lincoln looked out the window. "I'm serious Kilroy! This makes us even."

Lieutenant Rice pointed out the location of the supply trucks on the map and Johnny and Jake jumped onto the truck's running boards.

"Follow the jeep." Johnny instructed Lincoln. The truck made a wide turn and followed the jeep north. West gave the boys a big thumbs-up.

The fog limited visibility to a few dozen yards. The two-vehicle convoy made decent time as it quickly traversed the few miles between Bastogne and the village of Foy. They slowed as they went through the deserted little village and picked up speed again on the other side of town. Noville was only a few more miles north and the men could hear the battle raging in and around the hamlet. A high ridge on the left side of the road gave way to a rolling pasture on the right side. A mile outside of Foy they saw the trucks.

There were ten two-and-a-half-ton trucks, five on each side of the road, parked with their open backs to the highway. Soldiers and drivers were busily milling around. The tail end of the 1st Battalion just cleared the supply trucks having acquired all the grenades and ammo they could carry. Beyond the trucks on the right side of the road was an M16 Gun Motor Carriage, called a halftrack. It had four .50-caliber machine guns arranged on a gun mount, pointing toward the sky. The GIs called the weapon the 'Meat Chopper'. The crew wasn't expecting enemy aircraft because of the fog so they helped with the unloading.

Lieutenant Rice barked some orders and the supply soldiers began moving ammo and weapons into the empty truck. Jake, Johnny, Lincoln and Chauncy lent a hand and in a few minutes the truck was bulging with guns, ammo and medical supplies. Rice left orders to provide the paratroopers with as much as they required and then, saying his farewell, headed north to Noville. The four GIs headed back to Bastogne and arrived in less than twenty minutes.

Chauncy drove the truck back through the columns of paratroopers. He U-turned the vehicle and pointed it back north. The four men jumped into the rear and began handing down boxes into the waiting arms of the desperate paratroopers.

Lincoln looked at Jake's nametag as they manhandled the boxes and crates over the tailgate. "Another Kilroy?"

"Yup!"

"Brothers?"

"Nope!"

When the truck was empty Johnny looked at Lincoln. "One more trip?" he pleaded.

"Last trip," Lincoln looked at both paratroopers for agreement.

Johnny nodded.

Lincoln hopped into the cab and started driving slowly out of town. The fog seemed to thicken as they worked their way through Foy. They crept along slowly since visibility was reduced to just a few yards. When they reached the supply trucks they were shocked. Nobody was there. The trucks had been abandoned. Where a few minutes before there was a beehive of activity it was eerily quiet as the four men walked along the road between the trucks. Jake pointed to a fresh set of tank tracks across the road. The supply detail had been run off or captured.

Johnny spoke first. "There's no way the four of us will be able to load the truck. Let's all take a truck back. Check for keys."

"We gotta' take our own truck back," Chauncy explained. "We're responsible for it."

Johnny nodded. "Okay, we'll spread out, find the trucks with the thirty cal and the grenades and drive them back." They began searching the trucks.

Chauncy turned his truck around and slowly headed back south into the fog while the other three worked from truck to truck to check the load and look for keys.

"Found one!" Jake called out.

The second truck pulled out of formation and followed Chauncy back toward Bastogne. Both trucks disappeared into the fog.

"Hey Kilroy," Lincoln whispered loudly. "Listen!"

Suddenly, a German flakwagon came over the ridge to the west. It had dual .20-millimeter cannons mounted on a light tank chassis. It stood there ominously for a few moments before opening up with a stream of tracers at the remaining trucks. The two Americans dove for cover behind the halftrack. After a moment the guns fell silent.

"Hey, Kilroy," Lincoln whispered. "Kraut flakwagon. We're screwed now."

"They don't even know we're here. We'll surprise them when they get closer."

At that moment a German Mark V Panther tank crawled to the top of the ridge from the opposite side. Its gun ranged from side to side, taking in the spectacle of partially laden American supply trucks arrayed defenseless before it. The German tank did not open fire on the vulnerable trucks, revealing the need to capture supplies. However, the armored halftrack represented a potential threat so the high velocity .75-millimeter gun swung over and zeroed in on the exposed vehicle.

"Can you drive this damn thing?"

"I'm a Red Ball driver. I can drive any fucking thing in this man's army."

"Then let's get the hell out of here."

The German tank fired. The shot was high and went over the top of the halftrack. It ripped into the ground with an explosive roar. Dirt and debris banged off their helmets, ripped into their faces and covered their clothing.

"Kilroy! Your face is bleeding!" Lincoln jumped into the cab and started the engine.

"It's nothing. Let's go, go, go!" he said as he jumped into the rear compartment.

Suddenly an incoming round landed near the Panther tank. An American Tank Destroyer had heard the distinctive sound of the German high-velocity cannon and fired a round in the general direction. While it was well wide of the mark, the Panther cautiously retreated to the opposite slope giving the M16 a brief opening to make a break. Lincoln punched the gas and the vehicle lurched ahead toppling the paratrooper to the floor. The German flakwagon came over the rise firing both cannons but lost the M16 in the fog.

"Pull over, Lincoln."

"What for? It won't find us in this fog. We need to keep going." The M16 hit a bump and both men were thrown in the air.

"Jeez, Lincoln. Pull up! Let me take care of this." The paratrooper pulled the charging handles of the four .50-caliber machine guns and strapped himself into the small seat in the Maxson turret of the M45 quad mount. Lincoln shut off the engine. The noisy diesel engine of the flakwagon could now be clearly heard not far behind them. The deadly accurate .20-millimeter cannons fired explosive shells. The Americans would be outgunned and had to make their first shots count.

"Get down."

Lincoln slumped on the floor of the driver compartment. "Don't miss, Kilroy!"

"Shh," he turned his head to pick up the sound of the flakwagon. The German vehicle moved closer and slowed to a crawl. The occupants were speaking loudly enough to be heard over the sound of the engine.

"What the hell are they saying?" Lincoln whispered harshly.

"Heck if I know," came the answer as he fingered the electrical traverse mechanism. The sound of the turret moving would give away their position. He would have to swing the turret around, get the guns on target and fire in one smooth, fast motion.

Lincoln peered out from the passenger side of the M16. If he could see the vehicle first, maybe he could help. His heart was pounding. He could feel it through his chest. His mouth was dry and his body was shaking. *So this is what combat is like?*

The high-pitched mechanical whine of the M16 turret startled him. The quad-fifty mount swung into position and opened fire. The entire halftrack shook with the recoil and the noise was deafening. Armor-piercing bullets were flung at the German vehicle at the rate of thirty-six rounds per second from the four synchronized machine guns. Lincoln heard glass shatter, metal rip and saw rubber and canvas pieces flying in all directions. The bodies of the four German crewmen were flung from the vehicle riddled with bullet holes. The vehicle caught fire and ammo began to explode. In less than ten seconds over 300 rounds were poured into the target, ripping flesh and metal alike. A smoking, twisted and charred pile of junk was all that was left.

"Let's go!"

Lincoln jumped up in the driver seat and started the engine. "Which way?"

"Head west. I don't remember the map. If we head toward our lines, we might make it back to Bastogne."

Lincoln turned the M16 and headed west through the fields. They traveled for a few minutes when they heard the frightening sound of squeaking bogey wheels off to their right. Lincoln instinctively turned the wheel to the left to avoid the perceived threat. Visibility was still poor but they were certain the tank they heard was not American. The Germans bypassed Noville and were about to encircle it.

Lincoln guided the M16 through the fog trying to avoid any ditches or sharp changes in the ground elevation. Both men strained their eyes to see in the mist. The sound of the tank faded off to their right, probably holding to the main road and advancing cautiously.

The M16 moved slowly and vigilantly. An opening in the fog revealed a small stone farmhouse in a bowl-like depression straight ahead.

"What do you think, Kilroy?"

"Looks abandoned. Pull in the back."

There was an empty open shed with a slanted roof directly behind the structure. It was just big enough for the M16 and Lincoln guided the halftrack into it just as the fog closed in again.

"I'll check the house," Lincoln announced and went in the back door.

He exited a few minutes later to see the rear of the M16 hidden by a stack of hay bales, covering everything below the quad-fifty mount.

"Good work, Kilroy. The house is empty."

The paratrooper waved Lincoln into the back of the M16. "We need to stay here until we can see better and know what's going on. Out there we're sitting ducks for the Krauts."

Lincoln nodded. "Just what I needed. Stuck out here with Whitey surrounded by Jerry."

"Give it a rest," he almost said 'boy' but caught himself. "You want to get out of this alive, we gotta' work together."

Lincoln nodded again. "Okay, so what's the plan, Kilroy?"

"I got no plan. If they attack we got this quad fifty." He slapped the ammo canister. "And we got this other fifty mounted behind the driver's seat. That's yours."

"Thanks a lot."

"Also we got these." He opened both cargo box compartments. "One Thompson. You can have that too." He flipped the submachine gun to Lincoln. "One .30-caliber M1903 Springfield rifle with sniper scope, three Carbines and a box of thirty-six grenades. We got what looks like ten thousand rounds of fifty-cal ammo and a couple of cans of gas. Thank God they loaded this halftrack up!"

"Great! Custer's Last Stand!"

"C'mon, Lincoln. We got no choice! What would *you* have us do?"

"We can hide. There's a crawl space under the house and we can squirrel ourselves away in there until the Krauts leave."

"No way. They could be here for days and I'm not going to get myself cooped up like that. Besides, we need to be able to move and fight. And one more thing, I'm not surrendering."

"And what if the tanks come, 'Sergeant York'?"

"You get in the driver's seat and we go like hell and make a break for our lines."

Lincoln shook his head. He had a splitting headache and was trying to gather himself after the adrenalin rush of obliterating the flakwagon. "Not my idea of a good plan but I guess we're stuck with each other. For now! Anything to eat, Kilroy?"

The paratrooper kicked around some more boxes. "Nothing here but a pair of binoculars and a medical kit. Let's look in the house."

The two men scoured the small farmhouse and came up with a jar of preserves and a stale loaf of bread. They stood watch at the windows while they ate in silence even though the ground fog limited their visibility to just a few yards. Lincoln watched his cohort bandage his forehead to stop the bleeding from a grazing wound. He easily resisted the fleeting temptation to help while he picked a small piece of shrapnel from his bleeding leg. He didn't want to be there and he wanted no part of this crazy, ballsy white paratrooper.

The deep rumbling sounds coming from Noville told of a fierce battle still raging. The booming sound of cannon fire could be heard echoing off the hills. Both German and American ordinance were identifiable to the trained ear. The battle raged on through the afternoon as the two Americans moved from window to window in a fruitless effort to observe their surroundings. Late in the day, gunfire erupted from near the town of Foy. That battle raged furiously for hours. There were Germans engaged in battles all around them. They were penned in with no place to go and would certainly be discovered in short order when the interminable fog finally lifted.

"We just gonna' stay here?" Lincoln finally blurted out after long hours of silence. The waiting was wearing away his resolve.

"For now. There's no place to go until we can see."

"And what if they find us here?"

"We fight our way out. That halftrack out there moves along pretty good."

"You a fucking crazy-ass cracker, you know that?"

"Drop the chip on your shoulder for once. Your attitude sucks. No wonder why they don't let you people fight!"

"You people? Oh, yeah. You try being a colored boy in this man's army and then tell me about motivation," Lincoln said through an angry grimace.

"If it's sympathy you want, go see the Chaplain or look it up in the dictionary next to syphilis. I ain't got none for you!"

"Fuck you, Whitey!"

"Right. Now it's 'fuck you, Whitey'. Back in London it wasn't our fight but we saved your ass anyway and now it's 'fuck you, Whitey.'" He pushed his webbed steel helmet up and back on his head. "You need to aim all that anger at the Krauts."

"I got enough to spread around pretty good."

The paratrooper wouldn't back down. "All I hear is how you boys are all pissed off they make you drive trucks, dig graves, and never let you fight. Well, ever since we've been together you've shown no willingness to fight. You complain but when you get the chance to prove yourselves, you got no balls!"

Lincoln took a step closer. "That's 'cause we're surrounded man and it's hopeless!"

"Get this once and for all, soldier." He took a step toward Lincoln. "I'm airborne. We're always surrounded. But we're not surrendering. And I didn't make the damn rules in this man's army. I'm not the one who says what colored troops can and can't do. I follow orders just like everybody else so don't take your damn shit out on me!"

Lincoln turned away but Kilroy continued. "Maybe they were right not letting you boys into combat if this is how you plan on fighting. What the hell's the point if you're ready to give up as soon as it gets rough?"

The Red Ball driver wheeled around and was about to say something when he was interrupted. "You think I want to be here, Lincoln? You think I'm not scared? If you want to surrender, go hide in the cellar and wait for me to get myself killed. Then you can wave a white flag and do whatever the hell you want!"

A strange calm came over Lincoln. He regained control of himself and smiled. "Go hide in the cellar? Like my granddaddy did when he hid from the Klan?" He reflected on the frightening stories his father told him when he was just a young boy. "If it's all the same to you, Kilroy, my people are done hiding in cellars. I'll fight with you!"

Chapter Sixty-Five

Washington, D.C. - January 27, 1998

"One deceit needs many others,
and so the whole house is built in the air and must soon come to the ground."

Baltasar Gracian (1601-1658)

Cynthia Powers walked into the condo after a long day of work to find J.P. sitting at the kitchen table staring blankly at his flowchart. He normally got home before she did and usually started dinner by the time she walked in. The two customary glasses of wine on the table were also missing. He was drinking Chivas Regal on the rocks. Something was wrong.

"Honey, I'm home," she mocked the oft-used greeting with a big smile.

He returned her greeting with a weak smile. Whatever was bothering him, she concluded, had nothing to do with her. Their relationship had become a bit more complicated. Her subtle hints for something more permanent failed to elicit any response from him. In spite of that, she enjoyed being with J.P. The sex was good, the conversations were stimulating and he made her laugh. She wasn't ready to admit she was in love with him yet but he would do for now.

J.P. was staring at a diagram he sketched of the relationships of all the men involved with his father. He drew a box for each person and connected them with lines drawn in black magic marker. The connecting lines each had a comment and through every box was a bold red line labeled "reunion-parade-1946". There were additional notes in the margins.

She stepped up behind him and began massaging his shoulders. He loved that. She intentionally saved it for special moments, to ease tensions, making up after an argument or the beginning of foreplay. He murmured softly.

"Do you almost have this figured out?" she glanced at the flowchart.

"It had me puzzled for awhile, especially Lincoln's relationship with Harley and Jake but the answer to the great mystery is not on this diagram."

"Really? You've spent so much time on it. How do you know that?"

"Because I figured it out." He took a sip of scotch.

"When?"

"Today. And it's just as well because I can't be wasting energy on this anymore. With the Lewinsky scandal breaking wide open I won't have the time. There's going to be a media feeding frenzy and I think there's more to it than a vast right wing conspiracy." He was clearly distressed.

"So, how did you figure it out? We haven't talked to anyone lately." He had made her a partner in his search for answers and she relished the job. But now he seemed to be withholding something from her.

"It was something you said. It struck me as odd at the time and it stuck in my mind."

"Really? What?"

"You said, 'it's kind of weird to know the day you were actually conceived."'

"Yeah, I remember that. It *is* kind of freaky."

"Well, I just couldn't get that out of my mind so I did something about it."

"Oh, shit." She stopped rubbing his shoulders. "What did you do?"

"I sent my father's DNA from a coffee cup I took in Bedford, along with mine, to a commercial lab for analysis."

"Oh my God! And?"

"And he's not my father, Cynthia. The DNA doesn't match." He emptied the glass of scotch and poured another.

She got herself a glass, pulled up a chair next to him and poured herself three fingers. He looked wounded and she felt the need to comfort him. "J.P. What does it matter? It doesn't mean anything. Whatever was between you and him doesn't change. He raised you. The good is not better and the bad is not worse. It's just biology."

J.P. nodded. He appreciated her effort to comfort him but he had a knot in his stomach since opening the lab report. "On one hand I'm happy to finally solve the mystery. On the other hand perhaps it would have been better if the secret stayed a secret."

"We'll never know, now. Will we?" She sipped her scotch. "Are you going to be okay?"

"Sure, but I can't help but wonder what the hell happened. Or how these four old men found out and banded together to keep it from me."

"It really doesn't matter any longer, does it?"

He continued without hearing her. "Or why my mother wanted me to know so badly before she died. That makes no sense."

"Stop! Maybe she was looking for forgiveness."

"And the sixty-four thousand dollar question is, who's my father?"

"Don't do this to yourself!"

"And why did Johnny...I can't call him my father any longer...go to Bedford? Did he make a promise to Jake he had to keep? Or did he find out my mother was unfaithful? That would certainly explain why he left us if he found out. And why did Lincoln send me back to him?"

"Let it go, J.P."

He took a deep breath. "You're right, Cynthia. I have to let it all go. I'm not sure that old man in Bedford who raised me even knows who my real father is. But those four old warriors, they wouldn't give up my mother, no matter what!" He smiled at the thought.

"Somehow they found out Johnny wasn't your father," she speculated. "Then they agreed never to tell anyone, especially you."

"Probably at that homecoming parade in forty-six. That was the only time they were all together." J.P. tapped the flowchart and pointed to the red slash he used to connect all of the boxes.

She took another sip of scotch. She would rather be drinking her wine but was trying to demonstrate some empathy toward J.P. in his time of need. "I'll help you as much as I can if you decide to try to find out who your real father is."

He smiled and pulled her closer to him. "I don't want to scare you away, Cynthia, but I think I'm falling for you. I may even be in love with you."

"You're so romantic," she chided. It was all she could do to stifle the cough in her throat. "Do you want my help or not?"

"I think I have to let go of what's left of this quest and focus on my job and on us."

Chapter Sixty-Six

Foy, Belgium - December 20, 1944

"Duty is ours; consequences are God's."

Lieutenant General Thomas "Stonewall" Jackson, (1824 - 1863)

A t dawn on 19 December, *General der Panzertruppen* Hasso Eccard von Manteuffel's XLVII *Panzer* Corps, having clawed its way out of the deep ravines and steep river valleys, was finally in open tank country. Three German divisions were now bearing down on Bastogne. The road hub town should have been his on the second day but the persistent Americans bravely resisted even when there was no hope of victory. They frustrated him, delayed his timetable and thwarted his plans. Just as he was poised to finally take Bastogne, the Americans pushed out probing forces on the roads leading into the city. Skirmishes ensued. Now the Germans would waste even more time dealing with these tenacious Americans, which now included paratroopers.

Manteuffel's 2nd *Panzer* Division had run into determined resistance at Noville while trying to approach Bastogne on the N-15 Highway. A small American force of paratroopers and armored infantry stubbornly held the village. The German *Panzers* outgunned the American Sherman tanks but not the American tank destroyers. The M36 with its .90-millimeter gun and the M18 Hellcat with its .76-millimeter long-barrel high-velocity gun made the *Panzers* pay dearly. On 19 December, outside Noville, thirty-two German tanks were destroyed. Lieutenant Colonel James L. LaPrade, who took command when Major William R. Desobry was critically wounded and evacuated, asked for permission to withdraw and awaited orders.

These were the sounds of battle the two isolated American soldiers heard from the fog-shrouded stone farmhouse, which remained in a clingy mist for the rest of the day. As the temperature dropped below freezing, both soldiers wrapped themselves in blankets against the cold. The fog would occasionally lift like a curtain rising from a stage, offering some brief moments of vision before crashing back down and smothering everything in a cloak of invisibility. In those brief moments of clarity the two men scanned all points of the compass. All that was discernible were the heaps of high haystacks spread across the rich farmland.

The Americans took turns trying to snatch some sleep. The constant noise of a battle raging around Noville served to deny them much needed rest. As both soldiers struggled with brief, fitful naps, it snowed through the night.

Shortly after dawn, on 20 December, the two soldiers were shaken by the sounds of .88-millimeter rounds smashing into Noville. The orange glow, acrid smell of gunpowder and smoke from burning vehicles served to remind them that the battle was still being fiercely contested.

Noises of tracked vehicles reverberated through the bowl-shaped plain. Small arms and cannon fire from the direction of Noville went on all day long. From time to time voices could be heard in the distance and they were always German voices. It was a miracle that they had not yet been discovered by enemy forces which flowed around them heading toward Foy and Bastogne.

It was shortly after 0800 hours when Foy again came under attack. The battle raged for hours while the fight for Noville was still underway. With enemy forces in their front and rear as well as surging around them they felt safer remaining in the farmhouse tucked into an undulation in the terrain and shrouded in the dense fog.

Both men heard the sound at the same time. It was an American jeep pulling up in the back. The driver brought the jeep to a halt. The two Americans stepped out of the back door; weapons trained on the four occupants.

"Hey, Mac. What outfit?" The jeep driver asked.

Lincoln circled the jeep and seemed to be studying it. The driver peered at him condescendingly. The other passengers sat quietly, hands on weapons.

"Who are you?" Kilroy finally asked.

"We're from the Twenty-eighth Division. We're heading for Bastogne."

"So is everybody else, it seems."

Lincoln came completely around the jeep and whispered, "They're stinking Krauts."

"You think?" he answered out loud and raised his weapon. "Easy everybody. Just empty your pockets. No sudden moves." Lincoln moved to one side of the jeep.

The driver was getting nervous. The other men began reaching into their pockets. One soldier pulled out some pound notes and dollars.

"Jeez, you're Krauts! Lincoln, tie them up!"

Suddenly one of the soldiers in the rear reached for his rifle. The two Americans reacted immediately. Both Thompsons roared and in less than three seconds the four German infiltrators were sprawled out in the blood-drenched jeep.

The two GIs stood for a moment, inhaling the acrid smell of cordite and the sweet smell of blood. They were both breathing hard. "How did you know, Lincoln?"

"Well, the markings on the jeep are all wrong. Also, we were ordered not to use hooded headlights. Either lights full on or completely off. Americans would know that." Lincoln smiled; satisfied he contributed with information only a driver would know. "How about you?"

"They were carrying pound notes and dollars. GIs only carry invasion money."

"Oh, these boys were screwed. I wonder what the hell they were up to?"

Before Lincoln received an answer, the sounds of motors and tracks became audible from the direction of the main highway. The engine noises became louder. They looked at each other.

"Sounds like our vehicles to me."

"You ought to know, Lincoln. Let's hope to God you're right."

The two men jumped into the halftrack. Lincoln backed it out of its hideout through the wall of hay bales. One bale fell into the back compartment. The halftrack pushed the stricken jeep aside and cleared the farmhouse. Lincoln proceeded slowly toward the sound of engines he prayed were American.

The deep voice pierced the fog. "Halt. Identify yourself. What's the password?"

The paratrooper jumped out of the back and approached the voice. "Corporal Kilroy. Easy Company, Five-oh-Sink." He used the nickname of his regiment to convince his challengers he was an American soldier.

A group of ragged, dirty paratroopers came out of the fog and surrounded them with weapons at the ready. "Yeah, how do we know you're for real and not lousy Krauts?"

They closed in, boots crunching the snow. Kilroy pointed to Lincoln who was standing in the cab. "Do the Krauts have any of these?"

There was some nervous laughter as the group of men recognized Lincoln as a colored soldier. They put up their weapons. "Nah, I guess not. Where you guys heading?"

"Bastogne."

A major walked into the small circle. "I'm Major Harwick. I'm in command."

"Colonel LaPrade?" Kilroy asked. LaPrade was well known in the regiment.

"Dead," he said without emotion. "This convoy is bogged down here right now. If this fog lifts we're dog meat. Where did you soldiers come from? What can you tell me?"

"We got separated yesterday while on a supply run. Lincoln and me have been holed up in a farmhouse waiting for this fog to lift. We just took out four Krauts in a jeep disguised as GIs."

The officer barely acknowledged the colored trooper. "We're conducting a fighting retreat from Noville. As soon as Third Battalion takes Foy we'll be moving forward again. You're welcome to join us."

"You look like sitting ducks out here, Major." The convoy was not moving, the grumbling engines idling anxiously in the misty fog.

"We have about thirty vehicles in this column. Most of them have wounded aboard. We lack maneuverability and we're low on able-bodied infantry. The few fighting tanks we have are up front. We're counting on them to kick the door open to get us into Foy."

"Flanks?"

"Wide open. It's like a wagon train in the old west except I can't circle them. We're road bound." The major nodded at the halftrack. "Since you're still mobile, we can use the extra firepower to protect our flanks."

"We can do that."

Just then small arms fire started peppering the column from the western flank. Some of the paratroopers returned fire even though they could not see far into the mist. The fire became more intense. It sounded like a large force of infantry was pressuring the flank.

The major pointed toward the gunfire. "There's a creek, some low ground and then a ridge. They probably came over the ridge. Can you push them back? Keep them off us?"

"Sure thing. Let's go Linc."

"Be careful son. There's a Panther tank roaming loose out here somewhere and I'm sure it wants to get a crack at this column."

Lincoln shifted gears and pushed the halftrack through a break in the column while Kilroy strapped himself into the quad-fifty mount. "Linc, let's go straight at them until we see muzzle flashes and then turn right and we'll sweep the line. Stay low."

The fire began to plink off the sides of the halftrack's half-inch armor plate. Kilroy grabbed the handlebar grips on the post between his knees. He knew the powered turret could sweep 180 degrees in three seconds. He waited for Lincoln to make the turn.

He saw the flashes and heard the crack of bullets whizzing by his head. Lincoln made the turn, ducked down and the trooper opened up with the quad-fifty. The noise was ear shattering as brilliant flashes of tracers shot off into the blanket of fog. The entire vehicle rocked and vibrated violently to the recoil. He struggled to keep the .50-caliber M2 machine guns on target while he continued to sweep back and forth. The screams and groans from behind the misty fog told him he was on target. The armor-piercing rounds severed limbs, split heads wide open and tore bodies in half. Flesh, bone and blood along with bits and pieces of uniform flew wildly in all directions. He continued to pour relentless fire onto the defenseless German infantrymen who were caught out in the open and quickly sliced to pieces by the withering fire of the Meat Chopper.

Lincoln reversed course and they swept the line again with a fusillade of bullets while heading back in the opposite direction. The shooting stopped when they ran out of ammo. Through a thinning fog they saw the carnage the armor-piercing rounds caused. It was once a reinforced platoon of *Panzergrenadiers* but now body parts of their dead and wounded were spread all over the field on both sides of the shallow creek. The few who survived were retreating back up to the ridge. For the moment this flank would remain secure.

Lincoln drove the halftrack back to the convoy. There was still intense fighting toward the front but the column began to creep forward slowly. Paratroopers were fanning out to the right and left to help dislodge the German defenders and find a way into Foy. As they pushed forward, the flanks became less protected. Kilroy busied himself replacing the four empty canister magazines on the quad-fifty with the last four full ones. Lincoln took the M1903 Springfield rifle and extra clips of ammo up in the front seat.

They worked in near silence save for the sounds of metal clicking on metal and the gunfire all around them. Then they proceeded to patrol first one side of the convoy then the other. The tracks of the vehicle made it easy for them to navigate the snow-bound terrain just off the macadam highway. On their first trip around the rear of the column they saw massive explosions in Noville. Before evacuating the town, the engineers of the 10th Armored Division set charges in the church basement. In one shot they denied the Germans the use of the steeple observation post and the main road through town.

Each time the halftrack came around the west side of the convoy, the side with the wooded ridge, they heard the squeaking bogey wheels of the elusive Panther tank. But the fog cloaked both forces. If the Germans could delay the convoy until the fog lifted, they could stand off at a distance and pick off the vehicles with deadly cannon fire. They continued to search for the column by launching their ghostly flares.

Kilroy was taking fragmentation grenades from the wooden box and passing some to Lincoln when two German scout cars came racing through the eerie light of the flares hanging in the fog. They were running parallel to the road. They began to pour small arms fires into the column while on the move. Kilroy threw two grenades as far as he could and the explosion of shrapnel stopped one of the scout cars. Lincoln emptied a clip from his Thompson into the same vehicle. Kilroy had just strapped himself into the quad-fifty when the second scout car came roaring back. The force of the .50-caliber volley was so powerful the scout car flipped end over end and crashed in a pile of junk and debris. A few walking-wounded paratroopers from the column scrambled out and finished off the survivors.

The column continued to creep toward Foy. The halftrack prowled the flanks in search of the enemy and, like an outrider in a cattle drive, stewarded the convoy toward its destination. Finally, they took up a position behind the last vehicle in the column. They would be in Foy in another twenty minutes if they kept up the pace. Suddenly, they heard the sounds of squeaking bogey wheels and tank treads slapping through the creek.

"Shut her down, Linc."

Lincoln turned off the engine so they could hear. A slight breeze came up and the fog began to dissipate.

"No, not now," the paratrooper whispered into the air.

"What do we do if they spot us?"

"Run like hell. Provide a diversion. Draw them away from the column."

"Don't sound like a good plan to me."

"We can't outfight him. We'll have to out maneuver and outrun him! You can drive rings around him, Linc. He'll never touch us!"

"I suppose." Lincoln popped up in the driver's seat. "Shit. Right there." He was pointing to a Mark V Panther coming down the hill from the wooded ridgeline. He fired up the engine.

"Let's haul ass," Kilroy yelled as he rotated the four .50-caliber machine guns toward the tank. "This ought to get their attention!"

He fired the four synchronized machine guns and the tracers created streaks of light in the smothering haze. Sparks flew off the tank's glacis plate and turret as the armor-piercing rounds ricocheted off of the thick body armor with sharp metallic clangs. The fog swirled as he poured hundreds of rounds at the tank in just a few seconds. The tank turret swerved toward them. Small arms fire began to hit the halftrack. "He's got infantry with him!" yelled Kilroy.

"Stop firing," Lincoln yelled as he punched the gas and the vehicle took off in the opposite direction from the convoy. "They're tracking back on your tracers!"

Kilroy let off the triggers and Lincoln changed direction. The tank fired its main gun. The round landed where the halftrack would have been had Lincoln not changed course. "You're right, damn it! They can't see shit either! He back-tracked our tracers!"

Lincoln guided the vehicle back down the road as the fog settled back in. The tank lost contact with the halftrack and began to move toward the convoy. It opened fire with its main gun again, this time aiming at the convoy.

"C'mon Linc, we gotta' distract him." he yelled as he unbuckled himself from the quad mount to get grenades.

Lincoln turned their vehicle to the sound of the cannon fire. He was moving fast through the translucent curtain of fog. Too fast! Suddenly the halftrack came over a rise in the terrain and down into a deep depression. The body of the huge tank loomed directly before him. Lincoln yanked the wheel sharply and punched the gas hard to avoid colliding with the tank. The centrifugal force of the sudden turn sent the paratrooper flying out of the rear compartment and onto the ground. His helmet came flying off as he tumbled along the snowy hardscrabble ground. He wound up sprawled out on all fours without a weapon. The halftrack sped away and disappeared into the gloom.

"Lincoln, come back you bastard," he yelled at the top of his lungs.

Before he could rise up from the ground, two *Panzergrenadiers* had him by the arms and were dragging him to the front of the tank. The turret on the panther popped open and a German officer began barking orders. Before he knew it, he was standing in front of the muzzle of the tank's .75-millimeter high-velocity long-barreled cannon.

"Dirty, yellow-bellied bastard," he mumbled to himself. He looked up at the muzzle aimed directly at him. *At least it will be quick and I won't become a prisoner.*

The tank engine shut down and the officer spoke loudly in stilted but passable English. "Ah, paratrooper I see. Screaming Eagle."

One of the *Panzergrenadiers* yanked off his dog tags and read his name to the tank commander in stilted English. "Corporal John Kilroy."

"Ah, yes. Corporal Kilroy. How many of your comrades in Bastogne?"

"You'll find out soon enough."

The two soldiers holding his arms stepped away and motioned for him to place his hands on his head. He complied. They quickly stripped him of his grenades and sidearm. "What outfit are *you* from?" The words came out spontaneously and were the product of his nervousness.

"Ah, you'll find out soon enough, Corporal. We are the Second *Panzer* Division and we plan to spend the night in Bastogne."

"Good luck with that!"

The German officer let out a brief hearty laugh. "So cocky, you American paratroopers. You devils in baggy pants. Not so tough now, ah?"

Kilroy stared at the gun. His heart was racing with fear. "Let's get this over with."

The officer's face contorted in confusion. Then his eyebrows lifted in understanding. "Ah, you think I mean to kill you with my main gun? No, no. We are not the SS. And besides, I would not waste an amour piercing round on you." He let out another brief grunting laugh. "No, you will be a guest of the Third Reich until we win the War."

"Sounds like a life sentence to me," he mumbled under his breath.

They heard the sound of the screaming truck engine simultaneously. It seemed to reverberate off the side of the massive tank. All eyes turned toward the high-pitched sound of a revving motor as it became louder and louder. Everyone stared in horror as the fog lit up in a curtain of bright flame and the halftrack, engine roaring, came flying over the embankment at great speed. The bale of hay was alight in the rear compartment and the open gas cans further fueled the fire. The driverless halftrack went airborne and came back to earth with a loud crash as its nose buried itself at the base of the tank's tread. The momentum pushed the halftrack over on its back spilling the burning hay and gasoline over the body of the tank. The commander barely got the hatch closed before a blanket of flames spread across the turret and deck of the tank.

Kilroy ducked to the ground at the appearance of the flaming halftrack. The Germans stood motionless, stunned by the sudden appearance of the driverless vehicle. The tank backed away, sending the overturned halftrack crashing to the ground.

Suddenly, one of the guards spun down with a bullet in the head, the shot muffled by the sounds of the tank's engine. Before the other *Panzergrenadier* could react, he too was cut down.

The tank continued to move in reverse trying in vain to douse the flames spreading on its hull. As the flaming liquid began pouring into the interior through the view slits, the crew tried to abandon the tank. The top hatch flipped open. The first one out, the commander, was shot in the chest. He slumped back into the turret. The backdrop of the flames made the targets clearly visible. As the next crewman climbed out, he was silhouetted in the light and shot. The ammunition began cooking off and explosions ripped the tank apart from the inside.

The young paratrooper lay frozen, hugging the ground, when he heard footsteps crunching on the frozen snow. He turned around to see Lincoln Abraham walking slowly toward him. He had the M1903 Springfield sniper rifle in his arms and the Thompson slung over his shoulder.

"What the hell took you so long?" he mockingly asked.

Lincoln helped his buddy off the ground and handed him the Thompson. "I couldn't find a match." Lincoln had a bloodstained field dressing on his forearm.

"What happened to your arm?"

"Bullet clean through. No broken bone," Lincoln answered.

"Where did you learn to shoot like that?"

"Back home in Michigan. I hunted a lot."

The paratrooper retrieved his helmet and dog tags from the body of a fallen German. They were both killed with headshots. "You're good!"

"It's got a scope. Could hardly miss at this distance."

They walked toward the road in silence for a few moments. Finally the relieved paratrooper put his hand on the driver's shoulder. "Thanks for coming back for me."

Lincoln kept walking, head down, and rifle ready. "You're welcome, man. You would have done the same."

"I know. But I wasn't sure *you* would."

They walked until they found the road in the mist and followed it toward Foy. It was getting dark and there was still fighting up ahead. The tracks in the snow led off to the right. The convoy must have taken a slight detour. The two men followed the tracks around the village of Foy to its northwest side. An officer appeared out of the fog.

"Is that you, Kilroy?" It was Captain Frank West.

"Yes it is, Captain!"

West grabbed his shoulders. "Am I glad to see you, son. Major Harwick told us a paratrooper and colored driver were providing rear guard for the convoy in an M16 halftrack. I figured it must have been you and the driver who went back for the supplies."

"Yup. We lost the halftrack. Sorry."

"Major Harwick told me how you shot up an enemy patrol and some flakwagons to allow the convoy to get through. Good work, men. We need to write you up for a medal."

"This scrawny little driver is PFC Lincoln Abraham. He was with me all the way. If you're going to recommend medals, he damn well earned one too, sir."

"Thanks, son. I'd be glad to write both of you up. What happened to the halftrack?"

"Lincoln smashed it into the Panther. Saved my ass and the convoy."

West looked at Lincoln who responded. "It was a team job. We both did what we had to do." He smiled. "We didn't feel like hiding in cellars and we weren't being taken prisoner. Right, Kilroy?"

The paratrooper nodded. "Did the convoy make it through?"

"Most of it," West replied. "We salvaged most of the vehicles and about half of the four hundred men from Team Desobry and two thirds of the six hundred paratroopers made it back. Also, fifty wounded were taken to Bastogne."

"Whew! Pretty stiff price, Captain. Was it worth it?"

"It's never worth it, son. Not one American soldier is worth it." West paused, letting his words sink in. "But if you mean was their sacrifice meaningful, I would tell you it most certainly was. Two battalions held up an elite armored division for two days. That's time the Krauts can never make up and time we needed to dig in." West put a hand on each of their shoulders. "We're going to stop the Krauts right here. They'll never take Bastogne. Their big counteroffensive will fail. And when history tells the story, I wouldn't be surprised if the battle for Bastogne was won because of the battle for Noville!" He stepped back. "Their sacrifice will not be in vain and your contribution will not go unnoticed."

"Thanks, Captain."

West looked at Lincoln and pulled a pencil and small pad from his breast pocket. "Tell me what happened out there tonight."

Chapter Sixty-Seven

Newport News, Virginia - December 24, 1944

"Our debt to the heroic men and valiant women in
the service of our country can never be repaid.
They have earned our undying gratitude.
America will never forget their sacrifices."

Harry S. Truman (1884 - 1972)

Macie Vance sat on the flight deck of the soon-to-be USS *Crown Point* *(CV-32)* with her back against the unfinished center-island superstructure. Nora Lee was beside her as they ate their lunch in silence. It was a rather warm day for December, temperature in the high fifties, and they took advantage of the soft onshore breeze to breathe in some clean, salty sea-air. It was a refreshing contrast to the pungent smell of the welding torches in the confined spaces below decks.

Macie was wearing her customary coveralls and knotted red bandana. Her welding helmet was at her side. She flipped open the lid of her lunch pail and pulled out the other half of her peanut butter and jelly sandwich and continued to eat in silence. It was Sunday and Christmas Eve. The "yard" would be closing early. It would also be closed on Christmas Day for the first time in four years.

CV-32 was the only Essex-class aircraft carrier hull still under construction in the Newport News Shipyard. At its peak in late 1943, the yard had five of the magnificent aircraft carriers under the welders' torches at the same time. They all had been completed, launched and commissioned. Only the USS *Boxer (CV-21)*, which had been launched on 14 December and was out for sea trials, had not yet been commissioned. That would take a few more months. Macie and her crew came over from working on the *Boxer* to the *Crown Point*.

As the orders for carriers dried up, workers were furloughed. The frenetic pace of construction in 1942 and 1943 had slowed to a more methodical tempo. It was clear America would eventually win the War. There was no longer a desperate need to build any more of these majestic behemoths.

The change in attitude came about slowly but steadily as the year 1944 unfolded. If 1942 was a year of survival and 1943 a year of stabilization, then 1944 was the turning point toward victory. The initiative was completely in Allied hands and the Axis Powers were forced into a reactive and defensive mode. Not that the battles were easy. But each fatality marked the road to the ultimate triumph and pointed to the end of this grueling War.

Macie kept up on world affairs but the change from struggle to imminent victory was so subtle she nearly missed it. The year began with small, hopeful signs the Allies were gaining control. On the Eastern Front, the Russians were continuing their push westward. They broke the siege of Leningrad in the north in January and recaptured the port of Sevastopol in the south in April. In the center, Russian armored forces pushed back Germany's Army Group Center and recaptured the Ukraine. The Germans were hard pressed everywhere to defend a 1,400-mile front. By the end of 1944, the Russian armies were sitting on the Vistula River across from Poland. They were re-supplying and consolidating forces for the final push to Berlin.

In Italy, the Allies were busy as well. The amphibious landings at Anzio in January signaled the Allied effort to break the stalemate. The Germans resisted stubbornly across the mountainous boot but the Allies eventually pushed them back and captured Rome in June.

The invasion of Normandy on 6 June 1944 was a momentous event that augured the return of the Allies to confront the Germans on French soil. Breaching the Atlantic Wall was arduous but with the breakout in July and the liberation of Paris in August, the Allies had the Germans in retreat and on the run. The surprise Nazi counteroffensive in December, which resulted in the Battle of the Bulge, was a huge setback for the Allies. But they recovered rather quickly. By the end of 1944, they too were approaching a river barrier, the Rhine, preparing for the final assault on the Third Reich.

In the Central Pacific, United States Marines recaptured most of the Marshall Islands in February against fanatical resistance. The next targets were the islands of Tinian and Saipan in the Marianas. The Americans attacked the islands in June, triggering one of the most one-sided battles in history. The Battle of the Philippine Sea, otherwise known as the Great Marianas Turkey Shoot, pitted what was left of the Imperial Japanese Navy's carrier fleet against the American Fast Carrier Task Groups. There had not been a major carrier battle of this scope for two years in the Pacific. Since the Battle of Midway, both sides were husbanding their resources and gathering strength. But the Japanese were not about to let this incursion by the Americans go unchallenged.

The Imperial Japanese Navy brought all of their might to bear on the Americans; five heavy and four light aircraft carriers plus land based planes from nearby islands. Their forces also included five battleships. The Japanese force had a strength of 673 planes, 473 carrier based and the rest land-based. The Americans brought fifteen fast carriers into the battle with new F6F Hellcat fighters on their decks. The Battle of the Philippine Sea was virtually all air combat. When it was over, more than 600 Japanese planes were downed. In addition, three of their aircraft carriers were sunk or damaged. The Americans lost twenty-three planes in air combat and another hundred ditching in the dark sea when they ran out of fuel returning from attacking the Imperial Japanese carriers.

It was a source of great pride to Macie and her co-workers at Newport News

Shipyard that the Japanese fleet was decimated with weapons forged and built with their own hands.

In October, the Americans invaded the Japanese-held Philippines and began the methodical process of evicting them from the islands. MacArthur had vowed to return two years prior when he was ordered to leave his troops and withdraw to Australia.

As the Americans closed the ring around Japan, their warships hunted Japanese shipping relentlessly. American submarines and aircraft carriers now roamed the seas with impunity. They regularly interdicted traffic between the Japanese Home Islands and their recently captured possessions. The Americans had Japan in a chokehold and continued to rack up big scores of shipping tonnage through all of 1944.

As the year came to a close, the news from all fronts was extremely encouraging. However, finishing the War would not be easy. The final conquests of Germany and especially Japan would be hard-fought and costly. The question was whether victory was near at hand or would the obstinate Japanese hold out for years?

Nora Lee brushed her recently cut short blond hair back under her baseball cap. She pulled the cap tight to her head against the breeze. "What are your plans after the War, Sweetie?"

Macie pulled her knees up to her chest and finished chewing. "I really haven't thought about it, Nora. I probably should with so many yard workers being let go."

"Well, I don't think they're going to let us do this." She waved her hand across the deck. "I certainly won't be able to find a job as a drill press operator. It's all over for us."

"Us?"

"Women, Macie. When this War is over they'll be shoving us back to be housewives."

Macie considered that for a moment. "The guys coming home are going to need the jobs, Nora. And I was thinking about raising a family anyway."

"With Derek?"

Macie looked directly at Nora and didn't answer.

"Buyer's remorse?" Nora pressed. Still, Macie wouldn't answer. She had been conflicted ever since she wrote Jake the Dear John letter. It was an issue she was still sorting out and she knew where Nora stood on the matter. Nora had lived the pain of losing men to the insatiable grinding gears of the War and wanted to spare Macie the same fate. Nora loved her as a sister and withheld judgment, just as Macie had with Nora's occasional impulsive, salacious behavior.

"Anyway, Sweetie, we shouldn't be forced out of our jobs now and we should be allowed to do what we want after the War. We should have choices. We earned the right to make the choice of family or career. It's not fair that we get pushed around."

"Nobody is pushing *us* around Nora. We still have jobs."

"Thanks to Derek, probably. Who do you think is being let go?" Macie didn't answer. "Mostly dames and the niggers! The big shots are already putting us back in our place!"

"I wish you wouldn't call them that."

"What? Dames or big shots?" Nora chortled at her own little joke.

"You know what I mean. Besides, Nora, do you really want to be a drill press operator for the rest of your life?"

"That's not the point, Macie. I want the choice. I *earned* the right to have a choice. So did you!" She motioned to a group of women having lunch a short distance away. "So did all of us. I like the financial independence. I like being part of a team. I love accomplishing things and the respect that goes with that. We helped build, what, eight big ships in two years? Didn't you feel proud that you personally accomplished something when those ships were launched?"

Macie nodded. Nora continued. "Besides, I've already proven I could learn a skill and be good at it. That should count for something after the War."

"You don't know what it's going to be like after the War. I'm worried about the layoffs, too. I left Derek a message…"

"Speak of the devil," Nora eyed Derek as he came through a doorway in the superstructure.

He approached the two girls looking somber. "They told me I could find you two up here." He looked at Macie. "You left me a message?"

"That was Friday, Derek." Macie's face-hardened, her voice firm.

"Sorry. Been a little busy lately."

"Laying off people?" Nora asked with obvious sarcasm.

Derek stepped back. "Is that what this is about? Look ladies, I'm not making these decisions. I'm not that high up on the food chain to decide who stays and who goes. I just do what I'm told."

"Why are we still here?" Macie asked. "Are you pulling strings for us?"

"I can only make recommendations. You both have seniority so keeping you on isn't so hard."

"What about the colored and the other women? Why are so many being let go?" Macie still had an edge in her voice.

"Same reason. Seniority. Last in, first out."

Both girls gave Derek a skeptical look.

"Look around, ladies. There's only one carrier under construction. It's obvious we don't need as many people as when we had five in the works. We had to let them go."

"Will they find jobs, Derek?" Macie's tone softened a bit.

"I called around. There are only seven carrier hulls under construction in the five shipyards in the country that can build them. No new hulls have been laid down since August and none are planned. I guess the navy only needed the twenty-four they ordered."

"So all those people are out of jobs?" Nora asked.

"Some factories in the North are still hiring. They may have to relocate. That shouldn't be a problem. Most of them moved here to get this job, like you two. I think they'll find work."

Nora scoffed. "I just think they're trying to shove us women back into the lives we had before the War."

Derek looked directly at Nora. "They may try Nora but nothing will be the same when the War ends. Society will be turned upside down. Everything will change. You'll see."

"I hope you're right, Derek. Women deserve better," Macie offered. She noticed some papers in Derek's hand. "What do you have there?"

Derek frowned. "It's not good news." He handed Macie the letter from Roxie dated 19 December. She began to read it softly out loud while Nora read over her shoulder. They read for a few moments and the letter came to an abrupt end. Derek fought back tears as he handed them another letter.

> December 21, 1944
> Dear Derek,
>
> You don't know me but I'm a close friend of Roxie Rawls. She left the attached letter on her writing tablet when she had to leave to ferry a plane. She never finished the letter because she never came back. I'm sorry to have to inform you that her plane went down in a storm and she along with her co-pilot are missing and presumed lost.
>
> I know you were close friends. She spoke of you often and was very fond of you. I thought the least I could do was forward her last letter to you and advise you of her fate. We here in the WASPs will miss her terribly. She was a loyal and caring friend and a great pilot. I'm so sorry!
> With deepest sympathy and regret,
> Dora Dougherty

Chapter Sixty-Eight

Bedford, Virginia - September 11, 2001

"Three can keep a secret, if two of them are dead."

Benjamin Franklin (1706 - 1790)

J.P. Kilroy pulled into the National D-Day Memorial at ten minutes to eight in the morning. The site was vastly different than what he remembered from his last and only visit over three years before. He drove around the empty circular parking lot that circumscribed the memorial and parked near an opening. He noticed how new and clean everything was as he walked to the ersatz shoreline and sat on one of the many smooth, shiny marble benches facing the water. There were only a few people walking about. His dad offered to give him and Frank West a personal tour of the memorial. As he waited, he reflected on the intervening years since his last visit to Bedford.

As far as J.P. was concerned, the last three years flew by in a flash. After finding out the man who raised him was not his biological father, he was convinced he discovered what the old men were hiding. Coupled with the last three years of a tumultuous presidency, a contested national Presidential election that went all the way to the Supreme Court and his complicated relationship with Cynthia Powers, J.P. had neither the time nor desire to chase down the identity of his real father. His mother had ample opportunity to consort with other men so he resigned himself to the probability he may never know for sure. J.P. also acknowledged that even his dad might not know, although it was likely he knew it was someone other than himself. He resisted the temptation to drag himself through those emotions once again and focused on his surroundings.

J.P. remembered the President of the United States just dedicated the D-Day Memorial two months earlier on the sixth of June. He could see it was laid out in a huge circle with a wide road surrounding it. The massive arch was the dominant feature as one approached through the main entrance. The word OVERLORD was inscribed across the top. Three huge white stripes on the arch represented the invasion stripes marked on every Allied plane that flew on D-Day. Under the arch the visitors would come face-to-face with a dark green statue of an Army Ranger scaling the cliff at Pointe-du-Hoc. His Thompson submachine gun was raised high over his head in a triumphant gesture having successfully scaled the dangerous heights. Looking out beyond the statue, the perspective was looking from atop Pointe-du-Hoc across the sea toward England.

Two inclined ramps, one on each side, led down from the "heights" to the next lower level and a tan colored depiction of a narrow sandy beach. Lying on the half-moon shaped beach were three dark olive drab bronze statues of soldiers.

One was lying lifeless. Another was dragging the inert body of a fellow GI inland. The lifelike scene was riveting and compelling.

Looking up from the beach toward the heights, one could see three more Rangers in bronze laboring mightily to gain the summit. Taught ropes, dangling feet and joined hands testified to the strain and struggle to breach the cliff.

Beyond the beach was the water, also shaped in a semi-circle to follow the contour of the beach. There were iron cross-shaped obstacles reaching up from the water representing the gripping danger that lurked where the waves touched the land. Another soldier in the water waded inland, rifle held high overhead. A granite landing craft with a lowered ramp dominated the center but the most striking aspect of the beach display was the simulation of bullets striking the water. At random intervals, sprays would leap out of the water at various points with a soft but definitive cracking sound. Even in the welcoming hills of Virginia, the Stonewallers could not escape the relentless gunfire of the invisible enemy.

Four marble steps led up from the pool to the land and were ringed by a series of low, flat marble benches. In front of the benches was a simple chain separating the steps from the rest of the memorial. *To keep the kids out,* he thought. Behind the benches was a vast, open circular area paved with large gray marble and granite tiles. This huge area represented the English Channel. The lines on the floor showed the sea-lanes taken by the vast armada of 5,000 ships. Encircling this vast, flat area was a low concrete wall adorned with plaques and flags honoring both individuals and units that participated in D-Day. There were hundreds of them. The plaques on the Necrology Wall listed the names of all Allied servicemen killed in action on D-Day, the only place in the world to do so.

Well beyond the wall, and directly opposite the beach, was a gray stone cupola covering a full-length statue of General Dwight David Eisenhower, the architect and leader of the greatest invasion in history. Between the cupola and the "sea" was a small garden with flowers arranged in shape and color to replicate the shoulder patch of SHAEF. The crescent shaped patch with the flaming sword and rainbow was recognizable to everyone who served in the European Theatre of Operations. The memorial, in all of its exquisite beauty, was framed beneath the backdrop of the majestic Blue Ridge Mountains.

J.P. pulled out a brochure. He followed the descriptions of the various parts of the memorial with his eyes. The vast open space could accommodate hundreds of chairs for an evening concert, speech or lecture. It was a marvelous facility with a clean, well thought out design and captivating bronze statues. The feeling was both eerie and comforting. It was a place blessed with an unexplained energy that elicited a visceral reaction. He felt his own hair standing on the nape of his neck. It was as if the spirits of the fallen had returned to revisit Omaha Beach in Bedford and were all around him.

J.P. attended Harley's wake and funeral the day before. It was a simple affair. The small quaint funeral home was filled with many friends and neighbors including members of the local American Legion and Veterans of Foreign Wars posts. Surrounding the casket were pictures of Harley as a youth in uniform. His face was young, fresh and proud. He had an expression of pride and fulfillment repeated in other youthful pictures of old veterans lying in funeral homes across the land. Frank had also informed J.P. that Lincoln was too ill to travel and Sky had passed away the year before. The old warriors continued to pass on at an unremitting rate.

J.P. shifted his weight on the hard marble bench. He agreed to meet the man who raised him as a courtesy. After all, the old guy did pay for school and appeared anxious to bring them closer together. But J.P. couldn't help but put more distance between them as time went on. Life intervened. Besides, he already knew the dark family secret so there was no reason to cultivate a closer relationship. To keep things cordial, J.P. continued to call him "Dad". They spoke from time to time but J.P. never revealed what he had discovered.

J.P. spotted the two old men at the top of the ramp. They walked slowly down the incline. Frank was wearing an American Legion cap strewn with patches and medals. His dad wore a baseball cap with the Screaming Eagle emblem. Both wore windbreakers. They made their way slowly to the bench and sat, one on each side of him. No one spoke for a long few minutes.

J.P. spoke first. "It's beautiful," he nodded toward the water and the statues.

"Harley came here every day," his dad finally said. "I'm glad he got to see it finished before he passed away." He breathed the words hard as he tried to choke back tears. He just stared at the beach in a near comatose state. The only noise was the popping sounds of the faux bullet splashes in the water.

Frank turned to J.P. "Bloody Omaha decimated the Stonewallers. The only thing that came close to that for us was Bastogne."

"The Battle of the Bulge?"

"Oh, yeah. We were surrounded and cut off and the Krauts wanted that town bad. Fortunately we collected a bunch of artillery units who were retreating and along with the Tenth Armored and a few scattered TD units, we gave the Krauts more than they could handle."

"Until Patton rescued you." J.P. paused. "I saw the movie."

Frank glowered at him. "Hollywood!" he growled. "We never agreed that we needed to be rescued!"

J.P. smiled. It was a source of pride among paratroopers that they never needed outside help from anyone. Frank went on. "We would have never surrendered but Bastogne was hell. It got very cold after we arrived and snowed every day. We dug in on the outskirts of town and the Krauts shelled us regularly with flat-trajectory eighty-eights. They would hit the trees and spread shrapnel and wood fragments down on us. The Screaming Eagles lost a lot of guys. Bastogne was our Omaha Beach."

J.P. looked over to his dad who stood up and began walking to the chain. The old man was transfixed on the bronze relief statue of the Rangers scaling the heights of Pointe-du-Hoc. J.P. looked back at Frank. "Tell me about it."

"After the retreat from Noville and Foy we gathered our forces in the woods outside of Bastogne called the *Bois Jacques* and dug in. I sent Lincoln back to the artillery park in the city to serve with a colored artillery outfit. Before I did that I told him about the Five hundred fifty-fifth, an all-colored parachute battalion forming up in the States. I told him I would provide a recommendation. He was happy about that and anxious to sign up. In the days that followed, I wrote both of them up for a commendation but it went nowhere. I guess someone in the chain of command pigeon-holed it."

"So, that's how you met Lincoln and how he found out about the Triple Nickels," J.P. concluded.

Frank nodded. "Good man, Lincoln. They both deserved that Medal."

"But you were saying about Bastogne?"

"It was cold and it was bloody. The Krauts shelled us every day. We were surrounded and cut off. The weather was too bad for aerial resupply. We ate pancakes every day because we had a huge supply of flour in town. I still can't eat pancakes." Frank took a deep breath. "We just stood there and took it, beat back every attack and denied them the city. Some of their armored elements bypassed us and continued to the Meuse River but without the roads through the city the Krauts couldn't supply them. But they kept attacking and we kept beating them back. We took tremendous casualties. We lost a lot of guys in that town. But we held. We never surrendered."

Frank paused. He became emotional. J.P. touched his knee with a compassionate tap of his fist. After a moment, Frank continued.

"Jake and Johnny were inseparable as usual. If one was ordered to set up an observation post, the other went too. If one was ordered to mount a patrol, the other volunteered to join the detail. If they were close before Bastogne they were inseparable during and after."

Frank paused and reflected. "Ike gave Monty command of all the American forces north of the Bulge. That pissed off the American generals to no end. The Eighty-second was part of that force. They hated Monty for making them retreat 'and tidy up the lines', as he put it. It was the first time in history that the All-Americans ever gave up ground. Sky told me more than once how they hated Monty for that."

"You guys seemed to have had a bit of a rivalry going."

"We did," Frank smiled. "But it was based on mutual respect. The Eighty-second was every bit as good as the Hundred and first and I'm not ashamed to admit it. Sky knew how I felt. If the Eighty-second had been at Bastogne, they would have done as good a job as we did.

"In any event, the glory of Bastogne fell to us. Around Christmas Eve the skies cleared and the Allied fighter-bombers pounded the Kraut positions and C-47s dropped supplies on the town. Two days later Patton's force broke through, the Kraut offensive petered out and we went on the attack. By mid January we retook Foy and Noville and were chasing the Krauts back to the Fatherland. Then they shipped us one hundred sixty miles to Alsace to stop Operation Nordwind, a Kraut attack to cover their retreat from the Ardennes. As if we weren't beat up enough. It took a month but we stopped them there, too.

"Finally, after spending a few weeks in the village of Haguenau on the Moder River, we were sent back to Mourmelon, France to rest and refit. Word was out that the division was to be awarded a Distinguished Unit Citation in the name of the President; the first time in army history the award went to an entire division."

"That must have been some moment," J.P. acknowledged.

"The guys were almost more nervous about the ceremony than going into combat. They spent hours spit shining boots, pressing uniforms, oiling rifle stocks, making brass gleam…I'd never seen them so frazzled. Finally, on a Thursday morning, 15 March 1945, Eisenhower himself inspected the ranks and made the award. Big, tough paratroopers were seen in tears. They were crying for their brothers who would never come back and whose bravery and dedication made the last stand at Bastogne a victory.

"By then the War was pretty much over for us, except Jake and Johnny were ordered to accompany Captain Lewis Nixon to observe the jump of the Seventeenth Airborne Division in Operation Varsity. Sky was transferred to the Seventeenth and was short of experienced jumpmasters so he called in some favors and had Jake and Johnny temporarily assigned to him. All three Screaming Eagles made the jump but were pulled out of the combat zone before they could become casualties. That's how the boys got their fifth combat-jump star."

A noise behind them attracted their attention. Both men turned to see an oversized golf-cart ferrying a group of visitors to the Necrology Wall. The memorial was waking up and the aging visitors were getting assistance from the attentive volunteer staff.

Frank continued. "The division absorbed replacements and were dispatched to the Ruhr Pocket along the Rhine River where a huge Kraut force was holding out. By April, we had reduced the pocket and were into Germany. That's when we found the camps…the concentration camps. I'll never forget how that felt. Jake and Johnny took it hard. Johnny was simply overwhelmed and Jake was madder than hell. He was ready to kill every German in the town. Cooler heads prevailed. By early May, we were in the town of Berchtesgaden where Hitler had his Eagle's

Nest retreat and the high-ranking Nazis had homes. We sat out the end of the War in relative comfort."

J.P. turned to Frank. "But if they both survived the War, how did Jake die?"

Frank swallowed hard. "I've already said too much."

J.P. sighed. He looked over at the back of the man he called dad and jerked his head up. "I already know the secret, Frank. That man is not my father."

Frank looked stunned.

"I know he raised me and I'll call him *dad* but the DNA test said he's not my biological father. I may never find out who is, but it's not him. Apparently, my mother was indiscreet."

A slow smile crept across Frank's face. He shook his head. "Things are not always as they appear. What you think you know may not always be correct."

J.P. was about to question Frank further when he heard a commotion behind them. One of the volunteers in the golf cart was holding a radio to his ear.

"What's going on?" J.P. asked.

The volunteer shook his head in disbelief. "Someone just crashed a plane into the Pentagon!"

Chapter Sixty-Nine

Kaprun, Austria - June 27, 1945

"Loyalty is the marrow of honor."

Field Marshal Paul von Hindenburg (1847 - 1934), *Out of My Life.*

Johnny and Jake Kilroy were standing in a line of paratroopers that snaked out the door of the Kaprun town hall and into the street. The building served as headquarters for the 506th PIR. The Divisional S-1, the Staff Officer for Personnel and Administration, was hearing appeals for reconsideration of the points assigned to each member of the division. Eighty-five points were required for immediate rotation back to the States and discharge. Points were credited to an individual for factors such as length of service, time overseas, marital status, campaigns fought, battle stars won, medals awarded and wounds received. Most of the 101st Airborne Division had not amassed sufficient points but some, particularly those who served with other units prior to the Screaming Eagles, were extremely close to the life altering magic number. Each came to plead his case to the high-ranking officer who was sent to adjudicate complaints, address discrepancies and render judgments.

The records were notoriously out of date. It was impossible for the paper trail to keep up with the lightning campaigns fought in Europe in the fall and winter of 1944-1945. Some of the paratroopers needed only to show a marriage certificate, a Purple Heart or some other proof of participation in a campaign to be awarded additional points. Officers from the 506th were present in the room to validate or deny the claims and assertions of their men. Those who received good news rushed back to their quarters to pack for home. All of these "high-point men" would be sent home the next day.

Jake and Johnny were near the end of the line, which moved surprisingly quickly. They inched their way steadily to the door of the interview room.

"This ought to be a snap," Johnny excitedly said to Jake. "We got enough points. We'll be home in a week." He rubbed his hands softly in anticipation.

After the division left Berchtesgaden, the day after the Nazis surrendered on 8 May, the 101st Division was assigned to the Zell-am-See area of Austria and the 506th occupied the town of Kaprun. Their duties became rather routine if not outright tedious.

Occupation duty was fine with Johnny. But high-strung paratroopers used to a steady adrenalin rush became bored and susceptible to mischief. There were accidents, brawls and all sorts of troublesome behavior. Captain Frank West worked equally hard to get both the civilian population and his own men under control. He relied heavily on both of the boys, especially Johnny and his language skills.

"Jake, remember that letter I gave you back in Bastogne?"

"Yeah."

"Let me have it back."

"Jeez, Johnny. I lost that letter." He hesitated. "Actually I burned it." Something inside Jake had told him carrying that letter invited bad fortune. Not that he was superstitious but with the War in Europe being over, he didn't see the need any longer.

"I know you did. So here's a new one. Clean and tightly wrapped." Johnny had a big smile on his face. He handed the white envelope to Jake.

Jake took the letter. "I'll humor you, Johnny. Since the War is over, I won't be giving this to Rose, ever."

Johnny chuckled. "Hey, there's still the Pacific. Rumor has it that anyone staying will wind up fighting the Japs. But if we pull this appeal off, when we're both back in the States, you can give the letter back to me."

"You're nuts, Johnny," Jake laughed.

They moved closer to the door until they were next.

"We go in together, right?" Johnny was becoming anxious. Getting enough points to go stateside was much more important to him than it was to Jake.

"Together, like always."

Captain West opened the door and they both entered the room.

"One at a time," the colonel behind the desk growled without looking up.

West intervened. "They joined my outfit at the same time, from the Eighty-second. I think that's the basis for their appeal."

The colonel shuffled some papers. "At ease. Both Kilroy? Brothers?"

"No sir," Johnny answered.

The colonel shuffled more papers. "I got the Eighty-second service on Sicily but you're still ten points short. The married one is only five short. Anything else?"

"What about Italy? The oil drum drop? On Salerno?" Jake asked.

The colonel turned some pages. "Nothing here about that."

Jake and Johnny looked at each other. They both realized their mission into Rome and the subsequent secrecy must have resulted in cleansing of their personnel files.

Jake was the first to react. "There must be some mistake," he said angrily. He looked for help from Captain West who just shook his head. Whatever happened in Italy was before his time.

"I don't think so, soldier, and besides…" the colonel looked, stopped in mid sentence and stared at Jake.

"Sir," Johnny interrupted. "We participated in the Italian Campaign. If you would just contact General Taylor, he can personally vouch for us."

"I'll do no such thing, Private." The colonel answered Johnny and then looked back to Jake. "Have we met before, Corporal?"

Jake stared back at the slightly crooked nose and pudgy face and immediately recognized the major he had punched and whose boots he had taken in Rheims. "No, sir. I don't believe we've ever met."

Johnny looked at Jake with a quizzical stare. Jake was beginning to sweat. He knew there was no way this officer was going to help them.

The colonel continued. "I think we have met, Corporal." He stamped their petitions, "DENIED" and threw the paperwork into a tray on his desk. "Too bad there are no battle campaign points for Rheims." The colonel's mouth twisted into a cynical smile. "Dismissed!"

The two men left the room and were back out on the street. An extremely disappointed Johnny spoke first. "What the hell was all that about?"

"Sorry, buddy. I am truly sorry."

"About what, Jake? What the hell was that crack about Rheims?"

"That colonel won't help us. We're screwed and it's my fault."

"What the hell are you talking about, Jake?"

"He used to be a major…"

"So?"

"A certain major in Rheims that I liberated a pair of jump boots from."

Johnny stopped. "You're pulling my leg!"

Jake shook his head. "I wish I were."

Johnny took a deep breath and exhaled slowly. "Jesus, Jake. Do you know what you did?"

Jake nodded. Letting his best friend down was the last thing on earth he ever wanted to do.

Johnny struggled to gain control over his rising outrage. He looked around and exhaled loudly. He saw that his friend was inconsolable and Johnny couldn't stand that. With an extraordinary force of will he suppressed his anger and put his arm around Jake's shoulder. "It's not your fault if that pansy-ass colonel doesn't have a sense of humor!" Johnny let out a faint laugh, trying to hide his disappointment.

"Thanks, buddy," Jake smiled. "I owe you big time."

"You owe me?" Johnny asked rhetorically. Then his face lit up with a huge grin. "Fine, you owe me so buy me a beer and don't ever lose my letter again!"

Chapter Seventy

Washington, D.C. - June 1, 2004

Rest easy, sleep well my brothers. Know the line has held, your job is done.
Rest easy, sleep well. Others have taken up where you fell, the line has held.
Peace, peace, and farewell.

Unknown

Twenty-one steps.

J.P. Kilroy counted the number of steps the soldier took before executing a precise ninety-degree turn to face the huge white marble sarcophagus. He paused for what seemed like twenty-one seconds before making another ninety degree turn. The guard deftly shouldered his bayonet-tipped rifle to the damp white-gloved hand facing the gallery before beginning his march back. J.P. watched intently as he stood at the entrance to the Tomb of the Unknowns.

The young soldier was not much over twenty but he moved with a smooth grace and dignity that defied his age. His army dress blue uniform was impeccable and he glided softly down the narrow black carpet, past the Tomb and down to the other end. Waiting there, next to a small green canvas guardhouse, was a sergeant and another physically perfect specimen of a soldier. They executed a series of precise moves, with muted verbal orders, until the second soldier had replaced the first and was "walking post" at the guard position. He would do so for thirty minutes. Though the amphitheatre was full of spectators, not a sound was heard. Even the birds and the breeze seemed to stop as the Sentinel continued his silent vigil in the sober stillness.

The Tomb of the Unknowns was a striking rectangular structure of white marble originally erected in 1931. The Sentinels, as they were called, guarded it continuously since 1937. Seven days a week, twenty-four hours a day, the sleek and trim young soldiers from the Third Infantry Regiment, The Old Guard, paid homage to the deceased warriors by protecting their resting place.

It was a rare privilege to become a member of the Honor Guard who accepted only twenty-percent of those who applied. They had to be formidable of mind and body and dedicated to the duty. Their training was rigorous and meticulous. They had to memorize the resting places of 175 notables within Arlington National Cemetery. To spend five hours each day preparing their uniforms and shining their equipment for duty was not unusual.

Although he lived in Washington, J.P. Kilroy had never been to the Tomb before. He read the pamphlet while he waited. The Third Infantry Regiment, stationed at Fort Myers, Virginia, was the oldest active-duty infantry unit in the army, serving since 1784. The Old Guard remained the army's official ceremonial unit and escort to the President. They also provided the Honor Guard for burials in Arlington National Cemetery as well as for funeral processions for dignitaries.

The most prestigious and desirable assignment for an enlisted person was to be accepted as a Sentinel. Their ranks were commanded entirely by enlisted men and women.

The view past the Tomb was spectacular. Below and beyond, in the distance across the Potomac River, was the city of Washington D.C. with all of its dazzling white monuments and memorials glistening in the brilliant sunshine. On this bright and clear June day the visibility was virtually limitless but J.P. had difficulty looking past the engraving on the tomb.

HERE RESTS IN
HONORED GLORY
AN AMERICAN
SOLDIER
KNOWN BUT TO GOD

The entire scene before him was a moving experience and J.P. felt himself choke up as he observed the reverence and respect the Honor Guard displayed toward their fallen brethren. He once heard someone say that a soldier does not die until he is forgotten. If that were true, he concluded, the Sentinels would assure their comrades in arms would live forever.

At that moment J.P. felt a tug on his sleeve. He turned to meet the smiling gaze of Frank West. The old soldier was wearing his Screaming Eagle windbreaker and American Legion cap festooned with medals and patches. A digital camera hung around his neck. He held one finger to his lips while he grabbed a sleeve and led J.P. down the path out of the amphitheatre. Frank was spry for his age but his short choppy steps were now aided by a rather sturdy bamboo cane with a carved Eagle's head for a handle. He looked older than the last time J.P. saw him. When they were out of earshot he grabbed J.P. and gave him a hug.

"It's so good to see you again, young fella'. Thanks for meeting me here. How long has it been? Two years since Lincoln's funeral?"

"Yes, Lincoln died in oh-two. Time flies. It seems like just yesterday that we met and talked in Bedford at the D-Day Memorial with Dad. September 11. I'll never forget that day."

"No one will."

J.P. continued. "Why did you pick this place to meet? It's a long walk up this hill."

"I always enjoy watching the Honor Guard. I never miss a chance to see them. Impressive, isn't it?"

"Very. I read somewhere that in order to serve in the Honor Guard a soldier must not speak to anyone for the first six months and swear to never drink or curse for the rest of his life."

Frank smiled at J.P. "Not true. They can do whatever they choose in their off-duty hours. But obviously any disgraceful conduct unbecoming would result in forfeiting their Honor Guard badge. And since there are only about four hundred of them in existence, that's a big deal. It's the best deterrent against bringing dishonor to the group and the mission."

J.P. looked confused. "What about the story that during Hurricane Isabelle last year the Sentinels were ordered to take shelter and not march but did so anyway?"

"It's a great story but that's not true either. They were never ordered to stand down but the safety of the troopers would override any ceremonial duties if it came to that."

"How do you know all this?"

Frank chuckled. "My grandson is a Sentinel. You were watching him back there. I came up here to see him and to pay my respects. That's why I called you."

"To what do I owe the pleasure?"

"Since I was in town anyway, I wanted to see you for two things, Mister Kilroy. First, I wanted to visit your father's grave. I'm sorry I missed the funeral last year. I screwed up my back and was in traction for a few weeks." Frank paused but got no reaction from J.P. "Would you show me where his grave site is?"

"Sure, it's down this way."

They walked in silence for a few minutes on a path named Wilson Drive until they came to a fork. The mature trees provided ample shade and the breeze seemed to pick up in the shadows.

J.P. led them to the right on Roosevelt Drive in front of, and well below, the Tomb. He couldn't help but consider that Frank was the last person alive who knew the secret. While J.P. tried hard to let that whole affair slip quietly into his past, every time one of the men died the whole experience came swirling back into his mind. He never got validation of the secret from any of the old men and he never sought to identify his biological father. It was an effort he was not inclined to commit.

Ever since he found out that his dad was not his biological father, he assumed he already knew what the old men were trying to keep from him. But Frank said something at the D-Day Memorial in Bedford that made him question his conclusion. The shock of September 11, along with the wars in Afghanistan and Iraq that followed, were more than enough to occupy his mind to the exclusion of most anything else. Cynthia Powers occupied any spare moments left in his life. But every time he came in contact with any of the conspirators, the old curiosity was resurrected and he found himself questioning his conclusion that the secret was already revealed.

They made a left on Porter Drive adjacent to Section 3 of the cemetery. They walked for a few moments when Frank came to a sudden stop.

"It's a little further up," J.P. advised.

Frank slowly took off his hat. He was staring at a simple white marble gravestone. A small cross was inscribed at the top.

ANTHONY C

MC AULIFFE

GENERAL

US ARMY

WORLD WAR I

WORLD WAR II

KOREA

JUL 2 1898

AUG 22 1975

Frank slowly saluted the marker. "I heard he was buried at Arlington with his wife, son and daughter. This was one great man."

"Who was he?"

"He took command of the division when we went into Bastogne. General Taylor was back in the States at the time. He gave the famous 'NUTS' reply when the Germans called for our surrender. It fired all the troops up."

Frank snapped a picture of the headstone and they began walking again. "Bastogne was hell," Frank continued. "That was where Lincoln won the Medal. I wrote the recommendations and got a bunch of eyewitness accounts, too. I told Lincoln about the all-black parachute battalion forming back in the States. I wrote a letter, got him in." Frank was repeating what he had previously told him but J.P. just let him continue.

"Go on," J.P. kindly encouraged.

"The Jerrys threw everything they had at us. Surrounded us, cut us off and pounded the crap out of our perimeter and bombed the town. Four or five divisions at one time or another, maybe more, who knows, but we stopped them and stacked bodies. It was freezing cold, snowed every day; fog as thick as smoke, and they kept coming and we kept putting meat on the table. Around Christmas the Jerrys gave him," Frank waved at the grave marker, "an ultimatum. Surrender or be destroyed. He answered with one word. 'NUTS'!"

J.P. smiled. He had heard the account either on the History Channel or the National Geographic Channel. It was an inspirational story. They continued walking.

"That boost in morale came at the right time. We were low on everything and Jerry was pressing us really hard. It gave us a rallying cry and pumped up our spirits. McAuliffe basically told the Germans to 'go to hell' with that answer."

483

As they walked, Frank was gazing into the distance as if trying to read the story from some far-away journal. "We held out for eight days. It was so cold. They say pain has no memory but I can still remember the cold and I get chills when I think of it. When the sun finally came out, we got supplies by air and our Thunderbolts and Mustangs gave the Jerrys hell, bombing and strafing their positions. Then we went on the offensive and kicked the crap out of whatever Jerrys were left. Kicked their asses all the way back to Germany. We lost a lot of guys in the Bulge. They were the bravest men I ever knew and they were mostly boys. By the spring of forty-five we were pretty much on occupation duty. After Hitler surrendered most of the high-point men were rotated back to the States. Jake and Johnny were a little short so they stayed on. We all expected to be fighting Japs by the summer."

J.P. jumped in before Frank could continue. "So, sometime after the War in Europe ended, Jake died. I'm still trying to find out how that happened." J.P. could not help himself. There were still some loose ends surrounding the conspiracy.

"Shit happens in the military, son. Let it go."

"It's something I really want to find out the truth about." J.P. stopped walking. "Here we go."

Frank stepped over the low chain and walked up to the headstone. He removed his hat and bowed his head. The top of the arched white stone had an engraved cross. The inscription read:

JOHN

KILROY

CORPORAL

US ARMY

WORLD WAR II

FEB 9 1924

OCT 15 2003

Frank handed his digital camera to J.P. "Would you mind?"

Frank walked up to the stone and struggled to kneel beside it. With his arm around the stone he motioned to J.P. "Get closer." J.P. moved in a few steps, snapped a few pictures and helped Frank to his feet.

"Thank you, son. I just had to pay my respects." They continued walking on Porter Drive.

"You said you were in town anyway. What for?" J.P. asked.

Frank looked at him as if he had three heads. "They dedicated the World War II Memorial this past Saturday. The place was packed with old veterans the whole Memorial Day weekend. I wouldn't have missed that for the world. Not for anything!"

"Of course." J.P. mentally slapped himself in the head. How could he have forgotten the official dedication this weekend even though the site had been open to the public since late April?

"You said you wanted to see me for two things. What was the other?"

Frank smiled. "I'm buying lunch today. It's just me paying off an old debt."

J.P. laughed. "There's no need to…"

"I insist. Besides, you'll be celebrating a birthday soon. Call it an early birthday present. How old? Of course, I know." Frank did some mental math. "Born on D-Day. That would make you an even sixty this year. Congratulations, young man."

J.P. smiled. To Frank he was a young man. Then why was he feeling so old? They came to another intersection and Frank led them left on Grant Drive. They continued walking.

"In that case, if you insist," J.P. smiled. "But I don't have a lot of time."

"Big shot reporter like you can grab a long lunch hour occasionally, I'm pretty sure," Frank stated emphatically.

"I suppose," J.P. agreed. "Are we going now?"

"In a few minutes, Mister Kilroy. Right after we pay a short visit to my old friend, Lincoln."

Chapter Seventy-One

Joigny, France - August 15, 1945

"Only the dead have seen the end of war."

Plato (c. 428 BC – c. 347 BC)

Finally, there was something to celebrate.

July had been a depressing and frustrating month for Jake and Johnny. After being denied their appeal to be sent home, they had to incur the indignity of saying goodbye to friends and acquaintances on their way back to the States. Over 800 of their fellow paratroopers and over 500 officers were transferred to the 501st PIR, which was to serve as a vehicle to transport all high-point men back to America for discharge. These fortunate troopers were to be replaced by low point men from other airborne divisions and newly trained replacements.

The word had come down the 101st Airborne Division had been classified as Category II, which meant they would be redeployed to the Pacific to fight the Japanese. Soon after, General Taylor announced the division was going back to the States into Strategic Reserve. The first move would be back to France. The men considered the most recent plan good news but unreliable. Circumstances had a nasty habit of changing drastically and rapidly in the army.

At the end of July, most of the 101st Airborne loaded onto "forty and eight", railroad cars and left Austria. The rest left by truck convoy for the three-day trip to the ancient Roman towns of Auxerre, Sens and Joigny. After the relative comfort of the hotels and billets in private homes in Austria, the paratroopers were appalled by the squalid conditions in France.

The 506th PIR was assigned to garrison the town of Joigny, the smallest of the three towns situated on the Yonne River between Sen and Auxerre. They bivouacked in abandoned French barracks and did their best to repair the broken windows and doors and clean up the area to make it passably livable. Their barracks were run down and the plumbing was inadequate and unsanitary. The impatient airborne troopers were already in a resentful mood and the living conditions did not help. Their officers initiated a stepped-up training regimen and an accelerated organized sports program but could not completely remedy the anxiety and disappointment of their men. They had survived the War thus far and just wanted to get home.

Given the circumstances, there was bound to be trouble and it manifested itself mostly in brawls in taverns in the towns. There were frequent fights among troopers and between the military and civilians. Divisional command acted promptly to squash the unruly violence. Passes were restricted and additional Military Police were assigned to patrol the towns. Airborne paratroopers were conscripted into military police duties, as rowdy paratroopers were slightly less likely to pick a fight with one of their own. It was not unusual for the number of duty MPs to be equal to the number of passes issued on any given night. Predictably, the violence subsided.

The news on 7 August garnered the attention of the world. A new super weapon, an Atomic Bomb, was dropped on Japan. The entire city of Hiroshima was destroyed. This news did not elicit any sympathy from the paratroopers. They had passed through Munich on their trip back and it was nothing more than one huge bombed-out ruin. There was no compassion for the foe who started the War and who killed so many of their friends. There was only astonishment that one bomb could demolish an entire city and thankfulness that America alone had it. When a second bomb destroyed the city of Nagasaki, the veteran paratroopers were confident they would never have to invade Japan. The survivors of North Africa, Sicily, Italy, Normandy, Holland, Bastogne, Alsace and Germany had no way of knowing America had already used all the special bombs it had manufactured.

When news of the Japanese surrender circulated through the ranks, the mood of the troopers was pure euphoria. They had survived the damn War and would make it safely home. Letters were hastily written, plans were solidified and celebrations abounded.

Jake and Johnny were drinking cognac as they celebrated the end of the War. Johnny was more enthusiastic. He had a family waiting but he tempered his delight so as not to make Jake feel any worse. Jake had been more subdued since Macie left him but appeared much happier tonight. Johnny assumed Jake feigned a measure of cheerfulness so as not to spoil the celebration.

Johnny tapped the bar and ordered two more cognacs. They already had too much. "I can't wait to get home to see my kid."

Jake downed the last of his drink and slammed the empty glass on the bar. "We made it, Yank. There were times I wasn't so sure."

"Yeah, we had some close calls, brother. But I think I'm going home the same guy who came into this War."

"You think so? Because I'm sure not the same," Jake disagreed.

"I'm pretty sure I didn't let anything I saw or did change me a whole lot."

"Well, Johnny, you're a better man than me. I can't wait to get back home and start over. There is way too much I don't know or understand so, like I said, I'm going back to school on that GI Bill."

"Good for you, Jake. You'll do great!"

The bartender poured two glasses. Jake picked up his. "Here's to all the guys who won't be going home."

"I'll drink to that."

They downed their shots and both slammed their glasses down. After paying the bill they headed back toward the barracks. It was a warm night and they were in no hurry. They talked about things soldiers talked about since the beginning of warfare. They talked about the chow, they talked about their friends and they talked about home.

Johnny noticed Jake was in an exceptionally good mood. Gone were the mood swings that dominated his personality since Macie left him. Whatever it was that changed his outlook and attitude, Johnny was confident he would hear about it soon enough.

As they neared the barracks compound, a paratrooper MP stepped out of the guardhouse.

"Let's see your identification and passes!"

Both paratroopers were taken by surprise. "Hey Mac," Johnny answered. "Aren't you supposed to keep guys from getting *out*? Not prevent us from getting back in?" He laughed at his own joke. Jake giggled along with him. They made a move to walk around the guard.

"Hey, I gave you an order. Show me your ID." The guard stepped in front of them.

"Okay General Patton, let me see what I can find," Johnny joked while he fumbled around with his pockets on unsteady feet.

Jake held Johnny up. "I'm with him." There were childish grins on both their faces.

After a moment Johnny turned to the guard. "Nope, I seem to have misplaced all my shit." He turned to Jake. "Do you have any shit to prove who we are?"

Jake shook his head vigorously. "We just need to get some sack. Check us in the morning." He took another step and the guard blocked him, placing his hand on the flap over his pistol.

Both paratroopers stopped laughing and tried to gather themselves. Jake noticed the guard was wobbling a bit. "Have you been drinking soldier?" Jake asked.

"You guys are drunk," the guard exclaimed.

"We're supposed to be drunk," Jake shot back. "But you're supposed to be sober." He pointed a finger in his chest. "Now get the fuck out of the way before I rip your arm off and shove it up your ass."

The guard stepped back and pulled out his .45.

"Whoa, slow down," Johnny pleaded. "No need for that shit. Call the duty sergeant. He can vouch for us."

The .45 was pointed down. The guard looked nervous and confused. He got himself into something he didn't know how to get out of. "You guys think you're so damn tough? You're not all that tough! You'll see. I'll show you!"

Johnny recognized the words. He studied the guard's face. He was a replacement but Johnny suddenly recognized the harelip.

"Didn't we meet in Bastogne?" Johnny asked.

The guard stepped back a half step to look at the paratroopers' faces. "Maybe."

"We know this guy?" Jake asked.

"Yeah, we do. Bastogne." Johnny kept his gaze on the guard. "He was going in the other direction. From the Golden Lions. Took off and ran out as I remember. Tom, isn't it?"

Tom English became indignant. "No I didn't. My regiment surrendered. Everybody knows that."

Jake answered. "Yeah, everybody knows they surrendered at noon on 19 December. But not everybody knows you were already in Bastogne with us at noon on 19 December." Jake was making quick calculations in his head. "So it seems like you had a pretty good head start getting back. Maybe you left the day before?"

English began to sweat nervously. "Yeah, maybe, but I stayed in Bastogne and fought. And I joined the paratroopers and that proves I'm no coward."

Jake became angry. "It proves nothing, you stupid one-day wonder. The bravest men I ever knew worked for months to earn that patch and jump wings and you sneak in the back door and get it all in one day? That's bullshit. And you think you're equal to us? You may wear the patch but you'll never be airborne to me, you candy-ass little pussy!"

Tom English raised the pistol but it was not the deterrent he had hoped for. He had angered Jake far too much. "And another thing you chickenshit, rat-bastard coward. Why the hell are you playing cop and hassling real paratroopers? I'm going to my captain and report what a sorry son of a bitch you are for drinking on duty. We'll see how long you keep that patch!"

Tom English raised the pistol and Jake lunged to disarm him. Before they came together, Johnny saw what was about to happen and leaped in for the pistol. The three struggled for a moment, twisting and turning in a tight scrum until the deafening crack of a pistol shot stilled the night.

Chapter Seventy-Two

Washington D.C. - June 6, 2007

"In peace, sons bury their fathers. In war, fathers bury their sons."

Herodotus (c. 484 BC - c. 425 BC)

"Happy Birthday!"

Cynthia Powers brought the small cake into the dining room of the condo. Two small number-shaped candles adorned the top, a six and a three. J.P. was already sitting at the table gathering up the dinner plates and silverware. He smiled as she approached.

"Where's my present?"

"Later," she nodded toward the bedroom.

"In that case..." he got up and quickly cleared the table.

After the dishes were in the dishwasher and Cynthia had poured two cups of steaming hot black decaf coffee, they sat down to enjoy thin slices of his birthday cake.

"I can't ever enjoy my birthday without thinking of my father," he hesitated. "I mean the man who raised me. D-Day, the sixth of June."

"Oh, that reminds me." She hopped off her chair and grabbed the pile of mail she hastily dropped on the hallway table. She flipped through it quickly until she found one particular manila envelope. It was addressed to J.P. She brought it to the table.

"I was so anxious to get the cake into the freezer I forget this was there."

J.P. looked at the return address. It was from Frank West's widow. J.P. had attended the funeral just two weeks prior. It was another touching ceremony at Arlington National Cemetery with full honors. He tore open the envelope. There was a handwritten note along with a picture.

> *Thank you for attending the burial Mr. Kilroy. Frank always spoke well of you. He asked me to send this to you after he passed. He said you would understand. I wish I could be more helpful but Frank didn't share much with me regarding you or your situation.*
>
> *Respectfully,*
> *Gilda West*

J.P. held the picture. It was one he took a few years ago at Arlington National Cemetery. Frank was kneeling at his father's gravestone. His right arm was on top of the stone. His left hand was gripping the side of the stone. J.P. studied it for a moment and handed it to Cynthia.

"Do you see anything here?"

She looked at it for a moment. "Just a man kneeling by a grave." She handed it back.

J.P. kept looking at the picture as he spoke. "Every time I feel like I got this behind me, something happens to stir it up again. More than once I was determined to let it go but Frank kept hinting I still didn't get it. Of all the guys, he seemed like the only one who really wanted me to know the truth. Even from beyond the grave he won't give it up but keeps sending me clues." J.P. shook his head in curious disbelief as he propped the picture up against the sugar bowl and continued to study it. "I'm getting too old to worry about this shit!"

Cynthia saw the writing on the back of the photo, reached across the table and read the comment. "When you see it, find Macie Vance. Frank."

"See what?" he said aloud.

Cynthia studied the picture of a white marble gravestone.

JOHN

KILROY

CORPORAL

US ARMY

WORLD WAR II

FEB 9 1924

OCT 15 2003

"Who is Macie Vance?" she asked.

"I believe she was Jake's girlfriend or fiancée before she sent him a Dear John."

Cynthia studied the picture. "It's got to be here. We're both staring at it. Whatever it is."

J.P. picked up the picture and held it up. Nothing! Then he flipped it upside down, still nothing. "At least he could have pointed me in the right direction," he finally said in desperation.

Cynthia took the picture. "Pointed? I think he did," she said. "Look at his index finger on the hand gripping the side of the stone. It's pointing between John and Kilroy."

J.P. studied the picture from that perspective. He let out a deep sigh. "Oh, my God!"

"You see something?" she asked.

"I think I do and I can't believe it." He leaned back in his chair, looked up and tapped his forehead with the heel of his hand. "Can you pull some strings for me and find Macie Vance?"

Chapter Seventy-Three

Charleston, South Carolina – June 20, 2007

"Women who stepped up were measured as citizens of the nation, not as women…this was a people's war and everyone was in it."

Colonel Oveta Culp Hobby (1905 - 1995)

J.P. Kilroy walked stiffly into a salty, brisk wind coming off a restless Charleston Harbor. The numerous American flags that flanked both sides of the concrete causeway snapped and fluttered in the vigorous, humid breeze. The walkway was about 700 feet long and led from the parking lot of the welcome pavilion directly to the wharfs and the ships. He walked inside the painted yellow line that separated the narrow walkway from the wider driveway. At the end of the causeway was the massive bulk of the aircraft carrier USS *Yorktown (CV-10)*. She was the 900-foot long centerpiece of the Patriot's Point Naval and Maritime Museum. What he had come specifically to see was situated on the hangar deck of the vintage World War II aircraft carrier.

J.P. Kilroy followed the signs that led to a series of switchback metal stairs. He ascended to a platform level with the hangar deck and stepped inside the cavernous space. The breeze was less forceful within the ship even though some of the sliding shutters that adorned both sides were raised open. In front of him was the visitor's Information Desk, a long counter staffed by three people, one elderly man, a middle aged man and an elderly woman.

While he waited his turn, J.P. stared off to his right down the huge hangar deck. There were numerous World War II aircraft on display as well as many exhibits and memorials with period pictures. There were tributes to the heroes of carrier aviation as well as aviation and space flight. He could barely see the theater at the bow and concluded it showed continuous documentaries of the ship and its collection of artifacts.

It was a weekday and there were not many people in attendance. Most of the tourists were older couples. Some of the men were very old, a few in wheelchairs. He observed them as they explored the ship and their own frail memories with obvious emotion.

When his turn came, J.P. stepped up to the man in the middle. The man wore a Vietnam Veteran baseball cap with a Military Police designation. J.P. did not recognize the four ribbons embroidered on the peak of the cap. While the man was sliding over a pamphlet, J.P. snuck a look at the baseball caps on the man and woman on either side. Both caps were black and simply said USS *Yorktown (CV-10)* in bright yellow letters. They looked old enough to have actually served aboard the ship in wartime except one was a woman.

"Welcome aboard, sir," the man broke J.P.'s concentration on the other hats. "We have six self-guided tours here on the *Yorktown* but if you don't have time for them all, I recommend tours number three and six, along with the hangar deck." He opened the pamphlet and pointed to the small map, which showed the starting places for all the tours.

J.P. lifted his head toward the area behind the Information Desk. "I'd like to start there," he said referring to the light blue structure trimmed in white stripes. The name over the entrance said simply, "Medal of Honor Museum".

"Of course," the man agreed. "It just opened last month. Very popular although you'll have it all to yourself today."

The museum was about a hundred feet wide and took up half the width of the huge hangar deck. J.P. pushed the entrance door open and stepped into the dark. The warm, moist air gave way to a dark, cool and dry space. It surprised him. He blinked to adjust his eyes. On the near right wall of this first room was a floor to ceiling rendition of the Tomb of the Unknown. The scene was comfortably familiar to him. A soldier facing the Tomb was holding a salute. The left wall revealed the history of the Medal of Honor. Continuing on the right wall were randomly placed flat screen televisions showing various pictures of Americana. The pictures were accompanied by a continual audio track of what it means to be free in America. There were many voices but J.P. recognized Tom Brokaw's voice immediately.

The next room was small and circular. Across the top of the room, close to the ceiling was a metal banner, which read "Medal of Honor Society". This society of living recipients was the curator of the Medal of Honor museum. On the right were replicas of the Medals of Honor for the three armed services of the United States. They all shared the common ribbon scheme of white stars on a blue field and differed only slightly in the design of the medal itself. Above the replicas was a quote from President John F. Kennedy.

> *A nation reveals itself not only by the men it produces,*
> *but also by the men it honors, the men it remembers.*

J.P. turned to exit this room and stepped into a corridor he would later learn was called the Combat Tunnel. It was a long darkened enclosed walkway with handrails on each side. Beyond the rails and at angles above and below the walkway were darkened battle scenes from a number of wars.

For the second time, J.P. was startled as a motion activated sensor lit up the screens on each side of him. As he walked, the sounds changed to match the pictures of that particular conflict. The noises ranged from musket and machine gun fire to aircraft engines and bomb explosions. The walkway was about thirty feet long and each panel lit up in turn with the accompanying audio sounds as J.P. made his way along. At the end of the Combat Tunnel was an exhibit honoring the youngest Medal of Honor winner, twelve year old William "Willie" Johnston in the Civil War.

J.P. then entered the Hall of Heroes with alcoves alternating left and right. He went from exhibit to exhibit, each one emphasizing a different conflict. He noticed the name Dr. Mary E. Walker who won her Medal during the Civil War, the only woman ever so honored. He recognized some household names as he passed through the various alcoves; names like Sergeant Alvin York, Audie Murphy, Eddie Rickenbacker, Teddy Roosevelt and Senator Daniel Inouye.

He finally found what he was looking for in the next room. It was a large round room with kiosks containing four touch screens encased in plastic and metal. They were obviously designed for rough use. He stepped up to one of the screens and touched it. It immediately lit up. On the left side of the screen was a list of search filters. He selected CONFLICT and then SECOND WORLD WAR. The next filter was BIRTHPLACE. He scrolled and selected NEW YORK. A list of names appeared and he used the touch screen to scroll to K. There was no Kilroy. He reset the screen and started over. Same result. He moved to another touch screen and repeated the process more deliberately. There was nothing between KIDD and KIMBRO. He stared at the screen, nodding his head. Then he reset the criteria by touching NEW SEARCH and repeated all the previous criteria. When he selected BIRTHPLACE, instead of selecting NEW YORK, his fingers hovered above VIRGINIA. He hesitated.

"Having difficulty? Maybe I can help." The woman's soft voice startled him. It was the elderly woman he had seen at the information desk; the one with the *Yorktown* baseball cap. She was tall, slim and rather striking for her age, which J.P. figured to be between seventy and eighty. Her hair was silver-white and well manicured. She carried a walking cane. There was a small mole on her upper lip.

"Ah...I don't know," he replied. "I don't think so..."

"Move over," she interrupted with a smile and nudged him over with her hip and shoulder. She then selected VIRGINIA.

"No, no," he corrected her.

"Shush," she answered and started scrolling down the names. She came to the name John Kilroy and pressed it. Up on the screen flashed a picture of his father. He stood there in silent bewilderment. Next to the picture was information on Birthplace, Rank in Action, Service Branch, Conflict, Unit and Occupation. He read the Citation quickly. Everything matched what he knew about his father except Birthplace. His suspicion was starting to gain traction.

"What just happened here?" he asked the woman.

"You probably never read your father's citation carefully enough or you would have found out years ago. They were all afraid you would." She appeared relaxed and confident.

"Found out what?" he asked, still totally in the dark. "Who are *they*?"

"All in good time, John." She slid her right arm under his left and clutched it with her free arm. "If you might help an old lady to a seat, I'll explain everything to you. You've traveled a long way and it's long past time you knew the truth."

"How did you know my name?"

"I was expecting you, John. I recognized you from your father's funeral although I had to lay low for the short time you were there. My name is Macie Vance."

J.P. was stunned. His knees buckled slightly and he dropped his pamphlet. He smiled sheepishly as he bent to retrieve it. "Nice to meet you."

She led him through the last few rooms of the museum, past the video testimonials of living Medal recipients and the large bronze memorial wreath and guided him out the exit and toward the stern of the big ship's hangar deck. They walked slowly in silence, her steps matching his. They headed toward the snack bar where there were a dozen large round wooden tables. She took a seat at one of them.

"You need to get me a nice hot tea, John," she smiled at him. "They don't like it when you just sit here and not buy anything."

"Of course," he sprang up to the counter and ordered two.

At last, after years of probing and searching, interviewing and interrogating, he would finally get some answers. He had buried his mother and his father and everyone else who knew his father in wartime and had all but lost hope he would ever get to the bottom of it all. After ten fast years in which he alternated between his own life and the search, he had metaphorically thrown in the towel after Frank West died. When they all passed on, all hope of fulfilling his mother's last wish was dashed. Now, at least, he just might find out what so many people conspired to keep from him. He would finally learn the truth. And then, perhaps, finally find peace.

He brought the two cups of steaming tea back to the table. He took a seat right beside her. Macie was waiting patiently.

"The Hall of Heroes is my favorite," she whispered as she tested the hot tea with a small sip. "Last month on May twenty-third they cut the ribbon, opened the new museum…forty live Medal recipients. NBC News and that Williams guy were here. Then we had a gala party on the flight deck. Quite a show."

"Yes, ma'am, I imagine it was quite a show." His impatience was tearing at him. He put some sugar in his tea and a dash of milk. He smiled at her and waited for her to continue. J.P. glanced up and noticed they were sitting directly underneath a B-25 Mitchell Medium Bomber hung from the hangar deck ceiling by thick cables. It was part of the Doolittle Raid exhibit. *Were bombs about to drop?* He watched her sip her tea. "You had something to tell me?"

She looked at him. "The man you knew as your father, the man who raised you was…John Kilroy of Bedford, Virginia. We all called him Jake."

Chapter Seventy-Four

Joigny, France - August 15, 1945

"Whom the gods love dies young."

Menander (342 BC - 291 BC)

The single shot echoed loudly through the night. For a few seconds everything was quiet. Johnny screamed and fell to the ground while Jake shoved Tom English violently out of the way. Johnny was holding the barrel of the .45, still pointing toward his stomach, his thumb stuck in the slide.

Paratroopers came running over from all directions. Jake knelt down beside Johnny and pulled the slide back on the pistol, releasing his thumb. He felt for the wound around Johnny's stomach and his hand came back covered in blood.

"I got ya' buddy. You're gonna' be all right." Jake took off his jacket and rolled it quickly into a pillow for Johnny's head. He then applied pressure to the hole in Johnny's jacket where he thought the wound would be. "Medic," he instinctively yelled. "Somebody call a medic!"

"What the hell happened, Jake?" It was Sergeant Christian's voice.

"That drunken dead-beat guard shot him." Jake didn't look up. He just nodded toward English as he tried to stem the bleeding.

"He's a dead man. We're gonna' fuck him up." Christian and two other paratroopers began stomping English before they dragged him off kicking and screaming.

Corporal Leland Brewer ran up to the scene.

Jake looked up. "Beerman! Am I glad to see you!"

Brewer felt around the wound. "Aw shit, Jake. This is bad. I don't have my stuff."

"Go get it!"

"Be right back." Beerman took off for the infirmary.

Johnny was breathing heavy, his eyes wide with anxiety. Suddenly he pounded the ground with his fist. "Shit! Goddamn it! I can't believe this!"

"Calm down, buddy. You're gonna' be fine."

"He pulled a pistol on us! I can't believe he did that. That little shit pulled his weapon on *us*."

"He pulled it on *me*, Johnny." Jake closed his eyes and shook his head. "Why'd you get in the way?"

"Where is he?"

"Some of our guys took him. They're kicking the shit out of him. I think they're gonna' kill him."

"Let me see," Johnny tried to raise his head. Jake was not sure if he wanted to look at the wound or English being dragged toward the barracks.

"Stay down. Stay calm. Beerman is getting his stuff."

"Beerman. Good man. Great medic. Gonna' be a doctor when he gets home." Johnny's breathing was labored and shallow.

"I need a meat wagon here," Jake yelled out. Some more troopers were gathering around. Someone dropped a towel and Jake used it as a compress.

"Oh, man. I almost made it. I almost made it home."

"You'll make it home. We're gonna' get you to the infirmary hubba-hubba and they're gonna' take care of you."

Someone dropped to his knees alongside Jake. It was Captain Frank West. "What the hell happened?"

"Trigger happy sentry, sir. The boys took him to the barracks."

West looked at Johnny. "Stay with us, son. Help is on the way."

Johnny's eyes calmed though his breathing remained rapid and strained. "Jake, brother." Johnny forced a smile. "Can you get off my legs?"

Jake looked down and then at West. Neither of them was on Johnny's legs.

"We have to roll him over," ordered West. He looked at Johnny. "Hang tough, trooper."

They rolled him partly on his side and West took out a flashlight. There was an exit wound on Johnny's lower back near the spine. They gently rolled him to his back.

"What's there?" Johnny asked anxiously. "What do you see?"

No one answered. Johnny took a deep breath and exhaled. "No one's kneeling on my legs. It's my spine right?"

"Don't give up on me, buddy. Don't quit. Hang on."

Johnny punched the ground again with his fist. "Don't rush, don't hurry. I'm not going home like this."

"Johnny, save your breath. Don't give up!"

"That's an order, son," West added. He turned to look for some help. About a dozen troopers had gathered around. The call had been put out for an ambulance and Beerman was off getting his supplies and trying to round up a doctor. But West could not see anyone racing toward the scene. Johnny was bleeding out and help was not imminent.

"Jake, come closer."

"I'll take that," West pointed to the towel. Jake took the pressure off. The towel was soaked blood red. Captain West began to apply pressure as Jake moved toward Johnny's head. He cradled his head in his arms. There still was a chance to save him if he could only get Johnny to want to live.

"You have a wife and son, home. You have to fight!"

"Do you still have my letter?"

"Sure, I still got it. I was giving it back to you tonight!"

"Good, you bring it to Rose… in person… like you promised… right?"

"Don't talk like that! Don't give up, for her sake. You're gonna' make it!"

"I don't want to make it. Not like this."

"Look, buddy, don't quit on me!"

"Jake, I don't have a lot of time. I don't want to spend what's left arguing with you. I love you like a brother. I need you to promise me something."

"Sure!"

"I need to ask you to take care of my family. I need to know they'll be in good hands."

Jake blinked. Tears began streaming from his eyes. "Jeez, I would do anything for you, buddy. You know that. But how am I supposed to do that?"

"I don't expect her to stay single forever. Bring her my letter. Use your charm!"

Jake looked at Captain West. His eyes asking *what do I do now? How do I deal with this?*

West nodded. His facial expression replied *tell him what he wants to hear.*

Johnny coughed. He was spitting up blood. He grabbed Jake's collar and pulled him close to his face. "C'mon brother. You can do this. You have nothing to go home to anyway. I need to know my family is…in good hands. In *your* hands!"

Jake smiled slightly. He wanted to reassure his dying friend; make his last moments bearable. He wanted to say he would try his hardest but it would be up to Rose. He never got to share the news he had a letter in his pocket from Macie asking him to come back to her. And now, at this moment, he knew he never would. Looking into the pleading and desperate eyes of the friend he loved, he could not bring himself to excuses or explanations. "Of course, buddy. I'll take care of them."

Johnny smiled back. His face instantly became relieved. "Is that a blood pact?" Johnny weakly raised a fist.

Jake tapped it with his. "You have my word."

"That's all I needed to hear. There's no one on this earth I would rather have raise my son and take care of my gal than you. No one!"

Johnny's hand slipped from Jake's collar. He leaned back on his makeshift pillow. He began to cry through labored breathing. "I feel cold…like Bastogne! It's so damn cold!"

Jake was crying. He reached down and cradled Johnny's head and shoulders in his arms. He hugged Johnny tightly to provide warmth, rocking him ever so slightly. Jake looked at West. All three men had tear-streaked faces. Jake held his friend tightly and gently rocked him until he expelled his last breath.

Chapter Seventy-Five

Charleston, South Carolina – June 20, 2007

"There is nothing on this earth more to be prized than true friendship."

Saint Thomas Aquinas (1225 - 1274)

Macie made the revelation with the calm conviction of someone who was certain of the truth.

J.P. folded his hands and looked at her. "I learned a lot from his buddies. I know they were both back in the States in September of forty-three and they stayed in my parents' apartment for one night." He hesitated, trying not to contradict this nice old lady. "Are you telling me my mother had an affair with Jake that night?" The words sounded foreign, like they were coming from someone else. "And I'm the result?" He pondered the unlikely thought for a moment. "Because I already know the man who raised me is not my biological father and if I were Jake's son, that would explain it. Is that the big secret everyone was trying so hard to keep from me?"

"No, silly!" she admonished. "You have it all backwards."

"Well, that's a relief," he exhaled. "And Frank said the same thing, that I had it upside down. But you said Jake was my father?"

"No, John, I didn't say Jake was your real father. What I said was the father you knew, the father you grew up with, *that* man was Jake Kilroy. John Patrick Kilroy was your biological father but he never made it home. *Jake* raised you."

J.P. nodded. He considered that possibility when he realized the name on the tombstone had no middle initial. That was either a mistake or the person lying there was John NMI Kilroy. However, there were too many unanswered questions to arrive at that conclusion. "This makes no sense, Macie. How can that be?"

"Let me explain," she took another sip of her tea. "It gets complicated so try to keep up." She smiled her disarming smile. "Johnny, your biological father, was killed in France in 1945, right after the War ended. Unfortunately, a drunken American soldier killed him. On his deathbed he asked Jake to promise to take care of you and your mother. Jake gave his word. And once Jake gave his word, it was written in stone! Besides, Jake always blamed himself for Johnny being killed over there. It was a guilt he never got over."

J.P. contemplated what Macie just told him. "So, that's why he failed the paternity test," he mumbled aloud. "So, why did he pretend to be my real father? Why didn't he ever tell me who he was or who my real father was?"

"Jake was too modest to tell anyone what he was doing. That he was giving up his own life to raise his friend's son. He didn't want anyone else to know. It was Jake who made everyone promise to keep the secret, even your mother. He certainly didn't want your mother embarrassed. Neither of them had any family. It was an easy ruse to pull off. So he stayed with you and your mother until you were grown and on your way in life and then he came home to Bedford and back to me. Then the Medal of Honor thing came up and he figured if he went back to Washington, he was likely to run into you, with the publicity and all. He was trying to avoid that. With Harley's help Jake pretended to be dead to avoid the ceremony. He wanted you to have the Medal. Harley just reminded everyone involved they made a pledge to keep Jake's secret. They didn't realize until later that your mother had sent you on the mission to reconcile with your father and find out the secret. It wouldn't have mattered. Even after your mother passed, it was a matter of honor for them to keep their promise." She touched his hand. "Jake always had your best interest in mind."

"But to do that? Give up his own life and dreams to keep a promise?"

"Let me explain. Jake and I were engaged when I sent him a Dear John letter. I was a confused kid," she smiled again. "When he got the letter he went a little crazy and wound up punching an officer. A few months later, when they each missed rotation back to the States by a few points, they went to appeal. The appeals officer was the one Jake hit. Of course, the officer denied them on the spot."

"The point is?" he asked.

"The point is Jake felt totally responsible for his friend not making it home. He never got over that guilt. They would have gotten the needed points on appeal but for Jake hitting that officer. Then the night your father was killed, Jake got into an argument with an armed sentry who was drunk. Your father tried to break it up and stepped in front of Jake and was shot and killed." She paused, her eyes welling up. "Jake was overwhelmed with guilt. In his own mind and heart, Jake caused your father's death and was honor-bound to keep his last request. For Jake, it was also a small piece of redemption."

"Unbelievable," J.P. shook his head.

"And your father believed Jake had no one to go home to anyway. He was wrong. Jake had me but he could never tell Johnny we had reconciled."

Chapter Seventy-Six

Marseilles, France - November 4, 1945

"Adapt yourself to the environment in which your lot has been cast, and show true love to the fellow-mortals with whom destiny has surrounded you."

Marcus Aurelius (AD 121 - AD 180)

Corporal Jake Kilroy leaned over the rail of the USS *Wooster Victory*, an American fast steam turbine troopship. He held the letter from Macie he had repeatedly read since receiving it in August. This time it hit him hard. The irony was so thick it was almost comical. *No*, he thought, *more like a Greek tragedy.*

He watched the wharf as the last of the American soldiers, barracks bags piled high on their shoulders, ambled up the gangway and onto the ship. Most wore the red, white and blue patch of the 75th Infantry Division. The division was scheduled for deactivation and high-point men from other divisions were transferred into the 75th for the trip home. Many of the transferees were from the 101st Airborne Division. It was distasteful for a paratrooper to belong to any unit other than an airborne unit, especially a straight-legged infantry outfit. Not that the 75th was a poor division. On the contrary, they were respected as a hard-fighting outfit. Their original nickname, the "Diaper Division", given to them because they were so new in the ETO, gave way to their ultimate nickname, "Bulge Busters". That moniker was hard earned as they fought fiercely for ninety-four consecutive days to help push the fanatical Germans out of the Ardennes and back to the Fatherland. Still, they weren't airborne!

As a matter of mild protest, the Screaming Eagles continued to sport their own Eagle patch despite orders to the contrary. Even the airborne officers defied the orders. The patch was sacred to the paratroopers and no one pressed the issue, as they were aware every single member of the Screaming Eagles of the 101st Airborne Division was in a particularly foul mood.

Captain Frank West walked over. "How are you doing, Jake?" West leaned over the railing alongside him.

"I'm okay, Sir. Not looking forward to getting home. Not as much as I thought I would be. Johnny and me…we were supposed to make this trip together. It's just not the same now."

West nodded. "For sure. That's a tall order Johnny left you with."

"Oh, don't get me wrong, Sir. I'll do it if I can but I can't imagine Rose letting me take care of her and the baby. There better be some magic in this letter Johnny wrote to her." He tapped the breast pocket of his combat blouse.

They leaned against the ship's rail in silence for a few minutes. The dock crane was pulling the gangway away from the ship. Glints of bright sunlight sparkled from the gleaming metal stairway. The seagulls, disturbed by the motion, complained loudly as they scattered in all directions into the clear Sunday sky.

West broke the silence. "Johnny was a great guy and an outstanding paratrooper. We're all going to miss him." West turned around and stared out to sea. "We're going to miss a lot of those guys, good guys who put themselves between their country and its enemies. All those great lives not lived, children never born." West choked up a little. "The world will never know what pieces of humanity are missing from it and our countrymen could never be thankful enough for what they sacrificed for our liberty."

Jake knew West took every casualty hard. He wrote to the family of every man he lost. Both of them, along with many others, suffered from survivor's guilt. They simply suppressed that emotion as deeply as they could and carried on. Jake leaned his back on the railing.

"I can't believe they're deactivating our division," Jake blurted out in a surly tone. "After what we did at Normandy, Holland and especially Bastogne. It's just not fair to the guys who didn't make it. I thought the Eagles would be an active division forever."

"You and everyone else, Jake. Nobody can believe what those stupid idiots in the War Department did." West had an edge in his voice. "When General Lee formed the division he told everyone we had no history but we had a rendezvous with destiny. That turned out to be Bastogne. We're the only division to get a Presidential Unit Citation in the history of the army. We created a legacy for future warriors to follow and a tradition to be proud of. And what do the damn pencil pushers do? They did what the Jerrys could never do. They wiped out our division! Dumb shits!"

The deck began to vibrate as the engines started up. Longshoremen released the lines and the tugs began to edge the ship from its berth. The long awaited journey home was finally at hand.

"What do you have there?" West asked pointing to the letter in Jake's hand.

Jake put a wry smile on his face. "This is what Johnny would call irony. Or maybe he would call it a Greek tragedy." Jake handed the letter to West.

It was short letter and West finished it quickly. He had a dumbstruck look on his face.

"Can you believe that, sir? Macie wants me back and I'm headed for New York City. Would you call that a tragedy, or what?"

West nodded. "It's certainly a twist the ancient Greek playwrights would appreciate. Shakespeare too. What are you going to do, Jake?" West handed back the letter. "Would you take Macie back?"

"Absolutely, with no questions asked. She's always been in my life. I thought she always would be my destiny. On the other hand, if I can convince Rose to keep me around, I'll keep my promise to Johnny. I'll take care of them." He paused.

"And I'll do my best to persuade her but if Rose throws me out, I have a place to go." Jake folded the letter and stuffed it in his pocket. "I'll answer Macie's letter after I know which way the wind blows in New York City."

West shook his head. "Good luck, Jake. I don't envy you." He pulled out a small notebook from his pocket and scribbled something. He tore the page out and handed it to Jake. "Here is my home address, Jake. If you need anything… anything at all just let me know. If I can help in any way, I owe it to you and Johnny. Remember! Anything at all."

"I'll remember that, Sir. And thank you."

"You can call me Frank." West smiled to himself. "Just don't call me Casper."

Just then the deep-throated ship's steam whistle blared a long note followed by a few short blasts. The gulls scattered again. The deck vibrations strengthened as the ship's propellers churned up the water in the stern. At last, they were finally heading home.

Chapter Seventy-Seven

Charleston, South Carolina – June 20, 2007

"What you leave behind is not what is engraved in stone monuments but what is woven into the lives of others."

Pericles (495 BC – 429 BC)

Macie Vance continued. "It didn't help matters any that I sent a letter to Jake apologizing and asking him to take me back. That was hard to do but not as hard as the first letter. Jake forgave me but he couldn't come home to Virginia after making that promise to Johnny. Like I said, he truly believed he caused Johnny's death. He was going to do everything he could to take care of his best friend's family. So, Jake moved in with your mother."

J.P. interrupted. "My father was a teacher and I know Jake was not an educated man. How can that be?"

"Jake reinvented himself. He went back to school on the GI Bill, hit the books and got his degree. As a part-time cabbie, he acquired a bit of a New York accent and attitude. When he graduated college, he became a teacher and helped Rose raise you. When you were through with school, he left New York and came home to me." She blushed a little. "I waited for him."

"Over twenty years?" he asked incredulously.

"Oh, I dated men. I tried to fall in love…to forget about him…but I couldn't find anyone with his character. He was pretty cute, too." Macie had a playful twinkle in her eye. "I never stopped loving him. Never got over him. He was what young people today call my *soulmate*. Any woman would have been proud to have him in her life. Time went by and I was still single. He fulfilled his obligation. He kept his promise. And he was proud of who you became. More importantly, he knew Johnny would be proud of you so he came back home with a clear conscience and a feeling of fulfillment." Macie touched his hand again. "He never stopped loving you, John. He followed your career, spoke proudly of you often. You were the son he never had. But he simply couldn't stay any longer."

J.P. nodded. "I can certainly understand his desire to go home and live his own life."

"We had some great years together after he came back. Besides, too many mothers and young girls in Bedford had men that never came back. That my man came back twenty years late was a small price to pay compared to what they lost."

"You understood what he was doing and why?"

"Yes. It was hard at first," she confessed, "but it was my fault. I left *him*. Your father would never have asked Jake to do it if I was still in Jake's life. For a while we each lived our own lives but kept in touch. We would write from time to time but nothing much ever came of it while he was with your mother. Jake had too much honor to cheat. I thought you should know that. For a time I actually thought they would just stay together but once you were on your way, he came back home to me."

J.P. was astounded. He would have never figured this out on his own. He shook his head, waves of emotion sweeping over him. "It still amazes me both why...and how he did it."

Macie sensed J.P. was overwhelmed by the revelation and started to explain. "The boys were very close. Jake asked your father to be his best man. Your dad asked Jake to be your godfather. That's how close they were...closer than the closest brothers. Jake loved your father. He admired him for being both smart and tough. He respected him for being a fighter who could also be decent and moral. But most of all he loved him for his loyalty. Jake believed there was nothing in this world that your father wouldn't do for him! And he felt the same toward your father." She paused. "Jake loved his friend so much he assumed his life."

"Unbelievable," J.P. shook his head again. It was yet another story of self-sacrifice and humility from this generation of people he had learned to respect and come to love. "I must confess that I believe the people from your generation are utterly amazing."

"That's a bit of an exaggeration, I always thought," she replied. "We were just trying to survive. Unfortunately, with the Depression and the War, we had many challenges to overcome." She hesitated while she finished her tea. "There is something to be said for the struggle you know. It builds character. Anything worthwhile is only valuable if you have to work hard for it." She gulped down the last of her tea. "But I will confess this much. Life was a challenge after the War. Can you imagine what it's like to be twenty-two years old and already know that you will never do anything more important for the rest of your life than what you've already done?"

J.P. reflected for a moment. "No, I can't."

"That was *all* of us," Macie continued. "Except Jake. He had a mission harder than anything he did in the War. Less dangerous but more difficult. He had to take care of a friend's family and raise his son. And he did a marvelous job!"

J.P. was embarrassed. "Thank you." He paused for a moment. "Do you have any children?"

"No children," she answered. "He considered you his son. We thought we were too old to start a family. Besides, we never officially married. He didn't marry Rose either." Macie pondered for a few seconds. "Despite his high standards for loyalty, Jake was a bit of a scoundrel." She chuckled. "Are you married, John?"

"No, I'm not." J.P. didn't want to explain Cynthia Powers though he had a feeling Macie already knew. He brought the conversation back on point. "And

I thought he left because I went to Canada to avoid the draft," J.P. shared that thought with Macie. "I heard about a promise and at the time I thought my father went to Bedford to take care of a promise he made to Jake. I figured it might have something to do with you or Harley. There *was* a promise to be kept but, like Frank said, I had it all backwards."

Macie continued. "Frank wrote us often. After Jake died he was tempted to share all of this with you. He couldn't bring himself to do it. Recently he wrote me that you might find your way here, someday. He asked me to be prepared to explain everything to you."

"However, you might not have all the answers," he countered. "For example, why would my mother agree to take Jake's help?"

"I certainly don't have all the answers but I can guess from a women's point of view. She was a young girl alone in a big city, with no family and a baby. It wasn't too hard to accept an offer of help and security. Especially from someone her husband trusted more than anyone in the world. I can understand how she could accept that simple idea at first and wound up accepting Jake later. He was easy to like and somewhat of a charmer. He definitely could get under your skin, in a good way."

"Do you think they were in love?"

"Now John, that's a touchy subject. One that I avoided asking Jake about for obvious reasons. I have my pride, too," she laughed. "I'm not sure about love but there certainly was a great deal of respect and affection. I would like to think that it was an arrangement of necessity fostered by a mutual love for Johnny. It certainly got more involved than they planned at the beginning. Obviously, something kept them together for over twenty years. Maybe it was what they felt for each other; or for you or a combination of the two. Like I said before, it's complicated." Macie reflected on what she said. She needed to give J.P. something more. "If Jake were alive today and you twisted his arm, I believe he would confess that he was actually in love with two women."

"No disrespect to you, Macie but from everything I witnessed growing up, they seemed to love each other. It also seems to me that convincing her to try this arrangement would have been the hardest thing to do. My mother had a bit of an independent streak so Jake must have been a *real* charmer to pull that off."

"Oh, he had help." Macie reached into her purse and handed him a letter. "Here. Read this letter from your dad to your mother."

Chapter Seventy-Eight

New York City - November 22, 1945

"A friend is, as it were, a second self."

Marcus Tullius Cicero (106 BC – 43 BC)

Jake Kilroy stood in the hallway facing the door to Rose's apartment. He was gathering himself, summoning the courage to knock. His barracks bag stood upright on the floor. It was opened at the top and he extracted two bottles of wine, a white and a red. Flowers or candy seemed too personal. Johnny would have brought wine when invited to dinner. He raised his hand to knock and froze in mid-air. *Why was this so hard?*

When he called Rose from Norfolk she was happy to hear from him. They chatted, exchanged pleasantries, mostly small talk. When he told her he had some of Johnny's personal items he would like to bring to her, she invited him to come to New York immediately. Jake was halfway there on the train when it suddenly occurred to him he would arrive at her place on 22 November, Thanksgiving Day. She surely would have a Thanksgiving dinner prepared. *We'll eat, I'll show her the letter, she'll throw me out and I'll be heading home before dark. Let's get this over with!*

Just as he was about to knock, the door opened. Rose stood there in a flowery print dress with her hair done up and a face made up moderately and tastefully. Her apron was discarded on the floor.

"I thought I heard something. Welcome Jake!" She nervously pressed her palms on her thighs and extended one of them to shake his hand.

Jake lifted his hands to show they were occupied. "Hi, Rose. It's great to see you."

"Oh," she looked at his hands and shook her head. Then she reached under his arms and hugged him tightly. He lowered his arms around her shoulders. "It's so good of you to come." They held each other for a moment.

Rose stepped back and took in the sight before her. Jake was in his army dress greens with a chest full of ribbons. His trousers were bloused into a shiny pair of Corcoran jump boots and he wore an overseas cap with the airborne insignia. The sight was too much for her and she broke into tears.

He reached for her but she stepped back, bent down to pick up her apron and wiped her tears with it. She struggled to gain control.

"Come in, Jake. Sit down."

Jake fingered the strap of a small canvas pouch and lifted it from his barracks bag. He kicked the door close, leaving his barracks bag in the hall. He handed her the wine and sat down at the table. The kitchen was comfortably warm with the odor of cooking and the scent of her perfume. She would have had Thanksgiving dinner alone if he had not come. Nevertheless, he felt awkward and was immediately at a loss for words.

She sat down across from him. "I'm sorry, Jake. I must look frightful. But the sight of you standing there reminded me…"

"It's alright, Rose. Nothing to apologize for."

She sniffled and straightened up. "I've roasted a nice chicken basted in honey with walnut and raisin stuffing. Some foods are still hard to get so I'm using my favorite *Betty Crocker* wartime recipes. We also have baked potatoes, that beer you liked and pumpkin pie for dessert."

"Sounds great. Thanks for having me." Rose was as pretty as he remembered, even with her mascara running down her cheek. He looked around. "Is anyone else coming?"

"It'll just be us and John Patrick when he wakes up. I even have some turkey flavored baby food for him." Rose smiled. She was regaining her composure. "Mrs. Geelan from upstairs might drop down for coffee when her family leaves. She does some babysitting for me from time to time but she's getting on in years."

"I'd love to see the boy."

"When he awakens. Let's go sit in the living room and you can show me what you brought," she pointed to the canvas pouch.

They went into the cozy living room and sat at opposite ends of a long, soft couch. Jake noticed the various pictures on the walls and furniture. They were all of Johnny and her before the War, except for two. One was of Johnny taken in a photo studio in Palermo, Sicily and the other was the picture of the three of them taken on the roof two years before.

"That was the last time he was home." Rose caught Jake staring at that picture. Then she changed the subject. "What do you have for me in that bag?" She forced a smile.

Jake unzipped the pouch, removed the items one at a time and placed them on the couch near her. Johnny's medals, ribbons and badges came out first. He explained each one to her. There were two purple hearts and a bronze star. The jump wings were new and now had the five combat jump stars. The records had been corrected since the War ended. She noticed Jake had almost the same awards on his chest. Then he handed her the dog tags. Next came three airborne sleeve patches and Johnny's wristwatch. Rose handled each item with tender respect before placing them back in the canvas pouch. She held the silk escape maps of Sicily and France to her cheek and smelled them before putting them back. She was still fighting to keep her composure. Finally, there was only one item left. It was a letter.

Rose picked up the sealed envelope. "What's this?"

"He made me promise to bring this to you if he didn't make it back."

Rose tore open the envelope and read the letter. Tears began streaming down her face. She wiped them away with her forearm as she continued to read, occasionally looking up at Jake. She finished the letter and put it down.

"Did you read this?" she asked Jake.

He shook his head.

"Do you know what Johnny is asking me to do?"

Jake took a deep breath and let it out slowly. *This is the part where he gets thrown out.* "I don't know what he wrote there," he pointed to the letter, "but I promised I would take care of you and his son for as long as needed." Jake looked at the floor and braced for the reaction.

Rose surprised him by calmly asking him a question. "And how exactly had you planned on doing that?"

"I haven't figured that out yet."

"Well, he did." She stood up and dropped the letter in his lap. "Excuse me, I need a moment." A touch of anger seemed to replace her sorrow as she walked to the bathroom and closed the door behind her.

Jake picked up the letter.

Dear Rose,

If you're reading these words, the worst has happened and Jake is sitting across from you. I made Jake promise to bring you this letter. Don't blame him. What I'm about to ask you is not his idea. It's driven by my undying love for you and my son. Here it goes! I want you to let Jake take care of you and John Patrick. It may seem unreasonable for me to expect him to take care of you and for you to accept, but he is the only man on earth that I trust with you and my son. If I had a chance to request this before I died, to take care of you guys, I know he would have said yes. If I didn't, I know he'll do it when you read him this letter.

I'm not expecting that you marry him, although I wouldn't be disappointed if that happened. I'm just asking you to give him a chance to look out for you, to watch over you and take care of you. It won't take long for you to see the loyal and honorable guy I fought with. All I'm saying is I want you to get to know him and give him a chance and open your heart to him. As for Jake, he's smart enough to see what a wonderful and swell girl you are. Besides, he has nothing to go home to. Before you get angry with me, please understand I'm trying to do the next best thing to me coming home. This request comes from my love for all three of you. What I ask may not be fair and it may not work out for any number of reasons. But please consider this and give it a chance.

With all my love, I'll be watching over you.
Johnny

"Is that what you signed up for when you made your promise to him?" Rose came back into the room, her voice breaking his concentration.

Jake let out a loud sigh. "He did ask me, with his dying breath. I said yes. I would do anything for him. It would be my honor to take care of you guys for as long as you need me to."

"This is not fair. Johnny shouldn't ask me to do this." There was a mild protest in her voice. "The idea that I'm being forced on you is almost as bad as you being pushed on me."

"I don't look at it that way…you being forced on me. In another time, if things were different…" he hesitated, not wanting to come on too strong although he certainly found her attractive. "I don't mind at all. But I understand if you feel like I'm being forced on you." He was doing his best to make it easier for her to decide. Then if she turned him down and he had to go home, he could do so with a clear conscience.

She studied his face. He was sincere and contrite. She looked away, avoiding eye contact. "I have a job. I'm a nurse's aide. I don't need that much help as it is. So, how would this work?"

"Oh, I don't know. It's awkward but I can get an apartment nearby, drop in on you and the boy. Make sure you're doing okay. I can baby-sit some if you have night shifts. Help out with heavy stuff and repairs when you need them." He was playing it by ear and found himself making sensible suggestions. "It would be strictly platonic. I learned that word from Johnny. Also, I'll be going to school on the GI Bill. I'll work part-time while I get my degree. Meanwhile, I'll check in with you guys regularly to make sure you're doing all right."

"Just until we get on our feet?" she asked putting a limit on any help she might accept.

Jake nodded his agreement.

She was impressed by his humility. "I think Johnny had a more ambitious plan in mind. And if I said no?"

Jake gulped. *Here it comes.* "I wouldn't force myself on you, but I'm asking you to please let me help."

She sat on the couch and thought for a moment. "I like you, Jake. I wouldn't mind having you around. It's this 'shotgun wedding' thing that has me upset." She buried her face in her hands. "I can't believe Johnny wants me to actually consider this!"

He smiled at her. "I understand. Look, we don't have to look that far down the road. That doesn't have to be part of the plan. We're two adults. We can work things out without getting too far ahead of ourselves."

Rose didn't want to appear too easy although she was warming to the idea. "Let's have dinner. This is all happening too fast. Let me think about it."

He carved and she served the bird right at the table. They ate and drank the wine and spoke mostly about Johnny and their adventures together. Jake sanitized the stories as best he could. The conversation was unforced and easy. Jake was a good listener and had a self-deprecating sense of humor. He was humble and a bit shy. She liked those qualities. After dinner, she woke John Patrick and fed him a small jar of turkey flavored baby food. She disappeared into the living room to change the baby while Jake cleared the table and did the dishes. After the baby was fed and changed, she came back into the kitchen to find the table cleaned and the dishes in the drying rack.

"I could get used to this," she joked.

"See," he smiled back. "This arrangement could have its benefits."

They had coffee and pie for dessert. Mrs. Geelan called to say she was tired and would not join them. Jake and Rose continued talking. He was also interested in how things were on the Homefront and Rose explained wartime America in great detail. They were getting along better than he had expected after her initial reaction to the letter.

Jake excused himself to use the bathroom and she disappeared into the living room for a few moments. When she returned to the kitchen, Jake was putting on his tunic.

"It's getting late. I should find a hotel room."

"Your real name is John, isn't it?"

He nodded.

She led him into the living room. The couch was made up with a pillow, sheet and blanket. "It's too late, John. You can do that tomorrow. Just don't get the wrong idea!"

Chapter Seventy-Nine

Charleston, South Carolina – June 20, 2007

"Humility must always be the portion of any man who receives acclaim,
earned in the blood of his followers and the sacrifices of his friends."

Dwight David Eisenhower (1890 - 1969)

"I think Jake brought me this letter from Johnny to convince me that living with Rose wasn't Jake's idea," Macie explained as J.P. placed Johnny's letter in his pocket.

"It wouldn't be a big deal today but living together back then was taboo, right?"

"Scandalous," she smiled. "And that was one reason for the secrecy." She hesitated for a moment. "Among others."

J.P. nodded. He decided to change the subject. "What brings you here to Charleston?"

"I live here now. I moved here after Jake passed," her eyes got watery again and she dabbed them with a dainty hanky. "Pardon me." She sniffled and looked up.

"But why here, at the museum?"

"Why, John," she smiled broadly. "I volunteer here. Didn't you know I built this ship?"

Somewhere embedded in all the stories, he was told Macie worked in the Newport News Shipyard. "Of course, how could I have forgotten?"

"It's comforting to know that I'm going to spend my last days in this place. A great ship that I helped build as a young woman. It's His divine master plan at work...this connection between my life and the life of this ship. It's hard to explain, but it's very comforting."

Two women about Macie's age walked over to the table and sat down. They wore the simple uniform of the volunteers; white shirts with blue jeans. The blonde woman had her baseball cap pinned lightly to her head so as not to disturb her hairdo. The redhead had her cap pulled tightly down. "And it's comforting to spend them with great friends. We're all volunteers here."

"Ladies," J.P. nodded.

"This is John Patrick Kilroy, the man Jake raised," she explained to the two women who smiled and nodded. "Pleased to meet you," the blond winked.

"And these are my good friends, Nora Lee and Roxie Rawls Edson. Nora built this ship with me. Roxie ferried and tested planes that flew from its decks. Some of them are right there." She looked down the hangar deck with its many planes on display.

"Of course, ladies. Pleasure to meet you."

Macie continued. "I was telling John here about how Jake raised him. He didn't know that until today."

"So, the boys never cracked?" Nora Lee quipped.

"Nope," Macie answered.

"Good for them," Roxie chimed in.

"Does everyone know about this but me?" J.P. half-jokingly asked.

"Just a close circle of friends that go way back," Macie assured him.

J.P. smiled. "I'm happy for you, Macie, and grateful for everything you shared with me. We must stay in touch. If there is anything I can ever do, please call. I'm in your debt." He handed her his business card.

"That's so kind of you, John."

J.P. reached into his pocket. He slid the case that contained the Medal of Honor awarded to John NMI Kilroy over to Macie. "This doesn't belong to me. It belongs to you or it belongs over there," he pointed to the Medal of Honor Museum."

She reached for the case as he slid it toward her. She slid it back. "Jake wanted *you* to have this. That's one of the reasons he had Harley tell Colonel Chase about you."

J.P. nodded and slipped the case back into his pocket.

"And I have something else for you." She took another folded letter from her purse. "Jake wrote this to you. Wait until you get home to read it."

"More letters?" J.P. quipped. "You must feel like a post office." He took the sealed envelope and slipped it in his pocket.

Farewell greetings were exchanged and it was time to go. But he had a last question. "One more thing, Macie."

"Of course."

"Why did those men keep this secret from me for so long? I mean, why were they so determined never to reveal what really happened?"

Macie reflected for a moment. "You met these men. You know what kind of integrity they had. When they gave their word or made a promise, it meant everything to them. They don't make men like that anymore."

"I've come to learn that."

"Well, John, I wasn't there but Jake told me this story many times. Jake, Harley, Sky, Frank and Lincoln met in New York after the War. It was January of forty-six. They attended a parade. Rose was there and so were you."

"Really?"

"Before you leave today, let me tell you this one last story."

Chapter Eighty

New York City - January 12, 1946

"It is not the oath that makes us believe the man, but the man the oath."

Aeschylus (c. 424 BC - c. 455 BC)

Jake, Rose and baby John Patrick stood on the sidewalk on the corner of Eighth Street and Fifth Avenue just off Washington Square Park in the shadow of the Washington Arch. They were dressed against the biting cold. One and a half year old John Patrick Kilroy was bundled into a furry snowsuit. Rose, with reddened cheeks and teary eyes, wore her black ersatz fur coat over two sweaters and gabardine slacks. Her black wool hat was pulled down firmly over her ears. She leaned on Jake for warmth as he held the baby against his flannel shirt buttoned over a heavy sweatshirt. He wore jeans and his baseball cap had a Screaming Eagle on the front and an Eighty-second Airborne crest on the bill. He wasn't cold. He could never be as cold as he was in Bastogne. Streaks of sunlight snuck through the canyons of the city to provide intermittent and much appreciated warmth.

Eager crowds lined both sides of the avenue in anticipation of the Victory Parade for the 82nd Airborne Division. Onlookers were twenty deep in places. It was the first and only time an entire division would be welcomed home from the War and honored for their service. Frank West and Jake's cousin, Harley Tidrik, were supposed to meet them on this corner. Lincoln and Sky would be marching in the parade. They all arranged to gather afterward for dinner at the famous Luchow's Restaurant on Fourteenth Street near Union Square Park.

Since arriving from Liverpool, England on the third of January, the 82nd had been absorbing replacements and practicing precision marching at Camp Shanks in Orangeburg, New York. Sky's responsibility was the assimilation of the 555th PIB (Colored), which had been administratively attached to the 82nd. That is how Captain Sky Johnson met First Lieutenant Lincoln Abraham, a company commander in the Triple Nickels. It didn't take much conversation before they realized they had common friends in the Kilroys and traced their meeting back to the brawl in the Queen's Bazaar Pub in London. The two young paratrooper officers worked well together to get the Nickels up to speed.

New class-A uniforms were issued to all personnel and any free moment not spent in marching drills was used to polish brass, boots and helmets to a dazzling shine. General James M. Gavin insisted the uniforms of all marching members of the division include the battlefield decorations and unit citations earned by the division. That order included the entire contingent of Triple Nickels.

The parade route was one hundred blocks long from lower Manhattan all the way to midtown. It would take the division over two hours to march the entire five miles. The parade route was choked with people. Veterans were particularly well represented on this Saturday afternoon as they prominently wore their field jackets, military caps or sported flags and placards identifying their units. Gavin would lead the march until he joined City Mayor William O'Dwyer and New York Governor Thomas Dewey among other notables on the reviewing stand. This was a big deal for both the city and the army.

Jake heard the deep rumbling of drums. At first it sounded like distant artillery. He looked south and could barely make out the honor guard leading the formation. The flags were fluttering and the paper and ticker tape began to descend from the tall buildings. Soon the air was filled with a snowstorm of paper fluttering toward the ground. The drumbeat became louder as the marchers closed the distance. People began to clap and cheer as they anxiously awaited the arrival of the first company.

The lead element marched into Washington Square Park. There were nineteen ranks of soldiers marching nine abreast in perfect unison. An officer and a trooper carrying a pennant led each company. There were four companies to a battalion, three battalions to a regiment and four regiments in the division. Including attached units and formations, over fifty companies marched that day, all with great exactness and skill. The marching music from one of the many marching bands was barely audible over the cheering crowd but the deep thrumming drumbeat remained clear and the paratroopers stepped smartly to the beat.

Finally, the first formation was marching underneath the Washington Arch and the crowd grew louder and more excited. General Gavin led the formation followed closely by his staff. Shouts of "Slim Jim" and "General Platoon Leader" could be heard emanating from the crowd. They were terms of endearment from men who loved Gavin and treasured serving under him.

Jake nudged Rose whose clapping was muffled by her thick gloves. He nodded toward the flag bearers behind Gavin. The American flag was flowing gently in the breeze alongside the divisional flag with its seven campaign ribbons and numerous battle streamers. The colorful sight was awe-inspiring.

As the leading company passed by, Jake noticed how precise their marching was and how picture perfect their uniforms were. Helmets gleamed, brass sparkled and boots reflected like mirrors. There wasn't a spot of lint on their Wool Field Jacket, M1944, commonly called Ike jackets, or a single wrinkle in their khaki trousers. The ranks and files were aligned flawlessly. The paratroopers marched with visible pride stamped on their cold, blushed faces. The multitude cheered its appreciation.

Company after company marched by. The throng never lost its enthusiasm. Names were hollered from the masses as discharged civilian veterans recognized old friends. The paratroopers continued to file by, one proud company in perfect formation after another.

Jake looked around. Harley and Frank were still not there and the sidewalks were packed right back to the buildings. Moving about was going to be difficult.

The men had agreed to meet at the Washington Arch the night before when they got together at McSorley's Old Ale House on Seventh Street and Second Avenue. Harley had come into town and Jake met him at Grand Central Station. Together they waited for Frank's train and after introductions and bear hugs, they took a cab to McSorley's. They grabbed a booth in the corner and waited for Lincoln and Sky.

McSorley's was a New York landmark made famous by its prominent clientele. Artists and writers frequented the place and made it legendary through their portraits and writings. Other celebrities of the arts followed and soon the pub attained icon status. The walls were covered with old dusty pictures faded brown with age. It was no more surprising to find a vintage oil lamp as the farewell picture of Babe Ruth or a wanted poster for John Wilkes Boothe. The bar had no stools and the handcuffs hooked to the bar rail were said to be once owned by Harry Houdini. The sign above the bar read "Be Good or Be Gone".

The only two alcoholic drinks served were light and dark ale. The three men ordered dark ale while they waited for their friends. Frank was extremely interested in how Jake was doing with Rose and Johnny's son.

"Things are going good, Frank. We found a bigger apartment and I moved in with her. She didn't want to live in her old neighborhood anymore once she took me in."

"I guess that's good. So what are you doing?" Frank asked.

"I'm registered for college. I start next week. The GI Bill is covering it and some living expenses. I'm also driving a cab part-time, when Rose is home and I'm not in school. We know it will get hard at times, with our schedules, but we'll work it out."

"And the boy?"

"Great kid," Jake smiled. "Just eats and sleeps. I can't wait to play catch with him."

"So, Rose is accepting this…help," Harley stated rather than asked.

"So far," Jake answered. "It's only been a few months but we get along great and I really like them both a lot. Not everyone would do what she is doing to make sure her son has a better life. I admire her for it."

"Not everyone would be doing what you're doing, either," Frank interjected.

Jake got embarrassed. "I'm not so sure. I bet a lot of other guys are doing the same thing. Helping out a buddy's family, I mean. But I don't want Rose's reputation to suffer and I think she's worried about that. That's why she wanted us to move."

Just then two men walked in the door. They wore civilian clothes but their high and tight haircuts indicated they were military. Sky was in front. He shook hands and embraced Jake, remembered Harley from London and was introduced to Frank.

The introductions continued. Lincoln was next and he shook Jake's hand. They stood for a moment, staring knowingly at each other, and then embraced in a long and warm hug.

"We're a long way from Foy," Lincoln reminded.

"And I wouldn't be here if it wasn't for you," Jake commented.

"Me neither," Lincoln reciprocated.

Harley reminded Lincoln he was also present for the brawl in the Queen's Bazaar but Lincoln confessed he was so scared he only remembered Johnny.

"Congratulations!" Jake told Lincoln. "You became a paratrooper!"

"Thanks to him." Lincoln pointed to Frank. He remembered him from Foy and thanked him profusely for the letter of recommendation, which helped him get into the 555th PIB.

"How many jumps?" Frank asked.

"Sixty-something," Lincoln answered smugly with a big smile.

"Is that a lot?" Harley asked.

"More than the rest of us combined," Jake speculated.

"Oh, yeah," Sky interjected. "Ask him how many combat jumps?" Sky was smiling. It seemed the two of them had had this exchange before.

"None, you know that," Lincoln smiled back. "But I'd like to see you jump into the blinding smoke of a burning forest on the side of a mountain with only a shovel and a prayer."

"No thanks," Sky joked back. "Give me Krauts shooting flak at my plane and swamps to land in anytime!"

"That many jumps? You were that busy?" Jake asked Lincoln.

"Yup. The Japs were sending balloon bombs over the Pacific and most of my jumps were made in the Northwest."

"Very impressive," Frank added. "You're in Master Parachutist territory."

They all sat down and ordered more ale.

"You're going to see the best freakin' division in the world marching tomorrow," Sky announced. "Right Linc?"

Lincoln nodded.

Frank responded. "How can that be? They deactivated the Screaming Eagles on twenty-six, November of forty-five."

"Oh no," Sky scoffed. "The Hundred and first is better known only because of Bastogne. If we were there, like we were supposed to be, we would have gotten all the credit and the fame. But we're the ones marching tomorrow." The ribbing seemed good-natured.

"But you *weren't* there. *We* were!" Frank responded. "Right, Jake?"

"Boys, boys. C'mon now. Both divisions were great! I should know. I served in both of them." Jake was sure Sky was just having a little fun but Frank seemed to be taking the exchange more seriously. "According to the newspapers, this division represents all the fighting men of all the services. This division is… what did they call it…symbolic of everyone who fought. In fact I read there are new guys and replacements marching that never even saw combat. Is that right?"

"That's right," Sky answered. "Gavin wanted a full division for the parade. I suppose we are representing everyone who fought or served but I need to tell Frank this story."

"Go ahead," Frank allowed.

"At the Bulge there was this lone private digging a hole for an outpost. This American tank comes hauling up the road and the commander asks this paratrooper if this was the front line. The paratrooper asked, 'Are you looking for a safe place?' The commander said, 'yeah'. So the trooper says, 'Well buddy, just pull your vehicle behind me. I'm the Eighty-second Airborne and this is as far as the bastards are going'. True story." Sky held up his right hand.

Frank stared at Sky. It was hard to get mad at him. He had a friendly grin on his face throughout the whole conversation. "I'm not saying your division was not a great one. Just don't try to tell me mine wasn't great either."

"I'm not. Two great divisions, I agree with that. But which one was better? Jake. You served in both. Which one was better?"

Jake looked at Frank and Sky as they both awaited an answer. "If I'm the referee then my decision is final. They were equal!"

"Fair enough. For today," Sky laughed. He looked at Frank. "We'll continue this another time," still laughing.

The waitress brought over the mugs of ale and Sky reached across and grabbed Jake's arm. "I heard what you're doing. How's it going?"

Jake explained to Sky and Lincoln what he had earlier told Harley and Frank. Sky listened with great interest. Sky loved Johnny, too.

"So, you're living together?" Sky probed.

"It's not what you think, Sky. It's platonic…so far. It's just more convenient this way."

"I don't think it's bad at all, Jake. What does she think about it?" Sky persisted.

"She's embarrassed, Sky. She doesn't want anyone to know. That's why we moved."

"Does she know that we know?" Sky circled his hand around the table.

"Yeah, but she'll never see you guys after tomorrow. I think she can live with that."

"You should have brought her. We could have made her feel better about it," Sky offered in support.

Jake cocked his head toward a sign near the bar, which said:

Good Ale
Raw Onions
No Ladies

Jake continued. "She's having dinner with us after the parade tomorrow. She wants to meet all of you. It's important for her to hear about Johnny from his closest friends. I talk about him all the time. It seems to help her accept it. If you want to make her feel better, tomorrow's your chance."

Sky thought for a moment. He reached out and grabbed Jake's arm. "Let me tell you what this looks like and I don't mean this in a bad way."

"Go ahead."

Sky clasped his hands and looked down at the table. "You came home to help out and it's almost like you replaced Johnny. Assumed his role and identity. Living out his existence. You're going to do that and take care of them, aren't you?"

Jake answered. "If that's what I have to do to keep my promise, then that's what I'll do. Besides, anyone who can, how did you put it, 'assume his role', should be proud that he could do it."

The drinks came. Each man grabbed a mug. Lincoln lifted his mug first.

"To Johnny. Let him never be forgotten!"

They clinked mugs to a chorus of agreement and drank.

Sky was next. "To Jake and the successful completion of his new mission."

They clinked mugs again, except this time Jake withheld his drink. They all looked at him curiously.

"Look, guys, I appreciate this but this is not about me. Someday that little boy is going to grow up. If I'm still around, I sure don't want any special credit for this. I don't want him wondering about who his father was or why his father would want a stranger to raise him. Most importantly, I don't ever want him to question his mother's motives or her morals in accepting me. If I'm there for two months, two years or twenty years, I don't ever want the boy troubled about what happened. He can never know."

Jake paused. All eyes were on him. "I don't know if there's a future for Rose and me as a couple but as long as I'm there, I'll act like his father and help raise him. In any event, I would prefer the boy never find out how his real father died or what anyone else did to make sure he was taken care of. I think these were Johnny's last wishes." Jake paused to let the logic sink in. He looked to Frank who was there when Johnny died and Frank nodded.

Jake continued. "We need to make a pact."

Sky smiled. "As long as we don't have to cut ourselves and spill blood," he joked. "I'll never reveal anything about Johnny's death and how his son was raised." He pushed his glass forward.

Everyone else followed until all the mugs were touching in the center of the table.

"Remember," Jake warned. "Some day we're all gonna' be feeble old men and be tempted to talk about this. When this boy becomes a man he might get a whiff of something and start asking questions. Since we're the only people in the world who know the truth, it will just take one of us to break in a weak moment to blow the whole damn thing. We have to keep this pledge and keep faith with each other and with Rose, no matter what!"

"Count me in, I promise," Sky spoke first.

"I pledge my silence until my dying day," Frank added.

"Never a word…on the soul of my mother," Harley intoned.

"My oath to the Lord," Lincoln signed himself.

"I swear never to reveal this secret," Jake concluded the declarations. "It's done!"

Everyone drank and then and there the oath was sealed.

Company after company filed by. Jake checked little John Patrick, who was snuggled in his snowsuit, and switched arms. The boy was sound asleep under the oversized hood, which protected him from the frigid breeze.

The 504th PIR began marching by and Jake started counting off the companies. When he got to H Company he recognized Sky at the front.

"Hey Sky," he yelled loudly as he raised his free arm and waved.

Sky turned toward the sound. He expected his friends to be slightly beyond the Washington Arch and was looking for them.

He spotted Jake in the crowd and gave the command, "EYES…RIGHT" and snapped off a salute while looking directly at Jake and Rose. All of the men turned their heads to the right and kept that position until the company passed. Sky then gave the order to resume eyes front.

"What was that all about?" Rose asked.

"That was Sky. You'll meet him tonight. That salute was in memory of Johnny."

She nodded, smiling through teary eyes.

The endless procession of companies continued. Neither the crowd nor the soldiers seemed to lose any enthusiasm. Each company seemed to march better than the last. The crowd got bigger and louder as more ticker tape and confetti filled the canyon between the tall buildings.

Rose grabbed Jake's free arm and held it tightly. She was crying and seemed to need his support against the cold as well as the memories.

The Triple Nickels were next through the arch. They seemed to be stepping livelier and more proudly than any other company. Black people in the crowd reacted immediately to the colored paratroopers with screams of joy and elation.

A few people ran out into the street to get a closer look and to touch them as if to make sure they were real. Fathers and mothers hoisted small children high overhead so they could see for themselves the dignity and grace of the black paratroopers. They responded to the adulation by standing taller, marching smarter and looking even more noble and self-assured.

"Here comes Lincoln's company," Jake pointed.

As the first company came through the arch, Lieutenant Lincoln Abraham ordered, "EYES…RIGHT" and 172 heads snapped to the right as one. They held the position until they were well past.

"Was that for Johnny, too?" Rose asked.

"I think that was for you."

Chapter Eighty-One

Henri-Chapelle, Belgium - July 27, 2007

"Go tell the Spartans, thou who pass by,
That here, obedient to their laws, we lie."

Simonides of Keos (c. 556 BC - c. 468 BC)
of the Spartans who fell at Thermopylae

J.P. Kilroy walked slowly past the building up the trail adorned by large beds of pink Polyantha roses. Cynthia Powers clutched his arm with one hand and held a small map in the other. She was reading the markers along the trail.

"Take a right here," she instructed and they turned onto another wide concrete footpath.

"Thanks for coming with me, Cynthia."

"Of course. You're welcome."

"I should have figured this out years ago. West was right when he said I had what I needed to find out the secret. And it's true. I just couldn't put it all together."

"Don't beat yourself up. It was an illogical conclusion to come to."

"I'm not beating myself up. But I should have figured it out."

"All you knew of your father was what you observed for your first twenty years. You had nothing to compare that to. Why would you have even suspected he wasn't your real father?"

"I didn't have anything to compare to at the time but the old men revealed a lot about both men that I should have picked up on. It was the innocent things they told me that contained all the information I needed."

"Like what?"

"Well, like what was Harley doing at the Medal ceremony? I should have suspected something from the start. Harley had little contact with my real father. But he did have a connection with Jake."

Cynthia reflected about that for a moment. "That's only obvious after you know the answer but not obvious enough to point you to the answer. Besides, no one was looking for proof that your father was your father? There were a lot of mysterious things that happened to them during the War. There was the secret mission to Rome, the suspicious death of Sergeant Bancroft, Harley killing prisoners, the unexplained souvenirs. The secret could have been associated with any of those bizarre things."

"You're right. Those things muddied the waters but when it came to the differences and similarities between Jake and Johnny, I was asleep at the switch. For example, Jake smoked and the guys told me Johnny didn't smoke. Another one…Johnny apparently didn't know how to swim. Jake taught me how to swim."

"But those are attributes that can change. People can smoke, then quit and smoke again. They can learn to swim. You can't identify a person by these characteristics."

"And what about the marked up Bible?" he continued undeterred. "If we would have read the marked passage of Luke chapter twenty, verse twenty-eight maybe we would have picked up on it."

Cynthia squinted as she tried to remember. "When a man's married brother dies the brother shall take the woman and raise the children for his brother." She deliberated for a few seconds. "Not exactly accurate but I think he may have marked it up after the fact. Probably to rationalize what he was doing."

They walked on in silence for a few minutes, Cynthia checking her map frequently. She looked up and took a breath of the clean summer air. On the near horizon were groups of Sperbian and Norway spruce mixed with Hawthorns. The weeping willows reverently guarding the perimeter were a poignant touch.

"Harley always said 'I'm Jake's cousin', not 'I was Jake's cousin'. He always spoke as if Jake were still alive. And if Jake was still alive…" J.P. left the sentence unfinished.

Cynthia turned them right onto a wide path in the grass and J.P. followed.

"And the man who raised me was smart but he *did not* have a photographic memory. But the real clincher was the citation. When Lincoln told me I had everything I needed to figure out the secret, he must have been talking about the citation. With the "entered service at" and "birth place" information, it would have been pretty obvious that the Medal of Honor was awarded to Jake Kilroy and not John Patrick Kilroy."

"We both missed that. We read right past it, never noticed it. It never really registered. Still, what happened was so implausible, so unbelievable, I'm not sure we could have figured it all out without Macie."

"Maybe you're right, Cynthia." J.P. paused for a moment. "I had a dream the other night. It was weird. I usually don't remember dreams but this one was so real."

"What was it about?"

"Johnny and Jake, my real father and his best friend who raised me, were young and walking together in full combat gear into a mist. Each had his arm around the other's shoulder. Then the mist cleared and all these other paratroopers in full jump gear were standing in front of the open door of a C-47, like they were waiting for the two men. I never saw these faces before but I knew who they were."

"Who were they?"

"Their names were Boothe, Angelo, Copping, Wolff, Gorham and Tedesco. Somehow I recognized Christian, Smith, Stockett, Goldbacher, Turnbull, Sosa, Zebrosky and Danny Boy. And of course I knew the younger versions of Frank, Sky, Harley and Lincoln. Some of these guys never came back and others died in their beds. I don't know how I knew them but I did. And they were all waiting for the Kilroys. When the plane's motors started they all began boarding. Someone yelled out, 'Hey Kilroys. Are you guys brothers?' The two men answered together. They said 'forever!' They all boarded and took off."

"That is a heart-wrenching dream."

"I know. It touched me. I woke myself up crying. But it's comforting to know they were somehow together for the last jump, even if it was only a dream."

They came to a bench and sat down for a moment, both winded from the walking. "Are you okay with this whole thing?" she asked him.

"I am after reading this." He handed her an envelope. She opened it. The letter was handwritten on yellowing paper with tattered edges. She read it carefully as some of the words were difficult to discern.

> *John Patrick,*
>
> *By now I'm sure you wish to understand why we went through such trouble to keep you in the dark. There are so many reasons. I didn't want to embarrass your mother even though as time went on she encouraged me to confess. You had a life to build and I didn't want to see you starting off with the mindset of a victim. That role stimulates some people but destroys others. I couldn't take the chance. I also didn't think it would be helpful if you learned exactly how your real father died. The circumstances were bizarre and I wouldn't want them to diminish all he accomplished before that. And I didn't want you to blame me even though I blamed myself every day of my life. When you add all this up, it just seemed better not to tell you. And we all entered into a pact to keep it that way. Please remember this was all done out of respect for your mother and love for you. I hope you can find it in your heart to forgive us, especially me.*
>
> *Love, Dad*

Cynthia handed back the letter without comment and they resumed walking. She took in the wide panoramic vista of the perfectly manicured fifty-seven acres of the Henri-Chapelle American Cemetery and Memorial. The marble headstones, each with a small American flag fluttering at its base, were arranged in precise concentric arcs sweeping across a broad green lawn that sloped gently downhill. She turned them to the left between two white crosses and walked up three rows. "It's right over there," she pointed and stepped back. They had found the exact monument they were looking for.

J.P. Kilroy dropped to his knees and touched the white marble cross.

JOHN P. KILROY
PVT 506 PRCHT INF REGT
NEW YORK AUGUST 15, 1945

"I know it took a long time for me to finally get here, Dad, but I'm here now."

He brushed his fingers lightly across his father's name and the tears began to pour in a torrent. J.P. tried to fight them back but he couldn't stem the flow as all the pent-up guilt and anxiety flushed out of his body. As he tried unsuccessfully to stifle his uncontrollable whimpering, he found himself staring through watery eyes at the small American flag.

Finally, he bent over and uttered a barely audible choking whisper. "I'm sorry...I'm so sorry." Then he slowly raised his head, wiped his eyes, forced a weak but sincere smile and gently touched the flag.

"Thank you Dad, for saving my country."

LaVergne, TN USA
30 March 2011

222198LV00001B/10/P